ADVENTURES IN TEHUATL

Author: Tom Knauss
Additional Design: Tim Hitchcock and Rob Manning
Project Managers: Zach Glazar and Tom Knauss
Editor: Jeff Harkness
Art Direction: Casey Christofferson
Layout and Graphic Design: Charles A. Wright
Cover Design: Charle A. Wright
Cover Art: Adrian Landeros
Interior Art: Julio de Carvalho, Adrian Landeros, Santa Norvaisaite, Terry Pavlet, Thuan Pham, Hector Rodriguez, and Erica Willey
Cartography: Robert Altbauer

FROG GOD GAMES IS:

Bill Webb, Matthew J. Finch, Zach Glazar, Charles A. Wright, Edwin Nagy, Mike Badolato, John Barnhouse

ADVENTURES WORTH WINNING

FROG GOD GAMES
ISBN: 978-1-943067-46-6

TABLE OF CONTENTS

THE RE-EDUCATION OF COYOTL

BY TOM KNAUSS

"THE ROAD TO BECOMING AN ADULT IS BEST NOT CIRCUMVENTED BY SHORTCUTS."

— AN AZTLI PROVERB

The Re-education of Coyotl is an adventure for four 2nd- to 3rd-level characters and introduces them to the lands and people of Tehuatl. The opening foray into the world of Tehuatl takes the heroes into a local calmecac, where the teenage boys and their newly anointed leader Coyotl appear to have taken control of the boarding school and now run amok in the absence of any instructors or other authority figures. Bloodthirsty canines and other horrors seemingly under the children's control roam the grounds, apparently performing the bidding of their power mad adolescent master. Although the adventure may be run as a standalone product, it offers an ideal opportunity to gradually present the people and cultures of Tehuatl in an adventure setting.

ADVENTURE BACKGROUND

Whether consciously or by sheer accident, Coyotl, the second son of a prominent Aztli family, always emulated the traits of the canine hunter who shares his name. From an early age, the wily little brother demonstrated remarkable resourcefulness and an aptitude for outwitting or tricking his opponents during any contest or game. These traits served the youngster well, as he desperately lacked the physical size and strength bequeathed to his older brother Ezel, who seemed destined to become a great warrior. Although separated by only 18 months, the brawny Ezel towered over his wiry, younger sibling, giving him a decided advantage in sporting events and the martial arts. When push came to shove in Coyotl's family, Ezel received preferential treatment from his parents who admired his combat prowess and athleticism over Coyotl's intelligence and cunning.

As the sons of a noble family, Ezel and Coyotl spent most of their childhood away from home at the local calmecac, which operated under the guidance of the local temple of Nonotzali and its high priest Aloc. It was there that they received their formal education. Despite being the younger sibling, Coyotl always bested his older brother in academic pursuits, a harsh reality that greatly rankled the fiercely competitive Ezel. Indeed, Coyotl frequently gloated about his scholarly achievements to further antagonize his larger rival in the controlled setting of the calmecac. Yet the tables ignominiously turned on Coyotl when he turned 15 and began his military training. Now firmly in his brother's domain, the older Ezel pounded his younger and significantly smaller sibling into submission on an almost daily basis. In addition to routinely meting out decisive beatings to his younger brother, Ezel copycatted his rival's behavior by crowing over his fallen foe. Naturally, Coyotl seethed over losing the upper hand in his lifelong rivalry against his older brother. He vowed to reverse his newfound fortunes and defeat his sibling by any means necessary.

Coyotl recalled overhearing Aloc and his acolytes occasionally speak in hushed whispers about Ozhuma, a hermetic magician who lived in a secluded cave east of the school. Although his instructors feared the dangerous man who allegedly communed with the spirits of the netherworld, the desperate young man brushed their warnings aside and visited the reclusive spellcaster. When he told the wizened old man his name, Ozhuma's eyes sparkled.

"The coyote runs deep in your blood," the magician uttered while he raised his index finger above his eye. With a deliberate motion, he dragged his outstretched finger across the boy's forearm and drew blood with his sharpened cuticle. "Now, release the beast residing within you," he cryptically muttered. After this brief exchange, the old man dismissed his young counterpart. He refused to speak any further, leaving Coyotl at a loss to interpret the magician's enigmatic words and deeds. However, their hidden meaning became abundantly clear when the full moon appeared in the heavens the following evening.

A cold sweat inexplicably overcame the young man while hunger pangs wracked his empty belly. He instinctually curled into the fetal position, where he watched fur suddenly sprout from his arms and claws emerge from his paw-like hands. His jaw elongated, and fangs tore through his bloody gums. Much to his horror and delight, he became a coyote. Ozhuma's words and actions now made sense. He embraced what he had become and over the next few months, he learned to control the transformations, even under extreme duress including during his one-sided sparring sessions with Ezel. During his fleeting metamorphosis, the vile god Itzcuin, a shapeshifter in his own right, crept into his troubled mind and filled his thoughts with images of carnage and slaughter.

While Coyotl developed the ability to trigger or end his ability to change forms at will, he could no longer contain the primeval rage fuming inside of him. One night, the angry flames burned too bright for him to repress any longer. Consumed with bloodlust, he snuck into the acolytes' living quarters and savagely mauled them to death while they slept. The furious beast then confronted Aloc atop the temple of Nonotzali. In the ultimate act of sacrilege, he knocked the priest unconscious, placed him atop the sacred altar, and ripped his heart from his chest with his teeth. Coyotl then roused his brother from a deep sleep, poking his wet nose against his flesh while slowly slobbering onto his skin. The startled man awoke from a pleasant dream and slipped into a terrifying nightmare. After briefly taunting him, Coyotl leapt onto his brother, sank his teeth into his neck, and tore out his arteries, veins, and muscles in a single bite.

With their adult supervision and authority figures out of the way, Coyotl gave the remaining pupils an ultimatum: Obey him or perish. The menacing circle of coyotes surrounding the bewildered and frightened students bolstered the half-man/half-beast's threat. Within minutes, the vast majority of young people acquiesced to his demands. The handful who openly resisted his call soon met a gruesome end as Coyotl and his loyal underlings tore them apart within minutes. By the following morning, a new hierarchy emerged within the calmecac. Without any structure or authority, the children and their leader established a new pecking order. Under the accommodating gaze of their self-appointed headmaster, Coyotl's ardent supporters abandoned Nonotzali's teachings and devolved into an unruly, savage mob devoid of rules or morality, where the strong bully the weak into utter submission.

Although he exercises absolute authority over the calmecac and the temple, the impulsively violent Coyotl never formulated any strategy to keep Teohuacan at bay. While Itzcuin blessed him with newfound magical abilities, the cunning lycanthrope realizes he and his followers lack the military might to subjugate the neighboring town. However, he also knows that the settlement is unlikely to launch a full-scale assault against their own children, giving him some time to devise a scheme to even the odds against his adversaries. In furtherance of this end, he is in the midst of conducting a depraved experiment on his less enthusiastic followers. In an attempt to unleash their inner beasts, he mixes ground cacao beans with saliva from rabid dogs and gives this lethal concoction to some of the calmecac's students in a deliberate effort to transform them into savage beasts. Despite these efforts, the petulant teenager truly has no grand plan other than to indulge his impulsive, violent whims. Even without a cohesive strategy, Coyotl's reign of terror claims numerous lives and threatens to envelop the neighboring town of Teohuacan in mayhem as fathers may ultimately have to do battle against their sons solely for Itzcuin's and the werecoyote's amusement.

Adventure Synopsis

The characters begin the adventure roughly three weeks after Coyotl staged his coup in the calmecac adjacent to the settlement. If they are traveling to Teohuacan from another locale, they may explore the areas surrounding the town, including Ozhuma's cave on Teohuacan's outskirts. When the adventurers arrive in Teohuacan, residents and visitors alike appear in a jovial mood with the rain harvest festival just a few days away. However, the calmecac has largely fallen silent. The strange events greatly trouble the ruling hierarchy, who want to simultaneously get answers to these burning questions without unnecessarily bucking the temple of Nonotzali's autonomy. Several days earlier, a covert team of jaguar warriors sent to investigate the activities at the calmecac never returned, fueling speculation that something untoward is taking place on the school grounds. The adventurers present the perfect opportunity to infiltrate the calmecac without directly challenging the administrators' authority or ruffling the feathers of influential parents whose sons may be involved in scandalous activities. Unbeknownst to the town's adult residents, several of Coyotl's loyal minions anonymously walk among the townsfolk, where they relish any opportunity to eradicate potential threats to his burgeoning regime.

When the characters arrive at the calmecac at the behest of one or more concerned parties, they find the grounds in disarray. Wild coyotes and other beasts freely roam through the compound, while unruly teenagers indulge their cruelest whims and vilest fantasies without restraint. During their interactions with the undisciplined youth, the characters realize some are voluntarily acting out their darkest impulses. On the other hand, some youngsters suffer from the early stages of the deadly rabies virus (see **Rabies** sidebar) that Coyotl deliberately transmitted to them through a contaminated cacao drink. During their investigation, the characters also discover that Coyotl is a werecoyote who butchered Aloc and his acolytes and then took control of the calmecac. His bestial nature and faith in Itzcuin captured the interest of several demonic minions who joined his ragtag band of followers. Despite Coyotl's absolute authority over the school, the characters meet a disorganized response as they make their way across its grounds into its residential structures.

After seizing control of the calmecac, Coyotl repurposed the temple of Nonotzali to serve as his command post, even though he has no coherent plan to combat Teohuacan's authorities. Nonetheless, the characters must wade through its bolstered defenses of loyal servants, demonic underlings, and insidious traps to reach its inner recesses where the horror and folly of Coyotl's scheme come into full view. The characters must bypass the formidable temple vault door to confront the teenager who perpetrated the calmecac's numerous atrocities. The wily lycanthrope hides behind his lackeys until he senses an ideal opportunity to ambush the unsuspecting adventurers, who must then vanquish him in this climactic battle to free the school from his and Itzcuin's baleful influence. If the characters defeat him, they and Teohuacan's authorities face the messy task of separating the guilty parties from the innocent children corrupted by Coyotl's tainted chocolate treat.

Starting the Adventure

For characters hailing from other locales within the Lost Lands, the adventure begins with a lengthy sea voyage from a distant port in Akados or Libynos. In this case, you must decide whether the heroes intentionally sailed for the shores of Tehuatl after perhaps hearing rumors about vast stores of gold or silver in these mysterious, unknown lands, or they got lost at sea and accidently landed on the large island's eastern beach. In either event, you may read or paraphrase the following description or recount their long days at sea with an original composition.

Characters indigenous to the lands of Tehuatl may omit the preceding sea voyage description and instead undertake an overland trek to the small town of Teohuacan for a specific purpose or on their way to another location.

Hooks

As the introductory adventure to the island of Tehuatl, the characters can become embroiled in the adventure in a multitude of ways. Characters originally from other areas of the Lost Lands, such as Akados, Libynos, or even the Razor Coast, must arrive here by sea. They can then stumble upon the town of Teohuacan by accident while wandering through the surrounding wilderness or receive some incentive to trek to the settlement, such as purchasing provisions in its marketplace or hearing a tale about its purported riches. Characters from Tehuatl may already live in Teohuacan or are traveling there from somewhere else to visit a relative, attend a ceremony, or participate in a local event. Alternatively, an individual residing in the town may summon the characters to the settlement for a different purpose. With the preceding ideas in mind, you may use one of the following hooks to draw the characters into the story or create a unique way to entice the heroes to make their way to Teohuacan.

Missing Dog

A hairless **dog** with light tan skin digs its paw into the ground. Standing roughly two feet tall at the shoulder and weighing approximately 50 pounds, the obviously distressed canine with bat-like ears repeatedly barks at the characters and then turns in the opposite direction, as if beckoning them to follow. The animal wears a leather collar adorned with blue and red stones around its neck. Pictographs inscribed onto the collar indicate the dog's name is Zot. If the characters accept the dog's invitation to join him, he leads them to his hometown of Teohuacan and then to the calmecac where he lived until Coyotl killed his master Patil, one of the acolytes. If a character can communicate with Zot, the dog tells him that he found his owner's body drenched in a pool of blood, though he is unaware of the circumstance's surrounding Patil's untimely demise. Fearful of the coyotes now freely wandering the school's grounds, the clever animal slipped past the wild beasts during the night, though his circuitous route completely bypassed the town.

Dog: HD 1; **HP** 3; **AC** 7[12]; **Atk** bite (1d3); **Move** 15; **Save** 17; **CL/XP** 1/15; **Special:** none. (*Monstrosities* 127)

Religious Festival

Communities dependent upon agriculture rightly fear nature's unpredictable whims. Excessive heat or an early frost can severely damage crops, but these perils pale in comparison to the trepidation accompanying a long dry spell. Without water, plants eventually wither and die. Three times per year, Aztli communities gather to partake in the rain festival celebration, where they beseech the rain god Quiahuitl to call water down from the skies to nourish the maize and grasses. The nearby town of Teohuacan hosts one of the largest celebrations in the area, drawing visitors from the neighboring settlements to the sprawling community. In this circumstance, the characters may already reside in or be traveling to Teohuacan to partake in the celebration firsthand, or **Mintoch** (see **Teohuacan**), the resident cleric of Quiahuitl, invited them to join him and his followers at the ceremony.

School Haze

In anticipation of the upcoming rain festival celebration, the temple of Quiahuitl usually dismisses its students to allow them to join their families for the revelry. However, the calmecac remains eerily quiet. Indeed, Aloc and his acolytes appear to have done nothing to prepare for the massive event. Meanwhile, the children attending the calmecac remain sequestered behind its walls, sparking concern from some worrisome parents. However, every time someone approaches the calmecac's entrance to inquire about their children, growling coyotes seemingly appear out of nowhere to block the way. While the temple stands silent, bloodcurdling screams periodically emanate from behind the school's impressive walls, prompting more cause for alarm. At the urging of the several concerned mothers, **Mintoch** (see **Teohuacan**), the high priest of Quiahuitl, sent four jaguar warriors into the compound under the cover of darkness to investigate the strange occurrences at the calmecac. None of these accomplished soldiers returned to report their findings.

Rumors

Characters spending at least several weeks at sea before arriving on Tehuatl's shores undoubtedly hear strange tales about the lands south of Akados and Libynos, if they were intentionally heading toward this foreign realm. Otherwise, adventurers who washed ashore by accident likely know nothing about this new world. Aztli heroes obviously have a far better lay of the land than a stranger. Regardless of their background, Ccharacters may learn gossip and rumors from third-party sources if they can effectively communicate with the individual and if the person has some knowledge of the area.

Roll a d20 once on the table below. Give the characters all the information with a target number equal to or lower than the number rolled.

TABLE 1–1: RUMORS

d20	Rumor
3	Three times per year, the temple of Quiahuitl in the town of Teohuacan holds the rain festival celebration. The next event takes place a few days from now.
4	The Aztli people represent the largest human ethnic group in the region. They worship a large pantheon of deities with Nonotzali being the most important of them. Lesser populations of Tlotls and Tulita live among them. The latter group of humans venerate different gods than the Aztlis.
5	Most inhabitants wield weapons crafted from bone, stone, and wood. The Tlotls tightly guard the secrets of forging iron and steel, though they sell some of their handiwork to those willing to pay their hefty prices.
6	Local residents have noticed an increase in coyote attacks and activity over the last few months.
8	A juvenile black dragon swims through the shallow channels and tributaries searching for a secluded spot to take up residence. (This is a false rumor.)

d20	Rumor
10	Gnolls have made a resurgence under a new chieftain they call Necapaluma. They plan to attack the small villages and towns in the near future. (This rumor is partially true. Gnolls have reappeared in the area under their new leader, though a large-scale assault is not currently imminent.)
11	The Tulita gather in the swamp during the rain festival celebration to practice their bizarre rituals dedicated to their strange gods. (This is a false rumor.)
12	The Tlotls originally descend from an Akadonian and his crew who came to Tehuatl centuries ago at the direction of a mysterious infernal being. Because countless generations have come and gone since their arrival, the Tlotls bear little resemblance to their forebears and appear more like the indigenous people than an Akadonian.
14	An old hermit named Ozhuma lives on the outskirts of town. Many residents fear the recluse, claiming he made a pact with a foul being from the underworld in exchange for his powers of foresight. (This rumor is mostly true. Ozhuma is a warlock with exceptional powers of observation, but he cannot see into the future.)
16	A crotchety swamp troll the residents derogatorily call Fish Breath occasionally butchers a local fisherman or child who strays too far into the swamp. The townsfolk have undertaken several efforts to get rid of the oafish brute, but to no avail.

Teohuacan Regional Map

The town of Teohuacan is the largest settlement in the sparsely populated and generally inhospitable Izmalli Swamp. It lies near the banks of the Elcomatl River and Lake Tlacuca, giving it access to a navigable waterway and bodies of water well stocked with fish. The water from the saline Elcomatl River is not potable. Therefore, the town's engineers built an aqueduct transporting freshwater from Lake Tlacuca into the community. Characters traveling to Tehuatl by sea arrive at the designated landing point on the map between the Elcomatl River and the path leading from shore to Teohuacan. If the adventurers are native to Tehuatl, they may begin their journey in one of the small settlements scattered throughout the area or at an intersection along a river or other landmark.

The following section describes the small towns and villages appearing on the local map. With a few exceptions, these settlements and geographical landmarks are generally too small to warrant extensive discussion in the *Tehuatl* sourcebook. Therefore, they are presented below for you to use if the characters hail from one of these locales or visit them during the course of the adventure.

Ameka River

Although the mangrove trees and hillocks encountered in the river's delta allow water to flow through these barriers, the tangle of branches, roots, and loose earth make it impossible to navigate a vessel larger than a canoe past this immovable obstacle. The strong current passing through its cataracts and rapids pose an even greater impediment to river travel. The Ameka River can be safely crossed only at a few points generally corresponding with the paths connecting the town of Milpachi to Ollitl and Teohuacan.

Comatl River

The gentle current funnels saltwater from the neighboring ocean into the swamp until the waterway joins forces with an even larger river farther inland. The river measures 30 feet across in most spots with some fluctuations in width ranging from nine feet in a few isolated locations to 58 feet at its widest point. However, the slow-moving river is remarkably shallow, reaching a maximum depth of eight feet with most sections averaging approximately 3–1/2 feet, making it easy to ford. The challenge in getting across the Comatl River lies in avoiding the numerous crocodiles inhabiting its murky waters.

Teohuacan Regional Map

Elcomatl River

Few locals refer to this river by its proper name. Instead, they call it "The Little" as its official moniker literally translates to Little Comatl.

Lake Tlacuca

Although found in a saltwater swamp, Lake Tlacuca displays features more typically found in a freshwater fen. The low-lying basin collects precipitation that falls in the immediate area, though groundwater seeping into the otherwise closed system mitigates the water's acidity.

Lake Zupil

This vaguely bean-shaped saltwater lake reaches a maximum depth of 25 feet near its center, though the waters along its edges are only a few feet deep. Brine shrimp are the dominant form of marine life in this otherwise desolate ecosystem. Mangrove trees and shrubs grow in the shallow water covering the lake's banks. Some birds also feed and wade in these waters. The Aztlis swear the lake is cursed, which causes them to steer a wide berth around its condemned waters. Other human ethnicities and humanoid races scoff at this notion, though they rarely, if ever, venture to its bleak shores.

Milpachi

Population: 464
Ruler: High Priest Ihcalzuma
Government: Aztli Confederation

Macabre images of dancing skeletons and festive corpses cover nearly every manmade surface in this small town. Despite the plethora of gruesome artwork bombarding the senses, the people paradoxically seem happy and lively, reveling in celebrating the lives of the dearly departed. Terraces cut into the face of a plateau house the mausoleums containing the earthly remains of the dead, while the temple of Micoateotl, the Aztli god of the dead, sits atop the elevated mound. Indeed, most wealthy Aztli families from other towns throughout the region make a pilgrimage here to bury their beloved family members, visit their graves on important religious holidays, or to commemorate a special day in the decedent's life such as the anniversary of their death or their birthday.

Milpachi's economy is built around its mausoleum and the steady influx of mourners that the tombs attract. Local florists design custom-made wreaths and other decorative items to adorn individual graves, while skilled artisans sculpt likenesses of the gods and the decedent onto monuments raised above their crypt or create funerary objects such as statuettes and jewelry to be interred with the body. Milpachi also offers the services of professional mourners known as chocas. Some specialize at carrying out hysterical displays of faux grief during the person's interment. Others offer to perform stirring eulogies at their graveside, while a small segment of this occupation engage in acts of self-mutilation or bloodletting as a sacrifice to the gods.

Namatl River

Rip currents scattered along the length of this narrow river make the waterway especially treacherous for swimmers and vessels alike. The swift yet unpredictable flow of water may impede humanoid travel, but it offers a boon to the shellfish and shrimp that live along the silty riverbed. Causeways placed at strategic locations allow travelers to safely cross the turbulent river.

Ollitl

Population: 386
Ruler: Jaguar Cuauhocelotl Imotica
Government: Aztli Confederation

Almost everyone in this community earns a living from the sea. Every morning, fishing boats set sail for the nearby ocean and return in the evening with the day's catch. Tulitas make up a significant percentage of the population, though Aztlis remain in the majority. Quell, the Tulitas' god of the sea, enjoys a widespread following in the community even among the Aztli who incorporated the deity into their pantheon of gods. The fusion of cultures is most evident in its unique cuisine, which blends maize-based dishes with seafood stews and gumbos. Despite sharing some aspects of their individual cultures, the village's leader, Jaguar Cuauhocelotl Imotica, strictly forbids Aztlis from marrying Tulitas. Although the prohibition does not explicitly preclude having a romantic relationship with a Tulita man or woman, a child produced from an unauthorized union between an Aztli and a Tulita never lives to see his or her first birthday. Under Imotica's supervision, the infant's young life ends as a sacrifice to Quiahuitl during the rain ceremony festival. Aztli mothers usually freely give up their newborns to appease their gods, deeming the infants' death as a small price to pay for engaging in taboo behavior. Conversely, Tulita mothers fervently cling to their illegitimate children. Some leave the village shortly after learning of their pregnancy to give birth in secret. Other common practices include entering into a sham marriage with a Tulita man to attempt to pass the infant off as their progeny and imbibing a malodorous cocktail known as moxtica to induce a miscarriage.

Sakatl

Population: 233
Ruler: High Priest Lacui
Government: Aztli Confederation

This small settlement benefits from the luxury of sitting atop an elevated parcel of land that allows its residents to plant crops without the incessant fear of losing them to flooding. The raised mound is also large enough to support the grazing needs of livestock animals, making Sakatl one of the few communities within the Izmalli Swamp to produce wool and milk. Because of the people's dependence upon rain to water their crops and nourish the grasses, humanoid sacrifices to Quiahuitl occur with frequent regularity. To satisfy the fickle deity's appetite for blood, his high priest Lacui offers cueyatls, gnolls, and orcs to his divine patron, though when supplies of these hated foes run low, the priest looks toward the villagers to make up the difference. Not surprisingly, Quiahuitl's followers give Lacui the least meritorious citizens for this dubious honor.

Traders from other neighboring towns and villages venture to Sakatl's farmers' market to barter for wool, milk, and maize. The merchants offer pelts, leather, and other commodities in exchange for Sakatl's rare items. Although they live in a remote community, the villagers are shrewd negotiators who rival any cosmopolitan peddler. They strike a hard bargain for their coveted wares. Sakatl's residents have no tolerance for an unscrupulous trader who tries to pull a fast one on their citizens, especially if the person is not of Aztli descent. On more than one occasion, an unsavory merchant got more than he bargained for when Lacui removed his still-beating heart from his chest while strapped to a sacrificial altar.

Xica

Population: 319
Ruler: Jaguar Cuauhocelotl Cipali
Government: Aztli Confederation

The people of Xica engage in a dangerous profession: crocodile hunting. Although they live far from a significant body of water, the aggressive reptiles thrive in the shallow streams and small tributaries surrounding their community. Some of these hungry beasts occasionally wander into Xica proper in search of a meal or for some other unknown purpose. Despite their expertise combating these creatures, fatalities still occur with alarming regularity. It is not uncommon to see a resident proudly displaying their battle scars from a disastrous encounter with a hungry croc or walking around the village with a missing hand or arm, which serves as a constant reminder of a rendezvous gone terribly wrong. However, the rewards gained from the perilous profession still outweigh the risks in the minds of most Xicans. The durable hide, meat, and other byproducts procured from the beasts fetch a handsome price from traders in neighboring communities, making their efforts worthwhile.

Although still predominately Aztli, many neighboring settlements equate Xicans with suicidal madmen. The Aztli warrior culture loathes fear, yet in their minds, combating an enemy warrior on the field of battle is a sacred duty. Wrestling a crocodile in a muddy stream seems like lunacy. Those engaging in this hazardous occupation have over time adopted a gruffer and less sophisticated demeanor than the townsfolk and villagers in neighboring settlements, giving the Xicans an undeserved reputation for being backward, even though they are just as well educated as their counterparts.

CONDITIONS IN THE IZMALLI SWAMP

The Izmalli Swamp is a semitropical saltwater swamp supporting many small streams and ponds as well as several rivers and lakes. Although it is currently the dry season in Tehuatl, the earth remains spongy where grass grows and soggy in areas lacking any vegetation. In wilderness areas, the ground is treated as difficult terrain in all locations. Teohuacan's drainage system keeps soil within the town firm and reasonably dry, allowing characters to treat the area as normal terrain.

THE WILDERNESS

Unless the characters begin the adventure in Teohuacan, they must spend some time trekking through the swamp surrounding the settlement before they reach their intended destination. When the adventurers enter the wetlands, read or paraphrase the following description of the area:

> Saplings, shrubs, and other woody plants protrude from the damp earth partially covered by pools of standing water and tiny streams in some isolated sections. Mangrove trees and shrubs tower over the shorter vegetation, though the arboreal giants lack the height and density to create a true canopy over the swamp. A faint yet seemingly omnipresent buzzing sound lingers in the background with an occasional crescendo indicating a winged pest's impending arrival.

The villagers and townsfolk always stick to the downtrodden paths winding a route through the foliage. These makeshift roads predominately connect the settlements to one another and other points of interest in the region. Despite hosting more traffic than the unspoiled wilderness, these thoroughfares offer no guarantees of safety. Wild animals generally prefer avoiding contact with humanoids, but the same cannot always be said of men and monsters. For every hour spent trekking through the untracked wilderness around Teohuacan, there is a 50% chance of encountering one of the creatures appearing on **Table 1–2**. If the characters exclusively remain on the paths, the chance decreases to 25%, but they encounter only humanoids or monsters. A rendezvous with an animal is rerolled until the adventurers run into a humanoid or monster. When the characters approach within five miles of Teohuacan, the detailed map of the area surrounding the settlement determines whether they participate in a set encounter based upon the route they choose or deliberately venture to the predesignated location.

TABLE 1–2: TEOHUACAN WILDERNESS RANDOM ENCOUNTERS

d10	Encounter
1	2d3 **Aztli hunters**
2	1d3+1 **Aztli jaguar warriors**
3	1d4+1 **beasts of Itzcuin**
4	1d4+1 **cadavers**
5	1d2 **cipatenhuas** plus a **cipatenhua disciple**
6	1d4 **crocodiles**
7	1d4 **gnolls**
8	1 **jaculus**
9	2d4 **orcs** plus an **orc sacrificial priest**
10	1d2 **swamp trolls**

AZTLI HUNTERS

These **Aztli hunters** from Teohuacan generally stay on the path until they spot prey from their vantage point on the road or deviate from the trail at a predesignated location where they have experienced past success. They give the appearance of nonchalantly going about their business, though they keep a very wary eye on outsiders. Characters can detect a note of apprehension in the hunters. If the characters earn their trust, the men tell the adventurers they must be constantly wary of the "fish-men" who roam the swamp. Otherwise, the hunters ignore the passersby and attend to their designated task at hand, while constantly glancing at strangers from another land.

Aztli Hunters (2d3): HD 2; AC 7[12]; **Atk** itztopilli (1d6); **Move** 12; **Save** 16; **AL** N; **CL/XP** 2/30; **Special:** none.
Equipment: tlahuiztli armor[B], itztopilli[B], hide bag containing 2 cacao beans.
[B] See **Appendix B: New Equipment and Magic Items**

AZTLI JAGUAR WARRIORS

Although the **Aztli jaguar warriors** from Teohuacan pounce on the opportunity to kill game wandering too close to them, the attentive armed soldiers predominately look out for monstrous denizens trespassing in what they consider their territory. Unlike the hunters, these seasoned warriors display no signs of fear. Furthermore, they aggressively confront any non-Aztli they meet, vigorously questioning the interlopers in their native Aztli tongue while refusing to converse in any other language. If the characters give them a concise, plausible answer — such as mentioning the rain festival celebration or visiting the calmecac — the jaguar warriors back down and allow them to continue on their journey. In the absence of a satisfactory answer, the jaguar warriors attempt to detain the trespassers or attack the characters if they resist. Characters who satisfy the jaguar warriors' inquiries may in turn ask them questions about recent events in Teohuacan. Under these circumstances, the jaguar warriors sheepishly admit four of their fellow warriors never returned from their mission to infiltrate the calmecac several days earlier to investigate the inactivity at the temple of Nonotzali and the inability to contact the children residing within the school.

Aztli Jaguar Warriors (1d3+1): HD 4; AC 6[13]; **Atk** macuahuitl (1d6) or javelin (1d6); **Move** 12; **Save** 13; **AL** N; **CL/XP** 4/120; **Special:** none.
Equipment: cipacahuipilli armor[B], macuahuitl[B], 4 javelins, hide bag containing 4 cacao beans.
[B] See **Appendix B: New Equipment and Magic Items**

BEASTS OF ITZCUIN

At first glance, these vicious canines appear to be mangy, oversized coyotes, but a closer examination reveals odd yet harmless deformities suggesting someone or something horribly altered these poor creatures. These mutations include grotesque underbites; elongated, flappy ears; mismatching eye colors; stubby tails; and other minor defects that solely affect its appearance and not its performance. Indeed, the vile god Itzcuin twisted these ordinary dogs into bestial abominations. Furthermore, their ability to verbally communicate among themselves and others immediately sets them apart from ordinary dogs. The **beasts of Itzcuin** dispense with pretenses and attack on sight, using their pack tactics to surround and maul one or more designated enemies. Although they speak Aztli, they refuse to converse with the characters unless compelled against their will. These beasts associate with the hermit Ozhuma and have no knowledge of the events at the temple of Nonotzali or the calmecac.

Beasts of Itzcuin (1d4+1): HD 2; AC 7[12]; **Atk** bite (1d3 + disease); **Move** 15; **Save** 16; **AL** C; **CL/XP** 2/30; **Special:** darkvision (60ft), disease (save or 1d4 damage per day, healing ends damage), misfortune (1/day, save or −1 penalty to hit and saves for 24 hours). (see **Appendix A: New Monsters**)

CADAVERS

The wilderness claims many victims, and few of them go gently into that good night or receive a proper sendoff. These **cadavers** number among them. The Aztli teenagers who transformed into these shambling undead abominations foolishly ingested saline swamp water while frolicking in a deep pond. The salt content made them delirious and dehydrated. When one of them fell into the pond and started to drown, the others leapt into the water and vainly tried to rescue him. In the end, they all perished and began their existence as cadavers. The cadavers burn with hatred and anger for all living creatures, especially adult humans who remind them of the lives prematurely denied to them. Despite their shared loathing, they never act in concert with their fellow monsters. Instead, each wildly rushes their opponent in a mad attempt to slash and bite them to death.

Cadavers (1d4+1): HD 2; **AC** 6[13]; **Atk** 2 claws (1d4 + disease), bite (1d6 + disease); **Move** 6; **Save** 16; **AL** C; **CL/XP** 4/120; **Special:** disease (1d4 damage, save resists), reanimation (regenerates 1 hp/round after death). (see **Appendix A: New Monsters**)

CIPATENHUAS

Cunning and clever, the predatory **2 cipatenhuas** and the **cipatenhua disciple** swim through the shallow, coastal waters searching for prey that blunder into their territory. Although they predominately hunt wayward vessels, the crocodilian, bipedal humanoids indiscriminately capture and kill any living creature unfortunate enough to enter their territory. They predominately stick to the rivers and streams bisecting their domain, though they occasionally take to land where their slippery, greenish skin blends into their surroundings remarkably well. The vicious humanoids never flee or surrender.

Treasure: Each cipatenhua carries a greatclub and keeps a pouch containing 1d4 decorative mussel shells (worth 10 gp each) on a belt wrapped around their waists. The disciple has two pink pearls (worth 100 gp each) in a pouch affixed to his belt.

Cipatenhuas (2): HD 3; **AC** 7[12]; **Atk** 2 claws (1d4) and bite (1d6) or weapon (1d6) and bite (1d6); **Move** 12 (swim 12); **Save** 14; **AL** C; **CL/XP** 3/60; **Special:** camouflage (1-in-6 chance to spot), cursed (must remain on wet land or 1d6 damage every 10 minutes). (see **Appendix A: New Monsters**)

Cipatenhua Disciple of Tsathogga: HD 6; **AC** 7[12] or 2[17] (missile) and 4[15] (melee) from *shield* spell; **Atk** 2 claws (1d4) and bite (1d6) or weapon (1d6) and bite (1d6); **Move** 12 (swim 12); **Save** 11; **AL** C; **CL/XP** 6/400; **Special:** camouflage (1-in-6 chance to spot), cursed (must remain on wet land or 1d6 damage every 10 minutes), spell-like ability, spells (4/2/2 MU), touch of madness (1/day, save or babble incoherently for 1d6+2 rounds). (see **Appendix A: New Monsters**)
Spell-like ability: 1/day—*polymorph self* (into giant frog)
Spells: 1st—*charm person, jinx*^c, *magic missile, shield*; 2nd—*invisibility, phantasmal force*; 3rd—*instill madness*^c, *hold person*.
^c See **Appendix C: New Spells**

CROCODILES

These reptilian predators lurk in the shallow waters, waiting for prey to enter their territory. The **crocodiles** remain underwater, using their stealth to quietly approach their victims before lashing out with their massive jaws. Like most wild animals searching for a meal, the beasts flee when seriously threatened or injured. They retreat below the water's surface and swim to safety.

Crocodiles (1d4): HD 3; **AC** 4[15]; **Atk** bite (1d6); **Move** 9 (swim 12); **Save** 14; **AL** N; **CL/XP** 3/60; **Special:** none. (*Monstrosities* 77)

GNOLLS

As the rumors suggest, the **gnolls** in the region are stepping up their game, though the scope of their activities seems modestly exaggerated. The aggressive humanoids lack the vision to consciously expand their footprint in the area, but their inability to grasp the big picture fails to abate their bloodlust. They forego any efforts to sneak up on their quarry and instead madly charge one or two designated opponents. They always concentrate their attacks on as few opponents as possible to increase the odds of quickly dropping that foe. Gnolls who are badly overmatched escape if possible. Characters who attempt to follow their tracks back to a lair lose the trail when the monsters trudge through several streams and other small bodies of water. The gnolls have no knowledge of Teohuacan's inner workings.

Gnolls (1d4): HD 2; **AC** 5[14]; **Atk** bite (2d4) or longsword (1d10); **Move** 9; **Save** 16; **AL** C; **CL/XP** 2/30; **Special:** none. (*Monstrosities* 209)
Equipment: longsword, 1d3 obsidian stones (10 gp each), 2d10 gp.

JACULUS

Although this small, light-brown dragon has feathered wings to propel it in flight, the creature is more adept at leaping than flying. The **jaculus** uses its powerful back legs to scale mangrove trees, where it makes its abode. While not brilliant by draconic standards, the monster exhibits tremendous cunning. When it spots a shiny object or other item that catches its fancy, the jaculus formulates its plan to steal the object from its unworthy owner. It may use its stealth and its darkvision to creep up during the night on a sleeping target and wrest the item from its possession while in a deep slumber. Alternatively, it can pretend to offer the characters assistance by relaying one or more of the prevalent rumors circulating throughout the region or fabricate a story the adventurers may want to hear. In this circumstance, the jaculus may provide the preceding information to acquire the object it covets as part of a bargain, or it may use the ruse to gain the characters' trust and make a bigger score after lulling them into a false sense of security. When forcibly confronted over its thievery, the jaculus stands and fights rather than making a futile attempt to outrun its adversaries or slowly fly to safety. The monster's bite and claws pack quite the punch for a creature of its small size. The naturally treacherous and suspicious jaculus never travels far from its arboreal lair carved into the trunk of a mangrove or other species of tree.

Jaculus: HD 5; **AC** 4[15]; **Atk** bite (2d6), 2 claws (1d6); **Move** 9 (fly 12, climb 9) or 30ft leap; **Save** 12; **AL** C; **CL/XP** 5/240; **Special:** charge (successful bite after 10ft move deals additional 1d6 bite damage, save avoids), darkvision (60ft), immune to electricity, leap (30ft). (see **Appendix A: New Monsters**)

Treasure: The jaculus keeps a *potion of healing* within an abscess inside the tree's trunk. It also stores three deep green jade stones (worth 100 gp each) and an amber brooch (worth 50 gp) in the same location.

ORCS

Orcs frequently imitate the bloody rituals conducted in other humanoid cultures. These cruel humanoids took to the practice of human sacrifice like ducks to water. The deadly rites performed by the Aztlis and other indigenous peoples carry an important religious significance, whereas the orcs seem to partake in this endeavor solely to satisfy their lust for violence. In furtherance of this end, an **orc sacrificial priest** accompanies his fellow **orcs** on their quest to find new victims to sacrifice. They gladly slaughter any sentient being as an offering to their gods, though they take fiendish delight disemboweling elves. Like most of their kind, these orcs retreat back into the swamp when seriously threatened by an obviously superior foe. They often target hunters and fishermen trekking through the wilderness to find game and a productive fishing hole, though they generally remain on the outskirts of town. Nonetheless, if compelled to speak, the orcs tell the characters that they noticed several strange beasts resembling filthy, oversized coyotes wandering through the swamp over the last few weeks.

Orcs (2d4): HD 1; **AC** 6[13]; **Atk** spear (1d6) or scimitar (1d8); **Move** 9; **Save** 17; **AL** C; **CL/XP** 1/15; **Special:** none. (*Monstrosities* 364)
Orc Sacrificial Priest: HD 4; **AC** 5[14]; **Atk** *+1 dagger* (1d4+1); **Move** 9; **Save** 13; **AL** C; **CL/XP** 4/120; **Special:** spells (2). (*Monstrosities* 364)
Spells: 1st—*cause light wounds, detect good*.
Equipment: *+1 ceremonial obsidian dagger* (150 gp), scroll (*detect magic, hold person*).

Swamp Troll

Despite its size, this **swamp troll**, nicknamed Fish Breath by the locals, moves through the shallow water and soggy earth with surprising agility. The large, hulking brute uses its long, thick arms and legs to propel it through the water, while the sharp, filthy claws at the end of its appendages give it added traction when walking and serve as highly effective weapons. The moss and fungus covering its body, in addition to its dark brownish-green hair, allow it to blend into its surroundings, giving the remarkably nimble monster an opportunity to ambush opponents at a predetermined site or more likely to sneak up on them while they slog through the difficult terrain. The giant generally keeps a healthy distance between itself and the town of Teohuacan. Therefore, any confrontation with the swamp troll likely occurs in remote wilderness areas. However, the brute is clever enough to stalk the paths and roads leading to and from the settlements scattered throughout the region, where it exhibits no qualms killing and eating an inhabitant who wanders into its territory. Regardless of the encounter's circumstances, the swamp troll beats a hasty retreat if the characters seriously threaten its wretched existence. Because it can move through the swamp without impediment, the swamp troll stands a good chance of outrunning its pursuers. Following its tracks back to its lair through the waterlogged terrain proves virtually impossible, because the giant frequently swims atop the waterways crisscrossing the landscape. However, if the adventurers discover its hillock lair, they also locate the bulk of its treasure.

Fish Breath, Swamp Troll: HD 3; AC 3[16]; **Atk** 2 claws (1d6), bite (1d8); **Move** 12; **Save** 14; **AL** C; **CL/XP** 3/60; **Special:** surprise (1–2 on 1d6), swamp dependent (suffocate after 10 hours away from water). (see **Appendix A: New Monsters**)

Treasure: The giant conceals an alderwood chest in its lair beneath a layer of silt and sediment on its hillock. The unlocked device contains a *potion of fire resistance* and four *+1 arrows* as well as a bronze Aztli statue (worth 150 gp).

Teohuacan Area Set Encounters

The adventure focuses on the town of Teohuacan and its calmecac, but other residents have established permanent lairs in the surrounding area. The most noteworthy of these structures is the cipatenhua stronghold just north of the Elcomatl River. The location appears on the regional map, but it is detailed in the supplemental adventure *The Hidden Shrine of Tmocanotz*, as it is not central to this story. Other creatures have also established smaller footholds in the untamed wilderness outside of the Aztlis' influence. The following section details these areas.

Area O: Ozhuma's Cave

The hermitic magician **Ozhuma** lives in a secluded cave 2–1/2 miles east of Teohuacan amid a dense tangle of mangrove shrubs and hillocks off the trail leading from Teohuacan to the coast. The devious warlock occasionally ventures to the island's shore to harvest food from the sea or to salvage treasure from the shipwrecks in the shallow depths near the beach. However, the infrequency of these jaunts and the conditions in the swamp make it extremely difficult to pick up the trail connecting his isolated cave to the path leading to the sea. The only other clue pointing toward Ozhuma's residence lies with the characters' knowledge of the area and their understanding of geology. A character has a 1-in-6 chance to recall an elevated rock formation ideally suited for an aboveground cave, if the character already reasoned that Ozhuma could not reside in a submerged cavern. Otherwise, adventurers seeking an audience with the reclusive man must bumble their way through the mass of shrubs, trees, and ponds surrounding his humble abode.

If the characters successfully locate Ozhuma's cave, you may read or paraphrase the following description:

> The soggy ground reaches a mild elevation and culminates in a formation of rocks and stones resembling a hemispherical mound. Periodic wisps of smoke rise out of its western face.

Characters facing the cave's western side obviously see the entrance into the small chamber, while those viewing the mound from a different direction likely deduce where to find the opening by following the trail of smoke emanating from the cavity. The wily Ozhuma keeps a hawk that always circles the area around his lair searching for prey and potential intruders. While awake, which is generally from noon until the early morning hours, Ozhuma intermittently telepathically communicates with the hawk or views his surroundings through the bird's eyes. Alternatively, if he hears someone or something approaching, he may cast *clairvoyance* to monitor the trespasser's activities. If the creature poses an obvious threat, he casts *hallucinatory terrain* just outside the entrance to his cave to slow their progress while still allowing him to escape his abode without hindrance. The hermit exercises extreme caution when strangers draw near, though he may not necessarily attack intruders. If the visitor interests him, he may converse with the creature to gain knowledge about outside activities or simply to pique his curiosity. He sets a tripwire at night to alert him if any large creatures pass within 30 feet of the cave entrance.

If the adventurers peer into his cavern, read or paraphrase the following description:

> The dying embers from a fire sporadically belch out puffs of smoke that dance into the musty air. A makeshift rotisserie stands above the small tongues of fire. Pools of groundwater seep to the surface, forming several small puddles on the soggy, earthen floor. Moldy scraps of leather and fur likely function as a crude bed. Niches cut into the walls contain the bleached skulls of several animal species, while an assortment of jars, beakers, and vials sits atop a circular bench along the far wall.

Characters who approach Ozhuma's cave with weapons drawn and spells at the ready force the recluse to take defensive actions. If he uses a potion to turn invisible and uses *ESP* to gauge the characters' intentions or, depending on the circumstances, he overtly threatens them. He is not keen on fighting the characters, though he does so if necessary, using his spells to fend off the intruders. Ozhuma only takes an interest in creatures with an affinity for animals, such as druids, rangers, and, of course, lycanthropes. He generally ignores everyone else and demands they leave his abode.

However, if the characters get his attention, the curmudgeon becomes surprisingly talkative, especially during discussions about animals. The normally reserved hermit divulges tales of mythical serpent warriors having no bearing on this adventure, though the rumor proves true in one of the later adventures in the series. If the subject veers onto Coyotl, the formerly gregarious Ozhuma returns to his aloof demeanor. He evasively responds to questions about the young man. Nonetheless, a character who persists may pry some information from Ozhuma to learn that the young man visited the hermit several months ago. He further reveals that the teenager suffered from lycanthropy, which gave him the power to transform into a coyote and an enhanced affinity to interact with the roguish canines. Ozhuma has no additional information about Coyotl's actions or whereabouts after their meeting several months ago.

Ozhuma, Male Aztli Hermit Magic-User (MU7): HP 21; AC 9[10] or 2[17] (missile) and 4[15] (melee) from *shield* spell; **Atk** *staff of striking* (2d6); **Move** 12; **Save** 9; **AL** N; **CL/XP** 8/800; **Special:** +2 save (spells, wands, staffs), spells (4/3/2/1), telepathic link with hawk familiar (up to 2 miles).
Spells: 1st—*light, magic missile, shield, sleep*; 2nd—*ESP, phantasmal force, web*; 3rd—*fly, lightning bolt*; 4th—*hallucinatory terrain*.
Equipment: hide robes, *staff of striking, ring of protection +1, potion of invisibility*, scroll of *wall of ice*.

Treasure: The jars, beakers, and vials (worth 150 gp) on the bench contain an eclectic variety of animal byproducts such as hair, powdered bone, assorted organ tissues, and blood collected from several species. Ozhuma also has three *potions of healing* interspersed among the other items, as well as a packet of *dust of sneezing and choking*.

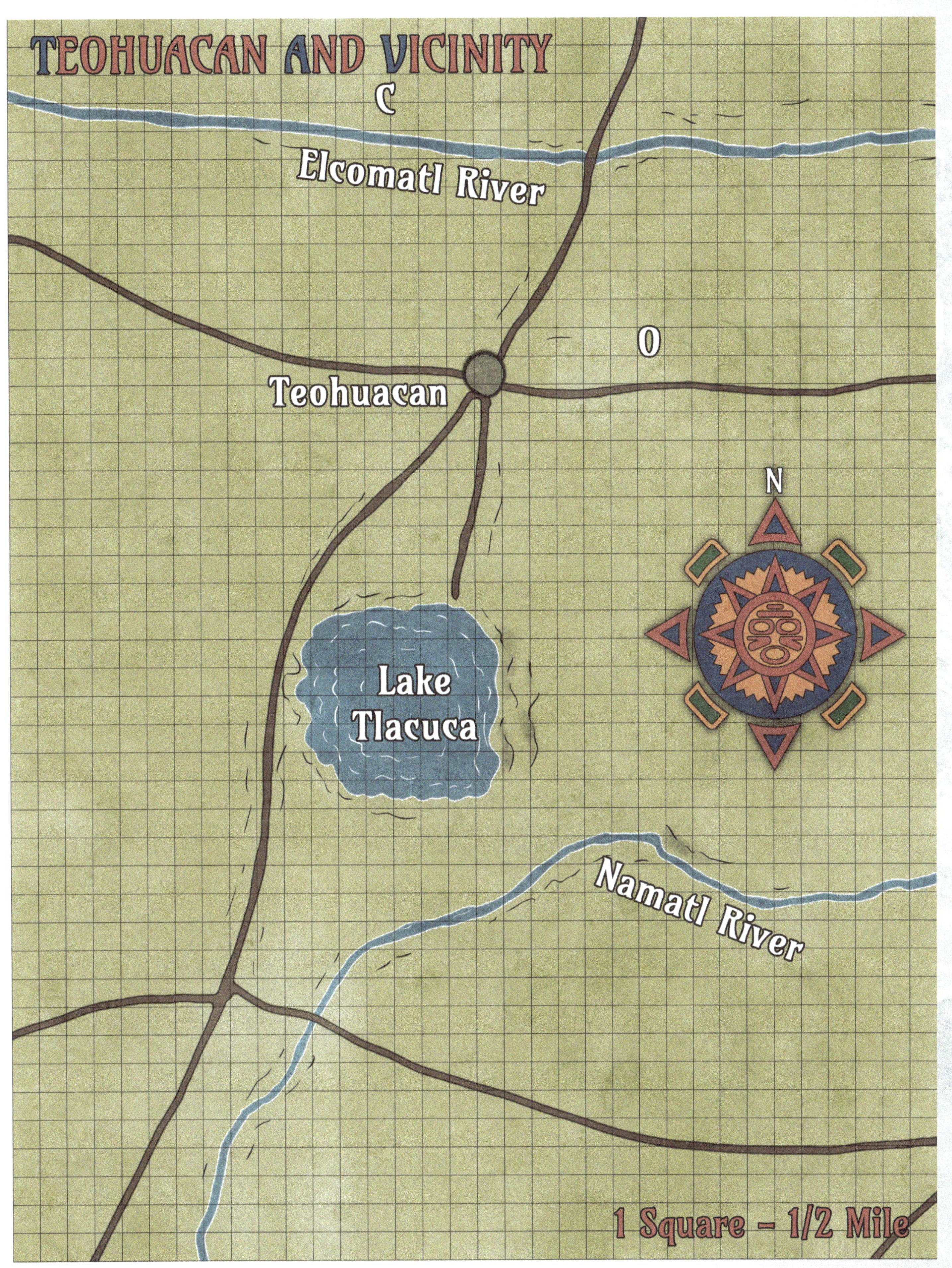

TEOHUACAN AND VICINITY
C
Elcomatl River
O
Teohuacan
N
Lake
Tlacuca
Namatl River
1 Square – 1/2 Mile

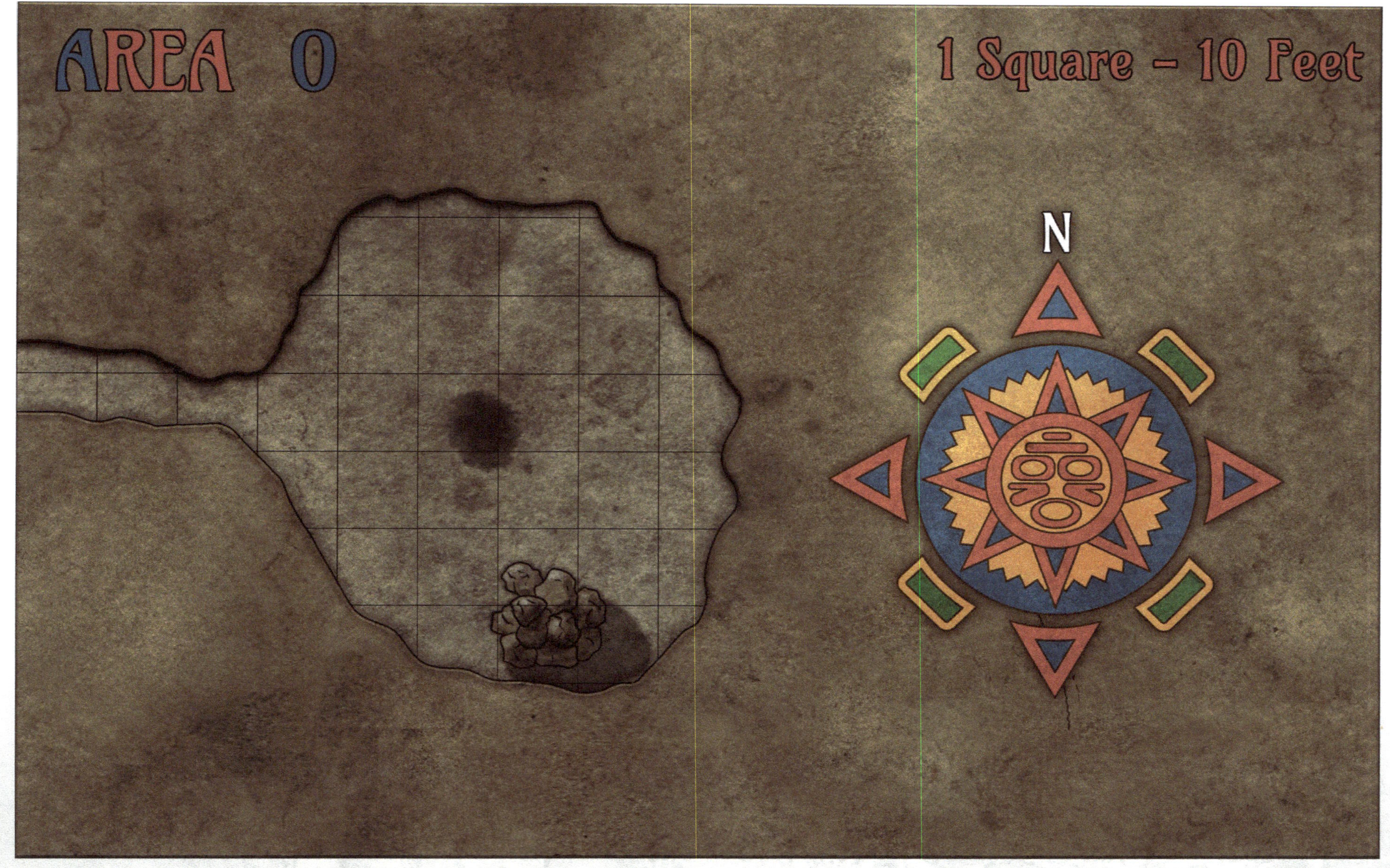

AREA 0
1 Square - 10 Feet
N

TEOHUACAN

Roughly 160 years ago, Aztli migrants founded Teohuacan atop the site of a drying lake bed. Local legends credit Teohuacan's birth to the visions of Caxto, an elderly priest of Quiahuitl. The tale claims the god directed his emissary to erect a temple in his honor on this site in his final, vivid dream before he passed on to the next world. Like many other Aztli communities, its ingenious builders used chinampas to lay the groundwork for their burgeoning settlement in a marginally hospitable land.

Today, Teohuacan is the hub of civilization in this section of the Izmalli Swamp. Situated near the Elcomatl and Namatl Rivers as well as Lake Tlacuca, the town of 1,102 residents is the largest settlement in the region. Aztlis make up a significant majority of the population, with a few pockets of elves, gnomes, and halflings living among their human counterparts. Most lead a frugal existence living off the land, harvesting maize, tomatoes, avocados, and squash in their gardens while supplementing their diets with fish harvested from the nearby lake and rivers as well as waterfowl and other domesticated birds such as chickens and turkeys. Although not peasants in the typical medieval sense, the farmers who till the fields do so on property theoretically owned by the distant Aztli Confederation. Despite working and living on the same land for generations, the families who dwell in the community have no legal rights to the ground beneath their feet.

While Teohuacan and the surrounding communities fall under the dominion of the Aztli Confederation, the quartet of ruling city-states exerts little influence over the remote settlement in the heart of an overgrown wetland. Instead, jurisdiction over legal, economic, and military matters falls upon the local authorities, most notably **Mintoch**, the high priest of Quiahuitl who serves as the town's spiritual and political ruler. The temple of Quiahuitl is a three-level step pyramid decorated with seashells and iconography associated with its divine patron. Religious ceremonies take place atop its highest level, which includes a stone arch resembling the boundaries of a tidal wave and an altar where the high priest and his underlings offer feathers, maize, seashells, and an occasional animal sacrifice to their chosen deity.

Mintoch, Male Aztli Priest of Quiahuitl (Clr6): HP 28; AC 8[11]; **Atk** club (1d4); **Move** 12; **Save** 10; **AL** L; **CL/XP** 6/400; **Special:** +2 save vs. paralysis and poison, banish undead, spells (2/2/1/1).
Spells: 1st—*cure light wounds, protection from evil*; 2nd—*bless, hold person.*
Equipment: ichcahuipilli armor[B], club.
[B] See **Appendix B: New Equipment and Magic Items**

Mintoch leads a force of **26 jaguar warriors** complemented by a retinue of **6 priests** who reside in large residences just outside the temple grounds. They primarily function as temple guards who enforce the temple's edicts and moral code throughout Teohuacan rather than serving as the backbone for a professional army. Every adult male in Teohuacan has some martial combat training. Therefore, these citizen-soldiers make up the vast majority of Teohuacan's military forces, though the jaguar warriors associated with the temple typically lead the town's citizens into battle.

Aztli Jaguar Warriors (26): HD 4; AC 6[13]; **Atk** macuahuitl (1d6) or javelin (1d6); **Move** 12; **Save** 13; **AL** N; **CL/XP** 4/120; **Special:** none.
Equipment: cipacahuipilli armor[B], macuahuitl[B], 4 javelins, hide bag containing 4 cacao beans.

Temple Priests of Quiahuitl (Clr2) (6): HP 12, 10x2, 9, 8x2; AC 7[12]; **Atk** mace (1d6); **Move** 12; **Save** 14; **AL** N; **CL/XP** 2/30; **Special:** +2 save vs. paralysis and poison, banish undead, spells (1).
Spells: 1st—*cure light wounds.*
Equipment: tlahuiztli armor[B], mace
[B] See **Appendix B: New Equipment and Magic Items**

Despite the looming rain festival celebration, the temple of Nonotzali located on the calmecac grounds has fallen silent, leaving Mintoch and his underlings to singlehandedly welcome citizens and visitors from other communities. This unexpected development sends the already irritable high priest into a grouchier mood than normal. The taciturn high priest appears at a loss for words about the situation, especially when the four jaguar warriors he dispatched to investigate the matter never returned. Although Mintoch has no verbal answers for the problems besetting Teohuacan, he has not sat still. He sent six jaguar warriors, whom he still awaits to return, into the surrounding wilderness to gather sacrifices for the festivities, including a jaguar. The high priest fervently believes that the offerings and freshly spilled blood will bring relief to the troubled settlement.

The temple currently serves as the town's seat of power, but most activity centers on the bustling marketplace. Business is usually brisk in Teohuacan's open-air shops. Local farmers, trappers, and hunters sell their products from makeshift stands, while professional traders dealing in exotic goods such as cacao, agave, and rare bird feathers occupy permanent stalls within the marketplace. The upcoming festival has the marketplace in a tizzy, as visitors and residents scour the shelves for the best deals. Shoppers with attentive ears can also overhear or solicit the town's juiciest gossip, especially as it pertains to events in the local calmecac.

RUMORS

Characters who interact with the peddlers or their customers may learn some useful information. Of course, the character must be able to effectively communicate with the person, and that individual must have some knowledge of current events within Teohuacan. Characters can sense the person's apprehension and nervousness when discussing events at the neighboring calmecac:

No one has seen or heard from their children in the calmecac for the last several weeks. Although the teenagers usually remain sequestered behind its walls, visitors approaching the institution's walls have been met with snarling coyotes and mysterious beasts who block entry into the calmecac.

The temple of Nonotzali on the calmecac grounds also fell silent. Aloc, its high priest, has had no contact with the temple of Quiahuitl regarding the upcoming rain festival, leading many visitors and residents alike to wonder aloud about the reason for the unexpected schism between the normally cooperative priesthoods.

Mintoch dispatched several jaguar warriors to infiltrate the calmecac. These experienced soldiers never returned. Some claim to have heard bloodcurdling screams only a few minutes after they scaled the compound's walls.

Although no one has set foot on the calmecac's grounds since the strange events began, residents occasionally hear humanoid voices and other sounds from inside the complex's walls.

If you keep your eyes and ears open, you may be able to purchase peyote in the marketplace.

DEALERS OR NO DEALERS

Aztli society frowns upon public intoxication, especially among women and children. Despite these stigmas, some believe ingesting the hallucinogenic cactus opens a channel to the Miquito (the domain of the dead) or the gods themselves. **Four jaguar warriors** patrol the marketplace to deter thieves from stealing wares off the shelves as well as to protect the buying public from price gougers and unscrupulous peddlers. Transgressors face a merciless legal system renowned for its cruel and unusual punishments ranging from barbaric forms of execution for egregious crimes to a lengthy stint in the peticalli, the Aztlis' notoriously harsh penitentiary. Minor or petty offenses may require the perpetrator to pay restitution to the aggrieved party or to become that person's slave.

Aztli Jaguar Warriors (4): HP 28, 27, 24, 20; AC 6[13]; **Atk** macuahuitl (1d6) or javelin (1d6); **Move** 12; **Save** 13; **AL** N; **CL/XP** 4/120; **Special:** none.
Equipment: cipacahuipilli armor[B], macuahuitl[B], 4 javelins, hide bag containing 4 cacao beans.
[B] See **Appendix B: New Equipment and Magic Items**

Despite these obvious hazards, four young men move through the marketplace subtly hinting that they may have peyote for sale. The four teenagers — Cuapac, Ichtli, Toltuma, and Yatli — are students at the calmecac who serve as Coyotl's operatives within Teohuacan. The young men discreetly avoid friends and family while disguised as traveling merchants. If the character has firsthand knowledge of the young men from living in the town or from spending a considerable amount of time in Teohuacan, he has a 75% chance to see through their disguise.

Cuapac, Ichtli, Toltuma, and Yatli, Male Aztli (Thf2): HP 5 each; AC 7[12]; **Atk** club (1d4) or sling (1d4); **Move** 12; **Save** 14; **AL** C L N; **CL/XP** 2/30; **Special:** +2 save bonus vs. traps and magical devices, backstab (x2), read languages, thieving skills.
Thieving Skills: Climb 86%, Tasks/Traps 20%, Hear 3 in 6, Hide 15%, Silent 25%, Locks 15%.
Equipment: leather armor, club, sling, 10 sling bullets.

The teenagers feign being peyote dealers because it gives them a pretense to lure a prospective buyer outside of town to conduct the illicit transaction. However, their main goal is to eavesdrop on conversations taking place within the marketplace to gauge the community's resolve regarding the mysterious events at the calmecac. When they overhear someone talking about the calmecac, the quartet subtly take interest in the conversation. Likewise, the sudden appearance of adventurers asking residents and visitors alike about the institution also attracts their full attention.

Toltuma, the oldest member of the group that ranges in age from 15 to 17, has a glib tongue and a shrewd mind. He suspects adventurers have no interest in buying peyote. Instead, he plays the role of double agent, claiming he has been secretly communicating with his brother who still resides in the calmecac. Naturally, Toltuma cannot discuss the intelligence he has gathered out in the open. If the characters want his intelligence, he insists on meeting them on the outskirts of town, where his cohorts wait to ambush them at a predetermined, overgrown swampy location. The site offers ample cover to the trio of spies who conceal themselves amid the dense vegetation surrounding a brackish, 40-foot-diameter pond of shallow water. Toltuma wades into the ankle-deep water that seems more like a nuisance than a hazard. However, the muddy water conceals numerous mangrove roots and branches. Any creature, including Toltuma, who moves into or within the pond must make a saving throw to avoid getting snagged and falling prone into the water.

Characters who thwart Toltuma and his cronies may interrogate the teenagers. Despite their youth, Coyotl's loyalists bite their tongues at every turn. Because of their steadfastness, they resist attempts to pry information from their lips. If the characters make them talk, the teenagers reveal that Coyotl, a shapeshifting coyote, murdered his upperclassman brother and then wrested control of the calmecac from the temple of Nonotzali's clergy. Students who pledged their loyalty to Coyotl and the institution's new divine master, Itzcuin, revel in their newfound liberation. Youngsters who openly defied Coyotl met a fitting end on the sacrificial altar, while those who seemed less than enthusiastic about the werecoyote's ascendance are supposedly going to be trained to be more bestial, though the quartet remain uncertain about the terminology's cryptic meaning.

Treasure: Toltuma and each of his associates carries a small leather bag filled with eagle feathers (worth 2d6 gp each) that they stole from the temple of Nonotzali within the calmecac compound. A character can identify the objects as being associated with Nonotzali. Toltuma also has a *rope of climbing*, a magic item he uses to scale the calmecac walls when necessary.

OTHER SITES

While the temple and marketplace attract the most attention from residents and visitors alike, the town boasts several other noteworthy sites. The tzompantli may be the most gruesome of these locales, especially for characters unfamiliar with Aztli culture. This device resembles an upright, modern tennis racket with a rectangular frame. The strings sewn into the object's brackets hold skulls belonging to fallen enemies, sacrificial victims, and notorious criminals, with as many as 15 of these heads dangling on a single thread. However, most of these macabre display pieces came from the team who lost a match in the neighboring tlachtli, the court used to play ullamaloni, the Aztli ball sport. The field is a long, narrow chute surrounded by high sloped walls culminating in a broad platform where spectators watch the festivities. Two teams participate in a sport similar to modern racquetball or tennis, where each side lobs a rubber ball back and forth until the ball bounces twice on one team's section of the playing field. The contestants cannot strike the ball with any body part above their waist, though some variations of the game allow players to hit the ball with a rounded, wooden paddle or a long, wooden stick. The excitement and thrill of competition makes the sport a popular pastime among the populace, who venerate its most successful and beloved competitors. Gamblers frequently wager on the contest's outcome. The sport's governing body of several noblemen and acolytes added a wrinkle into the game to safeguard its integrity, with a randomly chosen member of their contingent drawing one of four tiles from a sealed bag at the end of each contest. Three of the ceramic tiles are blank, while the remaining tile bears the image of a skull. Whenever this tile is chosen, the temple of Quiahuitl sacrifices the members of the losing team to their god. The organizers believe this disincentive prevents bettors from bribing participants to intentionally lose a game.

Matches always begin at noon. The typical day's card features two contests, but with the impending rain festival ceremony, visiting teams from other communities have swelled the participants' ranks to allow for five individual contests. One of these includes a visiting team from neighboring Ollitl. Their entourage includes an amoral scoundrel named **Nezcapa**. A **card shark** accompanies him. This strange, shapeshifting creature can take the form of any small object. Earlier in the day, the monster assumed the likeness of the death tile before being placed into the bag. Prior to the match featuring the Ollitl team, the card shark polymorphs into an ordinary tile, thereby eliminating any chance of selecting the death tile and removing the potentially dire consequences for intentionally throwing a match. With his scheme in place, Nezcapa bets heavily on the visiting team from Ollitl, whom he has bribed to intentionally lose their match in dramatic fashion to their presumably inferior opponents, giving the cagey gambler an even larger payoff.

Nezcapa, Male Aztli Thug: HP 37; AC 7[12]; **Atk** club (1d4+1) or shortbow x2 (1d6); **Move** 12; **Save** 13; **AL** C; **CL/XP** 4/120; **Special:** none.
Equipment: leather armor, club, shortbow, 20 arrows.

Card Shark: HD 3; HP 20; AC 6[13]; **Atk** card slice (1d4); **Move** 6; **Save** 16; **AL** C; **CL/XP** 4/120; **Special:** drain host (with each use of luck, initial 1d4 damage), immune to sleep and charm, luck (host has 95% chance of success at games of chance), shapechange, spell-like abilities, vulnerable to fire (200% damage). (see **Appendix A: New Monsters**)
Spell-like abilities: 1/day—*invisibility*.

Characters observing the contest have a 5% chance per level to sense that Ollitl's participants oddly seem complacent and unafraid considering the high stakes. Furthermore, a character who observes Nezcapa during the match has a 1-in-6 chance to notice that he exudes overconfidence in his response to the action unfolding on the ball court. His attitude would be logical if his hometown team were comfortably winning, yet he seems certain his team is going to lose despite their opponents' lesser abilities. Despite risking everything he owns on one game, Nezcapa acts too nonchalantly for the situation when considering he bet his entire fortune on the prohibitive underdogs.

Suspicious and clever adventurers may thwart Nezcapa's ruse in creative ways. For instance, a *detect magic* spell cast on the contents of the leather bag reveals the presence of a sentient mind among the inanimate objects. The character may also examine the tiles in the bag, though the intelligent card shark transforms into the death tile when it becomes aware of the characters' intentions by perhaps overhearing them discuss their plans or by emptying the bag's contents in an unexpected manner. Fighting is not the card shark's forte. When caught in a bind, the wily creature blames its unwitting host for the deception, implying that it is a mere pawn in its dubious game. Of course, it gladly offers its services to a potential new host. When faced with an unreceptive audience, the card shark flees at the first opportunity by leaping onto a passerby and disguising itself as an ordinary personal item.

With his scheme in tatters, Nezcapa feigns ignorance, claiming he had "inside knowledge" about the game's predetermined outcome, though he denies using the card shark to rig the contest. Unfortunately for him, the card shark happily throws its co-conspirator to the wolves to save itself. When weighing the evidence, the game's organizers focus on motive. The card shark gained no direct benefit from its role, while Nezcapa made a fortune on his wagers. In the end, Nezcapa faces swift and merciless Aztli justice for his crimes, along with the complicit team members.

The Calmecac

Teohuacan develops its future warriors, leaders, and artisans within the imposing walls of the community's premiere learning institution, which sits roughly one-quarter mile beyond the eastern edge of the town proper. The Aztlis built the calmecac on this sequestered piece of land surrounded by streams and rivers to reinforce the students' notions of independence from their friends and families outside the school. The stone walls surrounding the complex add to this ideal. The barriers are intended to prevent external teachings from influencing its students, which in turn allows its teachers to impart a uniform, uncorrupted curriculum regarding Aztli religious beliefs, ideals, and morality. The 10-foot-high outer walls surrounding the calmecac primarily serve a symbolic rather than a military purpose. When the characters approach the locale, read or paraphrase the following description:

entrance cut into the south wall offers a glimpse inside of the compound. The constant drone of buzzing insects drowns out most sounds, though an occasional bark or howl emanating from behind the compound's walls occasionally pierces the monotony.

Only a handful of trees and bushes surrounding the complex reach a height of more than 30 feet, but these woody giants provide ample cover for the **3 mobats** concealed amid the tangle of twisted branches, leaves, and roots. The monstrosities occupy these perches only during daylight hours. Because they have ample time to hide, characters have a 1-in-6 chance to spot the monsters even from close range. The mobats circle the skies around the calmecac at night. Because they rely upon echolocation rather than sight to detect prey, invisibility has no effect on the mobats.

Mobats (3): HD 4; HP 30, 26, 21; AC 3[16]; **Atk** bite (1d8); **Move** 9 (fly 15); **Save** 13; **AL** N; **CL/XP** 6/400; **Special:** sonic screech (3/day, 20ft spread, fail or stunned for 1d3 rounds). (see **Appendix A: New Monsters**)

The semi-intelligent mobats defend the calmecac at the behest of Coyotl and his divine patron Itzcuin. However, the creatures have no profound loyalty to either individual. If the battle turns against them, the winged beasts take to the skies and flee deeper into the swamp, likely never to return here again. Although the characters may perceive the mobats as guards, the calmecac's disorganized residents view them as creatures of opportunity. The commotion of a battle raging outside their walls fails to rouse the unorganized students from their self-imposed stupor.

After defeating or circumventing the mobats, the characters may approach the calmecac's outer walls. The 10-foot-high obstacles are more symbolic than practical lines of defense. The wooden gate on its southern face is the only portal that grants passage through the wall. A character can climb over this impediment or force it open with a successful Open Doors check.

When the characters enter the compound or peek through the gate, read or paraphrase the following description:

Calmecac Encounters

The characters' incursion onto the school grounds triggers multiple responses from the inhabitants who roam through the courtyard at various points during the day and night. The best way to adjudicate these reactions is to present them in waves. Although the numbers may initially seem overwhelming, some of the combatants are likely to flee at the first sign of adversity or pose very little real danger to seasoned adventurers. By staggering the encounters, the characters get an opportunity to recoup and regroup between battles rather than be inundated by seemingly endless horde of enemies to fight. This approach gives the characters an opportunity to explore their surroundings and learn more about the calmecac between engagements without any consequences for doing so.

CALMECAC

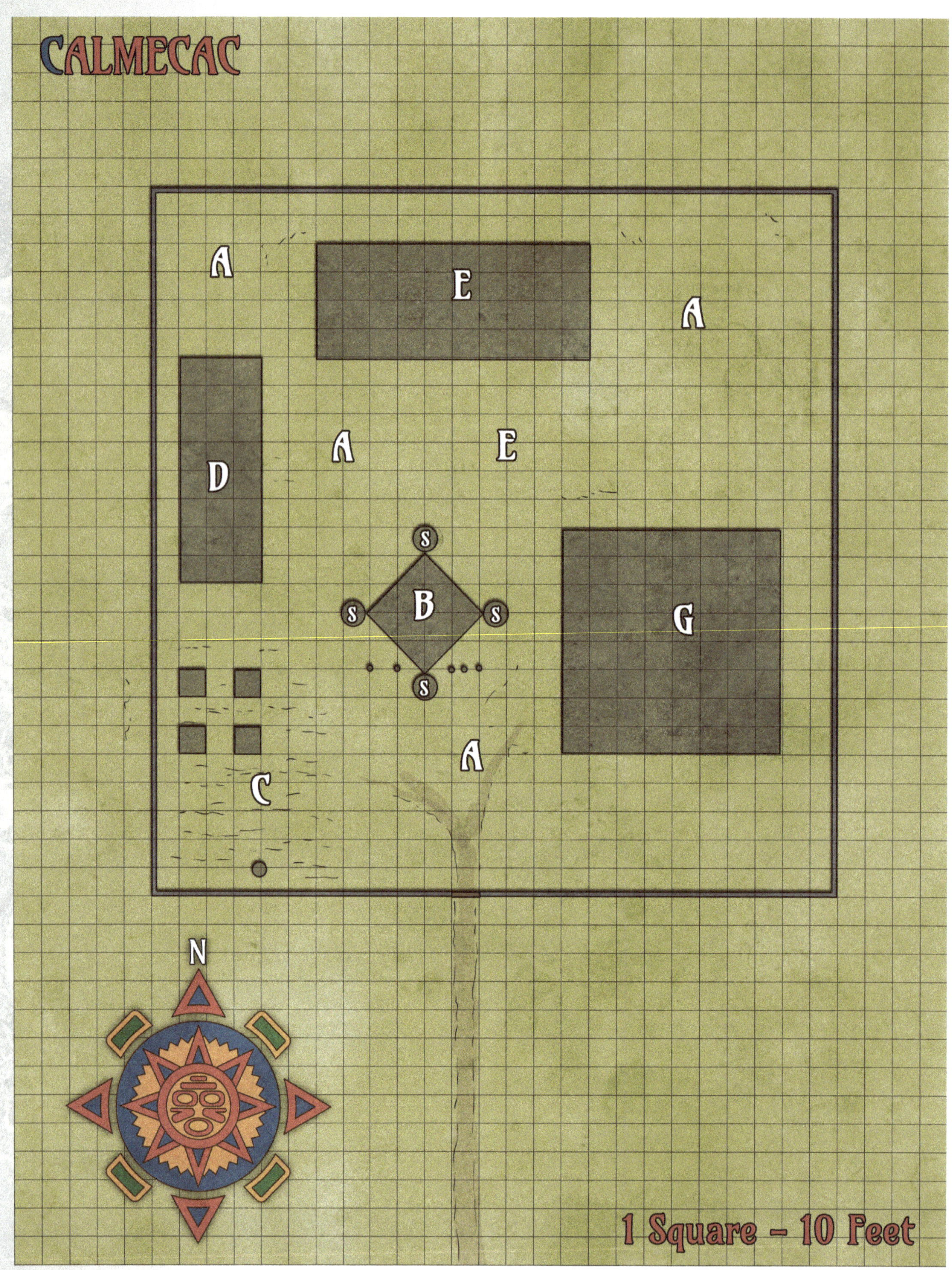

While circumventing the barrier poses little problem for adventurers, the gates and walls are not wholly unattended. Two packs of **6 coyotes** roam the grounds searching for intruders. When the animals detect an unfamiliar scent or see someone they do not recognize, the beasts loudly yip, bark, and howl. The canines attack the trespassers, though the coyotes hastily retreat after sustaining a wound. The ruckus attracts the attention of **3 beasts of Itzcuin** that arrive on the scene within 1d4 rounds to investigate the disturbance.

Coyotes (6): HD 1; HP 7, 6x2, 5, 4x2; AC 7[12]; **Atk** bite (1d3); **Move** 16; **Save** 17; **AL** N; **CL/XP** 1/15; **Special:** none.

Beasts of Itzcuin (3): HD 2; HP 14, 12, 11; AC 7[12]; **Atk** bite (1d3 + disease); **Move** 15; **Save** 16; **AL** C; **CL/XP** 3/60; **Special:** darkvision (60ft), disease (save or 1d4 damage per day, healing ends damage), misfortune (1/day, save or –1 penalty to hit and saves for 24 hours) (see **Appendix A: New Monsters**)

In addition to the animals and beasts wandering around inside the compound's walls, **4 students** who submitted to Coyotl's will immediately after his takeover of the school haphazardly oversee the calmecac's defenses. The youngsters have some combat training, though they are not as adept as Coyotl's operatives in Teohuacan. The teenagers' most noticeable features are their disheveled, bestial appearances and the wild expressions on their faces. The outwardly feral children lurch and gallop around the area as if they were emulating the gait of the animals moving among them. Instead of summoning reinforcements, the students violently confront the characters, charging at them with greater abandon than the beasts of Itzcuin.

The four males — Ayohua, Cequi, Nayohua, and Palan — range in age from 11 to 14. Despite their noble upbringing, they behave more like crazed dogs than Aztli scions. They bark, growl, and yip like their canine counterparts, while interspersing some coherent speech amid their bestial sounds. During their brief moments of lucidity, they shout, "Bite the hands and necks that feed you!" Unlike their coyote counterparts, these youngsters never retreat even in the face of imminent death. If the characters capture any of the boys, they sit down and intentionally lapse into a near-catatonic state. They say absolutely nothing and are content to sit still for hours. However, the characters can possibly pry information out of the reluctant child.

If intimidated or convinced to talk, the frightened teenager finally breaks down. He admits that Coyotl, whom he describes as a man-beast, murdered the acolytes and Aloc, the high priest of Nonotzali. They now worship Itzcuin, Nonotzali's younger, bestial brother. He also grudgingly admits that Coyotl's serves a cacao drink to his most reluctant followers in the belief that the liquid will instill bestial qualities in the young boys and men.

Ayohua, Cequi, Nayohua, and Palan, Male Aztli youths (4): HP 3 each; AC 9[10]; **Atk** club (1d4) or sling (1d4); **Move** 12; **Save** 18; **AL** C; **CL/XP** B/10; **Special:** none. (**Monstrosities** 254)
Equipment: club, sling, 10 sling bullets.

Characters who linger too long in the compound's courtyard unexpectedly meet one of the calmecac's latest terrors: a malevolent **wahuapa** that dwells among the ordinary maize plants. This bloodthirsty plant creature is a new addition to the calmecac, joining the compound's ranks after blood poured onto the soil around the maize plant triggered its transformation into a wahuapa. Itzcuin aided the strange creature's metamorphosis, ensuring its allegiance to the dark god. The sentient creature patiently watches and waits for an ideal time to strike, preferably while the characters are distracted investigating other areas of the courtyard or if they fortuitously wander into its territory. Alternately, the wahuapa may also entangle the characters to preoccupy them. Despite possessing some intelligence, the monster cannot effectively communicate with other creatures. It obeys simple commands, but it cannot converse with the characters.

Wahuapa (Maizefolk): HD 7; HP 46; AC 7[12]; **Atk** 2 claws (1d6 + blood meal); **Move** 9; **Save** 9; **AL** N; **CL/XP** 8/800; **Special:** blood meal (save or additional 1d4 damage, wahuapa gains hit points equal to damage), camouflage (1-in-6 chance to spot while standing still in maizefield), entangle (3/day, plants grow in 10ft radius within 60ft range, save or restrained, Open Doors check to escape). (see **Appendix A: New Monsters**)

The sounds of another combat are unlikely to evoke any coordinated response from Coyotl's subjects. They are either too lazy or disinterested to quickly investigate any disturbances in the courtyard. Nonetheless, 4d6 minutes after entering the compound, **4 teenage boys** finally emerge from the northern building, leisurely bouncing a rubber ball against the ground. These boys also charge headlong into the fray, though this time, they loudly call for aid from the **black skeleton** standing atop the apex of the neighboring temple of Nonotzali. When summoned in this manner, the black skeleton abandons its station and rushes to engage the enemies without emitting an alarm. Azcatl, Cualne, Milice, and Zintli — the teenagers in this encounter — react in the same manner as their previous counterparts.

Teenage Students, Male Aztlis (4): HD 1; HP 8, 7x2, 5; AC 7[12]; **Atk** club (1d4) or sling (1d4); **Move** 12; **Save** 17; **AL** C; **CL/XP** 1/15; **Special:** none. (**Monstrosities** 254)
Equipment: club, sling, 10 sling bullets.

Skeleton, Black: HD 6; HP 41; AC 4[15]; **Atk** weapon (1d6) or 2 claws (1d4); **Move** 12; **Save** 11; **AL** N; **CL/XP** 6/400; **Special:** shriek (30ft radius, save or flee in fear). (see **Appendix A: New Monsters**)

CALMECAC GROUNDS

The calmecac's structures look intact absent some early signs of neglect and numerous empty jars and ceramic cups of pulque scattered around the area, but order has completely broken down. Schedules have been thrown out the window, and classes are no longer in session. None of the youngsters adheres to any of the school's previous rules. The children generally fall into two different camps — those who reject traditional Aztli beliefs and are now fiercely loyal to Coyotl's new order, and those children who begrudgingly went along with the werecoyote's unplanned revolution. The adolescents and teenagers belonging to the first camp behave like spoiled brats, unrestrained by social restrictions or norms. They often emulate canine mannerisms by barking, yipping, and exhibiting a pack mentality. The individuals in the latter group have been repeatedly exposed to the rabies virus through Coyotl's contaminated drink, making them either sick and lethargic or wild and unpredictable.

AREA A: OUTER COURTYARD

This area refers to the open spaces between the major points of interest in the calmecac.

During the school's heyday, the staff carefully attended to the grounds comprising its outer courtyard. Coyotl does not share their enthusiasm for the endeavor. Nonetheless, the residual fruits of their labors keep the vegetation in check with the exception of several bush and tree saplings making some headway in the outer courtyard. Creatures moving through the outer courtyard may do so without penalty or impediment.

AREA B: SPARRING GROUNDS

The calmecac's teachers instructed their pupils in the arts of war atop this square patch of earth. Young men learned the art of wielding the club, spear, and other Aztli weapons, though Coyotl's unmotivated and largely directionless underlings spend little to no time honing their combat skills. A character searching through the debris littering the ground easily finds pieces of shattered obsidian and wood on the ground, as well as chunks of copper just beneath a fine layer of dirt.

However, the characters' attention likely shifts toward the macabre displays facing the gate. A character who examines the decapitated heads determines the heads were removed from the spinal column in an imprecise manner rather than with single, sharp cuts. Coyotl, in his coyote form, chewed through their necks and sliced through their vertebrae with his fangs rather than cutting or sawing through their spinal columns with a sharp instrument or weapon. The skulls belong to Aloc and the four jaguar warriors sent to investigate the events at the calmecac. However, the exposure to the elements, especially the high humidity, and the carrion-eating insects make it impossible to identify the individuals even though scraps of flesh still cling to their bones. However, a character who examines the bugs covering these decomposing faces can confirm that the presence of maggots on four of the skulls indicates they have been here no more than a week. The remaining skull (Aloc's) has sat on display for at least two weeks.

Area C: Cultivated Field

The fruits and vegetables harvested in the calmecac's garden serve as a primary food source for the students, though a character who inspects the plants notices that the edible parts of many plants are rotting on the vine or appear overripe. More importantly, characters who wander into the garden may run afoul of the resident **wahuapa**. The maizefolk perfectly blends into its surroundings, where it stands concealed among the ordinary maize plants.

Wahuapa (Maizefolk): HD 7; HP 46; AC 7[12]; Atk 2 claws (1d6 + blood meal); **Move** 9; **Save** 9; **AL** N; **CL/XP** 8/800; **Special:** blood meal (save or additional 1d4 damage, wahuapa gains hp equal to damage), camouflage (1-in-6 chance to spot while standing still in maizefield), entangle (3/day, plants grow in 10ft radius within 60ft range, save or restrained, Open Doors check to escape). (see **Appendix A: New Monsters**)

Despite its carnivorous nature, the wahuapa ignores the ducks and turkeys confined to the pens. The birds lack the coordination and digits to free themselves from their captivity, though a character may easily spring them from their wooden pens. A character who examines each pen also discovers that each cage contains 1d3 unharvested eggs. The slaves from **Area D** occasionally dump human and animal waste onto the soil as crude fertilizer.

The honeybees at the southern edge of the field only attack visitors who disturb their honeycomb or who stray within five feet of their nest. The **swarm of bees** emerges from the hive's inner recesses to assault the unwelcome trespasser. The swarm pursues transgressors up to a distance of 100 feet from its abode, at which point, it ceases the assault and retreats back to its hive.

Swarm of Bees: HD 2; HP 13; AC 7[12]; **Atk** swarm (1d6); **Move** 6 (fly); **Save** 16; **AL** N; **CL/XP** 3/60; **Special:** immune to all but blunt weapons.

<<Insert Area D and Area F Map>>

Area D: Food Production

The typically impulsive Coyotl realized hunger can derail even the most idealistic revolt. He spared the lives of the compound's four Poqoza slaves who tend the gardens and prepare meals for the residents. The structure's walls and foundation are constructed from adobe bricks. Packed dirt makes up its floor, while the eight-foot-high pitched ceiling is made from wood and straw. The wooden door granting access into the mess hall is always kept ajar to allow light into the building and to let heat escape. The kitchen generally operates from dawn to dusk, though the servants toil for several hours before sunrise prepping for the next day's meals, and for an hour after sunset to clean. The staff leaves a few light snacks, such as uncontaminated cacao drinks, tortilla chips, and salsas, on a table during the overnight hours to accommodate stragglers looking for a quick meal.

D1: Kitchen and Dining Area

When a character peers into the room beyond the ajar door, read or paraphrase the following description.

The **4 slaves Atexa, Cahuitl, Inexca,** and **Tahuauta** have no love lost for the Aztlis and certainly no fond feelings for Coyotl and his bratty cohorts. They never mourned for Aloc and his acolytes, but they fear the calmecac's cruel and unpredictable new master who revels in death and carnage far more than his predecessors. They bemoan the upstarts' obnoxious attitudes and disrespect toward them. A character who converses with the slaves notices that Inexca appears sullen and upset while her counterparts vigorously bash Coyotl and the boys. If questioned, she sheepishly admits to having a clandestine romantic relationship with Coyotl for almost eight months. During her conversations with the teenager, he frequently spoke about his jealousy and hatred toward his older brother Ezel, who had bullied his physically weaker younger brother. Despite their age and size differentials, Coyotl vowed he would one day become the family's patriarch.

Inexca brushed his boasts aside, yet as their forbidden relationship grew stronger, Coyotl abruptly changed. He began ranting about learning the secrets of tapping into his inner beast. One night during an argument, the enraged Coyotl manifested into an upright coyote. His metamorphosis terrified her, especially considering she was now carrying his unborn child. The older and infinitely wiser young woman kept her pregnancy a secret from her fellow slaves and most importantly, from Coyotl, for as long as she could until he finally realized the truth. Eager to please Itzcuin, Coyotl forcibly extracted the unborn child from her womb and sacrificed the fetus to his divine patron in the ultimate display of fidelity to his ungodly master. Under the bestial deity's urging, Coyotl even devoured the girl's flesh and poured some of the child's spilt blood onto the maize plants, giving birth to the wahuapa now inhabiting **Area C**. After relaying her tragic tale, Inexca and the other slaves fall silent until they slowly return to the tasks at hand.

The slaves use the cooking implements scattered around the kitchen to make tortillas from ground corn dough, tamales from peppers, pozoles, and warm cacao drinks to feed and nourish the boorish residents. They have no knowledge about the contaminated cacao drinks spiked with saliva harvested from rabid dogs. The comallis — the clay discs resting atop the stones — are used to heat the tortillas, while the stone bowls are used to grind, mix, and serve the soups, known as pozoles, as well as salsas and other cold dishes.

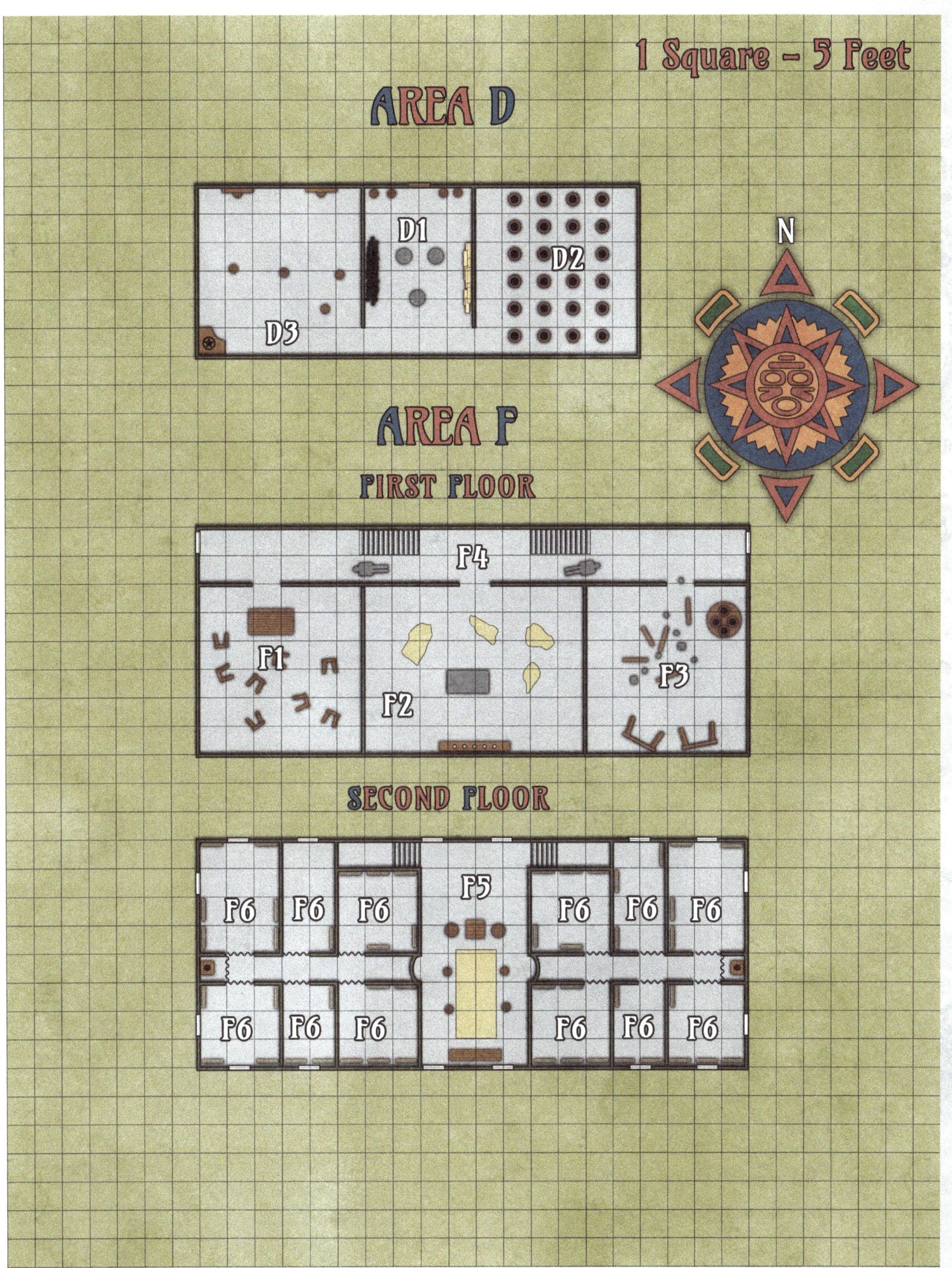

1 Square – 5 Feet
AREA D
D1
D2
D3
N
AREA P
FIRST FLOOR
F1
F2
F3
F4
SECOND FLOOR
F6
F6
F6
F5
F6
F6
F6
F6
F6
F6
F6
F6
F6

Atexa, Cahuitl, Inexca, and Tahuauta, Female Poqoza Half-Elf Slaves (4): HP 2 each; AC 9[10]; **Atk** strike (1hp); **Move** 12; **Save** 18; **AL** N; **CL/XP** B/10; **Special:** none. (*Monstrosities* 254)

D2: FOOD STORAGE

Numerous sealed clay pots rest upon the floor. Some of these containers bear images of maize and other gourds.

The slaves store food inside the three-foot-tall clay pots. Eight clay pots emblazoned with images of maize are filled with dried kernels, while the four pots decorated by depictions of gourds contain squash and pumpkins. The remaining unadorned 12 clay pots hold an assortment of other fruits and vegetables, though two of these pots contain urine collected to dye and wash textiles. A character who drinks the urine must make a saving throw or be nauseated for 10 minutes (–1 to hit and saves). To safeguard their food supply, **3 cats** patrol the area. The friendly animals greet visitors with an enthusiastic meow and purr at the slightest provocation.

Cats (3): HD 1d4 hp; HP 3, 2x2; AC 8[11]; **Atk** 2 claws (1hp); **Move** 12; **Save** 18; **AL** N; **CL/XP** B/10; **Special:** none.

D3: SLAVES' QUARTERS

Two looms stand near the far wall where bundles of leaves and other plant fibers are piled on the floor next to them. Four colorful mats are on the floor. Clothes rest atop a stool near each of the mats. A small, wooden statue of a handsome humanoid man with a lithe physique and long, upright rabbit ears rests upon a pedestal in the near corner.

In addition to feeding the calmecac's students, the slaves also use the looms to weave blankets and clothing, though most residents arrived with their own garments. The slaves sleep here during the overnight hours. A character who examines the plant fibers near the looms identifies them as maguey leaves. The wooden statue sitting atop the pedestal serves as a makeshift shrine to Tlatlcolli, the Poqozas' patron deity.

AREA E: WELL

Several underground canals connected to Teohuacan's main water system supply the calmecac with its life-giving liquid.

A five-foot-diameter brick-and-mortar shaft burrows into the ground. A clay pot tethered to a rope floats atop the water's surface, roughly three feet below the well's lip. A square-shaped piece of wood with a hole cut out of the center rests against the side of the well.

The water retrieved from the well is potable and safe to drink. However, over the last few hours, a **purple slime** has infiltrated the subterranean network of channels feeding the cistern. If a slave accompanies the characters to the well, the person tells them that the clay pot is usually stored upright on the ground rather than left bobbing in the water. This unusual change in protocol may alert the adventurers to potential danger. The unintelligent, yet cunning ooze has already claimed one victim, a student who tried to drink from the well, which explains the clay pot's strange location. The purple slime floats on the water's surface. When it senses an approaching creature, it makes a spike attack against the trespasser. The mindless creature attacks until destroyed.

The water reaches a depth of 20 feet. The channels flowing into and out of the well are four feet wide yet narrow with a maximum height of only six inches. A character who can access such a tiny opening may travel westward back to Teohuacan or in a southeasterly direction into another cistern in **Area G9**. To prevent accidental drownings, numerous handholds and footholds jut

from the walls. The youngsters occasionally use the well as a basket for their athletic competitions. They sometimes place the wooden board with a cutout hole on top of the well to make the game more challenging.

Purple Slime: HD 5; AC 8[11]; **Atk** 2 spikes (1d8 + 1d6 acid); **Move** 9 (climb 9, swim 9); **Save** 12; **AL** N; **CL/XP** 5/240; **Special:** acid (additional 1d6 damage with strike, save avoids), immune to acid and cold. (see **Appendix A: New Monsters**)

AREA F: SCHOOL COMPLEX

The two-story brick and mortar building adjacent to the northern outer wall houses the calmecac's classrooms on the first floor and its dormitories on the second floor. The building is 20 feet high with a sharply sloped roof constructed from wood and plant fibers. The ceilings on each floor are nine feet high, while the internal doors are made from wood. Natural light trickles into the first-floor corridor through the doors, though the classrooms remain dark unless currently occupied. The two-foot-wide, roughly one-foot-high second-floor windows allow natural light into the dormitories during the day, yet dim light prevails on moonlit nights, with darkness enveloping the building on moonless or cloudy evenings. A character squeezing through the window must make a saving throw to shimmy through the tight opening without falling face first when it gets inside or getting stuck midway. Read or paraphrase the following description when the characters lay their eyes upon this edifice:

The rectangular, two-story brick building features a door on its eastern face and another on its western face. Small rhomboid-shaped windows dot portions of the second floor. Faded, painted images of classrooms adorn the structure's outer walls. Indecipherable sounds periodically emanate from inside the building.

With no classes in session, Coyotl's underlings and his minions freely roam through the building at their leisure. The unsupervised children often remain awake well into the wee hours of the morning and sleep off their excesses until noon. Characters moving through the building have a 30% chance of encountering **1d4 teenage students** for every 10 minutes spent within the structure's confines. The youngsters carry a lantern when encountered in normally unlit areas within the building. There is a 50% chance that a **beast of Itzcuin** accompanies them.

Teenage Students, Male Aztlis (1d4): HD 1; AC 7[12]; **Atk** club (1d4) or sling (1d4); **Move** 12; **Save** 17; **AL** C; **CL/XP** 1/15; **Special:** none. (*Monstrosities* 254)
Equipment: club, sling, 10 sling bullets.

Beast of Itzcuin: HD 2; HP 12; AC 7[12]; **Atk** bite (1d3 + disease); **Move** 15; **Save** 16; **AL** C; **CL/XP** 2/30; **Special:** darkvision (60ft), disease (save or 1d4 damage per day, healing ends damage), misfortune (1/day, save or –1 penalty to hit and saves for 24 hours) (see **Appendix A: New Monsters**)

F1: SOCIAL STUDIES CLASSROOM

Images painted on the walls depict several distinct events. These include numerous humans digging a massive trench, the burning of a major city, a gathering of three royal figures and a serpent-like creature, and the depiction of a legal proceeding. Twelve overturned, damaged wooden stools are strewn about the floor in varying states of disrepair. A wooden desk adjacent to the near wall is nearly intact, though the four codices resting atop it exhibit extensive wear to their bindings and pages.

The artwork adorning the walls depicts several seminal events in Aztli history, including the building of the Great Canal, the formation of the Aztli Confederation, and the destruction of Xacota. A character indigenous to Tehuatl might recognize these major moments from Aztli history. Likewise, the codices on the desk include three history texts focusing on Xacota, while the remaining tome is a legal treatise on Aztli law. A character who can read Aztli may identify the texts' subjects. Someone who examines the codices and cannot comprehend Aztli writing must use magic or some other means to gain a basic understanding of the subject matter. Only four wooden stools remain functional. The remaining eight are missing 1d4 legs.

Treasure: The three history codices (worth 150 gp each) are fairly rare. They describe several important yet obscure facts from this period of Aztli history. The codices were written on deer hide, making them relatively durable from a structural integrity standpoint, though they are still vulnerable to extreme humidity and temperature. The legal treatise (worth 50 gp) scribed onto plant fiber is more common and less sturdy, making it less valuable than its counterparts.

F2: Religious Studies

Aloc taught religion and, to a lesser extent, medicine within these walls. Students sat or kneeled on the colorful linens while the high priest and his acolytes imparted divine inspiration from the Aztli gods. However, Coyotl and his disciples smeared feces and dried blood from Aloc and his acolytes on the walls' painted images of Nonotzali and Quiahuitl. His minions also dug deep grooves onto the stony surfaces with rocks, stones, and bronze tools. The altar and the obsidian dagger also suffered the same fate. In an ultimate act of sacrilege, Itzcuin raised one of the acolyte's corpses as a **mummy**. The undead monstrosity lies atop the slab only to rise when a creature enters the room without uttering the password "Itzcuin." If the creature fails to say the word, it attacks. The mummy speaks Aztli and recalls portions of its past life, though it now venerates Itzcuin and refuses to converse with the characters unless they magically compel it. Under those circumstances, it reveals that Coyotl murdered him several weeks ago and that the teen can transform into a coyote.

Mummy: HD 5+1; HP 34; AC 3[16]; Atk strike (1d12); Move 6; Save 12; AL C; CL/XP 7/600; Special: +1 or better magic weapons to hit, rot (prevents magical healing, wounds heal at one-tenth normal rate, *remove curse* lifts curse). (*Monstrosities* 340)

Treasure: The vials on the shelf are three *potions of healing*, a *potion of extra healing*, and a *potion of undead control*. The medical codex is *Cahuotl's Journal*, a nonmagical diary written in Aztli that describes advanced diagnostic techniques. Whenever a character spends 48 hours over a period of six days or fewer memorizing the book's diagrams and following its diagnostic protocols, a character has a 10% base chance + 5% per level to learn how to properly bandage a wound so that it heals 1d6 points of damage. This bandaging can be used on a character once per day if needed. On a failed save, the character learns nothing from the experience and cannot try to read the book again for one year. After one year lapses, the character may reread the book.

F3: Artisan's Studio

The instructors used the raw materials and ingredients to teach students the arts of sculpting and painting as well as engineering. Not surprisingly, they used these newfound skills to adorn the walls with graphic depictions of Itzcuin. At the moment, **4 teenage students** are honing their craft, adding gory details to the earlier paintings. These older students obviously disavow Aztli traditions. They appear unkempt and exhibit a blatant disregard for the calmecac and its principles by further desecrating the building and the gods who supported it. The young men openly speak ill of Aloc, the acolytes, and Teohuacan as a whole. The fanatics never willingly speak to the characters. They do so only if magically compelled or if a character successfully intimidates one of them.

Teenage Students, Male Aztlis (1d4): HD 1; AC 7[12]; **Atk** club (1d4) or sling (1d4); **Move** 12; **Save** 17; **AL** C; **CL/XP** 1/15; **Special:** none. (*Monstrosities* 254)
   Equipment: club, sling, 10 sling bullets.

A character has a 1-in-6 chance to spot a codex underneath the overturned table against the far wall. If retrieved, the book contains numerous geometrical diagrams along with numerical values used for the study of engineering.

Treasure: An Aztli architect and engineer named Quintin wrote the engineering codex (worth 200 gp) that was predominantly used to build the neighboring temple of Quiahuitl as well as several other important sites in nearby Teohuacan. The room also contains two complete sets of carpenter's tools, three sets of mason's tools, and four complete sets of painter's supplies.

F4: Corridor

The rambunctious students defaced the artwork on the walls, replacing the scenes associated with Nonotzali's instructor with depraved images of Itzcuin's canine servants. Despite conveying their intention, the latter artwork appears primitive and juvenile in comparison to their predecessors. After overthrowing the calmecac's administration, the boys toppled the statues of Nonotzali, causing them to break apart. The decapitated statue and the other sculpture, which broke into three pieces as shown on the map, portray Nonotzali.

F5: Common Room

During the day, light filters into the room from the windows on the north and south walls. The **4 teen students** who occupy the common room spend their free time playing patolli, a game played on the cross-shaped board resting atop the table. The dried, red beans function as the game's playing pieces. Like the other residents, these boys behave in an unruly manner, display no interest in maintaining their personal appearance, and immediately attack intruders. They repeatedly refer to the trespassers as "blasphemers" amid other crude insults about the characters' appearances and characteristics. Under questioning, they react in the same manner as the children in **Area F3**. In addition, an **elusa hound** reclines on the carpet alongside the boys. Coyotl uses the beast to sniff out spellcasters disguised as students. When the monstrosity detects a magical aura, it exclusively focuses its attacks against that target. In typical pack fashion, the elusa hound nonverbally encourages the boys to attack the same foe.

Obviously, the sounds of combat from **Area F5** may evoke a response from the residents occupying **Area F6**. Under these circumstances, you may increase the chance of an encounter taking place from once every 10 minutes to once every minute while the characters are engaged in battle. When the commotion ends, the chances of a random encounter return to normal.

Teenage Students, Male Aztlis (1d4): HD 1; AC 7[12]; Atk club (1d4) or sling (1d4); **Move** 12; **Save** 17; **AL** C; **CL/XP** 1/15; **Special:** none. (*Monstrosities* 254)
    Equipment: club, sling, 10 sling bullets.

Elusa Hound: HD 3; HP 20; AC 7[12]; Atk bite (1d6+1); **Move** 15; **Save** 14; **AL** N; **CL/XP** 3/60; **Special:** detect magic. (see **Appendix A: New Monsters**)

Treasure: The furnishings in the room are sturdy yet ordinary. The carpet (worth 10 gp) consists of plant fibers, deer skins, and feathers from birds of prey. Students use the mats (worth 5 gp each) near the entrance for short naps or brief relaxation.

F6: DORMITORY

Each of the dormitory rooms houses between three and six students. Upperclassmen traditionally occupy the larger corner rooms, while the underclassmen dwell in the small and more crowded interior rooms. During the day, natural light filters through the windows into the rooms with an exterior wall. Students use bundles of sticks to illuminate the interior areas and during the overnight hours on moonless or cloudy nights. When the characters enter one of the dormitories, you may read or paraphrase the following description, adjusting it as necessary for the room's unique circumstances.

> A blue, red, and green curtain hanging from a rod suspended in the doorway serves as a makeshift door. Heaping mounds of soiled clothing, food scraps, and torn pages from codices litter the floor. Colorful, linen mats are rolled up onto a bar against the wall. Niches built into the near walls display religious iconography, though most of the images are now covered by writing, dirt, and other materials.

When Aloc and his acolytes held sway over the calmecac, the student dormitories resembled military barracks in terms of order and cleanliness. In the absence of any formal discipline, the students wallow in sloth and filth. They rarely, if ever, wash the piles of dirty linens strewn about the floor, pick up leftover food, or read from their codices. As previously discussed, the youngsters usually stay awake until the wee hours of the morning and do not stir until at least noon. When exploring these rooms, you may consult the follow table to determine whether an individual room is occupied, and if so, what the occupants are doing at the time.

TABLE 1–3: DORMITORY OCCUPANTS BASED UPON TIME

d6	Early Morning to Noon	Noon to Sunset	Overnight Hours
1	Occupied, sleeping	Occupied, awake	Occupied, awake
2	Occupied, sleeping	Occupied, awake	Occupied, sleeping
3	Occupied, sleeping	Occupied, sleeping	Occupied, awake
4	Occupied, awake	Unoccupied	Unoccupied
5–6	Unoccupied	Unoccupied	Unoccupied

If the room is occupied, the residents' reactions depend upon whether they are Coyotl's loyal followers, who enjoy more privileges, or if they belong to the camp of indifferent followers succumbing to the ravages of rabies from Coyotl's tainted cacao drink. Fanatical devotees immediately attack intruders, while infected students behave in accordance with the effects of the disease.

RABIES

When saliva from an infected creature enters a beast or humanoid, the creature must make a saving throw or become infected with the disease. Symptoms manifest 6d6 days after infection and include a sore throat, fever, and nausea.

Each day, an infected creature must succeed on a saving throw or exhibit signs of confusion, increased aggression, and dysphagia. The creature cannot swallow, which prevents it from drinking any liquid, including potions. Whenever the infected creature must make a saving throw, the creature becomes agitated (50% chance) or confused (50% chance) for one minute. While agitated, the creature randomly attacks any target it can see. It can take no other action while agitated. The creature moves at up to its speed toward the target. A confused creature behaves as if under the influence of a *confusion* spell.

Left untreated, rabies has a nearly 100% mortality rate. It can be cured only by a *cure disease* spell.

In general, the number of students in the room is equal to or less than the number of beds. The **upperclassmen** occupy the corner bedrooms, while the **underclassmen** reside in the interior rooms and smaller exterior dormitory rooms. Upperclassmen have a 75% chance of belonging to Coyotl's loyal henchmen. His loyal devotees respond to questions in the same manner as their fanatical counterparts. The underclassmen, on the other hand, have a 75% chance of suffering from rabies.

If the characters encounter infected students, searching their quarters locates a clay cup containing a foul-smelling cacao residue. Interrogating Coyotl's less-enthusiastic residents yields better results, especially if the characters cure the disease ravaging their bodies. Otherwise, all attempts to gather information from infected students automatically fail as their diseased minds are incapable of recalling any details. If cured, the students reveal that Coyotl forced them to regularly imbibe a presumably doctored cacao drink to "unleash their inner beast." He brewed and administered the concoction to them within Nonotzali's converted sanctum within the temple. They also tell the characters that Coyotl killed the students who initially resisted him and that a few of their classmates almost immediately took ill after ingesting the cacao drink and have not been seen since they exhibited signs of sickness.

Teenage Students, Male Aztlis Underclassmen: HD 1; AC 7[12]; Atk club (1d4) or sling (1d4); **Move** 12; **Save** 17; **AL** C; **CL/XP** 1/15; **Special:** none. (*Monstrosities* 254)
    Equipment: club, sling, 10 sling bullets.

Teenage Students, Male Aztlis Upperclassmen: HD 4; AC 7[12]; Atk macuahuitl (1d8); **Move** 12; **Save** 13; **AL** C; **CL/XP** 4/120; **Special:** none. (*Monstrosities* 254)
    Equipment: tlahuiztli armor[B], macuahuitl[B].
[B] See **Appendix B: New Equipment and Magic Items**

To prevent the characters from monotonously going through one identical room after another, consult the following table to add random details or treasures to each different area in **Area F6**. Do not give the characters the same discovery more than once, with the exception of the tlachtli ball that the characters may receive more than once. If die roll generates the same result a second time, reroll the die only one more time and give them that discovery instead. If they already unearthed the next discovery, they receive nothing.

TABLE 1–4: AREA F6 RANDOM DISCOVERIES

1d8	Discovery
1	Cacao beans
2	Eagle feathers
3	Golden idol
4	Macuahuitl
5	Mysterious drawing
6	Pulque
7	Silvery earrings
8	Tlachtli ball (can be generated more than once)

Cacao Beans

A calmecac resident hid 16 cacao beans (worth 1d4 gp each) in a pouch concealed among the clothing. A character has a 1-in-6 chance to spot the pods inside the gigantic mess.

Eagle Feathers

Four eagle feathers (worth 1d3 gp each) are rolled inside one of the linen mats. It is impossible to locate the feathers without unfurling the mat.

Golden Idol

This golden statue of a pouncing jaguar (worth 300 gp) is four inches high, six inches long, and weighs roughly two pounds. Its owner stuffed the valuable object inside of a shirt, yet an observant character can spot the object's outline among the linens. If the characters are from Teohuacan or are very familiar with the settlement, they recall hearing about this golden idol being stolen from Nonotzali's temple in the neighboring town roughly one year earlier, well before the current events that befell the calmecac.

Macuahuitl

This fearsome club laced with obsidian shards hangs from a bracket embedded in the wall. The *+1 macuahuitl* is wrapped inside of a linen cover to prevent accidental lacerations from anyone touching its keen edges. See **Appendix B: New Equipment and Magic Items** for details on the weapon.

Mysterious Drawing

Before Coyotl's ascendancy, a student devoted to Nonotzali doodled a cryptic drawing onto a ceiling's whitewashed surface. The image depicts a feathered serpent wrapping its coils around a wild-eyed coyote. Surprisingly, none of Itzcuin's followers defaced nor erased the remarkably well-done piece of artwork.

Pulque

A sealed jar contains roughly one gallon of pulque (worth 10 gp). The alcoholic beverage fermented from the sap of the maguey plant is a popular drink among the Aztli.

Silver Earrings

Before his transformation into a werecoyote, Coyotl planned to give this exquisite pair of silver earrings (worth 150 gp) to Inexca (see **Area D1**). After this plan fell by the wayside, the irate young man tossed the earrings into the well, where one of the students later retrieved them.

Tlachtli Ball

This round, leather ball rests in the far corner of the room. The students use it to play the ball game in the courtyard (**Area A**), using the well (**Area E**) as the goal.

Area G: Temple of Nonotzali

Pictographs of geometric shapes and colorful paintings of feathered serpents adorn the step pyramid's adobe brick walls. A 10-foot-wide staircase with one-foot-high and one-foot-deep steps built into the structure's southern face ascends 40 feet onto a square shrine atop the temple of Nonotzali, which grants access to the temple complex within the pyramid. Perfectly symmetrical 10-foot adobe brick cubes form the foundation and building blocks of the temple. Creatures who forego the staircase can scale the walls to reach the next level. In addition to repelling intruders, the dense material also prevents light from entering into the temple's interior sections, which feature eight-foot-high ceilings and smooth walls decorated with carvings and paintings depicting storm clouds and the harvest. When the characters approach the temple, read or paraphrase the following description:

> Vibrant pictographs of geometric shapes with tick marks and paintings of feathered serpents adorn the step pyramid's exterior and culminate in a limestone shrine at the building's apex, just beneath a staircase that ascends along the structure's southern face. An altar chiseled from speckled red and gray stone stands outside the shrine enclosure atop the step pyramid. Several chunks of broken stone and loose scraps of maguey paper litter the base of the steps.

The objects and artwork adorning the pyramid's exterior are commonly associated with Nonotzali, who is depicted in several paintings of the feathered serpent. Six of these drawings adorn the pyramid's walls. Characters who examine the broken stones and scraps of maguey paper can confirm that they were once small limestone statues depicting serpentine creatures. The pieces of paper contain bits and pieces of mathematical ratios associated with geometric objects. Nonotzali's priests would have offered items associated with learning to their deity as a sacrifice.

G1: Apex Level

> Two wooden statues of coiled feathered serpents flank a stone slab carved from speckled red and gray stone. A black dagger crafted from stone rests atop the altar, which occupies the space in front of an enclosure dominated by a meticulously detailed bronze statue of an odd humanoid figure.

Unless previously summoned, a **black skeleton** stands vigil behind the altar. Before taking its post, the undead monstrosity wandered the surrounding wilderness until it sensed Itzcuin's presence in the former temple of Nonotzali. The evil guardian, who frequently sparred against Nonotzali's worshippers during his wicked mortal existence, freely offered his services to Coyotl's fledgling regime. The black skeleton immediately attacks any creature who fails to recite its safe word, "Itzcuin." If someone utters the passcode, the monster allows that person and their allies to proceed without hindrance. Otherwise, the creature hacks at its enemies with merciless precision. Although the serpent statues adjacent to the altar are also carved from wood, these objects keep their silent vigil without stirring to life.

Skeleton, Black: HD 6; HP 41; AC 4[15]; **Atk** weapon (1d6) or 2 claws (1d4); **Move** 12; **Save** 11; **AL** N; **CL/XP** 6/400; **Special:** shriek (30ft radius, save or flee in fear).

During the temple's heyday, Aloc sacrificed objects and an occasional animal to his divine patron atop the granite altar. With the exception of Aloc who perished atop the sacrificial altar, Coyotl and his minions have refrained from butchering animals on the hardened stone, though mercy plays no

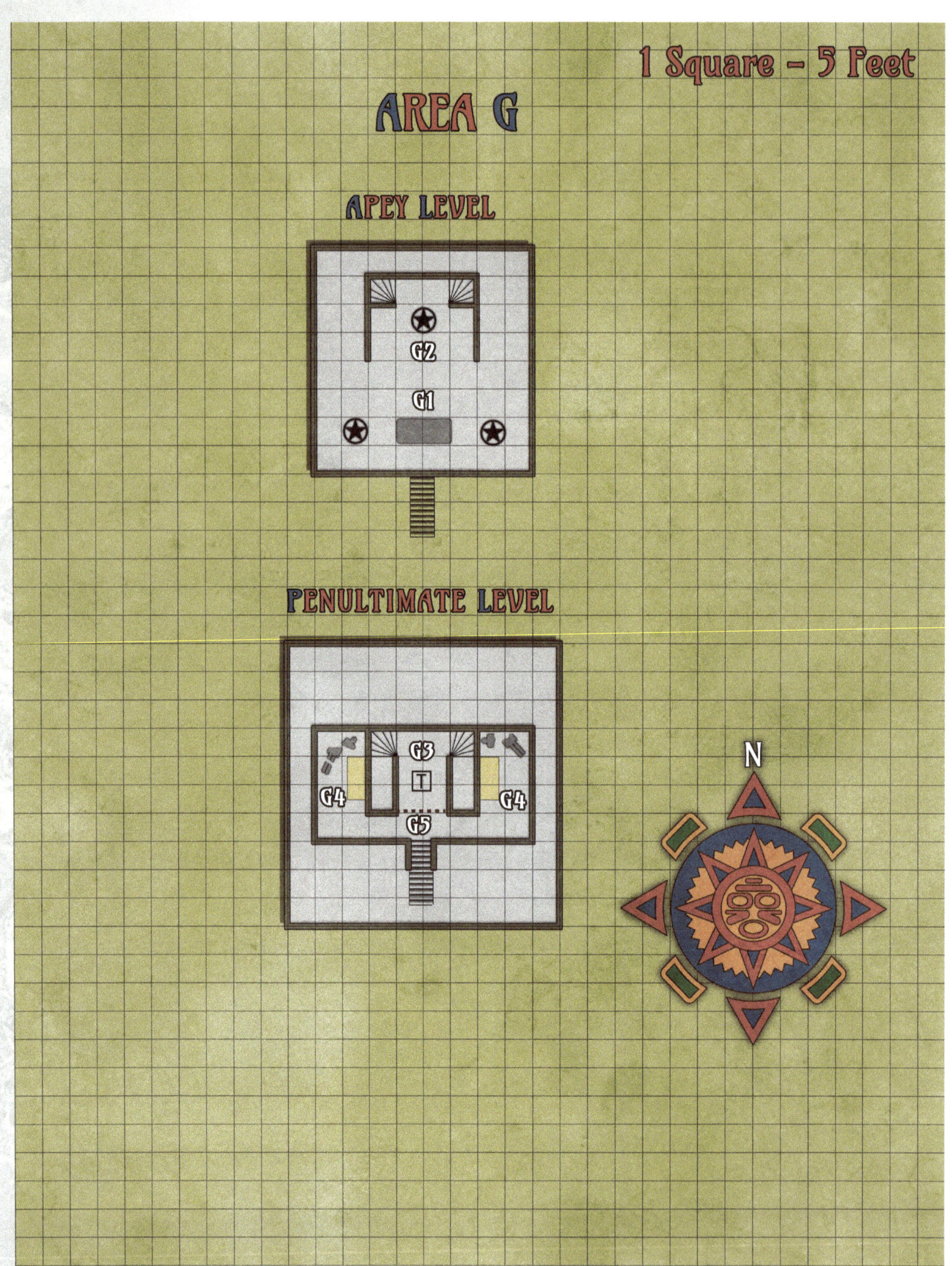

1 Square – 5 Feet
AREA G
APEY LEVEL
G2
G1
PENULTIMATE LEVEL
G3
T
G4
G4
G5
N

part in their decision. The impulsive young man and his followers lack the discipline to adhere to the ceremonial killing's rigid protocols and instead prefer to immediately indulge their bloodlust rather than prolong the misery. It is impossible to distinguish the high priest's dried blood from previous animal victims slaughtered atop the altar.

Treasure: The serpent statues (worth 100 gp each) are carved out of oak. They stand 2–1/2 feet tall and weigh 40 pounds. The obsidian dagger (worth 500 gp) on the altar is extremely sharp and wondrously decorated with unique carvings. While it cuts through flesh with ease, it is too brittle and fragile to be an effective weapon. If wielded in combat, the dagger shatters into pieces when the wielder rolls a natural 1 on a melee or ranged attack made with the weapon.

G2: Shrine of Nonotzali

The statue dates back to the temple's founding more than a century ago. Forged from bronze, it depicts Nonotzali in meticulous yet interpretive detail during the war of liberation against Tlatoani. When Aloc presided over the temple, visitors and students would leave offerings at the statue's feet to beseech the god to acknowledge their intellectual breakthroughs and curiosity. In his aftermath, Coyotl encouraged his supporters to deface the statue with vulgarities; draw disgusting, juvenile images of extra genitalia; urinate on its base; and smear human and animal feces onto its formerly smooth, polished surface. A character with a sense of smell immediately identifies the malodorous substances covering it.

The seashells dangling from strings attached to the wooden beams in the thatched ceiling belong to a variety of marine species. A creature who examines them identifies them as clam, scallop, and oyster shells. The staircases leading down are steep and narrow yet structurally sound and safe. They lead into **Area G3**.

Treasure: Sixty-eight strands of seashells (worth 1 gp each) are affixed to the ceiling. Characters can carefully remove one strand without damaging them. A character who attempts to remove more than one strand at a time must succeed on a Delicate Tasks check to avoid dropping the strands on the floor where they break into pieces rendering them worthless. A thief has a normal chance of success; non-thieves can make a Delicate Tasks check at half the thief's chance equal to their current level. A creature who tries to simultaneously remove more than five strands suffers a –2% chance to the check per strand above the fifth (so an additional –6% penalty for trying to remove eight strands). It is impossible to remove more than 10 at once.

A small edible sphere containing a *potion of heroism* is glued onto an oyster shell hidden among the ordinary shells. A character who takes the time to examine the shells has a 1-in-6 chance to spot it from afar, though a character who takes the time to examine the individual strands has a 3-in-6 chance to notice the sphere. Likewise, a *detect magic* spell successfully locates the concealed sphere.

G3: Penultimate Level Landing

The stairs against the far wall connect this level to the apex level, specifically in **Area G3**. The artwork adorning the walls dates back to the temple's creation roughly 160 years earlier and are obviously fading, chipping, and peeling away

from the surface. Worshippers seeking counsel from Nonotzali's priests would wait in this vestibule before discussing their current field of study or debating the merits of a formative hypothesis. After slaying Aloc, Coyotl repurposed an alarm formerly used to alert the priests to the arrival of visitors into a juvenile yet potentially harmful trap.

Pressure Plate Trap

The pyramid's builders added a pressure plate to the floor covering the entire space between the dotted lines. When a creature weighing 50 pounds or more steps onto the plate, two bronze plates imbedded into the space beneath the floor emit low chimes that lasts for six seconds before ending. Fortunately for the characters, the alarm functions more as a courtesy rather than a loud, general alert. There is a 50% chance at least one occupant in **Area G4** hears the noise, though they do not necessarily respond to the chime as an immediate call to arms.

However, the chime's purpose is now twofold. The sound now alerts the occupant to deactivate the second portion of the trap contained in the ceiling within 12 seconds. Coyotl thought it would be funny to conceal the shutoff switch in an obscene manner by requiring the trespasser to press a switch hidden in the painting of a priest's backside. A character who examines the paintings on the wall spots the switch, while anyone who inspects the ceiling detects a trapdoor.

If no one presses the switch within the allotted timeframe, the trapdoor opens, dropping roughly 20 pounds of moldy refuse and excrement into the center of the room. Creatures within five feet of the trapdoor must succeed on a saving throw or be covered in the debris. The falling garbage deals no damage, but an affected creature must make a saving throw or contract sewer plague (1d4 points of damage per hour; a heal spell or *cure disease* ends the ongoing damage).

In more pressing matters, the occupants of **Area G4** arrive on the scene to presumably mock whom they believe to be one of their fellow associates who activated the trap. Their jest soon turns to anger when they realize trespassers have entered their domain.

G4: Acolytes' Quarters

Nonotzali's acolytes occupied these humble quarters during their stay at the temple. While intact, the oak statue of Nonotzali stood four feet high. However, Itzcuin's worshippers hacked the limbs from the torso and decapitated the sculpture's head, leaving it in sundered pieces across the floor. Even in this state, characters can identify Nonotzali as the statue's subject. Unlike the artwork, the acolytes' linen mats, which served as their beds, survived Coyotl's onslaught, though the textiles conceal a gruesome discovery. Moving the mats from their current position reveals a thick pool of dried blood, the grisly aftermath of Coyotl's bloodthirsty assault against Aloc's assistants. Although the characters cannot identify the blood's source, it is obvious that the congealed substance is blood. The acolytes kept the sloughed snakeskins as religious objects supposedly harvested from one of the first snakes in the region. The veracity of this claim is dubious at best.

A **coyote warrior** and a **beast of Itzcuin** now occupy each of these quarters (for a total of 2 coyote warriors and 2 beasts of Itzcuin). These young adult males are fanatical devotees of Itzcuin. They excelled in the sparring ring during their tenure at the calmecac, prompting Coyotl to reward them with their new lofty positions and a disgusting pet. Each coyote warrior and their beast focus their attacks against one opponent. Like their counterparts, the coyote warriors fiercely resist any attempts to force their surrender or divulge information about the complex. If they crack under the pressure, the coyote warriors reveal that Coyotl plans to release a virulent contagion upon Teohuacan in the coming days. Although they cannot relay how he intends to set this scheme into motion, they believe dogs somehow play a role in his devious plans.

Coyote Warriors, Male Aztli Warriors (2): HD 5; HP 37, 32; AC 7[12]; **Atk** club (1d6+2) or dagger (1d4+2); **Move** 12; **Save** 12; **AL** C; **CL/XP** 5/240; **Special:** power strike (3/day, triple damage with strike).

Equipment: club, 2 *potions of healing*.

Beasts of Itzcuin (2): HD 2; HP 14, 12; AC 7[12]; **Atk** bite (1d3 + disease); **Move** 15; **Save** 16; **AL** C; **CL/XP** 2/30; **Special:** darkvision (60ft), disease (save or 1d4 damage per day, healing ends damage), misfortune (1/day, save or –1 penalty to hit and saves for 24 hours). (see **Appendix A: New Monsters**)

Treasure: One of the warriors carries a pouch containing 19 cacao beans (worth 10 gp each), while the other carries a *pumpkin seed* (see **Appendix B: New Equipment and Magic Items**).

G5: Vestibule

> A T-shaped intersection connects three adjoining chambers to a staircase.

The vestibule connects the penultimate level to the third level via a staircase connecting **Area G5** to **Area G6** in addition to linking **Areas G3** and **G4** together.

G6: Observatory

> The likeness of a humanoid face bristling with teeth occupies the center of a circular carving teeming with cryptic symbols, celestial bodies, and anthropomorphic creatures. The artwork contains finely detailed and colorful etchings carved into the limestone floor. Four equidistant cylindrical stone pillars with a borehole surround the object adorning the floor. Paintings of the sun moving across the sky adorn the walls, with depictions of men and women laboring in the fields interspersed among these images.

The pyramid's initial blueprints only planned for creating three levels, which would have placed the Aztli calendar and observatory outside as originally intended. However, Nonotzali's arrogant high priest Mocentini later decided to add two more levels to the pyramid in a deliberate effort to outshine the temple of Quiahuitl in neighboring Teohuacan. This amendment accomplished its desired goal, though it also relegated the calendar to the structure's interior sections. A character who examines the etching quickly confirms the diagram represents the Aztli calendar. The undecorated, one-foot-diameter pillars' exact purpose is less obvious. They bear no obvious clues, yet the paintings covering the walls, which were also a later addition after the level was enclosed, provide some insight. The boreholes carved midway through the six-foot-high obelisks descend at a sharp angle instead of being level, while the panorama on the walls depicts the changing of the seasons. A character who examines the calendar, the pillars, and the paintings determines that the pillars coincide with the seasonal equinoxes. Sunlight passes through the borehole and illuminates the corresponding point on the calendar associated with the season shown in the neighboring paintings.

Nonetheless, Coyotl remains convinced that the calendar harbors some additional meaning or secrets he is yet to unravel. In furtherance of his theory, three of his devotees, **Ciuatl**, **Pachoa**, and **Tzona**, carefully study the objects. Although they are in earshot of any combat taking place in **Areas G3**, **G4**, or **G5**, the determined students attribute any commotion to their fellow residents getting too rowdy rather than participating in a life-and-death struggle. The trio jots hand-drawn diagrams and notes about the calendar onto a leather-bound tome containing pages made from maguey leaves. When they spot the intruding characters, they drop the journal and try to quickly neutralize as many adventurers as possible. Like their counterparts in **Area G4**, the trio never surrenders and actively resists any attempts to extract information from them. If forcibly compelled to speak, the trio discusses their research on the calendar, divulging that they have found no hidden meanings or purpose to the etchings on the floor or the paintings on the wall. When pressed about details regarding Coyotl's activities or plans, they confirm he currently occupies the chambers one level below this one where he ruminates about ways to spread Itzcuin's influence to the neighboring towns and villages. His latest scheme uses dogs, though they are short on any specific details.

Ciuatl, Pachoa, and Tzona, Male Aztli Cultists (Clr6) (3): HP 33, 30, 26; AC 8[11]; **Atk** club (1d4); **Move** 12; **Save** 10; **AL** C; **CL/XP** 6/400; **Special:** +2 save vs. paralysis and poison, banish undead, spells (2/2/1/1).
   Spells: 1st—*cure light wounds* (x2); 2nd—*hold person, speak with animals.*
   Equipment: ichcahuipilli armor[B], club.
[B] See **Appendix B: New Equipment and Magic Items**

Treasure: The book (worth 50 gp) contains a surprisingly in-depth analysis of the Aztli calendar as well as the paintings adorning the walls. One also carries two scrolls (*floral bouquet* [C], *wall of smoke* [C]), while another has one spell scroll (*clairvoyance*).
[C] See **Appendix C: New Spells**

G7: Aloc's Quarters

A thick, gray curtain made from linens hangs from a rod imbedded in the doorframe. A character can walk through the curtain, but is blinded until the character moves more than five feet from the entrance or brushes the curtain aside.

> The partially decomposed remains of a snarling, mangy, wild dog with bloodshot eyes and foam around its lips stares maniacally toward the curtain. A wooden statue of a handless Aztli man strikes a bizarre pose with one of the subject's thumbs stuffed into the figure's mouth with the other thumb inserted into its rectum. An ornate grayish-black linen mat rests against the far wall while a portal opens into a steep staircase presumably descending deeper into the pyramid's interior.

After desecrating Nonotzali's temple, the deranged Coyotl became obsessed with others embracing the inner beast. To that end, he became fascinated with the canine disease the Aztlis refer to as the "Drooling Sickness," which he associated with Itzcuin. The almost always fatal illness, commonly known as rabies (see **Rabies** sidebar), also infects humans with equally deadly precision, a fact lost upon Coyotl. The preserved corpse of his first test subject now occupies Aloc's former chambers. A character who examines the dog confirms that the canine suffered from rabies.

Coyotl sawed the hands off of the oak statue depicting Aloc in his youth and inserted the thumbs into two of the statue's orifices. The crudely carved sculpture bears only a faint resemblance to its subject. Wracked by his lycanthropy, Coyotl rarely uses the linen mat Aloc slept on during his stay in the temple. Instead, **2 geruzous** now dwell here. Read or paraphrase the following description of these fiendish beings:

> Two four-foot-tall humanoid creatures with horned, equine heads constantly secrete ooze and slimy mucus onto the floor beneath them. Oversized fangs protrude from their mouths, while membranous wings extend from the creatures' spines. Their hands and feet end in sharpened claws.

At the first sign of intruders, the demons spit slime and then rush forward to attack with their claws. The monsters telepathically communicate with characters, urging them to indulge their bestial natures and revel in carnage. Conversation is a one-way street for the demons, who never respond to the characters' inquiries nor reveal any details beyond "Itzcuin sent them here." They have no knowledge of what lies at the bottom of the staircase nor of Coyotl's ultimate intentions.

Geruzou Demons (Slime Demons) (2): HD 4; HP 27, 22; AC 4[15]; **Atk** 2 claws (1d4), bite (1d6); **Move** 12 (fly 15); **Save** 13; **AL** C; **CL/XP** 6/400; **Special:** +1 or better magic weapons to hit, goo spit (20ft range, save or slowed for 6 rounds; save avoids), immune to electricity and poison, magic resistance (10%), spell-like abilities, telepathy (100ft). (see **Appendix A: New Monsters**)
   Spell-like abilities: at will—*darkness 15ft radius*; 3/day—*ESP, invisibility*; 1/day—*fear, mirror image.*

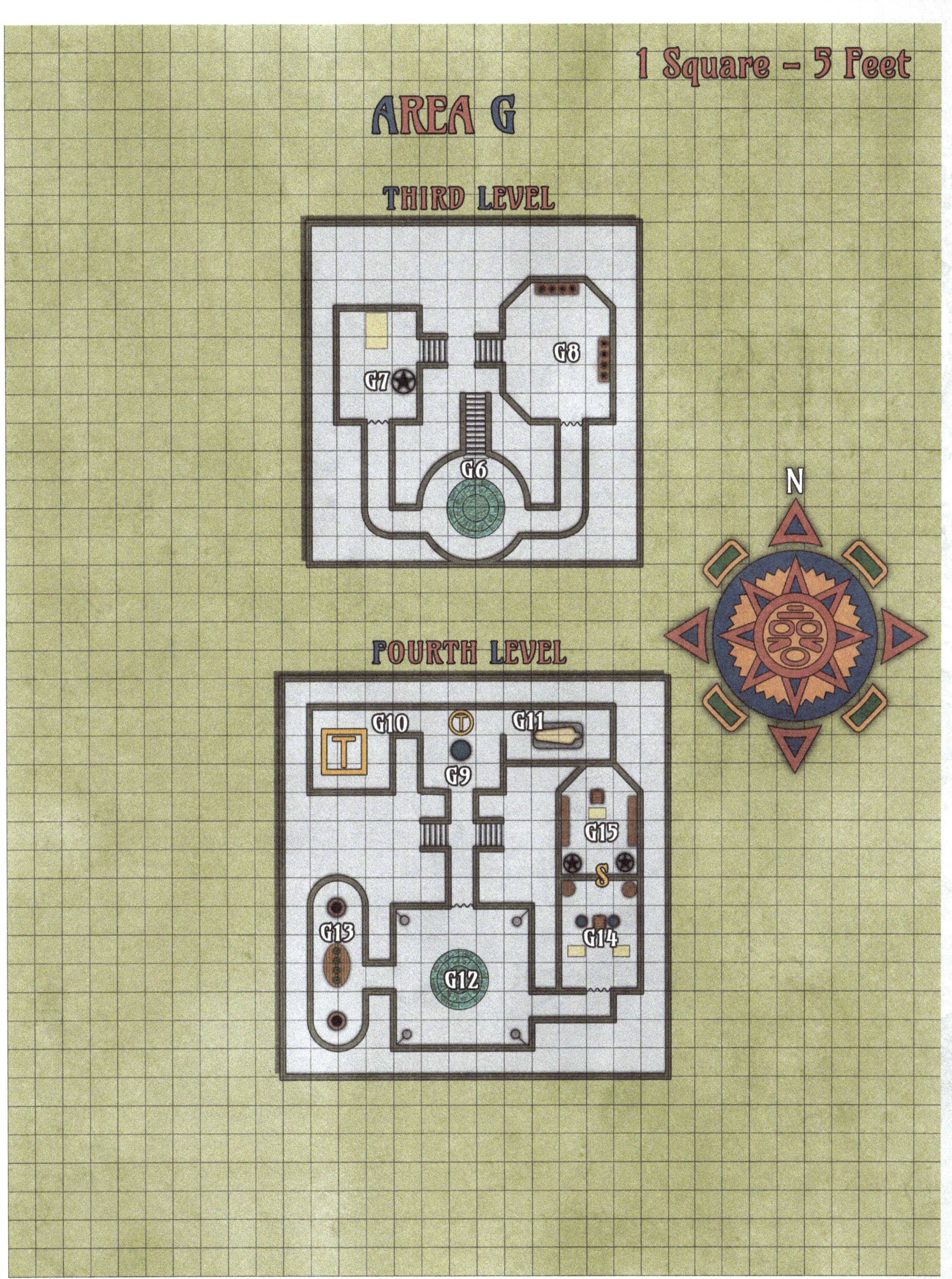

AREA G
THIRD LEVEL
G8
G7
G6
N
FOURTH LEVEL
G10
T
G11
G9
G15
S
G13
G14
G12

G8: Scriptorium

A thick, gray curtain made from linens hangs from a rod imbedded in the doorframe. A character can walk through the curtain without a check, but is blinded until the character moves more than five feet from the entrance or brushes the curtain aside. A character who listens hears intermittent snarls, yelps, and other animal sounds behind the curtain in addition to smelling a rancid stench.

> The foul odor of feces, urine, and drool combine to bombard the olfactory senses. The disgusting stink comes from four mangy, snarling dogs of various sizes confined in blatantly inhumane cages. Bowls beneath each of their frothing mouths collect their saliva as its seethes out of their clenched jaws and into the receptacle beneath it. Several codices, eagle feathers, and clay pots of pigments rest atop a table against the near wall and the far wall. A portal opens into a pitched staircase that descends into darkness.

Coyotl deliberately infected these unfortunate dogs with the deadly rabies virus (see **Rabies** sidebar). He uses the bowls to collect their contaminated saliva, which he adds to the calmecac's cold cacao drinks to unleash the beasts inside his remaining followers. For their part, the tragic canines horrifically suffer from the final stages of the lethal virus. Although it appears to fit in with its diseased counterparts, a **retch hound** freely roams about the chamber, waiting for its inhabitants to expire so it can feast on their diseased flesh. However, the surly beast truly savors the taste of humanoid meat, prompting it to immediately exhale acidic bile at its potential prey before sinking its teeth into the tender morsels. The animal works in concert with **2 beasts of Itzcuin** also wandering around the converted scriptorium. The trio coordinate their attacks to give the retch hound advantage while it waits for its retch ability to recharge.

Six codices sit atop the tables. Five of them are vestiges from the temple's former masters, but one codex details Coyotl's experiments on his captive hounds. A character may flip through the work of crude sketches and contemporaneous notes. A character who spends 10 minutes on this activity realizes Coyotl adds the infected saliva to the cacao drinks he serves his subordinates to whip them into an animalistic frenzy. His studies indicate that the dogs eventually died from the contagion. The misinformed Coyotl initially seemed to believe the disease would turn his human subjects into wild beasts without killing them. His research appears to end at this point.

Retch Hound: HD 3; HP 21; AC 5[14]; **Atk** bite (1d8); **Move** 18; **Save** 14; **AL** N; **CL/XP** 4/120; **Special:** Breath weapon (1/round, 10ft cone, 2d6 damage, save for half), stench (30ft radius, save or nauseated, −1 to hit and saves). (see **Appendix A: New Monsters**)

Beasts of Itzcuin (2): HD 2; HP 13, 11; AC 7[12]; **Atk** bite (1d3 + disease); **Move** 15; **Save** 16; **AL** C; **CL/XP** 2/30; **Special:** darkvision (60ft), disease (save or 1d4 damage per day, healing ends damage), misfortune (1/day, save or −1 penalty to hit and saves for 24 hours). (see **Appendix A: New Monsters**)

Treasure: The five codices (worth 100 gp each) are rare works of Aztli poetry and song praising Nonotzali.

G9: Ceremonial Font

> Painted images of feathered serpents adorn the walls surrounding an elevated basin sculpted from blue stone with green and black flecks interspersed across its surface. A bronze ring is attached to a trapdoor built into the floor.

Shortly after consecrating the temple, Nonotzali's priests and worshippers collected ink and deposited the liquid within this turquoise receptacle. Despite the passage of 160 years, the stone basin remains half-full and the ink remains viable. During the Summer Solstice, Nonotzali's clergy used a few drops of the precious to chronicle local events that occurred in the prior year.

The trapdoor built into the floor adjacent to the north wall connects to the underground tunnels supplying water to **Area E** outside. The wooden door opens with nominal effort. The temple's architects attached a 25-foot-long rope tethered to a bronze pail to the inside of the trapdoor, allowing the user to retrieve water through a two-foot-diameter shaft below the trapdoor that descends 20 feet into a small cistern.

Cursed Ink Trap

When a creature removes the font from this chamber or more than two vials of ink from the receptacle per day, all creatures within five feet of the font must succeed on a saving throw or be cursed for one hour. While cursed, the creature takes 2d4 points of damage when it eats or drinks, including imbibing potions and magical elixirs. A *remove curse* spell ends the effect. Destroying the font permanently removes the trap.

Treasure: The turquoise font (worth 1,000 gp) rests atop a limestone pedestal. It weighs 200 pounds, though removing it from the temple is considered a sacrilege in the eyes of Nonotzali's devout followers.

G10: Pit of Bones

> A heavy wooden trapdoor with an obvious locking mechanism and a sliding eye panel occupies a large portion of the floor in an otherwise featureless room.

After rare animal sacrifices, Nonotzali's priests dumped the remains into the pit beneath the trapdoor. It takes a successful Open Doors check to pry the locked door open through brute force. If the characters bypass the trapdoor, read or paraphrase the following description:

> Bones litter the floor of a 40-foot-deep pit with earthen walls beneath the trapdoor.

The skulls, long bones, and vertebrae contain a mixture of humanoid and animal bones sacrificed to Nonotzali over the last 160 years, as well as Coyotl's recent additions to the pit. The students who resisted the vicious lycanthropy as well as Aloc's torso and the missing acolyte were dumped into the pit after he and his minions savagely butchered them. From the surface, it is impossible to discern the type, age, or number of skeletons in the pit, though the bones are roughly one to three feet deep in most spots. The characters may circumvent this obstacle by using a rope to raise or lower adventurers into or out of the pit. A character who examines the recent skeletons confirms that they are almost all adolescent and teenage human males with the exceptions of Aloc and his acolyte who are both middle-aged human males. A character who explores the bottom of the pit serpent bones accounting for a significant percentage of the animal skeletons.

While many of the skeletons are decades old, the uppermost layer are relatively recent additions almost completely stripped of their skin and muscles. The heat and humidity partially explain the rapid skeletonization of these earthly remains, yet the **ghast** and **3 ghouls** picking through the bones are mostly responsible for the rapidly vanishing flesh.

The undead scavengers are recent additions to the complex. They are typically content to remain in the pit where they can freely pick the meat from the bones of the recently departed. However, the prospect of a fresh kill proves too irresistible to ignore. The cunning monsters know the best route to use when climbing out of the pit. They have no information about Coyotl, as their attention is squarely focused on their next meal.

Ghast: HD 4; HP 24; AC 4[15]; **Atk** 2 claws (1d3), bite (1d6); **Move** 15; **Save** 13; **AL** C; **CL/XP** 5/240; **Special:** paralyzing touch (3d6 turns, save avoids), stench (10ft radius, save or suffer −2 penalty on attack rolls). (***Monstrosities*** 189)

Ghouls (3): HD 2; HP 14, 12, 9; AC 6[13]; **Atk** 2 claws (1d3 + paralysis), bite (1d4); **Move** 9; **Save** 16; **AL** C; **CL/XP** 3/60; **Special:** immunities (charm and sleep), paralyzing touch (3d6 turns, save avoids). (***Monstrosities*** 191)

G11: Priest's Tomb

Nonotzali's priests laid the temple's founder Caxto to rest near the heart of the pyramid he designed and built. They wrapped his mummified body inside the preserved jaguar skin that serves as his crude coffin, using vines to seal it shut on both ends. It is impossible to unravel the skin without severing or removing the vines that bind the skin.

Summon Celestial Trap

Dealing at least one point of slashing damage to a vine instantly severs the magical bond keeping the makeshift sarcophagus intact. However, doing so immediately summons a **couatl** solely charged with the task of defending Caxto's corpse from defilement and theft. The couatl demands an explanation for the transgression. If the characters apologize for their actions and agree to leave the body undisturbed, the guardian allows them to leave unharmed, though the couatl keeps a watchful eye on the characters' future actions to ensure they keep their word. Otherwise, the couatl attacks.

Couatl: HD 8; HP 56; AC 4[15]; **Atk** bite (2d6 + poison), tail (1d6 constrict); **Move** 12 (fly 24); **Save** 8; **AL** L; **CL/XP** 11/1700; **Special:** poison (save or die), polymorph (at will), spells (3/2/1). (*Monstrosities* 73)
  Spells: 1st—*charm person, magic missile, sleep*; 2nd—*invisibility, phantasmal force*; 3rd—*lightning bolt*.

Detect magic cast on the coffin detects the presence of magic on the vines. Alternatively, the characters may bypass triggering the trap by untying or carefully removing the bonds without severing them. It takes a successful Delicate Tasks check to manipulate the delicate bonds without breaking them. A non-thief character can attempt the check at half the chance of a thief of the same level. On a failed check, the character inadvertently snaps the vine, triggering the trap.

Characters who successfully bypass the trap and unravel the coffin discover the withering, decomposed corpse of an elderly man. The decedent still wears a gold ring on each hand and a lapis lazuli necklace around his neck. He holds a dried husk of maize in his clenched fingers.

Treasure: The corpse wears a gold ring (worth 500 gp) on his right hand, and another gold ring (worth 250 gp) on his left hand. The gold rings bear no symbols or images, which makes them unique. However, the lapis lazuli necklace (worth 700 gp) bears a striking resemblance to a snake wrapped around a giant eagle, making it easy to associate the piece of jewelry with a priest of Nonotzali.

G12: Kennel

A thick, white curtain made from linens and decorated with an embroidered depiction of a feathered serpent hangs from a rod imbedded in the doorframe. A character can walk through the curtain but is blinded until he or she moves more than five feet from the entrance or brushes the curtain aside. Furthermore, a character who listens hears intermittent snarls, yelps, and other animal sounds behind the curtain in addition to smelling a foul odor.

Open wounds perforate the skin and fur of **3 dogs**, each outfitted with a harness that is attached to a rope affixed to one of the stone hooks. These animals suffer from the early stages of rabies, which leaves them feverish, lethargic, and obviously sick. In this condition, they barely react to the unexpected intrusion. The characters can release the dogs from the harnesses by undoing the straps keeping the harness in place. These animals are eventually slated to replace those in **Area G8** when those tragic creatures finally succumb to rabies.

Coyotl leaves the animals' bodily waste on the mosaic floor out of pure laziness and his crass need to debase Nonotzali and his worshippers. If the characters remove the excrement and vomit from the floor, they discover a magnificent tile mosaic. The grand artwork depicts Nonotzali in his humanoid form striking a serpent-headed humanoid with a lightning bolt.

The occupants in neighboring **Area G13** expect some noise from the dogs, though any sounds with obvious humanoid origins, such as voices or a concerted effort to clean off the mosaic prompt these individuals to investigate the activity in the adjoining area.

Rabid Dogs (3): HD 1; HP 5, 4x2; AC 7[12]; **Atk** bite (1d3 + rabies); **Move** 15; **Save** 17; **CL/XP** 1/15; **Special:** rabies (save or infected [see **Rabies** sidebar]). (*Monstrosities* 127)

G13: Cacao Storage and Brewing

Aloc stored dried maize and other nonperishable goods in this repository. Coyotl unceremoniously disposed of those foodstuffs with the exception of the cacao beans, which became an integral part of his fiendish plan to unleash the inner beast in his surviving charges. To that end, **Cuxta** and **Quezatl** grind cacao beans into a fine powder to be mixed into their deadly concoction. Two teen boys named **Elzatl** and **Teuatal** sit on the floor holding a clay drinking vessel in their outstretched hands. If the characters create a commotion in **Area G12**, Cuxta and Quezatl temporarily abandon their post to look into the matter. Each carries a cup containing cacao powder as well as their weapon. Regardless of where they encounter the characters, they throw the ground material from the cup into the characters' faces to blind them. The powder can be thrown 10 feet but there is only enough powder for one attack. A creature hit by the powder must succeed on a saving throw or be blinded. Like their fellow fanatics in **Area G4**, the duo remains tight-lipped about Coyotl's plans.

Cuxta and Quezatl, Male Aztli Cultists (Clr6) (2): HP 30, 24; AC 8[11]; **Atk** club (1d4); **Move** 12; **Save** 10; **AL** C; **CL/XP** 6/400; **Special:** +2 save vs. paralysis and poison, banish undead, spells (2/2/1/1).
  Spells: 1st—*cure light wounds* (x2); 2nd—*hold person, speak with animals*.
Equipment: ichcahuipilli armor[B], club.
[B] See **Appendix B: New Equipment and Magic Items**

Elzatl and Teuatal, Teenage Students, Male Aztlis (2): HD 1; HP 7, 5; AC 7[12]; **Atk** club (1d4) or sling (1d4); **Move** 12; **Save** 17; **AL** C; **CL/XP** 1/15; **Special:** none. (*Monstrosities* 254)
Equipment: club, sling, 10 sling bullets.

The younger boys surprisingly watch the battle unfold without interfering. So far, they are fortunate enough to have avoided contracting rabies from the contaminated cacao drink, which proves to be an imperfect method of quickly transmitting the virus. The duo, who have been best friends since childhood, have no knowledge of Coyotl's plans. They admit they did not speak out against Coyotl after his coup, but they never supported his violent takeover either. Since then, his ardent followers have forced them to come to the temple for their daily serving of his cacao drink. They believe the concoction is designed to make them more obedient, though they are concerned that several of their friends exhibit symptoms of a virulent illness or seem to have lost their minds.

Treasure: The two clay pots hold a substantial quantity of cacao beans (worth 400 gp). Cuxta wears a turquoise ring (worth 100 gp), while Quezatl carries three *potions of healing* and *blue war paint* (see **Appendix B: New Equipment and Magic Items**).

G14: AUDIENCE HALL

A thick, gray curtain made from linens hangs from a rod imbedded in the doorframe. A character can walk through the curtain but is blinded until the character moves more than five feet from the entrance or uses brushes the curtain aside.

> Two linen mats lie on the floor before an ornately carved oak chair decorated with etchings of feathered beasts. Two small clay basins containing water sit on each side of the chair. A small round table is in each of the far corners. An ornate painting of a grand library runs across the entire wall. Pictographs cover the face of a stone door against the far wall.

Aloc and his acolytes entertained visitors and guests in this understated audience chamber. The high priest sat in the oak chair, which bears carvings of feathered beasts along its back and legs. The water in the clay pots appears stagnant and cloudy. Aloc would normally sprinkle the water onto guests and visitors as a blessing or to wash their hands between morsels. The priests served food on the lightweight tables that they moved from the far corners and placed next to the chair and linen mats.

The pictographs on the stone door granting access to **Area G15** are arranged into five vertical rows. (The horizontal rows are obviously off-center.) Going left to right, each carving depicts the same feathered serpent. The first row contains four carvings, the second row has three, the third row has one, the fourth row has five, and the fifth row has two. Scrawled across the top of the carvings is another depiction of the feathered serpent followed by a horizontal line and two dots. Although the carvings look the same, a character who carefully examines the carvings notices that the top carving in each vertical row has a slightly raised indentation that functions as a crude button near the base of the creature's tail.

The code is a mathematical formula. The horizontal bar represents the number five, and the two dots represent the number two. Therefore, the correct sequence is to push the top button in the fourth vertical row, which has five carved serpents, followed by the top button in the fifth vertical row, which has two. Alternatively, the door can be forced open, though it takes a herculean effort to bypass this formidable barrier. However, a character who succeeds on an Open Doors check with a –3 penalty (minimum 1) can push the door open.

VAULT TRAP

If a character presses a button in an incorrect sequence or forces the door open without using the correct code, the images of the suns on the door's face emit a blinding flash of light in a 20-foot cone. Each creature in the cone must succeed on a saving throw. On a failed saving throw, the creature takes 5d6 points of damage and is blinded for 1d4 + 1 rounds. Once triggered, the trap is rendered inert until it resets 1d4 rounds later.

G15: VAULT

> Two bronze statues of Aztli warriors stand in the near corners with their outstretched spears pointed toward the door. Wondrous objects and open bags of coins sit atop two shelves lining the surprisingly undecorated walls. A luxurious linen mat adorned with feathers and preserved snakeskin rests on the floor in front of a sturdy oak chair.

Hardly renowned for his bravery, **Coyotl**, has taken up residence in the vault housing the temple's treasury, the complex's most secure locale. The uprising's cowardly leader broods in his quarters, disappointed in his plan's lack of visible and obvious progress. Two adolescent boys bound by heavy ropes foam at the mouth while they helplessly twitch and convulse. The rabies virus quickly overwhelmed these two young boys. They rapidly progressed through the disease's initial stages without transforming into the killing machines Coyotl desired. Instead, they quickly cycled into deathly ill children who now suffer through rabies' horrific death throes. When Coyotl and his loyal minions saw the disease's effects firsthand, they removed these two individuals from the populace and kept them hidden to keep Coyotl's failure private and to prevent panic from spreading through the calmecac.

Behind the claws and fangs, Coyotl is a selfish young man obsessed with his sense of self-importance and resolving old scores. Despite his formidable combat abilities, he shies away from fighting an opponent who poses a realistic threat to his safety. If the characters' actions in **Area G14** gave Coyotl any warning of their arrival, such as triggering the vault trap or pounding on the vault door, Coyotl sits on the oak chair and casts *phantasmal force* to conjure ropes around his arms and chest to make it appear as if he is being restrained. A character who physically interacts with the ropes discovers it to be an illusion.

Coyotl assumes a catatonic appearance to blend in with the other victims of the virus. In this case, Coyotl cautiously watches from his seat while the **3 beasts of Itzcuin** fight the intruders. Coytol unexpectedly rises from his seat and joins the fray when the beasts hit more than one character or render a character unconscious. He transforms into his hybrid form and attacks the unsuspecting adventurer with his claws and bite. Alternatively, he may grab a club from the nearby shelf in lieu of his claw attacks.

If the beasts fare poorly, Coyotl pretends to be in an irreversible stupor. An astute character who examines him can discover that the young man is faking his current condition. Of course, if the characters attempt to restrain him, touch him, or say anything remotely threatening, Coyotl immediately snaps out of his catatonia and goes on the offensive. Surrender is not an option for the werecoyote. Left to the whims of Aztli justice, he would assuredly die a horrifically gruesome death on a sacrificial altar or a prolonged incarceration in the notoriously brutal prison system. While he cannot undo the murders he already committed, the cagey werecoyote blames his corruption on Itzcuin and Ozhuma who unleashed his lycanthropy. He offers permanent exile as the only alternative punishment for his crimes. He rejects any other option, knowing full well that any other choice gives him no hope for the future. If negotiations break down, Coyotl still has some tricks up his sleeve. Depending on the circumstances, he may cast *dimension door* to slip past the characters and potentially outrun them into the wilderness. If flight does not appear to be a viable option, Coyotl casts *mirror image* and attempts to slug it out with the characters using his melee attacks or spells.

Coyotl, Male Aztli Werecoyote: HD 6; HP 43; AC 5[14]; **Atk** bite (1d8), 2 claws (1d6) or club (1d4) or spear (1d6); **Move** 12; **Save** 11; **AL** C; **CL/XP** 8/800; **Special:** +1 or better magic or silver weapons to hit, lycanthropy, shapechange (into human, coyote, or hybrid forms), spells (4/3/2/1).
  Spells: 1st—*detect magic, magic missile* (x2), *sleep*; 2nd—*darkness 15ft radius, mirror image, phantasmal force*; 3rd—*flay skin*[C], *haste*; 4th—*dimension door*.
Equipment: olli armor[B], club, spear, *potion of invulnerability*, pouch containing eight pearls (100 gp each).
[B] See **Appendix B: New Equipment and Magic Items**
[C] See **Appendix C: New Spells**

Beasts of Itzcuin (3): HD 2; HP 12, 9; AC 7[12]; **Atk** bite (1d3 + disease); **Move** 15; **Save** 16; **AL** C; **CL/XP** 2/30; **Special:** darkvision (60ft), disease (save or 1d4 damage per day, healing ends damage), misfortune (1/day, save or –1 penalty to hit and saves for 24 hours). (see **Appendix A: New Monsters**)
Rabid Male Aztli youths (2): HP 2 each; AC 9[10]; **Atk** bite (1d3 + rabies); **Move** 12; **Save** 18; **AL** C; **CL/XP** B/10; **Special:** rabies (save or infected [see **Rabies** sidebar]). (*Monstrosities* 254)
Equipment: club, sling, 10 sling bullets.

Treasure: The shelf along the southern wall holds a *+1 itztopilli*[B], a spell scroll (*falling logs*[C]), and a *death whistle*[C], in addition to ordinary objects including a bronze statuette of a pouncing cat (worth 150 gp), a collection of seashells (worth 75 gp), and 23 bloodstones (worth 10 gp each). The shelf on the northern wall holds 2,534 sp and 1,002 gp in open leather bags. The two bronze statues (worth 250 gp each) stand 5–1/2 feet high. Each statue weighs roughly 1,000 pounds. Eagle feathers and tufts of jaguar fur adorn the linen mat (worth 100 gp).
  [B] See **Appendix B: New Equipment and Magic Items**
  [C] See **Appendix C: New Spells**

Concluding the Adventure

With Coyotl dead or otherwise neutralized, the characters face the dilemmas of what to do with the calmecac's infected residents, many of whom remain symptom-free. *Cure disease* offers a cure, but those left untreated face a tragic descent into delirium and ultimately death. However, Coyotl did not act alone. The characters and local authorities must also decide the fates of the young boys and men who willingly joined Coyotl's cause and helped put his diabolical plan into motion. Aztli justice often lacks mercy, but the notion of summarily executing the town's potential next generation of leaders and warriors generates political ramifications for Mintoch and the ruling nobility. In the end, the town likely punishes only a small handful of ringleaders as an ominous warning to the more malleable calmecac residents who fell prey to Itzcuin's empty promises.

Meanwhile, Quiahuitl's priest presides over the critical rain harvest festival that takes place in the outer courtyard of the temple of Quiahuitl within Teohuacan. The townsfolk naturally invite the heroes as honored guests, as some families express their gratitude by offering them a host of gifts ranging from the mundane (maize, squashes, trinkets, and similar baubles) to the extravagant (family heirlooms, tracts of arable land, and even marriage proposals from family patriarchs). If the characters did not explore the cipatenhua stronghold earlier in the adventure, Mintoch may ask the adventurers to investigate several recent kidnappings or ambushes involving the cunning monsters. From here, the characters may also travel to the neighboring Tepepan Mountains to begin ***Gargoyle Pet Sematary***, the next adventure in the series.

Gargoyle Pet Semetary

By Rob Manning

"Tepetzin towers over us all! Hail to the stairway of the hero-gods!"

— A Mountain Dweller saying

"The silver of a sprig of chachacomo is worth more than real silver to me."

— Aztli boast heard throughout the lands

"Miquiztli icuhea or Death comes quickly."

— The motto in the mountains

Gargoyle Pet Sematary is an adventure for four 3rd- to 5th-level characters that introduces the heroes to the Tepepan Mountains in central Tehuatl where Aztli and dwarven cultures partially merge. When the characters arrive at the village of Alataq, they soon discover something is amiss within the settlement as several of its steadfastly loyal gargoyle servants appear to have gone rogue. What feels like an isolated incident turns out to be far more sinister as the architects behind the insidious plot have grander designs and greater horrors to unleash upon an unprepared world unless the adventurers stop them.

Adventure Background

There are no coincidences for the Aztlis. While fate may not be preordained, omens and signs frequently portend what the future holds. On this occasion, a chance meeting between a debonair demon named Chupura and a cunning night hag named Aytasina led to love at first sight for the smitten pair. The devious and alluring Aytasina had previously spent her lonely, forlorn existence wandering through the Tepepan Mountains perpetrating isolated murders and minor corruptions while dabbling in the pseudoscience of altering living creatures and studying arcane magic. At first, Chupura tried to convince his beloved hag to leave the small island for greener pastures and greater conquests. However, when the demon learned about the Aztli god Itzcuin's interest in canines and gnolls, he too came to believe that their encounter represented part of a divine destiny in Tehuatl.

Despite the demon's sincere belief in the couple's newfound destiny, the apathetic Itzcuin felt the need to test the fidelity of his neophyte disciples. To prove their worth, he appeared to the pair in cryptic visions, beseeching them to find the Lost Temple of the Twins hidden within the Tepepan Mountains. With nowhere else to turn for information or even hints about its whereabouts, Aytasina consulted her divination magic. Her spells and research led her to an obscure man named Hiuaui who lived in the village Alataq. The ambiguous clues pointed toward the secret being linked to a mysterious object in his possession associated with the settlement's unusual tukkuru gargoyles who serve and obey their humanoid masters as pet animals.

The connection between the item and the creature remained elusive, but the malevolent duo came upon a brilliant idea. They saw an opportunity to maximize their investment by exploiting the citizens' dependence and absolute trust in their generally benevolent and loyal servants. With these wicked thoughts in mind, they located and ventured into the tukkuru gargoyle graveyard within the mountain range where they began the process of corrupting these faithful creatures into conniving, evil, killing machines masquerading as stalwart friends. After several fits and starts, Aytasina sent prototypes to Hiuaui's home to spy on the old man and to discover where he hid the object of their mutual desire. To their chagrin, Hiuaui remained tightlipped about the item despite the monsters' cajoling and coaxing.

Frustrated by the lack of progress toward achieving their objective, the impatient demon and his lover ordered their minions to murder the old man and then torture his old gargoyle pets to reveal the location where he hid the object. Hours of agony and excruciating pain could not break Hiuaui's devoted gargoyle pets. Although they failed to accomplish their intended goal of retrieving their target, they wildly succeeded in their endeavor to build legions of deadly, innocent-looking creatures to wreak havoc throughout the Tepepan Mountain and beyond. They now stand on the precipice of unleashing mayhem upon the Aztlis and dwarves unless someone intervenes to stop them.

Adventure Synopsis

The adventurers' travels take them into the unruly Tepepan Mountains where Aztli and dwarven cultures collide in bizarre manners. During the initial foray into this rugged terrain, the characters are free to explore the region where they may engage in several random encounters with its indigenous denizens or become embroiled in the activities at the Obsidian Vault or the machinations brewing inside the quirky town of Aruapa. From there, the trail leads to the village of Alataq, where the adventurers arrive during a funeral for an elderly resident who died under very mysterious circumstances. After some inquiries, Calcata, the man's son approaches the characters and asks them to retrieve several items from his deceased father's house. Although this appears to be a curious request for such a minor task, Calcata tells them that he fears going to his father's residence because of recent unsettling events in the home.

When the characters arrive, they find the scene in disarray. With the evil gargoyles gone, the vile monstrous allies of Chupura and Aytasina torture Hiuaui's loyal servants to learn where he hid the object the demon and his lover desire. Fortunately, the characters appear in the nick of time to spare the tukkuru gargoyles any further suffering and retrieve the objects his son requested. After inspecting one of the items, they realize a maguey paper concealed inside Hiuaui's scepter leads them to the gargoyle graveyard where Chupura and Aytasina are ramping up production of their evil tukkuru assassins.

During this segment of the adventure, a benevolent tukkuru gargoyle may accompany the characters on its way to join its fellow gargoyles in the afterlife. When the characters arrive, they see troubling signs of the evil duo's recent insidious activities. The adventurers' investigation reveals that the two parties plan to extend their influence even further by courting potential discontent among the Firebrand dwarves. Their exploration first leads them to an encounter with the charming Chupura who attempts to procrastinate while trying to telepathically summon aid from his lover. If the distraction fails, he fights the characters until forced to flee. The characters then delve deeper into the complex where they encounter a crude alteration center for the modified tukkuru gargoyles as well as the ancient gargoyle graveyard itself. After navigating through these hazards, the characters meet the plot's mastermind within her secure vault where she and potentially her healed lover wait to deal with the trespassers infringing on their plans. The characters must defeat the pair to halt their production of the devious pet gargoyles and to restore solemnity to the somber gargoyle cemetery.

With the immediate threat neutralized, the characters return to the village where they learn the original message also contained an encoded map directing them to the hidden temple within the Tepepan Mountains. Although the malevolent locale poses no imminent danger to the region, its mere presence warrants taking action to prevent others from finding and using its power to spread Itzcuin's baleful influence across the land at a later date.

STARTING THE ADVENTURE

By Lost Lands standards, the island of Tehuatl and the Tepepan Mountains are a mere fraction of the size of most kingdoms in Akados and Libynos. The characters may begin the adventure along the southern edge of the mountain range that dominates the island's interior. The characters are free to be on their way to a location within the mountains such as the village of Aruapa or to travel directly to the settlement of Alataq, which is the main jumping-off point for this story. Because the distances between these points are relatively short, you can determine how far you want the characters to venture to reach their destinations. The following sections contains adventure hooks and random encounters you can throw at the adventurers during their trek through the mountains, as well as several fixed site encounters.

ADVENTURE HOOKS

You have several options to entice the characters to partake in this tale. You may use one of the following hooks or create one of your own. If you are using this adventure as a continuation of *The Re-education of Coyotl*, their discretion and valor in handling that situation may lead Kharu Amayana and Jark'iri from the town of Aruapa to request the characters' assistance in dealing with their bedeviled, small outpost.

THE SCRIPT

The Library of Alataq is renowned for its repository of knowledge and for offering sagacious advice to those seeking it. The characters recently acquired a curiosity that defies magical insight even though it appears completely nonmagical. The object is an ancient, weathered scrap of maguey paper containing faint drops of ink made from an unknown substance that form strange symbols and pictographs. The item is a coded message written in a cipher system that functioned as a precursor to the Aztli alphabet. Although the piece has no intrinsic value, the library's sages fawn over the rare piece, as they believe it was written by Nonotzali himself during his mortal lifetime. They appraise the item as being worth 500 gp for its value as a religious relic. The characters' journey to the mountain settlement then embroils them in the plot centering around Hiuaui.

THE GARGOYLE MESSENGER

Although the character has not seen him in years, a distant relative named Hiuaui (see **Alataq**) has one of his **tukkuru gargoyles** deliver a message to the character expressing his concerns about strange events taking place in his home. He asks the character to visit him to investigate his suspicions. The message conveys no specific details regarding his misgivings other than to vaguely allude to his lack of trust in others, and enemies murmuring behind his back. The dispatch seems coherent in parts and rambling in others, but the character recalls Hiuaui to be a remarkably sharp man before his advanced age apparently took its toll on him. If the characters respond to the summons, the gargoyle leads them back to its master's home, which is now a crime scene in utter disarray.

Tukkuru Gargoyle: HD 3; HP 18; AC 6[13]; Atk 2 claws (1d3), bite (1d4); Move 9; Save 14; AL N; CL/XP 3/60; Special: +1 or better magic weapon to hit. (see **Appendix A: New Monsters**)

FIREBRAND AGENTS

If one of the characters is a dwarf of the Firebrand Clan, the influential and powerful Garunt Firebrand approaches the characters to investigate a rumor about an evil entity attempting to make contact with disloyal members of the clan. Details about the plot are scant, but the source believes answers may be found in the mountain town of Alataq, where they believe some of the group's agents are currently active. Under questioning, Garunt reveals that he has no further information other than what he fortuitously overheard two patrons of unknown origin discussing in a tavern within Alataq. He never saw the parties before, and he has not seen them since, though he believes they were really otherworldly creatures in disguise. He also swears he heard one of the individuals mumble the name Itzcuin in an otherwise indecipherable language.

Garunt Firebrand, Male Dwarf Warrior (Ftr10): HP 67; AC 4[15]; Atk *+1 flail* (1d8+3); Move 9; Save 5; AL L; CL/XP 10/1400; **Special:** +2 to hit and damage strength bonus, multiple attacks (10) vs. creatures with 1 or fewer HD.
Equipment: *+1 chainmail*, shield, *+1 flail*, *ring of fire resistance*.

THE TEPEPAN MOUNTAINS

Through it all, the Tepepan Mountains survived. The cataclysm that laid waste to nearly all of the southern continent spared the northern tip that ultimately became the Tepepan Mountains. For generations, the humanoid populations crammed into this small corner of the world. When the island expanded and the waters ebbed, the Aztli people left the rugged peaks for the reborn grasslands and forest growing in the stony giants' shadows. While the Aztlis maintained some presence in the Tepepan range, the lonely peaks came under the Firebrand dwarves' dominion, giving the region a unique character that combines elements from both cultures. While the dwarves enjoy a great deal of autonomy, the Aztli Confederation still demands their literal and figurative pounds of flesh from the dwarves to keep their mighty armies at bay.

Despite the tropical conditions on the island, the mountains are a climate all their own. The elevation and comparatively dry air keep the temperatures mild and the humidity low during the daytime hours. When the sun sets, the air rapidly chills, dropping below freezing at the higher altitudes. Indeed, permanent snowcaps coat the tops of the tallest mountains, though nearly the entire area experiences some frozen precipitation over the course of the year. The onshore flow of air also pushes fierce winds through the peaks and valley, which makes the cool temperatures feel even colder.

The harsh environment and rugged terrain conspire to keep settlement populations low in comparison to communities with more accommodating weather and soil. With the exception of Balandrur, there are no major cities in the Tepepan Mountains. The hardscrabble people who make a go of life under these challenging circumstances tend to dwell in small, self-sufficient communities that are easier to clothe and feed than giant metropolises reliant upon trade. See the Tepepan Mountains map on page 70.

MOUNTAIN ENCOUNTERS

The rugged, unforgiving terrain gives adventurers little respite from the natural and unnatural dangers that abound here. In the absence of any clearly discernable paths or trails, the characters must trek through trackless areas for much of their journey into the foreboding peaks. The extreme altitude in some spots makes travel difficult and harrowing to say the least. For every hour spent trekking through the untamed wilderness, the adventurers have a 25% chance of participating in one of the encounters found on **Table 2–1**. The encounters include a mix of combat and opportunities to explore the characters' surroundings in greater detail. These short encounters are also easily dropped in when you need a mountainous encounter in any campaign.

TABLE 2–1: TEPEPAN MOUNTAINS RANDOM ENCOUNTERS

1d12	Encounter
1	The Faeries and the Footman
2	Mummy Dearest
3	The Wyrmlings
4	Devilish Flames
5	The Church of Seeping Death

1d12	Encounter
6	The Squid and the Whale
7	Rash Decisions
8	Wolves in the Distance
9	Hair of the Dog
10	Lightning Crashes
11	Orc Vision Quest
12	Drunken Dwarf Avalanche

THE FAERIES AND THE FOOTMAN

Once, a small coterie of elves under the orders of a high-level wizard made a home and observatory in the Tepepan Mountains. Only the first floor of the stargazing tower and one outbuilding remain. The wizard built two constructs to protect her library, and they are the only remnants of the expedition, save for a single book written in elvish in the library. When the characters come within visual range of the mostly razed structure, read or paraphrase the following description:

> A roofless, single-story rock building and a toppled stone tower dominate this plateau. Wind swirls across the flat surface and pushes anything in its path against the buildings and eventually over the edge. The roofless building looks empty and is open to the sky, but the barricaded door to the tower bars clear sight into what lies behind its walls. A long, yet narrow six-inch-wide, four-foot-high crack in the tower's foundation allows the elements to penetrate the interior.

When the characters move close to the observatory tower, **2 phookas** hiding in the ruins of the roofless outer building attempt to ambush them. The duo discovered the library in the tower some time ago and their mischievous nature wouldn't allow them to leave without gathering the seemingly burning book resting atop the floor. The footman drove them back and now they wait, nearly invisible in the ruins of the other building, where a large tree now grows. After surprising the characters, they try to lure or steer the combat toward the library and the **2 monolith footmen** that guard the entrance. Charged with the sole task of preventing intruders from entering the tower, the constructs attack only if a living creature moves within 10 feet of the tower's perimeter.

A character who peeks through the crack can see the book. If the combat or another ruse distracts the constructs, they can slip into the library uncontested through the crack and steal the book from its place on the floor. If the monolith footmen become occupied with attacking the characters, one or both phookas step into a nearby tree to stride into a tree close to the building and then run through the crack and into the tower to retrieve the book and escape with their prize.

Phookas (2): HD 4; HP 28, 23; AC 5[14]; Atk dagger (1d4); **Move** 6; **Save** 13; **AL** N; **CL/XP** 5/240; **Special:** alternate form (mountain lion or wolf), magic resistance (16%), spell-like abilities, tree stride (50ft range). (see **Appendix A: New Monsters**)
Spell-like abilities: 3/day—create dancing lights.

Monolith Footmen (2): HD 6; HP 44, 39; AC 5[14]; Atk longsword (2d6) or slam (1d8+2); **Move** 12; **Save** 11; **AL** N; **CL/XP** 8/800; **Special:** +1 or better magic weapons to hit, fey flame (3/day, enhance longsword with additional 1d6 fire or cold damage), immunities (charm, fear, and sleep), vulnerable to blunt weapons (natural 20 destroys footman). (see **Appendix A: New Monsters**)

Treasure: One phooka holds an onyx figurine of a wolf worth 200 gp in a small pouch. If the characters recover the book, they confirm the book's cover has been enchanted with a magical flame similar to *continual light*. The book is a diary containing personal accounts of the wizard's life in excruciatingly droll, boring detail. However, the book also conceals two spell scrolls (*slither*, *wall of smoke* [see **Appendix C: New Spells**]).

Mummy Dearest

Many tribes of gnolls thrive in the high mountains. The humanoids preserve the bodies of their deceased for the afterlife by removing all the major internal organs, wrapping the bodies in a huddled position with shellacked hides, and burying them in narrow crevasses high on the mountainsides. The Anu Khunu were one of the most devout tribes, and some of their dead still wander the area above the timberline. At the beginning of this encounter, read or paraphrase the following description:

> *"Swirling snow betrays its depth."* This old adage proves true in this valley where the sun fights to shine. A keening howl from above sets the nerves on edge as waist-high snowdrifts await. Bare patches of rock peek from the snow ahead, promising easier travel once attained. Ahead, two mounds of snow seem to creep closer.

The lack of visibility and deep snow might give the **3 mummies** enough leeway for the pair in front to close in to attack. A third mummy delays its attack for a round or two before approaching the adventurers from behind. The three mummies have no regard for their personal wellbeing. They just want to kill any living creatures that cross their path.

Gnoll Mummies (3): HD 5+1; HP 37, 34, 30; AC 3[16]; **Atk** strike (1d12); **Move** 6; **Save** 12; **AL** C; **CL/XP** 7/600; **Special:** +1 or better magic weapons to hit, rot (prevents magical healing, wounds heal at one-tenth normal rate, *remove curse* lifts curse). (*Monstrosities* 340)

Treasure: If the characters find the crevasse where these gnolls were once entombed, they discover a *ring of jumping* (see **sidebar**) entirely carved from a large opal secreted among the paltry treasures left in the preservation jars. Characters must traverse up to the bare patches of rock ahead of them to locate the crevasse.

New Magic Item
Ring of Jumping

A *ring of jumping* is similar to *boots of leaping*. It allows the wearer to make a 10 foot leap upward or a 30-foot horizontal leap.

The Wyrmlings

Some species of dragons in the Tepepan Mountains are nearly flightless. Their wings are underdeveloped, and their bodies are longer, more lupine, and sinewy. Their altered physiques help them to swiftly move through the narrow caverns beneath them. These youngsters usually set their sights on dwarves, but as this trio of immature beasts has learned, food comes in all shapes and sizes. At the beginning of the encounter, read or paraphrase the following description:

> A slight skittering across the crumbling rock surface is the only sound above the wind before a swift shadow blots out the sun.

The **3 immature white dragon** attack in concert. One wyrmling tumbles into the largest group of enemies to bite, while the other two wyrmlings blast the characters from afar with their cold breath attack as they jump around the melee. Their mother, an adult white dragon, lumbers through the subterranean caverns hunting dwarves. She is too far away from her offspring to hear their cries or help them. However, if the characters kill her progenies, they earn an eternal enemy.

Immature White Dragon (3): HD 5; HP 15; AC 2[17]; **Atk** 2 claws (1d4), bite (2d8); **Move** 9; **Save** 12; **AL** C; **CL/XP** 5/240; **Special:** breathes frost (3/day, 70ft cone, 15 damage, save for half). (*Monstrosities* 141)

Treasure: The skin and teeth of the trio are worth 50 gp per dragon if the characters take the time and effort to remove these items from the corpses. Their lair is also nearby but difficult to find as several pillars of ice camouflage the opening at the base of an ancient, ice-covered waterfall. The dragons have amassed only a small cache of silver and gems worth 450 gp and a gold-filigreed breastplate worth 550 gp. If the mother dragon learns of the characters' identity through whatever means, she exacts her revenge later when the characters have the wherewithal to defeat or at least survive an encounter with the irate mother dragon. You may use the dragon to remind them of their time in the Tepepan Mountains, even if they are in a different climate.

Devilish Flames

This encounter occurs either aboveground or below. When it begins, read or paraphrase the following description:

> What seemed a trick of the mind soon becomes evident that this is no illusion. The air is getting warmer. Actual permeable soil supporting succulent plants covers the ground. An apple tree, a group of irises, and lush grass dazzle the senses with thoughts of eternal spring. Ahead, a cracked vent made of basalt sports an intense yellow flame that shoots three feet into the air.

This vent has burned for centuries. Natural gas and the right combination of elements created this small oasis in the mountains where it continues to thrive to this day. Any snowfall here quickly turns to mist or rain. Just below the surface, **2 fire phantoms** gloomily sulk in the eternal flame. They rarely rise above the vent's lip but do so if the characters have any magical light source or if they camp here for any length of time. Fire phantoms who leave their subterranean refuge attack trespassers with unbridled fury.

Fire Phantoms (2): HD 6; HP 41, 37; AC 6[13]; **Atk** slam (1d4 + 1d6 fire); **Move** 6; **Save** 11; **AL** C; **CL/XP** 7/600; **Special:** fire blast (every 1d4 rounds, 30ft range, 2d6 damage, save avoids), immolation (1/day, 6d6 damage to all within 10ft radius, save for half, kills phantom if it fails save or extinguishes flame for 1 round if successful), immune to fire. (see **Appendix A: New Monsters**)

Treasure: Nestled among the topiary are some rare spices (cinnamon, cardamom, and mustard). If harvested, they are worth 150 gp.

The Church of Seeping Death

This encounter occurs underground in a shrine to the star spawn that brought forth chaos in centuries past. The shrine's power associated with the outer planes has weakened over time, though the imagery still evokes the fear of the Nights of Sillu and Claw. Gnoll cults used to worship here, offering blood and bone to the uncaring star spawn. If the characters happen upon this locale, read or paraphrase the following description:

This shrine once held high ceremonies to summon creatures from other dimensions. Most have moved on to wreak havoc in the mountains or to spread even farther across Tehuatl. The characters swear they can still hear the chattering of the insects in their minds as they observe the intricate carvings dedicated to the ancient evil overlords.

However, the chapel is not abandoned, as **8 grey oozes** remain here to this day. They appear as moist patches of stone, with some clinging to the 50-foot-high ceiling, some near the shrine, and some just inside the door. They swarm the intruding characters and attack from all sides with no plan other than to kill. If one adventurer falls, the surviving ooze moves to another combatant. Each hit from a melee weapon causes an ooze to pop with an audible sound and causes pustules of jellied, infected fluids to spray out.

The shrine radiates evil and chaos. A cleric or other good-aligned character who destroys the shrine by blessing the area or who smashes the altar into pieces gains a 400 XP story bonus.

Grey Oozes (8): HD 3; AC 8[11]; **Atk** strike (2d6); **Move** 1; **Save** 14; AL N; **CL/XP** 5/240; **Special:** acid (dissolve metal [save resists]), immunities (blunt weapons, heat, cold, spells). (**Monstrosities** 229)

Treasure: A *+1 tecpatl* (see **Appendix B: New Equipment and Magic Items**) lies near the altar — also covered with the sickly sheen of the endless travels of the oozes across the surface of the entire chapel.

The Squid and the Whale

Shortly after the great cataclysm, this comparatively low-lying area was completely underwater. In a remote area high in the mountains, a strange remnant of those primordial times still exists. If the characters begin this encounter, read or paraphrase the following description:

Centuries ago, this site hosted a great battle. A massive mysticeti whale swallowed a large squid whole. Unwilling to cede dominance to its rival, the squid forced its tentacles back out of the gullet through the mouth, and the two beasts killed each other simultaneously. Their remains, which were once deep below the sea, now lie atop this peak. The only evidence of the squid to survive is the beak, buried under the snow midway between the whale's skull and its tail.

This locale is now the lair of Achila, a **spirit naga**. She remains invisible as she thoroughly evaluates their strengths and weaknesses before launching her assault. The sword buried in the eyehole is a *phantasmal force* the naga previously cast. Achila attempts to charm any heavily armored or equipped character first. If successful, she commands the enthralled victim to quickly run back down the mountain, taking a chance that the character falls hundreds of feet to their doom off the steep, icy cliff near her lair. It takes a successful saving throw to avoid such an ignominious fate. If this attempt fails, she may then command her subject to throw their gear, including a weapon or shield, over the cliff. Magic-wielding characters are her second choice. She tries to get them to cast their most potent spell

Non-Combat Encounters

The following set of encounters are designed to give you an opportunity to throw something different at the players to keep them on their toes and engage their paranoia. You do not want the players to automatically start saying things like, "I cast *detect magic*," or something similar every time you roll dice. The Tepepan Mountains are a dangerous place, but not every encounter is a life-or-death struggle. Feel free to add monsters or intriguing non-player characters to beef up the combat encounters or use treasure found during one of these encounters to get a group back on track to help them refocus on the story you want to tell.

against a fellow adventurer. She saves her *lightning bolt* until two or more enemies are in a line in front of her.

If the characters struggle with this encounter, you may have the whale's long dead spirit momentarily appear to distract Achila to allow the characters an opportunity to flee the area or disrupt one of her spells. After she dies, Achila rejuvenates three days later, unless magically compelled to not reappear.

Spirit Naga: HD 9; HP 65; AC 5[14]; **Atk** bite (1d3 + poison); **Move** 12; **Save** 6; AL C; **CL/XP** 13/2300; **Special:** charm gaze (as *charm person*), lethal poison (save or die), spells (MU 4/2/1; Clr 2/1). (**Monstrosities** 344)
Spells: 1st—*cause light wounds, detect magic, magic missile* (x2), *protection from good, sleep;* 2nd—*hold person, invisibility, phantasmal force;* 3rd—*lightning bolt*.

Treasure: One of the smallest whale bones, located under the massive skull, functions as a *wand of cold* (12 charges).

Rash Decisions

This encounter may reoccur several times over the course of the adventurers' travels. In addition, you may add the effects of this encounter to any others below the timberline. While venturing across the Tepepan Mountains, the characters run across the flowering herb poison chachacomo. This poisonous variety closely resembles chachacomo, its non-poisonous relative, which vaunted mountain climbers and explorers greatly covet. The poisonous version is an irritant that grows more abundantly at a lower altitude. Characters who run across a patch of poison chachacomo must make a saving throw or take a –2 penalty to hit, damage, and saving throws for 2d6 hours, or until they wash thoroughly to remove all traces of the herb from their skin and clothing.

Wolves in the Distance

To set the mood for this scene, read or paraphrase the following description:

Animals and humanoids use this valley to traverse the area. The slide happened a long time ago and poses no immediate danger. As the characters start to move through the area, a pack of wolves intermittently howls in the distance. It is best to keep the number of wolves in the group indeterminate as well as concealing their exact location. While the encounter lasts, the animals neither draw closer to the characters nor move farther away. Furthermore, the beasts' verbal exchanges periodically occur in noisy but brief spurts between long periods of silence.

Hair of the Dog

Read or paraphrase the following description to set the action into motion:

This was once a small inn called Chichi auh Mazatl. It used to be a wooden, two-story structure that catered to travelers seeking shelter in the rugged mountains. The building is long gone, with only a few stones left to mark where it stood. The remaining hall served as the inn's kitchen and dining room. A small pile of chopped wood and pine needles lies near a recently used fire pit. A great fire consumed the inn several decades ago, but many travelers still recount strange tales of mysterious events taking place during an overnight stay in the rough-and-tumble lodge owned by an eccentric Tlotl who allegedly scoured the nearby mountains looking for something.

Lightning Crashes

Mountain weather is frequently unpredictable and subject to change at a moment's notice. Read or paraphrase the following description when the storm clouds suddenly gather overhead:

Storms form quickly in the highlands. Most blow over in a matter of minutes, but some pack a significant wallop from rapid drops in temperature, fierce winds, and torrential downpours or snow squalls in freezing conditions. The precipitation and swirling winds often wash or blow away any evidence or tracks, making it difficult to pursue prey in this challenging environment. While such weather events are likely not deadly, they may force the characters to use resources to cope with the horrific conditions.

Orc Vision Quest

Read or paraphrase the following description of this locale:

In a rite of passage, young orcs must spend a week in this cave to further strengthen their resolve to conquer the sun-drenched lands. Every initiate must be awake before the sun breaks over the horizon, shouting to their god for the sun not to rise. The devotee partakes in the consumption of special fungi to aid them as they begin to understand the universe and their place in it. No brave warriors are here when the characters arrive, though a shaman and a daring orc youth may appear at any time.

Orc: HD 1; HP 5; AC 6[13]; Atk spear (1d6) or scimitar (1d8); **Move** 9; **Save** 17; AL C; CL/XP 1/15; **Special:** none. (*Monstrosities* 364)

Orc Shaman (Clr4): HD 4; HP 24; AC 6[13]; Atk flail (1d8); **Move** 9; **Save** 13; AL C; CL/XP 4/120; **Special:** spells (2/1). (*Monstrosities* 364)

Spells: 1st—*cure light wounds, purify food and drink*; 2nd—*bless*.

Drunken Dwarf Avalanche

Dwarves continuously mine the mountains, looking for silver and gems. Sometimes, they dig a little too close to the surface and the resulting avalanche has a lasting effect. Some of these mishaps can be catastrophic, and they create a new tunnel leading to the dwarven lands below the surface.

A group of **11 drunken miners** are responsible for the rockslide. The men harbor no ill will and are truly sorry for the havoc their negligence caused. The avalanche poses no threat to the characters who are close enough to see, but are not in its direct path. If the adventurers move toward the avalanche, they must make a saving throw or take 4d6 points of damage, be knocked prone, and be buried beneath the debris on a failure, or evade the avalanche's effects in its entirety on a success. A buried creature may make an Open Doors check to escape or others can dig the character out of the debris.

Regardless of whether the characters avoid the avalanche, the dwarves leave a silver ingot worth 30 gp and a *potion of healing* on the path ahead as recompense for their negligence. If forced to fight, they try to run back to the depths and rile the guards on duty or a patrol of dwarven soldiers from outposts connected to the Firebrand Clan as soon as possible.

Drunken Dwarven Miners (11): HD 1; AC 4[15]; Atk pick (1d4); **Move** 6; **Save** 17; AL L; CL/XP 1/15; **Special:** darkvision (60ft), detect attributes of stonework. (*Monstrosities* 149)

Side Treks in the Tepepan Mountains

This section presents two side treks the characters can partake in while exploring the Tepepan Mountains. The first is a short encounter involving events around an obsidian mine, while the second takes place in the unusual town of Aruapa.

Side Trek 1: The Obsidian Vault

This vault is in a small cavern system just below the surface of one of the mountains. Recently exposed due to seismic shifts, an enterprising gnoll named Anuqara discovered the crevasse and has been harvesting obsidian to bring back to Aruapa, a village a few miles away. Anuqara and her pack of minions are oblivious to any outside intruders. Luckily for them, a gang of plaresh demons roam around with them and should help the pack realize they are under attack before it is too late.

Area ST1-A: The Maws and the Bats

> A fluttering cloud of bats flits around a narrow slit in the side of a cliff. An odd pyramid of writhing worms snaps into the cloud. The worms coalesce into the shape of a mouth and a sticky pseudopod covered with a filthy mucous to entrap the bats. Soon, a second wobbling mass emerges from the cave, and they contentedly eat their fill.

The strange worms are **2 plaresh demons** that eat from the seemingly endless parade of bats for four rounds before returning inside the cave as the stream of bats tapers off. If the characters attack the monsters, they summon two more of their kind from **Area ST1-B**.

Plaresh Demons (2): HD 4; HP 30, 26; AC 4[15]; **Atk** bite (2d6 + poison); **Move** 12 (burrow 12, swim 12); **Save** 13; **AL** C; **CL/XP** 6/400; **Special:** immunities (charm, poison, sleep), infect corpse (destroy body and cause new plaresh demon to rise in 1d4 rounds), magic resistance (10%), poison (save or additional 1d4 damage), resistances (cold, electricity, fire, slashing weapons, 50% damage). (see **Appendix A: New Monsters**)

Area ST1-B: Vented Maw

> A crunching sound echoes from inside the mountain and away from the near-constant wind. The cavern slopes down steeply as it goes deeper into the mountain.

The stench of bat guano fills the air. The remaining **2 plaresh demons** feast while thrashing about in the 14-inch-deep guano pile. The decomposing waste emits methane gas that explodes when exposed to an open flame, spark, or any suitable ignition source. Creatures and objects within the chamber must make a saving throw or take 5d6 points of fire damage on a failure, or half as much damage on a success.

The demons are mostly mindless, but they do chant "wilanchana" (bloody ritual) as they attack.

Anuqara tasked a **gnoll** to retrieve these demons, and he is approaching from the other direction when the characters enter this area. His name is Lakin and though he is not extremely vigilant, the sounds of combat or an explosion immediately notify him to the presence of intruders. Lakin thought he was on a foolish errand. When alerted to the presence of intruders, he waits one round and then retreats to the vault to warn his mistress.

Lakin, Male Gnoll: HD 2; HP 12; AC 5[14]; **Atk** bite (2d4) or battle axe (1d10) or spear (1d6); **Move** 9; **Save** 16; **AL** C; **CL/XP** 2/30; **Special:** none. (*Monstrosities* 209)
Equipment: battle axe, 3 spears.

Plaresh Demons (2): HD 4; HP 32, 27; AC 4[15]; **Atk** bite (2d6 + poison); **Move** 12 (burrow 12, swim 12); **Save** 13; **AL** C; **CL/XP** 6/400; **Special:** immunities (charm, poison, sleep), infect corpse (destroy body and cause new plaresh demon to rise in 1d4 rounds), magic resistance (10%), poison (save or additional 1d4 damage), resistances (cold, electricity, fire, slashing weapons, 50% damage). (see **Appendix A: New Monsters**)

Area ST1-C: The Vault

Long ago, an ancient eruption deposited this formation of snowflake obsidian (speckled with flecks of white star shapes in the caramel-colored obsidian through cristobalite clusters). Anuqara only recently discovered the vault. She now endeavors to retrieve the stone and bring it to Aruapa. If Anuqara returns with this load, her queen promised her a promotion and a village of her own for her pack.

The vault itself is almost a hundred yards from the bats' room. There are no major splits in the cave and no dangerous drops, though the trail is continually going downhill as it delves deeper into the mountain. The following description assumes the characters have a light source, as Anuqara and her gang work without light, using their darkvision to complete their tasks. The loading process takes nearly three hours before the gnolls are ready to travel to the river to send the obsidian on the next leg of its journey.

> The now familiar satisfied grunting, lip-smacking sound echoes down the hall as the cavern widens in the distance. The room slopes upward and to the left 30 feet, where another of the monstrosities gnaws on the remains of a humanoid corpse. Wooden boxes lie scattered all around. Some lie open, their lids leaning against the edge. Some are stacked against the wall with their lids nailed shut. All have shards of obsidian in them. More of the black stone grows from the far wall, glinting in the light.

If the characters surprise the gnolls, you may add or paraphrase the following description. Change the number to three humanoids if the characters somehow killed Lakin, the gnoll from **Area ST1-B**, before they approach this room.

> Four tall humanoids are working in pairs, bent over the boxes. They load obsidian into them as fast as they efficiently can.

In addition to the **plaresh demon**, there are 2 (or 3 if Lakin is with them) **gnolls** working under the cruel eye of **Anuqara**, a **gnoll slaver**. If caught unaware, the gnolls fight with their pair of spears. They throw one of their spears and then rush into melee combat. The demon uses its infest corpse ability to spectacularly consume the dead gnoll in a burst of slime and offal, bringing forth a new **plaresh demon** in the bloody remains as the gnoll's soul goes to its next destination. The pair wades into melee as soon as the gnolls attack. Anuqara fires her longbow from cover at the other exit from the room. She concentrates all her attacks on a single intruder, while the gnolls throw and attack in pairs. If Lakin made it here, all three warriors arm themselves with bows, and they cling to the piles of boxes to use as partial cover.

All of Anuqara's gnolls sport brands on nearly every inch of exposed flesh. She enjoys the branding process and keeps many metal tools in a pouch to create her "art." If Anuqara is reduced to less than half her maximum hit points or if any three of her pack falls, she flees. She quaffs up to two *potions of healing* during her escape. If the character capture her and compel her to speak through magical means, she reveals that the obsidian is bound for the town of Aruapa to be delivered to its queen.

OBSIDIAN VAULT

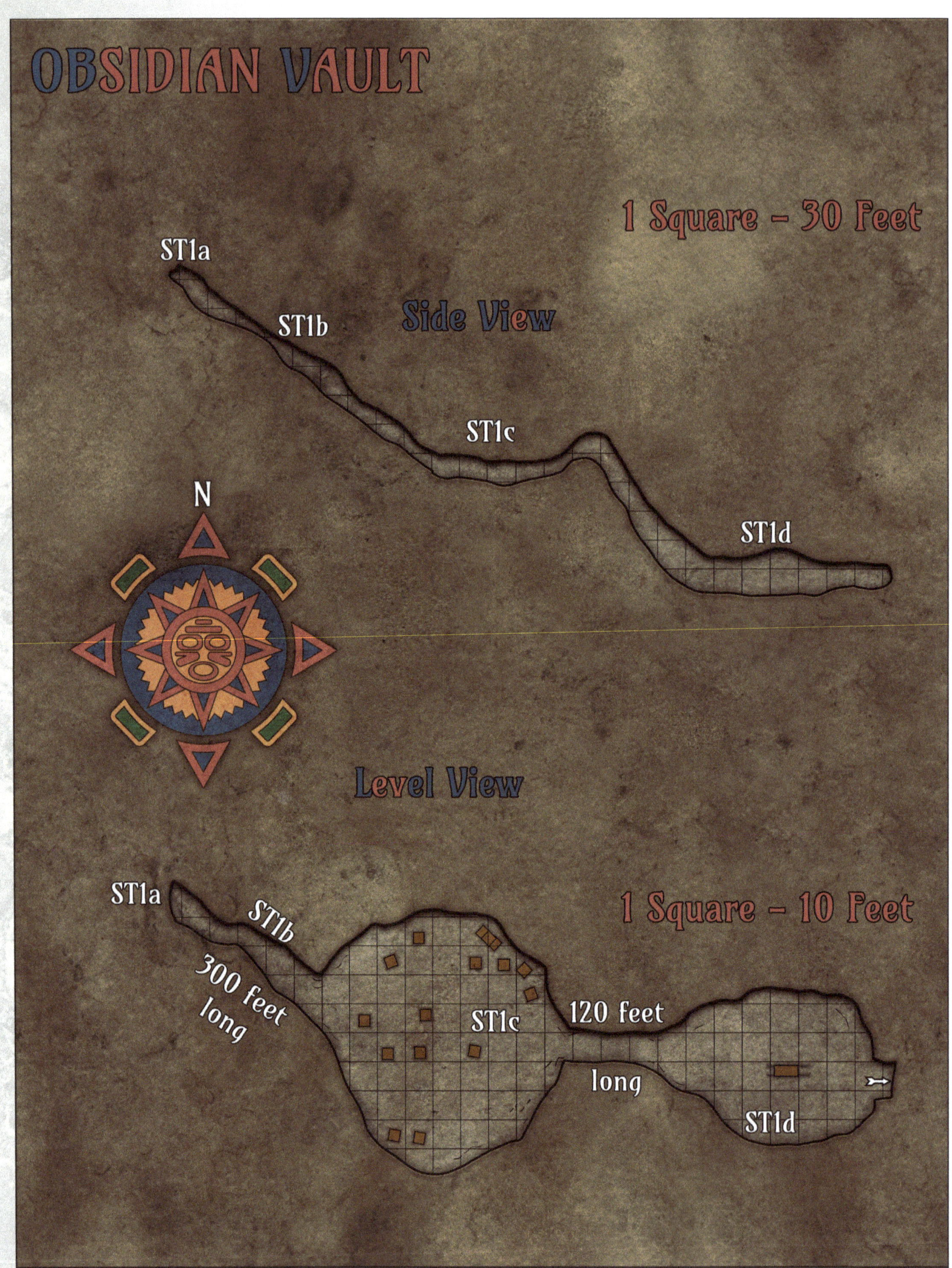

Gnolls (2 or 3): HD 2; HP 12, 11, 10; AC 5[14]; **Atk** bite (2d4) or battle axe (1d10) or spear (1d6) or longbow x2 (1d6); **Move** 9; **Save** 16; **AL** C; **CL/XP** 2/30; **Special:** none. (*Monstrosities* 209) **Equipment:** battle axe, 3 spears, longbow, 20 arrows.

Anuqara, Female Gnoll Slaver: HD 5; HP 35; AC 5[14]; **Atk** bite (2d4) or longsword (1d10 +1) or longbow x2 (1d6); **Move** 9; **Save** 12; **AL** C; **CL/XP** 5/240; **Special:** none. (*Monstrosities* 209) **Equipment:** longsword, longbow, 20 arrows, 2 *potions of healing*, metal branding tools, 2d6 gp.

Plaresh Demons (2): HD 4; HP 28, 23; AC 4[15]; **Atk** bite (2d6 + poison); **Move** 12 (burrow 12, swim 12); **Save** 13; **AL** C; **CL/XP** 6/400; **Special:** immunities (charm, poison, sleep), infect corpse (destroy body and cause new plaresh demon to rise in 1d4 rounds), magic resistance (10%), poison (save or additional 1d4 damage), resistances (cold, electricity, fire, slashing weapons, 50% damage). (see **Appendix A: New Monsters**)

Treasure: The obsidian collected here is worth 1,000 gp.

Area ST1-D: Burrows and Barks

The narrow, winding corridor connecting the vault to this cavern slopes down until it widens again into a level loading area. Scratches and footprints tell the tale of the gnolls' use of the passage. Anuqara directed her pack to load the boxes of obsidian onto a waiting sledge device pulled by a team of **4 hairless dogs**. If she passes through here, the dogs are riled and wandering aimlessly. If she has not fled, they stand staged and harnessed to the nearly full sledge.

Blood covers two of the four excessively branded dogs. Another gnoll corpse lies nearby. The reason for the dead gnoll and the current bloody dogs is the unexpected arrival of an oafish **hill giant** that stumbled upon the fresh meat and treasure. The brutish humanoid is an opportunist who surprised the gnoll and is not sure whether to eat the dogs or use them to pull the sledge back to his lair. When he spots the characters, the giant swings its massive greatclub to batter his opponents into submission. The giant is not bright, but he knows well enough to retreat if his life is seriously threatened.

Hairless Dogs (4): HD 1; HP 7, 5x2, 4; AC 7[12]; **Atk** bite (1d3); **Move** 16; **Save** 17; **AL** N; **CL/XP** 1/15; **Special:** none. **Hill Giant:** HD 8+2; HP 52; AC 4[15]; **Atk** club (2d8); **Move** 12; **Save** 8; **AL** C; **CL/XP** 9/1100; **Special:** throw boulders (2d8 damage). (*Monstrosities* 198) **Equipment:** club, leather sack containing 429 gp.

Treasure: The piled boxes of obsidian are worth 2,000 gp.

The trail of the previous sledges leads away from the cavern and directly to a fast-moving river about a mile away. Anuqara follows her shipment downstream and rejoins her final pair of gnolls. They are stationed at an ox-bow in the river almost eight miles from the point of entry. They fish the boxes of obsidian from the stream and have them packed and ready for Anuqara's return. The characters can catch up to her at some point solo or at the ox-bow with her minions if she is swift enough. If the characters confiscate any of the uniquely patterned obsidian and try to sell it in the area, Kharu finds out and sends a small task force to track down the thieves.

Side Trek 2:
Gaunt Whispers in Aruapa

You can run this side trek separate from the others or in conjunction with the previous excursion. If the characters encounter the town of Aruapa first, they hear of Anuqara the slaver, but not necessarily of her mission.

Aruapa is a settlement of misfits, made up of outcasts from communities across the island. They fled their homes and resettled here for various reasons. Some out of fear, some out of guilt, and some out of desperation. Here at Aruapa and other remote mountain villages, people can reinvent themselves. Aruapa boasts humanoids of Tosca descent, Tlotls from various cultures in Akados and Libynos, as well as other people displaced from communities in Tehuatl. Half-orcs, gnolls, gnomes, and elves make up nearly half of the population, and half-bloods of all combinations thrive in the settlement. Aruapa welcomes new arrivals (sometimes pressing new recruits into "freedom" from caravans that pass too close to their village). Loyalty to The Queen curtails racial animosity quickly here. Old enemies such as orcs and dwarves live peacefully in the same dwelling.

Aruapa is fairly civilized but harbors a deep distrust of Chacuina, another nearby outpost with a similar background. This distrust stems from an incident where warriors from Chacuina crept into Aruapa's holy place and stole a figurine of the hero-god Zipe-Toteque, also known as Xotite among the dwarves. Ithapina, the outpost's leader at the time, credited the statue for Aruapa's luck in the growing season. When it was stolen, it created the lasting rivalry with the Chacuina villagers.

The main reason for the current extended stretch of harmony in Aruapa is Kharu Amayana and Jark'iri. These two elf women rule the settlement and root out dissension before it has a chance to fester. Kharu is "The Queen" and Jark'iri, a couatl, acts as her counselor. Jark'iri took elf form to be closer to the object of her desire. Tattoos of moths decorating their bodies from neck to calf symbolize their loyalty to each other. Anuqara (see **Area ST1-C**) serves as Kharu's enforcer. When Jark'iri warns her Queen of treacherous thoughts among the villagers, Kharu sets her gnoll slaver to work. Sometimes, Anuqara presses the unruly citizen into her war band, and sometimes the unfortunate soul "accidentally" falls off a cliff. Jark'iri warns Kharu only if she detects murderous thoughts. She numbs herself to most other thoughts, including Kharu's. The couatl knows hers is an unrequited devotion, but her heart tells her she cannot live without the elf.

Fortunately for the couatl's potential redemption, Kharu rarely abuses her power. She spreads the wealth of their outpost's acquisitions among her people almost evenly, and she keeps Anuqara on a short leash. Nonetheless, she realizes she is losing control over her gnoll slaver and is growing wary of her rough manner. She has promised Anuqara her own tribe and her blessing to move on after she makes her final delivery of obsidian.

One of Aruapa's main exports is silk gathered from a colony of moths brought here and cultivated by a Tlotl family whose ancestors escaped their homeland in distant Libynos generations ago. Most villagers work in some way to further the silk trade here. Some tend the lichen surfaces and mulberry orchards where the moths feed, while others boil the cocoons and harvest the silk. Specialists dye and weave the product, and a few transport and sell it to neighboring Aztli villages that covet the unusually strong and luxurious material.

Unfortunately, when the characters first arrive here, Aruapa is in a state of panic. Ch'usuyana, a spökvatten, recently gave birth to Ikanp'akiri, her ice maiden daughter. Although the fey would normally stay on the outskirts of town, she and her ghastly child decided to use the villagers' suspicions about the neighboring settlement of Chacuina against them. The evil fey used her to guile and charm to plant stories about Chacuina spies infiltrating the village to kill its normally trustworthy citizens. After she and her daughter killed their first victims under this pretense, the terrified citizens' imaginations took hold. They saw traitors in their midst as mass hysteria swept through the village. Meanwhile, the alluring Ikanp'akiri quickly enthralled two vagabonds of Aruapa. One man's true love chased her beau through the driving snow and dragged him back to civilization with a determined kiss and saved his soul. The other thrall is still with Ikanp'akiri in a nearby hovel on the outskirts of Aruapa. For now, Ch'usuyana watches the spectacle of violence and suspicion unfold from the safety of the town's tavern as she tries to ensnare others into her devious web of lies and false accusations.

Imata, the gate guard used to be praised for his bravery and keen sight. He served as a guard for nearly his entire adult life. Ch'usuyana triggered childhood fears in him, and he sees the approaching strangers as otherworldly terrors from his youthful nightmares. If the characters allow him to fully retreat, he finds his way to the tavern, where he tells his tale to the frightened throng.

Imata, Male Elf Gate Guard: HD 3; **HP** 17; **AC** 5[14]; **Atk** spear (1d8); **Move** 12; **Save** 14; **AL** Any; **CL/XP** 3/60; **Special:** darkvision (60ft), detect secret doors (4-in-6 chance).
Equipment: spear.

The outpost of Aruapa consists of 18 small homes and the large warehouse built into the side of the mountain. Up to six people occupy each house at this time, though some homes are abandoned while others are cramped. Terror grips most villagers as they cling to improvised weapons in the vain hope that the evil that has descended upon their community might move elsewhere. They never willingly open their doors. The warehouse has a tavern attached to the front where 11 people chug pulque from clay containers. Only Kharu and Jark'iri sit on the large work floor of the warehouse. They are preoccupied with trying to figure out what has happened to their village and are trying to devise a means to stop it.

Encounter ST2-A:

The Hovels of Aruapa

Each two-story building measures 10 feet by 20 feet and has a steeply sloped roof. Small, shuttered windows keep the chilly breezes out, and villagers bolt the sturdy front doors from the inside against intruders. Most of the villagers avoid any conversation with the characters. Trespassers hear a few snarled threats when they get too close to a house containing scared villagers. Some villagers left their homes to stay with others as evidenced by seven abandoned homes. Only a simple latch secures those doors. Even within the occupied homes, distress and rancor rule over the huddled villagers, as they rediscover how to trust no one. Ch'usuyana's plot has torn at the façade of camaraderie in Aruapa.

Within 30 minutes of the characters' arrival, two of the homes experiencing suspicion turn to bloodshed and murder as one frightened occupant turns on another terrified villager. When this occurs, **6 villagers** approach the characters and beg for them to end the terror. Most of the remaining 66 villagers are commoners as well, though there are 11 more experienced warriors and two civil authorities. This oasis of hope teeters on the edge of anarchy unless the characters restore their faith in others.

Villagers, Male and Female Humans and Elves (53): HD 1d6hp; **AC** 9[10]; **Atk** weapon (1d6); **Move** 12; **Save** 18; **AL** Any; **CL/XP** B/10; **Special:** darkvision (elves only). (*Monstrosities* 254)

Male Human and Elf Warriors (11): HD 3; **AC** 5[14]; **Atk** spear (1d8); **Move** 12; **Save** 14; **AL** N; **CL/XP** 3/60; **Special:** darkvision (60ft) (elves only), detect secret doors (4-in-6 chance) (elves only).

Dwarf Authorities, Male Dwarves (2): HD 4; **AC** 4[15]; **Atk** war hammer (1d4+1); **Move** 6; **Save** 13; **AL** L; **CL/XP** 4/120; **Special:** +4 save vs. magic, darkvision (60ft), detect attributes of stonework. (*Monstrosities* 149)
Equipment: chainmail, shield, war hammer.

Encounter ST2-B: The Tavern Uana

If Imata successfully left the characters behind at the guardhouse, he points a shaking finger at them when they enter. Read or paraphrase the following response:

Although it seems as if everything is back to normal, the patrons watch the characters with great interest. Iquina, the barman oversees the activities of **7 patrons** (four male Aztli humans, one male orc, and two male dwarf **commoners**) and **2 druids**. There are **7 more patrons** (four male and two female Aztli humans and one male orc, and a dwarf soldier outside Iquina's supervision). A female Aztli jaguar cuauhocelotl oddly accompanies the soldier, though this woman is really **Ch'usuyana**, the **spökvatten** polymorphed into an Aztli woman. She used her powers of persuasion to convince the soldier of her love for him. Although not magically charmed, he swears to defend his new acquaintance at any cost.

Iquina, Male Orc Bartender: HD 5; **HP** 35; **AC** 6[13]; **Atk** battle axe (1d8); **Move** 9; **Save** 12; **AL** N; **CL/XP** 5/240; **Special:** none. (*Monstrosities* 364)
Equipment: battle axe, leather apron.

Bar Patrons, Male Aztlis (8): HD 1d6hp; **HP** 7, 6x3, 5x2, 4, 3; **AC** 9[10]; **Atk** club (1d4); **Move** 12; **Save** 18; **AL** N; **CL/XP** B/10; **Special:** none. (*Monstrosities* 254)
Equipment: club.

Bar Patrons, Female Aztlis (2): HD 1d6hp; **HP** 6, 5; **AC** 9[10]; **Atk** dagger (1d4); **Move** 12; **Save** 18; **AL** N; **CL/XP** B/10; **Special:** none. (*Monstrosities* 254)
Equipment: dagger.

Bar Patrons, Male Dwarves (2): HD 1; **HP** 6, 5; **AC** 4[15]; **Atk** club (1d4); **Move** 6; **Save** 17; **AL** L; **CL/XP** 1/15; **Special:** darkvision (60ft), detect attributes of stonework. (*Monstrosities* 149)
Equipment: club.

Druid Bar Patron, Male Aztli Druid (Drd2): HP 9; **AC** 7[12]; **Atk** dagger (1d4); **Move** 12; **Save** 14; **AL** N; **CL/XP** 2/30; **Special:** +2 save vs. fire, banish undead, identify pure water and plants, move through non-magical undergrowth, spells (2/1).
Spells: 1st—*faerie fire, purify water*; 2nd—*cure light wounds*.
Equipment: leather armor, dagger.

Druid Bar Patron, Male Dwarf Druid (Drd2): HP 9; **AC** 7[12]; **Atk** sickle-shaped sword (1d6); **Move** 12; **Save** 14; **AL** N; **CL/XP** 2/30; **Special:** +2 save vs. fire, banish undead, darkvision (60ft), detect stonework, identify pure water and plants, move through non-magical undergrowth, spells (2/1).
Spells: 1st—*detect snares and pits, locate animals*; 2nd—*heat metal*.
Equipment: leather armor, sickle-shaped sword.

Bar Patrons, Male Orcs (2): HD 1; **HP** 7x2; **AC** 6[13]; **Atk** spear (1d6) or scimitar (1d8); **Move** 9; **Save** 17; **AL** C; **CL/XP** 1/15; **Special:** none. (*Monstrosities* 364)

Soldier, Male Dwarf: HD 3; **HP** 18; **AC** 4[15]; **Atk** war hammer (1d4+1); **Move** 6; **Save** 14; **AL** L; **CL/XP** 3/60; **Special:** +4 save vs. magic, darkvision (60ft), detect attributes of stonework. (*Monstrosities* 149)
Equipment: chainmail, shield, war hammer.

Ch'usuyana, Spökvatten: HD 8; **HP** 54; **AC** 5[14]; **Atk** cold touch (2d4 + paralysis); **Move** 12 (swim 12, fly 12 [mist cloud only]); **Save** 8; **AL** N; **CL/XP** 10/1400; **Special:** cold touch, darkvision (60ft), icy fog (3/day, 15ft cone, 6d6 damage, save for half), immune to cold, paralysis (save or frozen for 1d4 rounds), shapechange (at will, cloud of mist, beast, or humanoid). (see **Appendix A: New Monsters**)

Meanwhile, several conversations take place around the tavern. The orc, an Aztli, and the dwarf pair tell bawdy tales as they try to outperform each other with their lies. One of the Aztli commoners sits alone, reading a thin tome and smoking a pipe. The soldier and jaguar cuauhocelotl appear well into their cups judging from the empties on their table as they smile at each other. The two druids give the characters a peace gesture before discussing their travels above and below the ground. The remaining patrons play a dice game in which a shooter rolls two six-sided dice, and then they bet on whether a third die's result will fall between the other two numbers shown. The characters are free to join in any of the discussions, though the participants are initially reluctant to accept the strangers into their midst, especially the polymorphed Ch'usuyana.

The conversations continue for almost 30 minutes before the chaos from outside crashes into the tavern. (If the characters leave beforehand, the following parties burst into the tavern as they prepare to leave.) A tumult accompanies **3 elves** and **3 gnolls** who enter the tavern, shouting at each other as they approach the characters. The elves approach the characters and irrationally demand the strangers prove they are not in league with the other community, while the gnolls dispute the characters' need to prove anything.

Male or Female Elf Guards (3): HD 3; HP 20, 17, 12; AC 5[14];
Atk spear (1d8); **Move** 12; **Save** 14; **AL** N; **CL/XP** 3/60; **Special:** darkvision (60ft), detect secret doors (4-in-6 chance).
Equipment: spear.

Gnolls (3): HD 2; HP 14, 12x2; AC 5[14]; **Atk** bite (2d4) or battle axe (1d10) or spear (1d6) or longbow x2 (1d6); **Move** 9; **Save** 16; **AL** C; **CL/XP** 2/30; **Special:** none. (*Monstrosities* 209)
Equipment: battle axe, 3 spears, longbow, 20 arrows.

When this confrontation diffuses or reaches a crescendo, someone outside screams, "Murder!" Ch'usuyana uses this distraction to move to the rear exit where she uses her icy fog attack in the tavern and then reveals her true form to Imata, who acknowledges her presence. She then grabs a torch from the wall and ignites the wood supply in the back room to set the tavern ablaze. In the main room, the dwarf soldier attacks the remaining patrons, and the enthralled Imata charges the characters. No one else within the tavern attempts to attack the characters. Iquina desperately tries to restore order within the tavern without harming any paying customers, though the confusion and panic from the growing fire and the slippery floor make for tough sledding within the tavern.

Although spökvattens normally lie in wait for their prey in lonely ponds, rivers, or streams, the birth of her ungodly child has spurred her to grander ambitions. She and her daughter now see the humanoids as their bountiful playthings whom they can devour at their leisure. However, the adventurers' unexpected arrival leaves her in a quandary. Until she can assess their abilities, her present goal is to return to her shack on the outskirts of town. Ch'usuyana jumps into a frigid stream and swims back to her residence as her pursuers likely struggle to pursue her on the ice and snow. Nonetheless, her footsteps leave a trail on the solid, yet yielding packed powder. In her haste to leave, Ch'usuyana makes no attempt to conceal her tracks.

If the spökvatten escapes without being followed, she hides in the shack while Ikanp'akiri, her **ice maiden** daughter, remains holed up inside with her **hostage**. The fey's ice maiden daughter attacks anyone who approaches the shack. Meanwhile, Ch'usuyana holds her hostage in one arm and attacks using her cold touch with her other free hand. The cornered spökvatten and her ice maiden daughter flee if an opportunity to do so presents itself. Despite their familial bond, neither is willing to risk life and limb for the others. On the other hand, if Ch'usuyana eludes pursuit altogether, she returns to the village after a few days in a new guise to continue to spread fear.

Ikanp'akiri, Ice Maiden: HD 5; HP 33; AC 7[12]; **Atk** ice dagger (1d4 + 1d4 cold); **Move** 12; **Save** 12; **AL** C; **CL/XP** 9/1100; **Special:** +1 or better magic weapons to hit, chilling presence (15ft radius, 1d4 damage per round [save avoids], 45% chance to dispel cold protection magics), flurry form (1/day, 20ft radius, whirling snow cloud for 3 rounds, 2d6 damage), immune to cold, invisibility (at will in snowy environments), kiss of the frozen heart (1/day, freeze heart of target to create servant, save avoids), magic resistance (15%), snowblind burst (1/day, 30ft radius, save or blinded for 1d4+1 rounds), spell-like abilities, vulnerable to fire (200% damage). (see **Appendix A: New Monsters**)
Spell-like abilities: at will—*detect magic, light*; 5/day—*fear, obscuring mist*; 3/day—*polymorph self, wall of ice*; 1/day—*ice storm*.

DESIGNER'S NOTE

You can run the evil fey's retreat as a moving battle, with her trying to give the characters the slip in the unfavorable conditions. If they defeat her on the trail before she returns to the shack, they can later follow the path to her abode and find the ice maiden and her kidnapped victim at daybreak, after the stormy weather moves on and the sun shines in the morning.

Hostage, Male Elf Commoner: HP 3; AC 9[10]; **Atk** dagger (1d4); **Move** 12; **Save** 18; **AL** C; **CL/XP** B/10; **Special:** darkvision (60ft), detect secret doors (4-in-6 chance). (*Monstrosities* 254)

Treasure: If the characters find the pair's shack, they discover the following items hidden throughout the building: *frozen concoction* potion, a *potion of giant strength*, and a pouch containing six amethysts worth 100 gp each.

If the characters defeat the fey and her maiden — and keep the hostage alive (or raise him from the dead) — the citizenry of Aruapa treat the characters to a drink or two before letting their queen lavish praise and gifts upon them.

ENCOUNTER ST2-C: THE QUEEN AND HER MAGE

Kharu Amayana and Jark'iri refuse to grant the characters an audience until they either deliver a sledge of obsidian to the village or defeat Ch'usuyana and Ikanp'akiri. If the characters attempt to barge their way in, the citizens unite to protect their rulers from the strangers, especially during these uncertain times. The mismatched duo appears as different as night and day. **Kharu** is tall and heavy for an elf, evidence of the human genes in her background. **Jark'iri** is a **couatl** disguised as an elf, and is small and slight with pale charcoal skin contrasting her companion's ruddy tan. While Kharu is curt during an initial meeting, Jark'iri goes out of her way to make everyone feel welcome. Several loyal **villagers** are in the room when the adventurers finally meet the two rulers of Aruapa.

Kharu Amayana, Female Half-Elf Queen of Aruapa: HD 8; HP 42; AC 7[12]; **Atk** flail (1d8); **Move** 12; **Save** 8; **AL** N; **CL/XP** 8/800; **Special:** darkvision (60ft). (*Monstrosities* 255)
Equipment: leather armor, flail.

Jark'iri, Couatl: HD 8; HP 51; AC 4[15]; **Atk** bite (2d6 + poison), tail (1d6 constrict); **Move** 12 (fly 24); **Save** 8; **AL** L; **CL/XP** 11/1700; **Special:** poison (save or die), polymorph (at will), spells (3/2/1). (*Monstrosities* 73)
Spells: 1st—*charm person, magic missile, sleep*; 2nd—*ESP, phantasmal force*; 3rd—*lightning bolt*.

Villagers, Male or Female Aztlis Commoners (as needed): HD 1d6hp; AC 9[10]; **Atk** weapon (1d6); **Move** 12; **Save** 18; **AL** Any; **CL/XP** B/10; **Special:** none. (*Monstrosities* 254)

The pair enters the room in a hush. An Aztli serves the pair a cup of pulque each, though Jark'iri asks for water. Their alluring butterfly tattoos are mesmerizing.

"So, did you bring us good news?" Kharu asks while scanning her audience. She throws the alcohol down her throat in one swift gulp. Jark'iri accepts the water proffered her and sips daintily.

"I would like to thank you for bringing us what we need."

After perfunctory greetings, the conversation varies depending on if they beat her gnoll slaver and brought pilfered obsidian into her village or if they defeat the duplicitous fey and exposed her devious plot to turn the villagers against each other. Kharu keeps the discussion light but pointed, never losing track of the direction of the questions. She outwardly flatters any obvious warriors. On the second round, Jark'iri begins using *ESP* to probe their thoughts.

If the characters have the obsidian, Jark'iri tries to find out what happened to Anuqara by sifting through the characters' thoughts. Kharu starts the negotiations to repurchase the obsidian at a low price but ultimately settles on something almost equivalent to what she promised Anuqara. The price of the lost slaver is worth the removal of her most stress-inducing villager under her protection. In the next few days, Kharu makes Iquina her new "muscle," and he splits his time as War-chief of Aruapa and tending the bar at his tavern.

If the adventurers defeated the fey and her minion, the elvish pair speak freely with the adventurers, though Jark'iri still tries to unmask anyone with murderous designs on her queen. The pair offer their guests pulque to drink.

Treasure: With either conclusion, Kharu bestows the deed to the obsidian vault to the character she deems most worthy. The characters can use the vault as a launching point for other adventures in the Tepepan Mountains.

If they defeated the hag and the maiden, she also gives an obsidian *+1 tecpatl* (see **Appendix B: New Equipment and Magic Items**) to the bravest fighter. Kharu Amayana grants the characters a week's stay as guests of the village for free as well (to rest and recuperate from their battles). The village presents each adventurer with fine silk clothing tailored to fit them perfectly (worth 20 gp each).

THE VILLAGE OF ALATAQ

When the characters arrive at Alataq, the village is the midst of a celebration. A day before their arrival, a resident died a peaceful death, and within hours of his earthly demise, Manq'awi Aicha, a priest of Micoateotl, arrived as if summoned. Everyone took this as a sign of a good death, and the living kin of Alataq began their revelries.

Because there are very few places to bury loved ones high in the Tepepan Mountains and precious little firewood and flammable oil to help dispose of the body, the priests who serve the Lord of the Dead engage in ritual cannibalism to avoid having to inter the corpse. This simultaneously passes on the decedent's good traits to the survivors who feast on the flesh. After consuming the meal, the priest arranges the bones in an ossuary box, and honors the deceased with chants and other rituals to help grant a speedy journey through Miquito. In most cases, the box is then placed under the floor in the decedent's home.

Only the wealthy and powerful are laid to rest in splendor in a multiroomed vault elaborately decorated with pyramids of skulls and candelabrums made of femurs and fibulae. Some villages keep only the skulls on labeled shelves. Slotted boxes near the entrance collect small offerings to pay for the shrine's maintenance or to serve as tributes for the dead. On the rare occasion when a priest of Micoateotl arrives in a community with no recent dead, the superstitious Aztli residents see it as a bad portent indicating that someone's journey on earth is nearing an unexpected end. The next few hours are tense as the villagers watch their infants and infirmed with an agonized eye. A pack of 2d4 giant vultures usually accompanies the priest. The vultures' appetites help with the ritual to come.

The death ritual celebration is only one of the many festivals Alataq's citizens witness on a regular basis. The village of nearly 400 people (66% Aztli, 20% dwarf, 10% Tlotl, 4% other) has a fete about every 13 days in accordance with the Aztlis' Tonalpohualli religious calendar, in addition to family activities celebrating weddings, births, and other momentous events.

Alataq is renowned within the Tepepan Mountains and regions beyond for its unusual architecture, which combines elements of Aztli, Dwarfish, and Tlotl designs. Originally constructed underground during the Nights of Sillu and Claw, the oldest tunnels are now mostly used as catacombs and storage in case of siege. Early settlers carved out the underground area with fortification in mind, and the passages are easily defended, with strategically placed arrow slits stocked with ammunition carved into the bunkers, along with tight passageways to facilitate a fighting retreat.

Aboveground, a family of Tlotl artisans imported their style of mysterious grotesques in the design of their buildings. The village of Alataq includes 50 structures. They are universally tall and narrow, with slate roofs and artful dwarven wrought-iron worked into the windows, doors, and guttering, though rust has taken a toll on some of the ancient metalwork. The masonry also defies conventional expectations. Fortified by enchantments, the stonework appears otherworldly, as the impossibly angled pinnacle designs could not withstand the structural forces without magical enhancements.

Alataq's other noteworthy marvel is the tremendous number of gargoyles incorporated into its architecture. Creatures carved from stone and clay appear everywhere. Some squat over drainage openings, fishing for coins or mice. Others spout water from rooftops. A few decorate the spindly towers around town. Their most wondrous feature is that almost all of the gargoyles move.

These sentient beings, known as the tukkuru gargoyles, go about their daily lives among the humanoids of Alataq. Elders do not know where they came from or why they even coexist with the villagers. They display no malevolence like most of their kin, and some even adopt families or individuals for whom they perform basic tasks such as guarding their homes, washing their clothes, digging, and tending a garden. If someone is lucky enough to garner the affection of a gargoyle, that person has made a companion for life. Like pets, these gargoyles usually have a shorter lifespan than the humans they befriend.

Most tukkuru gargoyles live about as long as a domesticated dog (2d6 + 2 years). They neither eat, drink, nor breathe. Given their limited requirements, no one can explain their short longevity, though no one has ever researched them in great detail. When a gargoyle in Alataq senses death is near, it treks up into the mountains during the night to rejoin its brethren in the gargoyle graveyard, from where it never returns. Although their companion's passing saddens them, no one from Alataq has ever gone looking for the graveyard or an explanation as to why the gargoyle left them.

A council of nine individuals rules the village of Alataq: five Aztlis, two dwarves, one Tlotl, and a dour half-orc. The Aztli Confederation rarely sends a delegation to visit the remote locale as long as the annual tribute of stone and rare metal pours into the alliance's coffers. Alataq features many of the amenities of any large village, including dwarven metalworkers and jewelers, a moneychanger and lender who loans and converts currency minted by the Aztli Confederation and the Firebrand Clan to prospective clients. Many visitors spend their fresh coins in one of three taverns with homebrewed beers, distilled pulque, a few hallucinogens, and beds to sleep off the stupor (even by the hour). A library with a pair of sages staggers over the upper end of the main road, and several shrines honoring the Aztlis' hero-gods — most notably Quiahuitl, Atoyatl, and Contlati — dot the landscape. Alataq is ensconced in a light fog 350 days of the year. Many tunnels lead underground, and heated, moist air billows forth from them. The slightly smoky tang emerging through these vents mixes with the chilled environment to create a hazy soup.

Chapter One: Dead Man's Party at Alataq

When the characters first arrive in Alataq, read or paraphrase the following description:

Transcendental visions of impossible architecture flourish in the village of Alataq. As the mist rolls away, cobblestones and charcoal pave a crude walkway through the settlement. Chunks of red granite veined with golden pyrite mimic sidewalks, separating the manmade trail from the charcoal and gray edifices of the town. Wrought-iron filigrees and subtly twisted bars reinforce and underscore the absurdity of the village. Shops line both sides of the street, their wares a dazzling display with reflected lights emphasizing each item for sale. Towers reach impossibly high into the heavens. Balconies lurch overhead, their guttering and waterspouts deftly moving the nearly constant mist from the roofs down to the channels running under the roads. The water flows in musical harmony with the constant pounding of the village smithy as it gurgles and tinkles and drips rhythmically through the waterworks. The people nearby shop, eat, and hold discussions or embrace each other while clothed in strange attire. Most dress in bright colors, accentuating their appearance with scarves and finery. They move toward an open area farther up the main road, as if drawn to the spot by the music resonating in the area.

More importantly, the gargoyles incorporated into the village's architecture freely move about, and no one here seems the least bit concerned. As a pair of the small creatures sweep debris from the road into a nearby sewer grate, another one crash lands on a store's awning, stirring up several ravens languishing there. The people of Alataq never give these creatures a second glance as they blissfully stroll toward their destination farther up the main road.

Three main paths lead to the village of Alataq — two aboveground and one below. The underground one eventually leads to the dwarven community of Balandrur, though many chambers and thoroughfares branch off to more remote destinations. Some of the caverns are not well traveled, and due to volcanism and earthquake activity, some of the neglected paths are prone to collapse. The two paths that meet in Alataq both head south to lower altitudes. One goes directly south through the grassland and forest before ending at the edge of the Great Canal. This trail, Malcu Aztana, once traversed the entire island from the northwestern beaches to the southern tip of the swamplands. Time, nature, and progress ravaged Tehuatl's thoroughfare, though the section from Alataq to the canal can still be followed with some extrapolation around the island's waterways. The other trail winds south and west and ends at Qana, a small fishing village on the coast.

The characters are not expected to join in today's festivities. Most shops closed their doors, but the tavern stayed open, and one of the smiths is hammering away on a piece of iron. The adventurers can visit with the few villagers not reveling in the death ritual or interact with the gargoyles on the street. Three of the creatures eventually notice the characters and approach. They are chubby and almost cube-shaped — 12 inches on a side. Their small legs and arms make them wobble, and they look up at the characters with inquisitive eyes. If given a metal coin, they jump and tumble about with glee. One consumes the coin with an audible metal-on-stone clanking noise.

The festival for the deceased takes place in Alataq's park and lasts for nearly an hour. Dancing and loud singing conveys the revelers' joy rather than their sadness over the loss. **Manq'awi Aicha** leads the throng as he escorts the elder's body up the mountain to the far end of the park, where it is laid to rest atop a simple, unadorned table surrounded by a curtain. The festival winds down after an hour of song and speeches. When its ends, the family of the deceased thanks every attendee whether they be friend or stranger. Manq'awi Aicha and his pack of **4 giant vultures** surround the table at the far end of the park, where he draws the curtain to separate the town from the next phase of the ritual. Etiquette and decorum prohibit anyone from observing the consumption of the body. Manq'awi Aicha eventually sends his birds into the sky with a flourish as the priest blows into a wooden whistle to signal the ceremony's conclusion and the beginning of the decedent's journey into Miquito. The man's skull remains on the table until the next time Manq'awi Aicha or another priest of Micoateotl visits the village. At that time, the priest and the family will inter the skull beneath their home. If the characters attend the ritual and act reverently, award them a story bonus of 50 XP.

Manq'awi Aicha, Male Aztli Priest of Micoateotl (Clr8): HP 40; AC 6[13]; Atk obsidian dagger (1d4); **Move** 12; **Save** 8; **AL** L; **CL/XP** 8/800; **Special:** +2 save vs. paralysis and poison, banish undead, spells (2/2/2/2/2).
  Spells: 1st—*detect evil, detect magic*; 2nd—*bless, speak with animals*; 3rd—*prayer, speak with dead*; 4th—*create water, cure serious wounds*; 5th—*commune, dispel evil.*
Equipment: cipacahuipilli[B] armor, obsidian dagger, wooden whistle.

Giant Vultures (4): HD 1; HP 8, 6x2, 5; AC 6[13]; Atk 2 claws (1d4 + disease), bite (1d6 + disease); **Move** 6 (fly 9); **Save** 17; **AL** N; **CL/XP** 1/15; **Special:** disease (save or 1d4 damage per day until healed).
[B] See **Appendix B: New Equipment and Magic Items**

The family of the man who passed fears returning to his home now that he is no longer there. Hiuaui lived in one of the houses built underground some distance away from the main village. He thought himself a guard of sorts. His family moves from the celebration of his death to the nearest tavern to help steel their nerves to go to Hiuaui's house. The characters can find them there or on their way to the house after drinking. The pair of men carry a lantern and wield a dagger. The smaller one seems to be braver and is leading the taller one. Eventually, the mourners summon the courage to engage the strangers in their town. When they do so, read or paraphrase the following description:

The taller man begins his tale. "I am Calcata. My father was the man who died yesterday. Has it been a full day? I don't know. We do not have much to pay you, but we would request that you come with us to gather his belongings. Hiuaui was a simple man who made friends with several of the gargoyles during his life, but in the last month he would tell us strange tales about something stirring within his house. We thought he was kidding."

He stops to take a drink of water as he ponders how to say the rest. He is obviously sad and distressed about his father's mental state, but he finally continues his tale.

"He previously told stories of other noises near his home. It turned out to be his own gargoyles completing his monotonous tasks. He was at our last feast just a few days ago. He did not have a scratch on him. This morning though …"

The man trails off, his eyes blurry from drink and fear. He says he hoped the priest would accompany the family to the house, but the priest made excuses, claiming that another village was about to have another death tonight, and he needed to be there in the morning.

Calcata is now the patriarch of his family after his father's death. He and his partner **Aqallor** fostered several orphans they consider blood relatives, but they have no children of their own. Calcata is bald and bespectacled with a chubby countenance. Aqallor is also beefy from his previous military service but appears to take care of himself a bit more. He attends to Calcata as he discusses what they want to retrieve from Hiuaui's house.

Calcata, Male Aztli Commoner: HP 4; AC 9[10]; **Atk** club (1d4); **Move** 12; **Save** 18; **AL** L; **CL/XP** B/10; **Special:** none. (*Monstrosities* 254)
 Equipment: tlahuiztli armor[B], club.

Aqallor, Male Aztli Commoner: HP 4; AC 9[10]; **Atk** ollitztli (1d6); **Move** 12; **Save** 18; **AL** N; **CL/XP** B/10; **Special:** none. (*Monstrosities* 254)
 Equipment: ichcahuipilli armor[B], ollitztli[B].

[B] See **Appendix B: New Equipment and Magic Items**

Chapter Two: Clearing House

This chapter takes the characters into Hiuaui's home to discover the circumstances surrounding his death.

Area A2-A: Entryway

The nearly hourlong trek to Hiuaui's house is uneventful. When the characters arrive, they find the narrow doorway to the house ajar. The lock and handle are shattered nearby.

Over the years, Hiuaui taught the gargoyles some Aztli phrases. They looked out over the caves nearby and gave him an early warning about intruders. Unfortunately for Hiuaui, a pair of unknown enemies sought something from him. They dispatched a squad of three demons and their diabolical leader to find what the old man was hiding. Hiuaui was mortally wounded by their minions and stumbled his way to Alataq to die.

The **3 tukkuru gargoyles** here are feline-themed in design. They are severely damaged and are afraid to fight. The demons tortured the stone beasts and broke pieces off them. The gargoyles ironically comply with Hiuaui's training, as they now warn the geruzou demons inside about the trespassers. If the gargoyles fail to warn the current occupants, the characters may attempt to slip by unnoticed.

The **3 geruzou demons** slink to the front of the house while the gargoyles hiss and screech. One demon spits slime from the open doorway. The rest wait inside the door to bite and claw anyone who enters the front room. The front room is a mess of splintered wood and smashed ceramics. A large cabinet and pile of debris block the doorway to the chambers beyond the entryway. The room is considered difficult terrain because of the clutter.

Geruzou Demons (Slime Demons) (3): HD 4; HP 30, 28, 24; AC 4[15]; **Atk** 2 claws (1d4), bite (1d6); **Move** 12 (fly 15); **Save** 13; **AL** C; **CL/XP** 6/400; **Special:** +1 or better magic weapons to hit, goo spit (20ft range, save or slowed for 6 rounds; save avoids), immune to electricity and poison, magic resistance (10%), spell-like abilities, telepathy (100ft). (see **Appendix A: New Monsters**)

They ask the characters to retrieve a ceramic scepter and a book of family history from the home. They have a nicer home in Alataq and have no interest in what happens to Calcata's father's property. Indeed, they offer to gift the home to the characters if they retrieve the two items from the building. Read or paraphrase Calcata's general description of the home:

If asked, Calcata and Aqallor are unsure how many gargoyles occupy the abode, but he had four the last time they visited. Aqallor gives the characters the key to the front door and says they will wait in the house in Alataq, praying for their safe return.

Spell-like abilities: at will—*darkness 15ft radius*; 3/day—*ESP, invisibility*; 1/day—*fear, mirror image*.

Tukkuru Gargoyles (3): HD 3; HP 1x3; AC 6[13]; **Atk** 2 claws (1d3), bite (1d4); **Move** 9; **Save** 14; **AL** N; **CL/XP** 3/60; **Special:** +1 or better magic weapon to hit. (see **Appendix A: New Monsters**)

Treasure: Hiuaui collected figurines and only one delicate obsidian panther worth 50 gp remains in the mess.

Area A2-B: Living Quarters

The furniture that once decorated this room (including the bed) dropped through the fissure and into the lower level. A character attempting to traverse the chasm without falling in must succeed on a saving throw. On a failure, the creature tumbles into the lower level, taking 1d6 points of damage from the fall and is knocked prone. A character who slips while attempting to climb down to the lower level suffers the same fate. The geruzou demons in **Area A2-C** beyond are too enraptured in their torture to notice anything short of an extremely loud commotion here.

Treasure: A large case lies unopened on a ledge, hidden among some other debris. Within lies the ceramic scepter as well as a half dozen books. Close examination shows that at least one of the manuscripts has to do with local history and may be the genealogy Calcata and Aqallor require. The case also holds a silver whistle with a trio of emerald chips embedded in its length inside worth 40 gp.

Area A2-C: The Mess Hall

This was Hiuaui's dining area. He prepared meals at a cooking station and ate at a rather luxurious table setting. He even fed his pet gargoyles, though they needed no sustenance. The geruzou demons are now torturing one of

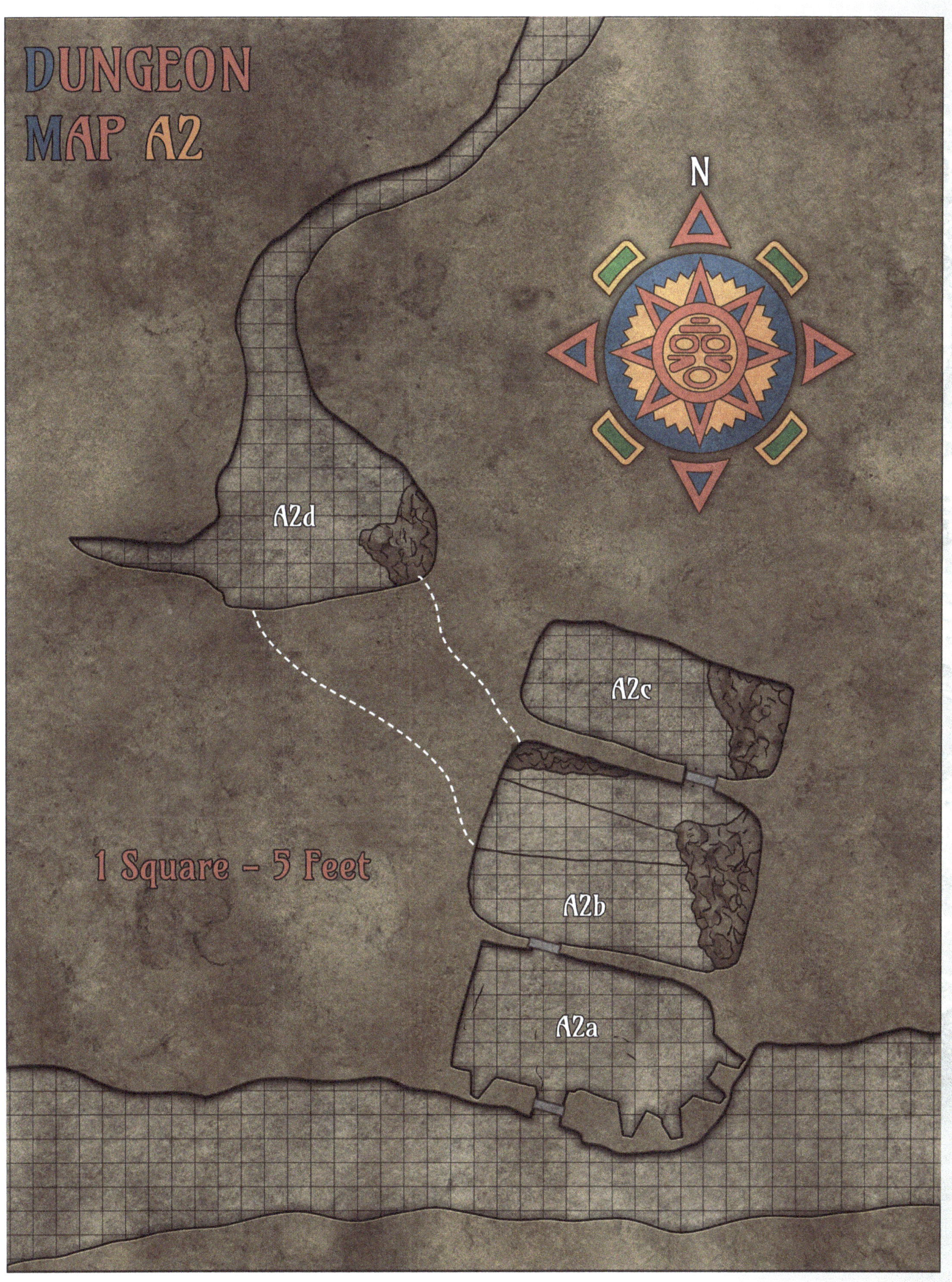
DUNGEON
MAP A2
N
A2d
A2c
A2b
A2a
1 Square - 5 Feet

Hiuaui's gargoyles in the oven. They heated the loyal servant to a temperature that cracked both its arms and one half of its face.

These **2 geruzou demons** rush forward to engage characters intruding on their fun. The home once had a "safe room" beyond this mess hall, but the collapse that brought the demons from below also crushed the small oubliette and the supplies stored within the room. The **tukkuru gargoyle** suffers from severe burns. If the characters rescue it from the demons' clutches, it thanks them profusely. Characters who can converse with the gargoyle discover that the demons kept asking it about finding the "twins," though Hiuaui's pet has no idea what they were referencing. The creature also swears they kept repeating the name "Itzcuin" throughout their interrogation, though the gargoyle once again cannot explain the correlation between the devious Aztli god and the demons' inquiries.

Geruzou Demons (Slime Demons) (2): HD 4; HP 29, 27; AC 4[15]; **Atk** 2 claws (1d4), bite (1d6); **Move** 12 (fly 15); **Save** 13; **AL** C; **CL/XP** 6/400; **Special:** +1 or better magic weapons to hit, goo spit (20ft range, save or slowed for 6 rounds; save avoids), immune to electricity and poison, magic resistance (10%), spell-like abilities, telepathy (100ft). (see **Appendix A: New Monsters**)
Spell-like abilities: at will—*darkness 15ft radius*; 3/day—*ESP, invisibility*; 1/day—*fear, mirror image*.

Tukkuru Gargoyle: HD 3; HP 2; AC 6[13]; **Atk** 2 claws (1d3), bite (1d4); **Move** 9; **Save** 14; **AL** N; **CL/XP** 3/60; **Special:** +1 or better magic weapon to hit. (see **Appendix A: New Monsters**)

Treasure: A wizard imbued the stove with magic, and it can generate flames to produce varying levels of heat by adjusting a lever on the front. Hiuaui inherited this item from his godfather. Despite its magical properties, its weight (100 pounds) makes it worth only 100 gp.

Chapter Three: Back to the Village

Any gargoyles who survive the geruzou demon attack croak and stutter their way through a conversation in broken Aztli with the characters. They tell their rescuers, "We must go home." All of the tukkuru gargoyles can sense their time on Tehuatl is nearly over, and when they are close to the end of that allotted time, they must make a pilgrimage back down to the heart of the mountains to the tukkuru graveyard. The characters can persuade the gargoyles to wait until they deliver the scepter and books to Hiuaui's family.

The citizens of Alataq stare at the damaged gargoyles with horror. Many adults approach, cooing and trying to crowd in close to pet the small creatures, offering support. A traffic jam forms around the characters, and one of the gargoyles gets to use its old warning voice to tell the gathered villagers to "back away." The villagers ultimately disperse with sympathetic smiles on their faces.

Calcata and Aqallor's house is near their bookshop. They usher the characters in, frowning at the state of their father's pets. Once settled, the couple accepts the case filled with genealogical materials and the scepter.

Area A2-D: Basement

The geruzou demons collected a big bruiser to help spread mayhem. K'ullarana, a **nalfeshnee demon**, is separated from his "chanaki" (little brothers) down here. He followed a **tukkuru gargoyle** back into the chasm below the house and is trying to chase it down and crush it with its huge hands. The gargoyle now hides in a narrow crevasse. Although the demon has extraordinary reach with its extended arms, it cannot grab the tiny gargoyle trying to elude its grasp. The gargoyle hisses and tells the fiend, "Go away!" as loudly as it can.

The demon prefers pulverizing its foes with its mighty fists and ripping through their flesh with its teeth.

K'ullarana, Nalfeshnee Demon, Fourth-Category Demon: HD 7d10; HP 61; AC 4[15]; **Atk** 2 claws (1d4), bite (2d4); **Move** 9 (fly 14); **Save** 9; **AL** C; **CL/XP** 12/2000; **Special:** +1 or better magic weapons to hit, +2 on to-hit rolls, immune to fire, magic resistance (65%), spell-like abilities, summon demons (60% chance, roll 1d6 for category). (**Monstrosities** 102)

Tukkuru Gargoyle: HD 3; HP 20; AC 6[13]; **Atk** 2 claws (1d3), bite (1d4); **Move** 9; **Save** 14; **AL** N; **CL/XP** 3/60; **Special:** +1 or better magic weapon to hit. (see **Appendix A: New Monsters**)

Treasure: If the characters search through the debris scattered here from the house above, they uncover *+2 chainmail armor* of obvious dwarven craftsmanship.

The tunnel leading away from Hiuaui's house travels deep into the Tepepan Mountains. A small pocket of geruzou demons lives in a small, dirty community almost 11 miles from this breach, though this is accessible only through many forks and divisions and chasms.

paper up from the shards. The pair unroll it and spread it out on the table. Ancient text and scrolled lettering are beautiful but indecipherable without closer examination or interpretation.

Map

If the characters did not rescue any gargoyles in the preceding encounter or were uninterested in visiting the tukkuru gargoyle graveyard, you can use this map leading to the location to spur their interest in doing so. Use the paper as a correction device if needed. Alternatively, it could also reveal the location of the obsidian vault detailed earlier in this adventure. If used this way, allow the characters to visit Quriana and Achtata, the elders in the library at the top of Alataq, in the morning to decipher the runes and legend to find where the characters travel next. If the characters are already committed to helping the gargoyles, the parchment refers to events in **Chapter Six: Where Eagles Dare**.

he couple explain that Hiuaui didn't have the heart to break the scepter, as he collected ceramic pieces almost religiously. When Calcata's father told them how he obtained the scepter, he warned them of what was inside. "It leads to great treasure and great danger." A traveler left it behind after disappearing mysteriously one night in a tavern Hiuaui used to frequent. The traveler regaled the tavern with outlandish tales of his journeys beyond the realms of men. He claimed that otherworldly beings — attracted to the silver thread with which he wove his life — followed him. The other tavern patrons thought him mad, but Hiuaui fed him leading questions, and they talked about other worlds until daybreak. When the traveler went to relieve himself, he never came back.

If any gargoyles are present, they nuzzle the characters and reiterate their need to "go home." Calcata and Aqallor understand and do not think themselves adventurous enough to try to find the treasure described on the paper, but they will talk to Quriana and Achtata, the elders in the library up the street while the characters are away. If the characters reach the destination appearing in the map and spirit away some of its riches, the pair tries to negotiate receiving a part of the treasure, but they make no concrete demands.

Chapter Four: The Tukkuru Gargoyl Graveyard

The gargoyles instinctually sense where they must travel and have only a limited vocabulary to describe the urge driving them forward, though they gladly accept any shoulder to perch on during the journey. These feline-shaped creatures weigh a few pounds and can just as easily rest in a backpack or cradled in someone's arms.

The trip takes several days. Feel free to use any of the random encounters from the previous sections to liven up the overland trek. When the characters make camp, the gargoyles harmonize great battle songs of previous generations. Some of the songs are ridiculously obscure. However, they gladly teach the words and melodies to anyone interested in ancient history. After the third day, the gargoyles nudge the characters toward a gaping maw in one of the mountains. This great cavern was once the lair of a huge skeletal dragon queen and her undead horde, but heroes vanquished her majesty and looted the caves long ago. After traveling a full day belowground, the characters find their first casualty.

Graveyard, Upper Section

The graveyard's upper section allows the characters opportunities to rest and recuperate between encounters as the adventure's main antagonists rarely, if ever, venture here. Unless otherwise noted, the surfaces are all carved from stone. Ceilings reach a height of 2d6 + 10 feet.

Area A4-A: The Outer Regions

Ahead, the characters spot a number of gargoyles, at least 30, that did not make it to their ancestral home without assistance. Furthermore, without

magic, the characters cannot carry them all. They can placate Hiuaui's pets by promising to deliver these statues to their final resting place after they are sure the way is clear. The gargoyles get nervous and jumpy whenever they get closer to their "home." They urge the characters to march faster. They even harmonize a batch of inspirational songs about adventurous exploits to encourage them to pick up the pace.

Area A4-B: Symbolic Entry

Hundreds of years ago, a strange wizard decided to modify this cavern to his own twisted vision. After spending a month fabricating this aperture with multiple spells, the wizard spent another three months casting protective spells in this gaping maw until he believed he got it right. The light comes from three *continual light* spells cast onto the walls.

Explosive Trap

The eccentric wizard scattered six magical traps around this chamber in random spots. Whenever a creature other than an elemental enters this area for the first time or ends its turn in this room, it has a 50% chance of encountering one of these traps, which is triggered by stepping onto an enchanted five-foot square. If a trap is triggered, it explodes. Creatures within 20 feet of the detonation point must make a saving throw or take 3d6 points of damage on a failure or half as much damage on a success. Once triggered, a detonated trap becomes inert for one minute until it fully recharges.

Another way into the graveyard exists, but it is one mile out of the way to the south of this main entrance. The gargoyles know about the second entrance, but their pride never allows them to enter through that gateway. If the characters need to enter through the alternate passage, the gargoyles promise to meet them inside. The gargoyles practically beg to be let down and walk this final way into the graveyard. They offer the characters their sincere thanks for bringing them this far before gleefully taking the final steps through the open maw.

Referee Tips

The following descriptions assume that the characters are escorting at least one gargoyle. If the group is exploring the graveyard without the company of a gargoyle, alter the descriptions to account for their absence. All the encounters within the upper part of the graveyard are spaced far enough apart that one denizen's realm of influence very rarely overlaps with another. Allow the characters to take a long rest between encounters (except for Irontooth's maze and lair [**Area A4-F** and **Area A4-G**], as one triggers the other), but throw in some sort of "color" as they rest. "You hear a scraping of stone on stone in the distance," or "A gust of super-heated air blasts through the cavern, nearly dousing the campfire." You can add other minor annoyances and incidents to keep the players on their toes without significantly taxing their resources.

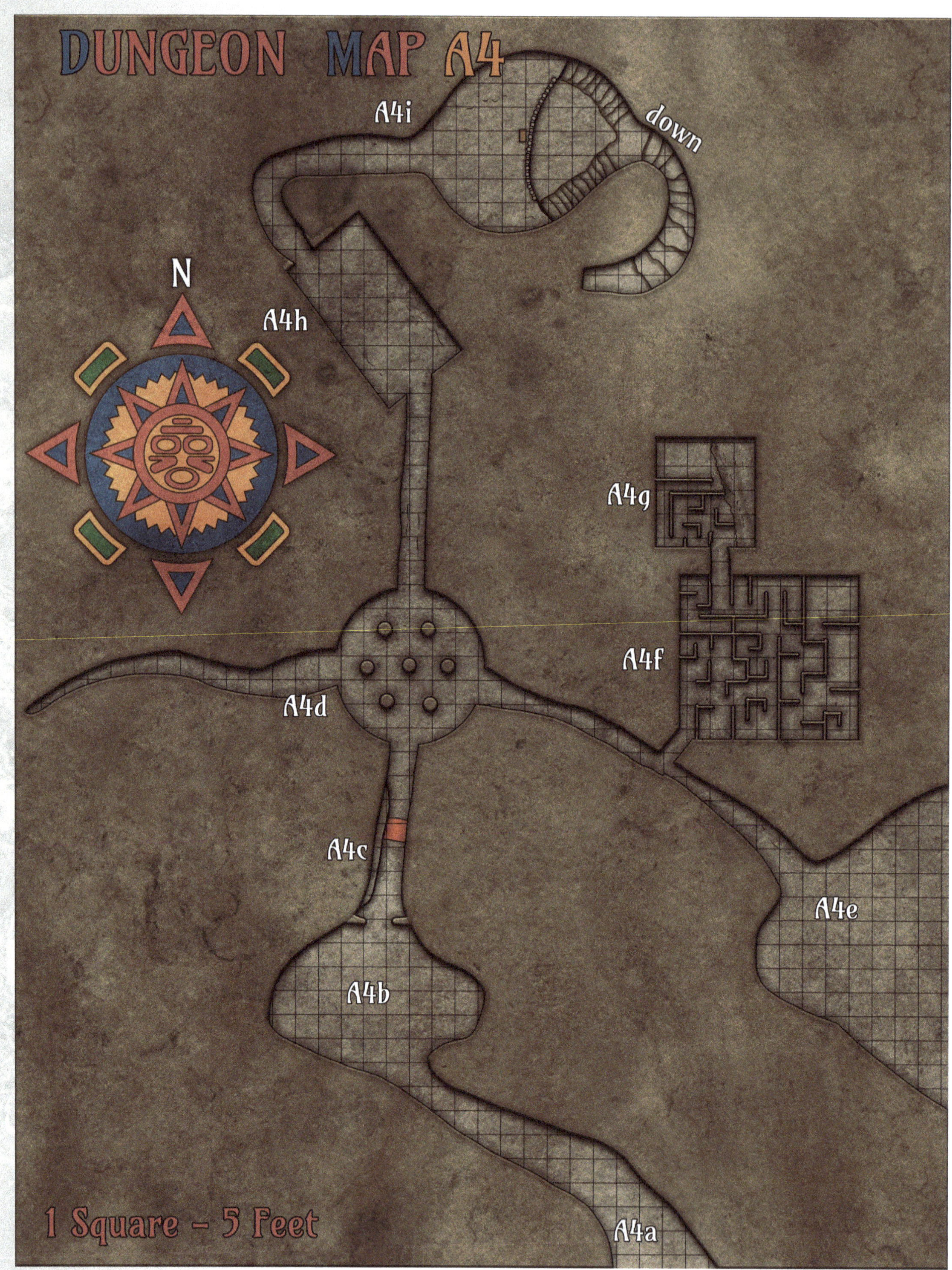

DUNGEON MAP A4
A4i
down
N
A4h
A4g
A4f
A4d
A4c
A4e
A4b
A4a
1 Square – 5 Feet

Area A4-C: Esophageal Lobby

Beyond the face in the side of the cavern wall, the path narrows to a throat, descending on a slope. The air is warmer here and moist. Heat shimmers up from the floor and reddish light pierces the darkness as a bubble of lava surfaces on the floor, flowing across the passage and disappearing under the wall.

A small ledge just a few inches wide rises up on the left wall about a foot above the flow. The gargoyles hop up and traverse the ledge relatively easily. Characters must roll below their dexterity on 3d6 to do the same. If a creature fails, it can make a saving throw to catch itself or suffer 1d6 points of fire damage as one of their feet comes into contact with the lava beneath the surface. A creature that catches itself does not fall in, but it must still succeed on another dexterity check to walk along the ledge. The lava flow covers about 10 feet of hallway floor. A creature that falls into the lava takes 4d6 points of damage per round.

Area A4-D: Front Hall

Cobwebs drape this ancient hall. Seven pillars hold the domed roof aloft with buttresses connecting them together in a beautiful symmetry. Crumbling husks of gargoyles lie on honeycomb-like shelves built into the walls and pillars. Some gargoyles are nearly unrecognizable from the decay. Many tunnels lead away, each pockmarked with shelves of gargoyles. Spiders, roaches, and beetles of many varieties crawl along the exposed surfaces.

The only area not covered with cobwebs is an area about 18 inches off the floor where gargoyles go through the area to the caverns deeper in this complex. As the characters disturb the webbing and move through the room, a **ghost** manifests near the ceiling. It is the apparition of a gnoll priest who used to preside over this area when the gargoyles first appeared. The ghost just wants all humanoids to leave and tries to horrify interlopers into leaving through any of the doors. The ghost will not chase creatures outside of this room nor will it leave here if compelled to do so. Unfortunately, it has been a long time since the ghost manifested and, in its absence, **2 insect swarms** infested the area. Characters frightened into near-paralysis by the ghost's fearful visage suffer the wrath of the newest occupants of this hall. The chittering horde of insects overruns one of the ghost's victims and burrows their mandibles and pincers into his or her flesh. A flood of chitinous pests flows under an intruders' protective armor and bites the vulnerable underbelly of those who try to pass. The ghost and the insects ignore the gargoyles, if present.

If constrained by a cleric powerful enough to sway it through faith and a holy symbol, the ghost retreats to its own remains. A small shelf near the floor in the central pillar holds a gnoll skull and a few bones resistant to time's decay.

Ghost: HD 5; HP 31; AC 0[19]; **Atk** spectral touch (1d6); **Move** 12 (fly); **Save** 12; **AL** C; **CL/XP** 7/600; **Special:** +1 or better magic or silver weapon to hit, fearful visage (20ft radius, save or immobilized by fear for 1d4+2 rounds), magic resistance (50%). (***Monstrosities*** 190)

Insect Swarms (2): HD 3; HP 20, 17; AC 7[12]; **Atk** swarm (1d6); **Move** 6; **Save** 14; **AL** N; **CL/XP** 4/120; **Special:** immune to all but blunt weapons.

Treasure: Nestled among the bones is a one-foot-long ivory tusk with scrimshaw along its length in the style of sharks. This device acts as a *wand of magic missiles* (18 charges).

Area A4-E: Second Entrance

The lifelike face carved into the main entrance appears familiar, but this effigy seems perverted and bastardized by a lack of focus. The eyelids above the doorway look rumpled, and the eyes themselves have a dazed look. The mouth still gapes wide enough to allow a large beast to ride through it, but there are no teeth showing, save one small grizzled point hanging down. This face's nose points down and almost touches the ground, dividing the entrance in two. A 10-foot-wide, five-foot-long trench lies just inside the entry, impeding the hallway beyond. Several flames light the entryway, casting eerie shadows over the carvings.

The 10-foot-wide trench completely divides the outer passage from the graveyard. The area is illuminated by three *continual light* spells. If the characters approach from the graveyard side, they may trigger the trap before they can investigate the pit. If they approach from the outside, they can see the visible pit is 10-feet deep. A second pit located one foot farther into the graveyard beyond the trench awaits new victims. The idea is for trespassers to leap over the first pit, only to land on the hidden trapdoor just beyond it.

Locking Pit Trap

The hidden trapdoor covering the pit is spring-loaded. Whenever a creature or object weighing more than 70 pounds rests on its door (marked with an X on the map), the trap triggers. After a creature falls into the 30-foot-deep pit, the cover snaps shut to trap its victim inside. A creature falling in this manner takes 2d6 points of damage. Two humanoid skeletons lie at the bottom of the locking pit. Their weapons and armor are rusted, and their other equipment is rotted and useless. One of the corpses is a halfling, and the other is a gnoll.

For characters who fall into the locking pit trap, it takes a successful Open Doors check to force the trapdoor open from inside the pit. Rescuers above can push open the trapdoor by placing at least 70 pounds on the trapdoor. A character in the pit can also attempt to open the door by disabling the spring mechanism from the inside with thieves' tools, provided the character can reach the mechanism. Those trapped in the pit can locate the locking mechanism hidden behind a secret panel. The secret panel is nine feet above the floor on the west wall.

Area A4-F: Irontooth's Realm

Long before the Aztli retreated into the depths of the earth, the Tepepan Mountains served as the home of a moon princess minotaur and her minions. The priestess led her progeny through her interpretation of the celestial bodies, especially the moon and all its phases. This civilization thrived for many centuries but died of a waterborne plague. In her hubris, she misread a premonition warning her of a melt, which came to pass. The event killed the entire minotaur population and collapsed their short passageway to the surface. However, four of her minions reanimated after death as skeletons. Irontooth assumed leadership by taking the priestess' silver axe and demanded fealty among the other undead. They follow Irontooth until he falls, then they scatter from this place, trying to go to their Great Beyond. Hiuaui's gargoyles know nothing of this area and, though they would rather have the adventurers carry them, they can walk through the maze underwater and out of sight.

The tunnel from the secondary entrance to the graveyard is fairly straight and narrow. Only one branch leads from the main thoroughfare. Sloping down and to the right, liquid floods the passage. The moldy water doesn't ripple, and the tunnel still has about three feet of air above the water's surface.

This flooded labyrinth holds between three and four feet of chilly water. Debris makes the floor uneven below the surface. The short cul-de-sacs are easily distinguished with a cursory glance. The hidden tunnel leading to Irontooth's lair is in the floor, under the water, at the square marked by an X. It is fairly easy to get to the northeast corner of the maze. In that corner, a trio of iron levers jut from a plaque on the east wall about two feet above the water level. The middle one is set to the uppermost position (designated with a full circle). The outer-left one is set to the lowest position (by a semicircle arc outline raised from the plaque). The rightmost one is slightly above level (just above a filled-in half circle on the plaque). The symbols stand for different phases of the moon. It also tells the character the current phase of the moon. Moving a lever also changes the layout of the labyrinth. As the walls shift, the movement alerts the remains of the minotaurs to the intruders.

The **4 minotaur skeletons** approach underwater and then burst from the muck to rush toward the characters to gore them. They try to surround the characters or isolate one or more adventurers. If Irontooth falls, the other three flee if possible.

Minotaur Skeletons (4): HD 4; **HP** 30, 26, 23, 19; **AC** 8[11]; **Atk** strike (1d8) or gore (2d6); **Move** 9; **CL/XP** 4/120; **Save** 13; **Special:** immune to sleep and charm spells.

Area A4-G: Irontooth's Lair

The tunnel connecting **Area A4-F** to **Area A4-G** is completely flooded and requires characters to hold their breaths as they swim or walk through roughly 12 feet of submerged tunnel to get from the labyrinth to the lair. Characters who cannot hold their breaths any longer while in the submerged tunnel ultimately suffocate if they cannot escape.

The maze continues onward after breaking through the water's surface. Unlike the tunnel, this section is completely above water, with stairs rising up to the dry land. No noise or light emanates from the area beyond.

This area is only half the size of the previous maze. Once, the labyrinthine tunnels were a way to pass the time during the reign of the moon princess, but now the layout is a shadow of its former glory. There were many entrances and exits, but the flood caved in the other passages, leaving only this small area intact. The northwest corner has a wide area with a raised dais supporting a throne. Tapestries decorate the walls behind the throne, but time has left them in worthless tatters. A few silks and pillows lie about, hinting at the opulence once heralded here. A large ornate box behind the throne is all that remains of the place's treasures.

Treasure: A crystal ewer of aromatic oil and a jug of ambergris worth a total of 300 gp are in an unlocked iron box behind the throne. The silks and pillows scattered around are worth 100 gp.

Crumbled stonework chokes passageways leading away from the labyrinth, but it would take a herculean effort to excavate the collapsed tunnels to explore the minotaurs' former glory.

Area A4-H: Historical Hall

Niches line this triangle-shaped hall. The base of the cavern is 20 feet across and rises to a height of nearly 60 feet. The two walls slope inward toward the top, resulting in a single seam as a roofline. The niches have sconces, plaques, and other decorative accouterments. Hundreds of flames in tiny iron braziers glow here, changing color in a rhythmic pattern. Violet stays lit the longest, with each color of the rainbow represented in a swirling arrangement, finally blinking on red before returning to violet. The small braziers stay red for only a moment. Twelve braziers near the ceiling begin to flash red for longer periods of time as the pattern continues until those dozen braziers radiate only red light.

Gargoyles of importance entombed themselves here. The plaques, written in Terran, reveal the name, birth date, and date of death for those laid to rest here. A few have a note of accomplishment, though there are only about 15 of the 200 plaques lauded in this manner. The caretaker of this room died long ago, and no new burials have transpired in this room since his death. The caretaker's niche is near the front, and a plaque identifies the gargoyle in charge of this room and reveals that he died 1,129 years ago. The flashing patterns are the work of the mad wizard who created the entryways to this place. He enchanted the braziers with *continual light* spells. These flames were once controllable by visiting gargoyles or other mourners, but the means of doing so have been lost as no one from the village has traveled to the graveyard for at least several generations. A visitor had to remember the gargoyle they wanted to visit and the lights would pulse and change colors to direct the bereaved to the final resting place. The light show is just that — a show. They pose no danger. If escorting any of Hiuaui's gargoyles through this area, they make reverent harmonies and quietly sing mournful dirges.

Area A4-I: The Grand Stair

The cavern opens wide ahead with four-inch-square tiles bearing ornate, colorful patterns paving the way. The wider passage slopes into a gentle staircase leading down. The broad steps have been polished clean of scratches and dust. Small flames dance in the eye sockets of the faces carved into the granite balustrade, which marks the end of the balcony before the twin staircases begin their descent. These two sets of stairs join below the balcony and continue to descend in a grand display. An open book, inkwell, and quill are on a pulpit near the balustrade.

If the characters wait at the balcony's edge for more than a few seconds, they hear the familiar hopping sounds of many small gargoyles coming up the stairs.

Phiskhuri the Dustman has kept this area nearly spotless for centuries. He is a fastidious **gargoyle** and defends the Lower Section from intruders. The book is a visitor's sign-in book. A mourner can record their name in the book and also describe whom they are here to grieve or visit. No entries are recorded on the previous pages. The book is magical. Each time Phiskhuri removes a page, a new one appears in the back of the book. A character who examines the book can see the outline of the last entry in the book; a character could copy that previous name in the book to avoid a confrontation with Phiskhuri.

If anyone attempts to descend the Grand Stair without writing a proper entry on the page, Phiskhuri attacks. He watches and listens from a small alcove 30 steps down the Grand Stair. A character who peers down the Grand Stair has a 1-in-6 chance to see him. As Phiskhuri flies up to attack, the characters notice the **13 tukkuru gargoyles** in this area are not the same as Hiuaui's pets. These little creatures have been re-carved with sadistic expressions etched onto their faces along with sharp, menacing teeth. The monsters aid Phiskhuri's attack by ganging up on the characters. All of the creatures here ignore Hiuaui's gargoyles.

If the characters inspect the tukkuru gargoyles after the attack, they notice that the thicker creatures are of the same species but are not as amiable as the ones all around Alataq. The gargoyles the characters are escorting find these creatures disgusting and remark that they do not know how these beasts came to be.

Phiskhuri the Dustman, Gargoyle: HD 4; **HP** 29; **AC** 5[14]; **Atk** 2 claws (1d3), bite (1d4), horn (1d6); **Move** 9 (fly 15); **Save** 13; **AL** C; **CL/XP** 6/400; **Special:** +1 or better magic weapon to hit. (*Monstrosities* 185)

Tukkuru Gargoyles (13): HD 3; **HP** 18x2, 16, 15x3, 12, 11, 10x4, 8; **AC** 6[13]; **Atk** 2 claws (1d3), bite (1d4); **Move** 9; **Save** 14; **AL** C; **CL/XP** 3/60; **Special:** +1 or better magic weapon to hit. (see **Appendix A: New Monsters**)

Treasure: The gold-leafed book is worth 200 gp.

GRAVEYARD, LOWER SECTION

The following entries describes the graveyard's lower and more difficult section.

AREA A4-J: MASS GRAVE WARD 1

Cracks and crevasses riddle the massive cavern ahead. The shifting quakes have not been kind to this room. One wide trench is an impromptu mass grave as several hundred gargoyle husks have accumulated to create a makeshift causeway for later generations to continue on to someplace deeper in the graveyard. The floor is slippery with mud, and warm, moist air condenses on the dirt walls and flows to the floor.

Another wave of **12 evil tukkuru gargoyles** are here, moving toward the surface. Cavorting in the deeper part of the muddy floor are **3 mudbog oozes**. These monsters try to engulf the characters if they attack the gargoyles; otherwise, they impassively watch the combat unfold. A character trying to traverse a crevasse must roll below their dexterity on 3d6. On a failure, the creature tumbles 25 feet to the bottom of the crevasse, taking 3d6 points of damage and falling prone.

Tukkuru Gargoyles (12): HD 3; HP 17, 16x2, 15, 14x3, 13, 9, 8x3; AC 6[13]; Atk 2 claws (1d3), bite (1d4); Move 9; Save 14; AL C; CL/XP 3/60; Special: +1 or better magic weapon to hit. (see **Appendix A: New Monsters**)

Mudbog Oozes (3): HD 3; HP 21, 17, 12; AC 5[14]; Atk engulf (save avoids); Move 3; Save 14; AL N; CL/XP 3/60; Special: acid (1d6 damage, dissolves organic material), engulf (automatic 1d6 damage per round), immune to blunt weapons. (see **Appendix A: New Monsters**)

Treasure: At the bottom of the crevasse is a silver *+1 trident* embedded into the skull of a gnoll. The entire weapon is made from a single piece of metal. An inscription on the shaft of the trident written in common reads, "Tartarus." A character who reads the inscription recognizes the name as an ancient great hero from a distant land lost to history.

AREA A4-K:
COMMON GRAVES WARD 2

This section and the next are vertically aligned. The characters must climb down the face of a cliff riddled with small shelves that hold tukkuru gargoyle husks (and some enemies). If attacked, the character must succeed on a saving throw to hold onto the handholds and footholds while moving down. Furthermore, the character can attack only with one hand while holding onto the wall. If the character attempts to use both hands to attack or to perform an activity other than climbing, the character makes the preceding saving

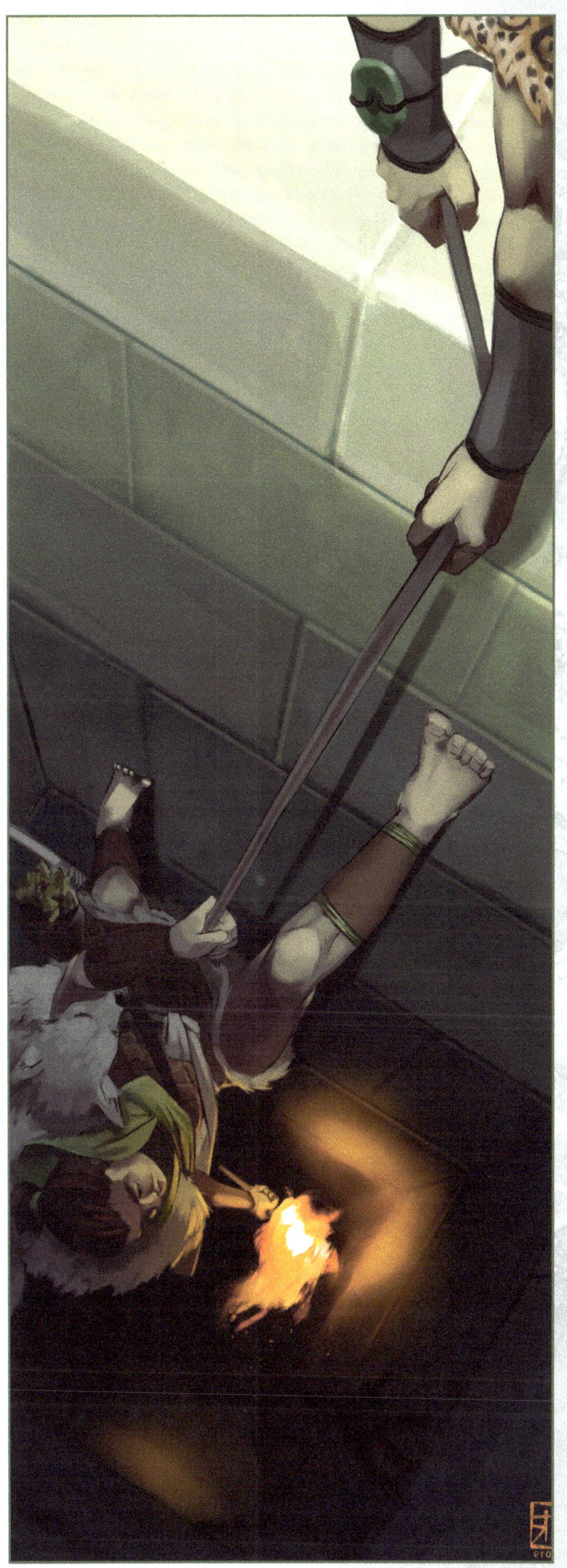

DUNGEON MAP A4

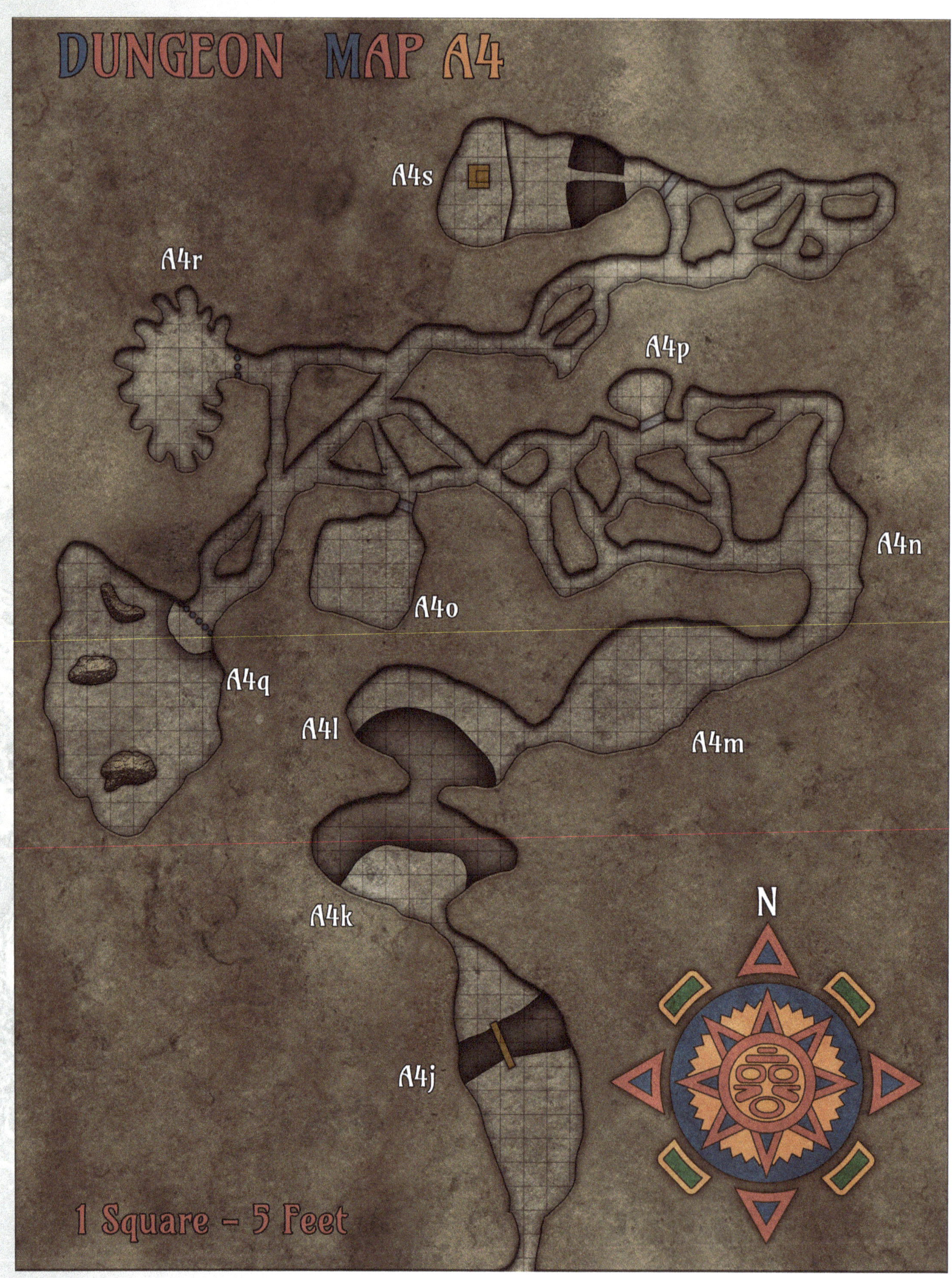

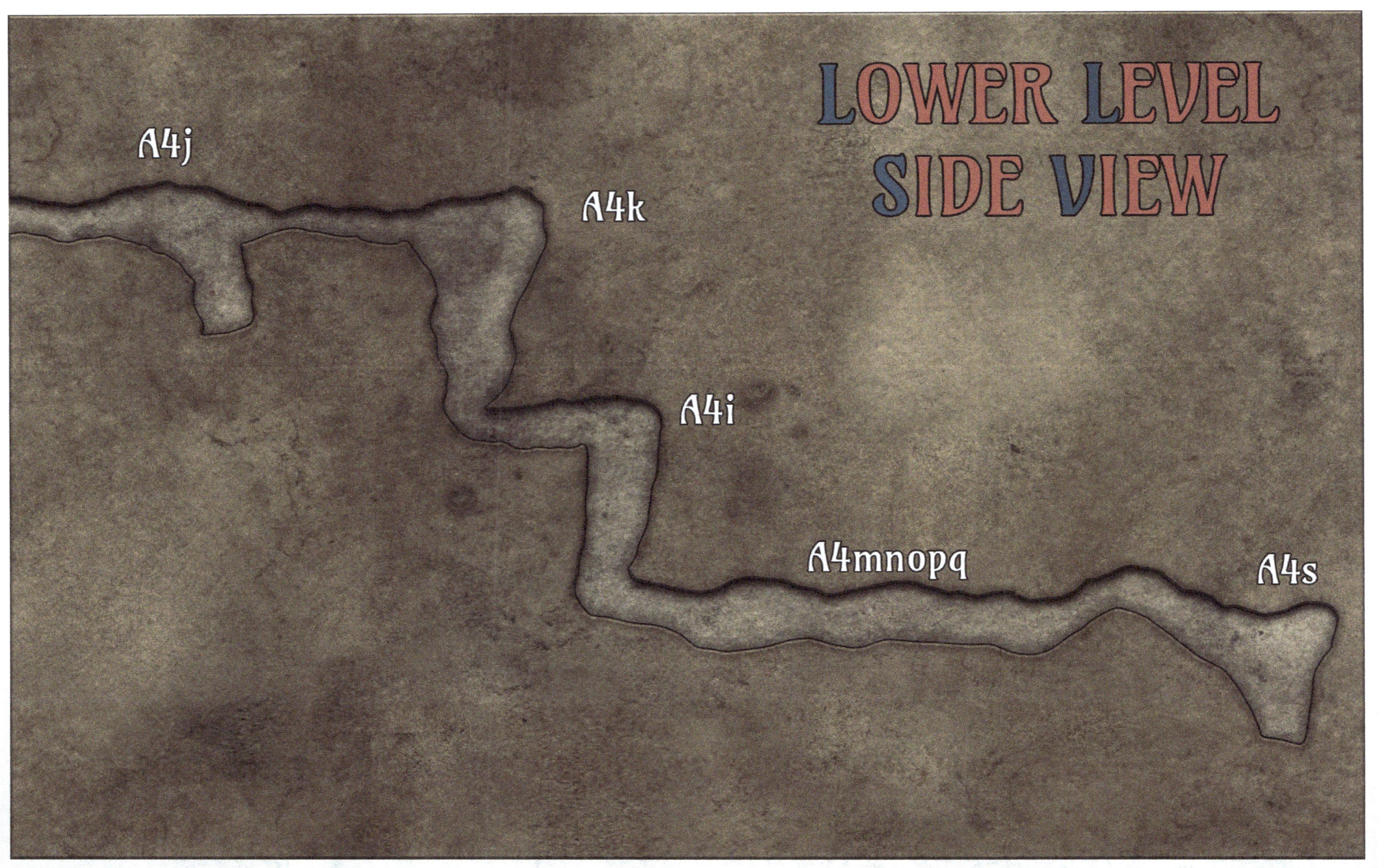

LOWER LEVEL
SIDE VIEW
A4j
A4k
A4i
A4mnopq
A4s

throw with a –2 penalty. The adventurers can take other precautions to avoid falling, such as securing themselves with ropes or by using other climbing implements. The entire cliff face is 80 feet tall from the lip to ground level. One small ledge juts out at 50 feet from the floor and has a small chance to break a fall, though doing so requires the character to make a saving throw.

This is where Hiuaui's pets leave the group. They vociferously thank the helpful characters and move over the edge to make their way to the nearest empty compartment. They confirm that they feel like they are about to rejoin the mountain as their ancestors did before them.

Hot air billows from below, and a character who listens hears a cackling echoing up from somewhere down in the darkness. Although the characters escorted the gargoyles to their final resting place as they requested, the sight of their evil counterparts greatly disturbs the gargoyle pets, and likely the characters as well who hopefully sense that something is amiss here. Nonetheless, the characters can turn back if they wish, though if they do so, Aytasina completes her ritual. The first wave of evil gargoyles makes its way out of the graveyard several days later, where they spread mayhem in neighboring areas. If the characters leave the region altogether, Aytasina discovers their identities by torturing Hiuaui's gargoyle pets. She publicly uses the characters as a scapegoat and blames them for unleashing the ensuing evil upon the world. With their reputations potentially ruined, the characters may ultimately have to decide to join her or defeat her.

The skin forming the gargoyles' final cocoon is malleable, created by the mountain itself in some sort of magical reclamation process. Creatures can use the shelves to climb up or down this cliff face as previously discussed. This section of graves, Ward 2, does not have any traps or enemies for the characters to fight. No treasure is located here either. If the players are trying to decide whether to climb down, have another **12 evil tukkuru gargoyles** appear in a pool of light and start their climb.

Tukkuru Gargoyles (12): HD 3; HP 20, 17x2, 15x4, 12, 9, 8x3; AC 6[13]; **Atk** 2 claws (1d3), bite (1d4); **Move** 9; **Save** 14; **AL** C; **CL/XP** 3/60; **Special:** +1 or better magic weapon to hit. (see **Appendix A: New Monsters**)

AREA A4-L: COMMON GRAVES WARD 3

This was the first area where the tukkuru gargoyles were "born" and then returned to be absorbed by the mountain. No one knows how the birthing began or the origin of the magic creating the stone beasts, but Aytasina warped and polluted the design during her time exploring this graveyard. When the gargoyles now emerge from the walls, they bear her hatred for the Aztlis and all other humanoids with them.

The dimensions of this area are nearly identical to the description of **Area A4-K**, though there is no jutting ledge for falling characters to land on or grab to break their fall. It is just an 80-foot-tall shaft from lip to floor. The entire area feels unsettling, though not in a distinctly tangible sense. However, the presence of **2 purple slimes** gives some credence to the uneasiness. These monsters root around this area, feeding on the amniotic fluids and whatever detritus is left behind in the hollows after the mountain gives birth to a tukkuru gargoyle. The first **tukkuru gargoyle** loiters around the top 20 feet of the vertical surface, nearly invisible as it flattens itself into a hollow. A second **tukkuru gargoyle** languishes in the drainage pool at the base of the cliff. They are devouring the husks left behind by the newest gargoyles. In addition, **6 recently birthed evil tukkuru gargoyles** sit in their individual hollows at various points along the cliff face. The gargoyles attack if the characters begin their descent; the slime on the wall attacks adventurers already engaged with the gargoyles. The slime at the base of the cliff attacks any creature, including a gargoyle, if it is unfortunate enough to fall into the 18-inch-deep lagoon of waste at the bottom of the cliff.

Tukkuru Gargoyles (8): HD 3; HP 21, 19, 10, 8x2, 7, 4x2; AC 6[13]; **Atk** 2 claws (1d3), bite (1d4); **Move** 9; **Save** 14; **AL** C; **CL/XP** 3/60; **Special:** +1 or better magic weapon to hit. (see **Appendix A: New Monsters**)

Purple Slimes (2): HD 5; HP 33, 28; AC 8[11]; **Atk** 2 spikes (1d8 + 1d6 acid); **Move** 9 (climb 9, swim 9); **Save** 12; **AL** N; **CL/XP** 5/240; **Special:** acid (additional 1d6 damage with strike, save avoids), immune to acid and cold. (see **Appendix A: New Monsters**)

Characters traversing from here into **Area A4-M** must trudge through this waste. The roof of the tunnel is only another 18 inches above the surface of the disgusting, slimy water. Taller creatures will need to crawl to get through to the next area. Wading through the sickening muck requires a successful saving throw. On a failure, the creature heaves and retches from exposure to the malodorous water.

AREA A4-M: THE WHEEL

When Aytasina arrived here, luminescent fungi covered the walls of this tranquil cavern, and the large wooden waterwheel centerpiece rotated from the runoff dripping down from an underground spring near the ceiling. The paddles of the wheel delicately delivered nutrients over a large area of colorful lichens. After her takeover, Aytasina quickly plugged the ceiling, shoving early prototypes of her gargoyles' bodies into the opening and softening them to seal the opening to the spring. Some of the gargoyles embedded into the ceiling move their appendages in feeble attempts to escape their hell. She completely repurposed the wheel, knocking it off its axis and setting up bindings to strap down newborn tukkuru gargoyles to spin them faster than humanly possible to teach the beasts to embrace their fear and follow her every command. As she perfected her training, she stopped using the wheel and unleashed a more direct psychological torture on the creatures before they are "buried." They now come out of their hollows as chaotic and evil as she is. After large patches of the ground cover died horribly from the fires and filth she caused, the lichens and fungi retreated below the surface. They hibernate until the raucous energies dissipate, at which time they can flourish again. There are no light sources in this area.

If the characters have a light source, read or paraphrase the following:

This is Aytasina's lover, **Charphu**, who is also a **kishi demon**. He set the dinner table to celebrate his mistress' successes so far in her bid to expand her influence over the Tepepan Mountains. He had been on a diplomatic mission to meet with dwarven representatives from Balandrur. The meeting quickly went sour when the dwarves discovered his true identity. The setback forced him to kill nine dwarves before escaping to safety. However, an Aztli warlock posing as a dwarven priest of Xotite (the dwarven version of the Aztli god Zipe-Toteque) contacted him telepathically and sought to establish an alliance. The warlock secretly worships Itzcuin. He is a member of a secret cabal seeking to infiltrate Balandrur's upper echelon. He explained to Charphu that he had magically observed the initial meeting from afar and would welcome cooperation between their two factions to remove the Firebrand dwarves — the clan that serves as the Tepepan Mountains' de facto ruler — from their position of power.

Charphu was sitting in the dark, thinking of the proper way to tell Aytasina this good news while preparing a dinner of seared, blackened dwarf hearts and dark blood wine. Unfortunately, he must now deal with the unexpected intruders in a slightly weakened state after his encounter with the hostile dwarves. He thinks he can use his abundant charm and suave demeanor to persuade the trespassers to join their cause. Just as his lover turned her misfortune of being shunted to this plane into an opportunity to gather forces for her eventual return to the underworld, he operates under the impression that he can do the same with his unexpected guests. Charphu masquerades as a charming gnoll draped in luxurious silk scarves and gold jewelry. The scarves cover his second face, which he believes is a blessing Itzcuin conferred upon him.

Charphu speaks at length, emphasizing his interest in what any female characters have to offer. He does not ignore male opinions, but deflects their ideas in favor of any females' plans. If women do not speak up, he still steals glances at them as he converses with the males. He tests the group by suggesting it is time for the gargoyles to return to the surface in the form they were meant to have.

"Surely," he says, "you have never seen such abominations as … this?" He produces a husk of a tukkuru gargoyle as he talks of how unnatural those gargoyles are. He wants to bring them back to the way they have always been. He tells them his research is nearing its conclusion, and the exhausted adventurers are welcome to partake of the meal he provides. Afterward, they could return to the surface to gather any stray beasts and send them down here to their home to integrate them into the new plan. Despite his outward friendliness, he is secretly trying to delay the characters for as long as possible until Aytasina joins him.

During their meeting, Charphu weaves his *suggestion* spells into the conversation by telling individual characters to leave their weapons down in the mud or to take off their armor and stay awhile. A character who drops an item into the mud must feel around in the muck to find it again. Charphu loves fighting alongside his paramour Aytasina, as the pair finds battle to be an aphrodisiac for both of them.

When Charphu finally attacks, he throws spears until the characters engage him in hand-to-hand combat. If there are no dwarf characters, he attacks with his magical spear and bite. If a dwarf is present, he taunts the characters with the scalps of his dwarven kin that are attached to his trophy shield. His pouch of 12 throwing spears lies near his feet by the table. He fights with his main weapon *Chuymani-Ari*, a *+1 flaming spear*, which has taken many lives during his existence.

Aytasina is very busy at this time. If Charphu successfully delays the characters for two minutes, she finally comes within range of the demon's telepathic pleas for aid. Aytasina (see **Area A4-S**) arrives on the scene 1d3 + 2 rounds later, using her ability to become incorporeal to pass through intervening objects. Charphu flees if he is reduced to fewer than half his hit points. He works his way to **Area A4-P**, where he uses his copy of the key and hides. He drinks as many *potions of healing* as he can in the interim. When fully healed, he tries to summon his uncle, Acwa Anchhicha, who is also a **kishi demon** (see **Appendix A: New Monsters**). Use the same stat block you used for Charphu, except he wields a *+1 longsword* instead of a spear.

Charphu, Kishi Demon: HD 8; HP 58; AC 3[16]; Atk *+1 flaming spear* (1d6+1 + 1d6 fire) and bite (2d6), or thrown spear (1d6); **Move** 15; **Save** 8; **AL** C; **CL/XP** 10/1400; **Special:** +1 or better magic weapons to hit, darkvision (60ft), resistances (fire, electricity), spell-like abilities, summon kishi demon (35% chance), telepathy (60ft). (see **Appendix A: New Monsters**)
Spell-like abilities: at will—*detect evil, detect magic, suggestion*; 3/day—*charm person*; 1/day—*confusion*.
Equipment: *Chuymani-Ari* (*+1 flaming spear*), 12 spears in pouch, 2 *potions of healing*, key to **Area A4-P**, gold links and rings (1200 gp total), gold scarab (600 gp).

Treasure: Charphu's mass of gold links and rings adorned with rubies and emeralds is worth 1,200 gp. A fine scarab made of yellow gold and six-pointed star-shaped rubies of the deepest crimson are woven into his headdress and is worth 600 gp.

AREA A4-N: CROSSROADS

This wide crossroads in the tunnels is now used as a staging ground as Aytasina sends her minions, the altered tukkuru gargoyles, to the surface or to other destinations farther abroad. She has sent very few of them underground toward Balandrur while her lover attempts to negotiate with the Firebrand dwarves. This area is naturally unlit, but if the characters can see, read or paraphrase the following description:

Aytasina could potentially run into the characters here on her way to her dinner with Charphu, but more than likely, this is an area for the characters to take a short rest before trying to defeat the demonic influence corrupting this once consecrated graveyard. This area is the first room without niches carved into the walls as it was only recently constructed.

AREA A4-O: THE LABORATORY

This is another encounter where Aytasina could interact with the characters, but is set as another reason for her final encounter to be fully buffed and ready for attack. She discovers the aftermath of this lab's destruction and then hunts down the defilers in her throne room.

The **6 Aztli and halfling servants** are working on different projects for Aytasina's gargoyles. They follow her blueprints to design the next upgrade to make them tougher and more durable. If one of them notices an intruder, the servant assigns that person a mundane task to perform. The servant shows the character the task once and then expects him or her to complete the repetitive job of chopping, cutting, pouring, lifting, or mixing until the character creates a refined pile of ingredients. The chemicals are caustic and dangerous. A character who spends one minute performing any of the tasks must make a saving throw or take 1d4 points of damage from an accidental spill on a failure.

The servants are accustomed to temporary slaves popping in unannounced. Therefore, they likely do not notice the characters' weapons at first. The servant eventually declares the weapon to be a safety hazard and demands the transgressor put it away and get to work. The servants do not initiate an attack against the characters, even if they openly defy their directions. Instead, they vow to report the incident to their superiors, whom they never name, and continue about their business. On the other hand, if the characters attack them, they fight back, using their spells first before pulling out maces.

Male and Female Aztli Servants (Clr4) (3): HP 21, 17, 13; AC 7[12]; **Atk** mace (1d6); **Move** 12; **Save** 12; **AL** C; **CL/XP** 4/120; **Special:** +2 save vs. paralysis and poison, banish undead, spells (2/1).
Spells: 1st—*cure light wounds, detect magic*; 2nd—*hold person*.
Equipment: tlahuiztli armor[B], mace.

Male and Female Halfling Servants (Clr4) (3): HP 19, 16x2; AC 7[12]; **Atk** mace (1d6) or sling (1d4); **Move** 9; **Save** 12; **AL** C; **CL/XP** 4/120; **Special:** +1 missile weapon bonus, +2 save vs. paralysis and poison, +4 save vs. magic, banish undead, spells (2/1).
Spells: 1st—*cure light wounds, light*; 2nd—*silence 15ft radius*.
Equipment: tlahuiztli armor[B], mace, sling, 10 sling bullets.
[B] See **Appendix B: New Equipment and Magic Items**

Treasure: The lab holds several labeled potions ready for transport. There are two *potions of fire resistance* and a *potion of gaseous form*. A vial labeled as a potion of growth instead contains poison (save or die). Another rack contains a *potion of levitation* and two *potions of giant strength*. The other philters are empty or just have partially completed recipes in them. Aytasina hopes to incorporate potions into a batch of gargoyles in the future. She has not fused the newer advancements she and her team have made into her growing army yet. She plans to experiment on new strength enhancements into a clutch of gargoyles hatching in 14 days.

AREA A4-P: THE SAFE ROOM

Only Aytasina and Charphu have the keys for this door. Otherwise, characters must bash the door open or pick the lock. Charphu hides here if he can retreat from the characters in **Area A4-M**. If possible, he locks the door from the inside and summons his uncle. If successful in this endeavor, his uncle scoffs at Charphu, smacks him upside the head disdainfully, and moves out into the corridors to find the characters who brought shame upon their demonic family.
Treasure: The small room beyond the door holds potable water (60 gallons), dried fruits and meats (16 meals worth of rations), eight blankets, three heavy coats of ermine worth 20 gp each, a six-foot-tall ladder, a light crossbow with 11 bolts, a drum, a lyre (nonmagical), four *potions of healing*, and one *potion of extra healing*.

AREA A4-Q: THE KENNEL

Aytasina houses another experimental creation in this area. A latched iron gate blocks the cavern, keeping her pets from wandering around. She used them in the excavation of this part of the catacombs, and she is breeding them as a gift to the Firebrand dwarves or the cabal they hope to be working with soon. This is where Aytasina starts when the characters encounter Charphu in **Area A4-M**.

After opening the gate, read or paraphrase the following description:

This cavern is 300 feet below the surface and serves as a repository for all the excess stone excavated while constructing the complex's network of tunnels. Aytasina uses **7 t'shanns** to maintain this area. She plans to mutate these creatures when she gets more time after her gargoyle project becomes self-sustaining. The creatures adhere to their normal protocol, burrowing about five feet below the surface while they wait for an opportunity to play with Aytasina. They recognize the sound of the grating iron in the tunnel above that signals her arrival. The creature nearest the entry relays the message of imminent excitement to its cohorts, causing them to all lay in wait for their master to arrive. Aytasina never brings anyone else into this room. Therefore, they immediately attack if they sense more than one creature moving around the sea of stones.

T'shanns (7): HD 4; HP 48, 43, 41, 37x2, 33, 28; AC 9[10]; **Atk** strike (1d4); **Move** 5 (burrow 5); **Save** 13; **AL** N; **CL/XP** 4/120; **Special:** alien thoughts (30ft range, save or affected by *confusion* spell; within 10ft, save or 1d4 damage), spew (10ft range, acid spray, 1d4 damage, save for half). (see **Appendix A: New Monsters**)

Treasure: A search reveals a cache of deep-green tourmalines worth 400 gp inside a cracked geode.

AREA A4-R: THE CELL

Aytasina trusts few beings on this plane. She must work with some who have skills she requires, but she never truly understands them. These include the acolytes in her laboratory, the t'shann excavators, and possibly the Balandrur dwarves. During her outbursts, Aytasina sometimes kills those who disappoint or frustrate her without a moment's hesitation. She binds and holds those who survive her violent fits in this dungeon until they prove their worth again.

The locked barrier has three keyholes. Each key — and by extension, keyhole — is slightly different in shape and thickness. Only Aytasina carries the keys to unlock this device. A creature can force the door open or pick the locks with thieves' tools.
She keeps her slaves in individual cells, but only two cells are occupied at the moment. The cells are minimalist at best — no bed, no chamber pot, and no food bowl. Simply put, she expects her captives to die rather than redeem themselves. Most of the individual cells have a hook embedded into the ceiling where she can string up a poor soul and flog them. Almost every cell has copious bloodstains on the walls and floor. There are 11 cells in all.
At the moment, Cell 4 holds **Avvisana**, a **unicorn**. Tehuatl has no horses, making unicorns an even greater oddity. Tragically, Aytasina found, captured, and painfully removed the noble beast's horn for fun and to keep Avvisana from teleporting. His beard has grown scraggly, and large patches of his once-luxurious coat have grown matted or fallen out. He has been here for months and strangely only remembers how to converse in elvish, though he can do so only using his telepathy. If an elvish woman is among the adventurers, Avvisana swears fealty to her if she can return his horn from "that usuchana," an insulting word he uses to describe Aytasina. The beleaguered unicorn apologizes for using such harsh language. He solemnly says that if that task is too great, the characters are welcome to put him out of his misery. If the characters heal Avvisana back to fighting condition, the unicorn relishes the chance to vanquish Aytasina from

this world either on his own or alongside the adventurers. He has no knowledge of her lover or their plans regarding the gargoyles.

Avvisana, Male Unicorn: HD 4; HP 23 (currently 6); AC 2[17]; **Atk** 2 hoofs (1d8), horn (1d8); **Move** 24; **Save** 13; **AL** L; **CL/XP** 5/240; **Special:** double damage for charge, magic resistance (25%), teleport, telepathy (60ft). (*Monstrosities* 494)

You are free to determine the exact means of reattaching or regenerating Avvisana's missing horn without using likely unavailable potent magic. At your discretion, you can make this a side quest requiring consultation with the elders of Alataq's library or with another suitable party to uncover a nonmagical method of restoring his horn. Aytasina carries the detached horn and uses it as a component of her spellcasting, even though it is not necessary to do so.

Cell 11, the one the farthest from the gate, holds a **giant ant**. Captured from an invading swarm, Aytasina hopes to use the creature as a nourishing host for invasive egg-laying. She is learning how to "impregnate" a living host to feed freshly hatched larva housed within them. All of these experiments have been fatal missteps so far. Aytasina used acid to drill holes through its exoskeleton, leaving open wounds in its wake. Leather straps restrain the ant to the floor. Its mandible is still intact.

Wounded Giant Warrior Ant: HD 3; HP 17 (currently 5); AC 3[16]; **Atk** bite (1d6 + poison); **Move** 18; **Save** 14; **AL** N; **CL/XP** 4/120; **Special:** poison (2d6 damage, save for 1d4 damage). (*Monstrosities* 15)

Area A4-S: Throne Room

> Across a gaping moat of lava, a beautiful throne dominates a raised dais. Gouts of flame erupt from the liquid stone surrounding the island of solid rock. Heat waves disrupt the view of the empty throne, warping the details of the island's contents. A small chest appears to peak out from behind the seat. The temperature in this area is sweltering. A single iron beam traverses the gap between the hall and the island where the throne sits. The beam is one foot wide and stretches 15 feet to the island.

This is where **Aytasina**, an **annis hag**, likely encounters the characters after she finds her lover's corpse, the dead acolytes, her slaughtered pets, or her prisoners freed. If she is aware of the characters' impending arrival, she uses the magic at her disposal to fortify her defenses and tries to summon her paramour to her side, provided he still lives. Enraged by the damage they have done, Aytasina strives solely to destroy the trespassers who may have foiled her intricate plans. Her location is her first line of defense, as the lava surrounding the island is an imposing natural obstacle. Characters must roll below their dexterity on 3d6 to traverse the narrow beam connecting the hall to the island. A creature who falls into the lava for the first time or starts its turn in the lava takes 6d6 points of fire damage. If she has enough warning, Aytasina tosses a pot of slippery grease on the beam to make it slippery, which requires characters to instead roll below their dexterity on 4d6 to walk across.

If she is prepared for her showdown with the characters, she uses the most advantageous magical gear among her treasure. She drinks a *potion of giant strength* from her stores to boost her already impressive physical might.

Poison Needle Trap

The lock built into the chest conceals a poison needle. Opening the chest without the key causes the needle to spring out and deliver a dose of poison. Triggering the trap extends the needle three inches straight out from the lock. A creature opening the chest takes 1d4 points of damage and must make a saving throw or die. A thief examining the lock can determine that alterations were made to the lock to accommodate the needle. Unsuccessfully attempting to pick the lock triggers the trap.

Aytasina, Annis Hag: HD 10; HP 76; AC 1[18]; **Atk** 2 claws (2d8), bite (1d8); **Move** 12; **Save** 4 (+1, *luckstone*); **AL** C; **CL/XP** 13/2300; **Special:** hug and rend (if 2 claws hit, hold and automatic claw and bite damage, Open Doors check to escape), polymorph self (at will), call mists (as *obscuring mist*), spells (4/4/3/2/2). (*Monstrosities* 237) **Spells:** 1st—*bumble* ᶜ, *charm person, magic missile, stumble* ᶜ; 2nd—*detect invisibility, invisibility, phantasmal force, web*; 3rd—*dispel magic, fireball, triplicate* ᶜ; 4th—*dimension door, wall of fire*; 5th—*passwall, transmute rock to mud*. **Equipment:** unicorn horn (taken from Avvisana in **Area A4-R**), keys to every lock in the complex, a *luckstone* (+1 to hit and saves), two spell scrolls (*fear, wall of stone*), *sandals of the mitote* ᴮ, soul bag containing the soul of a wicked sorcerer who served Itztliteotl.

ᴮ See **Appendix B: New Equipment and Magic Items**
ᶜ See **Appendix C: New Spells**

Aytasina appears as a blue-skinned, black-haired fiend wearing a sweeping cloak. The look of absolute hatred she aims toward her enemies seems permanently etched onto her chiseled features. Aytasina bolsters her defenses when an opportunity presents itself, casting *invisibility* on herself or Charphu. If her lover accompanies her, they coordinate their attacks on one or two individuals rather than spreading them out over the characters. She may use a magical *wall of fire* to separate the party into smaller groups. When one of the paramours falls in battle, the other surprisingly disregards their personal wellbeing and uses their movement to race to their fallen lover's side to exchange their final farewells.

If defeated, Aytasina disappears in a flash of painfully bright light. She leaves no trace of her existence behind other than the objects she carried on her person. After her defeat, the characters sense a sea change in the overall mood filling the graveyard. The ominous feeling of sin and corruption gives way to a reverent solemnity for the gargoyles laid to rest here. Furthermore, with Aytasina's scheme foiled, the scourge of evil gargoyles plaguing the land comes to an end.

Treasure: The chest contains 4,520 sp and a jeweled tiara made of silver and emeralds worth 1,500 gp. The paranoid Aytasina built a false bottom into the chest to confound thieves in addition to wasting their time searching for it. Beneath it are five rings. Two of them are magical. One silver band with a turquoise gem is a *ring of regeneration*. Another ring, carved from a single opal, is a *ring of protection +2*. A matching pair of thin gold bands are nonmagical but worth 100 gp each. The last ring is a thick palladium band carved from the metal of a meteorite that is worth 400 gp.

Designer's Note

If the characters want to roleplay the transfer of gargoyle husks into the proper burial niches, go ahead and tell them about the long process of finding the individual husks, moving them into the graveyard, and finding a vacant niche for the mountain to reclaim them. It takes a 1d2 + 2 weeks of hard work (40 hours per week) to complete the task. If they spend the time, give them a story award of 400 XP.

Chapter Five: Back to the Village, Part II

The characters return to Alataq on a clear, warm day to find the citizens once again in the midst of another celebration — the feast of the maize harvest honoring Tonacayotl, the Aztli god of maize. Tiny booths have popped up all over the village, with most concentrated in the park. Seventy-five different dishes containing at least some maize capture the grain's remarkable diversity, while masks, woven mats, and a large maize-*máché* dragon puppet crafted from husks, leaves, and even eaten cobs adorn many of the awnings outside these stands. Several people maneuver a green dragon puppet from booth to booth, sampling the food in a grandiose ritual to give thanks to Tonacayotl for the bountiful harvest. Songs of praise resonate throughout the settlement, but the joyous voices grind to a screeching halt when the characters come into view.

The raucous celebration abruptly ceases as everyone stares in unison. Children race out to greet the heroes who ended the scourge of evil gargoyles. The elders smile, nod assertively, and display non-verbal gestures signaling approval. Everyone wants to touch the people they call the "Ahillita." Shouts of congratulations and adoring smiles flow through the crowd. The Aztlis bring food and ask about Calcata and Aqallor, while pushing through the mob and toward the quaint house where the excursion began. The couple are waiting there, waving from the front door, and gesture for them to step inside. They shut the door behind you to give you a moment's peace.

"We have found out part of what the document in the scepter means … Oh, wait. Welcome back to Alataq, friends!" With that, Aqallor finds a decanter of pulque and pours a glass. They salute you with raised glasses and ask if you need a bath and a bed.

The Aztlis intently listen to the characters' tales about the gargoyle graveyard with rapt attention, asking questions and delighting in the harrowing story. They tell the characters that no one has seen any of the evil tukkuru gargoyles. They also have contacts with different shop owners who may be interested in purchasing some of the treasures the adventurers found. If the characters mention it, they also have ideas on how to aid the unicorn missing its horn. They claim to know a druid in the lowlands who performs miracles. "If anyone knows how to make this fine creature whole, it is her."

Eventually, they begin their story of the research they made on the map their father left them.

"It took a long time to establish this was not a map, by itself," Calcata begins, producing the document. "The beautiful rendering of the mountains is a gorgeous depiction, but neither we nor the elders of the library could discern a specific location." Aqallor lays the paper on their table and anchors the corners with the art side facing down.

"Look here," Calcata says, pointing to a series of dots on the back of the document. "These splashes of ink tell a tale." He explains the seemingly innocent ink marks and imperfections in the page itself on the back of the document correspond to a cipher system the ancient Aztlis developed thousands of years ago that ultimately fell out of favor.

"The elders had a series of scrolls that helped decipher the code. The basics, anyway. There was some extrapolation to gather what we have." Aqallor produces a second folded piece of weathered maguey paper from his pocket. "This is what those marks say. 'Look to the rise of our blessed night orb from the top of the tallest peak. After she changes from umber to pale white, removing colors from your sight, you will know. Ome guide you. Monk is key.'"

"Ome means duo or two in that language, so we think it has to do with Chachacua Cahxatana, known as the mountain between men."

The reference to the tallest peak refers to the mountain that gave rise to Tehuatl itself, the stratovolcano Tepetzin. Chachacua Cahxatana is an otherwise unremarkable, 7,000-foot-tall mountain renowned for only one thing — being the reputed site of the Lost Temple of the Twins, Itziuhqui and Tlahuizcal. Because it has no features that distinguish it from the other surrounding peaks, the mountain's precise location has also fallen into the realm of speculation. Calcata advises the characters that they must scale the range's tallest mountain to find the presumably long-abandoned religious site. The cryptic portion afterward indicates that Chachacua Cahxatana's hidden location can be revealed only by observing the moon's change in color while it travels across the night sky.

If you wish to have the characters explore this section, but they do not stumble upon it themselves or with Calcata's assistance, you may have the library's resident scholars track down the adventurers, or you may gently encourage the adventurers to visit the library and then relay this information to them instead.

The trip into the mountains in search of Chachacua Cahxatana follows the script for the characters' previous excursions into the wilderness. You may challenge them with some of the random encounters presented earlier in this adventure or allow them to pass through the untamed landscape without hindrance. Trekking to the top of a perilous mountain is not an easy task. At various points along the way, the characters have a 30% chance of losing their bearings (20% if a ranger is in the party) and finding the best route to climb up the mountain. If the characters lose their way, add several hours to their trip. In addition, at several critical points the adventurers must climb challenging vertical surfaces without falling. Falling causes the climber to fall 1d6 x 10 feet onto a hard surface. A falling character takes 1d6 points of damage for each 10 feet fallen. Characters can find a suitable guide to navigate them up the mountain for a 50-gp fee. While traveling with the guide, the characters know the best route to the summit and do not get lost.

CHAPTER SIX: WHERE EAGLES DARE

This section begins after the characters scale Tepetzin, which allows them to set their sights toward their destination.

The flash of light comes from the mouth of the temple of Itziuhqui and Tlahuizcal. Built roughly halfway up the mountainside at a height of about 4,200 feet, a giant-sized moonstone inexplicably levitates with every moonrise. Carved from a single meteor originally from the satellite currently orbiting the planet, the object crashed into the sea shortly after the cataclysm devastated the entire continent. The meteor longs to return home. Therefore, every time the moon is within sight of the stone carved from its remnants, it strains to rejoin its former partner. Of course, gravity wins this contest, though the boulder nonetheless rises five feet and stays there while the moon remains visible in the night sky. It takes roughly four hours to conventionally traverse from the summit of Tepetzin to the opening. If the characters can fly to the site or travel there by another means, it takes significantly less time to get there. When the moon finally disappears, the stone falls back to the ground,

essentially sealing the temple's entrance and crushing anything underfoot. According to legend, one night in the future, when the moon rises blue and stays that shade during its entire nightly passage, the statue will break free of its earthy bonds and rocket back up into the heavens to rejoin the moon, free from its isolation on this world.

AREA A6-A: TEMPLE ENTRANCE

At one time, the moonstone was carved into the likeness of an Aztli priest, but time eroded the statue into an indistinguishable, upright oblong stone. While the stone floats above the ground, the entrance is accessible. When it descends back to the earth, it is virtually impossible to move it or squeeze past it. The light illuminating the hallway comes from six *continual light* spells cast in niches cut into the wall at roughly eye level. This was the source of light that the characters saw from the top of Tepetzin.

The decedent is a poor soul who could not escape the falling stone. If a character suffers the same fate of being beneath the stone when it descends to the ground, that person must make a saving throw to get out of the way or take 10d6 points of damage and be buried underneath the stone on a failure. A buried creature takes 4d6 points of damage each round it remains buried. A character must make an Open Doors check to escape.

AREA A6-B: THE NAVE

During the temple's brief heyday, worshippers cleansed themselves in the pool, which has remained remarkably pristine. Fed by the waters from an underground, volcanic spring, the warm water emits steam. The twins' priests would routinely consecrate this sacred water, but the magic of this place is long gone just like the gems and flecks of precious metals that the worshippers tore out of the recesses in the walls and ceiling before abandoning this place forever.

AREA A6-C: THE CHAPEL

THE TALE OF THE TWIN GODS

The winners write history, and the hero-gods are no exception. The nascent rebellion had many unsung heroes, and Itziuhqui and Tlahuizcal were two of the bravest and least fortunate. They served under the devious Itzcuin during the conflict against Tlatoani. When the war ended in victory, the pair attained godhood, though their tenures as deities were short-lived. The scheming Itzcuin urged the twins who were gods of the east to directly challenge Notonatiuh and attain his more prominent role as the god of the sun. Yaocteotl saw their gambit as a threat to his hegemony. In response, he and Notonatiuh utterly destroyed the two gods and forbid their worship throughout Tehuatl. Nearly all their priests and followers quickly abandoned their temple as the pair virtually vanished from history.

TWIN GODS' TEMPLE

monkey adorn the walls along with painted images of Aztli warriors.

One wall depicts numerous beasts bowing before the sun and moon, though decorative pieces that were attached to the painting are now missing. Numerous white dots set against a black background adorn the ceiling. The image of a ring and a triangle are also visible. A hastily drawn image on the wall behind the altar shows a pair of Aztli warriors hurling javelins from their atlatls at the rising sun. The artwork appears unfinished, as the painting's fine details were never completed. The painting fills the surface surrounding a detailed calendar, which has numerous charcoal markings along its edges.

A character can identify the artwork decorating the ceiling as an image of the night sky, though the ringed planet and triangle are anomalous features in the heavens. The charcoal marks around the calendar's edges also bear images of the ringed object and the triangle. However, a detailed examination reveals no clues as to their purported meaning.

A character who examines the artwork surrounding the calendar identifies the two figures hurling the javelins are Itziuhqui and Tlahuizcal. If the character learns their identities, the character also recalls the pair unsuccessfully challenged Notonatiuh for his position as the god of the sun. The character remembers the complete Tale of the Twins from the earlier sidebar and also believes the triangle and ring represent the twins' positions in the night sky.

The animal bas-relief sculptures have no special significance, though rotating the monkey's tail in a clockwise direction causes the altar to swing in a counterclockwise direction to reveal a sloping passage leading into darkness. A character who examines the altar has a 3-in-6 chance to detect the secret door. Opening the hidden portal without engaging the mechanism on the monkey's tail requires the character to pivot the massive and heavy object into the opened position. A character who locates the secret door believes there must be a device that opens the door. The riddle in Hiuaui's document about the "Monk is key" offers a clue. If a character asks to review the riddle or document again, give the player an opportunity to figure out the solution on his or her own. If the player does not recognize the significance, give the character a percentage chance to succeed (chosen by you depending on how much help the party might need). On a success, the character focuses on the riddle's play on words.

Area A6-D: Tilt-O-Whirl

Painted images adorning the walls depict two radiant Aztli men exchanging pleasantries with supplicants and participating in leisurely daily activities. At the midway point, the artwork takes an ominous turn. The scenes occur in darkness as a hairless dog seems to whisper in the pairs' ears and accompanies them while the two Aztlis from the paintings before the midway point engage in despicable acts of cruelty and violence.

The artwork depicts the twin gods' transition from benevolent deities to gods corrupted by Itzcuin. They portray the deities interacting with their newfound Aztli worshippers before Itzcuin transformed them into malevolent beings, though the transformation is moderately exaggerated. The paintings were completed shortly after the twins' destruction as an effort to placate the angry hero-gods who vanquished them. The hairless dog in the images is a representation of Itzcuin. Figuring out his corrupting influence is up to the characters.

A pressure plate is poorly concealed just inside the entrance. The pressure plate activates nothing and is solely intended as a ruse to make thieves and trespassers think that they outsmarted the defenders. The real trap awaits ahead.

Tilting Floor

This insidious trap turns the floor into a steep ramp. The floor rests on a pivot at the midpoint in the hallway, much like a seesaw. The first portion of the floor rests on a solid stone foundation. The latter half of the hallway sits atop a 40-foot-deep pit lined with spikes. When the weight beyond the hall's midpoint exceeds the weight before the midpoint, the floor tilts on its pivot at a severe slope. A character on the floor at that time must succeed on a saving throw to grab hold of the floor or wall to avoid sliding down into the pit. A character who fails the saving throw slides down into the pit unless he or she can fly or otherwise avoid falling. The creature takes 3d6 points of damage from the fall into the pit and lands on 1d4+2 spikes for 1d3 points of damage each. A character can climb out of the pit provided that the floor is still tilted at an angle that allows the trapped creature to escape. Faint grooves mar the wall's surfaces at the near end of the hallway, hinting at the danger of the tilting trap. The trap can be circumvented by keeping a sufficient counterweight on the near end of the corridor. A character can also disarm the trap by preventing the hallway from tilting. The twin gods' priests and worshippers used the former method to circumvent the trap and avoid falling prey to it.

Area A6-E: The Twins' Cavern

The twins' worshippers and priests almost unanimously abandoned the destroyed gods, but two of the acolytes refused to leave. They painted the images on the cavern walls to commemorate their patron deities in bleak fashion. To punish them for their insolence, Yaocteotl transformed them into **2 wraiths**. The hateful monstrosities attack any creature who trespasses on their sacred grounds. If the characters serve an Aztli god other than Itzcuin, they focus their attention on that individual. They curse and hiss at them throughout the combat. Despite their sad condition, they remain steadfastly loyal to their former masters, proclaiming that Itziuhqui and Tlahuizcal deserved the greatness Yaocteotl denied them. The artwork on the walls are the final depictions of the fallen twin gods becoming feebler and sicklier just before Yaocteotl utterly destroyed them.

Wraiths (2): HD 4; **HP** 29, 25; **AC** 3[16]; **Atk** touch (1d6 + level drain); **Move** 9 (fly 24); **Save** 13; **AL** C; **CL/XP** 8/800; **Special:** +1 or better magic or silver weapons to hit, level drain (1 level with hit). (*Monstrosities* 518)

Area A6-F: Collapsed Crematorium

A crematorium operated at this site while the temple was active. However, neglect and seismic activity caused shifting earth to bury the entrance to the crematorium's chute and gas flame. The deceased were lowered into the chute buried beneath the rubble and then incinerated by the gas flame. Loved ones retrieved the ashes from the grated chute and interred them here in the room's mausoleum section or spread them at another location significant to the decedent or the surviving family members.

Continual light spells cast onto the walls illuminate this area. When the characters reach the upper landing, read or paraphrase the following description:

The lock and chain are merely for show. The lock opens with the press of a button, which releases the chain. The twin gods' connection to the sun prompted their worshippers to incinerate most of their dead in this crematorium using natural gases from fissures beneath the crematorium for fuel. Of course, with the flame extinguished and the colorless, odorless gas still seeping into the room, it makes for a volatile combination. If a character spends at least one minute in this room, the character must make a saving throw or take 1d6 points of damage. The character must repeat this saving throw for each additional minute spent in the room. To make matters worse, the gas is flammable. If an open flame, spark, or any other plausible ignition source comes into contact with the gas, it explodes in a 40-foot radius centered on the ignition source. Creatures within the blast radius must make a saving throw or take 6d6 points of fire damage on a failure or half as much damage on a success.

Treasure: The silver rails are worth 300 gp each but are nearly 15 feet long. The silver lock and chain are worth 400 gp.

Area A6-G: Vault's Interior

The coffin bears no images and appears cracked and warped in spots. Despite its obvious state of decay, it takes a combined strength of 26 to pry off the coffin's lid. Inside, the characters find strips of moldy linens. More importantly, the characters see that the floor beneath the coffin opens into a passage from which the horrible smell originates.

Area A6-H: Dead Mass

The shaft beneath the coffin descends 20 feet at a 60-degree angle until it opens into this area. All creatures larger than a halfling must crawl through this narrow shaft. Even while crawling, the creature must succeed on a saving throw to safely drop from the shaft and land on the ground eight feet beneath it. On a failed save, the creature falls prone on the ground but takes no damage.

When the characters see the room, read or paraphrase the following description:

The creature is a **derghodemon**, otherwise known as a cockroach demon that the two priests from **Area A6-E** summoned thousands of years earlier. The dimwitted monster has tried to escape on numerous occasions to no avail. After centuries of boredom, the prospect of killing living creatures invigorates the diabolical monster. The demon wades into combat with its spells, savage claws, and ferocious bite. The monster fights until destroyed. The bodies it feasts on are those disloyal worshippers who turned their backs on the twins after their demise. The two stalwart priests who never renounced the twins deemed those who abandoned them as traitors. They consigned these unfortunate souls to a certain death in the cavern beneath the crematorium.

The two priests were unaware that the high priest interred in **Area A6-G** took a vital secret to the grave with him. Like his two counterparts, a priest named Iaqito never renounced the twins. He stepped into the coffin, wrapped his body in fine linens, and then swallowed a lethal dose of poison. Iaqito, a contemporary of Itzcuin and his twin brother Nonotzali, scrawled a scandalous, firsthand pictograph account of Nonotzali sleeping with his sister Quetzalpetlatl during a drunken stupor onto a stone tablet buried with him. If the characters search through the bones and other debris, they find the faded stone. While the stone has no monetary value, the ancient drawing corroborates the rumors surrounding the event, which were largely dismissed as Tlatoani's handiwork or Poqoza propaganda at the time. Iaqito believed the drawing along with his eyewitness testimony could force Nonotzali to intervene on the twins' behalf, but his uneasiness cooperating with Itzcuin and his minions led him to rethink his plan. He opted instead to take his secret with him to the grave. While its revelation would have been a bombshell after the hero-gods' victory, the vulgar images have lost their impact on the god's status within the Aztli pantheon.

Derghodemon (Cockroach Demon): HD 10; **HP** 71; **AC** –2[21]; **Atk** 5 claws (1d4) or 2 claws (1d4) and 3 swords (2d6); **Move** 15; **Save** 5; **AL** C; **CL/XP** 16/3200; **Special:** +1 or better magic or silver weapons to hit, immune to acid and poison, magic resistance (50%), spell-like abilities, telepathy (100ft). (see **Appendix A: New Monsters**) **Spell-like abilities:** at will—*darkness 15ft radius, detect invisibility, fear, sleep*; 2/day—*feeblemind* (30ft range)

Treasure: The derghodemon had no interest searching the dead for any valuables, which gives the characters an opportunity to search through these items themselves. There are 16 pearls worth 100 gp each, a *figurine of the golden lion*, a vial of *green war paint*[B], a suit of *+1 ollixalli armor*[B], and a *+1/+3 vs. giants tepoztopilli*[B]. Iaqito's stone tablet is worth 1,500 gp.

[B] See **Appendix B: New Equipment and Magic Items**

WRAPPING UP THE MOUNTAINS

It is almost eerie returning to Alataq without a festival or jubilee in full swing, but the town is quiet save for a few of the villagers who smile and nod at the characters' fresh wounds and new equipment. Calcata and Aqallor greet the characters at their door with open arms, escorting them inside to hear the tales. The couple congratulate the characters on their good fortune and expertly weave the conversation to those less fortunate. They tell of them of the Bloodmoon's imminent appearance and the harbingers it foretells. If you are continuing along the adventure arc, you may segue the conclusion of this adventure into the next one, *Seven Year Harvest*.

Seven Year Harvest

By Tim Hitchcock

When the spring moon rises,
We honor your voice, that of wind and sun, and rain.
When the spring moon rises,
We honor your flesh, that of the soil and the seed.
When the spring moon rises,
We honor your children, the gourds, the beans, the maize.
We honor you in the dance of our ancestors,
With the flames of the sun,
With the blood of the ocean,
With the passing of this life unto the next.
And with the passing of the next back into the now.
— *A Tehuatl Harvest Prayer*

Seven Year Harvest is an epic adventure designed for four 5th- to 7th-level characters who must enter the Gretat Void bordering the Realm of the Dead to retrieve the soul of a young boy and undo a terrible curse that has fallen upon his small village.

Adventure Background

This adventure takes place in the village of Cintlipetl within the Cuahtla Forest region of Tehuatl. The events occur at the end of the Seven Year Harvest Season a few days before the rise of the Bloodmoon. The Bloodmoon is an auspicious holiday whose coming is predicted by the Xiuhpohualli, a calendar that runs tandem to the Tonalpohualli used to count the passing of days and years.

Character Options

This adventure contains a few character options to help instill the players with a deeper sense of immersion. You or the players can tie one or more of these choices to the characters' backgrounds or create similar options to help them feel invested in the village, its people, or the situations that befall them.

The Local

This character either hails from the village or has family in the village.

Icnoyotl the Herdsman. Icnoyotl is either your brother or brother-in-law, as well as the uncle or aunt of his young son Itoxo. He always has a warm bed and food for you for as long as you stay in the village.

Xotaxtl the Sorcerer-Priest. Xotaxtl was either a close friend or cousin. He is something of a loner. He now serves as the headman's chief advisor and holds a fair amount of prestige in the town. Still, you know his real name is Citlalli, the girl's name his father gave him before he learned magic from Coaxoch.

Coaxoch the Medicine-Witch. The medicine-witch had no children but fortunately was gifted with the knowledge of magic from her grandmother. As a child, you may have studied magic or herbalism with her, or she may have been a family friend after treating them through a sickness.

Camaxtl the Headman. You are either the beloved grandchild of the headman or a warrior who earned his confidence and respect in some earlier trial. He trusts your word and respects your judgment, enough so that he feels entitled enough to ask you to fulfill certain obligations. Likewise, should he ask something of you, you would feel obliged to fulfill the request to uphold your name and honor.

Aluxes and the Forgotten Gods

Some of the creatures and gods appearing in the adventure **Seven Year Harvest** predate the ascendance of the hero-gods and even Tlatoani. The proto-humans known as the aluxes are the most prominent remnants of these bygone eras. The aluxes and their contemporaries speak Primordial Notoan, a distant ancestor of the current Aztli language. These beings and their deities — sometimes known as the Forgotten Gods — existed during the Age of Man and the Age of Strife as described in **The World of the Lost Lands** campaign setting book from **Frog God Games**. Displeased with the aluxes' progress and actions, the Forgotten Gods brought about the destruction of the Four Suns that all but wiped out the aluxes and their kin, leaving only a few, scattered survivors in their destructive wake. However, Aztli scholars and the hero-gods themselves dispute these accounts, believing the suns to be figurative expressions symbolizing the dawn of a new era rather than the literal recreation of a new sun. They counter that the Forgotten Gods directed their wrath solely at the aluxes and their counterparts rather than devastating the entire world. According to their argument, the northern continents of Akados and Libynos would have also seen the same wholesale devastation of their lands, yet the Tlotls cannot corroborate the aluxes' version of prehistory or even acknowledge the creatures' existence in their distant past.

Regardless of where the truth lies, it is impossible to refute that Tlatoani turned the tables on the Forgotten Gods during his rise to power. On the road to attaining utter supremacy, Tlatoani obliterated some of them outright, exiled others to distant worlds beyond the stars, and hurled the remainder of the Forgotten Gods into the Great Void, where they presumably waited to greet him when the gods of Boros subjected Tlatoani and his minions to the same fate.

Although the Forgotten Gods have long faded from Tehuatl's collective memory and have no known humanoid worshippers on the island, some vestiges of their existence remain as evidenced by their presence in the nether regions bordering Miquito, the Land of the Dead, and within pockets of the Great Void. The aluxes and their continued devotion to these Forgotten Gods likely play a significant role in preventing these fallen deities from completely slipping into oblivion and allowing them to affect the Material Plane. These deities include Auyinah, the goddess of dreams, Chalatihuatl, the goddess of sacrifice, and Iquixilli, the god of justice. While no longer present in the mortal world, their living or dead essence, depending upon your perspective, still endures in the ethereal realm.

The Outsider

The villagers distrust your intentions because you hail from a rival town or practice a religion that follows a set of ideals the villagers find distasteful or immoral. Alternately, you could simply be the black sheep of the town whose views and conjectures have always challenged the status quo.

Adventure Synopsis

The adventure begins in the village of Cintlipetl while the villagers scramble to prepare for the Seven Year Harvest festival correlating to the anticipated rise of the Bloodmoon. At the height of the ceremony, the villagers must sacrifice several peccaries to appease the hero-gods' demands for blood. However, the unanticipated and mysterious slaughter of the local herdsman's ritual offerings strikes panic throughout the village, prompting the town council to organize a small party of willing adventurers (the characters) to capture the peccary slayer, for fear that the harvest offerings will be ruined and the village will be cursed until the rising of the next Bloodmoon roughly seven years later.

The characters track down the peccary slayer to discover it is an alux, a supernatural human-like creature from the era before Tlatoani's downfall. Unsure of the implications of finding such a creature, the villagers confine it in a cell while the town council conducts a hearing to determine its fate. The characters may voice their opinion during this debate. Before its fate is determined, the sunrise brings ominous news. A chom has been sighted within the town, perched near the alux's prison hole. These mystical bird-like creatures are ancient bearers of ill-omen.

As if in response to the omen, the villagers discover the alux dead in its cell, apparently from eating a poisoned rat. A quick investigation determines the killer is the herdsman's young son who reacted to his father's distress. However, the son has fallen ill. The cause? A chom stole his soul as payment for the murder and is taking it to face judgment in Miquito, the Realm of the Dead.

After informing the council, the members blame the misfortune on the soured advice of Xotaxtl, the headman's chief advisor sorcerer-priest. They direct him to lead a party into Miquito to save the child's soul and determine proper payment for the death of the alux.

The characters venture through the Corpsewood, a small sliver of the Cuahtla Forest bordering the Tepepan Mountains, to seek passage to the Obsidian Spire at one of the gates of Miquito, which lies beyond the Great Void. There they must enter the sacred mines to procure the jadeite beads they need to pay passage into Miquito. Once they have the beads, they must find the place within the mountains' shadow where they can locate the first portal and perform a ritual that opens it so they can enter the Great Void. From there, they must then take the correct path to the Obsidian Spire, where they must then pass through several fabled challenges before confronting the judge who holds the child's soul. The judge demands the soul of the first individual who started the events as payment: the headman's advisor Xotaxtl. Unfortunately, Xotaxtl's soul has also been stolen after being consumed by a monstrously deformed giant alux during a brutal fight in the jadeite mines.

In the final section of the adventure, the characters return to the land of the living to confront the giant alux who, after consuming the sorcerer, gained access to his powers. The alux now calls himself Xotaxtl Nitlocati and uses his powers to lead a horde of aluxes against the village seeking to reclaim the world that humanity stole from them after the gods destroyed their world with the great cataclysms. The adventure ends when the characters defeat Xotaxtl Nitlocati, restore peace, and allow the people to restore the festival of the Seven Year Harvest.

Chapter One: On the Rise of the Bloodmoon

Starting the Adventure

The adventure begins during the last few days of the harvest season in the village of Cintlipetl. It is the year of the Bloodmoon, an auspicious time when the people of Cintlipetl hold a weeklong festival to honor the bounties bestowed upon them by the gods. Like everyone else in the village, the characters are slated to attend the festival. Skipping the festival is viewed as an insult to the gods and is likely to bring bad luck upon the village. Therefore, attendance is virtually mandatory.

The adventure gets underway when the village's Headman Camaxtl calls for a town gathering at the temple to discuss and ready the upcoming events. Read or paraphrase the following passage to describe the opening scene:

You have been called to attend a meeting to discuss the upcoming Harvest Festival at the village temple, a large structure of neatly stepped stone located in the heart of the settlement. Here, the headman holds court. The people come to celebrate the rise of the sun and the moon, and the priests bless the harvest and give thanks and sacrifices to the gods who have individual shrines within the structure.

You enter with a small crowd of villagers and find seats on the woven cloth mats laid across the floor. Slowly, more villagers drift in, quietly taking their places before the headman's great chair. Seated on the left of the headman is a man decorated with feathers and bones, the headman's sorcerer-priest and chief advisor. Next to the sorcerer-priest sits a woman dressed in a colorful cotton gown, a bald man wearing red paint and an ocelot skin sash, a man with dark skin and a complete set of gold teeth, and a woman dressed in a bright purple cloth gown embroidered with thousands of beads. On the right sits a man in a cloak with a feathered collar, a woman wearing a gold pendant and large golden ear spools, and an older warrior wearing a jaguar mask. At the far right sits a withered, gray-haired woman dressed in simple clothing, but wearing a collection of small cloth satchels indicating her power as a medicine woman. All of these people wear large jade lip plugs that identify them as members of the town council. The headman raises his hand and the crowd goes silent, waiting to hear him speak.

Before the proceedings can even begin, a terrified man dressed in simple common clothing rushes into the temple waving about a wooden crook and shaking in terror. He begs to speak with the headman on a matter of utmost urgency. Before anyone has time to react, four warrior guards spring forth, seize the man, search and strip him to his loincloth, and have him crawl forward before the headman.

While to some this act might seem cruel, such humiliation and prostration ensure Camaxtl's safety in the event the man is an assassin. Such procedures are normal and expected under such conditions. Once the characters are content to let the drama unfold, continue with the following scene.

Camaxtl the headman looks down upon the fearful commoner and utters a single word,

"Speak." He lets the full weight of his gaze bear upon the villager.

The villager speaks in a fear-filled whisper.

"Headman Camaxtl, my name is Icnoyotl. I am but a simple herdsman. I came here to warn you that I fear a terrible pox may fall upon our harvest. This morning I found lying in the fields several of my peccaries, each brutally slaughtered with its throat torn out and its hide savagely stripped from its flesh. Surely this bears upon us an ill portent, for those were the same peccaries I had

---

marked for the harvest sacrifice."

"And upon whom do you cast blame for this crime?" asks the headman.

"Of those within our village, none would commit such a crime. ... Therefore I shall assume the burden and serve as an offering. I ask only that my son be cared for and taken under the tutelage at the telpochcalli to be trained as a warrior to help repay my family's debt."

Upon finishing his plea, Icnoyotl the herdsman falls quiet and lowers his eyes as he awaits the headman's judgment.

At this time, the characters can intervene or ask questions. However, their input is uninvited in the court and causes them to suffer the headman's disfavor.

The headman turns to the sorcerer-priest, his chief advisor, and nods. He informs the crowd that he is postponing the village meeting and tells them to return to their homes for the time being. Once all have cleared the room, he calls for his advisor, the herdsman, and the town council to remain to discuss matters. He then commands the warrior-guards to seal the entrance and prevent anyone else from entering.

The characters are also asked to remain, depending on their background. If they share a connection to members of the council, they are invited to stay as they may well be needed for their expertise. If they are related to the herdsman, he requests they stay for similar reasons. If they chose the outsider option, the sorcerer requests they stay as he suspects they may have something to do with the slaughter of the peccaries. Once the room is secure, the headman turns to the sorcerer and asks him for his thoughts.

The sorcerer tells all in attendance the following legend. Read or paraphrase the following section:

"Last night I saw the coming of the Bloodmoon, a deep red rime around Ihueltiuh. This is an auspicious sign, but one that can either bring us years of prosperous harvests or lay our fields fallow. We must make the proper sacrifices or our fields will wither and our people starve to death. However, whoever has done this must face the judgment of this council so we can make amends with the gods, or we shall be cursed for seven years until the coming of the next Bloodmoon."

CONCLUDING THE INTRODUCTION

The council quickly concludes that for the good of the entire village, whoever has slain the peccaries must be caught and brought to face their judgment. Of all those present, the characters are most qualified to hunt and capture the perpetrator. Allow the characters to prepare themselves, gather whatever equipment they need, and then meet with the herdsman to survey the crime scene.

CINTLIPETL MAP KEY

During this portion of the adventure, the character may roam around the town to speak with villagers about what they may have seen or simply take in the local sites to get a better feel for the task at hand. Each numbered location on the accompanying map of Cintlipetl corresponds to the following legend.

1. Temple of The Sun. This temple is devoted to several gods, most notably Yaocteotl, the Aztli God of War and the Sun. The headman frequents the temple, and most of the time it is where he holds court. It is also used as the main communal temple for public assemblies and open town council meetings. The Temple of the Sun is the town's most important structure and the focal point of the settlement.

2. Temple of the Moon. The second-largest temple is primarily dedicated to Itztliteotl, the Aztli God of the Night, though small shrines to other gods can be found here. While the Temple of the Sun serves some secular purposes, this structure is solely devoted to housing the priesthood and conducting religious ceremonies. It is frequently used for more intimate or personal worship and rituals, as well as for special ceremonies to celebrate private events, such as weddings and funerals.

3. Sacred Courts. The council uses the courts to mete out swift and terrible justice. Death is a frequent punishment for those who defy the hero-gods' will. Individuals condemned to serve a prison sentence do so in the Aztli Confederation's brutal penitentiaries, which many believe to be a fate worse than death.

4. The Arena. These structures are used for outdoor performances, festivals, and sporting competitions, most notably the ball game.

5. Temple of the Harvest. This temple pays homage to Quiahuitl and the lesser gods and goddesses who provide the citizens rain, good harvests, abundant fishing, and healthy livestock. Those looking for meals can find them here provided they leave a donation or provide the temple with a sacrifice or service.

6. West Crossing. A packed earthen road wanders up the plateau and leads to a small section of modest homes facing toward the distant sea.

7. Lower Square. Several paths merge near this small square. Its buildings consist of several merchant shops and homes. People come here to trade for grain, pottery, cloth, soap, flowers, and other mundane items.

8. The Point. A series of larger communal homes make up the Point. Laborers, farmers, and other families not of noble birth pool their resources to reside in these spacious yet cramped residences.

9. The Clay Pits. This collection of caves provides the village with clay for pottery. Potters, other crafts folk, and laborers make up a large number of residents in this neighborhood.

10. Telpochcalli of the Ocelot. This martial school trains students in the arts of combat and strategy. Scholars live in the dorms and practice their trade almost nonstop.

11. East Ridge. A long switchback road runs the length of this ridge. At the end stand the broken ruins of several houses. They were torn down several years ago, and it remains taboo to build there. Some say this is because the people living there were dirty and carried the plague.

12. The Medicine-Witch's House. Coaxoch lives toward the west end of the north market community. She is an important member of the community and frequently gives them advice or represents them at the temple or court.

13. North Market. A tangle of small streets runs past modest homes and shops that sell wares such as wool, meat, pottery, cloth, and medicines. The area sits above the lower plateau with a view of the temples.

14. Herdsman's Home. The herdsman lives toward the upper edge of the plateau on the outskirts of town facing the woods and mountains to the west. The community here consists mostly of woodcarvers and hunters, along with other herdsmen who graze their animals in the fields along the woods.

CINTLIPETL
1 Hex = 300 Feet
N
SEVEN YEAR HARVEST | 69

CENTRAL TEHUATL
Cuahtla Forest
Minnalin
Xacota
Caya Grasslands
Teotlachco
Frowl
Hillamati
Quimichin
Onacatoya River
Ateztecatl
Darl
Tepepan Mountains
Hrawrg
Citlitoch
Atinaquina
Uolli
Tepetzin
Octli
Turew
Aliqtana
Kurn
Nepalta
Ixtla
Domladur
Kulm
Kulgan
Balandrur
Ipaconoytl
Cepual Desert
Node 226
Otimpo
Nochtli
Quannaqa River
Xalpit
Mactli
Ouatulli Lake
Omiex
Droomph
Teocua
Cuahtla Forest
Yoaltica Ilaquiloz
N
Necocyaotl
1 Square –
20 Miles
The Great Canal
Quizaloa
Amilotetl
Huitzineo
Azuato
Ixchicta
Zacatl
Ahuacua
Good fortune
Ezhuacoza
Quitlacatl
Cotza
Toxana
Mimicapoli
Blibleblup
Ezhuitotl
Tolzolotli
Hilaya River
Cuiateotl
Toctli Forest
The Spring
Mototoloa
Ixnenatl

Tracking the Peccary Slayer

When the characters secure their provisions and any additional equipment that they may need, they are ready venture over to the herdsman's small hovel so he can take them to the crime scene.

The Herdsman's Hovel

The herdsman lives with his young son in a small, single-room hovel just outside the village. He has just finished making a bowl of corn mash and beans for his son when the characters arrive. Upon seeing them, he quickly grabs his crook and a light cloak before leading them on the two-mile walk to the fields where he grazes his peccaries. The fields sit along a small rocky outcropping that stands near the edge of the Corpsewood, a transitory section of the Cuahtla Forest bordering the Cepual Desert, the Caya Grasslands, and the Tepepan Mountains roughly 35 miles due north of Teocua.

The herdsman directs the characters to the ghastly scene where the disemboweled bodies of more than a dozen peccaries stain the grass black. Massive wounds torn through their skins are plainly visible, and dried blood and rotting entrails litter the ground.

A character who examines the corpses confirms that a sharp instrument or object created the gaping lacerations on the bodies of the peccaries. The character also finds evidence of blunt force trauma injuries.

In addition, the meat is shredded, pierced, and torn, yet very little of it is missing, indicating the perpetrator ate very little of it. In a more disturbing development, the peccaries are missing their hearts.

A character who searches the area for tracks notices a pair of bloody footprints heading west. The trail disappears into the neighboring forest.

The bloody footprints lead a short way into the forest. There, a path left by bent twigs and trampled underbrush leads to a small spying hutch used by the peccary slayer before it made its attack.

E1: The Spying Hutch

A character who investigates locates telltale signs of peccary scraps, fur, and skin, along with a couple of small bones and some blood scattered about the encampment. The alux left the sack behind to ensnare the unwary. While the stains on the sack are peccary's blood, the creature placed several small stones of no value and an extremely venomous snake from the Land of the Dead inside the bag. The **Miquito adder** immediately bites anyone reaching into the bag to feel what might be inside. If a character opens the bag and looks into it, the snake gains a +1 to-hit bonus against that character. Conversely, if the character dumps the contents of the bag on the ground, the snake slithers out and attacks as normal. The sack is secured by a drawstring that requires an action to open or close.

Miquito Adder: HD 2; HP 13; AC 5[14]; **Atk** bite (1d8 + poison); **Move** 12 (swim 12); **Save** 16; **AL** N; **CL/XP** 4/120; **Special:** poison (save or die). (see **Appendix A: New Monsters**)

A character who examines the odd carving can identify the figure as a mythical creature known as the alux, a deformed humanoid creature said to be the last of the proto-humans slaughtered during a prehistoric cataclysm. Folktales describe the creature as an aggressive monster renowned for the savagery of its attacks. Nearly every recorded encounter with an alux took place deep within the forest, especially in the areas around Teocua, though it is said the creature occasionally wanders into human lands to feast on turkeys, dogs, and peccaries when its normal prey becomes scarce.

The aluxes were described as a race of proto-humans whom the Forgotten Gods destroyed during the ages of the Lost Lands before Tlatoani's ascendance, although there is some question to the accuracy of the tales. The more prevalent folklore derives from the latter revelation, but the more popular version better serves its intended purpose of scaring children from wandering into the forests.

Surveying the surrounding area uncovers footprints belonging to a humanoid-like creature. The tracks head northeast to what appears to be a shallow hole dug into the ground. Anyone inspecting the hole immediately detects the distinct stench of dung. From this point, the tracks continue onward north toward the Corpsewood, a sallow land that most people deliberately avoid. Any character re-examining the area notices another set of prints returning. Following these tracks east leads characters to **Area E2.**

E2: The Buried Shrine

A character who examines the stones believes the buried stones to be a shrine or older temple dedicated to a prehistoric nature deity.

The flowers are unusual and rare. A character can identify them as zac nicte. Some practitioners of ancient magic and healing consider them sacred, but they have no special properties.

This site harbors the buried remains of an ancient shrine devoted to a goddess of dreams worshipped in the time before the hero-gods and even the emperor. Like most of the ancient structures, it was destroyed when the seas swallowed most of the land. Still, the alux refused to forget the goddess, prompting it to pay her tribute before journeying onward.

Despite the obvious neglect, the shrine is not unattended. A **fey drake** watches over the locale. When it hears trespassers approaching, it quickly *polymorphs* into a small field mouse and hides among the nearby tree roots to monitor their activities. The fey drake is shy and does not reveal its presence unless the characters attempt to take the goddess's tribute. If this happens, it returns to its normal form and confronts the thieves, accusing them of stealing the goddess's tribute.

Although it is a capable combatant, the drake is willing to listen to reason. Nonetheless, it dislikes people and is extremely wary of their intentions. It never initiates an attack, preferring to turn invisible again to avoid a confrontation. However, if pressed into a corner or if the characters destroy or otherwise desecrate the shrine, the fey drake defends itself and the sacred ground against defilers. If the characters manage to gain its trust by returning the tribute and possibly adding to it, the drake entertains some of their questions, though it remains as aloof and obscure in the details as possible.

The drake can tell them an alux passed by the shrine and left the tribute. It knows the alux is one of the beings of humanity whose race was destroyed

TEOCTLAN
The Eye of the World
C4
Corpsewood
Jadeite Mines
C3
Iztaccihuatl
Popocatepetl
Gate to the Great Void
C2
Cuauhtenco
C1
E3
E1
E2
Crazing Fields
To Cintlipetl
N

by the Forgotten Gods during the prehistoric cataclysm and that it worshiped Auyinah, a peaceful goddess of dreams to whom this shrine was dedicated. She is one of the hundreds of gods these creatures once worshipped who are now lost to the annals of time. He knows the alux was returning home when it passed the shrine, and he wished the creature good fortune and fair omens before it departed. It knows only these few details but requests the humans not forget the goddess and attempts to get them to promise to one day return to pay her tribute.

Fey Drake: HD 5; **HP** 33; **AC** 2[17]; **Atk** bite (1d6 + confusion); **Move** 9 (fly 18); **Save** 12; **AL** N; **CL/XP** 6/400; **Special:** bewildering breath (3/day, 15ft cone, save or charmed), confusion (as spell, save avoids), spell-like abilities.
Spell-like abilities: at will—*invisibility*; 3/day—*locate animals, phantasmal force, suggestion*; 1/day—*polymorph self*.

E3: River's Edge

The second set of tracks leads to the edge of the Cuauhtenco River, a small, shallow waterway nearly 20 feet across that serves as the unofficial boundary between the Cuahtla Forest and the looming desolation of forbidden lands known as Corpsewood. The tracks run cold at the water's edge. However, a quick scan of the river reveals a small, crudely constructed raft beached on the opposing riverbank, about 100 feet downstream.

Characters who enter the Cuauhtenco River find it to be rather shallow, with a depth of five feet at the center with a gentle current. Being a minor tributary of the Quannaqa River, the waterway is inaccessible to vessels larger than a small canoe. Swimming through the lazy waters are **5 piranha swarms** that immediately respond to any noticeable disturbance and immediately race into the waters to feast upon the unlucky trespasser. The bloodthirsty, aggressive fish never disperse. They attack until they either eat their fill or eat their last meal.

Piranha Swarms (5): HD 4; **HP** 30, 26, 25, 20, 17; **AC** 7[12]; **Atk** swarm (1d6); **Move** 24 (swim); **Save** 13; **AL** N; **CL/XP** 4/120; **Special:** none. (*The Tome of Horrors Complete* 531)

Sabotaged Raft Trap

To stop pursuers, the clever alux tampered with the raft after crossing the river. It loosened several of the knots on the raft's bindings so that if more than one Medium-sized creature attempts to use it, the bindings slowly pull loose and cause the raft to come apart in the middle of the river. A character who examines the raft has a 1-in-6 chance to notice the sabotaged bindings. The raft can be repaired before being pushed into the river. However, if the characters operate the raft without repairing it, there is a 50% chance each round that the bindings come undone, causing the raft to fall apart. The raft can hold three creatures at a time without sinking into the river and capsizing, spilling its riders into the stream.

Along the eastern side of the river, characters find the alux's tracks. The trail leads up the shoreline and then eastward into the Corpsewood.

The Corpsewood

Across the Cuauhtenco River stretches a fallow and desolate land of dry, rocky soil and leafless trees whose dull gray bark constantly peels and flakes off, exposing an eerily flesh-colored wood beneath it. The Aztlis believe Yaocteotl fashioned these trees from the remains of warriors who fled during battle.

The Corpsewood stretches north and eastward, climbing into a series of low, rocky hills on the outskirts of the Tepepan Mountains.

Dozens of caverns bore into the surrounding hillsides. Those who have spiritually passed on but whose physical bodies still endure take refuge in these caverns. Within this dank land, they spend their final, lonely days contemplating the mysteries of the universe until their physical bodies eventually die. Some individuals succumb to natural causes, though many ultimately take their own lives rather than exist for another day in this dreary realm. Other times, aluxes that occasionally travel here eat them on their way to collect souls seeking passage to Miquito.

When the characters approach the Corpsewood for the first time, they spot a small copse of trees covered with ebon leaves. Moving closer to investigate, they soon realize that what first appeared to be leaves are really a flock of strange and silent black-feathered birds. If the characters approach within 300 feet of the **chom swarm**, the birds quickly take wing and race off. The winged monstrosities have no interest in fighting the characters at this time. Therefore, their sole inclination is to flee unless the adventurers force them to fight.

Characters can recall stories of black-feathered birds called choms whom the Forgotten Gods punished for their meddling and dishonesty by stripping away their bright plumage. It is believed that the gaze of a chom is an ill omen.

Chom Swarm: HD 5; HP 31; AC 5[14]; **Atk** swarm (1d8); **Move** 4 (fly 18); **Save** 12; **AL** N; **CL/XP** 7/600; **Special:** cast omen (1/day, targets meeting gaze of flock, save or –1 to hit, saves, and damage for 24 hours), mimicry (simple sounds), soul steal (against incapacitated or sleeping foe, soul is stolen and held within the flock, save avoids). (see **Appendix A: New Monsters**)

C1: The Canals

The characters enter a section of the Corpsewood that stands upon the ruins of an ancient aqueduct. The stone bricks once made up canals that led water to the fields and villages that existed here during the Third Sun, a prehistoric epoch before the ground shook and cracked them beyond recognition.

As the characters continue, the area slowly transforms into a wide and murky glade. Although traveling upon the bricks is safe, the mire covers nearly everything, thus hiding deep spots along the center of the canals or areas where the water flooded into the earth and turned it to quicksand. In this area, characters have a 10% chance of being able to move 30 feet across the bricks without impediment, and a 20% chance of being able to move 15 feet across the bricks without impediment. Once in the swampy glade, the characters lose all trace of the peccary slayer's tracks.

Despite the inhospitable conditions, **3 black puddings** lurk in the canal searching for living prey to envelop. The instant they sense creatures moving through the murk, they slither forth to attack. They blend in perfectly with their dark, soupy background.

Black Puddings (3): HD 10; HP 71, 65, 58; AC 6[13]; **Atk** slam (3d8); **Move** 6; **Save** 5; **AL** N; **CL/XP** 12/2000; **Special:** acidic surface (dissolve weapons, armor, etc.), immune to cold, divides when hit with lightning (splits into two puddings with equal hit points). (***Monstrosities*** 46)

C2: The Alux

When the characters approach this section of the Corpsewood, characters hear a rough, guttural voice quietly chanting strange words in an unknown language. They can attempt to draw close enough to see the creature speaking this seemingly alien tongue. If they are noticed, the disturbance interrupts the creature.

At this sacred site, the **alux of the Second Sun** has once again stopped to make offerings and pay homage to the Forgotten Gods. If the characters confront the alux, it turns to them wild-eyed and full of rage for daring to interrupt the ceremony. The strange creature spits out a foul and guttural language unknown and unheard of by modern mortals, then it clenches its stony fists and grits its sharpened teeth.

The alux first attempts to intimidate the characters and scare them off. As the alux snarls, one of the black-feathered birds lands on its shoulder and chatters something directly into the creature's ear. The alux looks quickly at the chom as if to acknowledge the message and then makes a quick gesture, which causes the bird to rapidly fly east.

Characters who previously identified the black-feathered birds recognize the bird as a chom.

A character can note the significance of the colored maize offerings as tributes made to the Forgotten Gods who watched over each of the four earthly kingdoms before Tlatoani's arrival.

The alux fights until subdued or killed. It begrudgingly surrenders if the characters reduce it to less than one-third of its maximum hit points. The creature is proud and angry but not stupid. It knows there will be dire consequences if the humans kill it, a fact it assumes they already know along with who it is and whom it serves. It does not understand why the characters interrupted its ceremony or attacked. It thinks they are crazy to perform such an act.

The alux is not a difficult opponent, and the characters likely have little difficulty subduing and capturing it. Hopefully, they do not kill the creature in the process. It might even be helpful to remind the characters that the headman sent them to capture the peccary slayer and not to kill it. Similarly, if they can determine that the creature is the alux, you can allow them to make a saving throw to recall that killing such a creature can afflict them with very bad luck.

Alux of the Second Sun: HD 6; HP 41; AC 7[12]; **Atk** weapon (1d8) or bite (1d6), slam (2d4); **Move** 12; **Save** 11; **AL** N; **CL/XP** 6/400; **Special:** backstab (x3), camouflage (80% chance to hide in hilly or mountainous terrain), darkvision (60ft), vulnerable to obsidian (200% damage). (see **Appendix A: New Monsters**)

Chapter Two: The Feast and the Omen

After capturing the alux, the characters should return to the village with the creature to present it to the headman. It is reluctant to travel with them, perhaps even fearful, but willfully accepts its fate. Regardless, the alux refuses to speak except for occasionally calling upon the Forgotten Gods in a harsh primordial language. No attempt to translate the speech yields any reward, for no creature of this world recalls how to speak its guttural and vile forgotten tongue without the use of some form of magic. Still, anyone attempting to decipher the creature's words determines they are loaded with anger and disdain. Most certainly the creature feels its captors are somehow ignorant, thus its physical struggles against its captors convey its defiance and pride rather make a desperate escape attempt or revenge retributive attack. The alux acts almost as if it expects someone or something to free it.

The headman meets the adventurers outside his house, where he walks around the beast in a circle, carefully observing it. Staring widely, it seems as if he cannot believe his eyes. After his third circle, he stops, pauses for a moment and then calls to a nearby warrior guard, "Quick, go and get the sorcerer."

While waiting for the sorcerer, a crow flutters down to perch in a nearby tree to watch. The crow seems almost thoughtful. The alux glances at it and utters a raspy whisper-scream. *"N'gah-tah!"* Upon hearing the strange syllabic noise, the crow immediately launches from its perch and wings off.

Anyone checking the direction of its flight knows it headed northeast toward the Corpsewood.

The characters, the headman, and the sorcerer are all free to interrogate the alux. However, it glares defiantly and refuses to speak with any of them. Unable to determine a clear course of action, the sorcerer suggests they lock up the alux, at least until he can research it a bit. It most certainly is a powerful creature and killing it might bring the village even more bad luck. The sorcerer can explain the following details about the legendary aluxes if the characters ask (although some of his details are suspect):

• The alux comes every seven years with the rising of the Bloodmoon.

• The alux can speak to the choms, once colorfully plumed birds cursed by an ancient deity who turned their feathers black and condemned them to eat only carrion.

• Killing the alux would certainly bring bad luck, especially during the Bloodmoon (partially true).

• The alux is a hideous, immortal creature and single survivor of the First Sun, the first cataclysm in which the Forgotten Gods summoned jaguars to feast upon the first men so that they might be built from their remains. The alux is the last of the first men, kept in Miquito as a model (partially true).

• The alux is a cannibal that only consumes hearts of mortals (partially true)

• The alux can carry souls to the gate of Miquito and tell them which path they must follow to live forever in the afterlife.

Running the Debate

There are only three choices for the alux's fate: The characters can execute the creature, set it free, or imprison it until more information about the creature and its intentions can be acquired.

Most of the meeting's participants lean toward prudence and want to keep the alux imprisoned, at least until they learn more about what happened.

Each NPC holds a certain number of votes, which they can exercise as three different verdicts: free, execute, or imprison. At the end of the trial, the votes are tallied and the council swiftly carries out the verdict to free the alux, execute him, or imprison him in a pit to delay his final judgment. At the start of the debate, each council member holds a specific position. Everyone has the opportunity to speak and persuade others to their position. After every member has spoken his or her piece on the matter, tabulate the final number of votes in each category. The most votes win, with any vote resulting in a tie resulting in the creature's imprisonment and retrial on the following day. Characters can also participate, but they have only a single vote.

The Characters

Each character gets a single vote, but more importantly, they also gain an attempt to sway the opinion of specific council members. A character can attempt to sway the opinion of only a single council member, though multiple characters can attempt to sway the opinion of the same council member.

You could play this out with each character presenting an impassioned argument for or against each option. If they present compelling arguments for one option, you could either assume that they win over the specific council member or assign a percentage chance based on their conviction.

The Headman. Camaxtl the Headman holds five votes and places all of them on imprisonment. The headman feels he lacks the information to make a prudent decision at this time. He is greatly influenced by the sorcerer and if the sorcerer's opinion changes, the headman can be swayed toward the sorcerer's decision by his total number of votes.

Camaxtl the Headman, Male Aztli Headman: HP 50; **AC** 5[14]; **Atk** club (1d4); **Move** 12; **Save** 9; **AL** L; **CL/XP** 7/600; **Special:** none. (*Monstrosities* 256)
    Equipment: olli armor[B], club.
[B] See **Appendix B: New Equipment and Magic Items**

The Medicine-Witch. Coaxoch the Medicine-Witch holds three votes and places all of them on immediate release. She cannot be convinced to kill the creature under any circumstances.

Coaxoch the Medicine-Witch, Female Aztli Shaman (Clr5): HP 26; **AC** 7[12]; **Atk** mace (1d6); **Move** 12; **Save** 11; **AL** N; **CL/XP** 5/240; **Special:** +2 save vs. paralysis and poison, banish undead, spells (2/2).
    Spells: 1st—*cure light wounds* (x2); 2nd—*bless, speak with animals.*
Equipment: tlahuiztli armor[B], mace.

The Sorcerer. Xotaxtl the Sorcerer seeks prudence and spends all three of his votes on keeping the creature imprisoned until the council can learn more about what happened. The sorcerer is a coward at heart. Therefore, he can be readily convinced to change his position.

Although a rather competent sorcerer-priest, Xotaxtl failed miserably at recognizing the alux as a servant of the Forgotten Gods, and the religious significance of the fey eating the peccaries' hearts. Xotaxtl worships the hero-gods, yet he is still familiar with some of the older traditions, especially being from this neck of the Cuahtla Forest that borders the Corpsewood. If he had understood the alux's true nature and its purpose, he would have vociferously argued to free the creature at once and allow it to return to Miquito to appease the Forgotten Gods. Instead, he meekly acquiesces to the will of others, sealing the alux's fate and eventually his own in the process.

Xotaxtl the Sorcerer, Male Aztli Magic-User (MU7): HP 23; AC 9[10] or 2[17] (missile) and 4[15] (melee) from *shield* spell; **Atk** obsidian dagger (1d4) or staff (1d6); **Move** 12; **Save** 9; **AL** N; **CL/XP** 7/600; **Special:** +2 save (spells, wands, staffs), spells (4/3/2/1).
Spells: 1st—*detect magic, magic missile, protection from evil, shield*; 2nd—*darkness 15ft radius, invisibility, ESP*; 3rd—*dispel magic, haste*; 4th—*polymorph self*.
Equipment: obsidian dagger, staff.

The Herdsman. Icnoyotl the herdsman holds a single vote that he places on killing the alux. His decision is unyielding and unreasonable, and he refuses to change it under any circumstance.

Icnoyotl the Herdsman, Male Aztli Commoner: HP 4; AC 9[10]; **Atk** dagger (1d4) or spear (1d6); **Move** 12; **Save** 18; **AL** N; **CL/XP** B/10; **Special:** none. (*Monstrosities* 254)
Equipment: bone-handled dagger, spear.

Town Council Members. The remaining council members consist of **6 nobles**. Ignorant of the nature of the old gods and the alux itself, they perceive it as a bloodthirsty and vengeful monster (it does, after all, eat people and serve some bloodthirsty Forgotten Gods). Half of them are ready to vote to kill the creature while the others opt for imprisonment. Any of the council members can be convinced to change their position in either direction. Roll 1d6 if you want to randomly determine how many vote with the characters.

Council Members, Male and Female Aztli Nobles (6): HP 12, 10x3, 9, 7; AC 7[12]; **Atk** tecpatl (1d4); **Move** 12; **Save** 16; **AL** N; **CL/XP** 2/30; **Special:** none. (*Monstrosities* 254)
Equipment: tlahuitztli armor[B], tecpatl[B].
[B] See **Appendix B: New Equipment and Magic Items**

When all the votes are tallied, the council makes its decision. Most likely the alux is sentenced to either imprisonment or death. In either case, it is sent to a prison pit, either to serve a sentence or to await a ritual execution at dawn. In the unlikely event that the council decides to release the alux, then there is a slight change of events. See the **Angry Herdsman** sidebar.

CONCLUDING THE COUNCIL

After the council determines the alux's fate, Camaxtl the Headman draws the meeting to a close, then calls for the feast to commence. At this point, the council members disperse to prepare for the celebration. Give the characters 20 minutes of game time to prepare, finalize plans, organize themselves, and plot a course of action before the festival begins. They can seek the advice or counsel of anyone else in the village, although they get just a few minutes as the person delays their preparations for the evening's festivities to speak with

them. When the allotted time expires, the person shoos them away to resume their preparations for the festival.

Most likely the members of the council determine that whatever fate the alux deserves, they should hold it captive until dawn before it faces it. They have no jail, as justice usually comes quickly and terribly, though the council remains undecided. Instead, several of the village warriors lead the alux to the Clay Pits, lower it into one of the pits and seal the opening with a wooden grate held fast with boulders. The village stations **2 guards** to keep watch at the entrance and switch out with new guards every four hours. Lest a worse fate befalls the village, no one is to speak of the strange creature or utter a word about the trial proceedings until the council reaches a verdict.

Guards, Male or Female Aztli Warriors (2): HP 6x2; AC 7[12]; **Atk** club (1d4) or longbow x2 (1d6); **Move** 12; **Save** 17; **AL** Any; **CL/XP** 1/15; **Special:** none. (*Monstrosities* 257)
Equipment: club, longbow, 10 arrows.

THE FESTIVAL

Entering into the center of town, the square has been transformed by lanterns and torches and drenched in colorful decorations of feathers, beads, and paper. Along the perimeter, a great feast is laid out upon long wooden tables laden with roasted corn, baked squash, beans, corn tortillas, tamales, spat rabbit, several whole roasted peccaries with their skin blackened and crisp from the coal pits, plank-smoked fish, and roasted frogs along with dozens of other delights. In the center, a wide circle of stones forms a tremendous fire pit stuffed with wood for the celebration pyre, and the surrounding earth has been swept clean to provide a smooth surface for the dancers and musicians.

The crowd mingles together, exchanging greetings and gifts and offering praise and thanks. Characters are free to engage with each other or others at this time, though only the council know about the recent troubling events and would scorn them for attempting to discuss them with others during the celebration. After some time passes and the moon peeks over the horizon, the music begins. Read or paraphrase the following description:

When the dancing dies down, the characters and villagers take their places for the feast as wood is gathered for the Great Pyre.

As the moon rises, the fire is lit in an attempt to have the fire roaring by the time the Bloodmoon reaches its apex. A murder of black-feathered birds flutters wildly across a blood-red moon, their ebon wings dancing like shadows. The event passes quickly and quietly, almost as if it never occurred, as most fail to remember or even acknowledge it.

Yet to those who know of the day's strange proceedings, the appearance of the black-feathered birds casts a strange and far more ominous omen. These individuals fall silent and deathly serious for a moment before trying to regain their composure to continue through the festival. The sighting is not something they want to see, or that they are going to speak of until the next day.

THE MORNING AFTER

At dawn, a murder of crows sits in the trees surrounding the village square, eerily watching all within their gaze. Yelling at them does little to scare them away. The villagers are afraid of the crows. They keep their distance and avoid meeting their gaze for fear of being cursed. If the characters approach the crows and physically attempt to shoo them off, the birds fly straight up into the sky, swirling together in a whirlwind formation, then head for the prison where the alux is being kept (see **The Clay Pits**).

THE CLAY PITS

About an hour after sunrise, a messenger seeks out the characters to inform them that they must hurry to the temple and speak with the headman's chief advisor. When they arrive, the sorcerer-priest quickly leads them inside. In a hushed and terrified whisper, he tells them that the alux is dead, poisoned in his pit during the night by an unknown assassin.

Upon inspecting the corpse, characters discover that the creature died after eating a rat that was first gutted and then had its stomach cavity stuffed with poison. The potion is a mixture of several highly toxic roots known as Eternal Sleep. It is known that the medicine woman uses the poison to help people or the mortally wounded die without pain.

If the characters seek out the medicine-witch, they find her at home, frantically searching through her shelves and jars of reagents. Upon seeing the characters, a horrified look washes across her face as she reveals her fear to them that someone has stolen a powerful poison from her.

If the characters decide to search her home for clues, they uncover a knife with a peccary-bone handle and a chipped blade in the garden near the front door. The weapon likely was used to pry open the sealed stone jars holding the medicine. The medicine-witch can tell them that the herdsmen commonly use such knives.

The knife suggests the herdsman Icnoyotl might know something about the murder. At first, his demeanor makes him appear guilty, but upon further interrogation, questions should arise about his involvement, although he does appear to be hiding something from the characters. If the characters search the house, they can find a rat stick and pouch of poison hidden beneath the sleeping pallet of his young son, Itoxo. If asked as to the location of his son, the herdsman pleads ignorance. He claims that when he arrived home, he found the door open, and his wife and son gone.

Unfortunately, Icnoyotl's lament was as ignorant as his son's actions. Killing the alux brings bad luck upon the village. The boy is found deathly sick, lying in his parents' bed, his mother soaking him with water to cool his raging fever. A lone chom flutters into the window and perches upon the sill, surveying the room. All fearfully avert their gaze to prevent the bird from locking eyes with them, for they know the chom curses those who gaze into the death-bird's eyes with foul luck. Coaxoch the medicine-witch notices the chom and makes some crazed gestures, then throws a handful of black and red corn seeds at the creature. In response, it cackles madly and flies off.

When Coaxoch turns to face the people in the hut, her eyes are rimmed with tears.

"The chom," the medicine-witch utters somberly, "it has taken the boy's soul."

The boy is scared and willing to talk to the characters for he is now desperate to undo his actions, as are his mother and father who encourage him to speak the truth. Characters who wish to speak to the child get him to reveal the following information.

Itoxo readily admits his crime, exclaiming that he hates the alux and blames it for the recent whirlwind of trauma and emotional upheaval that plagues his family since the peccaries were found slain. He tells the characters that the day before, he overheard his father lamenting that he had caused a bad omen to befall the village and dark curses to sallow future harvests for the next seven years. In his rant, Icnoyotl blamed the alux for cursing his family and their fields and wished death upon the hideous and loathsome creature. Upon overhearing his father's lament, the child determined to do something to help him. During the excitement and commotion of the festival, he slipped away to the medicine woman's hut and snuck off with the poison. He then stuffed a significant quantity of the poison into the gut hole of a large rat and went to see the alux. He simply told the guards he was there to feed it (a festival gift!) and dropped the rat into the pit. The guards did not bother to question the child's intention, though they can easily testify to the fact that he showed up with a rat and dropped it into the alux's cell.

After speaking, Itoxo tires and soon passes out in a feverish sweat. Coaxoch attempts to cast several spells and applies her salves and potions to help the boy, but her attempts prove futile. As the moon rises, the child suddenly stirs and speaks in a voice no longer his own. In his feverish state, he utters a haunting prophecy.

You shall all be cursed, your crops will not grow, plagues and fire.

You have denied the master your offerings and slain one of the ancients.

You have forgotten!

The short memories of mortals have forgotten the ceremonies, forgotten their ancestors, and forgotten me. I shall take this boy as payment, and upon his death, his soul shall forever reside in the Great Void! He shall never pass on to the afterworld.

At the end of the speech, the child collapses and falls still. Characters can determine he is barely alive and will likely perish in a few short days if nothing is done to save him.

Conversely, upon hearing the blackbird's prophecy, Xotaxtl becomes enraged and horrified as the terror of being cursed flood his thoughts. He knows that the headman and his fellow villagers will rightfully blame him for misinterpreting or outright missing the omens and signs portending these events. In his defense, he rattles off numerous potential dooms and at some point has an "I told you so" moment in which he starts tossing around accusations of guilt at the characters for being outsiders (whether this is a truly accurate statement or not) and for being the only unexpected change to the otherwise perfect harvest celebration preparations. Regardless of his rants, he is easily silenced by anyone that reminds him that capturing the peccary slayer was in fact, his idea. At the accusation, he pauses, turns pale, and defiantly pleads that he never intended for the creature to be killed. Still, deep down, he knows that the alux's death is on his hands, not the child's.

With the village cursed and the herdsman's young son doomed, the council once more meets in the temple to discuss a solution. As the headman and council listen, Coaxoch takes the floor and does her best to interpret their situation.

"The chom has the child's soul. However, few might benefit from such a prize, and fewer still whom the chom would be foolish enough to bargain with, for nearly all beings hate the chom. They are liars and cheats; all gods and demons know this. Of its path, I can guess, for it flew eastward, and in this direction, we know lies the Great Void and further beyond Miquito, the Land of the Dead, and the land where lie the bones and flesh of the first men, the alux. I am certain it went there.

However, it must have first passed the Oracle of Moons. She alone can pass judgment over who enters Miquito and who does not. The boy's soul must receive her judgment, and therefore so too must we seek her out. Only she can decide the boy's fate. Only she can release his soul. Even if she agrees, the cost of seeking her will be great and likely she shall require us to make some sort of amends in the form of a sacrifice that is at the least equal, if not greater than the damage we have wrought."

The medicine-witch then reveals that the Oracle of Moons resides in a towering black mountain called the Obsidian Spire that lies within the Great Void and marks the third gate to Miquito.

At this juncture, the characters are free to ask questions of Coaxoch or any other council members.

Once the characters' voice their questions and all understand the gravity of the situation, the headman appeals to those in attendance for brave individuals to undertake the journey to the Land of the Dead.

Coaxoch shakes her head. "I am too old for this quest; it is not of my fate. If we leave this tragedy undone, the boy is doomed and the village shall be cursed."

Allow the characters to respond and offer their services. If they attempt to decline, the headman requests it of them as their sacrifice to the people.

After the characters accept the quest, the sorcerer-priest interjects. "But how will they approach the oracle? All know none may safely approach the oracle without the proper payment?"

All realize the sorcerer is correct. Common knowledge holds that upon death, a disk of sacred jadeite is placed upon the tongue of the deceased as tribute for safe passage.

The headman replies, "Thank you for reminding me of such. Your priests are responsible for these payments and make them from the jadeite you collect in the sacred mine, which you keep secret. As the only one among us who knows the location of the secret mines, I appoint you to accompany the group to their location and procure for them the payment they require."

Xotaxtl starts to protest, then realizes quickly that the headman has given him no choice in the matter. Upon finishing, he draws the council to a close.

At this point, the characters can gather their things and begin their journey. Xotaxtl asks when the characters intend on leaving and asks for at least one hour to gather the items he requires for the trip. Unfortunately, one of the items he decides to take is several fingers from the alux, which he threads through a cord and tosses into a belt pouch, believing he might need them later to help guide him in the mines. Characters are free to spy on him, rest, or gather their own supplies. When they are ready, they meet at the edge of the border and venture east toward the Corpsewood to get jadeite from the mines before seeking passage to The Land of the Dead.

Chapter Three: Return to Corpsewood

The characters can return to Corpsewood the way they came during their first excursion into this domain. In most likelihood, they used the raft to cross the waterway and beached it on the western shore. Assuming they safely cross the river, they are free to venture in whatever direction they prefer. If they seek jadeite to pay for an audience with the oracle, Xotaxtl readily informs them the Jadeite Mines lie somewhere to the northeast. If pressed further about their location, the sorcerer-priest admits he has never seen the mines but assures the characters he has memorized the sacred signs and markings that his sacred order uses to mark the path.

A few miles into the Corpsewood, the terrain climbs upward, the trees thin, and the plain rises into Teoctlan's low and rocky hills. Scores of caves and caverns crack through these hills where the sacred Jadeite Mines are hidden. Whenever the characters reach an X on the map, they arrive at a random cave site. Use **Table 3–2** to determine what is in the cave. If you generate the same roll twice, ignore it and roll again. You can also use the table to beef up the exploration with more encounters or as additional locations if the characters decide to explore the region more extensively.

Table 3–1: Corpsewood Caves

2d8	Results
2	**Pitfall.** The entrance to this cave is protected by a deep natural ravine concealed by sticks and leaves covered with soil. A creature who falls into the pit takes 1d6 points of damage from the 10-foot plunge.
3	**Shallow Cave.** This cave goes only about two feet into the earth and then narrows to a thin crack, offering the characters little shelter. If they thrust a stick or torch or some other kind of probing object into the cave, they rile up a swarm of bats. While the swarm of bats poses little threat if the characters accidentally drive them out of the cave mouth, the sudden disturbance draws the attention of others lurking in the forest. A patrol of **4 gnolls** riding **4 giant hyenas** spots the swarm of bats and the opportunistic raiders rush to investigate activities near the cave. They arrive in 1d6 + 4 minutes, approaching stealthily. If the characters left the area before they arrive, the gnolls search for tracks and attempt to purse them until they catch up, at which point they attack.
4	**Empty Cave.** Currently, nothing occupies this cave though it bears evidence that someone once lived here. Long ago someone stenciled a series of handprints on all the walls. *Treasure.* A character has a 1-in-6 chance each round to find a small trinket made up of a feather, a snail shell, and three human finger bones strung together. The trinket is a set of *lucky fingers* (see **Appendix B: New Equipment and Magic Items**).
5	**Cave of Doom.** A hunched-over skeleton sits propped in front of a woven basket of dried corn in this cave. If the characters attempt to take the corn, the skeleton stands then topples into a pile of bones, animating as a **bone swarm**. It rushes to attack the characters to defend its bounty.
6	**The Ghostly Boar.** This large cave serves as the home to a hermitic **boarfolk**. Aluxes sometimes form alliances with these creatures that also originate from the Land of the Dead.

2d8	Results
7	**Nhatyol.** This small cave sits high along the ridgeline. An **alux of the Second Sun** named Nhatyol sits near the mouth of the cave having a conversation with three choms. The small, black-feathered birds visit her to bring her messages and updates of recent developments. they just brought her news of tragic events at the nearby village. Still, she is not foolish enough to trust the choms. She waits for news from a more reliable source. Despite her curiosity, if she spots the characters approaching, she attempts to hide, fearing that if the humans find her, they might murder her.
8	**Abandoned.** A small round pit has been dug near the entrance of the cave. The bottom of the pit is caked with potash. Nestled deep in the back of the cave is a pallet of dried grass. A thick layer of spider's webs blankets the fire pit, the cave, and its contents. Hidden in the pit beneath the webs is a small wooden box with a sunstone carved into its face that is worth 350 gp. The box holds six feathers and three small polished gemstones, each carved with a different image. A pale white moonstone with an image of the goddess Atoyatl (165 gp), a piece of polished lapis with the image of the goddess Cualliteotl (150 gp), and a piece of turquoise with the image of Contlati (175 gp). The feathers are from a great heron and are worth 10 gp. A deeply faded image sketched into the stone depicts two mountains.
9	**The Deep Cave.** This cave descends into the hillside for several dozen yards and eventually slopes downward into a small pool of foul-smelling, stagnant water. Characters who attempt to climb to the pool must roll below their dexterity on 3d6 to navigate the slippery rock. The pool is only five feet deep. Anyone drinking the water must make a saving throw to avoid being nauseated for 10 minutes (–1 to hit and saves).
10	**Hermit Cave.** This cave shows signs of recent use. There is a sleeping pallet, a peccary skin blanket, and a wooden table holding three clay jars, two of which are filled with water while one holds cornmeal. A message written on the dirt floor with a stick says, "Leave Me Alone!" in Aztli. An old **tribal warrior** lives here and keeps a vigilant watch over what he considers his territory. If the characters approach, he quickly shuffles off to hide in the nearby brush and waits patiently for them to leave. If they spot him, he yells at them to go away and leave him to his contemplations. He is annoyed by their company but can give them one or two hints about what's nearby if they promise to leave his home and give him back his peace.
11	**Empty Cave.** The cave floor is littered with dried dung, snapped bones, and pawprints. It reeks of wet dog. As one might expect, this cave is the home of a pack of **12 hyenas.** The ravenous canines are currently hunting and drinking water, though if the characters wait long enough, they return in about two hours. The hyenas attack any creatures they encounter in their cave without hesitation.
12	**The Stash.** The cave extends only about 10 feet before a pile of stones wall off the passage. Digging out the stones takes about 20 minutes and reveals a small alcove that contains a parcel wrapped in cornhusks. The parcel contains a set of four ancient obsidian knives worth 30 gp each and two ear spools of polished bone inlaid with gold in the visage of a serpent worth 300 gp.

13	**Mushrooms.** Anyone entering this cave is assaulted with a potent sour, earthy smell. Hundreds of tiny gray-brown mushrooms cover the cave floor. The mushrooms are edible and can be used to brew six servings of foul-tasting liquid that ironically removes the effects of nausea. In a popular folktale, the hero Temoaco used such a potion to ward off hallucinations on his voyage to the Great Void. Gathering and preparing the liquid takes 30 minutes. The solution lasts only for three weeks, after which it turns rancid and has the opposite effect.
14	**The Third Sun.** Loud slamming and hideous chomping sounds echo from this cave. Shortly after, a towering and obese ogre-like creature squeezes from the entrance, its mottled skin and mousy black hair spattered with gore. It clutches a still-beating heart in its fist, which the creature greedily pops into its mouth, after which it lets out a deafening belch. The creature is an **alux of the First Sun** that has just finished devouring the heart of an old mystic to take it back to Miquito. Inside, the creature ransacked the man's meagerly furnished dwelling. His broken body lies crumpled amid his torn blankets and crushed wooden tools and utensils. If the characters capture the alux alive, they can attempt to interrogate it. Still, the stupid creature knows little, claiming it is here only to gather souls of those seeking to travel safely to the afterlife. If pressed for what kind of creature it is, the alux responds only that it is like its captors, though most modern humans have trouble seeing or believing this and view all such creatures as monsters.
15	**The Ominous Bones.** A collection of bones litters the floor in this cave. The bones are human and are all oddly cracked with strange scratches on them. The markings are consistent with teeth marks, implying that the inhabitant was eaten.
16	**Empty Cave.** The cave smells dry and is entirely empty except for dust. A small crawlway is in the back of the cave. Characters attempting to use the crawlway must lie prone and squeeze through it. The crawlway continues for about 20 feet before it opens into another cave about 15 feet in circumference that is lit by a small crack in the ceiling. Around the perimeter of the cave are the propped-up forms of five humanoids curled into the fetal position and wrapped with cloth strips. Each is sprinkled with petals of dried flowers. The small cave is a grave, and characters entering its sanctity are obligated to make a sacrifice to its occupants. Characters automatically recognize it is their obligation to make an offering to the dead. Characters failing to pay tribute are cursed and suffer a −2 penalty to attacks and saving throws until the next sunrise.

Alux of the First Sun: HD 10; HP 72; AC 7[12]; **Atk** bash (2d6); **Move** 15; **Save** 5; **AL** Any; **CL/XP** 10/1400; **Special:** camouflage (80% chance to hide in hilly or mountainous terrain), darkvision (60ft), immune to fear, trigger rockslide (3/day, create 10ft wide rockslide, 3d6 damage, save for half), vulnerable to obsidian (200% damage). (see **Appendix A: New Monsters**)

Boarfolk: HD 6; AC 7[12]; **Atk** club (1d8+3) or gore (3d6); **Move** 12; **Save** 11; **AL** N; **CL/XP** 6/400; **Special:** darkvision (60ft). (see **Appendix A: New Monsters**)

Bone Swarm: HD 10; AC 6[13]; **Atk** swirling bones (2d6); **Move** 9 (fly 18); **Save** 5; **AL** N; **CL/XP** 10/1400; **Special:** immune to sleep and charm, resist slashing weapons (50% damage). (see **Appendix A: New Monsters**)

Giant Hyenas (4): HD 5; AC 6[13]; **Atk** bite (2d6); **Move** 18; **Save** 12; **AL** N; **CL/XP** 5/240; **Special:** none. (*Monstrosities* 260)

Gnolls (4): HD 2; AC 5[14]; **Atk** bite (2d4) or longsword (1d10); **Move** 9; **Save** 16; **AL** C; **CL/XP** 2/30; **Special:** none. (*Monstrosities* 209)

Hyenas (12): HD 1; AC 7[12]; **Atk** bite (1d3); **Move** 16; **Save** 17; **AL** N; **CL/XP** 1/15; **Special:** none. (*Monstrosities* 259)

Nhatyol, Alux of the Second Sun: HD 6; HP 41; AC 7[12]; **Atk** weapon (1d8) or bite (1d6), slam (2d4); **Move** 12; **Save** 11; **AL** Any; **CL/XP** 6/400; **Special:** backstab (x3), camouflage (80% chance to hide in hilly or mountainous terrain), darkvision (60ft), vulnerable to obsidian (200% damage). (see **Appendix A: New Monsters**)

Old Tribal Warrior, Elderly Male Aztli Warrior: HP 19; AC 7[12]; **Atk** club (1d4) or longbow x2 (1d6); **Move** 9; **Save** 14; **AL** N; **CL/XP** 3/60; **Special:** none. (*Monstrosities* 257)
Equipment: club, longbow, 10 arrows.

OHTLI

During their wanderings in the Corpsewood, the characters capture the attention of another alux named **Ohtli**, who is an **alux of the Third Sun** and of more recent origin than those the characters previously encountered. He was tasked with finding the alux the villagers unwittingly slew. When he spots humans wandering through the Corpsewood, his curiosity gets the better of him and prompts him to follow them to gather whatever intelligence he can. He stays out of sight for as long as possible. He remains hidden until the characters spot him or until he overhears them discussing the details of their doings, at which point he steps forth of his own accord.

Ohtli, Alux of the Third Sun: HD 7; HP 52; AC 7[12]; **Atk** macuahuitl (1d8) or 2 claws (1d4+1); **Move** 12; **Save** 9; **AL** Any; **CL/XP** 7/600; **Special:** darkvision (60ft), summon chom swarm (100%, arrives in 1d4+2 rounds), thieving skills. (see **Appendix A: New Monsters**)
Thieving Skills: Climb 89%, Hear 4 in 6, Hide 30%, Silent 40%, Locks 30%.
Equipment: macuahuitl[B].
[B] See **Appendix B: New Equipment and Magic Items**

Ohtli can speak broken Aztli at best. He explains in his best faltering Aztli that his name is Ohtli and that he has been looking for his kin, an alux of the Second Sun named Noycotl whom he believed inadvertently wandered into Cintlipetl seeking the seven year harvest sacrifice for the Forgotten Gods.

If the characters do not connect Ohtli's tale to recent events, give the characters an opportunity to correctly infer that he refers to the alux that died under the villagers' watch. If the characters share their story with Ohtli, he struggles to understand them but listens thoughtfully. Telling him the news greatly saddens him, and he grimly informs the characters that without the gifts, the Forgotten Gods will most certainly be angered and curse the village. He shudders as he recalls the cataclysm that the Forgotten Gods used to destroy his world and his people.

Ohtli then offers to help the characters, sharing his belief that since the child is made from the remains of his ancestors, he is also his kin. Ohtli believes that aiding the humans might help restore the balance of hostility and violence that has infested his people and help move them in a direction back toward achieving some measure of humanity.

Ohtli can serve as the characters' advisor or guide to the Gate to the Great Void. He explains as best as possible that mortals cannot travel into the next world as long as their bodies possess a soul. To pass through the gate, the characters must leave their souls behind in the land of the sun. Ohtli offers to care for them and promises to keep them safe until their return. However, he warns them that if they die in the Great Void or in Miquito, he must immediately surrender their life sparks to the gods. If they die in either locale, they cannot come back. Ohtli speaks the truth on this subject, and characters can recall several scriptures forbidding the living from entering the Great Void or passing into the afterlife. Those who defy the word of the gods suffer all manner of violent tortures.

If the characters accept Ohtli's offer, he claims he can perform the ritual at any time, but further stresses that he needs them to understand that if he takes their souls, he must go into hiding to ensure their safekeeping. If he dies, the characters die as well. If the characters return to the village with Ohtli, the headman offers to hide and protect him. The medicine-witch makes it clear to him that should any ill-fate befall Ohtli, those whose souls are in his possession would instantly perish.

When the characters are prepared to journey into the afterlife, Ohtli provides them with verbal instructions on how to reach the Void Gate, a mystic portal opening to the Great Void from whence they can follow the causeways anywhere in the universe. The Void Gate lies hidden within the valley of two sacred mountains known as the lovers, which lie east of Corpsewood, near the center of the world. Ohtli is forbidden to write or draw instructions showing the path to the Void Gate, for it is only for the dead and he would be flayed alive and his flesh fed to the choms if it came to light that he had revealed it. Similarly, he requests they not record his instructions and reminds them that his fate is now theirs until the matter is resolved. He whispers the instructions in the form of a sacred verse (see **Ohtli's Sacred Verse** sidebar).

C3: The Jadeite Mines

The location of the jadeite mines has been a long-kept secret passed on through whispers and secret chants from one generation to the next. Those blessed with this esoteric knowledge maintain the responsibility to care for the mines and the first humans who watch them — those made by the gods during the dawn of the world, which the gods then cast aside or destroyed as each coming age passed. Still, it is these creatures that hold the secrets to Miquito, the realm of the dead, and its safe passage. Jadeite, the most precious of stones, serves as a gift to those who dwell in the realms beyond. When the sacred stone is worked into beads or plates and placed into the mouths of the deceased, the dead are given passage and allowed to venture across the bridge of souls to face judgment. The damned dare not interfere with those bearing gifts and tribute to the lords of the dead. The Aztlis and their relatives believe it is taboo to venture into the mines. Stern warnings fill their ancient tales regarding those who would steal from them, for they consider jadeite as a tribute to Miquito. The sorcerer knows of the mines but holds many superstitions and fears about them.

Along the northeast border of the Corpsewood rises the tightly cramped, dry and rocky hills of Teoctlan. They seem to grow together to form a tightly bound cluster that creates a broad impasse. Little exists in the way of passage beyond; however, a ranger, dwarf, or elf can discern several paths of least resistance through the range. The rough, crudely formed trails are steep and covered with scree and other loose matter, making them difficult to traverse. Characters must make a saving throw for every 100 feet they climb or slip and fall, taking 1d6 points of damage as they slide 1d10 feet down the rocky slopes.

The hill reaches its crest at around 600 feet, where it empties onto a worn, wide plateau that runs for miles in either direction. On the opposite side, the plateau drops sharply into a wide chasm consisting of several levels of stepped cliffs that collapse into an open maze of wide gouges hacked into the earth.

Mine General Features

The mines consist of a series of open ravines, so technically one can enter them from any point. The ravines are leveled into two terraces, with the lowest about 30 feet below the ground level. Sunlight penetrates into portions of the mines, but the light is dim at best. Atop the first step, a narrow walkway encircles the entire mine. Creatures on lower levels cannot see the activities of creatures on the levels above them. To the south, an upper tier surrounds **Areas M6** and **M7**, completely blocking them from sight. When it rains, the mines collect water and sometimes flood, leaving the ground muddy.

M1: The Mine Entrance

Despite its appearance, the ladder is well built and sturdy. Still, it serves as the main entrance to the mine and therefore the aluxes have sought to protect the entrance against trespassers by boobytrapping several of the rungs. About halfway down, a 10-foot length of knotted hemp rope dangles from a metal spike pounded into the cliff face. The rope is within easy reach of the ladder. The knots make climbing the rope easy. Using the rope allows the aluxes (or anyone else) to safely bypass the trap.

Exploding Ladder Rung Traps

When a character steps on one of these rungs, it immediately snaps, triggering an alchemical explosion that splits the ladder down the middle, causing it to collapse. Creatures and objects within the 20-foot-radius blast area take 3d6 points of damage from the fiery blast. The creature can grab hold of a handhold or ledge with a successful saving throw. Otherwise, the creature falls to the bottom of the mine where it takes 1d6 point of damage for every 10 feet it fell. The loud explosion alerts every alux in a quarter-mile radius.

The first to hear the alarm is an **alux of the Second Sun** that is hiding in the southeast corner. It waits to see which way the characters go when they reach the bottom. If the characters begin moving toward him or make it obvious that they saw him, he suddenly breaks cover, screams out a warning to alert the other aluxes in a strange tongue, and then rushes to **Area M2**. A wide, worn passage, trampled by years of priests and their secret allies who mined the hills for jadeite and other precious metals, is at the bottom of the ravine.

Alux of the Second Sun: HD 6; HP 39; AC 7[12]; Atk weapon (1d8) or bite (1d6), slam (2d4); Move 12; Save 11; AL Any; CL/XP 6/400; Special: backstab (x3), camouflage (80% chance to hide in hilly or mountainous terrain), darkvision (60ft), vulnerable to obsidian (200% damage). (see **Appendix A: New Monsters**)

M2: Bridges in the Sky

If the characters did not catch the alux in **Area M1**, he waits here, hiding in the curved passage just a short dash from the knotted climbing ropes. He keeps a sharp eye out for the characters. The moment he spots intruders or otherwise learns of their presence, he lets loose another screech and then dashes for the climbing ropes as he attempts to ascend to the plateau as soon as possible. When he reaches the top, the foul creature teases and taunts the characters. Should the characters pursue the alux up the cliffs, the creature waits until they are a little more than halfway up and then calls for out for Xoctlzti. On the next round, Xoctlzti, an **alux of the First Sun**, rushes to the edge of the cliff and begins pounding on it to target climbers by triggering a rockslide over them. Xoctlzti waits with his Second Sun ally and attempts to kick invaders off the plateau.

Xoctlzti, Alux of the First Sun: HD 10; HP 71; AC 7[12]; Atk bash (2d6); Move 15; Save 5; AL Any; CL/XP 10/1400; Special: camouflage (80% chance to hide in hilly or mountainous terrain), darkvision (60ft), immune to fear, trigger rockslide (3/day, create 10ft wide rockslide, 3d6 damage, save for half), vulnerable to obsidian (200% damage). (see **Appendix A: New Monsters**)

1 Square = 10 Feet
M1
M2
M3
M8
M7
M6
M4
M5
N
JADEITE MINES

M3: The Carcass

A half-eaten carcass of a forest deer blocks the middle of the passage.

The kill was recent, despite the large swarm of flies feasting on it. There are no signs that the animal was dragged here or that any tracks are around it. It almost appears as though it simply fell out of the sky.

Further inspection of the walls discovers a series of small alternating gouges ascending the rock wall that are likely used as climbing handholds. Characters can use the handholds to make the easy 15-foot climb up to the plateau to the north without having to succeed on a check. A rope bridge connects the plateau to the ledge that circles the perimeter of the mines.

M4: The Mounds

Extensive excavation created a tangle of interlocking rifts that weave through several pick-worn mounds of earth.

This area was heavily mined and then abandoned. Numerous footprints cover the area, all human size or slightly larger. The most heavily trafficked paths lead south.

M5. The South Passage

The passage widens at a point where it makes a slight curve that snakes between two towering steps that rise 30 feet on either side.

A band of **3 aluxes of the Second Sun** and an **alux of the First Sun** wander down this passage. The creatures are bold enough to attack intruders, but realize they lack the numbers to win the fight. During combat, they slowly retreat to the dead-end in **Area M6** where their kin have prepared an ambush.

Alux of the First Sun: HD 10; HP 68; AC 7[12]; **Atk** bash (2d6); **Move** 15; **Save** 5; **AL** Any; **CL/XP** 10/1400; **Special:** camouflage (80% chance to hide in hilly or mountainous terrain), darkvision (60ft), immune to fear, trigger rockslide (3/day, create 10ft wide rockslide, 3d6 damage, save for half), vulnerable to obsidian (200% damage). (see **Appendix A: New Monsters**)

Aluxes of the Second Sun (3): HD 6; HP 45, 42, 34; AC 7[12]; **Atk** weapon (1d8) or bite (1d6), slam (2d4); **Move** 12; **Save** 11; **AL** Any; **CL/XP** 6/400; **Special:** backstab (x3), camouflage (80% chance to hide in hilly or mountainous terrain), darkvision (60ft), vulnerable to obsidian (200% damage). (see **Appendix A: New Monsters**)

M6: The Ambushers

A gaping passage to the east reveals broad gouges ripped into the plateau that form a massive, cave-like hollow. In the north, a narrow pathway climbs between taller mounds, emptying into another partially exposed ravine.

Anyone searching the ravine to the north finds a series of handholds cut into the stone that allow a character to easily climb to the top of the plateau.

An ambush awaits the characters as **4 aluxes of the Second Sun** and **2 aluxes of the First Sun** have taken up strategic positions. The aluxes of the First Sun are above the characters on the top tier, where they use their abilities to create rockslides or to toss opponents from the hill. If the characters retreat, they advance to the first tier and try to hold the higher ground while continuing the fight. The aluxes of the Second Sun strategically maneuver themselves into spots where they can surround an enemy, if possible. The monsters deliberately focus their attacks on the sorcerer Xotaxtl.

Aluxes of the First Sun (2): HD 10; HP 65, 60; AC 7[12]; **Atk** bash (2d6); **Move** 15; **Save** 5; **AL** Any; **CL/XP** 10/1400; **Special:** camouflage (80% chance to hide in hilly or mountainous terrain), darkvision (60ft), immune to fear, trigger rockslide (3/day, create 10ft wide rockslide, 3d6 damage, save for half), vulnerable to obsidian (200% damage). (see **Appendix A: New Monsters**)

Alux of the Second Sun (4): HD 6; HP 44, 39, 34x2; AC 7[12]; **Atk** weapon (1d8) or bite (1d6), slam (2d4); **Move** 12; **Save** 11; **AL** Any; **CL/XP** 6/400; **Special:** backstab (x3), camouflage (80% chance to hide in hilly or mountainous terrain), darkvision (60ft), vulnerable to obsidian (200% damage). (see **Appendix A: New Monsters**)

If the sorcerer takes a few significant hits, his cowardice kicks into high gear. On his next turn, he polymorphs into the form of a peccary and flees up the steep rocky mine walls only to be plucked up at the last moment by a monstrous hulking primordial alux that snaps his spine, tears him to pieces, and gluttonously devours the entire animal in under a minute. After finishing his macabre feast, the creature wipes its gore-smeared face with a meaty arm, screams something unintelligible, belches, and then dashes off, vanishing down the opposite hillside.

M7: The Jadeite Boulder

A massive boulder sits propped up on its side between two large stumps. The rind is partially chiseled away to reveal the smooth greenish-blue mineral inside it.

The boulder has some monetary worth, but unfortunately, it weighs nearly 400 pounds. It is also sacred and therefore its handling should be left for the priests. Stealing it or removing the jadeite without performing the proper rituals would bring one great dishonor and likely a potent curse.

Luckily several flecks of jadeite lie on the ground around the boulder. **Treasure:** There are five detached chunks of jadeite worth 25 gp each. One chunk of jadeite can be transformed into 1d4 beads or plates with the same

Xotaxtl's True Colors

In this section of the adventure, the characters suffer a fearsome attack that reveals the sorcerer's true colors. Halfway through the encounter, his fears get the better of him and cause him to use his magical powers to transform into a peccary to flee. The sorcerer plays a very important role in the development of the plot of this adventure. Not only is Xotaxtl the cause of the curse, but he also serves as its solution. For events in the adventure to unfold as intended, an alux of the First Sun must eat the sorcerer and assume his mantle of power.

If the characters somehow prevent the sorcerer from taking this course of action, there are other ways to assure the sorcerer gets eaten. The alux could pick him off with a trap, a sneak attack of some sort, or grab him during the night while the characters are resting. Alternatively, he could sneak off in the night after witnessing something horrific or after getting into an argument with the characters. However he meets his fate, make sure you give the alux an opportunity to eat his body. The two most difficult scenarios involve the characters taking the body with them (forcing the alux to steal the sorcerer's body from them) or burning the body.

If the latter situation unfolds, the pyre stinks so profoundly that it threatens to draw attention to their actions, encouraging them to vacate the area to avoid detection. Once the characters leave, the alux returns to claim the scorched meat. Prepare to be creative to make sure events unfold as intended, but do your best to not make the situation feel forced. While the plot has some railroad tracks, in this case you are forcing the actions of an NPC and not those of a character.

value. The characters can use this jadeite to gain access to the Great Void and the realms that lie beyond it.

M8: Tool Stockpile

In the corner of this wide alcove, animal hide tarps cover a large unknown pile, tied down with rope strung through spikes hammered into the ground.

The tarp covers a stockpile of crude mining equipment fashioned from stone wood and iron. The tools are primitive but effective. There are also a few hemp ropes and coarse cloth blankets. Most of the equipment is covered in dust.

Treasure: Among the tools are a chisels and hammers and a bundle of moldy cotton cloth containing a stash of raw gold nuggets worth 100 gp.

C4: Cave of the Old Master

The cave of the Old Master is the key to accessing the Eye of the World that leads the characters on the path to the Gate of the Void. It lies in the mountains a little more than a week's journey into the rugged terrain. As the characters proceed closer to the heart of the Tepepan Mountains, the altitude increases and it becomes colder. The jungles and lowlands often reach sweltering temperatures above 90° Fahrenheit by midday. For each day of travel deeper into the mountains, the increasing altitudes drop temperatures by 2d4 degrees. The steady decrease should serve as a warning for characters used to the warmer climates of the tropical forest to get ready for chillier days ahead. By the time the characters reach the foothills surrounding the Eye of the World, the temperature averages 50° Fahrenheit, which is chilly for anyone dressed in light robes or a loincloth.

At this location, a small winding path through the rocks leads to a steep crevasse cut into the mountain face. A small clearing is near the crevasse. Nearby, a 30-foot-long wooden shaft carved from a young tree lies on the ground; the shaft is old and worn smooth. Several bits of old and dirty cloth are tied tightly around the shaft and continue along its full length at one-foot intervals.

The crevasse is steep and deceptively slippery as it is slicked with water. A non-thief character has a chance equal to half the Climb Walls check of a thief of his or her level to climb the crevice. The hermit built the shaft to use as a climbing ladder and adds a +10% bonus to the check if the character uses it.

The climb leads to a narrow ledge that is less than three feet deep and five feet wide. The crevasse continues upward. A faded carving on the rock depicts what appears to be a stylized eye and an arrow pointing up the crevasse. As with the first climb, a non-thief character has a chance equal to half the Climb Walls check of a thief of his or her level to scale the crevasse, though using the shaft once again grants the climber a +10% bonus if used. Sixty feet up, a small opening in the rock leads to a hollow shaft with handholds cut into the surrounding stone. These handholds ascend another few hundred feet to a wider ledge, about 20 feet across, that faces another footpath continuing farther up the mountain. The footpath winds for several hundred yards and then empties into a dark, deep cave face.

Environmental Factors

The temperature drops as the characters continue their ascent until it is 3d6 degrees colder by the time they reach the cave opening.

A small cave opening enters into the side of the mountain. Above the entrance, someone carved a stylized depiction of an eye into the stone. An X-shaped symbol is carved in the pupil of the eye.

Next to the cave entrance is a petrified tree with seven limbs. Each limb is wrapped with a different colored cloth, though the colors are long faded.

Characters who examine the eye discover the X as having four stages, with each representing the apocalypses, but possibly also interpreted in this context as meaning "The World."

Not long after the characters arrive, a single chom lands on the withered tree and curiously stares at them. In its beak, it clasps a small leather satchel. If approached, it tilts its head and stares, waiting to be engaged in some sort of conversation. If it senses hostility, it simply drops the satchel and wings off quickly. If any character attempts to communicate with the chom, it nods and drops the satchel, spilling the kernels inside on the ground. It then wings down, eats one of the kernels, and uses its beak to gesture to a character, pushing another kernel toward that individual as if suggesting they eat it too.

The satchel contains nine pieces of dried corn and a plate of jadeite carved with a grinning skull. The kernels are magical; the jadeite plate is not. Creatures ingesting a single kernel (or more) gain the ability to speak to others or animals. The effect lasts for 10 minutes.

Characters who eat the magic kernel can communicate with the chom (as can any character that speaks Primordial Notoan).

The chom tells them they have found the cave of the old master that holds the secrets to the Eye of the World. From its peak, one can interpret how to get to any location in the world. Despite its great height, it is not as much a lookout as it is a sort of compass for determining points and directions.

The chom does not know how to use it, but its dead master does. However, the chom assures the characters that its master can speak to them from beyond the grave if they place one of the kernels along with a bead of jade in his mouth.

If asked why he is helping them, he claims he is neutral in their affairs and curious as to what will happen if the characters actually get to Miquito. It knows of their affairs because all choms know. After all, they never hold their tongues and spread secrets like the wind. After giving them the corn and answering as few questions as possible, the chom excuses itself and flies off, wishing them good luck and telling them to keep the corn and the jade before departing.

Although they are legendary liars, this chom speaks the full truth, as it faithfully serves the old master. It chooses its words carefully and deliberately, but avoids going into detail. It is not lying, and the characters can follow its instructions to speak with the Old Master …

The cave opening leads to a dry and dusty entrance centering on a stone-lined fire pit filled with gray ash. A neatly piled stack of kindling and twigs leans against one of the corners, and there is a wooden bucket, two reed baskets, a polished walking stick, and a moth-eaten sack of moldering grain. Two archways branching off on either side lead to smaller caves, both are blocked by peccary-hide draperies.

The Master

The passage leads to a slightly larger cave. Within the room stand a collection of painted urns and pottery, a bunch of them worn and damaged. In the center of the floor is another X painted in a mixture of what is likely soot and lard. Wooden bowls sit in each section of the X. The skeletal remains of a long-dead wise man sit propped in the back of the cave wrapped in a faded wool blanket woven with designs that resemble daggers.

Anyone inspecting the wooden bowls notes that some contain traces of colored powder. The first bowl is empty; the second has an eagle feather; the third has traces of feline fur (likely jaguar); and the fourth has traces of marigold seeds. The bowls obviously held offerings, and any character can recall the following associations between deities and their preferred offerings: the eagle feather with Notonatiuh; jaguar with Itztliteotl; and marigolds with Quiahuitl.

The Old Master lies dead. If anyone takes the chom's advice and attempts to talk to him by placing the kernel and the jadeite into his mouth, they are in for a rude awakening … literally. Performing this act causes the creature to rise from the dead, transcending his bound corpse as an **unresurrected wraith**, and while truthfully it can talk, it is furious. It accuses the characters of being blasphemous heathens who have disturbed its rest for taboo purposes.

Unresurrected Wraith: HD 6; HP 43; AC 3[16]; **Atk** spectral touch (1d6 cold + level drain); **Move** 18 (fly); **Save** 11; **AL** C; **CL/XP** 9/1100; **Special:** +1 or better magic or silver weapons to hit, breath of the dead (3/day, 30ft line of mist, 3d6 damage, save for half), immune to sleep and charm, level drain (1 level with touch, save resists), resistances (cold, electricity, 50% damage), spell-like ability, vulnerable to sunlight (1d6 damage per round, no save). (see **Appendix A: New Monsters**)
Spell-like ability: 1/day—*finger of death*.

Treasure: The mummified corpse in the back of the cave is the Old Master who is thoughtfully wrapped with the *blanket of daggers*. The blanket is magic and when wrapped around one's body like a shroud, the individual can safely pass through the **Wind of Daggers** (see **Chapter Five: Beyond the Pale Portal**) without a scratch. Otherwise, it has no magical properties.

THE EMPTY CAVE

The pitcher and cups are empty, while cornhusks and silks fill one of the baskets. Another holds a pile of dirty wool and eight spools of spun yarn. The third basket holds several bolts of wool cloth (about eight yards worth), and the last basket holds an arrow and a collection of sticks of various sizes easily identified as measuring sticks. One is a land-rod, the other is an arrow, and there are three hands and six hearts.

A thorough inspection of the rocks discovers that each one is painted with a name, a number, and a symbol. After investigating several of them, a few of them register as common names of various places in Tehuatl. Many of them are contemporary, though some are older and less familiar. A small number of them bear names of places believed to have once existed in the ages before the cataclysms.

The character can use the rocks to solve the mystery of the Eye of the World as described in the **Eye of the World** section below. One of the stones bears the icon for Popocatepetl and another the icon for Iztaccihuatl. Popocatepetl is marked with the symbol for water and the number 8. Iztaccihuatl is marked with the symbol for Death and the number 9. Characters have a cumulative 10% chance per round to locate the stones if they search. You may even wish to have the characters find one of the mountains by "accident" if they seem stuck and you need to nudge them forward.

Characters searching the room find a concealed exit. Behind one of the baskets hides a cramped and unlit crawlway with a narrow, two-foot-square opening. To enter the crawlway, characters must lie prone and squeeze their way through it. If the characters go through the passage, read or paraphrase the following description:

Upon emerging here, the characters notice another drop in temperature. It gets 1d6 degrees colder at the base of the stairs, then another 1d6 degrees even chillier halfway, and finally 1d12 degrees colder at the summit.

Similarly, the wind also increases, which is already factored into the cooler temperatures. The winds start at light speed (13 mph) and increases by 1d6 mph at the halfway point and another 1d8 mph at the top. You may also want to determine the chance of precipitation along the way.

The stairs climb another 2,500 feet up the mountain until they reach the apex where the top of the mountain has been shorn off and transformed into the Eye of the World, an elaborate tool for determining every location in Tehuatl.

THE EYE OF THE WORLD

Perhaps even more intriguing than the view is the strange carvings set into the platform floor. They consist of a great disk from which protrude four lines in a cross, each marked with one of the cardinal directions. Four symbols run the length of each of the directions. A second circle runs the perimeter of the disk, similar in appearance to a sunstone. The perimeter circle is divided evenly into 20 even, numbered sections.

A small pile of stones, similar to those found in the caves below, is near the entrance. While all have similar markings, none of these contains the names of mountains the characters seek.

SOLVING THE EYE

The Eye of the World can be used to determine the location of almost any location in all Tehuatl. To use the device, one stone must be placed upon the correct icon marking a specific point along one of the cardinal directions. The individual then rotates until they face the correct number along the perimeter. Following a straight line from the stone's location to the number gives the viewer a directional sighting point to the location they seek. If the path to the location is between two points (such as the location the characters seek), the individual reading the Eye of the World uses the intersection of the two points to make a new cross-section and uses that to determine the location by looking through that cross-section from the center of the Eye.

If characters correctly find the locations of both mountains, they can use them to make a new cross-section and then line it up with the center of the eye. This gives them the precise direction to travel to reach the location of the Shadow Where the Earth Touches the Void (aka the Gate to the Great Void).

TRAVELING TO THE GATE

The vale that hides the gate is a good distance east of the eye. The journey consists of approximately 50 miles of travel through rough, mountainous terrain. Unless the characters have some magical ways of transporting themselves, the trip takes at least several days, depending on events. At the start of the journey, the mountain weather is relatively cold, but temperatures quickly warm as they descend in the valleys. The west side of the mountains tends to get less rain, but no less wind. The rains and lush greenery return as the characters reach the valley. At first, the vale thrums with the sounds of life, but as they draw closer to the shadows of the Twin Mountains, things quiet down, and the number of animals and birds slowly dies out until, by the final day, they detect none. At this time, they see the mists ahead and know they have reached the site where the gate is hidden.

If you want to play out the journey, you can flesh it out by running any of the following encounters.

TRAVEL ENCOUNTERS

Upper Mountains: Amid the blue sky, characters see a dark form winging in the distance. Little by little, the creature approaches and soon its massive form

blots the sun. It is a **roc**. The bare and barren slopes offer them few places to take refuge, and the loose scree and pitched landscape make movement difficult.

Roc: HD 12; **HP** 86; **AC** 4[15]; **Atk** bite (3d6), 2 claws (2d6); **Move** 3 (fly 30); **Save** 3; **AL** N or L; **CL/XP** 12/2000; **Special:** none. (*Monstrosities* 399)

Lower Mountains: The characters cross paths with **2 stone giants** on their way south to the hunting lands. They seek prey much large than the characters and do not want to be bothered with a confrontation. However, they are willing to trade items and three pieces of jadeite for water (at least 10 gallons per piece) or a common magic item. Characters can use the jadeite to make additional beads should they still require payment for the oracle of Miquito. Conversely, the giants threaten those who offend them and fight if attacked.

Stone Giants (2): HD 9; **HP** 67, 54; **AC** 0[19]; **Atk** club (3d6); **Move** 12; **Save** 6; **AL** C or N; **CL/XP** 10/1400; **Special:** throw boulders (3d6 damage). (*Monstrosities* 200)

Into the Valley: While walking into the valley, randomly determine which one of the characters accidentally stumbles into a colony of flying, stinging insects, which constitutes **3 stinging insect swarms**. The character has a 2-in-6 chance to spot the strange colony before stepping on it. If the character fails, his or her foot breaks the hive and the hive gets stuck on it, reducing the individual's movement by half. The swarms of insects viciously attack that individual as they try to free their foot. It takes a round to remove the hive, but during that time, the character cannot do anything else.

Stinging Insect Swarms (3): HD 3; **HP** 21, 19, 14; **AC** 7[12]; **Atk** swarm (1d8); **Move** 9 (fly); **Save** 14; **AL** N; **CL/XP** 4/120; **Special:** immune to all but blunt weapons.

Early Valley: As evening falls, a herd of **3d6 deer** suddenly rushes from the wood and scatters across the trail. Seconds later, a sacred **jaguar** bounds out of the brush in pursuit. For a moment, it stops and stares at the characters and then bounds off. Have each character roll a d20. The character who roll

highest receives good luck for spotting it first. Award the character a +1 bonus to attacks, damage, and saving throws for 24 hours. If the character instead decides to hunt and kill the creature, the sky opens up upon its death and a downpour immediately begins. The torrential rains last for the next three hours.

Deer (3d6): HD 2; **AC** 6[13]; **Atk** 2 hooves (1d4) or gore (1d6); **Move** 15; **Save** 16; **AL** N; **CL/XP** 2/30; **Special:** surprise (1–2 on 1d6). (*The Tome of Horrors Complete* 625)

Panther: HD 3; **HP** 21; **AC** 6[13]; **Atk** 2 claws (1d3 + rake), bite (1d6); **Move** 16; **Save** 14; **AL** N; **CL/XP** 4/120; **Special:** rake (if both front claws hit, rake with rear claws for additional 1d6 damage). (*Monstrosities* 370)

Later Valley: As the characters work their way deeper into the valley, they pass through a forest of strange trees, their thick trucks warped and gnarled. Hiding in the trees are **4 shambling mounds** that drop from the branches to attack and devour any living creatures they encounter.

Shambling Mounds (4): HD 7; **HP** 51, 46, 42, 36; **AC** 1[18]; **Atk** 2 fists (2d8 + enfold); **Move** 6; **Save** 9; **AL** N; **CL/XP** 10/1400; **Special:** enfold (if two fists hit, save or suffocate in 2d4 rounds), resists cold and weapons (50% damage). (*Monstrosities* 419)

Edge of the Mists: Three creatures guard the edge of the Shadow Mists and know the location of the Gate to the Great Void. The **guardian naga** introduces herself as **Imitlapia** and the **2 couatls** as **Cuezali** and **Icoatzin**. If characters convince them of their good intentions, the naga claims to know the location of the gate and offers to lead them directly to it, provided they prove themselves worthy. Imitlapia requests the seeds of the giant purple-blossomed cocoxochitl. The sacred flowers once grew here in great abundance, but her two evil sisters poisoned the flowerbeds and stole the last remaining seeds for themselves. Her **2 spirit naga** sisters live 12 miles to the north, near a river that runs along the base of the mountain. If the characters recover the seeds for Imitlapia, she leads them to the gate. However, she doesn't know the secrets of opening it. Such knowledge is forbidden to her,

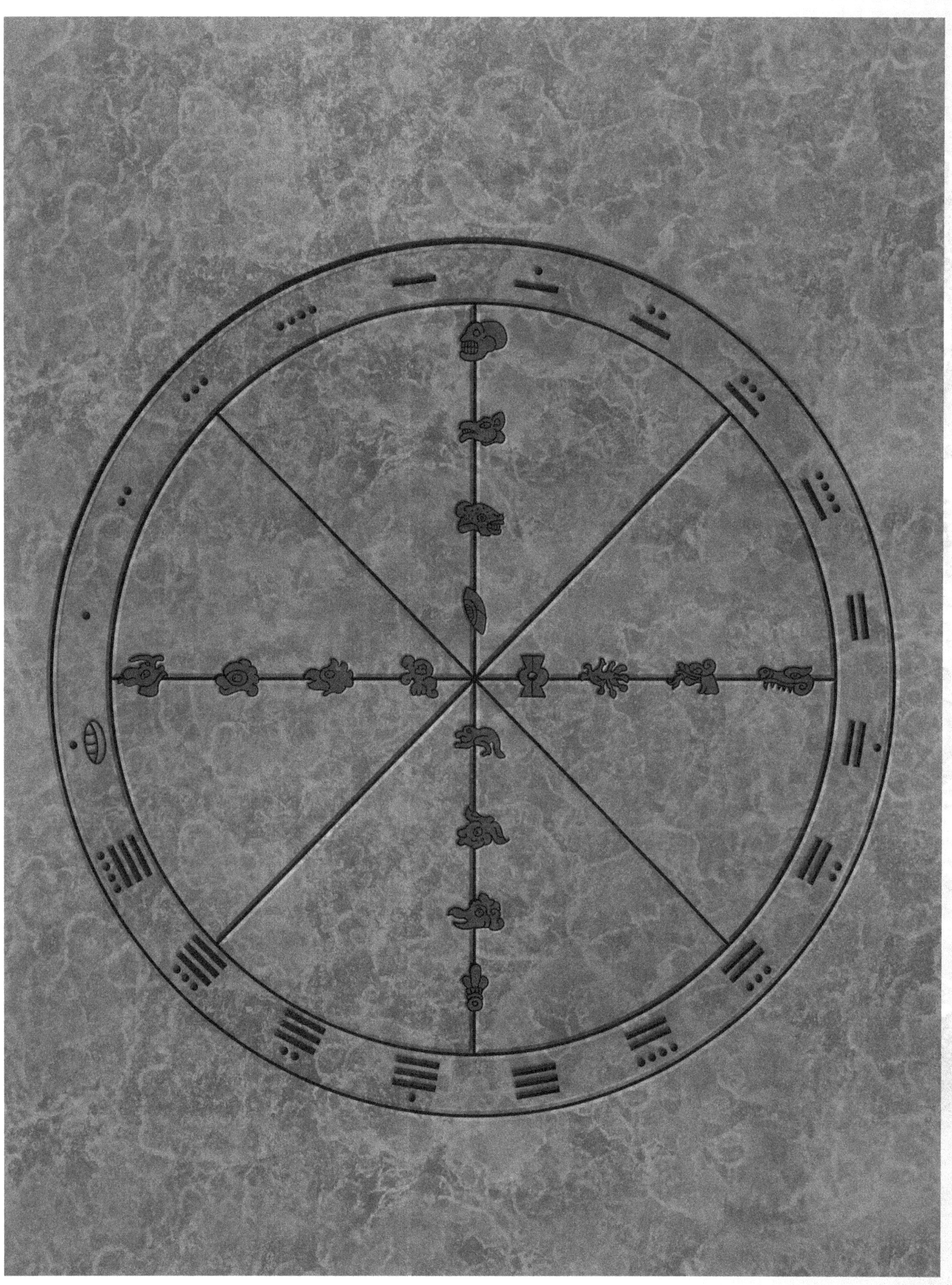

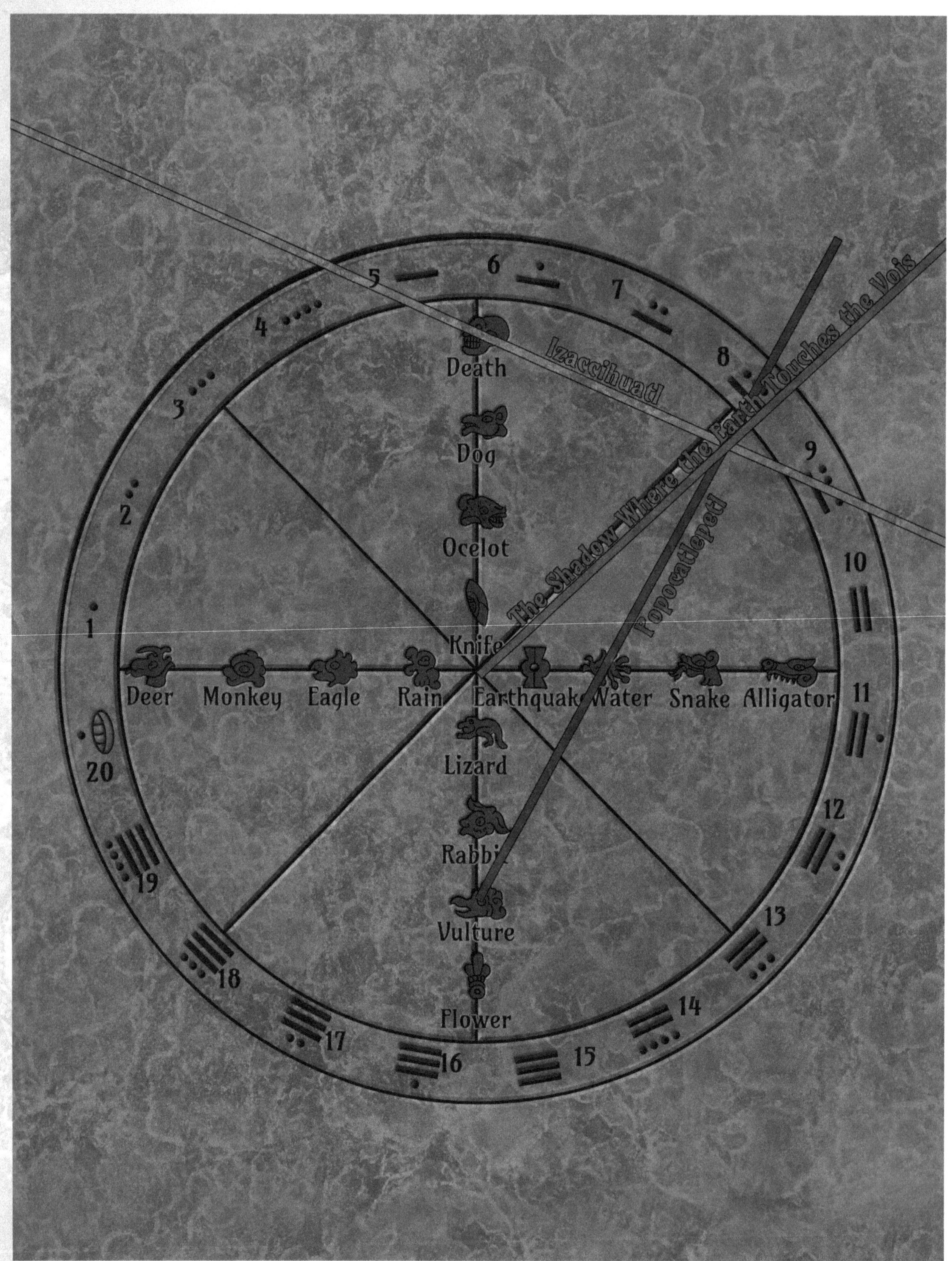

1
2
3
4
5
6
7
8
9
10
11
12
13
14
15
16
17
18
19
20
Death
Dog
Ocelot
Knife
Deer
Monkey
Eagle
Rain
Earthquake
Water
Snake
Alligator
Lizard
Rabbit
Vulture
Flower
Izaccihuatl
The Shadow Where the Earth Touches the Vois
Popocatlepetl

as is helping the characters any further. Upon completing her promise, she immediately departs.

If characters complete this challenge, they can offer the names of any of the guardians to the couatls watching over Ohtli as partial proof of their intentions.

Imitlapia, Guardian Naga: HD 11; **HP** 76; **AC** 5[14]; **Atk** bite (1d6 + poison), coils (1d8 + constrict), spit (poison); **Move** 18; **Save** 4; **AL** L; **CL/XP** 13/2300; **Special:** constrict (automatic 1d8 damage after coils hit), lethal poison (save or die), spells (2/2/1/1). (**Monstrosities** 342)

Cuezali and Icoatzin, Couatls (2): HD 8; **HP** 60, 53; **AC** 4[15]; **Atk** bite (2d6 + poison), tail (1d6 constrict); **Move** 12 (fly 24); **Save** 8; **AL** L; **CL/XP** 11/1700; **Special:** poison (save or die), polymorph (at will), spells (3/2/1). (**Monstrosities** 73)
Spells: 1st—*charm person, magic missile, sleep*; 2nd—*ESP, phantasmal force*; 3rd—*lightning bolt.*

Spirit Nagas (2): HD 9; **HP** 66, 51; **AC** 5[14]; **Atk** bite (1d3 + poison); **Move** 12; **Save** 6; **AL** C; **CL/XP** 13/2300; **Special:** charm gaze (as charm person), lethal poison (save or die), spells (MU 4/2/1; Clr 2/1). (**Monstrosities** 344)

CHAPTER FOUR: THE GATE TO THE GREAT VOID

The entrance to the gate to the Great Void lies in the mist-drenched vale that hides between the two mountains known as the lovers Popocatepetl and Iztaccihuatl. The Gate of the Void is unguarded, for it does not exist in the earthly realm and the living must coax it from its slumber with sacred rituals. Only the dead (or an entity without a soul) can call forth the gate with impunity, for the Great Void serves as the entrance to the paradises of Ilhuicac and the land of the dead, Miquito. Mortals are forbidden from performing the ritual and just uttering the words to call the gate forth is punishable by eternal imprisonment under Micoateotl's direct supervision. If a mortal performs the ritual, they stand marked for judgment and must pay for the consequence of their action upon facing the Oracle of the Empty Moon.

The characters searching the valley will find the spot where the shadows of two mountains meet.

This phenomenon takes place only when the sun slips above the edge of the eastern horizon near dawn. The shadow marks a small spot upon the earth where an ancient sunstone nearly five feet in diameter is buried a few inches below the surface. To perform the ritual that opens the gate, the sunstone must first be cleared, which takes a few hours, though it can be completed before the sun is high. When they finish, they reveal a large stone disk carved with a snarling face sticking out a bladed tongue. A carving of twin serpents encircles the face, and numerous numbers and images representing animals, elements, flowers, and gods are inscribed into the circles. The characters easily recognize the disk as a massive sunstone, a device their people use to measure and record the cosmic motion of the universe. It is used to determine sacred days, lucky and unlucky signs, and to predict future events. This sunstone also functions as a portal to the afterlife.

Characters can use Ohtli's verses to perform the ritual that opens the portal. A priest or other character with a religious background has a 75% chance to recall the circumstances and order of each cataclysm as well as determine the names of the goddesses and gods that keep them balanced and what they might require as a sacrifice. All other characters have a 40% chance. A character must make four checks to decipher the verses in their entirety. Spells such as *legend lore* and similar magic may offer the characters useful insight (and add a 15% bonus to the check). A character who fails to decipher a part of the sequence takes 1d4 points of damage as the gods take a blood sacrifice, and he or she must start over at the beginning of the ritual. Once a character learns all of the sequences of the ritual, they automatically know what objects they must offer to which deity.

In the shadows cast across the narrow valley by the two mountains, dust begins to swirl above the great stone calendar. Whirling faster and faster, it blurs out the horizon, revealing another world within its eye. Looking deep within, the ghostly image of a long causeway leading across still black waters becomes visible. Deep within your chest, you feel it beckon with a cold, hollow emptiness known only by those who step into the arms of death.

The characters have opened the portal to the Great Void, yet they have little time to enter before it closes again. They have only one minute to decide whether or not to step through it.

RITUAL SEQUENCE AND OFFERINGS

1. Jaguars caused the first great cataclysm. When the provider of the shadow soul is Itztliteotl, the god quells the jaguar.

Offering: An offering to Itztliteotl must be placed upon the image of ocelotl (the jaguar) to appease him. The god accepts sacrifices of obsidian or precious metals and gemstones stolen from others.

2. Winds caused the second great cataclysm. When the provider of the elemental soul is Nonotzali, then the wind falls still.

Offering: An offering to Nonotzali must be placed upon the image of ehecatl (the wind) to appease it. The god accepts sacrifices of artwork and objects created by hand.

3. Fire caused the third great cataclysm. When the provider of the Spirit Soul is appeased, his fires birth life.

Offering: An offering to Contlati must be placed upon the number Ce (1). The god accepts offerings of seared meat or turquoise.

4. Floods caused the last great cataclysm. When the provider of the Temporal Soul is appeased, the waters subside.

Offering: An offering to Quiahuitl must be placed upon the image of Quiahuitl (the rain). The god can be appeased with marigolds or heron feathers.

INTO THE VOID

Stepping through the portal, you find yourself standing at the intersection of two long causeways. Paved with stone and packed earth, lit torches line each path. The causeway sits several feet above black waters whose still surfaces glisten in the torchlight. They seem to stretch forever into blackness.

The characters stand at the center of the Great Causeway, a path that stretches between the four realms. While the characters are unable to determine the cardinal directions in the void, anyone studying the torches can determine slight differences in the colors of their flames.

The torches in one of the causeways flicker with dull orange flames that leak foul-smelling crimson haze. In another, the torch flames have a cold, purplish-green tint and leak a steady stream of black soot. In the third passage, the flames give off a faint, pale white glow and spit thin wisps of gray smoke. Along the last causeway, the torches crackle with bluish sparks that occasionally spit out and sizzle when they hit the water.

The colors possess great significance and allow each traveler to determine their correct path in the afterlife. Each color is associated with one of the

Void Checks

After a character has been in the Great Void for more than one hour, they must begin making void checks every 1d6 x 10 minutes. To do so, the character must succeed on a saving throw. On a failure, the character hears faint sounds and voices and experiences feelings they cannot quite grasp. On a success, the character hears and experiences nothing.

The character must make a new void check when called upon, regardless of whether the character succeeded or failed on a previous void check. If a character fails a second void check, the sounds grow louder and start to resemble voices spoken in unknown languages or perhaps many languages. Alternatively, a character can voluntarily fail its void check to hear these sounds and experience the strange feelings. If they do so, the character adds +2 to the Voices in the Void roll for each void check intentionally failed.

After spending more time in the void, any character who failed two previous void checks must succeed on a third and final saving throw. If the character fails, the sounds become clear. Determine the results of specific sounds using **Table 3–3: Voices in the Void**. If the character succeeds on the void check, the sounds do not escalate and the character hears what was heard in the previous stage.

cardinal directions and the four points that lead to the realms of the gods. The colors corresponding to the cardinal points are as follows:

1. The red flames mark the east, and its causeway leads to Tlahuizlampa.
2. The purple flames leaking black soot mark the north, and its causeway leads to Mictlampa.
3. The white flames mark the passage west to Cihuatlampa.
4. The blue flames mark the south and the passage to Huitzlampa.

Characters interpreting the signs and colors know that if they wish to find the Obsidian Spire, they must take the causeway that leads to the north.

The Void and Hallucinations

Journeying through the Great Void is long and timeless. Except for the characters and the seemingly eternal causeway, there is no sound, no depth, and no volume. Mortals exposed to the Great Void have an extremely difficult time coping with its vastness and the number of unknown energies traveling through it at any given time. Energies, souls, lifesparks, and thoughts race freely through the void. When they strike mortals, they erupt within their minds, unleashing emotions and desires, words and ideas, revelation and epiphanies, none of which truly belong to the mortal. When a mortal first enters, they are barely perceptible, but over time they slowly increase. Distractions dissolve thoughts, voices call from worlds unknown, emotions of forgotten entities express their longing to connect, and loved ones and gods offer power, acceptance, and immortality. The effects of all this are sometimes mind-shattering. Use Void Checks to determine the extent of the void's effect on the characters.

Special: Characters who possess beverages brewed from the fleshy mushrooms growing in the cave in Corpsewood can consume them to gain a +1 bonus on void checks made to resist the mental effects caused by exposure to the Great Void.

Table 3-2: Voices in the Void

Roll 2d8 to determine what happens to a character who fails or forfeits three void checks.

Die Roll	Effect
2	*Voices.* "Come into the void. Return my child, we await you. We are timelessness. We are one with eternity." The character responds by leaping into the void, traveling in a straight line at a speed of 60 feet per round.
3	*Voices.* "Feel your strength from within, do not burden yourself with the lies of materialism. You are greatness, release that which is not you." The character tosses a random magical item or weapon into the void. The item travels at a speed of 120 feet per round and vanishes at the end of the round with a loud pop.
4–6	*Voices.* "Offer yourself to the void, it is your flesh, heart, and blood. Bond with us and share our strength." Characters deal 2d6 points of slashing damage to themselves, spilling the blood into the void. The hit points cannot be healed until the character returns to the Material Plane.
7–9	*Voices.* "The knowledge of the void is infinite. You share all of this knowledge with us and we all with you." The character's thoughts fill rapidly, flooded with overwhelming amounts of vast knowledge. They find it difficult to think and suffer a –2 penalty on saving throws for as long as they remain in the void. When they leave the void, the character gains a +1 bonus to any stat (player's choice) to a maximum of 18.
10–14	*Voices.* "The void is boundless; it is everywhere at all times. We see all. We see through forever." The character's eyes widen as they stare deeply into the void until their irises merge with their pupils, eclipsing into vacant black pools. Thereafter, until they leave the void, the character is blind and suffers a –4 penalty to attacks. After leaving, their pupils turn starry and they gain the ability to cast *commune* once per week.
15	*Voices.* "We are the same. You cannot exist without us, and we cannot exist without you. We are forever merged." The character blurs for a few moments and then winks out of existence. The character becomes ethereal, and no one senses their existence for the duration they are in the void. Upon leaving the void, the character returns to normal and thereafter can cast *invisibility* once per day.
16+	*Voices.* "All that has, is, and ever will be now fills you. You are the inevitable. You are the cataclysms." The character returns to normal. Nothing happens. Let the paranoia begin. At some point in the distant future, the character becomes certain that the void is telling them "Now is the Time," and they believe with all certainty that they are at the dawn of the next cataclysm, and that the gods have once again prepared to clear the slate of existence.

The City that Sleeps upon the Doorstep of the Evening Flame

After traveling for some time in the Great Void, the causeway eventually leads the characters to an archipelago of four small floating islands, each populated by those wanderers denied passage into the Realms of the Dead. As the characters approach, read or paraphrase the following description:

Ahead in the distance, the causeway leads toward what appears to be several islands drifting across in the great starry void, sprawling like blackened clouds blotting the distant stars. Atop the colorless islands rise temples of unknown gray stone surrounded by fields of withered gray shafts of empty cornstalks. As you draw nearer, you spot people walking through the fields, yet they too are colorless, with gray flesh and gray clothing, silent, cold, and peering into the void with stone gray, nearly lifeless eyes. They watch your approach yet show no sense of enthusiasm or curiosity.

THE GREAT VOID
1 Hex – 150 Feet
V1
V2
V3
V4
V5

Unless they decide to turn back, wait, or jump from the causeway, the characters have little choice except to approach the strange city. The causeway appears to lead directly into a large area, dipping through a broad stone archway as if passing through a tunnel. Only when one draws close does it become apparent that the causeway ends several feet shy of the arch, and that what first appeared to be a shadow is a 10-foot gap between the causeway and an open drawbridge blocking the entrance.

The somber gray people appear to be of human descent, but from what age or ages one cannot tell. If the characters attempt to call out or otherwise communicate with the people, they offer no response and only stare.

VI. The Forgotten Ones

The drawbridge connects to a causeway on the other side that leads directly into a towering stepped temple. As with everything here, the temple and all that surrounds it appear dull gray and completely devoid of color.

Characters can either attempt to lower the bridge themselves using magic, by pulling it open with ropes and grappling hooks, or by convincing the gray people to lower the bridge. Any of these methods easily succeed, leaving characters to wonder if there is even a point to having a drawbridge.

The Faded

As soon as the characters cross the bridge, droves of gray-fleshed people surround them. Their expressions appear sad and curious but always steeped in desperation. When the characters first arrive, the Faded slowly approach and huddle around them, reaching out to touch their bodies and begging for their warmth. All are lost souls, perhaps waiting to continue, but going mad. Some cannot afford the fare, others are too scared to continue, and many cannot even remember how long they have been here. For many, this time has been infinite.

These lost souls call themselves the Faded. They cannot remember their names, their truths, or their past. All of this has faded from them. They barely remember their memories and hunger for the memories of others who still possess them. They long to be told tales and rituals, long to hear of color and sun and the moon, the rain, and the gods they hope might one day return to save them from the endless void. They are cold to the touch, near lifeless, and cast no shadows. Their curiosity with the newcomers is short-lived, and swiftly the throng begins to swell with paranoia, fear, and panic. The Faded start pulling at the characters, frantically whispering things such as "We must leave now," "It's not safe," "*They* will be coming soon," "You must get to Teotlachimalli before the shadows fall," and "Quickly! Quietly."

The Faded do not converse or answer outside the temple, but promise to explain everything once everyone is safely inside.

If threatened or attacked, the Faded take defensive postures and flee to the temple. They have no weapons and do not fight back. Characters' weapons pass harmlessly through the Faded.

The Temple of the God's Shield

Teotlachimalli is what the Faded call the temple. The name means something like "god's shield." However, the temple is unadorned and washed clean of all colors and symbols, so it remains unclear which god the shield might belong to. The Faded mass in and around the temple where they feel safe. It consists of a single large room where the people either walk in circles around a wooden post muttering prayers and wards of protection or cower in small groups crowded against the walls and corners, shivering beneath colorless threadbare woolen blankets.

If characters attempt to speak with the Faded, it is readily apparent that they have little to offer. The Faded believe they worship a god of protection and fear leaving the temple for they "know what lies beyond." Unfortunately, they are not entirely clear on "what lies beyond" and only stress something is out there and that the "something" is to be feared.

If characters question the Faded about what lies beyond the next two causeways, they can glean some insight. They call one of the causeways the **Bridge of Hearts (GV3)** and the other causeway the **Bridge of Bone (GV2).**

Bridge of Hearts

"Across the Bridge of Hearts lies the island bearing another temple. It belongs to a goddess of death, though I cannot recall her name. Once she was powerful and held vast armies and all worshipped her, but I suppose even gods must fall. The cataclysm is the only power and the only truth. Its inhabitants rip out their hearts as offerings, but it serves no purpose. It has lost its power and mysticism. … The people remain, like us except none of them have hearts, just empty holes in their chest cavities. Many cry endlessly, but they cannot say why. I have watched people from this island venture across the bridge, determined to get to Miquito, determined to make their sacrifices as they stand atop the temple, cut out their hearts and throw them still beating into the Great Void. It is madness, you know. … It is all madness."

Bridge of Bone

"Across the Bridge of Bones lies desolation. There is nothing, and any who go, disappear."

While characters have no problems entering the temple, should they attempt to leave, the crowd panics and blocks the exits, screaming and crying for them to stay, fearful for their deaths outside the temple. They grab and pull, grapple, and block the characters' movements to the best of their abilities. They clearly are not attacking and instead act out of extreme fear.

Anyone caught in the panicked throng or attempting to move through the throng is grabbed and held, although the characters can roll below their strength on 4d6 to break free. However, the Faded usually release a character after 1d4+1 rounds. Characters crawling through the tunnel are prone and treat the area as if they were squeezing through a tight space. The shouts and screams of the Faded also make it nearly impossible for characters to communicate with each other by normal means. To escape, the characters must blindly force their way through the throng and out the main entrance. Once they leave, the throng pleads for them to return to safety, but they are too overcome with fear to stop them. Instead, they stand there weeping and sobbing uncontrollably.

The Cornfields

The perimeter of this island and most of the other is filled with sweeping fields of gray lifeless corn. Dried and withered upon the stalk, it stands as if forgotten. The Faded avoid the fields for venturing into them means oblivion. However, when the madness takes them, some walk into the fields of their own accord and never return. More eerily, the details of such actions are quickly forgotten, only to have the memories replaced by a constant unending sense of dread. Numerous walkways wind through the cornfields and allow characters to traverse them freely and without constraint. Traveling through the maize proves slightly more difficult, and those attempting to move through it must use their action to clear pathways through the plants while the area is considered to be lightly obscured. What the Faded do not know is that the cornfields are overrun with shadows patiently waiting to take the Faded when they fade completely. Those who lose their memories become prey after they forfeit their fear, walk into the fields, and disappear to the creatures lurking in the corn.

Characters might encounter several challenges when traveling through or around the cornfields.

The Walkways

The walkways consist of pathways cut through the corn. Corn shafts cover the floor of each walkway. The many shadows lurking in the rows take advantage of this when laying their traps to snare travelers. It is also worth noting that the shadows can alter the shape of the walkways and the surrounding cornfields in a limited fashion.

Pit Traps

The shadows place the pit traps strategically along the walkways to capture their prey, then rush from the surrounding fields and swarm victims trapped within them. While the pits are only simple traps, the Faded do not possess memories of the pits and simply remember that those who travel the walkways suddenly disappear.

When traveling the walkways, each time the characters enter a new hex, roll 1d6 to determine the location of the pit trap. A roll of a 1–2 means it's near where the characters entered the hex; a 3–4 means it's somewhere in the middle of the path; and 5–6 means it's near where the path exits the hex. The shadows use these **hidden pit traps** covered with shafts of corn. Characters have a 1-in-6 chance to discern something odd about the pathways. If a character falls into a pit trap, **1d4 shadows** rush to attack.

Shadows (1d4): HD 2+2; **AC** 7[12]; **Atk** touch (1d4 + strength drain); **Move** 12; **Save** 16; **AL** C; **CL/XP** 4/120; **Special:** +1 or better magic weapons to hit, strength drain (1 point with hit, death at 0 strength). (*Monstrosities* 418)

In the Fields

Soon after any living creature leaves a walkway and enters the fields, they attract the attention of a group of **1d4 shadows**. The creatures surround targets and attempt to isolate them by driving them into pit traps and confuse or entangle any stragglers.

To determine where the shadows strike, each time the characters enter a new hex, roll 1d6 with a roll of 1–2 indicating the ambush happens as they enter the hex; 3–4 in the middle of the hex; and 5–6 as they leave the hex.

Shadows (1d4): HD 2+2; **AC** 7[12]; **Atk** touch (1d4 + strength drain); **Move** 12; **Save** 16; **AL** C; **CL/XP** 4/120; **Special:** +1 or better magic weapons to hit, strength drain (1 point with hit, death at 0 strength). (**Monstrosities** 418)

V2. Well of Empty Promises

Characters crossing the causeway the Faded call the Bridge of Bones enter a massive cornfield growing upon the ruins of what appears to be an aqueduct. The cornfields are dense, as if no one has traveled here for countless eons. The ground consists only of dry gray dust and broken bone that spills into the empty aqueduct's cracked stone channels. Determine the encounters in this region using the **In the Fields** section above. If you feel like you want to increase the challenges in this section, add **1d4 shadows** to each encounter.

The Desiccation

In addition to the cornfields and shadows, the Well of Empty Promises saps water from the environment. Every time the characters travel a distance of one hex, all water (mundane or magical) is mysteriously reduced in volume. Living creatures whose bodies rely on water must succeed on a saving throw or take 1d6 points of damage. Any water they carry is also reduced by one pint. Potions and other magical fluids are also subject to this effect. For each hex the characters enter, roll a d20 to determine if the item has lost enough water to become nonfunctional. A roll of 1 means the potion or item is desiccated and becomes useless.

V3. The Temple of Hearts

The causeway here leads through a path cut into the cornfields. In the distance, toward the middle of the island, a long, rectangular temple of dark grayish stone rises from the cornfield. Two rows of Faded stand on the opposite side of the bridge. However, these individuals hold spears and shields. They stare intently at the causeway, their expressions still and stoic.

As the characters draw closer, they quickly confirm the gruesome rumors told to them by the people of Teotlachimalli. These people have gaping holes in their chest that expose where their hearts have been torn out.

Halfway across the causeway, a Faded woman calls out to the characters, "Have you brought us the jadeite!"

If the characters answer "no" or something similar that denies they have any jadeite, the Faded one responds, "We need jadeite to enter the Realm of the Dead. Do not return until you have brought the sacrifice."

If the characters respond by giving any indication that they have jadeite, the Faded responds extremely favorably. The crier again calls out, "Honored champions, we have waited for your coming since the dawn of eternity. Come!

Designer's Note

The Faded stuck on this island do not possess the jadeite they need to cross into Miquito. They are not asking for the jadeite to allow the characters proper passage, but seek to take the jadeite for themselves. If the characters give them their jadeite, they may not have enough to make an offering to the oracle.

And let all the spoils of the Temple of Hearts be your blessing!" As the Faded finishes speaking, the others watching the causeway lower their arms and bow, throwing husks of corn into the pathway in celebration and to honor the characters.

At this point, the characters are free to cross the causeway and enter the island. The Faded who had been speaking rushes to meet them. She introduces herself as Cimoya and tells them that meeting them is her greatest honor.

If asked why, she responds with a broad smile and tells them, "Because you are our saviors, of course." She then attempts to usher them into the temple.

If the characters go to the temple, go to the **Incident at the Temple of Hearts** section below. If they refuse, go to the **A Moment of Truth** section.

The Incident at the Temple of Hearts

The temple is several hundred feet long and stepped with three large sections all splattered with dark black stains that dried in dripping formations down the gray stone walls. A long flight of steps ascends the face and enters it through an archway at the top step. On either side of the staircase, a steady line of people hefting sacks on great wooden yokes laboriously tread up and down in a stream that runs out of the entrance and around the temple toward another road leading down a pathway through the corn to somewhere off in the distance.

If the characters enter the temple with Cimoya, she shows them their gift, a great pool of blood collected from the hearts of thousands of lost travelers who have made an offering to the God's Shield in a desperately misguided effort to summon his agents to bring them jadeite.

Steps lead through a towering arch of stone opening into the temple. On either side of the staircase, the unadorned walls bear hundreds of dark, splatter-shaped stains. The workers on one side lug their loads as they carry them out of the temple, while others climb the opposite side of stairs with empty bags presumably to refill them and carry them back out again.

Atop the stairs, an archway flanks a stone landing overlooking a massive stone pool filled with viscous black liquid. About five feet above the surface of the pool, a walkway traces its perimeter. Webbing hangs from various points along the walkway, and smaller causeways traverse the pool and lead to several pillars rising from the murk. Atop each of the pillars is a stone altar with a ceremonial obsidian dagger resting on its center, presumably to cut out the hearts of human sacrifices.

At this point, the characters likely realize that the Faded do not want the jadeite as their payment, but instead have some sort of need for it themselves. The gift that Cimoya offers the characters is the blood, for she believes they have come as representatives of the God's Shield who has finally come to accept their sacrifices in exchange for the jadeite they need to bring them to their final resting place. Should Cimoya discover this is not the case, she becomes angry and turns on them. Go to the **A Moment of Truth** below.

A Moment of Truth

Cimoya at first becomes confused, asking the characters why they do not want to receive their blessings. When it becomes clear that the characters are not their saviors, she becomes angry and demands they hand over the jadeite they need to finish their journey. If the characters deny these people jadeite, the heartless people beg for jadeite. They weep and prostrate themselves before them, blocking their path as others slip behind to rummage through their possessions in a desperate attempt to steal anything resembling the precious sacred stone. As soon as they find anything resembling jadeite, they greedily grab it and flee toward the last causeway. Those denied jadeite or pushed back by the characters howl and curse them as demons and torturers.

Characters can flee Cimoya and her allies by exiting from whence they came or by taking **The Blood Baggers' Path** that appears below. They can also duck into the surrounding cornfields. While the Faded will not pursue them out of fear of the shadows, the shadows eagerly attack mortal trespassers. Again, determine their actions using the **In the Fields** section above and add **1d4 shadows** if necessary

THE BLOOD BAGGERS' PATH

Consumed with their toil, the blood baggers pay no mind to the characters taking this route and do nothing to help or hinder their journey. Instead, they work tirelessly to appease their god, walking the long journey from the Temple of Hearts to the temple on the last island. They do not stop and refuse to be interrupted. If forcibly stopped, they attempt to push back and complete their efforts. However, if they drop their loads and spill any of the black fluids, they scream hellishly and run straight for the edge of the islands. If they do not disappear into the corn and reach the edge, they then jump off, flinging themselves into the Great Void to drift off into infinity. The black fluid is blood, though in the void it has changed its consistency, scent, and color to something duller and far less lifelike.

As the characters travel down the path, the final Void Island comes into view. To describe it, read or paraphrase the following text:

V4. DISCIPLES OF THE DYING GOD

The temple holds a great hollow sarcophagus carved from the surrounding rock, in which his form has been reconstructed from cornstalks and clay, along with those parts they managed to recover, along with blood and other sacrifices taken from the Faded and other travelers who unwittingly passed through their domain. For centuries, the god's devoted followers have been trying to restore him by siphoning materials from other islands, the last little bit of life and hope to which they still cling.

The last island in this archipelago once served as a peaceful resting place for at least some of the Forgotten Gods that Tlatoani presumably hurled into the Great Void. Throughout the cornfields are the remnants of dozens of crumbling monuments, battered totems, defaced images, and ancient obelisks, all of which are toppled and smashed. These gods were captured and slain just centuries after their arrival. Logic suggests that Tlatoani is likely responsible for the carnage, but no vestiges of Notos' former divine ruler have ever been found in the Great Void. Whoever or whatever destroyed the Forgotten Gods and their faithful worshippers ultimately ground them into a sludge that now pollutes the River Miquiatoyatl.

The island also hides several pieces of the god of justice Iquixilli, whose body was dismembered and scattered through the void when the other Forgotten Gods met their unfortunate end. For thousands of years, his followers have searched the void, seeking these remains in hopes of restoring him. Upon discovering this location, they erected a great temple and seek to pump life back into them presumably to exact justice against the entity who destroyed him along with the other Forgotten Gods and their devout followers.

The followers of Iquixilli are strange, bluish-colored humans that the Faded refer to as sightless servants. These sightless servants keep their ever-bleeding eyes wrapped in bandages and believe that by restoring Iquixilli, their god will avenge his death and reveal to them the secrets of attaining godhood in reward for their actions and devotion.

A single **sightless servant** stands posted every 100 + 1d20 feet along the perimeter of Blood Bagger's Road. While they supposedly keep a sharp lookout for trespassers, they have grown lax in their duty. They remain in their lackluster state of attentiveness until they spot at least one intruder.

Sightless Servant (varies): HD 8; **AC** 6[13]; **Atk** macuahuitl (1d8); **Move** 12; **Save** 8; **AL** N; **CL/XP** 9/1100; **Special:** life drain. (see **Appendix A: New Monsters**)
Equipment: macuahuitl[B].
[B] See **Appendix B: New Equipment and Magic Items**

Entering the heavily guarded temple is near impossible. Nonetheless, stealthy characters able to ascend to the fourth level can see into it from several small openings. Far below, the god's great sarcophagus lies in the middle of the chamber as blood spills down from the pool above, soaking into the clay-and-cornstalk form. The runoff from this gory ritual flows out the back of the temple, traveling between two cleared cornfields and toward a strange opening surrounded by brambles. While the void continues beyond the opening, the opening appears to pierce the void, traveling into it, or through it, rather than across its expanse.

V5. THE MIQUIATOYATL

The next passage leading to Miquito is located where the brambles open. Here, the characters find the entrance to Miquiatoyatl, the Black River that marks the border between the Great Void and several of its adjacent planes. How the characters navigate the river falls upon them; however, the most likely means of transportation is a boat or raft.

Characters attempting to collect resources to make a boat must be industrious, as there is not much material available for them to use. Plenty of dried cornstalks can be used to make lashings and such, though they are not reliable or strong. Rope proves a far better option. Some characters might carry items such as blankets to help with the construction. The blood baggers' yokes are wood and can easily serve as planks, though if characters rob or slay more than 10 + 1d4 of the laborers, they can expect a group of **1d3 + 1 sightless servants** to investigate their disappearances. The characters may also attempt to gather wood from other sources such as the drawbridge (or parts of it), weapons, buckets, or magic. Feel free to encourage and reward characters for being industrious.

Sightless Servant (1d3+1): HD 8; **AC** 6[13]; **Atk** macuahuitl (1d8); **Move** 12; **Save** 8; **AL** N; **CL/XP** 9/1100; **Special:** life drain. (see **Appendix A: New Monsters**)
Equipment: macuahuitl[B].
[B] See **Appendix B: New Equipment and Magic Items**

When the characters figure out a way to travel the Miquiatoyatl, introduce the next section with the text below. Note, however, that although the black river hides within the strange living brambles, it is still another causeway within the Great Void. Any conditions characters acquired within the void remain active during this section.

Characters can avoid all contact with the thorny tendrils by keeping to the center of the river where the tendrils cannot reach them. The tendrils qualify more as a trap than as a monster. They cannot move except for their vine-like branches, which can be damaged and destroyed.

Tendril Vine Trap

The tendril vines are plainly visible. If a character moves away from the center, the **tendril vine** lashes out at the creature. The tendrils attack as a 5HD creature and have a reach of 10 feet. If a tendril hits a target, it does 1d8 points of damage and has a 50% chance of wrapping around the target and squeezing each round thereafter for an automatic 1d8 points of damage.

Despite the thickness of the water, its current flows at a brisk speed approaching 15 mph.

While swimming through the river may be the characters' only option, living creatures in direct contact with the water take 1d4 points of damage while in the water. On occasion, the waters bubble and splash, spitting the caustic murk into the air. When this happens, they splatter onto one randomly determined creature. Characters can avoid taking 1d4 points of damage by dodging the splatter with a successful saving throw.

If a character shines light upon the murk, it reflects off hundreds of pale broken branches floating in the mire which, on closer inspection, turn out to be hundreds of bones that churn like schools of fish in the hideous muck. Although the water's blackness prevents characters from visually determining the river's depth, they can estimate from the diameter of the tunnel that the center is near 30 feet deep.

More importantly, the waters are not uninhabited. An ancient and immortal guardian known only as the **beast from below the black** dwells in its depths. This tremendous crocodilian creature lurks below, waiting to suddenly surface and pound anyone foolish enough to trespass in its territory. It can easily crush the hull of any vessel bobbing atop the water's surface, which it does so if the characters travel aboard any type of watercraft during this leg of the journey. After ramming the vehicle, the crocodilian fiend lashes out to bite and then tail slap creatures knocked overboard by its attack on the boat.

After their encounter with the beast, the characters feel as if numerous hours pass as they lazily glide forward on the slow, churning current. Whatever lies ahead in the darkness remains unknown.

Beast from Below the Black: HD 10; **HP** 75; **AC** 3[16]; **Atk** bite (3d6) and tail (1d8); **Move** 12 (swim 18); **Save** 5; **AL** C; **CL/XP** 10/1400; **Special:** breach hull (25% chance to toss boat into the air and splinter hull). (see **Appendix A: New Monsters**)

Children of Quamaxotz

Descending on the characters, **6 bat swarms** viscously attack. They create so much noise and obscure the characters' vision that they steal their attention away from the much greater threat of the waterfall looming ahead.

Bat Swarms (6): HD 3; **HP** 22, 19, 17x2, 15, 10; **AC** 8[11]; **Atk** swarm (1d6); **Move** 3 (fly 18); **Save** 14; **AL** N; **CL/XP** 3/60; **Special:** disease (20% chance).

Leap of Faith

The line is caused by light reflecting off the edge of the water, which typically means the water ends, either at a shoreline or the edge of a cliff. Since the line is straight, it is likely a cliff.

At this point, the characters are 120 feet away from the edge of a sheer cliff into which the river empties. The waters begin to flow faster, and each round the craft gets 30 feet closer to the edge, which means the characters have only three rounds to act before their craft breaches the lip of the tunnel and plummets into oblivion.

Fortunately, just opposite the waterfall about 10 feet away stands a stone ledge, nearly 30 feet across, that sits atop a column occupying the center of the cavern. The pale glowing disk stands in the center of the ledge. Characters can use whatever means they have at their disposal to traverse the gap between the tunnel and the ledge. If they can fly, that likely serves as their best option. Turning gaseous or applying similar magics also work, as does simply leaping across, which can be accomplished by rolling below their dexterity on 3d6. Those who fail are in serious trouble as the drop descends thousands of feet deep into the lowest reaches of Miquito. Any character that falls into the chasm perishes.

CHAPTER FIVE: BEYOND THE PALE PORTAL

Characters who successfully make it across the chasm find themselves on a wide stone ledge suspended within a massive cavern. A pale glow shines in the distance. As the characters approach, they notice a path of small, glimmering white stones leading toward the circle.

> The path of glimmering white stones continues forward up a stone dais and into a gaping arch carved entirely from a single block of pale white jade. In the center of the arch, a cloud of thick gray mists swirls slowly in a counterclockwise direction and obscure any from seeing beyond the arch. The mists give off a faint glow while waves of frigid air intermittently roll from the portal entrance.

A pair of divine sisters keep vigil before the Pale Portal. They are **2 xoco tepeyollotl**, the daughters of the Great Jaguar who watched the mountains during the age of the Forgotten Gods. These battle-scarred jaguar-headed priestesses paint their faces to resemble bestial skulls and wield huge macuahuitls whose jagged teeth tear at their foes with the biting coldness of death.

To pass through the portal, the characters must somehow win their favor or rush past them without getting stopped, for they hold the energies keeping the portal open. If they are slain, the Pale Portal immediately closes, forcing them to find some other means of traveling beyond it or to head back to the village unsuccessful in their attempt to reach the Judge of the Dead. The pair enjoy a great deal of autonomy in their decision-making, leaving them open to reason or granting passage to accomplish a noble purpose.

Xoco Tepeyollotls (2): HD 9; HP 47, 41; AC 4[15]; **Atk** weapon (1d8+2) or bite (1d8); **Move** 15; **Save** 6; **AL** N; **CL/XP** 11/1700; **Special:** +1 or better magic weapons to hit, fearful visage (30ft radius, save or flee as *fear* spell), immune to charm and fear, Jaguar God's sacrifice (the heart of slain being has a 45% chance of exploding and healing xoco tepeyollotl for 1d8 hit points), magic resistance (20% and reflects spell back at caster), spell-like abilities, telepathy (60ft). (see **Appendix A: New Monsters**)
Spell-like abilities: at will—*detect evil, ESP, phantasmal force*; 3/day—*nohpalli*[C], *jaguar spirit*[C]; 1/day—*palpitating heart*[C], *teleport*.
Equipment: macuahuitl[B].
[B] See **Appendix B: New Equipment and Magic Items**
[C] See **Appendix C: New Spells**

THE WIND OF DAGGERS

As the characters step through the Pale Portal, it contracts and collapses in upon itself, disappearing in a matter of seconds.

After passing through the portal, the characters exit the Great Void and now stand on the edge of one of the outermost layers of Miquito, the Realm of the Dead. Any afflictions they acquired from exposure to the void now fade and any post-Void effects now become active.

The characters detect a strange ringing sound in their ears that translates as a message of some sort that says, "Pain beyond pain to the living is but nothing to the dead." Immediately, the characters experience a 15-degree drop in temperature.

> The portal opens into a 20-foot-wide circular tunnel that continues straight for some distance until it becomes too dark to see beyond. A faint droning howl ushers from somewhere ahead.

Characters can note that the coldness comes from a steady current of air that wafts up from the tunnel and escapes out of the portal. If a character recognizes this, that individual notices that the howling winds seem to grow louder and that the temperature keeps dropping. Characters who took the *blanket of daggers* from the cave of the ancient holy man can wrap it around themselves to gain immunity to the wind's effects.

> At this point, the sound grows so loud that it makes it difficult to hear speech above the howling winds. What must be the source of the sound lies ahead: a vertical wall of whirling, razor-sharp blades made of magical energy that fills the tunnel, blocking it entirely.

The characters have reached the fabled Wind of Daggers. Legend says that the dead suffer unimaginable pain from passing through the wind and that mortals are ripped to shreds. To pass safely, there is a shroud that protects those on their death journey. This is why the dead are cloaked in blankets, though only a priestess can imbue it with the power it needs to resist the wind, and the powers which she instills must come from the dreams and heart of the deceased individual making the journey.

If the characters possess the blanket, they can use it to pass safely through the Wind of Daggers.

While the characters are within the Wind of Daggers, they must succeed on a saving throw each round or take 3d6 points of damage. On a successful save, the creature takes half as much damage. The Wind of Daggers fills 120 feet of the tunnel.

The Wind of Daggers is a permanent magical effect of godlike power that can temporarily be suppressed or bypassed, but not dispelled. Characters could attempt to *teleport* to the other side, which is still a risky proposition, or increase their speed to quickly race through the Wind of Daggers even though they cannot tell how long the tunnel extends without additional magical insight.

Emerging from the Wind of Daggers, the characters enter a haze of crimson mist so thick that they can see only the faint shadows of their allies. The mist seems near-impenetrable and cannot be cleared beyond small, 10-foot areas that quickly refill with mist the moment an effect keeping them at bay ends. The passage continues for approximately a quarter of a mile, at which point the characters detect the unmistakable stench of rotting corpses filling the air. Characters who continue for another 100 feet emerge into Innetotcayan, a vast plane surrounding the Obsidian Spire that writhes with a sea of ravenous walking corpses.

INNETOTCAYAN

> Stepping from the mist, you emerge onto a small ledge that rests nearly 60 feet above a vast plane that seems to continue for miles in every direction. Whether the plane exists in the world or elsewhere cannot be determined. The horizons and whatever reaches above, cavern or sky, are all completely masked in a crimson mist.
>
> Far below, a vast sea of desiccated corpses meanders in an eerie, lifeless circle around a huge obsidian spire resting upon a carpet of crushed bones. They shuffle slowly, occasionally plowing over others that stumble or fall to the ground where the horde tramples them to pulp. Elsewhere, more dead rise, their arms thrusting from the muddy walls as they pull themselves from the earth entirely reformed, only to again join the throng as they plod onward, over and over in a slow-moving circle around the obsidian spire.

Sitting upon the ledge overlooking the throng of the dead is a small howler monkey wearing various amulets: a skull icon carved from bone, a jade jaguar, and a sharpened obsidian shard. He wears a cloak of colorful feathers and clutches a wooden staff hardened by flames and topped with the skull of a small animal. A deep firepit filled to the rim with white ash is near him. The monkey remains nearly silent when the characters enter, and if they do not immediately spot him, he shushes them away scornfully and tells them to keep it down lest the dead find out they arrived. If the characters introduce themselves, he politely replies and gives his name as **Mocayahua**.

Mocayahua, Male Howler Monkey: HD 6; **HP** 41; **AC** 7[12]; **Atk** staff (1d6) or 2 claws (1d6); **Move** 15 (climb 12); **Save** 11; **AL** N; **CL/XP** 8/800; **Special:** +1 or better magic weapons to hit, darkvision (60ft), spell-like abilities, telepathy (60ft).
Spell-like abilities: at will—*magic missile, invisibility*; 3/day—*confusion, mirror image*; 1/day—*teleport* (to the Obsidian Spire or to the Ebon Portal only).
Equipment: cloak, staff, amulets (20 gp total).

Mocayahua's name means, "He deceives, mocks, or makes fun of," which provides an accurate description of his intent. His purpose is to watch over the entrance to Innetotcayan and dissuade the living from entering. Still, as an agent bound to maintain the cosmic balance, Mocayahua must remain somewhat neutral. This means he can barter with the characters and will not stop them from entering of their own free will nor prevent them from taking the ash. However, he does not readily help or aid them unless they attempt to barter or trade with him. While he may feign interest in several treasures or items, he is most interested in musical instruments, ancient poetry, games of chance, or riddles.

If the characters seek his counsel, he offers them the following riddle:

The answer, of course, is ash. Mocayahua has a pit full of ash — bone ash to be precise — that he created by burning the bones of the dead. As previously noted, characters can freely take the ash and use it as they wish. However, it is most effective if the characters cover their entire bodies with the ash to disguise themselves from the skeletons.

MICQUINEMI HORDE

The number of undead in the Land of the Dead is incalculable. For every walking dead that gets destroyed, more rise up and fill the void. If the characters enter the Graveyard, the horde immediately senses them and rushes to devour their living flesh. While they can attempt to fight their way through (most likely a suicidal plan), they have another option. They can join the dead and pass through the horde unharmed by covering their bodies with lard or fat and rolling in the ashes of the first race of humans. In the event the characters must fight their way through the horde, refer to the **Fighting the Horde** sidebar.

As Mocayahua informed them, the characters can use the bone ashes to mask their mortality from the dead. Characters who paint themselves with bone ash can move through the horde without immediately attracting the zombies' attention. Characters moving through the horde must shove their way through the current of lumbering corpses and are forced to move at half their normal movement. Characters can increase their movement by hacking away at the horde. However, if they attack the horde, they risk revealing themselves and being attacked. Attacking the horde allows the character to move normally.

In addition to contending with the dead roaming the ground, **4 chomtzitzimitls** circle the skies above, using their detect life ability to scan the crowd. Although Mocayahua divulges clues as to how to use the ash to bypass the horde of undead, he holds off divulging anything to the characters about the chomtzitzimitls. Instead, the impish little trickster keeps their presence secret until the characters get about halfway to the spire then yells loudly, "Oh I forgot to warn you about the chomtzitzimitls. … They can sense you just fine. … You might want to hurry it up!"

The monkey's yelling also catches the chomtzitzimitls' attention, if the characters did not already do so on their own.

Mocayahua cannot resist one last taunt. When he spots the chomtzitzimitls closing in on the characters, he jeers loudly, "Stupid humans! Did you really think you out-vexed me by solving that obviously simple riddle?"

Once the chomtzitzimitls spot living creatures, they swoop down and mercilessly attack. Badly injured characters begin to bleed or wash off their ash disguises, allowing other dead to begin to recognize them. This awakens their hunger, at which point they too start attacking the characters and forcing them to focus on moving the remaining distance to the spire before the hordes and demons shred them.

FIGHTING THE HORDE

Running a combat between the horde of shuffling corpses and the characters may seem like a daunting task, though it is not quite as difficult as you may imagine. Remember, the horde is a flavor event, with the actual combat and greatest threat coming from the chomtzitzimitls.

If the characters' disguises start to fail, or if they insanely try to plow through the horde, only calculate the damage per round. Because the horde is so tightly packed, most of the undead cannot close ranks to attack. If the characters stick together in some sort of formation (such as surrounding their weaker members or clumping together), they reduce the hordes' ability to surround an individual. Use the following table to calculate the damage the horde deals each round, dividing the damage done each round among all of the characters:

TABLE 3–3: HORDE DAMAGE PER ROUND

1d20 Roll	Damage
1–5	4
6–12	6
13–14	10
15–16	12
17–18	14
19	18
20	20

INNETOTCAYAN

Chomtzitzimitls (4): HD 6; HP 45, 40, 39, 32; AC 7[12]; Atk 2 claws (1d8 + bleeding); **Move** 9 (fly 15); **Save** 12; **AL** C; **CL/XP** 7/600; **Special:** bleeding (1d3 damage per round after successful claw attack, save resists, healing ends ongoing damage), darkvision (60ft), detect living (60ft line of sight, 60% chance). (see **Appendix A: New Monsters**)

When the characters near the spire, read or paraphrase the following description:

A character has a 3-in-6 chance to spot a jade bridge that spans the ravine, arching up to the great obsidian spire. Curiously, the bridge is clear and unoccupied by any dead.

The hordes are unable to occupy the bridge because none of them possesses the necessary fare to cross. They are damned without payment. At this time, the characters need to place the jadeite bead or plate beneath their tongues to pay the fare. Otherwise, when they reach the center of the bridge, they trigger the trap.

FARE COLLECTION

If the characters have not defeated the chomtzitzimitls yet, the demons spot them the second they step onto the bridge and swoop in to make a final attempt to prevent them from crossing. If they defeated the demons and place the fare beneath their tongues, they are free to cross. However, if anyone did not first remove their soul before entering beyond this point, they immediately die unless they succeed on a saving throw with a –8 penalty to jump back at the last minute. Nonetheless, a successful saving throw reduces characters to half their current hit points from the near-death experience.

The characters cannot speak during the final passage and must carry a jade bead or plate in their mouth. Each mortal must offer its jadeite bead or plate to the oracle as payment.

THE ORACLE OF THE EMPTY MOON

The huge woman seated on the throne is a **Daughter of Chalatihuatl**, one of the goddess's many daughters who in turn serve as the Oracle of the Empty Moon. The misanthropic humanoids are **20 lemures**, failed reconstructions of humans fashioned from the remains of those fallen in each of the cataclysms.

Daughter of Chalatihuatl: HD 15; HP 110; AC 0[19]; Atk +3 *flaming spear* (3d6+3 + 1d6 fire); **Move** 15 (fly 18); **Save** 3; **AL** N; **CL/XP** 20/4400; **Special:** +2 or better magic weapons to hit, cry of the damned (at will, screech causes *confusion* [as spell] for 2d4 rounds, save resists), immune to cold and fire, magic resistance (25%), spells (6/6/6/5/5/2). (see **Appendix A: New Monsters**) **Spells:** 1st—*cure light wounds* (x2), *detect evil* (x2), *detect magic*, *light*; 2nd—*bless, heat metal, hold person, silence 15ft radius, speak with animals, warp wood*; 3rd—*call lightning, continual light, plant growth, prayer, remove curse, speak with dead*; 4th—*cure serious wounds, hallucinatory forest, neutralize poison, dispel magic, insect plague*; 5th—*commune, control winds, finger of death, quest, raise dead*; 6th—*blade barrier, word of recall*. **Equipment:** +3 *flaming spear*.

Lemure Demons (20): HD 3; HP 17 each; AC 7[12]; Atk claw (1d3); **Move** 3; **Save** 14; **AL** C; **CL/XP** 4/120; **Special:** regenerate (1hp/round). (*Monstrosities* 99)

The characters now face overwhelming odds. However, they have been sent to speak with the oracle and hopefully know better than to fight her. If they resort to violence over reason, refer to the **This Means War!** sidebar below.

The oracle knows why the characters have come, though she believes them to be arrogant and foolish to have gone through the trouble, especially without having brought her a proper sacrifice. Throughout their interaction, she remains aloof, possibly amused and perfectly willing to let the mortals play out their dramas. In the end, she has the child's soul and is content to present that to her mother as their offering.

If the characters question her about the boy, she can tell them that much. She makes it clear that the herdsman offered her a sacrifice, and she is pleased with the boy he presented.

If told that the boy is not the sacrifice, she seems unfazed and perfectly willing to keep him anyway. Characters can continue to discuss the matter

THIS MEANS WAR!

It is hoped that the characters realize that the oracle is an extremely powerful entity who is quite capable of destroying them. However, if they do not, they can certainly attempt to fight her, but this course of action likely results in their deaths. If the characters defeat her, the hordes of the dead and the chomtzitzimitls surrounding the spire are now free to pursue the characters. If this occurs, their death is certain. The oracle is only one of many daughters of Chalatihuatl, and another one of them quickly steps in to serve in the position. As for the characters, the oracle or Chalatihuatl is so bemused by their effort that the characters do not die but instead awaken in the grave-pits. They all have splitting headaches and horrible nightmares reminding them that the Goddess of Sacrifice demands Xotaxtl as her payment. While the characters do not have quite as much information as if they had conversed with the oracle, they are free to attempt to finish the adventure.

with her, as she is not toying with them and cares only that she has a suitable sacrifice to present to her mother at the start of the festival.

If the characters offer one of their own souls as a sacrifice, she accepts the exchange and hands them a small jade bead containing the boy's soul. If they return, they must place the soul beneath the child's tongue, wash him in the temple bath, and wait until his skin returns to a normal color. They must then crush the bead and spill its dust upon the gate to the Great Void. The sacrificed character remains in Miquito forever.

Alternately, if the characters question the oracle for other means of aiding the boy, she tells them they can undo the curse by delivering the soul of the sorcerer who failed to recognize the omens and the coming of the alux as a sign that the Forgotten Gods had accepted the herdsman's peccaries as a suitable sacrifice despite his intentions for the beasts. She looks at the characters sternly and emphasizes that Xotaxtl's failure alone created the current chain of events and that means he alone must pay the cost of recompense. The characters likely witnessed an alux devour Xotaxtl, which may lead them to believe his soul has already passed into the next world. However, the Oracle of the Empty Moon assures them that Xotaxtl's soul still resides within the alux who ate him and thus can be brought to her for judgment.

CHAPTER SIX: FINAL FRONT

In this section of the adventure, the characters return to Cintlipetl to discover it is under siege by a horde of renegade aluxes whose leader Xotaxtl Nitlocati rallies his kin to take back the world from the human usurpers. He seeks to conquer the villagers and turn them into slaves for his new empire.

Events that Transpire During This Time: After a violent lumbering alux of the First Sun killed and ate the sorcerer, its mind and body were flooded with innate and bloodborne arcane powers that transformed the creature into a higher version of itself that demands its followers call it Xotaxtl Nitlocati. Using its powers, Xotaxtl Nitlocati began seeking out other aluxes and preaching to them to help him carry out the prophecy it believes it was rebirthed to lead: the reclaiming of the Material Realms that the Forgotten Gods stole from its kind during the earlier cataclysms. In its first order of attack, it leads a horde of aluxes on a raid upon Cintlipetl in which its kin do what the Forgotten Gods did to them, by either slaughtering or enslaving everyone.

THE SIEGE OF CINTLIPETL

If the characters agree to bring Xotaxtl to face her judgment, the Oracle of the Empty Moon offers to return them to the land of the living but warns that if the debt is not paid, all of them are obligated to assume it. If the characters accept, she marks all of them on the forehead with a single smeary line of black soot. Make the characters aware that they have until the calendar shifts to complete their task, a time equivalent to approximately six days. If they do not complete the task, she immediately slays all of them and takes their souls as payment.

When the characters settle on a course of action with the oracle, she summons a massive swarm of choms that descend upon the ledge. A small flock grabs each of the characters and wings them straight into the searing sky, hundreds of feet upward to where a single hole directly above the spire pierces the red mists. The light beyond is blinding. At this point, all of the surviving characters pass out, drawing this section of the adventure to a close.

GRAVE AWAKENINGS

Climbing from their grave-pits, the characters immediately note that they are decorated in funerary trappings and all have unusually pale, corpse-like complexions. The pallid skin is a secondary effect from their journey, and it does not return to normal until they retrieve their souls.

Checking their surroundings, they determine that they are back at the edge of the Corpsewood. The sun is just rising. They have no idea how long they have been gone, though it feels as if they are still within the Harvest Season.

Characters soon catch the last glimpse of the Bloodmoon dipping below the horizon, confirming that only a day or two has passed.

The village lies about a day's walk to the west.

The characters have little time to stop the siege before the entire village is wiped out. Unfortunately, they are wildly outnumbered and a direct assault seems suicidal, especially without their souls.

Run the siege by allowing the characters to use strategies to stop the siege by addressing specific events individually. As they successfully handle each of the events, they gain points that help them in the final conflict against Xotaxtl Nitlocati.

CONTAIN AND QUELL FIRES

Many of the homes in the village have thatched roofs, particularly the smaller hovels of the common folk who live along the perimeter. The alux assailants began their attack by setting several of these homes on fire across the main roads leading into Cintlipetl. Winds now spread the conflagration across open ground as the arsonists attempt to direct it toward the center of the village.

When the characters first arrive, three separate bands of arsonists have set several rows of buildings ablaze in **Areas 6**, **7**, and **8**. They continue to set additional buildings on fire each round, and the combined power of the arsonists and the wind set an area of 30 square feet of flammable buildings or materials ablaze each round. Each band of arsonists defeated decreases the spread of fire by five square feet. The characters can also attempt to douse flames using magic or ingenuity, such as by smothering areas with water or soil. If the characters defeat all the arsonists, they save this section of town and allow several of the village's warriors to help them with the fighting. In this case, **4 Aztli fighters** join them. They can direct them to create distractions or fight forces in other sections of the village to help the characters complete further tasks. If the characters contain or extinguish the fire and successfully prevent it from spreading through the rest of the village, feel free to award one of the characters with Inspiration.

Aztli Fighters, Male or Female Aztli Warriors (4): HD 5; AC 7[12]; **Atk** club (1d4) or longbow x2 (1d6); **Move** 12; **Save** 12; **AL** N; **CL/XP** 5/240; **Special:** none. (*Monstrosities* 257)
Equipment: club, longbow, 10 arrows.

TABLE 3–4: ARSONIST BANDS

1	**Torchers. Three aluxes of the Second Sun** and **2 aluxes of the First Sun** rush through the middle of the street hurling jars of alchemist's fire and lit torches.
2	**Bowyers. Two aluxes of the Second Sun snipers** shoot lit arrows wrapped in oil-soaked rags at buildings while **2 aluxes of the First Sun** spur **2 agitated dogs** on a wild rampage up the streets with flaming stalks of corn tied to their tails. They attack any villagers in their way as they unwittingly create a wake of flames.
3	**Barrels. Three aluxes of the First Sun,** each carrying a barrel of flaming coals, shuffle down the street. They take the coal barrels and roll them at houses or at characters attempting to stop them. When rolling, the barrels spill coals that deal 2d6 points of damage and scatter the coals across the street where they burn for one minute. Rolling barrels travel in a straight line and move 60 feet per round for 1d6 rounds until they hit an object and shatter, dealing 3d6 points of damage from the burning coals. Any character who makes a successful saving throw avoids taking damage from the coals altogether.

Alux of the First Sun: HD 10; AC 7[12]; **Atk** bash (2d6); **Move** 15; **Save** 5; **AL** Any; **CL/XP** 10/1400; **Special:** camouflage (80% chance to hide in hilly or mountainous terrain), darkvision (60ft), immune to fear, trigger rockslide (3/day, create 10ft wide rockslide, 3d6 damage, save for half), vulnerable to obsidian (200% damage). (see **Appendix A: New Monsters**)

Alux of the Second Sun: HD 6; AC 7[12]; **Atk** weapon (1d8) or bite (1d6), slam (2d4); **Move** 12; **Save** 11; **AL** Any; **CL/XP** 6/400; **Special:** backstab (x3), camouflage (80% chance to hide in hilly or mountainous terrain), darkvision (60ft), vulnerable to obsidian (200% damage). (see **Appendix A: New Monsters**)

Alux of the Second Sun Sniper: HD 6; AC 7[12]; **Atk** longbow x2 (1d6+2) or bite (1d6), slam (2d4); **Move** 12; **Save** 11; **AL** Any; **CL/XP** 6/400; **Special:** +2 bonus to hit and damage with missile weapons, backstab (x3), camouflage (80% chance to hide in hilly or mountainous terrain), darkvision (60ft), vulnerable to obsidian (200% damage). (see **Appendix A: New Monsters**)

Dog: HD 1; AC 7[12]; **Atk** bite (1d3); **Move** 15; **Save** 17; **CL/XP** 1/15; **Special:** none. (*Monstrosities* 127)

FREE THE CAPTIVES

When the invaders first attacked, they snuck into homes and captured many of the villagers while they were resting or otherwise unprepared. Those captured, particularly warriors or others who might put up a fight, were brutally beaten and bound and then taken to nearby pits where they are now being held captive. The aluxes have scattered 14 prisoners throughout the Clay Pits (see **Area 9**). They paired or grouped some together, while others of greater threat are kept isolated.

To prevent any escapes or rescue attempts, **6 chom swarms** keep watch around the perimeter of the pits. When they spot intruders, they warn **3 aluxes of the Second Sun** and an **alux of the First Sun** that stand guard over the pits.

Alux of the First Sun: HD 10; HP 61; AC 7[12]; **Atk** bash (2d6); **Move** 15; **Save** 5; **AL** Any; **CL/XP** 10/1400; **Special:** camouflage (80% chance to hide in hilly or mountainous terrain), darkvision (60ft), immune to fear, trigger rockslide (3/day, create 10ft wide rockslide, 3d6 damage, save for half), vulnerable to obsidian (200% damage). (see **Appendix A: New Monsters**)

Alux of the Second Sun (3): HD 6; HP 42, 34, 26; AC 7[12]; **Atk** weapon (1d8) or bite (1d6), slam (2d4); **Move** 12; **Save** 11; **AL** Any; **CL/XP** 6/400; **Special:** backstab (x3), camouflage (80% chance to hide in hilly or mountainous terrain), darkvision (60ft), vulnerable to obsidian (200% damage). (see **Appendix A: New Monsters**)

Chom Swarms (6): HD 5; HP 36, 32, 27, 21; AC 5[14]; **Atk** swarm (1d8); **Move** 4 (fly 18); **Save** 12; **AL** N; **CL/XP** 7/600; **Special:** cast omen (1/day, targets meeting gaze of flock, save or −1 to hit, saves, and damage for 24 hours), mimicry (simple sounds), soul steal (against incapacitated or sleeping foe, soul is stolen and held within the flock, save avoids). (see **Appendix A: New Monsters**)

Pit 1: *Family Tied.* This pit holds a small family consisting of a man, a woman, and their two young children. The man is bound and unconscious, and bleeding from a head injury. The woman is unbound, but her arm is broken. The mother desperately attempts to keep her two terrified children from crying.

Aztli Adults (2): HD 5, 3; AC 9[10]; **Atk** club (1d4); **Move** 12; **Save** 18; **AL** N; **CL/XP** B/10; **Special:** none. (*Monstrosities* 254)

Aztli Children (2): HD 2, 1; AC 9[10]; **Atk** none; **Move** 12; **Save** 18; **AL** Any; **CL/XP** A/10; **Special:** none. (*Monstrosities* 254)

Pit 2: *Naxutilli.* This pit holds two bodies, one recently slain from having his neck broken when the aluxes pushed him into the pit. The second is a muscular woman decorated with numerous ritual scars. She has two black eyes and a swollen nose from being struck in the face while sleeping. Her injuries have reduced her to 3 hit points. Her name is Naxutilli. If healed, she eagerly joins the fight to save her village.

Naxutilli, Female Aztli Warrior: HD 5; HP 36 (currently 3); AC 7[12]; **Atk** club (1d4) or longbow x2 (1d6); **Move** 12; **Save** 12; **AL** N; **CL/XP** 5/240; **Special:** none. (*Monstrosities* 257)
Equipment: club, longbow, 10 arrows.

Pit 3: *Council Secrets.* This pit imprisons **3 middle-aged men.** All are bound and gagged. They are wearing fine clothing that denotes their status as either pochtecas or nobles. They were captured outside the temple by the first wave of aluxes that snuck into the village to clear the streets before the main attack. One of these men is Atlysis, the husband of Cothoti, one of the women serving on the town council. If the characters free him, Atlysis joins their fight and can direct them to where the headman and council members are holed up.

MOLYATL'S HUT

The hut is located somewhere in the village not overrun by fire. You can have the characters discover it before saving Molyatl or even if they do not manage to find or rescue the warrior. Read or paraphrase the following description:

> The inside of this small hut shows signs of an intense struggle, with much of the furniture and other contents toppled over or smashed.

Any character who scans the contents and décor of this small hut determines it is the residence of a powerful warrior blessed by the gods of the village to protect it. Any characters who search the hut can uncover some items wrapped in cloth that are stashed in a shallow dugout beneath the sleeping pallet.

Treasure: The cloth-wrapped items are a macuahuitl that turns out to be a *macuahuitl of Quiahuitl* (see **Appendix B: New Equipment and Magic Items**) and a wooden mask carved to resemble a jaguar covered with gold trim and jadeite inlays that is a *mask of Quiahuitl* (see **Appendix B: New Equipment and Magic Items**).

Aztli Nobles, Male Aztli (3): HD 6, 3x2; AC 9[10]; Atk club
(1d4); Move 12; Save 18; AL N; CL/XP B/10; Special: none.
(*Monstrosities* 254)

Pit 4: *Favored of Quiahuitl.* The aluxes took no chances with this warrior.
They chopped off one of his legs, and he is now swiftly bleeding to death.
Upon discovering him, the characters quickly realize he is unconscious
and bleeding out. He must receive magical healing. Otherwise, he dies. If
characters save him and bring him back to consciousness, he tells them his
name is Molyatl. He is one of the chief warriors from his village. He cannot
fight in his condition. However, he tells the characters where he stashed his
macuahuitl and helmet, both of which are blessed by the gods. If the characters
go to Molyatl's hut, they find the items.

Molyatl, Male Aztli Warrior: HP 34 (currently 3); AC 7[12]; Atk
macuahuitl of Quiahuitl (1d8) or longbow x2 (1d6); Move 12; Save
12; AL L; CL/XP 5/240; Special: none. (*Monstrosities* 257)
Equipment: *macuahuitl of Quiahuitl* [B], longbow, 10 arrows.
[B] See **Appendix B: New Equipment and Magic Items**

Pit 5: *The Scorpions.* Three villagers frantically cling to the pit walls,
desperately attempting to remain as still and silent as death.

Scorpion Death Rig Trap

The sadistic aluxes rigged an insidious trap in which they tied a scorpion to
the backs of all three prisoners, and then lashed the tails of the **3 large scorpions**
together with three long strings. At present, the victims are positioned so that
all the strings are just taut enough to prevent the scorpions from stinging them.
If any of the strings break or if any of the villagers change their position and
cause the strings to go slack, the scorpions can sting them with their tails. The
prisoners are too scared to move or speak. The secret to freeing the individuals
is to simultaneously incapacitate or kill all three scorpions.

If the characters defeat the guards and help the individuals escape, one of
them gives them a small carving hidden in their robes.

Aztli Adults, Male or Female Commoners (3): HD 6, 4x2; AC
9[10]; Atk club (1d4); Move 12; Save 18; AL N; CL/XP B/10;
Special: none. (*Monstrosities* 254)

Large Scorpions (3): HD 2; HP 14, 10, 8; AC 6[13]; Atk 2 pincers
(1d4), sting (1d3 + lethal poison); Move 12; Save 16; AL N; CL/XP
3/60; Special: lethal poison (save or die). (*Monstrosities* 411)

Treasure: The carving gifted to the players is a *figurine of the onyx dog.*

Pit 6: *The Warriors.* Two warriors anxiously pace the bottom of this pit.
Both put up a good fight, and the aluxes barely managed to imprison them.
The aluxes had such difficulty capturing them that they were unable to bind
them first. To remedy the situation, they called a **chomtzitzimitl** to keep watch
at the mouth of the pit to prevent the warriors from getting out. The demon
concentrates on teasing and harassing the victims in the pit. Therefore, until
it is attacked or until someone creates a huge distraction, the sadistic creature
doesn't notice the characters.

If freed, the **2 warriors** are eager to get back to fighting.

Chomtzitzimitl: HD 6; HP 43; AC 7[12]; Atk 2 claws (1d8 +
bleeding); Move 9 (fly 15); Save 12; AL C; CL/XP 7/600; Special:
bleeding (1d3 damage per round after successful claw attack, save
resists, healing ends ongoing damage), darkvision (60ft), detect
living (60ft line of sight, 60% chance). (see **Appendix A: New
Monsters**)

Male Aztli Warriors (2): HD 5; HP 33, 28; AC 7[12]; Atk club
(1d4) or longbow x2 (1d6); Move 12; Save 12; AL N; CL/XP 5/240;
Special: none. (*Monstrosities* 257)
Equipment: club, longbow, 10 arrows.

Rescue Camaxtl

After the first wave of attacks hit Cintlipetl, Camaxtl led Coaxoch, a few of
the council members, and a small group of **6 warriors** to the courthouses to
muster a quick defense. Unfortunately, the alux forces were too well organized

and flooded into the city with such efficiency that Camaxtl and his allies
became trapped in the building before they could lead a counterattack.

Male and Female Aztli Warriors (6): HD 5; HP 36, 32, 30x2, 27; AC
7[12]; Atk club (1d4) or longbow x2 (1d6); Move 12; Save 12; AL N;
CL/XP 5/240; Special: none. (*Monstrosities* 257)
Equipment: club, longbow, 10 arrows.

Xotaxtl Nitlocati believes Camaxtl the Headman is hiding Ohtli, whom
he refers to as the Betrayer. He sent four alux warbands to surround the
courthouse, seize Camaxtl, and drag him to the temple so he can torture him
into revealing the location of the Betrayer and then destroy him and all his
opponents in a single act. Each of the warbands lays siege to one of the sides
of the courthouse as described below.

1. North Side. A row of five windows runs the length of this side of the
courthouse, but there are no ground-level entrances. An **alux of the First
Sun** and **2 aluxes of the Second Sun snipers** monitor this side, trying to
sniff out any potential escapees and sniping at anyone nearing the windows.
Additionally, **3 chom swarms** fly overhead. They issue an alert when anyone
other than an alux approaches.

Alux of the First Sun: HD 10; HP 58; AC 7[12]; Atk bash (2d6);
Move 15; Save 5; AL C; CL/XP 10/1400; Special: camouflage (80%
chance to hide in hilly or mountainous terrain), darkvision (60ft),
immune to fear, trigger rockslide (3/day, create 10ft wide rockslide,
3d6 damage, save for half), vulnerable to obsidian (200% damage).
(see **Appendix A: New Monsters**)

Aluxes of the Second Sun Snipers (2): HD 6; HP 45, 37; AC 7[12];
Atk longbow x2 (1d6+2) or bite (1d6), slam (2d4); Move 12; Save
11; AL C; CL/XP 6/400; Special: +2 bonus to hit and damage with
missile weapons, backstab (x3), camouflage (80% chance to hide
in hilly or mountainous terrain), darkvision (60ft), vulnerable to
obsidian (200% damage). (see **Appendix A: New Monsters**)

Chom Swarms (3): HD 5; HP 33, 28, 22; AC 5[14]; Atk swarm (1d8);
Move 4 (fly 18); Save 12; AL N; CL/XP 7/600; Special: cast omen
(1/day, targets meeting gaze of flock, save or −1 to hit, saves, and
damage for 24 hours), mimicry (simple sounds), soul steal (against
incapacitated or sleeping foe, soul is stolen and held within the flock,
save avoids). (see **Appendix A: New Monsters**)

2. West Side. On the second floor, a narrow balcony frames a series of
windows that overlook the plateau. Dug into the ground, a cellar door allows
access to a basement. **Three aluxes of the Second Sun snipers** watch the
windows, while **2 aluxes of the First Sun** wait near the cellar door with
their backs pressed against the building. **Two chom swarms** watch from the
window balconies and squawk alarms if they spot anyone approaching.

Aluxes of the First Sun (2): HD 10; HP 60, 48; AC 7[12]; Atk bash
(2d6); Move 15; Save 5; AL C; CL/XP 10/1400; Special: camouflage
(80% chance to hide in hilly or mountainous terrain), darkvision
(60ft), immune to fear, trigger rockslide (3/day, create 10ft wide
rockslide, 3d6 damage, save for half), vulnerable to obsidian (200%
damage). (see **Appendix A: New Monsters**)

Aluxes of the Second Sun Snipers (3): HD 6; HP 47, 41, 35; AC
7[12]; Atk longbow x2 (1d6+2) or bite (1d6), slam (2d4); Move 12;
Save 11; AL C; CL/XP 6/400; Special: +2 bonus to hit and damage
with missile weapons, backstab (x3), camouflage (80% chance to hide
in hilly or mountainous terrain), darkvision (60ft), vulnerable to
obsidian (200% damage). (see **Appendix A: New Monsters**)

Chom Swarms (2): HD 5; HP 34, 27; AC 5[14]; Atk swarm (1d8);
Move 4 (fly 18); Save 12; AL N; CL/XP 7/600; Special: cast omen
(1/day, targets meeting gaze of flock, save or −1 to hit, saves, and
damage for 24 hours), mimicry (simple sounds), soul steal (against
incapacitated or sleeping foe, soul is stolen and held within the flock,
save avoids). (see **Appendix A: New Monsters**)

3. South Side. A loud rhythmic pounding comes from this side of the
building where **4 aluxes of the Second Sun** repeatedly slam against a
reinforced wooden door with a large log they are using as a makeshift battering

ram. A single round window is above the door on the second floor. Every so often, rocks and other debris fly out the window, pelting the creatures as they try to break down the door.

When the characters become aware of this encounter, give the alux door bashers another two minutes (game time) before they break the door down and gain entrance to the courthouse and its occupants. In addition, **3 chom swarms** fly overhead, keeping watch and issuing an alert if they spot anyone other than aluxes approaching the area.

Aluxes of the Second Sun (4): HD 6; HP 42, 36, 34, 28; AC 7[12]; Atk weapon (1d8) or bite (1d6), slam (2d4); **Move** 12; **Save** 11; AL C; **CL/XP** 6/400; **Special:** backstab (x3), camouflage (80% chance to hide in hilly or mountainous terrain), darkvision (60ft), vulnerable to obsidian (200% damage). (see **Appendix A: New Monsters**)

Chom Swarms (3): HD 5; HP 31, 26, 22; AC 5[14]; Atk swarm (1d8); **Move** 4 (fly 18); **Save** 12; AL N; **CL/XP** 7/600; **Special:** cast omen (1/day, targets meeting gaze of flock, save or –1 to hit, saves, and damage for 24 hours), mimicry (simple sounds), soul steal (against incapacitated or sleeping foe, soul is stolen and held within the flock, save avoids). (see **Appendix A: New Monsters**)

4. East Side. This is the main entrance to the courthouse. It has two reinforced doors and two large circular windows on the second floor. An encampment of aluxes holds a defensive formation in front of the building as a larger alux yells angrily at the courthouse as if making demands. Anyone capable of understanding Primordial Alux understands that the creatures are demanding the surrender of the individuals inside, one of them being Camaxtl the Headman. The small encampment consists of **3 aluxes of the Second Sun**, an **alux of the First Sun**, **2 aluxes of the Second Sun snipers**, and a **boarfolk warrior**. In addition, **4 chom swarms** fly overhead, keeping watch and calling an alert if they spot anyone other than aluxes approaching the area.

Reaching the headman and his allies is difficult. The characters can attempt to fight each of the warbands on their own by splitting them up and diverting their attention. Similarly, they might create a distraction using freed villagers and warriors to pin down the aluxes elsewhere, giving them an opportunity to enter the courthouse and free the headman. You may need to lower the number of creatures encountered at one time to keep them from overwhelming the characters.

Successfully rescuing Camaxtl provides the characters with two additional advantages in their fight against Xotaxtl Nitlocati. First, if Camaxtl accompanies the characters to get Ohtli, then they can readily bypass the couatl guardians (see **Recover their Souls**). Second, while Xotaxtl Nitlocati holds the Temple of the Sun, Camaxtl knows how to access a series of secret subterranean tunnels leading into the temple. Originally designed as an escape route, those entering them from the opposite direction can slip into the main room undetected, entering into a secret chamber hidden directly under the throne (see **The Final Confrontation**).

Alux of the First Sun: HD 10; HP 56; AC 7[12]; Atk bash (2d6); **Move** 15; **Save** 5; AL C; **CL/XP** 10/1400; **Special:** camouflage (80% chance to hide in hilly or mountainous terrain), darkvision (60ft), immune to fear, trigger rockslide (3/day, create 10ft wide rockslide, 3d6 damage, save for half), vulnerable to obsidian (200% damage). (see **Appendix A: New Monsters**)

Aluxes of the Second Sun (3): HD 6; HP 42, 34, 33; AC 7[12]; Atk weapon (1d8) or bite (1d6), slam (2d4); **Move** 12; **Save** 11; AL C; **CL/XP** 6/400; **Special:** backstab (x3), camouflage (80% chance to hide in hilly or mountainous terrain), darkvision (60ft), vulnerable to obsidian (200% damage). (see **Appendix A: New Monsters**)

Aluxes of the Second Sun Sniper (2): HD 6; HP 47, 39; AC 7[12]; Atk longbow x2 (1d6+2) or bite (1d6), slam (2d4); **Move** 12; **Save** 11; AL C; **CL/XP** 6/400; **Special:** +2 bonus to hit and damage with missile weapons, backstab (x3), camouflage (80% chance to hide in hilly or mountainous terrain), darkvision (60ft), vulnerable to obsidian (200% damage). (see **Appendix A: New Monsters**)

Boarfolk Warrior: HD 6; HP 41; AC 7[12]; Atk club (1d8+3) or gore (3d6); **Move** 12; **Save** 11; AL N; **CL/XP** 6/400; **Special:** darkvision (60ft). (see **Appendix A: New Monsters**)

Chom Swarms (3): HD 5; HP 33, 28, 22; AC 5[14]; Atk swarm (1d8); **Move** 4 (fly 18); **Save** 12; AL N; **CL/XP** 7/600; **Special:** cast omen (1/day, targets meeting gaze of flock, save or –1 to hit, saves, and damage for 24 hours), mimicry (simple sounds), soul steal (against incapacitated or sleeping foe, soul is stolen and held within the flock, save avoids). (see **Appendix A: New Monsters**)

Recover their Souls

Characters likely recall that Ohtli still possesses their souls and until they recover them, they risk having their souls lost or destroyed if they fall in the final conflict. To recover their souls, the characters must find the alux. Achieving this course of action ensures that the characters do not permanently die if killed. The headman hid Ohtli in the grain cellars beneath the temple.

Coaxoch summoned **4 couatls** to protect the alux. The spirit serpents stand guard over the entrance to his chamber and deny access to any who approach it without the medicine-witch. To reach Ohtli, the characters must convince the four couatls (named Iquiza, Nepantia, Onaqui, and Youal) to let them pass. The creatures are powerful and sworn to guard the alux with their lives. If necessary, they are willing to fight to the death to keep him safe. Killing the sacred creatures brings extremely bad luck. If they fight and kill a couatl, whoever participates in performing such an act suffers a –1 penalty to attacks, damage, and saves until they perform the proper sacrifice ritual to undo the damage of their actions. The ritual should involve some sort of additional quest. However, the details of such penance are not covered in this adventure.

Couatls (4): HD 8; HP 58, 55x2, 46; AC 4[15]; Atk bite (2d6 + poison), tail (1d6 constrict); **Move** 12 (fly 24); **Save** 8; AL L; **CL/XP** 11/1700; **Special:** poison (save or die), polymorph (at will), spells (3/2/1). (*Monstrosities* 73)
Spells: 1st—*charm person, magic missile, sleep*; 2nd—*ESP, phantasmal force*; 3rd—*lightning bolt.*

If the characters are in the company of Coaxoch or Camaxtl, all they must do to pass freely is to convince the couatls that the individuals they travel with are authentic. If not in the company of either of these individuals, gaining access to Ohtli is a little more challenging.

Characters could also prove they do not have souls by providing evidence that they have been to Miquito (which one cannot do with a soul). There are numerous ways to convince the couatls, but a single piece of evidence alone is not enough to convince them (neither is the testimony of a chom). For each piece of evidence the characters provide, they gain a 10% bonus to convince the couatls of their intentions. Evidence may include (but is not limited to) items taken from Miquito, accurate descriptions of some of the encounters, the *blanket of daggers*, an accurate explanation of how to work the gates, or any lasting effects a character might have from being in the Great Void.

If the characters get stuck, you can opt to have the couatls test them by offering the characters a trial by combat. The characters should, of course, refuse the trial on the grounds that if they lose, death will immediately claim their souls. Characters contemplating the gravity of this loss in front of the couatl might also aid in convincing the serpents of the sincerity of their intentions.

Once the characters gain an audience with Ohtli, he returns their souls. Ohtli offers to aid them in their fight, and he can also help them turn some of the aluxes from enemies to allies by convincing them that Xotaxtl Nitlocati's actions are misguided and as angry and capricious as the treatment they received at the hands of the Forgotten Gods. He still holds the belief that for the aluxes to prove their humanity, they must show they are human and not capricious monsters.

Similarly, the couatls offer to aid the characters in defending their village. You should decide whether they fight alongside the characters or fight against some other threats while the characters confront Xotaxtl Nitlocati at the temple in the final scene.

The Final Confrontation

After completing some or all of the tasks, the characters can finally confront Xotaxtl Nitlocati.

The would-be emperor sits on the throne in the temple overlooking his allies as they deface the walls by hacking at the sacred images and using blood and mud to paint crude and gory depictions of their own gods over the holy artwork. Xotaxtl Nitlocati delights in gorging himself on the spoils of the sacrifices and offerings intended to appease the gods during the Seven Year Harvest Festival. He commands the aluxes to throw them into a large bonfire that burns in the center of the room. A ring of large wooden posts are driven into the earthy floor around the fire. A villager is lashed to each post, including three of the council members, the herdsman's son, and his mother. The herdsman is nowhere to be seen. Swarms of choms sit high in the rafters and ledges, gazing down in the flickering light as multiple aluxes rampage and dance, feast, and fight in a bestial frenzy of elation and gleeful violence.

As noted in the description, **Xotaxtl Nitlocati** sits upon the throne. He uses **2 chom swarms** to keep watch and squawk warnings if they spot intruders. They then swoop down to attack. The rest of his entourage includes **3 aluxes of the Second Sun** and an **alux of the First Sun**. As soon as they detect intruders, they rush to attack, allowing Xotaxtl Nitlocati to use spells from a distance.

Xotaxtl Nitlocati, Alux of the First Sun: HD 10; **HP** 73; **AC** 7[12]; **Atk** bash (2d6) or macuahuitl (1d8); **Move** 15; **Save** 5; **AL** C; **CL/XP** 10/1400; **Special:** camouflage (80% chance to hide in hilly or mountainous terrain), darkvision (60ft), immune to fear, spell-like abilities, trigger rockslide (3/day, create 10ft wide rockslide, 3d6 damage, save for half), vulnerable to obsidian (200% damage). (see **Appendix A: New Monsters**)
Spell-like abilities: at will—*magic missile, darkness 15ft radius*; 3/day—*animal summoning I* (goat only), *plant growth*; 2/day—*fear, flesh to maize*[C].
Equipment: macuahuitl [B].
[B] See **Appendix B: New Equipment and Magic Items**
[C] See **Appendix C: New Spells**

Alux of the First Sun: HD 10; **HP** 71; **AC** 7[12]; **Atk** bash (2d6); **Move** 15; **Save** 5; **AL** C; **CL/XP** 10/1400; **Special:** camouflage (80% chance to hide in hilly or mountainous terrain), darkvision (60ft), immune to fear, trigger rockslide (3/day, create 10ft wide rockslide, 3d6 damage, save for half), vulnerable to obsidian (200% damage). (see **Appendix A: New Monsters**)

Aluxes of the Second Sun (3): HD 6; **HP** 45, 42, 36; **AC** 7[12]; **Atk** weapon (1d8) or bite (1d6), slam (2d4); **Move** 12; **Save** 11; **AL** C; **CL/XP** 6/400; **Special:** backstab (x3), camouflage (80% chance to hide in hilly or mountainous terrain), darkvision (60ft), vulnerable to obsidian (200% damage). (see **Appendix A: New Monsters**)

Chom Swarm (2): HD 5; **HP** 36, 30; **AC** 5[14]; **Atk** swarm (1d8); **Move** 4 (fly 18); **Save** 12; **AL** N; **CL/XP** 7/600; **Special:** cast omen (1/day, targets meeting gaze of flock, save or −1 to hit, saves, and damage for 24 hours), mimicry (simple sounds), soul steal (against incapacitated or sleeping foe, soul is stolen and held within the flock, save avoids). (see **Appendix A: New Monsters**)

Early in the fight, Xotaxtl Nitlocati targets either one of the council members or the most physically combative of his opponents with a *flesh to maize* spell (see **Appendix C: New Spells**). If the victim fails the saving throw, the alux calls out to the chom and commands them to swoop down and devour the victim. As the fight drags out, Xotaxtl Nitlocati commands his alux allies to start beating on the captives and yells at the intruders to surrender before he has them killed. He is not bluffing. If his allies start to drop, Xotaxtl Nitlocati also commands one of the chom swarms to break off and get help. Each round thereafter, determine if reinforcements arrive by rolling 1d6, with a roll of 5–6 indicating they found **1d3 aluxes** to aid in the melee.

As long as their leader remains strong enough to command them, the aluxes continue to actively participate in the fight. Conversely, if the characters fell Xotaxtl Nitlocati, the remainder of the aluxes panic, break from combat, and attempt to flee. If the characters defeat Xotaxtl Nitlocati, the fighting slowly subsides as word spreads of his defeat. Villagers drive off the remaining attackers while others readily surrender and beg for mercy. The choms ask for no quarter or forgiveness, but simply fly off chattering and laughing as if mocking the folly of the entire event.

CONCLUDING THE ADVENTURE

Xotaxtl Nitlocati's death frees Xotaxtl's soul from its earthly prison, sending it on its journey to the Oracle of the Moon for her judgment.

The Daughter of Chalatihuatl then appears to the characters in a vivid vision, where she accepts the sorcerer-priest's soul as recompense for the slain alux and the insult to the Forgotten Gods. The herdsman's son regains his soul, and the characters have fulfilled their end of their bargain with the Oracle of the Moon.

In the wake of the attack, there is much to do to restore and rebuild the village, especially with the Harvest Festival looming. Characters are free to help rebuild the village and participate in the festival where they are lauded as heroes. Camaxtl thanks Ohtli for his bravery and understanding. The alux is extremely moved by his gesture and returns his thanks. That night by the fire, Ohtli spins epic and dramatic tales of the third cataclysm and moves the audience to tears. In the morning, he bids his goodbyes and heads off to the Corpsewood to seek to restore order to his people. Not all ends well though. Many are dead, including the herdsman. His orphaned son weeps inconsolably and blames himself for the tragic events. Thereafter, Coaxoch the medicine-witch offers to take him on as her apprentice. If the characters choose to stay, the headman offers them property and housing as well as seats upon the village council. If not, he gifts them with some treasure.

Treasure: The headman gives the characters 11 large disks of gold (200 gp each), a *+2 shield*, a *necklace of firebaubles*, and whatever mundane equipment they require. Coaxoch adds a few more gifts to their stash: three *potions of extra healing* and a *potion of invisibility*. Lastly, the herdsman's son gifts them with a small peccary's hoof whistle he carved for his father. "For when you are in trouble," the boy tells them. "This time I shall listen."

After their experiences, the characters are ready to progress to the next adventure in the series, **Rider on the Storm**, which takes them out of the Aztlis' lands and into Poqoza territory across the Great Canal.

RIDER ON THE STORM

BY ROB MANNING

"YAHUITAMOTL IS HERE! DOOM UPON US!"

— COMMON SAYING DURING A THUNDERSTORM

SEASON OF THE QALLUCHA

Once the child is of the age, they must enter the Mulla Chanacu.
There, they will find their way. Embrace their true nature.
Fear not — revelation is at hand.

— The Way of the Quata Maque

Can't go over the grass. I'm not a toucan.
Can't go under the grass. I'm not a paca.
Must swim through the grass.

— Children's rhyme

Rider on the Storm is an adventure for four 7th- to 9th-level characters that takes them on an open-ended, whirlwind tour of the Caxcalli Grasslands in the heart of Poqoza territory. Here, they must face the dreaded Storm Rider and an otherworldly entity threatening to disrupt the Poqozas' way of life and bring them under its proverbial thumbs.

ADVENTURE BACKGROUND

Thousands of years ago, long before the hero-gods' ascendance, a meteorite streaked across the Tehuatl sky before it crashed into earth and created a massive crater in its wake. Although time largely healed the island's wound, the cosmic body brought a tiny organic hitchhiker along for the ride, a fungus known as shori huasca. Incredibly, the organism survived the harrowing trek across space and the devastating crash landing that followed. For countless centuries afterward, the fungus flourished in the depths of the earth, where it basked in the meteorite's residual cosmic energy that it needed to survive.

The fungus would have gone unnoticed if not for the ambitions of one Poqoza man — Elix Cucita. The bohemian explorer and his entourage found the strange plant and naturally began experimenting with its intoxicating properties. Much to their hedonistic delight, ingesting the fungus spawned wild hallucinations and transcendental experiences. Elix constructed a laboratory on the location's outskirts to further study the fungus. In time, Elix and his inner circle achieved the presumably impossible. Their consciousnesses escaped their physical bodies and entered the Great Beyond where they encountered a cabal of unexpected inhabitants — a small band of nihileth aboleths intrigued by their humanoid visitors. Much to the aboleths' horror, Elix and his associates resisted their mental powers, allowing them to reach a truce with the normally dominant monsters. At a standstill, the parties agreed to negotiate an agreement to share their knowledge. To ensure their mutual safety, one member of each delegation would reside in the others' home world until they completed the exchange. To conclude the bargain, one nihileth aboleth traveled to Tehuatl and remained hidden beneath the surface, dormant while it waited for its instructions.

The undead monstrosity waited there for centuries until it received a signal from its counterparts to reawaken. Meanwhile, word of the fungus's hallucinatory properties spread throughout the land. The Poqozas dubbed the site and its caverns as the Mulla Chanacu. In time, all adolescent Poqoza boys and girls traveled to the isolated locale as a rite of passage into adulthood. While the caverns of the Mulla Chanacu stayed active, Elix's research facility fell into neglect and disrepair until a new occupant arrived on the scene. Yahuitamotl, a bored and corrupted storm giant, entered the complex. He soon came to the realization that the location's unusual properties gave him an unnaturally long life. What seemed like a blessing soon became a burden as the isolation and ennui ate away at his soul and psyche. To amuse himself, the capricious giant summoned massive storms and foul weather to terrify the populace, earning him the moniker of the Storm Rider. Yahuitamotl remained directionless until a celestial occurrence set current events into motion.

Roughly once every 1,000 years, an enormous rogue gas giant planet passes through the solar system, creating a prolonged solar eclipse. After centuries of inaction, the nihileth aboleth took the event as its signal to reactivate. Over the next several weeks, the undead abomination began to enslave the unsuspecting teenagers venturing to the Mulla Chanacu, transforming the vibrant youngsters into a zombie horde. The monster then struck a bargain with the increasingly evil and destructive Yahuitamotl, who agreed to be his herald of the apocalypse and spread death and destruction across the Caxcalli Grasslands. The nihileth aboleth now gathers intelligence about the people and lands of Tehuatl to prepare an invasion force from the Great Beyond. Despite its efforts, the uneasy truce between Elix and the aboleth's kin devolved into a bitter conflict. Hurling terrible magic and frightening weapons, the combatants vanished into Oblivion, never to be seen nor heard from again. Although the aboleth has not received a response to any of its reconnaissance information, the monster proceeds full steam ahead on its dream of conquering the Poqozas with its undead army and adding the island to its vile race's inventory of conquered territories. That is unless characters intervene and stop these dire events from happening.

ADVENTURE SYNOPSIS

The characters arrive in the Caxcalli Grasslands where they embark on a series of encounters involving the Poqozas' social groups: the Thalus (farmers), the Thayanas (hunters), and the Alaxpachas (the craftspeople). During the course of these events, the characters increase their goodwill among these stratas within Poqoza society by saving lives, protecting property, and ridding their homes of evil. After winning the people's trust and admiration, an elder from the group asks the characters to assist them in a matter pertaining to their interests. After completing this task and again earning their gratitude, the characters learn of the Storm Rider who has been terrorizing Poqoza communities for many years. The weather activities in the area lead them to an ancient, largely abandoned laboratory where the bored Storm Rider laments the folly of existence and his self-proclaimed godhood. The Storm Rider's removal does not eradicate the threats looming over Tehuatl. The reawakened nihileth aboleth now poisons the land surrounding the Mulla Chanacu where young Poqozas experience visions to guide them into adulthood. Over the past several weeks, he has killed and raised many of them as zombie thralls under his command. Furthermore, the adults sent to check on their well-being also fell prey to the monster that now swims in the muck at the bottom of the Mulla Chanacu crater. The characters must destroy the malevolent creature to rid this wicked threat from the land once and for all.

OVERVIEW OF THE CAXCALLI GRASSLANDS

The grass is the lifeblood of the Caxcalli lands. It provides nourishment, clothing, shelter, and more for the people and beasts who call the grasslands home. The land is a sea of green and tan grasses, some reaching heights of five feet with stunted and twisted acacia trees dotting the landscape. The coarse blades are sharp, and the grains produced in the fields range from maize in the east (especially near Zacatl) to quinoa in the west (nearer to the Toctli Forest). Bamboo grows in abundance in the southeast, and the Thalu spread its use for construction and medicinal purposes across the countryside. Caxcalli experiences a wet and a dry season. Seven long months of minuscule rainfall strip the grasslands of most of its color, and nearly every year wildfires cleanse the land of brush and eliminate the weaker of the species. Five months of rejuvenating rains bring the grasslands back to a vibrant palate of green.

Kurn Domladur
Turew
Octli
Ixtla
Tamazoli
Nepalta
Shassal
Balandrur
Ipaconoytl
Cepual Desert
Nochtli
Xalpit
Quannaqa River
Hana'aloa
Mactli
Omehual River
Ouatulli Lake
Omiex
Droomph
Teocua
Cuahtla Forest
Yoaltica Ilaquiloz
Necocyaotl
Quizaloa
Amilotetl
The Great Canal
Huitzineo
Azuato
Ixchicta
Zacatl
Ezhuacoza
Good fortune
Cotza
Toxana
Mimicapoli
Quitlacatl
Blibleblup
Ezhuitotl
Ahuacua
Hilaya River
The Spring
Cuiateotl
Mototoloa
Ixnenatl
Zinacan
Xoxoquetzpali
Moyome
Atoyaxalli
Tlococua Marsh
Mauhque
Iachacina
Hamachi
Ixtama
Yolqui
Yoyoliton
Temetzin River
Cuanintli
Hualcitzen
Mulla Chanacu
Nezcatayotl
Xicotli
Onacina
Eei
Rommpf
Caxcalli Grasslands
Yuri
Tlahapina
N
CAXCALLI GRASSLANDS
1 Square - 20 Miles

The Poqozas who inhabit the grasslands divide their society into social strata based upon their lifestyle. The three primary strata of this adventure are the Thalu, Thayana, and Alaxpacha. These strata are more akin to medieval guild membership. While everyone identifies as a Poqoza, they subdivide their society based upon their profession. Regardless of which strata they belong to, all submit to the wiles of Chuxuntana, "The Sea of Green."

The Thalu are the farmers. These sedentary people learned to grow and manipulate plants to meet their needs. The Thalu mostly dwell in small villages and towns across a wide swath of land bisecting the grasslands from east to west, starting at the edge of Lake Moyome. They build chinampas atop a large freshwater lake on the eastern edge of the grasslands where it butts against the trackless swamp farther east. Simple and honest, the Thalu are a humble people who pray for good crops and peace.

The Thayana are the hunters. They follow the deer herds and know nearly every watering hole in the entire grasslands. Familial and loyal, these Poqoza band together in small groups that are usually led by a powerful ranger or druid. These self-sufficient nomads carry their homes on their backs in their constant pursuit of prey. More primal than their domesticated cousins, the Thalu, the Thayana acknowledge some of the older nature spirits, though they still place Tlatlcolli at the top of their religious hierarchy.

The Alaxpacha are the stargazers, the artists, and scholars of the Caxcalli. Their minds never rest. Many become wizards and rogues who congregate in the city of Zacatl and other urban centers, though some seek solace in isolated places toward the southern shore where the sea's salty breezes tame the tallgrass. The hills grow a bit taller just north of the sandy beaches, allowing the Alaxpacha better opportunities to study the inky expanse of the night sky. The Alaxpacha believe they have a better understanding of the workings of the planes and worship knowledge over all else.

For many generations, these three groups have harmoniously coexisted in the Caxcalli Grasslands. Occasional squabbles break out from time to time, but the participants generally accept such disputes as part of the grand plan without holding grudges or bad blood. Each Poqoza tries to further their life's experience by contributing all they can to the betterment of their people.

When couples bring forth new life into the Chuxuntana, their children eventually reach the age where they must go into the Mulla Chanacu and find their way in the barbarous wastes. Caves riddle the landscape, and strange fungi grow in the steamy earth. Shamans of each tribe encourage the adventurous youngsters to imbibe a variety of these mushrooms to help unlock their inner spirit and embark on a transcendental experience. After a month or more, the young person leaves the wild Mulla Chanacu and travels to meet members of their new profession and social strata. A Thayana youth might emerge as a Thayana, or an Alaxpacha, or some other profession completely, depending on what the spirits told them. The Poqozas have other smaller subsets of social strata who are offshoots of the three major groups. A few youths have left Mulla Chanacu to completely forsake the grasslands and move to another territory entirely. All Poqozas born in the grasslands must face their fears and enter the caverns to complete their transition from childhood to adulthood. The visit happens at different times for different individuals, but most enter around age 13 to 15. There the adolescents must partake in the tradition of ingesting the shori huasca, the fungus that guides them on their journey from childhood to adulthood.

HOOKS

You are free to use any of the following ideas to draw the characters into the story or create one of your own.

CANALS AND CONTRACTS

A powerful group of Aztlis calling themselves the Achni contacts the characters to set up a meeting with them in a luxurious audience hall in a metropolis of your choice, though it most likely takes place in Zacatl. The gist of the meeting is to ask them to explore the Caxcalli Grasslands. The Achni have been speaking with several Poqozas interested in developing a secondary canal running north to south that would help facilitate trade between the former archenemies. Before they undertake such a massive undertaking, they want to ensure that tales of the savage grasslands are just that — stories borne from overactive imaginations. The group grants the characters an advance of 1,000 gp to purchase any provisions necessary for the exploratory expedition they expect could take several weeks or even months.

SKULLS

Dangerous beasts roam the Caxcalli Grasslands. A wealthy, retired Aztli hunter regrets he never got the opportunity to hunt in Poqoza territory. Therefore, he contacts the adventurers and gives them a list of skulls he needs to complete his trophy collection. The list covers most of the basics: a rhinoceros, a caiman, a paleolithic specimen, and most notably at the bottom of his list a single word, "Achachila," which means the "one that got away." The hunter tracked his quarry up to the edge of the Tlacocua Marsh before he lost it. He never truly saw the creature other than catching glimpses of a vicious pair of eyes, a lone, clawed footprint, and a fleeting shadow. The beast strikes only at night and has legendary status among Aztli and Poqoza alike. Few have seen it and lived to tell the tale. Indeed, the descriptions of the beast vary from one person to the next. Although he desires to acquire all the missing skulls, he really cares only about one — that of the AchachilasanacaAchachila. Remember, the AchachilasanacaAchachila is not a specific creature, so feel free to use a suitable monster of your choice for this quest.

MEDICAL MISSION OF MERCY

Hucksters come in all shapes and sizes. An evangelist who arrived on the southern edge of the Caxcalli Grasslands began a tyrannical conversion therapy camp to force the Poqozas and Aztlis he encountered to renounce their faith and accept his one true, foreign god. He placed those who refused to convert into a brutal, forced labor compound he built on the back of the Poqoza living there before his arrival. Within its stone walls, he and his acolytes indoctrinated the unwilling participants in his religion. In addition to breaking the will of the free Poqoza living there, they also spread a coughing disease among the locals. The evangelist and his retinue are allegedly immune to the pox, but the Poqoza they imprisoned are not. The cough transforms into a choking fever after a few days, followed shortly thereafter by exhaustion, incapacitation, and ultimately death unless properly treated. The characters hear of this outbreak and must travel to the southern edge of the Caxcalli Grasslands to fight the spreading sickness, even as it moves farther north from village to village, and tribe to tribe. The characters come equipped with the proper treatment, a sulfuric powder that when mixed with water and imbibed provides immunity against the contagion or cures an infected person of the ailment.

SETTLEMENTS OF THE CAXCALLI GRASSLANDS

The Caxcalli Grasslands south of the Great Canal provide nearly ideal living conditions for most forms of life. Vast herds of deer and antelopes graze on the abundant grasses under the watchful gaze of predatory cats and canines alike. The biome is almost perfectly designed to support nearly every variety of flora and fauna, including maize, the lifeblood of the Aztlis and their offshoots, the Poqozas. Maize and other wild cereal grains thrive under these conditions, making this region ideal for agriculture and to maintain fertile hunting grounds. During the course of this adventure, the characters are likely to travel vast distances, potentially bringing them into contact with multiple settlements along the way. If you are using the **Tehuatl** sourcebook from **Frog God Games** along with this adventure compendium, you may use the settlements in that guide to aid you in populating the wilderness with suitable settlements. Nevertheless, the preceding work cannot detail every community within the grasslands, especially considering that some are only transient settlements established by nomadic people.

For each day of travel across this verdant landscape, you may consult **Table 4–1** to determine if the characters encounter a settlement during the course of their journey. We recommend you use these locations to give the adventurers an opportunity to rest, restock their provisions, and gather rumors or information from the inhabitants. Cities do not appear on this table as they appear on the Tehuatl main map and are not intended to be randomly generated.

1d20	Settlement Found
1–4	No settlement
5–7	Transient settlement
8–15	Village
16–18	Small town
19–20	Large town

As previously discussed, the Poqoza essentially divide their society in strata along the lines of city dwellers (Alaxpacha), sedentary rural inhabitants (Thalu), and nomads (Thayana). This section describes their populations within each of the following settlements:

Transient settlement: Lean-tos, huts, and other portable shelters comprise a transient settlement almost exclusively made up of Thayanas, with a few elves or even renegade Aztlis tagging along with them. These are a hardy people who live off the land and know nature's cycle like the backs of their hands. If they win their trust, characters who encounter these folks can expect to share a meal, and they are the best source of gossip for news throughout the area, including information about the Storm Rider. However, they are generally short on supplies and have little in the way of magic. Transient settlements have **2d8 x 10 residents** with a leadership cadre of **2d4 elders** and **1 chieftain**. For a fee of 2 gp per day, the characters can hire one of the residents to serve as a guide across the Caxcalli Grasslands. In the company of the guide, the characters have no chance of getting lost.

Poqoza Commoners, Male or Female Half-Elves (2d8 x 10):
HP 1d6hp; AC 9[10]; Atk spear (1d6); Move 12; Save 18; AL Any; CL/XP B/10; Special: darkvision (60ft). (*Monstrosities* 254)

Poqoza Elders, Male or Female Half-Elves (Drd3) (2d4): HP 3d6; AC 7[12]; Atk club (1d4); Move 12; Save 13; AL N; CL/XP 3/60; Special: +2 save vs. fire, darkvision (60ft), identify pure water and plants, move through nonmagical undergrowth, spells (3/1).
Spells: 1st—*detect magic, faerie fire, locate animals*; 2nd—*cure light wounds.*
Equipment: tlahuiztli armor[B], club.

Poqoza Chieftain, Male or Female Half-Elf: HP 5d8; AC 4[15]; Atk macuahuitl (1d8) or tecpatl (1d4) or sling (1d4); Move 12; Save 12; AL Any; CL/XP 5/240; Special: darkvision (60ft). (*Monstrosities* 256)
Equipment: ollixalli[B], macuahuitl[B], tecpatl[B], sling, 10 sling stones.
[B] See **Appendix B: New Equipment and Magic Items**

Village: This small community generally consists of several families living together in communal housing or in huts scattered across a wide area. Thalus make up the bulk of the population, though some Thayanas may use the village as a temporary base of operations between hunting expeditions. Most villagers spend their days working the land by either tending to the fields or minding the livestock, usually consisting of turkeys and occasionally goats. Poqozas make up the majority of the population, though some elves and halfling may cohabitate the village alongside these people. Characters who visit one of these settlements can expect temporary shelter from the accommodating residents as well as some provisions and news about the outside world. A village always has at least a minor temple dedicated to Tlatlcolli, where characters can find some magical healing as well as stores of alcohol and hallucinogenic agents including shori huasca. The typical village has **2d10 x 10 permanent residents**, **2d10 transient residents**, and a leadership council made up of **2d6 religious elders**.

Poqoza Commoners, Male or Female Half-Elves (2d10 x 10):
HP 1d6hp; AC 9[10]; Atk club (1d4); Move 12; Save 18; AL Any; CL/XP B/10; Special: darkvision (60ft). (*Monstrosities* 254)

Transient Poqoza Commoners, Male or Female Half-Elves (2d10): HP 1d6hp; AC 9[10]; Atk spear (1d6); Move 12; Save 18; AL Any; CL/XP B/10; Special: darkvision (60ft). (*Monstrosities* 254)

Poqoza Religious Leaders, Male or Female Half-Elves (Clr4) (2d6): HP 4d6; AC 6[13]; Atk macuahuitl (1d8); Move 12; Save 12; AL Any; CL/XP 4/120; Special: +2 save vs. paralysis and poison, banish undead, darkvision (60ft), spells (2/1).
Spells: 1st—*cure light wounds, purify food and drink*; 2nd—*bless.*
Equipment: cipacahuipilli armor[B], macuahuitl[B].
[B] See **Appendix B: New Equipment and Magic Items**

Small town: Individual homes, farms, and a town square are the hallmarks of this larger settlement. Although many people still work the land, some have the resources to hire transient laborers to harvest their crops and maintain their livestock, which usually consists of dogs, turkeys, and some goats. Thalus remain the most populous social strata within a small town, though Thayanas who may also double as traders, furriers, and merchants are frequent visitors. In addition, several Alaxpachas may take up residence in town to serve as sages, artisans, and skilled craftsmen. A small town is a good source of information about events in surrounding areas and has a well-stocked inventory of provisions for travelers, including commonly found magic items, some adventuring gear, weapons, armor, specialized equipment. Commerce is generally conducted in the town square. Furthermore, most small towns have a small military force to fend off incursions by their less hospitable humanoid neighbors. Poqozas are the dominant people in most small towns, with some elves, gnomes, halflings, and more exotic races scattered among the generally tolerant populace. Guest houses, inns, and other businesses accommodating travelers as well as a temple dedicated to Tlatlcolli can also be found in a small town. The temple always has ample supplies of intoxicating substances, including shori huasca, on hand for religious festivals. The typical small town has **10d10 x 10 permanent residents**, **8d10 transient residents**, a military force of **6d10 soldiers**, and a leadership council made up of **2d6 religious elders**.

Poqoza Commoners, Male or Female Half-Elves (10d10 x 10):
HP 1d6hp; AC 9[10]; Atk club (1d4); Move 12; Save 18; AL Any; CL/XP B/10; Special: darkvision (60ft). (*Monstrosities* 254)

Transient Poqoza Commoners, Male or Female Half-Elves (8d10): HP 1d6hp; AC 9[10]; Atk spear (1d6); Move 12; Save 18; AL Any; CL/XP B/10; Special: darkvision (60ft). (*Monstrosities* 254)

Poqoza Soldiers, Male or Female Half-Elves (6d10): HD 1; AC 7[12]; Atk tepoztopilli (1d10) or sling (1d4); Move 12; Save 17; AL Any; CL/XP 1/15; Special: darkvision (60ft). (*Monstrosities* 257)
Equipment: tepoztopilli[B], sling.

Poqoza Religious Leaders, Male or Female Half-Elves (Clr4) (2d6): HP 4d6; AC 6[13]; Atk macuahuitl (1d8); Move 12; Save 12; AL Any; CL/XP 4/120; Special: +2 save vs. paralysis and poison, banish undead, darkvision (60ft), spells (2/1).
Spells: 1st—*cure light wounds, purify food and drink*; 2nd—*bless.*
Equipment: cipacahuipilli armor[B], macuahuitl[B].
[B] See **Appendix B: New Equipment and Magic Items**

Large town: Although not quite a city, a large town has almost every amenity found in a great metropolis. The town square dominates this community as fewer people earn their livelihoods directly from the land. The Thalus inhabit the arable land on the settlement's outskirts, while Alaxpachas earn their keep producing manufactured goods and engaging in a myriad of academic studies. Thayanas also sell some of their fresh kills in the bustling marketplace, which serves as central hub for all activities within the town. Otherwise, the large town has the same general features of a small town except in greater supplies along with a larger percentage of Alaxpacha inhabitants than a small town. It may also house several shrines devoted to the deities of its non-Poqoza inhabitants, most notably its elvish population. Poqozas are still the dominant people in most large towns, though elves, gnomes, halflings and more exotic races share the same space. It is also not unusual to find an insular Aztli neighborhood within a small town. Although they tolerate the humans' presence, the Poqozas strictly forbid them from establishing shrines and temples within their communities. Some Aztlis may go figuratively and literally underground to honor their deities, yet doing so risks expulsion from the dominant Poqozas if they learn of such activities. A large town has **10d10 x 50 permanent residents** (minimum 1,000), **20d10 transient residents**, a military force of **20d10 soldiers** commanded by a retinue of **2d4 officers**, and a leadership council made up of **2d6 religious elders**.

Poqoza Commoners, Male or Female Half-Elves (10d10 x 50):
HP 1d6hp; **AC** 9[10]; **Atk** club (1d4); **Move** 12; **Save** 18; **AL** Any;
CL/XP B/10; **Special:** darkvision (60ft). (*Monstrosities* 254)

**Transient Poqoza Commoners, Male or Female Half-Elves
(20d10):** HP 1d6hp; **AC** 9[10]; **Atk** spear (1d6); **Move** 12; **Save** 18;
AL Any; **CL/XP** B/10; **Special:** darkvision (60ft). (*Monstrosities*
254)

Poqoza Soldiers, Male or Female Half-Elves (20d10): HD 1; **AC**
7[12]; **Atk** tepoztopilli (1d10) or sling (1d4); **Move** 12; **Save** 17; **AL**
Any; **CL/XP** 1/15; **Special:** darkvision (60ft). (*Monstrosities* 257)
Equipment: tepoztopilli[B], sling.

Poqoza Officers, Male or Female Half-Elves (2d4): HD 3; **AC**
5[14]; **Atk** ollitztli (1d6) or tecpatl (1d4) or sling (1d4); **Move**
12; **Save** 14; **AL** Any; **CL/XP** 3/60; **Special:** darkvision (60ft).
(*Monstrosities* 256)
Equipment: olli armor [B], ollitztli [B], tecpatl [B], sling, 10 sling stones.

**Poqoza Religious Leaders, Male or Female Half-Elves (Clr4)
(2d6):** HP 4d6; **AC** 6[13]; **Atk** macuahuitl (1d8); **Move** 12; **Save** 12;
AL Any; **CL/XP** 4/120; **Special:** +2 save vs. paralysis and poison,
banish undead, darkvision (60ft), spells (2/1).
Spells: 1st—*cure light wounds, purify food and drink*; 2nd—*bless*.
Equipment: cipacahuipilli armor[B], macuahuitl[B].
[B] See **Appendix B: New Equipment and Magic Items**

Chapter One:
Event Encounters

These encounters do not directly tie into the story of Yahuitamotl
or the adventure's main protagonist. They are designed to give the
characters an opportunity to explore the Caxcalli Grasslands and win
the favor of one of the three strata within Poqoza society. The events
can be run in any order. At the end of each event, the characters gain
goodwill points for resolving these situations in a manner favorable to
one of the three groups. If the characters accumulate four goodwill points
for a particular group, the adventure proceeds to **Chapter Two: Social
Business** and the corresponding strata's final encounter before moving
onto the adventure's main storyline. Of course, news spreads swiftly in
the grasslands as the characters' reputation grows with each triumph or
sinks with every failure.

None of these events takes place in the Mulla Chanacu. The tallgrass
hides the area well, and the priests who supply the shori huasca try not
to reveal its true location. Of course, the characters might try to cajole,
bribe, or threaten their way to the Mulla Chanacu, or someone else
there. If the characters explore that area, proceed to **Chapter Four: The
Nihileth Assault.**

The Legend of Yahuitamotl

Every community in the Caxcalli Grasslands knows the legend of
Yahuitamotl. No one has details on the appearance of the Storm Rider, but
all have a connection to an encounter of some sort. Yahuitamotl appears only
under a cloudy sky, sometimes in mist or dense rain. The Poqoza always
encounter the Storm Rider at a distance. The legends say that his voice is
commanding, but only at a whispering volume, even in the midst of a torrential
downpour. Yahuitamotl is fickle, unpredictable, and temperamental. Most
people leave offerings of food and other treasures for the being when it arrives,
though many speculate that Yahuitamotl cares little about these tributes as he
has sometimes taken them into their entirety and on other occasions left them
untouched. When the characters ask Poqozas about the Storm Rider, you can
provide them with any or all of the following rumors.

"Our cousin in a nearby village saw the Storm Rider just after dawn the
other day. As the mist of the morning rolled away, there Yahuitamotl stood,
towering 25 feet tall. My cousin tried to run, but fear froze her to the spot. The
Storm Rider asked how many Poqozas were in her village, and she responded
quickly. She did not take into account the outliers and field workers, and now
she is deathly afraid Yahuitamotl will return to beat her for her miscount. The
village has left extra portions of food in their shrine to make up for her folly."

"No one sees the Storm Rider. You only hear him as he rides the lightning
down from the heavens above and strikes the ground with such force!"

"Yahuitamotl made an entire village disappear! Where we used to set up
camp, Yahuitamotl found us on ground we think was sacred to him. The
world shook from his anger as he called down lightning to destroy our huts
and scatter us to the winds. I have not seen any of the other hunters from
that pack since."

"Yahuitamotl warns us of a coming doom! All who live in the tallgrass fear
this change. He whispers of the spirits of our ancestors rising from the very
ground to strike us down. We must prepare, but how? Most Poqoza just live in
fear and hope it doesn't come to pass."

"The winds knocked me down. By the time I regained my feet, Yahuitamotl
had already come and gone."

The tellers of these tales fully believe them to be true.

Event Encounter 1:
The Lady in the Iron Coffin

A small crowd gathers around a team of Poqozas
shoveling mud out of a massive hole in the ground
measuring almost eight feet on a side. Another team
assembling a pulley system with hemp cables that dangle
down into the cavity appears to be trying to overtake the
digging team. Excited onlookers munch on snacks and
give unsolicited advice.

These Poqoza are almost all Thalus. A farmer digging up a field near a
crossroads stumbled upon some ancient religious relics, including wooden death
whistles and small figurines of indiscernible identity. The chance discovery
spurred him to keep digging to figure out what lies buried beneath his crops.
After several hours of excavation, he discovered an iron sarcophagus four feet
below the surface. Excited by the find, he summoned his family and friends
to help him disinter the coffin. Almost everyone who sees the coffin feels an
inexplicable desire to liberate it from the cold earth and reveal its contents. None
can explain their rationale for this seemingly irrepressible feeling.

When the characters arrive, the farmer **Yacha Tol** and his closest family
explain their desire to remove the coffin from the ground to **Aqi Ciqana**, an

Alaxpacha priest from a neighboring village. Despite the priest's inexplicable curiosity, he warns the farmer about the dangers of meddling in affairs beyond his understanding. When Yacha sees the characters, he beckons them to join him and assist in the efforts.

Yacha Tol, Poqoza Farmer, Male Half-Elf: HP 5; AC 9[10]; **Atk** club (1d4); **Move** 12; **Save** 18; **AL** N; **CL/XP** B/10; **Special:** darkvision (60ft). (*Monstrosities* 254)

Aqi Ciqana, Poqoza Half-Elf Priest (Clr4): HP 20; AC 6[13]; **Atk** macuahuitl (1d8); **Move** 12; **Save** 12; **AL** L; **CL/XP** 4/120; **Special:** +2 save vs. paralysis and poison, banish undead, darkvision (60ft), spells (2/1).
  Spells: 1st—*cure light wounds, purify food and drink*; 2nd—*bless*.
Equipment: cipacahuipilli armor[B], macuahuitl[B].
[B] See **Appendix B: New Equipment and Magic Items**

The coffin houses the still living remains of **Aukka Castigas**, a female **black orc high priest of Orcus**). Tlatoani's snake advisors attempted to negotiate an alliance with the treacherous priestess, but her unwillingness to abandon Orcus and accept the Immortal Sun as her divine patron sealed her fate. Fearful of angering another god by killing one of his steadfast servants, the cunning serpents deceived her into willingly allowing a magic-user to cast a *time stop* spell on her. The spell placed her in a state of suspended animation that allowed them to seal her within the iron sarcophagus, which they buried deep beneath a crossroads to prevent someone from accidentally stumbling upon her burial site.

Over the last several thousand years, the ground shifted as weather events and seismic activity brought the coffin closer to the surface. Furthermore, a *wizard lock* spell cast on the coffin was accidentally dispelled during a magical duel between two sorcerers that took place on this very spot several hundred years earlier. Nonetheless, the iron coffin still radiates magic, though in this case, it amplifies the emotion of any creature within 20 feet of it who fails a saving throw. Those who fear it become frightened of it. Curiosity- and treasure-seekers greatly desire to open it and discover its malevolent contents.

When the characters arrive, the coffin is nearly free of the mud. Yacha Tol approaches, pushing aside the wizard as he and the others in the crowd beg for someone to crack open the lid and bask in its treasures. The numerous voices sound like a mad cacophony as each individual begs them to hear their side of the story. Suspended about halfway out of its hole in the ground, the featureless iron sarcophagus dangles in a mass of ropes and scaffolding in the light rain.

Feel free to allow the interaction between the characters and the crowd to play out as much as you want. A few individuals, including the magic-user and a village elder, demand that the villagers re-inter the coffin, while the farmer and the majority demand to see it opened.

With the coffin exposed to the elements, Orcus may sense the presence of a long-buried servant or a spiteful Aztli god such as Itztliteotl or Itzcuin may see an opportunity to spread mayhem among their former worshippers. Regardless of the cause, a wild, unanticipated lightning bolt strikes the ferrous object, awakening the long-slumbering servant of Orcus from her sleep. The suddenly rejuvenated black orc bursts forth from her coffin to rain death upon any who stand in her way.

Aukka Castigas, Black Orc High Priest of Orcus: HD 7; HP 52; AC 4[15]; **Atk** flail (1d8) or two-handed sword (1d10); **Move** 9; **Save** 9; **AL** C; **CL/XP** 9/1100; **Special:** spells (3/3/3/3/3).
  Spells: 1st—*cure light wounds* (x2), *detect magic*; 2nd—*bless, hold person, speak with animals*; 3rd—*cure disease, prayer, speak with dead*; 4th—*cure serious wounds* (x2), *sticks to snakes*; 5th—*finger of death, insect plague, raise dead*.

Goodwill Points: Destroying the evil within the coffin earns the characters one goodwill point with each of the three groups — the Alaxpachas, the Thalus, and the Thayanas. If the mage survives the encounter, he tells the story to anyone willing to listen, giving the characters one more goodwill point for the Alaxpacha. If the characters keep the farmers alive and restore at least one slain farmer back to life, the Thalus praise the characters, earning them one more goodwill point with the Thalus. If the characters refuse to heal any injured Poqozas or raise at least one of the dead Poqozas, the characters lose one goodwill point.

EVENT ENCOUNTER 2: THE PLAGUE OF TEETH

The characters catch up to a traveling band of Thayana to learn of the surrounding lands. One of the hunters warns the characters to step away. In the distance, the characters hear the wailing and pleading of the rest of the small group.

The hand signals are part of a regional sign language known as Hunter's Argot. The Thayana use the silent form of communication while hunting prey. The code contains only a handful of words and phrases pertaining to the hunt. The language has its roots in thieves' cant. Someone versed in that language has an 80% chance to understand Hunter's Argot.

The vague admonitions and warning can be attributed to the ancient curse the Alcati family stumbled upon in the high grass when traveling near Mulla Chanacu. They are growing an extraordinary number of teeth not just in their mouths, but on their fingers and toes, and more recently on their torsos. Several family members have died from the curse.

If the characters ignore the warning and investigate, they encounter a **lone sentry**. The characters can slip past the concerned guard or persuade him to let them pass.

Poqoza Soldier, Male Half-Elf: HP 5; AC 7[12]; **Atk** tepoztopilli (1d10) or spear (1d6); **Move** 12; **Save** 17; **AL** N; **CL/XP** 1/15; **Special:** darkvision (60ft). (*Monstrosities* 257)
  Equipment: tepoztopilli[B], spear.
[B] See **Appendix B: New Equipment and Magic Items**

If the characters view the gathering, they see a tormented family huddled together in a tight circle. A man and a woman equipped with a small chisel and hammer move from person to person. Using these implements, they chip the teeth loose from the skin in a sickening scene of blood and gore. They throw the extracted teeth into the fire with a plaintive prayer asking for relief from Tlatlcolli.

Poqoza Elders, Male and Female Half-Elves (Drd3) (2): HP 17, 15; AC 7[12]; **Atk** club (1d4); **Move** 12; **Save** 13; **AL** N; **CL/XP** 3/60; **Special:** +2 save vs. fire, darkvision (60ft), identify pure water and plants, move through non-magical undergrowth, spells (3/1).
  Spells: 1st—*detect magic, faerie fire, locate animals*; 2nd—*cure light wounds*.
Equipment: tlahuiztli armor[B], club, chisel, hammer.
[B] See **Appendix B: New Equipment and Magic Items**

The characters find the family grateful for any assistance they can offer. Removing the teeth is a straightforward yet painful process requiring the character to succeed on a saving throw to remove 3d6 teeth. After extracting the teeth, the two healers tell the characters to throw them into the fire. Some family members have 100 extra teeth, while others have up to 600. Most are molars, though some incisors and canines also protrude from the raw skin. An extraction causes a popping sound that leaves a small pool of blood and a fading, throbbing pain until the next tooth pops through to add to the torture.

There is no monster to fight during this encounter. It takes time to calm the **41 remaining Alkatiri tribespeople** as they work to help ease the suffering. Before the curse, the Alkatiri numbered a little over 300. Now they are a shadow of their former selves. The ones left behind offer tears, songs, and prayers to Tlatlcolli to end the misfortune. The healers tell the characters that anyone who grows more than 1,000 teeth dies an agonizingly horrific death.

The teeth grow from the nails of the outer extremities first, then move to sprout out of the head and mouth. In the final stages, the canines and incisors mostly emerge from the torso around the belly.

Alkatiri tribespeople, Male or Female Poqoza Half-Elves (41): HP 1d6hp; AC 9[10]; Atk spear (1d6); Move 12; Save 18; AL Any; CL/XP B/10; Special: darkvision (60ft). (*Monstrosities* 254)

The curse they suffer is from wandering too close to the baleful effects the nihileth produces in the Mulla Chanacu, but they think they have offended Tlatlcolli or even one of the older Aztli gods by slaying an albino deer. The Thayana elder **Illa Qullqi** still holds the skull and pelt of the beast in his pack. He is trying to commune with the gods to find the way to pay penance for their misdeed.

The characters can help Illa Qullqi and the two healers with the removal of the protruding teeth and alleviating the curse against their band. A character with the ability to cast *remove curse* or spells with similar effects can rid one person of the curse. Magical healing that cures hit points rids the person of a number of teeth equal to 10 times the number of hit points healed. If the spell rids the person of all their teeth, the curse is lifted.

Illa Qullqi's stubbornness and insistence upon performing an atonement for the slain albino deer clouds his judgment. If the characters have some type of magic to commune with the gods, they learn that the curse can be either magically removed or by drinking a tea brewed from the stems of the totencaxihuitl plant, which the characters can locate. Despite the breakthrough, any magic short of a *wish* spell does not reveal the true source of the curse.

Illa Qullqi, Male Poqoza Half-Elf Priest (Clr5): HP 26; AC 6[13]; Atk macuahuitl (1d8); Move 12; Save 11; AL L; CL/XP 4/120; Special: +2 save vs. paralysis and poison, banish undead, darkvision (60ft), spells (2/2).
Spells: 1st—*cure light wounds* (x2); 2nd—*bless, speak with animals.*
Equipment: cipacahuipilli armor[B], macuahuitl[B].
[B] See **Appendix B: New Equipment and Magic Items**

Goodwill Points: If the characters save more than half of the group, award them one goodwill point for the Thayana. If the characters rid the people of the curse in its entirety, award them an additional goodwill point for the Thayana

EVENT ENCOUNTER 3: HERDING THE CAIMAN

The caimans live along the eastern edge of the grasslands where the marshes bleed over into the Sea of Green. Grassland residents use the scaly beasts for food and leather products. The characters become embroiled in a rigorous dispute over who has the right to the largest pelt any of them has ever seen.

> The smell of meat sizzling over an open flame dances in the air. Six men work around a large fire, rotating the skewered smoking carcasses to ensure that they cook evenly. The men grumble in pairs while working until they take notice of the intrusion
>
> "Not going to add another claim, are you?" one of them shouts. He laughs as he shakes hands with his partner. They both stop working to stare.
>
> "We can sell you some meat, but the skin is *ours!*" emphasizes another one. His friend echoes the last word as loudly as he can and slaps him on the back.
>
> The last pair are packing a smaller amount of meat into a large rucksack on a travois as they polish a few huge incisors. One holds the tooth by the root and makes sweeping motions as if he wants to make it into a weapon.

A pair of representatives from each of the three societal strata of the grasslands all lay claim to the deathblow that felled the mighty caiman they are cooking. The beast was 37 feet long and had killed many humans and other humanoids during its long life. However, the crocodilian's luck finally ran out

as it happened to be in the wrong place at the wrong time. Each pair of Poqozas has a legitimate claim on the skin.

The **first pair** are Alaxpachas who ventured to this location to kill the massive reptile to study its anatomy and use parts of it in their magical experiments. They portended the beast's appearance in this very spot by correctly interpreting the omens in the sky. They struck the beast down with a mighty *lightning bolt* that singed the high grass near the bank of a languid creek.

The **second pair** are Thalus. They normally would not venture into the grasslands to hunt caiman, but the father and son used the opportunity as a bonding experience. They used an old hunting technique the older man learned from his father when he was a boy. They cornered the caiman into a garrote they laid where they knew it had to go. The rope anchored the beast as they closed in with knives.

The **third pair** are Thayanas who have extensive experience capturing and killing these reptilian beasts. They know what these creatures are thinking before they do. They tracked the caiman to this spot and threw their javelins to strike the beast in one of its great yellow eyes, effectively blinding it.

Alaxpachas Mages, Male Poqoza Half-Elf Magic-Users (MU6) (2): HP 17, 14; AC 9[10] or 2[17] (missile) and 4[15] (melee) from *shield* spell; Atk staff (1d6) or dagger (1d4); Move 12; Save 10; AL N; CL/XP 6/400; Special: +2 save (spells, wands, staffs), darkvision (60ft), spells (4/2/2).
Spells: 1st—*charm person, detect magic, magic missile (x2)*; 2nd—*darkness 15ft radius, web*; 3rd—*lightning bolt, monster summoning I.*
Equipment: staff, dagger,
Note: One of the mages carries a magical stone that can teleport the pair.

Thalus Hunters, Male Poqoza Half-Elves (2): HP 5, 3; AC 9[10]; Atk spear (1d6); Move 12; Save 18; AL L; CL/XP B/10; Special: darkvision (60ft). (*Monstrosities* 254)
Equipment: spear, rope.

Thayanas Hunters, Male Poqoza Half-Elves (2): HP 4, 3; AC 9[10]; Atk javelin (1d6); Move 12; Save 18; AL N; CL/XP B/10; Special: darkvision (60ft). (*Monstrosities* 254)
Equipment: 6 javelins

The three factions cajole the characters to take their side in this dispute over the course of the evening. Each tells the tale from their perspective, treating the other individuals as if they were not there at all. The Thalus and Thayanas dismiss the lightning strike as a minor distraction and even claim that it was a natural event rather than a manmade occurrence. The Thayanas downplay the garrote as a mere nuisance that got in the way of their javelins. They also scoff at the notion that foolish novices had any chance in Miquito of killing the creature. The Thalus are still feeling the adrenaline surge from their first successful hunt.

The arguments drag on well into the night. The character may offer any commentary or judgment they want including presiding over the discussion as if it were a legal matter. Without the characters' intervention, the trio of groups ultimately agree to divide the skin into equal shares. Everyone partakes in the delicious meal, with the Thalus complementing the dish with maize flour tortillas, while the Alaxpachas add herbs and spices to the meat to further enhance its flavor. With the night and fire winding down, the Alaxpachas nonchalantly walk over to the skin to admire it. As soon as an opportunity presents itself, one uses the stone they carry to *teleport* themselves and the skin to escape with their prize. The Alaxpacha pair live in a large town far from this location. The stone is paired to an item from their intended destination to ensure that they arrive on target.

The *teleport* stone requires only a verbal command, which makes it difficult to notice what the mages are up to by the skin. However, if they are close enough, the characters have a 1-in-6 chance to stop the mages from escaping. While the mages can likely best the Thalus and Thayanas, the characters present a significant challenge. They attempt to weasel their way out of a sticky situation by claiming they were going to return the skin intact after showing it to their colleagues or by concocting another plausible yet false explanation. The Thalus and Thayanas naturally want to punish the treacherous pair by forcing them to relinquish their share of the skin or teach them a brutal lesson. Nonetheless, none of the participants believes the skin is more valuable than someone's life, forcing them to ultimately reach a mutually agreeable resolution to the situation.

Goodwill Points: If the characters prevent the mages from stealing the skin, award them one goodwill point for both the Thalus and Thayanas. The two groups then come to an agreement between themselves over who gets to take home the skin. Preventing the Alaxpacha from taking their prize causes the loss of one goodwill point for the Alaxpachas as they retreat. If the characters aid the Alaxpacha plan, they gain one goodwill point for the Alaxpachas. Of course, siding with the Alaxpachas causes the loss of one goodwill point with the Thalus and Thayanas unless the characters' intervention in the matter goes unnoticed by both or either party.

Treasure: If the characters end up with the caiman skin, it is worth 800 gp. The skull also completes part of the list for the earlier **Skulls** adventure hook.

EVENT ENCOUNTER 4:
THE DEVIL OF THE MERCHANTS

Aitayna made a name for himself by robbing merchants. He and his growing band of gnoll underlings have taken down quite a few pochtecas in their time. Some traders go so far as to take out "Aitayna insurance" when shipping large quantities of grain from one place to another.

The Alaxpachan train is not the normal grain shipment he is used to, and Aitayna knows it. The defenders used powerful magic and killed a few of his gnolls before the devil killed the pochteca escorts with a *lightning bolt* from a scroll he had socked away for years. Aitayna is a **salt devil** and is becoming supremely confident with his efforts at building his small, portable empire. A foolish warlock summoned him to the "green place" a decade ago, and he has remained here ever since. Unwilling to share his loot or his power with his infernal kin, Aitayna never called for aid from other devils. He would rather die a prince than live as a commoner. In furtherance of his ambitions, Aitayna soon took over a gang of gnoll raiders that feast on travelers and merchants in the grasslands' numerous pockets of lawlessness.

In this case, the avaricious devil feels obliged to take everything of value from these merchants because they forced him to use a scroll he had been saving for a rainy day. For this score, Aitayna changed his routine and decided to rob this band of merchants traveling south from Zacatl on a rarely used trail through the grasslands. After discussing the situation with his **gnoll lieutenant**, they agreed that a group trekking along such a backwater trail likely carried something of great value or illicit goods, which are likely one and the same. Along with the **8 gnolls** who now accompany them, they picked off several guards and now have the survivors surrounded. Aitayna is about to cast *darkness* over the defenders when the characters first arrive. The gnolls are lying on the ground waiting for their salt devil leader to plunge the defenders into darkness.

Discipline keeps the gnolls from attacking until the devil's signal, but if the characters interfere, all bets are off. The gnolls currently have their longbows in hand, readying an attack for the moment they see a defender emerge from the darkness. The defenders include **2 Poqoza guards** and a **Poqoza druid**. The **8 laborers** with the group are laden with goods, making them ineffective for combat. If the characters come to the group's rescue, the Poqozas fight alongside the characters. Characters who foolishly opt to assist the gnolls and salt devil encounter fleeting allies who turn on their benefactors the first chance they get, which is whenever the characters suggest getting any spoils from the raid.

Aitayna, Salt Devil: HD 11; HP 79; AC 5[14]; **Atk** *+1 longsword* (1d8+1) or 2 claws (1d6); **Move** 12; **Save** 4; **AL** L; **CL/XP** 12/2000; **Special:** +1 or better magic weapons to hit, immune to fire, magic resistance (15%), spell-like abilities. (see **Appendix A: New Monsters**)
Spell-like abilities: at will—*darkness 15ft radius*; 1/day—*disintegrate, teleport.*
Equipment: *+1 longsword.*

Gnoll Lieutenant: HD 4; HP 27; AC 5[14]; **Atk** bite (2d4) or longsword (1d10) or longbow x2 (1d6); **Move** 9; **Save** 13; **AL** C; **CL/XP** 4/120; **Special:** none. (*Monstrosities* 209)
Equipment: longsword, longbow, 20 arrows.

Gnolls (8): HD 2; HP 15, 14, 12x2, 11, 10x2, 9; AC 5[14]; **Atk** bite (2d4) or longsword (1d10) or longbow x2 (1d6); **Move** 9; **Save** 16; **AL** C; **CL/XP** 2/30; **Special:** none. (*Monstrosities* 209)
Equipment: longsword, longbow, 20 arrows.

Poqoza Guards, Male or Female Half-Elves (2): HP 19, 15; AC 5[14]; **Atk** macuahuitl (1d8); **Move** 12; **Save** 14; **AL** C; **CL/XP** 3/60; **Special:** darkvision (60ft). (*Monstrosities* 256)
Equipment: olli armor [B], macuahuitl [B].

Poqoza Druid, Male Half-Elf (Drd6): HP 30; AC 7[12]; **Atk** spear (1d6); **Move** 12; **Save** 10; **AL** C; **CL/XP** 6/400; **Special:** +2 save vs. fire, darkvision (60ft), identify pure water and plants, immune to fey charms, move through non-magical undergrowth, shape change, spells (3/2/2).
Spells: 1st—*detect magic, detect snares and pits, predict weather;* 2nd—*cure light wounds, produce flame;* 3rd—*cure disease, hold animal.*
Equipment: tlahuiztli armor [B], spear.

Poqoza Laborers, Male or Female Half-Elves (8): HP 8, 7x2, 6x3, 4x2; AC 9[10]; **Atk** spear (1d6); **Move** 12; **Save** 18; **AL** N; **CL/XP** B/10; **Special:** darkvision (60ft). (*Monstrosities* 254)
[B] See the **Appendix B: New Equipment and Magic Items**

Goodwill Points: Destroying Aitayna earns the characters one goodwill point for the Thalus. The characters soon discover the Alaxpacha druid and guards are minions of a wealthy landowner to the south who belongs to a seedier criminal cartel in Zacatl that traffics in psychoactive plants, tobacco, and some deadly poisons. If the characters help the Poqozas escape this dicey situation, the characters gain one goodwill point for the Alaxpachas. If they help deliver the merchandise, they gain one more goodwill point for the Alaxpachas. However, the Poqozas in this encounter are inherently evil, which creates its own moral dilemma for good characters, especially exalted heroes and those in the service of a good deity.

Treasure: The goods include six jugs of pulque worth 100 gp each, eight jugs of honey wine worth 20 gp each, six crates of tobacco worth 100 gp each, three doses of lethal poison, two doses of truth serum, and one dose of wyvern poison.

EVENT ENCOUNTER 5:
FIRE IN THE DELL

A rare day without rain feels like a minor blessing, until the smell of black smoke chokes the air. A raid on a hunters' camp leads to animosity between two groups.

This is the site of a Thalu potato farm run by the Qinaya family. Hinayana Qinaya, the leader of this farm, captured and killed several hunting dogs of a Thayana hunting party that trespassed on his property and dug up his potatoes. Hinayana and his fieldworkers issued several warnings to the dogs' owners to stay away from potatoes and their prized rat terriers renowned for their ability to sniff out vermin and other pests. However, the untrained dogs and their owner refused to heed the warnings, which ultimately forced Hinayana's hand.

The hunters did not take the slight lightly. Instead of targeting Hinayana directly, they chose to attack his prized possession — his landmark villa. The two-story structure made from wood imported from the neighboring Toctli

ENCOUNTER 5
1 Square – 10 Feet
N

Forest is an architectural marvel. Indeed, the magnificent home attracts the interest of sightseers and architects alike. In an act of revenge, the Thayanas tossed a torch onto the back of the home in a deliberate attempt to burn it and its occupants to the ground.

The wood burns slowly, but the flames capture the attention of **4 fire phantoms** that venture from the Plane of Fire to partake in the conflagration. The monsters immediately incinerate the stunned arsonists, while the remainder of their company flee for their lives. Meanwhile, Hinayana and his family members desperately try to douse the blaze before it destroys the home in its entirety. They feverishly lower a bucket into a well behind the property and are poised to splash its contents onto the timbers as quickly as possible. However, the fire phantoms stand in their way. The characters have two minutes to defeat the fire phantoms, which would give the firefighters enough time to save the home from certain destruction. Of course, if the characters have a means of extinguishing the conflagration through magical means, they may attempt to do so as well. In addition to saving the residence, two young, frightened children remain trapped in the building, unable to escape because of the blinding smoke starting to fill its hallways and rooms.

Fire Phantoms (4): HD 6; HP 47, 45, 40, 36; AC 6[13]; Atk slam
(1d4 + 1d6 fire); **Move** 6; **Save** 11; **AL** C; **CL/XP** 7/600; **Special:**
fire blast (every 1d4 rounds, 30ft range, 2d6 damage, save avoids),
immolation (1/day, 6d6 damage to all within 10ft radius, save for
half, kills phantom if it fails save or extinguishes flame for 1 round if
successful), immune to fire. (see **Appendix A: New Monsters**)

Goodwill Points: Defeating the fire phantoms earns the characters one goodwill point for the Thalus. If the characters save the home and the children, they gain one more goodwill point for the Thalus.

Treasure: If the characters succeed at these tasks, the family invites them to attend a victory feast. Before the celebration ends, Hinayana presents them with *+1 ollixalli* armor (see **Appendix B: New Equipment and Magic Items**). This armor is made from hardened rubber rather than metal. It is a family heirloom that has been handed down for generations, much like the villa the characters saved.

EVENT ENCOUNTER 6: THE LOST CHILDREN OF THE CHUXUNTANA

The emaciated boys greet the characters with a distilled liquor made from fermented walnuts in tiny cups woven from the grass. The one pouring from the flask tells them his name is Cachana, and the other two are his cousins, Ziegler and Zemsky. They have lived their entire lives in the tall grass. They beg for information about the outside world, which they happily exchange for stories about this area. The boys have intimate knowledge of the region and its history, teasing the characters with the tale of a big cat that murders Poqozas in their sleep.

The boys tell the characters whatever they want to hear, moving from one tall tale to the next with the greatest of ease. Despite their propensity for telling fibs, the boys have no talent for making their stories sound true. However, they are so engrossed with the conversation that they make it uncomfortable for the characters to discreetly terminate the conversation and leave. While the characters talk to them, tiny thorns grow out of the boys' chubby, cherubic faces. In addition, their eyes, which initially looked hazel, now resemble polished pieces of wood.

The boys are not menacing in any way, though they act right on the edge of disturbing. Ziegler plays with a small knife, stabbing in quick succession between his fingers splayed out wide on the dirt. However, he sheathes the knife when politely asked to do so. Zemsky keeps looking outside, giving the impression he knows exactly when and where the next lightning bolt will strike. Cachana smiles good-naturedly and continues to pour out small draughts of the intoxicating liquor — if only for himself.

Cachana is the most gregarious of the group. He truly wants to know about the outside world. He trades stories of his mother deeper in the tallgrass, and how she does not like strangers around here. He offers to lead the characters out of this area of tallgrass and away from his mother, though he refuses to elaborate on his offer or provide any details about his mother. He leads characters who unquestioningly accept his offer past his "Mother" in the upcoming **Encounter Event 7: Mother of the Tallgrass** to a safe location in the grasslands where he and his cousin harmlessly part ways with the characters. However, if the characters discuss any terms of his offer with him, he casually rescinds the bargain, telling the characters he was only joking as he is just a boy. During the course of the conversation, he eventually puts his foot into his mouth when he tells them about the dead tree where his father died, and how his mother loves the tree more than any of her children. He awkwardly smiles while he conveys that unpleasant detail.

While the boys tell stories, the characters notice more of the thin boys emerging from the tallgrass into the trampled clearing. They sit out in the rain with smiles on their faces, catching the falling raindrops on their tongues and drinking them. When there are 14 boys in the clearing, read or paraphrase the following description:

At this juncture, the characters now stare down **14 children of the briar**. During the combat, the boys click in a foreign tongue as they assess the characters' potential strengths and weaknesses. They then attempt to entangle the characters as soon as possible while spitting thorns at them.

Children of the Briar (14): HD 2; HP 15, 14, 13x3, 12x2, 11x4,
10, 9, 8; AC 5[14]; Atk 2 claws (1d6); **Move** 9 (climb 6); **Save** 16;
AL C; **CL/XP** 2/30; **Special:** entangle (if both claws hit, save or
held, automatic 2d4 damage per round), spit thorns (60ft range,
1d6 damage, save avoids), vulnerable to fire (200% damage). (see
Appendix A: New Monsters)

Goodwill Points: The mischievous boys have attacked many of the surrounding farms and game animals. If the characters bring proof of the death of a child of the briar to any nearby Thalu farm or Thayana hunting party, award them one goodwill point for that group. The characters can gain a goodwill point from both groups. This encounter feeds directly into **Event Encounter 7: Mother of the Tallgrass**.

Treasure: The flask Cachana pours the liquor from is made using a rare and presumably lost technique. It is worth 100 gp.

EVENT ENCOUNTER 7: MOTHER OF THE TALLGRASS

the air. A grass curtain functions as portal into a thorny dome 300 feet across and nearly 30 feet high. The thorny vines part, and the visage of a waifish woman comes into view. She screams as a mass of vines wrap around her body and drag her deeper into the dome. She disappears over the edge of a pit of dark, raw earth.

"Mother" is a **duskthorn dryad**. The characters' natural instinct may be to rescue the woman being dragged into the dome. However, the vines are intended to drag her into a better defensive position within the area. To further the ruse, she may attempt to charm a character into saving her or suggest that a character follow her into the dome. Mother uses her magical abilities to remain out of sight by turning invisible or obscuring the characters' vision by filling the air with mist. She leaves the melee combat to her guardian, a **vine troll skeleton** (see **Appendix A: New Monsters**) that lies in wait just inside the grass curtain. It lashes out at the characters when they pass through the curtain.

If the characters present her with any evidence of the child of the briar's demise, she appears upset for a moment before quickly moving on from the tragedy.

Mother of the Tallgrass, Duskthorn Dryad: HD 8; **HP** 52; **AC** 6[13]; **Atk** dagger (1d4); **Move** 12; **Save** 8; **AL** C; **CL/XP** 10/1400; **Special:** control vines, speak with plants and animals (at will), spell-like abilities, tree stride, vulnerable (must stay near tree and vines or take 1d6 damage per hour), wall of thorns (thorn wall as a *wall of stone*). (see **Appendix A: New Monsters**)
Spell-like abilities: at will—*faerie fire, sleep;* 3/day—*charm person, invisibility, magic missile;* 1/day—*dispel magic, obscuring mist, suggestion.*

Vine Troll Skeleton: HD 7; **HP** 51; **AC** 6[13]; **Atk** 2 claws (1d6), bite (1d8); **Move** 12; **Save** X; **AL** N; **CL/XP** 8/800; **Special:** immune to sleep and charm, regenerate (3hd/round). (see **Appendix A: New Monsters**)

Goodwill Points: If the characters tell anyone in the Caxcalli Grasslands that they defeated the Mother of the Tallgrass, they are welcomed into the person's home or business, where they receive food, drink, and a bed, if available. In addition, they gain one goodwill point with the individual's group. They can retell the tale to each of the three strata, though they never receive more than one goodwill point from a single strata.

The base of "Mother's" main tree, the one with origins of her creeper vines that infest the area, holds a locked chest trapped with a poisoned thorn (save or die).

Treasure: The chest contains gold ingots worth 2,400 gp and a set of jade and amber chess pieces. Each piece is two inches across at the base and nearly four inches tall. One bishop and one queen are missing. Each piece is worth 20 gp for a total of 600 gp. The two missing pieces and the board are in **Area 1-D**.

EVENT ENCOUNTER 8: STRANGE WEATHER

Clouds gather in the east as the sun is about to set in the opposite direction. A storm appears to be brewing. As night falls across the land, the first raindrops hit the ground. Several minutes later, a subtle yet noticeable sizzling sound accompanies the precipitation. In an even more disturbing development, odd croaking sounds now drown out the rain.

The effects of the nihileth on the rain patterns in the southwest are unearthly. Acid rain falls nearly every time a storm develops in the lee of the Mulla Chanacu. The acid rain deals no damage to creatures, but 10 minutes of exposure to the caustic liquid deals 1 point of damage to nonmagical objects. The grass in this area has adapted to the change in weather. It is hardier and

more resistant to the acid than typical grass species in the region. The fauna is also very limited, with burrowing animals making up the majority of its population.

This freakish storm also picked up some small travelers: **5 swarms of poisonous frogs**. The winds lifted the tiny amphibians roughly 40 feet in the air. The roiling mass of poisonous frogs attacks anything in their path, biting living creatures with reckless fury. After 1d4 + 1 rounds, the creatures break off the assault and make their way to the closest puddle of standing water.

Poisonous Frog Swarms (5): HD 4; HP 36, 31, 28x2, 23; AC 8[11]; **Atk** swarm (1d6 + poison); **Move** 9; **Save** 13; **AL** N; **CL/XP** 4/120; **Special:** poison (save or die). (see **Appendix A: New Monsters**)

Goodwill Points: No goodwill points are available for this encounter.

Event Encounter 9: Strange Weather II – The Reckoning

Torrential rain sometimes spawns flash flooding in the grasslands. In this case, a sudden deluge combined with saturated ground and swollen rivers gives birth to a raging flash flood.

> Rain pounds the earth, drowning out all sound or so it would seem. A dull roar emanating somewhere in the distance rapidly draws closer. Moments later, a wave of four-foot-high water surges across the land as several panicked animals feebly try to outrun the onrushing water.

The raging waters are four feet high and measure 180 feet wide as the mindless body follows the path of least resistance across the intervening terrain. When the characters first notice the water, it is roughly 1d3 x 100 feet away and traveling at a speed of 100 feet per round. Any creature caught in the floodwaters must succeed on a saving throw or take 2d8 points of damage and be pushed back 1d10 x 10 feet in the same direction as the current. On a successful saving throw, the creature remains upright in the same spot and takes no damage. A character swept away by the current takes 1d8 points of damage each round spent in the floodwaters. Furthermore, the creature must hold its breath while underwater. A creature can regain its footing with a successful saving throw. If the creature regains its footing, it is not prone nor being swept away by the current that round.

The floodwaters automatically sweep away any loose, unattended objects in their path. The deluge has carried off a frenzied **giant weasel**, **2 giant scorpions**, and a **swarm of poisonous snakes** that attack any nearby creatures, including the characters.

Giant Weasel: HD 3+3; HP 23; AC 6[13]; **Atk** bite (2d6 + blood drain); **Move** 15; **Save** 14; **AL** N; **CL/XP** 4/120; **Special:** drain blood (automatic 2d6 damage until released). (*Monstrosities* 506)

Giant Scorpions (2): HD 6; HP 36, 22; AC 3[16]; **Atk** 2 pincers (1d10), sting (1d4 + lethal poison); **Move** 12; **Save** 11; **AL** N; **CL/XP** 7/600; **Special:** lethal poison (save or die). (*Monstrosities* 411)

Poisonous Snake Swarm: HD 3; HP 19; AC 6[13]; **Atk** swarm (1d6 + poison); **Move** 9; **Save** 14; **AL** N; **CL/XP** 3/60; **Special:** poison (save or additional 1d4 damage).

Goodwill Points: No goodwill points are available for this encounter.

Event Encounter 10: I am the Rat God

Capybara, nutria, cavies, and chinchilla roam the grasslands, destroying crops in civilized lands, but providing protein for creatures further up the food chain. These rodents usually gather in small groups of their own and feed on plants and grains they can find. One larger group follows and worships an ichneumon, a massive weasel who sometimes eats its followers, but mostly scares away larger predators to allow the ordinary rodents a near paradise in a warden of small burrows away from civilization.

> The trail becomes very narrow ahead, almost as if nothing taller than 24 inches travels through here.
>
> After wading through the thick grass, a dun-colored honeycomb of tunnels dug into the side of a large berm becomes visible. A cornucopia of rodents stand guard around the complex, as still as statues while they survey their surroundings. After a few moments, the crowd disperses as a handful of rodents take the initiative to scurry back into their burrows.
>
> A few moments later, the tall grass on the far side of the clearing past the berm shuffles. Something large moves behind the grass.

The **ichneumon** disappears into one of the hundreds of burrows riddling this area. The large beast can only enter the honeycomb's larger tunnels, though these passages ultimately connect to the smaller one the rodents use during the course of their daily travels.

The monster and the **5 rat swarms** under its sway are not itching for a fight against the characters. It waits below, hoping to detect the presence of a dragon, its ancient blood enemy. In the interim, the creature relies upon its rodent spies to gather intelligence about the unexpected trespassers. The rodents periodically emerge from their holes to keep tabs on the characters. They use high-pitched shrills and other sounds to communicate their findings to each other and the ichneumon.

If the characters attempt to explore any tunnel or attack a rodent, the reluctant ichneumon emerges from its hiding spot and attacks the aggressor. As previously mentioned, the creature does not relish a confrontation with the adventurers. If seriously wounded, it retreats into a tunnel, hoping the characters opt not to follow it.

Ichneumon: HD 9; AC 5[14] or 3[16] from mud armor; **Atk** 2 claws (1d6), bite (3d6); **Move** 15; **Save** 6; **AL** N; **CL/XP** 10/1400; **Special:** mud armor (mud coating grants +2 AC bonus), resistances (acid, cold, electricity, fire). (see **Appendix A: New Monsters**)

Rat Swarms (5): HD 5; AC 6[13]; **Atk** swarm (1d6 + disease); **Move** 12; **Save** 6; **AL** N; **CL/XP** 5/240; **Special:** disease (automatic 1d6 damage per day until healed, save avoids).

Treasure: If chased underground and cornered, the ichneumon nonverbally offers the characters a green dragon egg to broker a truce. The egg is nearly ready to hatch. The ichneumon uses its rodent followers to incubate the egg until the wyrmling inside hatches. The ichneumon considers the tasty treat a rare delicacy. If the characters accept the ichneumon's offer, the egg is worth 2,000 gp.

Goodwill Points: If the characters defeat the ichneumon, the hunters of the grasslands soon find out about the death of one of their wily foes. Grant the characters one goodwill point for the Thayana.

Chapter Two: Social Business

When the characters accumulate four goodwill points for a single group, a coterie of representatives from that group approaches them. If the characters complete all the event encounters without garnering four goodwill points, they are met by members of the group with the most goodwill points

A contingent of four finely dressed Poqoza men and women stand at a crossroads up ahead. The group takes notice and bows as one of them wearing a magnificent jaguar fur addresses the audience.

"Blessing of Tlatlcolli upon you," he says in a reverent tone. "Your deeds have traveled far and wide across our land, like grass seeds on the wind, O great Calanca."

They move aside to reveal a long table laden with fresh fruits, bowls of cooked grain, tortillas, tamales, and roasted turkey.

"We humbly beseech you to join us at our table," he says, gesturing for his guests to take their seats.

The Poqozas taste samples of all the dishes to reassure the characters that they are not poisoned. The hosts reiterate that they are here to praise their honored visitors rather than harm them. The Poqozas refuse to sit at the table until the characters do so first. The man who first introduced himself explains to them that his name is Oacce. He leads a small community in the area that has fallen on hard times. He and his people require the expertise of brave heroes to eradicate the blight plaguing their lands. The nature of the evil depends upon which strata the representatives belong — the Thalus, the Thayanas, or the Alaxpachas.

Oacce, Male Half-Elf Noble: HP 25; AC 5[14]; Atk tecpatl (1d4); Move 12; Save 12; AL C; CL/XP 5/240; **Special:** darkvision (60ft). (*Monstrosities* 256)
Equipment: olli armor, tecpatl[B].

Alaxpacha Final Encounter: Invaders! Within and Without

Characters partaking in the **Medical Mission of Mercy** hook may be surprised to learn that some of the rumors are true. A hobgoblin warship from distant Akados landed on these shores after their fellow goblinoids expelled them from their native homeland of Exor because of their heretical beliefs. To make matters worse, the Irpanuqana hobgoblins already met with the Achnis from the **Canals and Contracts** hook. The hobgoblins took their charge to explore the Caxcalli Grasslands as free rein to explore and conquer the region under their own banner. As they made their way inland, they used a combination of the Poqozas' proclivity for experimentation and an elixir of potent hobgoblin mead to sway some to their cause. The hobgoblins beat those Alaxpachas who refused to willingly forsake Tlatlcolli and embrace the invaders' newfangled religion. After several rounds of torture, they conscripted the resisters into forced labor camps where they toil day and night to build their fabled highway to riches outside the compound.

An unusually charismatic hobgoblin evangelist named Banc commands the military and religious expedition. The new faith he espouses is his belief in his own divinity, and he resorts to any means necessary to propagate his belief, including unspeakable acts of cruelty and barbarism. As proof of his godhood, he demonstrates his ability to cast powerful spells, an act he could not achieve without divine intervention. Of course, the arrogant Banc is a charlatan who cannot explain how he obtained his priestly powers. Unbeknownst to him, the Aztli god Itztliteotl took an interest in the conniving

huckster. He grants the hobgoblin his magical powers to amuse himself and indirectly to spite the Poqozas and Tlatlcolli. Many Poqozas, including some of Tlatlcolli's priests, fell prey to his abundant charms and brutal tactics. As punishment for their lack of faith, the angry god condemned his former priests to an undead existence as huecuvas who are partly to blame for the illnesses afflicting the Poqozas.

The characters can get involved in this storyline in several ways. Characters who embarked on the **Medical Mission of Mercy** hook may actively be searching for victims and could even arrive here by canoe. Alternatively, the characters could run across sick Poqozas who either fled the evangelist's compound and its horrendous working conditions or were infected by the huecuvas' diseased claws. Despite their poor health, the infirmed Poqozas get squirrely discussing how and where they may have contracted the disease. None wants to tell their fellow half-elves about their dalliance with the hobgoblin's warped faith after they abandoned Tlatlcolli either willingly or through coercion. Oacce may directly ask the characters to investigate or corroborate the stories coming from the hobgoblin compound. The characters could potentially encounter a hobgoblin patrol (see **Area E1-B** and use that opportunity to infiltrate the compound by claiming to be new converts or people who want to learn more about the evangelist and his burgeoning religion.

Regardless of how the characters get to the hobgoblin compound, read or paraphrase the following description when they arrive:

Garish paint, gold leaf accoutrements, opulent carvings, and images of a hobgoblin striking a regal posture adorn the outer surface of a wooden barrier surrounding a compound. Every square inch of ground inside the palisade appears spotless, and four Poqoza laborers meticulously sweep the sand into peaceful swoops of uniform design and groom the grasses into a luxurious green carpet. Otherwise, all seems quiet.

The **4 Poqozas laborers** obviously seem underfed and overworked. A character who examines one of the workers notices they conceal scorch marks and burns beneath their loose-fitting clothing. The men are terrified of the hobgoblins and their leader Banc. They refuse to converse with the characters unless compelled to do so, possibly through magic. Otherwise, they pontificate ad nauseum about the one true god — an individual they identify as Banc the Resplendent, Master of the Seas and Lord of the Lands. Other than prattling on about Banc's might and greatness, they cannot provide any details about the tenets of his religion. The grounds are currently quiet as the laborers in the field toil to construct the evangelist's roads and the patrols monitoring them search for fugitives and more converts.

Poqoza Laborers, Male Half-Elves (4): HP 3, 2x2, 1; AC 9[10]; Atk club (1d4); Move 12; Save 18; AL Any; CL/XP B/10; **Special:** darkvision (60ft). (*Monstrosities* 254)

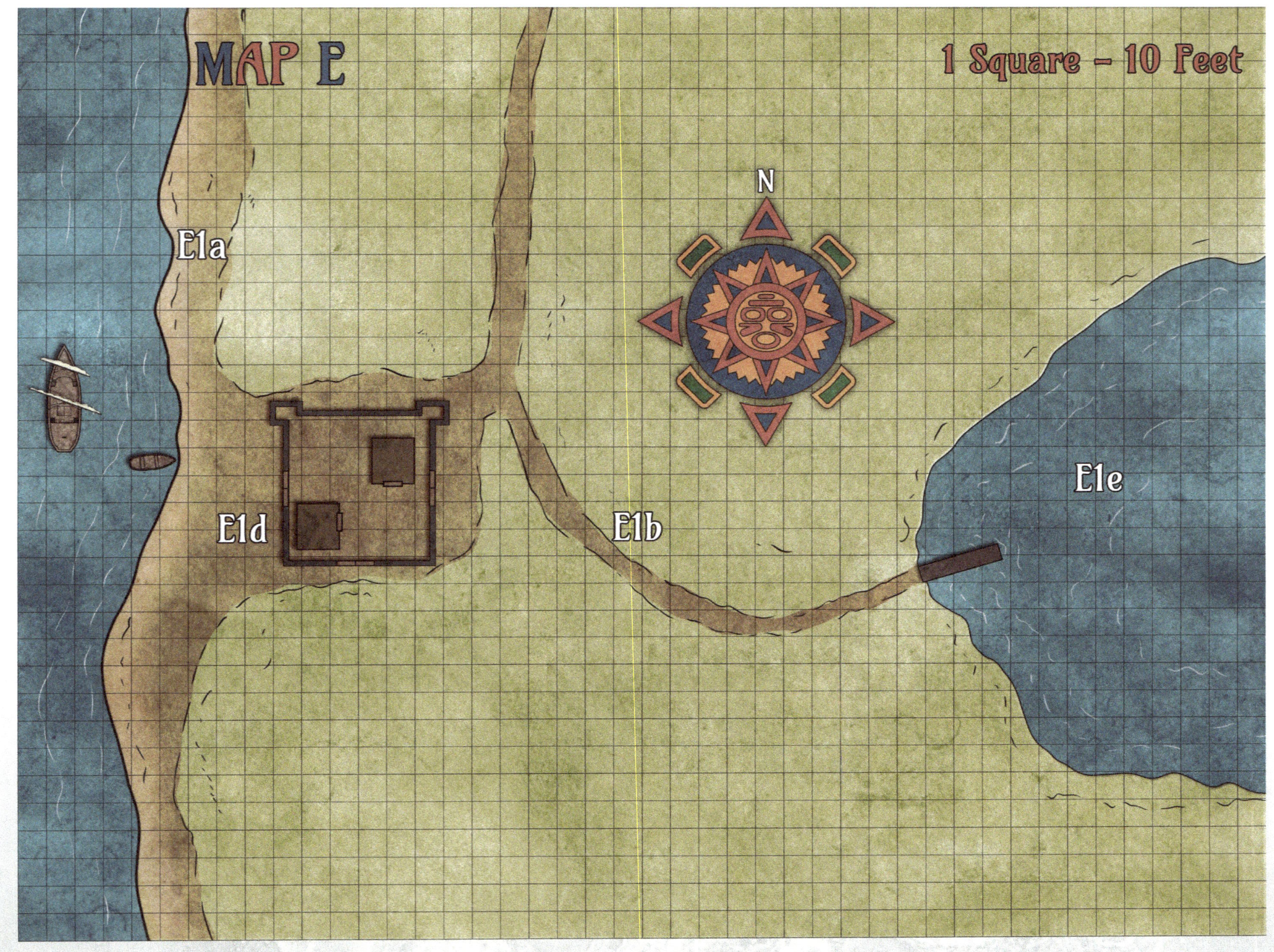

MAP E
1 Square = 10 Feet
E1a
E1d
E1b
E1e
N

Area E1-A: The Beach

The Poqoza on the beach is the Alaxpacha who used to be in charge of the community. If the characters approach him, he tells of his deep sorrow.

> "At first, we could not even see them. We did not know what to look for. We trained our eyes on the stars most of the time. The Irpanuqana were invisible to us. We did not recognize them or their wooden ship until it was too late."

Niya Qachana, the former Alaxpacha leader, sits on the beach every day lamenting his loss. The hobgoblins left him a broken man after their brazen pre-dawn raid, which caught him and his followers literally napping. The Irpanuqana hobgoblins led him to believe that they burned his spellbook and other possessions. However, the hobgoblins stole these objects along with the rest of his and the other Poqozas' possessions, which they now store in the compound's main building. The evangelist left him to wallow in his self-pity. Unless the characters rouse his spirits, he seems content to take no actions other than to blubber about the loss of his people and his magical powers.

Niya Qachana, Former Alaxpacha Leader, Male Poqoza Half-Elf Magic-User (MU6): HP 19; AC 9[10] or 2[17] (missile) and 4[15] (melee) from *shield* spell; **Atk** none; **Move** 12; **Save** 10; **AL** N; **CL/XP** 6/400; **Special:** +2 save (spells, wands, staffs), darkvision (60ft), spells (4/2/2).
Spells: 1st—*charm person, light, magic missile (x2)*; 2nd—*darkness 15ft radius, phantasmal force*; 3rd—*fly, lightning bolt.*
Equipment: staff, dagger,
Note: Niya Qachana has no spells currently memorized as he has been away from his spellbook for a while.

Area E1-B: The Road to Nowhere

After taking over the Alaxpacha compound, the evangelist immediately began constructing two roads. The first thoroughfare stretches north of the sand dunes on the southern beach and travels west toward the Toctli Forest, following an ancient, well-worn path. The trail is fairly flat with cobblestones marking its edges. The Poqoza laborers who toil on these endeavors use this first road to haul supplies and materials for the highway Banc believes is destined to lead him to fame and fortune. The evangelist took the Achnis' offer as described in the **Canals and Contracts** hook, yet he interpreted their offer to mean he had free rein not just to explore the Caxcalli Grasslands but to conquer it. Being an impulsive leader, the evangelist never bothered to survey his surroundings. Instead, he decided to build a path to Xicotli the instant he learned about the Poqoza city and its longstanding rivalry with his hobgoblin kin. Unfortunately for him, his path heads straight toward a vast swath of grass teeming with poison ivy. Despite the warnings from the Poqoza laborers familiar with the area, the evangelist dismissed their concerns out of hand as he declared that no patch of itchy weeds can stop him and his god. Those who express their opposition to his plans quickly vanish to an unknown fate.

The characters can intersect either of the six-foot-wide paths at any juncture along their route. At this point, the roads are merely earthen paths bordered by cobblestones. The laborers remove any debris, vegetation, and stones from the trail. The evangelist wants only to reach Xicotli to find more worshippers and exact his brand of hobgoblin revenge against the city's inhabitants. He cares not how he and his followers get there.

A team of **20 laborers** languish at these miserable tasks. It is evident that they live in utter squalor, often sleeping on the dirt and eating meals unfit for livestock. To prevent them from escaping during the night, their captors bind their hands and feet. During the day, a patrol of **6 hobgoblin guards** direct their activities while preventing any from escaping.

Poqoza Laborers, Male Half-Elves (20): HP 1d6; AC 9[10]; **Atk** club (1d4); **Move** 12; **Save** 18; **AL** Any; **CL/XP** B/10; **Special:** darkvision (60ft). (***Monstrosities*** 254)

Hobgoblin Guards (6): HD 2; HP 16, 15, 13, 12x2, 10; AC 5[14]; **Atk** battle axe (1d8); **Move** 9; **Save** 16; **AL** C; **CL/XP** 2/30; **Special:** none. (*Monstrosities* 250)
Equipment: battle axe, whistle on a leather strap.

In addition to monitoring the laborers under their command, they keep a watchful eye for fugitives, vandals, and potential new converts. If the characters attack them or attempt to free the laborers who are bound together by heavy ropes, the hobgoblins blow whistles attached to a leather strap dangling around their neck. When they sound the alarm, there is a 30% chance that another hobgoblin patrol of **6 guards** arrives 1d4 minutes later to investigate the disturbance. In any event, the characters never encounter more than 18 hobgoblins in this manner. The patrols' leader is a brutal taskmaster named **Achima**.

Achima, Hobgoblin Taskmaster: HD 6; HP 43; AC 2[17]; **Atk** battle axe (1d8+3) or whip (1d6+3); **Move** 9; **Save** 11; **AL** C; **CL/XP** 6/400; **Special:** none. (*Monstrosities* 250)
Equipment: battle axe, whip.

Hobgoblin Guards (up to 12 additional): HD 2; AC 5[14]; **Atk** battle axe (1d8); **Move** 9; **Save** 16; **AL** C; **CL/XP** 2/30; **Special:** none. (*Monstrosities* 250)
Equipment: battle axe, whistle on a leather strap.

Almost all of the Poqoza laborers and a handful of elves with them are malnourished, diseased, injured, or a combination of these conditions. When liberated, the emaciated laborers crowd around the adventurers as if they were Tlatlcolli himself, whom they credit for sending the adventurers to rescue them. Some suffer from the disease the huecuvas spread while others have fallen ill with influenza and several other contagions normally associated with filth, starvation, and fetid sanitary conditions. If the characters participated in the **Medical Mission of Mercy** hook, they may administer the powder they received at the beginning of the adventure to cure the Poqoza stricken by the disease spread by their former priests who fell under the evangelist's influence. Otherwise, the characters can use their magic, medical skills, and any supplies they have to tend to their wounds, feed them, and cure them of any ailments. If the characters do not have any powder on hand, residents of neighboring villages in the hobgoblins' future path provide them with a fresh supply of powder. In any case, you may award the characters a 500 XP story award for fulfilling their obligations to assist the sick and infirmed Poqozas.

Area E1-C: The Acolytes

Although labeled as an area, this encounter is intended to be a precursor to the characters' rendezvous with Banc. Therefore, its exact location depends upon the circumstances. If the characters explore the surrounding area, they encounter Ampeyo and Paysh, the acolytes, somewhere during their travels in the surrounding wilderness. If the characters proceed directly to **Area E1-D**, they meet them outside of the compound. The **2 hobgoblin acolytes Ampety** and **Paysh** loyally serve Banc as his trusted lieutenants, but the pair secretly pray to Kakobovia while outwardly professing their faith in Banc as a self-proclaimed deity. They suspect that Banc does the same, though they naturally fear raising the subject with him. Their doubts in Banc's divinity do nothing to lessen their enthusiasm and devotion to his grand plan and overall vision. The hobgoblin acolytes carry out their orders with ruthless efficiency.

At the moment, the pair is using their magic to discern what lies ahead for the hobgoblins in their adopted homeland. They seem concerned about the portents they recently witnessed, and the characters' arrival does nothing to temper their fears. When they notice the intrusion, the acolytes command the **6 hobgoblins** accompanying them to attack the trespassers. The pair never surrenders, even in the face of superior opposition. The acolytes are intimately familiar with Banc's plans to build a road to Xicotli to facilitate its downfall. The characters may already be familiar with this plan too. On the other hand, they likely do not know that the hobgoblins plan to supplement their force with their hobgoblin kin already living on the island and are preparing to make overtures to the indigenous gnolls to join forces with them. Unfortunately for Banc and his hobgoblin allies, the gnolls would never willingly forsake Itzcuin for what they perceive to be an imaginary hobgoblin deity.

Ampety and Paysh, Hobgoblin Acolytes (2): HD 8; HP 61, 56; AC 5[14]; **Atk** *+1 flail* (1d8+1); **Move** 9; **Save** 8; **AL** C; **CL/XP** 8/800; **Special:** spells (2/2/2/2/2). (*Monstrosities* 250)
Spells: 1st—*cure light wounds, detect magic;* 2nd—*bless, hold person;* 3rd—*cure disease, prayer;* 4th—*cure serious wounds* (x2); 5th—*finger of death, insect plague.*
Equipment: *+1 flail.*

Hobgoblin Guards (6): HD 2; HP 15, 14x3, 12x2; AC 5[14]; **Atk** battle axe (1d8); **Move** 9; **Save** 16; **AL** C; **CL/XP** 2/30; **Special:** none. (*Monstrosities* 250)
Equipment: battle axe, whistle on a leather strap.

Treasure: The acolytes carry three jars containing *potions of extra healing* as insurance against contracting any disease, *black war paint* (see **Appendix B: New Equipment and Magic Items**), a pouch containing six pearls worth 100 gp each, and a small bag holding 18 pp.

Area E1-D: The Evangelist

The Irpanuqana hobgoblin evangelist **Banc** spreads death and controversy wherever he goes. Before his arrival in Tehuatl, Banc was a revered and respected priest of Kakobovia and served in Exor's armies in their endless battles against the dwarf clans in the Stoneheart Mountains. Banc grew weary of waging a repetitive war of attrition against these hated foes and lost faith in his god's narrowminded vision. Inspired by the warlord Grugdour and his ascendency, Banc took a page from his playbook and renounced his faith in Kakobovia. In his place, he declared himself to be a god.

Unlike Grugdour's ploy, Banc's fell flat on its face. He temporarily lost his ability to cast spells, and his heresy earned him the swift wrath of Exor's traditionalist ruler, Teth Khan. In his haste to escape, Banc fled the city with his devoted entourage and headed for the coast, where he stole the moored vessel, *The Aviary*, and set sail on the open seas. He initially forced the ship's halfling crew to man the craft until he marooned them on a deserted island and took command himself. The novice navigator and his hobgoblin charges spent six months sailing *The Aviary* across the ocean with periodic stops along the way to "redistribute" supplies they found in far-flung ports of call before finally landing on Tehuatl's shores where they encountered the Achnis. By this time, Banc had regained his priestly powers thanks to Itztliteotl's intervention. Before departing for the southern coast of Tehuatl, he and his men burglarized a temple of Tlatlcolli and killed some of its clergymen in the process. The authorities used their magic to speak with those slain during the crime, giving them an accurate description of the perpetrators. Buoyed by the surprising restoration of his priestly powers, the deluded Banc now believes he can amass enough followers and coins to allow him to comfortably retire in the Caxcalli Grasslands, where he can lead a leisurely life of wanton excess.

When characters encounter him, Banc is dramatically preaching to a new batch of **17 Poqoza followers**. These enthralled worshippers hang on Banc's every word, as they are unable to resist his persuasiveness and enchantment magic. Banc immediately responds to the intrusion by attempting to charm as many enemies as possible. He uses his new thralls as human shields, imploring them to run interference for him, while **4 hobgoblins** defend him against attacks. While survival is naturally first and foremost on Banc's mind, he secondarily wants to add more followers to his retinue rather than outright kill the characters. Nonetheless, if left with no other choice, Banc favors death. Although the hobgoblin evangelist believes himself to be a god, he is unwilling to find out for sure if he is reduced to fewer than 30 hit points. He pleads for mercy and offers to serve the characters if necessary. Unfortunately for the characters, Banc is a habitual liar who betrays them at the first opportunity. If the characters confront him about the rampant diseases spreading across the area, he admits the huecuvas are responsible for spreading some of the contagions while the others arose from the squalid conditions.

Banc, Male Hobgoblin Evangelist: HD 12; HP 78; AC 5[14]; **Atk** *staff of beguiling* (1d6) or condemning touch (2d6 + fear); **Move** 12; **Save** 3; **AL** C; **CL/XP** 14/2600; **Special:** fear (flee as *fear* spell if condemning touch hits, save resists), proselytize (3/day, 30ft radius, as *charm person*, save resists), spells (4/4/4/4/4/1). (*Monstrosities* 250)
Spells: 1st—*cure light wounds* (x2), *detect magic, protection from evil;* 2nd—*bless, hold person, silence 15ft radius, speak with animals;* 3rd—*cure disease, locate object, prayer, remove curse;* 4th—*create water, cure serious wounds, neutralize poison, sticks to snakes;* 5th—*commune, dispel evil, finger of death* (x2); 6th—*blade barrier.*
Equipment: *staff of beguiling,* chainmail armor, 2 *potions of extra healing.*

Hobgoblin Guards (4): HD 2; HP 15, 14x3, 12x2; AC 5[14]; **Atk** battle axe (1d8); **Move** 9; **Save** 16; **AL** C; **CL/XP** 2/30; **Special:** none. (*Monstrosities* 250)
Equipment: battle axe, whistle on a leather strap.

Poqoza Followers, Male and Female Half-Elves (17): HP 1d6; AC 9[10]; **Atk** club (1d4); **Move** 12; **Save** 18; **AL** Any; **CL/XP** B/10; **Special:** darkvision (60ft). (*Monstrosities* 254)

Treasure: Banc has a *staff of beguiling* in his arsenal along with two *potions of extra healing* he keeps on hand to ward off disease. His ship *The Aviary* is anchored 100 feet offshore. The vessel is barely seaworthy and would require extensive repairs and maintenance to bring it up to snuff. Nonetheless, it is worth 4,000 gp, though it is rightfully owned by a halfling family in Akados. It is currently defended by **6 hobgoblins** who fight to the death. Banc keeps the spoils he burglarized from the temple of Tlatlcolli in a chest in his private quarters. The container holds 3,204 cacao beans worth 1 gp each, 602 gp, 1,923 sp, and a bronze figurine depicting the Poqozas' sole god Tlatlcolli that is worth 1,500 gp. While there is no way to trace the cacao beans and coins back to the temple, selling the figurine south of the Great Canal is a dicey proposition that is likely to attract the interest of the god's worshippers looking for Banc and the pilfered loot.

Hobgoblin Guards (6): HD 2; HP 16, 14, 13, 12, 10x2; AC 5[14]; **Atk** longsword (1d8); **Move** 9; **Save** 16; **AL** C; **CL/XP** 2/30; **Special:** none. (*Monstrosities* 250)
Equipment: longsword.

AREA E1-E: STAGING AREA

In one of the strangest and perhaps worst-planned plots, Banc and the hobgoblins plan to export the **8 huecuvas** gathered here by sea to numerous areas throughout Tehuatl. So far, his scheme sounds plausible. However, with *The Aviary* on the brink of falling apart, Banc needed to find an alternative means of getting them to his targeted destinations. The hobgoblin evangelist thinks he can charm animals to do his dirty work, in this case **2 killer whales**. Because the huecuvas are already dead and cannot drown, he plans to charm or train the killer whales into performing this task. So far, his efforts have proven unsuccessful. Meanwhile, Tlatlcolli's unfaithful undead priests attack the characters when they approach this area.

Huecuvas (8): HD 2; HP 16, 14, 13x3, 12, 10x2; AC 2[17]; **Atk** 2 claws (1d4+1 + disease); **Move** 12; **Save** 16; **AL** N; **CL/XP** 5/240; **Special:** +1 or better magic or silver weapons to hit, change self (3/ day), disease (save resists initial onset; symptoms appear 1d3 days after failed save, 1d3 points of constitution and 1d3 dexterity loss each day, save at −3 penalty to overcome ongoing damage).

Killer Whales (2): HD 12; HP 90, 82; AC 4[15]; **Atk** bite (3d10); **Move** 24 (swim); **Save** 3; **AL** N; **CL/XP** 12/2000; **Special:** None.

THALU FINAL ENCOUNTER:
THREE DAYS OF DARKNESS

Oacce tells the characters a tale of woe. He describes a rattling wail of unearthly origin that came from the tallgrass surrounding his village. His people thought it was the coming of Yahuitamotl. They set out offerings for the Storm Rider, hoping he would take them and move elsewhere. However, when the wailing moved toward the village and the destruction began, they knew Yahuitamotl had not paid them a visit. The costumed villagers ask the characters to rid them of the malevolence tormenting their community. The village is a few days' travel from the feast, where Oacce and his fellow villagers wait until the adventurers expunge the evil from their lands.

Centuries ago, a doomsday Alaxpacha cult created a golem to exact their revenge against a village elder, now long deceased. They programmed the monster to attack when the sun disappeared from the sky, but the deranged cult's leader proved to be a better magician than an astronomer. The solar eclipse he predicted never came to pass before his and his quarry died. The sun's prolonged disappearance is attributable to a total solar eclipse caused by a massive gas giant that orbits the sun in a wide, elliptical path that causes this eclipse once every 345 to 1,235 years. The planet's enormous size completely blocks the sun and causes some gravitational shifts that alter weather patterns and plunge the land into darkness for three consecutive days.

While the predicted darkness has finally come to pass, the doomsday cult's **witch-doll golem** finds itself in the right place at the wrong time. With its intended target nowhere in sight, the construct attacks anyone and anything that gets in its way with its fists and needles. The monster appears doll-like with human skin stuffing, buttons for eyes, and crude stitching for a mouth. It wears rags and has a hangman's noose around its neck. Pins and needles protrude from its body where its vital organs would normally be found.

The Alaxpacha predicted the eclipse, calling it "Tucuchana Ithuithu." A character who recently interacted with an Alaxpacha may have learned of the impending eclipse (1-in-6 chance) and recognizes the phenomenon as a solar eclipse. The enormous gas giant is the planet Nemini. Its appearance is also sometimes associated with the coming of a new sun.

Witch-Doll Golem: HD 10; HP 65; AC 2[17]; **Atk** 2 fists (2d8); **Move** 10; **Save** 5; **AL** N; **CL/XP** 10/1400; **Special:** +1 or better magic weapons to hit, immune to most spells (all but fire spells), linked damage (additional 1d8 damage to chosen foe, which also takes half damage done by others to golem [except fire damage]). (see **Appendix A: New Monsters**)

Treasure: The designers wove gold filaments into the golem's body. Harvesting the bands takes 30 minutes, but the materials are worth 1,000 gp.

THAYANA FINAL ENCOUNTER:
GHOST DANCE

Oacce tells the characters about a malevolent spirit that possessed his family's ticitl, a practitioner of traditional Aztli medicine. The ticitl named Amacaina and Oacce's hunting party recently captured the leader of a rival hunting party that habitually trespassed on their lands and even tried to steal their kills on several occasions.

Amacaina told the family she intended to terrify the captive leader by performing an ancient ritual her grandfather taught her decades ago that opened the gates to the realm of spirits, something Oacce and his counterparts greatly feared and warned against performing. Nonetheless, Amacaina proceeded with her idea despite the potentially dire consequences of doing so. Oacce now appeals to the characters to save their ticitl as well as their rival to avoid escalating the situation and unleashing something none of them can stop or control. While Oacce believes their rivals gravely offended his people and need to make reparations, he also thinks Amacaina is taking the feud too far.

DESIGNER'S NOTE

If you want to run this encounter without the preceding introduction, allow the characters to enter the scene when lightning strikes the ground from the ticitl's ritual or while the shadow demons emit an unearthly chill as they siphon the victim's lifeforce from the ritual.

Ixana, a **lamia**, has sporadically kept tabs on the ticitl for years. She has slowly converted Amacaina to embrace evil thoughts and vile inclinations. The transformation was subtle at first, but over time Ixana has charmed her way into exerting greater influence over Amacaina's actions, culminating in her first murder of a warrior from the rival hunting party. She lured the warrior into the wilderness with the promise of a tryst and then ambushed him with a garrote that she used to strangle him. Amacaina collected some blood and hair and tried to animate the dead body using her grandfather's ritual, but she lacked the skill to restore the slain warrior to an undead existence. Frustrated by her failure, she buried the corpse in a shallow grave near a creek bed. Fortunately for her and Oacce's family, a hungry jaguar smelled the fresh kill and partially devoured the unearthed body, which led to the hunting party blaming the big cat for the tragedy.

The rival Thayana parties have a long history of animosity from sparring over the same hunting grounds. The conflict has spurred minor raids and other petty acts of vengeance, yet neither group seems willing to cede the coveted territory to their foes and move into unknown lands elsewhere. Oacce almost convinced his group to leave once, but Amacaina talked them into staying. A week ago, their rivals finally crossed the point of no return when they accidentally killed Amacaina's son in a surprise attack while he was sleeping. When she saw her son's lifeless body, Amacaina swore to avenge his death. Ixana overheard her furious mutterings and blasphemous cries to the heavens and saw the perfect opportunity to convince her protégé to fully embrace her evil side.

This morning, Amacaina captured **Amriuhu**, the rival group's leader, and keeps him hogtied inside her abode. She spent the day sewing hides together and chanting over him as she sliced his flesh more than 200 times as part of a gory ritual long forbidden within her culture and by Tlatlcolli. When the sun set, she wrapped Amriuhu in her cinched hide bag and dragged him over a roaring fire so the heat could evaporate the moisture in the hides and crush the tortured person wrapped inside the bag.

The characters arrive on the scene as Amacaina calls down bolts of lightning from the clouds as she dances in a contorted manner to a melody only she can hear. The wounded Amriuhu struggles to breathe inside the bag, hastening the torturous ritual. Amacaina is also not alone, as **2 shadow demons** who share her interest in spreading chaos and evil hover nearby in the shadows beyond the fiery light. Their dark wings seem to capture and suppress some of the radiance emanating from the flames as they seem to taste the victim's lifeforce ebbing from him.

Ixana also gleefully watches from the darkness. She feels her time with her ticitl is drawing to a close. She waits to say goodbye to Amacaina after Amriuhu finally succumbs to the pressure of the shrinking hides and the heat. She swears she heard several bones snapping and faint, wracking wails over the crackling of the flames caressing the hide bag as it dips lower into the blaze.

When the characters arrive, the rest of the villagers are nowhere to be found. Amacaina's grisly ritual and her demonic associates scared everyone away except for one young Poqoza woman who bizarrely smiles at the spectacle. She is Ixana, who is disguised as a female humanoid. The participants are so engrossed in their ritualistic killing that they don't immediately spot any intruders. The characters can interrupt the ritual by physically preventing Amacaina from performing her frenetic dance. If they do so for more than three rounds, the lightning stops and the cloud dissipates. Amriuhu takes 1 point of damage per round during the ritual. If the characters fail to stop the ritual quickly after they first see Amacaina, Amriuhu dies (in six rounds) and is reborn as a **cinder ghoul**.

Naturally, the demons, the lamia, and Amacaina do not take kindly to the intrusion. They immediately attack the characters. The shadow demons hide in the darkness then lash out at their foes with their sharp claws. Ixana casts *mirror image* on herself and then rakes her adversaries with her claws and dagger. **Amacaina** is a less-formidable combatant than her counterparts. She tries to keep her distance from the characters while striking at them from afar. Ixana's primary goal is self-preservation. She may attempt to bargain with the adventurers for mercy. The demons and the now-disgraced Amacaina fight to the bitter end.

Ixana, Lamia: HD 9; **HP** 64; **AC** 3[16]; **Atk** 2 claws (1d6 + wisdom drain) and tecpatl (1d4) or longbow x2 (1d6); **Move** 24; **Save** 6; **AL** C; **CL/XP** 12/2000; **Special:** spell-like abilities, wisdom drain (1 point with touch, save resists). (***Monstrosities*** 284)
Spell-like abilities: 1/day—*charm monster, charm person, lightning bolt, magic missile, mirror image, polymorph self, suggestion.*
Equipment: tecpatl, longbow, 20 arrows.

Shadow Demons (2): HD 7; **HP** 51, 43; **AC** 4[15]; **Atk** 2 claws (1d6), bite (1d8); **Move** 15 (fly); **Save** 9; **AL** C; **CL/XP** 12/2000; **Special:** immunities (electricity, poison), incorporeal, shadow blend (1–5 on 1d6 to surprise), spell-like abilities, telepathy (100ft), vulnerable to sunlight (powerless). (***The Tome of Horrors Complete*** 151)
Spell-like abilities: 3/day—*darkness 15ft radius, fear*; 1/week—*magic jar.*

Cinder Ghoul (if needed): HD 6; **HP** 37; **AC** 4[15]; **Atk** slam (1d8 + 1d6 fire + level drain); **Move** 12 (flying); **Save** 11; **AL** C; **CL/XP** 8/800; **Special:** fire (additional 1d6 damage, save or catch fire), level drain (1 level with hit). (see **Appendix A: New Monsters**)

Amacaina, Female Half-Elf (Drd8): HP 39; **AC** 7[12]; **Atk** tecpatl (1d4) or spear (1d6); **Move** 12; **Save** 8; **AL** C; **CL/XP** 8/800; **Special:** +2 save vs. fire, darkvision (60ft), identify pure water and plants, immune to fey charms, move through nonmagical undergrowth, shape change, spells (4/3/2/1).
Spells: 1st—*detect magic, faerie fire, predict weather, purify water*; 2nd—*cure light wounds, heat metal, obscuring mist*; 3rd—*call lightning, plant growth*; 4th—*cure serious wounds.*
Equipment: tlahuiztli armor [B], tecpatl [B], spear.

Amriuhu, Male Half-Elf Rival Leader (Thf7): HP 22 (currently 6); **AC** 7[12]; **Atk** tecpatl (1d4); **Move** 12; **Save** 9; **AL** N; **CL/XP** 7/600; **Special:** +2 save bonus vs. traps and magical devices, backstab (x3), darkvision (60ft), read languages, thieving skills.
Thieving Skills: Climb 91%, Tasks/Traps 45%, Hear 5 in 6, Hide 40%, Silent 50%, Locks 40%.
Equipment: tlahuiztli armor [B], tecpatl [B].

[B] See **Appendix B: New Equipment and Magic Items**

If the characters save Amriuhu, they may attempt to finally resolve the long-standing dispute between the rival hunting parties. Characters who drive off the lamia, demons, and Amacaina can find Oacce and tell him his home is now safe. Read or paraphrase the following description of this interaction:

Chapter Three: Telling the Tale of the Storm Rider

Oacce is pleased as he enthusiastically shakes the characters' hands. He gently bows while he profusely thanks the heroes for freeing his community and people from the menaces that threatened their lives. He is not a wealthy man by any means, though he does have a trick up his sleeve or — more accurately — tethered to his shoulder. He unstraps a leather case containing eight stoppered vials.

"These are for you," Oacce says as he hands over the case. "A token of our gratitude for all you have done. You brought hope where despair reigned. You restored life where death ruled. You made dreams come true and nightmares cease. A curious man gave me this satchel many years ago in an odd place he called a laboratory. He seemed much like you in some ways. He never said how he came upon the case, though he told me to save it for the darkest of nights when even Tlatlcolli would hesitate to walk among us."

Treasure: The stoppered vials are a *potion of clairvoyance*, a *potion of diminution*, a *potion of extra healing*, a *potion of fire resistance*, a *potion of giant strength*, a *potion of invisibility*, a *potion of invulnerability*, and a *potion of levitation*.

If a character searches the case itself, that individual finds a hidden compartment within the case that contains an ornate *ring of regeneration* carved from bone in the likeness of an open-mouthed skull.

Before Oacce and the villagers depart, they have one more request. Read or paraphrase the following:

Oacce steers the conversation toward Yahuitamotl. He begins by kissing his right hand and pointing his forefinger and middle finger to the sky.

"Not long ago, the storms that pass through during the wet season gained a rider. This god-man whips through the torrents, leaps among the downpours, and slinks in the drizzle. No rain is gentle anymore. He arrives just as an event is dispersing. If he is displeased with our offerings, he razes everything in his path, doing more damage than any tempest ever could. Who defies the storm god? Not us! All Poqozas leave something for him. We hope the quality pleases him and that he leaves us alone until the next storm."

Oacce extends his outstretched hands toward the heavens.

"Yahuitamotl is here! Doom upon us!" The other villagers recite the chant several times to appease the god-man as a plea for him to spare village.

"It has come time that the god-man must move on. His arrival signals that the end times and the next sun are coming soon. Food no longer satisfies him. He now demands an arm from three people as tribute. We cannot give away such a great price. If we do not, he says he can blot out the sun. We do not know why he has cursed us. We have fed him several times, even when we did not have much to give. The strange man who found the case discovered it near Yahuitamotl's lair. The storm activity there when I was exploring is a sign from above. I am too old and too weak to conquer such as those who would ride on a storm, but you … you might have what it takes to deliver us from this oppression."

Oacce and the villagers must devote their energies to rebuilding their communities and cannot take a prolonged overland trip to the center of the Caxcalli Grasslands. However, they know how to get to the mysterious laboratory where the odd traveler found the leather case and claimed the storm activity was the greatest. They also convey a brief history about the Mulla Chanacu and its otherworldly origin. Every young Poqoza must venture there to transition from a boy into a man or a girl into a woman.

The trip to the laboratory goes uneventfully unless you want to spice up the journey with some early encounters that the characters previously missed. Although the monstrous activity seems low, the same cannot be said about the weather. The winds howl and the rain falls with greater intensity as the characters get closer to the laboratory.

The sun reappears after being gone for three full days. The rain thins to its normal consistency, and the ground warms with the first rays of light. A birdsong shatters the still and awakens the harmonious nature of the tallgrass. Soon, the pace of life resets, and life in the grasslands returns to its normal tempo, balancing the violent nature of the food chain and the peaceful grandeur of untouched beauty of the savanna.

Area 1-A: Laboratory Entrance

The laboratory of Elix Cucita lies on the southwest corner of the Mulla Chanacu. Elix established the facility on the principle of sharing the shori huasca. He designed the structures and grounds asymmetrically, with scrolling curved themes and sculpted molding with theatrical pastel colors to create surprise and the illusion of motion. Very soft edges and natural curves, eroded over time, emphasize the childlike wonder of the compound.

The storm breaks in full fury as Elix Cucita looms ahead. Lightning flashes across the sky, followed quickly by the peal of deafening thunder. The smell of ozone is thick in the air from repeated lightning strikes concentrated on a thick iron rod in the middle of a beautiful courtyard. The front doors stand wide open, beckoning visitors to step inside.

Elix built the laboratory into the side of a hill. The exposed area outside covers about 1,600 square feet of gated courtyards where Poqozas under the influence of the hallucinogenic fungi sit and converse about esoteric subjects and transcendental thoughts while still protected from the elements. Colorful tents and refreshing fountains took up the courts Elix did not fashion into gardens. Isolated shreds of fabric and crumbled stonework represent all that is left of that earlier time. The courtyard is completely devoid of life, including the omnipresent insects. A small, roofless outbuilding in the southeast corner of one of the courts is empty. The doors leading into the laboratory are 15 feet tall and made of thick oak. They are flung open.

If the characters survey the surrounding landscape, they have a 2-in-6 chance to see a hidden cave located in another low hill roughly one-half mile away. Strange tracks make deep impressions along a muddy trail from a lagoon on the outskirts of the Mulla Chanacu into the laboratory's back entrance (**Area 1-G**). Yahuitamotl lets a small outpost of cueyatls live here to protect his lair and to worship and care for his mount.

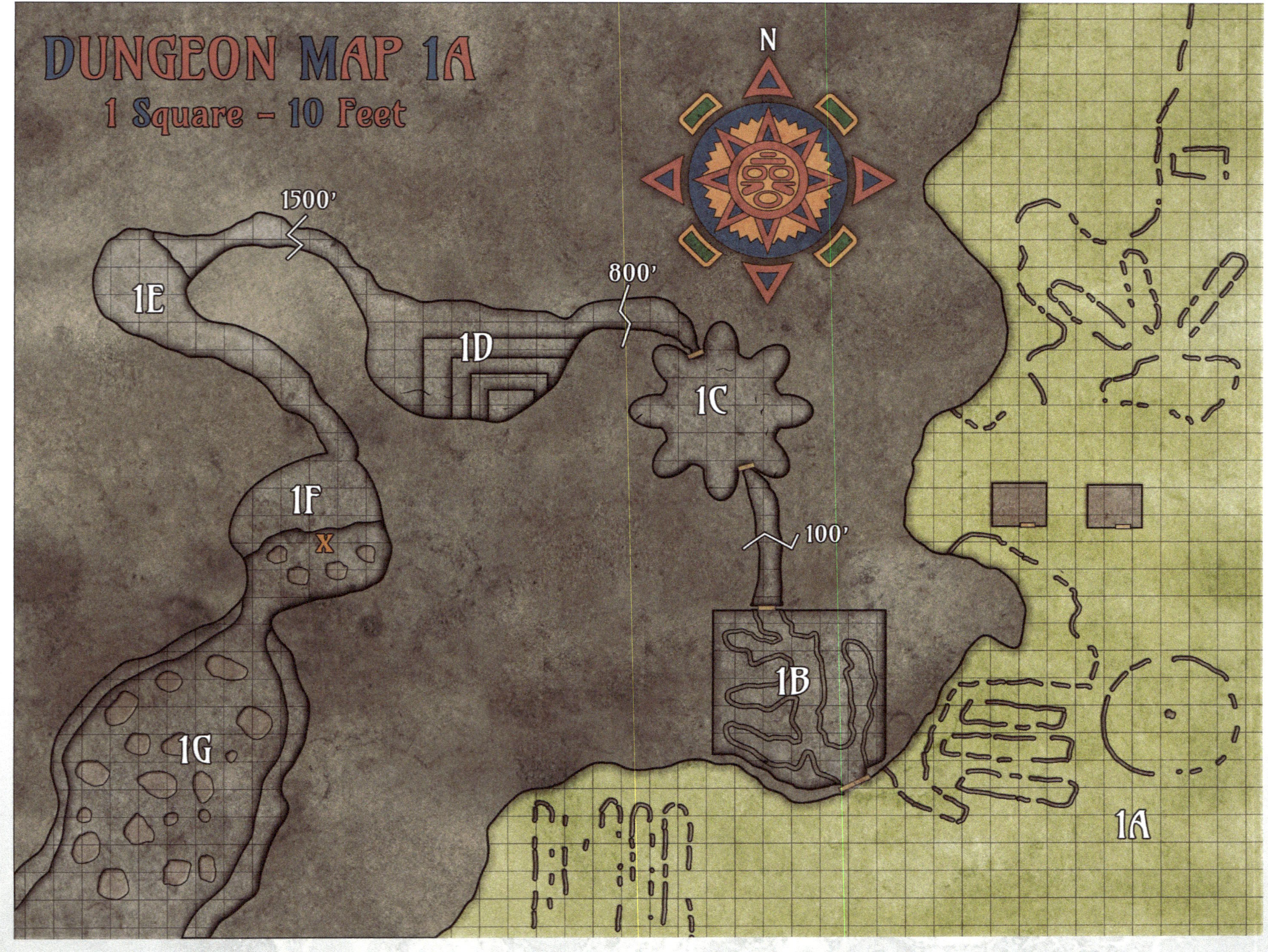

DUNGEON MAP 1A
1 Square – 10 Feet
N
1500'
800'
100'
1E
1D
1C
1F
X
1G
1B
1A

AREA 1-B: INNER LOBBY

Low padded sofas and bland, background artworks decorate the space, which obviously served as a waiting room. Although presumably abandoned, flames burn in several braziers affixed to the walls, illuminating the room in a soothing yellowish hue that extends into the back of the large area. Clay and bamboo pots hold rows of renegade hostas and other plants that grow unchecked, spilling over the sides of their containers. What once appeared to be a comfortable and well-kept area now resembles a steamy jungle greenhouse.

Vegetation and warmth overrun this once-welcoming chamber that is still bathed in the light of *continual light* spells cast on the braziers. The combination provides a perfect environment for the **8 violet fungi** now inhabiting the room. The mindless, purplish mushrooms slowly slither across the floor, attacking any living trespassers who enter the room. They ignore the almost equally dimwitted **7 zombies** cohabitating the area alongside them. None of these monsters ever leaves the room.

Violet Fungi (8): HD 3; **HP** 23, 21x2, 19, 17, 16, 14, 11; **AC** 7[12]; **Atk** 4 tendrils (rot); **Move** 1; **Save** 14; **AL** N; **CL/XP** 4/120; **Special:** tendrils cause rot (save or flesh rots for 1d4 damage per hour; *cure disease* ends damage). (*Monstrosities* 183)

Zombies (7): HD 2; **HP** 15, 13, 12, 10x3, 8, 5; **AC** 8[11]; **Atk** strike (1d8); **Move** 6; **Save** 16; **AL** N; **CL/XP** 2/30; **Special:** immune to sleep and charm. (*Monstrosities* 529)

Treasure: This room is where the mysterious stranger found the leather case containing the potions. The explorer he took the case from is still here as one of the zombies. This undead monstrosity still wears a belt pouch containing 70 sp and a silver locket worth 100 gp. A silvered short sword is under a nearby potted plant's foliage.

A simple lock and a pile of heavy crates bar the door to **Area 1-C** from the other side. A character must push the heavy crates back from behind the door to gain entry into **Area 1-C**.

AREA 1-C: THE LABORATORY

Elix and his inner circle of followers conducted controlled experiments on the users of the shori huasca within this laboratory as they sought to explore the depths of their own inner spaces rather than looking outward to the stars. They believed the fungi could potentially mutate ordinary people and unlock their hidden possibilities in a vein similar to the ascension of the hero-gods Micoateotl and Itztliteotl. They believed the legends about the Lord of the Dead making contact with temporal travelers and otherworldly beings as well as the God of Night tapping his inner potential for mystical energy. They wished to follow in their footsteps using the fungi to free their consciousness and transcend their mortal bodies. After years of experimentation, Elix and his inner circle succeeded, taking their knowledge and experience with them while their mortal bodies slowly withered into nothingness. Later generations attempted to duplicate their success but to no avail. Many believe Elix and several others currently wander another plane of existence, though no one has ever confirmed this controversial theory.

Only a few tables remain intact along with a bank of shelves attached to the walls. Scrolls and glassware are scattered throughout the room. Twenty-two fiery vents brightly bathe the chamber in cool, white light. A massive painting on the domed ceiling exquisitely details the cosmos. Five stone statues stand evenly spaced along the outside edge of this room, apparently poised to cast a spell or incantation, while a sixth obsidian statue depicts a hulking man with a jaguar's head emitting pinpoints of blue light from its eyes. The same obsidian statue also stands at the due west compass point. The spot designated as true north holds a mirrored sphere roughly four feet in diameter that basks in blue light. A door is on the northern edge of the northwest quadrant.

The fiery vents and the blue lights are all magical flames. Five of the six stone statues along the outer edges are artistic renditions of Micoateotl and Itztliteotl during their mortal existence. A character who views the statues can identify them as such. A character who searches the Itztliteotl statue closest to the entrance discovers a bone tube tucked into the stone. In addition to the magical writing inside of it, the tube also contains a scrap of weathered maguey paper. The medium contains the following message written in an archaic form of Aztli: "Here we come! Loving the trip! Elix." A character who reads the message recalls hearing of Elix and his attempts to free his mind and consciousness from his mortal body.

DESIGNER'S NOTE

At your option, you can include another message in the bone tube that might give the characters additional insight about a loose end they are having trouble closing.

While the stone statues are ordinary, inanimate sculptures, the obsidian statues are **2 obsidian minotaurs** with the slight alteration in their appearance. The monsters immediately respond to the intrusion by lowering their horns and charging toward trespassers. Elix and his followers programmed these two constructs to protect the laboratory in the event they decided to return here at a later time. Their sole task is to kill everyone not in the company of Elix. They have no regard for causing damage to the laboratory. Yahuitamotl attempted but failed to reprogram the two guardians. Therefore, he never visits this location and has not been here for years as well.

Obsidian Minotaurs (2): HD 12; **HP** 87, 68; **AC** −2[21]; **Atk** 2 claws (2d8 + 1d6 fire); **Move** 9; **Save** 3; **AL** N; **CL/XP** 16/3200; **Special:** breath weapon (every 1d4+1 rounds, 10ft cloud of gas, save or *slow* as spell), burn (after hit, save or take additional 1d6 damage that continues for 1d4+1 rounds), immune to magic (*transmute rock to mud* slows it for 2d6 rounds; *transmute mud to rock* heals all damage; *stone to flesh* negates its immunity to other magic for 1 round). (see **Appendix A: New Monsters**)

Treasure: The bone tube contains five scrolls (*continual light, confusion, haste, passwall, war cry* [see **Appendix C: New Spells**]).

AREA 1-D: LIVING QUARTERS

The **Storm Rider Yahuitamotl** waits here for a new challenge to alleviate his ennui. The **storm giant** also contacted the same mysterious, extraplanar entity that Micoateotl contacted long ago. The being granted Yahuitamotl the ability to stop aging while he remains here, but the loneliness and boredom that set in over the centuries since he acquired this "gift" changed his alignment from Lawful to Neutrality (bordering on Chaos). His longevity and the insight he gained from his discourses with the otherworldly entity convinced him that he is indeed a god in his own right. In the past, he used his time traveling outside the complex judiciously. Confident in his immortality, Yahuitamotl cares little about wasting any precious time and now endeavors to compel others to worship him as a capricious god. The whimsical giant uses the Poqozas' offerings as a tool to intimidate and frighten them into submission. He has no real interest or need for their sacrifices. Instead, he views his interactions with the terrified people as an amusing game, just like the chess board he keeps in his personal quarters. When the characters first encounter Yahuitamotl, read or paraphrase the following description:

"You have come!" the purplish-skinned man excitedly proclaims.

"I knew it would be you. Your deeds have reached my

ears. Many in this miserable land grovel at your feet. How many followers do you have? How many worshippers? Would any of them give you their right arm? Their wife? Their last kernel of maize? I have gathered many to my fold. As you have seen, no doubt. Puny mortals, you are not gods like me!" He gestures to a frog-like humanoid resting on one of the cushions. "They give of themselves so freely."

The man bids his guests to take their seats. There are many comfortable pillows scattered about, including a nest of plump cushions surrounded by gauzy veils. A library of scrolls and hardbound books illuminated by three lights spans the height of the wall. Trays of fresh fruits and breads are served at different stations throughout the cozy lounge, which features several pyramid-shaped tiered with six three-foot-high risers at each ascending level.

If the characters are not outwardly hostile, Yahuitamotl gauges their strength. If they came in through the front entrance, he gives them a low evaluation, whereas characters who slogged their way through the cueyatl side earn his respect and trepidation. In the former case, the storm giant seems at ease engaging them in conversation mostly about the futility of existence, the foolishness of mortals, and the vanity of the hero-gods to believe they are the only divine beings in Tehuatl. In the latter circumstance, Yahuitamotl errs on the side of caution with the characters and attacks at the first sign of trouble. The **cueyatl warrior** joins in the fight alongside Yahuitamotl, but the storm giant shows no concern for the creature's wellbeing. If the cueyatl is in the line of fire from one of his spells or abilities, Yahuitamotl makes a matter-of-fact comment about the cueyatl being no great loss to the world.

If faced with imminent defeat, the storm giant accepts his fate with resignation. He laments the loss of such a wonderous individual, greater than any other who ever set foot in Tehuatl while he vows to defy death and return as an immortal deity. He never surrenders and refuses under any circumstances to give the characters any credit for their astounding victory.

Yahuitamotl, Storm Giant: HD 15+5; **HP** 101; **AC** 1[18]; **Atk** treetrunk club (7d6); **Move** 15; **Save** 3; **AL** N to C; **CL/XP** 16/3200; **Special:** control weather (as spell), throw boulders (7d6), spell-like ability. (*Monstrosities* 201)
Spell-like abilities: 3/day—*lightning bolt* (5d6 damage).

Cueyatl Warrior: HD 5; **HP** 33; **AC** 8[11]; **Atk** battle axe (1d8) and bite (1d4), or 2 claws (1d6) and bite (1d4); **Move** 12 (climb 9, swim 12) or leap (20ft); **Save** 13; **AL** C; **CL/XP** 5/240; **Special:** amphibious, camouflage (85% chance to hide in jungles), darkvision (60ft), leap (20ft horizontal leap), slimy (half damage from fire). (see **Appendix A: New Monsters**)

Treasure: The storm giant's library holds many ancient, sacred texts worth 2,200 gp. The liquors stored in the nest are mostly gallons of common peppery red wines or ordinary tequila worth 200 gp, but a delightfully potent pulque decanted in a crystal bottle contains 11 ounces of the beverage worth 30 gp per ounce. Stored here are the two missing chess pieces and the chess board worth 1,750 gp that Yahuitamotl confiscated from **Event Encounter 6: The Lost Children of the Chuxuntana**.

Area 1-E: Dragon Roost

Several years ago, Yahuitamotl took an aspiring black dragon named Kullana under his wing. The storm giant uses the winged beast to perform aerial reconnaissance and underwater exploration before he leaves his compound to spread terror across the grasslands. The pair work well together, though the bombastic Yahuitamotl can sometimes be overwhelming. The partnership is not entirely altruistic, as Kullana covets coins and treasure more than his counterpart. He plans to amass a hoard worthy of winning the hand of an older and even more avaricious black dragon mate he has had his eyes on for the last two decades. Kullana has some measure of loyalty to the storm giant but would never compromise his safety to save Yahuitamotl in a pinch. He has a similar attitude toward the cueyatls, as he sees them as his playthings

and fodder to help ensure his safety. Likewise, he enjoys spreading misery and suffering to the Poqoza communities that Yahuitamotl devastates. Although he stays in the background during the assault, the dragon mops up any stragglers who stumble across him in the chaos. Kullana now rests among the coins filling his lair.

A staggering number of coins made from various materials are piled into hills and valleys that choke this wide cavern. The clinking sound made by shifting coins echoes against the wall and ceiling, while plopping noises can also be heard as some coins slide down a mound and fall into a puddle of water covering portions of the floor. Thousands of bugs crawl along the damp, earthy floor that is littered with bones and other refuse. A strong, pungent scent hangs in the foul, dank air.

Kullana, an **adult black dragon**, naps most of the day away. He burrows beneath one of the mounds of coins, though portions of his tail and body can be seen beneath his metallic camouflage. When he senses trespassers in his lair, he pushes the coins aside and unleashes a line of acid in the most advantageous direction before engaging the characters with his claws and bite. Kullana ultimately prioritizes his life over his treasure. He reluctantly bribes the adventurers to leave his lair with some of his riches in exchange for sparing his wretched life. Kullana may alternatively barter information about Yahuitamotl if the characters broach the subject. In that case, he divulges details about the storm giant in the same manner as a shrewd merchant negotiating a suitable price for his wares.

Kullana, Adult Black Dragon: HD 7; **HP** 28; **AC** 2[17]; **Atk** 2 claws (1d4), bite (3d6); **Move** 9 (fly 24); **Save** 9; **AL** C; **CL/XP** 9/1100; **Special:** spits acid (3/day, 60ft line, 28 damage, save for half). (*Monstrosities* 132)

Treasure: Although numerically impressive, Kullana's hoard contains a disproportionate number of copper and silver coins. He has 20,128 cp, 5,230 sp, and 902 gp. There is also a silver scepter worth 100 gp, a ceramic chihuahua statue worth 35 gp, an elaborately beaded headband worth 60 gp, and an expertly carved conch horn worth 150 gp.

The passageway leading from this cavern to the living quarters of Yahuitamotl is partially concealed by a luminescent column of stalactites and stalagmites.

Area 1-F: Cueyatl Queen

A sliver of open sky peeks through the ceiling of this enormous cavern, allowing moonlight and rain to enter the chamber. Lush vegetation sprouts from the roof and dangles down in verdant flowered curtains. Thick, sticky mud cakes the floor alongside standing pools of murky water of indeterminate depth. Several boulders on the muddy floor offer some respite from the dank, soggy ground. Hundreds of small bats circle through the air and cling to the ceiling.

A host of frog-like humanoids with purplish skin croak among themselves. Four of these spear-toting creatures move an enormous frond of the draping vines to reveal a pale blue creature with studded leather armor and a massive flail in her fist.

"How dare you come here," she exclaims. "You are not welcome. Turn back or die!"

Chaxtata, the **cueyatl moon priest**, thinks the characters are here to see their patron saint, the dragon Kullana. Even if they enter here from the dragon's room, she tries to usher them out of the cavern system while also demanding a monetary tribute for passing through the cueyatls' territory. She recognizes the characters as a serious threat to her and her people. She wants to avoid a fight with them while not appearing weak in the process. In sharp contrast, her **4 cueyatl warriors** are itching for a fight and a chance to prove their worth. They bravely thrust out their chests in defiance and stamp their spear butts into the muck. Chaxtata can barely control the quartet, who react violently to the slightest provocation. She hopes to keep the characters away from her clutch of eggs that is poised to hatch into three dozen new cueyatl tadpoles near her nest on the western edge of this cavern.

The sounds of battle reverberate through the empty space, ensuring that the cueyatls in **Area 1-G** hear the ruckus. Half of their number respond to the noise, joining in the melee 1d4 + 1 rounds later. The **piranha swarm** from **Area 1-G** follow shortly thereafter, though they must remain in the roughly two-foot-deep pools of standing water. They attack only if the characters get into the water at the point designated with an X.

If pressed into battle, Chaxtata orders her thralls to attack in groups. The cueyatls gang up on a single character, while a pair of warriors also try to isolate a lone combatant. Despite her reservations about engaging in combat with the characters, she and her people give no quarter nor expect to receive any from the interlopers.

Chaxtata, Cueyatl Moon Priest: HD 10; HP 71; AC 7[12]; **Atk** flail (1d8) and bite (1d4), or 2 claws (1d6) and bite (1d4); **Move** 12 (climb 9, swim 12) or leap (20ft); **Save** 5; **AL** C; **CL/XP** 12/2,000; **Special:** amphibious, camouflage (85% chance to hide in jungles), darkvision (60ft), leap (20ft horizontal leap), night's chill (3/day, 30ft radius, 2d6 cold damage, save for half; *dispel magic* in 30ft radius), slimy (half damage from fire), spells (2/2/2/2/2). (see **Appendix A: New Monsters**)
Spells: 1st—*cure light wounds, light*; 2nd—*bless, hold person*; 3rd—*cure disease, prayer*; 4th—*create water, cure serious wounds*; 5th—*finger of death, insect plague*.
Equipment: flail.

Cueyatl Warriors (4): HD 5; HP 35, 31, 26, 22; AC 8[11]; **Atk** battle axe (1d8) and bite (1d4), or 2 claws (1d6) and bite (1d4); **Move** 12 (climb 9, swim 12) or leap (20ft); **Save** 13; **AL** C; **CL/XP** 5/240; **Special:** amphibious, camouflage (85% chance to hide in jungles), darkvision (60ft), leap (20ft horizontal leap), slimy (half damage from fire). (see **Appendix A: New Monsters**)

Piranha Swarm: HD 4; HP 27; AC 7[12]; **Atk** swarm (1d6); **Move** 24 (swim); **Save** 13; **AL** N; **CL/XP** 4/120; **Special:** none. (*The Tome of Horrors Complete* 531) (see **Area 1-G**)

Treasure: Each cueyatl warrior carries a small pouch with 2d10 cacao beans worth 1 gp each. One also wears a silver ring worth 100 gp. Chaxtata has a small cache in her nest of 20 gp, a leather collar with seashell sewn into its surface worth 30 gp, and a leather-bound maguey paper book gifted to her by Yahuitamotl. She cannot read it, though she leafed through it nightly. The book, which is written in Aztli, contains a detailed history of the laboratory that is worth 100 gp. Its pages contain the background information about Elix and his inner circle as described in **Areas 1-A** and **1-C**.

AREA 1-G: FROG ROOM

The characters are not the only new arrivals on the scene. Several days earlier, the cueyatls butchered a troupe of entertainers traveling across the grasslands to perform at a funeral. The men did not take the unanticipated cancellation of their performance lightly. Instead, they rose from the grave and now seek revenge on the creatures who cut their musical careers short.

This locale has several moving parts to it. The **7 cueyatls** and **5 cueyatl warriors** encountered here were fishing for piranha in the deeper end of this room. Of course, if they rushed to the aid of their priestess in **Area 1-F**, adjust the cueyatls' numbers accordingly. While the cueyatls were hunting individual fish, the school is actually a **piranha swarm** that attacks any creature entering the water, which floods the uneven floor in this area to a depth of 1d8 + 4 feet at any given spot.

If the cueyatls responded to the racket from **Area 1-F**, at least half remain here to fend off the **2 allips** at their doorstep. The incorporeal, flying allips are unfazed by the water or any other physical obstacles in their way. The undead spirits exclusively attack the cueyatls until no cueyatls are left to fight. If that occurs, they turn their anger toward the adventurers.

Allips (2): HD 4; AC 5[14]; **Atk** strike (no damage, drain wisdom); **Move** 6 (fly); **Save** 13; **AL** C; **CL/XP** 7/600; **Special:** +1 or better magic or silver weapon to hit, drain wisdom (1d4 points with hit), hypnosis (as suggestion spell). (***Monstrosities*** 10)

Cueyatl (7): HD 3; HP 20, 18, 16x2, 15, 13, 9; AC 8[11]; **Atk** club (1d6) and bite (1d4), or 2 claws (1d6) and bite (1d4); **Move** 12 (climb 9, swim 12) or leap (20ft); **Save** 14; **AL** C; **CL/XP** 3/60; **Special:** amphibious, camouflage (85% chance to hide in jungles), darkvision (60ft), leap (20ft horizontal leap), slimy (half damage from fire). (see **Appendix A: New Monsters**)

Cueyatl Warriors (5): HD 5; HP 37, 34, 30, 28, 20; AC 8[11]; **Atk** battle axe (1d8) and bite (1d4), or 2 claws (1d6) and bite (1d4); **Move** 12 (climb 9, swim 12) or leap (20ft); **Save** 13; **AL** C; **CL/XP** 5/240; **Special:** amphibious, camouflage (85% chance to hide in jungles), darkvision (60ft), leap (20ft horizontal leap), slimy (half damage from fire). (see **Appendix A: New Monsters**)

Piranha Swarm: HD 4; HP 27; AC 7[12]; **Atk** swarm (1d6); **Move** 24 (swim); **Save** 13; **AL** N; **CL/XP** 4/120; **Special:** none. (***The Tome of Horrors Complete*** 531) (see **Area 1-G**)

Treasure: Each cueyatl and cueyatl warrior carries a small pouch with 2d20 sp. The water conceals a *+1 shield*. One of the cueyatl warriors also has a cylindrical tube containing 18 rubies worth 50 gp each and *gem of seeing*.

Chapter Four: The Nihileth Assault

After the Storm Rider's defeat, the palpable sense of unease gripping the Caxcalli Grasslands subsides. The storms still come, but the overwhelming dread that once accompanied their appearance is gone. Yet the elation is short-lived. Within days, the rain regains its slimy, viscous coating and blood-like consistency that started with the eclipse. Yahuitamotl's destruction certainly caused a setback to the nihileth aboleth's plans. However, the monster's corruption of the Mulla Chanacu grows only stronger. Without its herald to spread the word of the coming of a new age, the nihileth is now concentrating on the next phase of its strategy to destroy the entire grasslands and usher in the Season of the Qallucha. While only farmers and scholars notice the contamination of the water supply on Mulla Chanacu's west side, the monster's corrupting effect on the tallgrass and the flora appears more obvious. The strange rain turns the soil into gooey muck in many places. Formerly healthy vegetation withers and rots in the fields, only to be supplemented by sickly weeds. The abomination's baleful influence spreads not just from above but also from below as the deconstructed earth supports only an invasive new species — the caustic thistle. This invasive weed covers much of the ground at the Mulla Chanacu and spreads in an outward wave from that central crater, expanding primarily to the south and west where the conducive rains and soil are more prevalent. However, as the wind picks up its lightweight seeds, patches of caustic thistle are starting to appear in other locations as well.

The plants are the nihileth's advance guard, but the teenagers and rescuers who ventured to the Mulla Chanacu are its army. The young Poqozas who set off from their homes to partake in the spirit quests quickly fell prey to the nihileth, who killed them and reanimated their corpses as zombies under its command. The nihileth also stalked the tallgrass to slaughter bandits, fugitives, and hunters to supplement its band of recruits. With its ranks of nihileth zombies rapidly swelling, it gave the undead abominations standing orders to kill two other creatures and then go into hibernation beneath the damp earth. Over time, the plot has created the zombie equivalent of a modern minefield with dozens or perhaps even hundreds of these creatures in this near state of suspended animation. After the characters defeat Yahuitamotl, the nihileth set off a chain reaction by ordering the zombies closest to him to reawaken themselves and the other slumbering zombies near them. Now, they rise! Now, they kill!

The nihileth stored the ethereal undead roughly 20 feet underground. It concentrated them around the Mulla Chanacu, with a few outliers stationed up to 20 miles away from the crater. With Yahuitamotl gone, the nihileth fears the heroes who defeated Yahuitamotl would soon come after it. Rather than stay strictly on the defensive, the nihileth disperses its zombie hordes across the area to kill neighboring villagers and keep the characters' attention focused elsewhere.

Event One: Lightning Flashing Across the Sky

The hill is the site of the meteorite crash that created the Mulla Chanacu and currently serves as the nihileth aboleth's lair. Although they do not realize it yet, the nihileth has dispatched its minions, and the current storm provides the perfect cover for this action. Across the area, the nihileth's zombie servants attack with reckless abandon. Meanwhile, the rains and the mutated soil encourage the rapid proliferation of the caustic thistle (see the **Caustic Thistle** sidebar). Anyone foolish enough to drink the standing water in this area must make a saving throw or take 1d6 points of damage as their skin becomes slimy and slightly translucent for 1d4 hours. The creature takes an additional 1d4 points of damage every time it is injured during thi.s time.

Naturally, a cluster of lightning bolts blasting a single location is sure to attract the characters' attention. The iron particles scattered throughout the crater account for the strange anomaly. With a prospective target in sight, the characters' approach to the nihileth's lair is treacherous. The rain and mud make the entire area into difficult terrain. Although the lightning poses no immediate danger to the characters, the caustic thistle and zombie hordes greatly impede the adventurers' progress toward their intended goal. The caustic thistle grows in wide rows 1d6 x 100 feet across and 1d4 x 10 feet thick. They almost appear as if their seeds were deliberately sown to create broad fences or palisades to protect a strategic location. Amid the chaos, a Poqoza tribesman named **Alaxa** sobs in a shallow ditch along the characters' path. He tried to singlehandedly defeat the nihileth to avenge what the monstrosity did to his son and daughter. Yet his fear and a small horde of **11 nihilethic zombies** got the better of him. The undead creatures are closing in on the broken man when the characters arrive. The zombies know Alaxa is near, but the characters appear to be a greater threat to their master than a lone person crying in a hole. If the characters defeat the zombies, Alaxa regains his composure and peeks over the edge of the ditch to presumably confirm the characters' victory. When the last one falls, Alaxa cries out for them to listen.

Nihilethic Zombies (11): HD 2; **HP** 15, 14, 13, 11x2, 10x3, 7, 6x2; **AC** 9[10]; **Atk** strike (1d8 + 1d6 withering touch [3/day]); **Move** 9 (swim 12); **Save** 16; **AL** N; **CL/XP** 3/60; **Special:** ethereal (+1 or better magic weapons to hit), immune to charm and sleep spells, withering touch (3/day, 1d6 damage, save resists). (see **Appendix A: New Monsters**)

Alaxa, Male Poqoza Half-Elf: HP 35; **AC** 9[10]; **Atk** spear (1d6); **Move** 12; **Save** 11; **AL** L; **CL/XP** 6/400; **Special:** darkvision (60ft). (***Monstrosities*** 254)
Equipment: spear.

Event Two: A Friendly Face in the Chaos

He tells the characters that the village ticitl sent him here to investigate the disappearance of the settlement's teenagers who never returned after their expedition to the Mulla Chanacu. Along the way, he learned that the children from other small communities were also missing, though some witnesses also claimed to have seen them rise from the grave as grotesque shambling corpses. Although the creatures are clearly wicked, even the bravest warriors hesitate to strike down a beloved child when faced with such grim reality. Alaxa begged the ticitl to accompany him, but he needed to defend the village and steel the people's nerves against the approaching doom. However, to aid Alaxa in this dangerous endeavor, the ticitl gave him a potion and a ring. Alaxa freely offers the items to the characters to help them fulfill his mission to defeat the evil and rid the Mulla Chanacu of the cancer eating away at its soul.

Caustic Thistle

This invasive plant species comes from an unknown planet somewhere in the Void. It occasionally hitches a ride to a new home aboard an asteroid, comet, or meteorite. Under normal conditions, caustic thistle cannot take root in Tehuatl. However, it thrives when embedded in foul, gooey, acidic soil, especially mud created by a nihileth aboleth, which naturally leads scholars to speculate that the monster and plant species may share some commonality in the Void. Caustic thistle quickly sprouts into a six-foot-tall stalk surrounded by one-foot-long razor-sharp, serrated leaves. Small nettles grow along the edges of the leaves, which secrete an acidic irritant to protect the base. The flower blooms into a puffy ball about four inches in diameter. The tufts from the flower fly away on the wind and reseed up to one-half mile away. The plant matures in 2d4 hours after being planted, and it can reproduce from seed to fully-formed plant indefinitely — as long as the soil is extremely acidic. Caustic thistle grows in dense patches, with each individual plant only inches apart from its neighbor.

Moving through a caustic thistle patch proves challenging. Characters can move only at a quarter of their movement through the caustic thistle. A creature entering the patch takes 2d4 points of damage, or half as much damage with a successful saving throw.

Designer's Note

There are no maps for this section of the adventure as the nihileth's lair can be of any size of your choosing. Although the nihileth can pass through earth and even stone to reach its abode, the characters must pass through the muddy channels descending into the earth unless they can reach the nihileth's lair by an alternative means such as a *teleport* spell or similar magic. If the characters must traverse through the channels and tunnels to reach their goal, you can make the journey as difficult or easy as you choose depending upon the characters' current condition and your style of play. For instance, if you want the characters to defeat the zombie horde aboveground and immediately thereafter take the fight to the nihileth belowground, use that idea. For a tougher descent, you can make them work their way past levels of nihilethic zombies stored in isolated oubliettes with rows of caustic thistles intermittently blocking their way. Also, the nihileth can use its illusions.

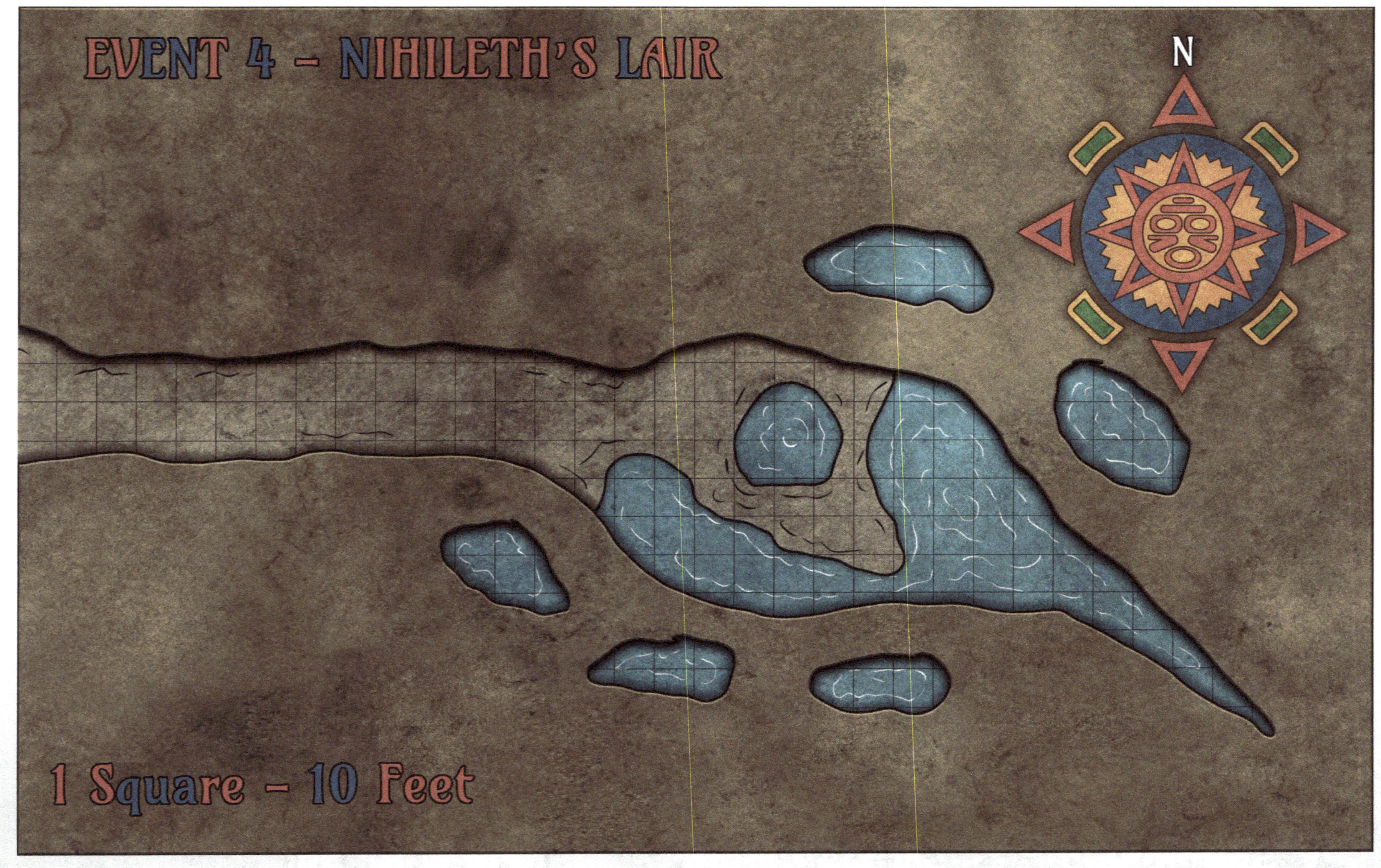

EVENT 4 – NIHILETH'S LAIR
N
1 Square – 10 Feet

Treasure: Alaxa gives the characters the *ring of poison resistance* and the *potion of giant strength* that the ticitl gave him. If they succeed at their given task, they are welcome to keep the items.

EVENT THREE: BUG HUNT

The sun still hides behind the billowing, charcoal-colored clouds, while the seemingly unnatural storm builds more energy, as if it were feeding off the energies of the netherworld. Lightning smashes the ground, while peals of thunder drown out all other sounds in the region. The acidic rain stirs up the yellowish mud, sending it out in rivulets to infect the surrounding area. The mud then washes away and exposes a huge crater.

Channels running away from the cavity transport the mud deeper into the earth. Amid the cacophony and dazzling light show, the storm suddenly ceases as a menacing, otherworldly clicking echoes through the crater, followed by a thick burbling laugh.

The sinister voice whispers, "You defeated my Storm Rider. Do you think it will be that easy to defeat me? He was merely my servant, and I was his master. Save your lives and flee this land. Let the land fester. If you refuse, only death awaits you."

The nihileth abruptly ends its telepathic communication with a disturbing chuckle. The nihileth then dispatches another horde of **16 nihilethic zombies** to the surface to attack the characters and drive them away from the crater. The concerned nihileth moves ethereally through solid stone to its lair 100 feet below the surface.

Nihilethic Zombies (16): HD 2; HP 16, 15, 14x3, 12x2, 11, 10, 9x2, 7x3, 6, 5; AC 9[10]; **Atk** strike (1d8 + 1d6 withering touch [3/day]); **Move** 9 (swim 12); **Save** 16; **AL** N; **CL/XP** 3/60; **Special:** ethereal (+1 or better magic weapons to hit), immune to charm and sleep spells, withering touch (3/day, 1d6 damage, save resists). (see **Appendix A: New Monsters**)

The channels leading to the nihileth's lair are large enough to accommodate an average-sized man, but the soggy ground makes it difficult. Furthermore, although the passages corkscrew into the ground at a relatively modest angle, any creature walking down the tunnel must periodically succeed on a saving throw to avoid slipping on the slick surface. On a failed check, the creature falls prone and slides 1d10 x 4 feet down the tunnel.

The nihileth left some areas under the Mulla Chanacu undisturbed. If you want to mix up the encounters on the way down to the nihileth's lair, you can allow them to explore a deserted, subterranean amphitheater infested by a group of **6 black puddings** or lead them into an underground archway defended by a **clay golem** and **6 flying swords** that leap off the walls to bar trespassers from proceeding through the archway. These interim conflicts give the ethereal nihileth an idea of the characters' strengths and weaknesses. Before facing the intruders in its lair, the ethereal nihileth observes the adventurers and uses its telepathy to gauge their mental fortitude. It then attempts to charm the mentally weakest character. If the ploy succeeds, the character shows no outward signs of being under the monster's influence. However, during the showdown with the nihileth, it forces its thrall to claw at its own face and shout, "Not safe! Not safe!" This causes 1d4 points of damage to the victim, but snaps them out of the effects of the charm.

Black Puddings (6): HD 10; AC 6[13]; **Atk** slam (3d8); **Move** 6; **Save** 5; **AL** N; **CL/XP** 12/2000; **Special:** acidic surface (dissolve weapons, armor, etc.), immune to cold, divides when hit with lightning (splits into two puddings with equal hit points). (*Monstrosities* 46)

Clay Golem: HD 10; HP 45; AC 7[12]; **Atk** fist (3d10); **Move** 8; **Save** 5; **AL** N; **CL/XP** 14/2600; **Special:** immune to slashing and piercing weapons, immune to most spells (harmed only by spells that affect earth; earthquake destroys). (*Monstrosities* 218)

Flying Swords (Animated Object) (6): HD 1; AC 5[14]; **Atk** 1d8; **Move** 15 (fly); **Save** 17; **AL** N; **CL/XP** 1/15; **Special:** none. (*Monstrosities* 13)

If the characters finally reach the nihileth's lair, read or paraphrase the following description:

EVENT FOUR: FIGHT FOR YOUR LIVES!

Liquid drips from the ceiling and seeps from cracks in the walls to flood this chamber to a depth of eight feet. Ripples show that something large lies beneath the surface. Six tentacles writhe up from the murky depths, sloshing water ahead of the quick-striking limbs.

This is the lair of the **nihileth aboleth's** (see **Appendix A: New Monsters**). It has spent a long time inconspicuously slumbering under the Mulla Chanacu, waiting for its time to come while transmitting intelligence reports back to its alien homeland. In this foreign land, it has a created a microcosm utopia for itself far below the surface. It seeks to make the landscape above its subterranean abode more habitable for its own kind as well after spending thousands of years confined to its underground realm.

While the rippling in the water is real, the tentacles protruding through the water are an illusion. The nihileth hopes the characters direct some of their firepower at the tentacles. The monster remains submerged but attempts to pull opponents into the water when they realize the tentacles are not real. If forced to leave the pool, it assumes its ethereal form. It also knows the location of **9 nihilethic zombies** concealed within pockets outside its lair. It uses these unfortunate creatures as a hit point reservoir to heal its injuries and return to its lair to rid itself of the pesky adventurers instead of using them as reinforcements.

The nihileth believes it has already fulfilled the requirements of its reconnaissance mission to gather data for its kin and signal the beginning of their invasion force. It believes the storm and lightning strikes are a beacon to summon more of its vile kin to this world to conquer it. However, the storm is a fortuitous coincidence for the characters, as it is the dying vestiges of the Storm Rider's residual energies rather than something of the nihileth's creation as it believes. Firm in this conviction, the nihileth would rather fight to the death to attempt to slay the characters and prevent them from derailing the invasion than flee to save its wretched life. Throughout the combat, the arrogant monster telepathically boasts about its brethren's imminent arrival and humanity's weakness. The creature remains supremely confident in its inevitable victory regardless of the circumstances and the characters' successes against the nihileth. If the characters kill the nihileth, it releases a bellowing laugh and utters the words, "Doom is falling" before its lifeless corpse turns into mush.

Aboleth, Nihileth: HD 10; HP 77; AC 3[16]; **Atk** 4 tentacles (1d6 + withering touch); **Move** 9 (swim 12, fly 12 [ethereal only]); **Save** 5; **AL** C; **CL/XP** 13/2300; **Special:** *charm monster* (3/day), drain zombie (heals number of hit points taken), ethereal form (at will), immunities (cold, charm, poison, sleep), *phantasmal force* (3/day), void aura (chilling cloud 5 ft. around aboleth; 2d6 damage and slowed [as *slow* spell]; save for half and not slowed), telepathy (100ft), withering touch (save or random limb withers). (see **Appendix A: New Monsters**)

Treasure: With the nihileth out of the way, the characters are free to explore its lair. Concealed within the muck at the bottom of its pool is an obsidian chest. Within the confines of the unlocked container, the characters find 4,230 gp, a *potion of giant strength*, a scroll (*raise dead*), a *wand of polymorph*, and a *helm of fiery brilliance*.

WRAPPING UP

When the characters leave the nihileth's lair and return to the surface, the storm is abating. Although the soil still wreaks, the rain now falling to the ground washes away the acidic liquid and makes the ground incapable of supporting the invasive caustic thistle. With the nihileth destroyed, the zombies under its command go dormant or mindlessly wreak havoc in Poqoza communities throughout the region.

Although this adventure implies that the nihileth failed to summon more of its kin to Tehuatl, you are free to adjust that conclusion if you wish. These creatures could also bring other alien invaders to the island.

Regardless of how you conclude the adventure, the disturbing thoughts swirling in the nihileth's mind torment the adventurers' during their sleep, filling them with horrific nightmares of strange worlds teeming with bizarre, vile creatures.

Poqoza communities throughout the region celebrate the characters. Feasts, games, and even marriage proposals from ambitious nobles follow them wherever they go. At your discretion, you may segue this adventure into the next and last one in the series — ***The Daughter of the Drowned Serpent***, where the Poqozas once again ask the characters for assistance or the characters learn about the attack on the Poqoza village near the Great Canal.

Daughter of the Drowned Serpent

By Tim Hitchcock

And the children, the little ones.
Those who barely walk, those who crawl.
Those still on the ground making little piles of earth and broken shards
*   of pottery*
The infants lashed to their boards and slats
All of them stare hollow-eyed.
Everyone knows anguish and affliction.
Everyone gazing upon torment; no one has been overlooked.
*   — Verse 18: The Commandments of The Serpent*

Daughter of the Drowned Serpent is an adventure for four 10th- to 12th-level characters in which the characters must investigate the forces behind the recent sacking and looting of several Poqoza villages. The raiders brutally slew numerous villagers, including a son of the tlamacazqui, the supreme priest of the southern half of Tehuatl. The attacks appear to be orchestrated by an alliance of humanoids and warriors from the neighboring Aztli city-state of Mactli. The elders and priests of the Poqoza villages now demand that the rulers of Mactli mete out justice for the victims and pay full restitution for the damages. The northerners deny responsibility for the attacks. Tension escalates as the Aztli city-state and Poqoza people prepare for an all-out war unless the characters can unmask the real culprit behind the attacks.

ADVENTURE BACKGROUND

After Tlatoani's defeat and the cataclysm that followed, those servants who remained loyal to the fallen ruler embarked on a mass exodus. Hunted and pursued at every turn, many fled to other planes of existence to avoid capture and certain death. Those who successfully escaped went into exile. For centuries they kept hidden until the day they would once again re-emerge to spread the word and power of their faith.

When tensions between mortals escalate, egos clash and individual desires for power become all consuming. The crafty Tlatoani has always known this, and his servants count on such mortal weakness to usher in his return. Mortals have short memories. Time dulls the recollection of the sufferings and trials their ancient ancestors faced. It obscures the foundations they laid for the betterment of their descendants. Good and evil share a commonality — a thread of non-duality in which both rely on each other for their existence. Only time and forgetfulness allow one to supersede the other. The serpent waits for these conditions to take hold.

The Poqozas have little regard or use for political leaders. Temporal authority painfully reminds them of the Immortal Sun's oppressive yoke, who in his mortal form once dominated the land as its unquestioned emperor. Instead, they refuse any type of centralized government and choose to live in autonomous communities that rely on the guidance and counsel of their elders and priests. To ensure that no settlement exerts no more authority than another, each priest serves only a single aspect of their god Tlatlcolli. All priests pledge loyalty to the tlamacazqui, who serves as the mortal representative of Tlatlcolli. The tlamacazqui has no dwelling and wanders the lands freely, staying within each of the villages for a few weeks before moving on. For this reason, many of the tlamacazqui's children live scattered throughout the Poqoza villages, each one serving as an act of solidarity and trust between their people.

The tlamacazqui's fifth and youngest son Metzpil resides in the small village of Atoyatetl, one of several settlements along the southern bank of the Acaotilihuei, (the waterway flowing through the Great Canal), where it serves as one of the main trade outposts for the rest of the Poqoza nation. Metzpil works on a trade barge and spends much of his time traveling and debauching himself in various ports. On a recent trip, he indulged in his first taste of a highly addictive mind-altering substance smoked by the violent warrior priests known as the Maldraht maht. Unbeknownst to Metzpil, he was deliberately given the substance by Tlatoani's demonic daughter to feed him dark dreams and manipulate him into seizing power. He became convinced that he would become Tlatoani's new host and through him would rule all of Tehuatl as its undisputed emperor.

In a few short months, Metzpil spiraled into a deep chasm of addiction and delusion where he believes himself to be the second coming of Tlatoani. To further his deranged ambitions, he began grooming a small group of disciples, all of whom share his addiction to Maldraht maht, which he refers to as the Serpent's Kiss. Seeking to create dissention among his people and incite them into a war against the Aztli people to the north, Metzpil and his disciples orchestrated several brutal attacks on Poqoza villages. He staged these attacks to appear as if Aztli jaguar warriors committed them. To carry out the attacks, Metzpil garnered the aid of a tribe of gnolls by promising them the raid's spoils in exchange for their help in the sacking and burning of the town. To further his ruse, he and his minions stole a black dragon's eggs, and he had his gnoll allies tell the furious beast that they saw the humans take them to their villages. Naturally, the conscientious gnolls offered to help the outraged beast exact its revenge on the human thieves to further solidify their alliance

Between the vengeful dragon, the gnolls, and Metzpil's depraved followers disguised as Aztli Jaguar Cuauhocelotls, the village of Atoyatetl stood little chance. The violence that fell upon the village tore it to shreds and sent its few survivors fleeing for their lives, taking with them horrific accounts of the devastation and murder.

ADVENTURE SYNOPSIS

Investigating the violent attacks of several villages along the Acaotilihuei, the waterway flowing through the Great Canal, the heroes must unravel a series of clues to figure out who perpetrated the murderous attacks. Several parties with their own motives committed the ghastly crimes, giving the heroes an opportunity to pursue each of these culprits to their base in a collection of sandbox style mini-adventures. These locales include three Poqoza villages, a riverside outpost occupied by hostile humanoids, a swamp hiding an outpost of ancient mummified warriors, a cavern complex that serves as a home to a brood of dragons, and a visit to a monstrous oracle living off the coast in an abandoned floating war-temple. After undertaking these related excursions, the characters likely have enough evidence to direct their investigation toward the southern human revolutionaries under the renegade son of the tlamacazqui, who has fallen under the baleful influence of an ancient evil. After defeating him, the heroes learn his puppeteer is none other than the demon daughter of the ancient serpent emperor Tlatoani who is seeking to restore her father onto Tehuatl's throne. In the final encounter, the adventurers square off against the demon-daughter in a heroic attempt to eradicate her and her diabolical parent from the world forever.

STARTING THE ADVENTURE

The adventure begins when the characters hear tales of the mysterious and violent destruction of a small Poqoza trading village known as Atoyatetl that rests along the southern shore of the Acaotilihuei, roughly halfway between the city of Zacatl and Azuato. Accounts tell of bodies burned by acid, villagers with their hearts torn out, and rumors of cryptic runes encircling the villages, all of which bear the hallmarks of the Aztli hero-gods Yaocteotl and Quiahuitl. Encourage the characters to travel to Atoyatetl to investigate the rumors. Make it clear to them that if the rumors prove true, such an act would sow the seeds of war between the Poqozas and Aztlis.

As a trading outpost, Atoyatetl is readily accessible via the Great Canal separating the Aztlis from the Poqozas. Additionally, four trails connect the village to surrounding Poqoza settlements. Two paths meander off to the south while the other two skirt along the edge of the canal in opposite directions.

As the characters approach the section of the canal where the village is located, they spot its precise location from the trail of thick black smoke rising up into the clear blue Tehuatl sky.

When the characters arrive at Atoyatetl, read or paraphrase the following description:

Walking the ruins are **12 Poqoza warriors**, each accompanied by a **war dog**. As soon as any of the characters enter the town, one of the Poqoza warriors spots them and demands they halt and identify themselves, or die. The warriors are particularly suspicious if the characters are not Poqozas and appear to be outsiders. However, defending against the attack has left them exhausted and several of them bear ghastly-looking wounds. They are not willing to risk an all-out fight, and the battered warriors are willing to stand down and listen to reason rather than engage in a physical altercation with the heroes. The warriors are obviously exhausted. Most sport significant injuries that inhibit their ability to fight.

Poqoza Warriors, Male or Female Half-Elves (Ftr4) (12): HP 26, 24, 21, 20x2, 19, 17x2, 16, 11, 10, 7; **AC** 5[14]; **Atk** macuahuitl (1d8+1 or 1d8+3 [maht user]) or tecpatl (1d4+1 or 1d4+3 [maht user]) or sling (1d4); **Move** 12; **Save** 11; **AL** Any; **CL/XP** 4/120; **Special:** +1 to hit and damage strength bonus, blood sacrifice (3/day, slice own chest for 1 point damage to gain +1 to hit and damage for 1d6 rounds), darkvision (60ft), multiple attacks (4) vs. creatures with 1 or fewer HD. (***Monstrosities*** 256)
Equipment: olli armor [B], macuahuitl [B], tecpatl [B], sling, 10 sling stones.

Guard Dogs (12): HD 2; **HP** 16, 14x2, 13, 11, 10x3, 9, 8x2, 6; **AC** 7[12]; **Atk** bite (1d6); **Move** 14; **Save** 16; **CL/XP** 2/30; **Special:** none. (***Monstrosities*** 127)

Characters who heal the injured warriors or civilians earn the Poqozas' trust. Similarly, characters assisting in the village's reconstruction or who help fortify against another potential attack also earn their confidence.

Once characters earn the warriors' respect and trust, the witnesses readily provide the characters with a detailed description of the attack.

After hearing the tale, the characters can attempt to discern more about the creatures or further question the warriors.

If asked what happened to the villagers, the warriors tell them that less than half of the people were able to escape. Some took to the roads, but others fled into the forest and grasslands.

The winged serpent described by the warrior is in fact a black dragon. If the characters attempt to figure out what the dragon took from the house, they can infer that the objects sound like they might be dragon eggs.

CHAPTER ONE: RUN THROUGH THE JUNGLE

If the players choose to follow the gnolls, the characters can easily follow their tracks along the west road. The tracks continue for approximately one-half mile until they reach an intersection where the main road bends south and a smaller footpath runs northward through the jungle. The gnolls' tracks clearly follow the northbound trail, likely headed toward the canal. Although technically part of the Tlococua Marsh that dominates Tehuatl's southeastern coast, trees and woody shrubs thrive along the banks of the Great Canal, making this wetland region into a combination of swamp and marshland.

At this point, allow any characters tracking the gnolls a 1-in-6 chance (3-in-6 for elves and rangers) to spot some curious tracks. If successful, the character notices that several sets of humanoid footprints break away from the road through the brush and into the forest, while the gnoll footprints continue along the road. If the characters pursue the gnolls, the tracks lead them to **The Children of Itzcuin**. If they instead break from the road to pursue the second set of prints, read or paraphrase the following description:

The children of Itzcuin are in fact gnolls.

If the characters ask where the dragon came from, the warriors say the serpent came from and flew off toward the swamplands on the northern side of the canal known as the Yoaltica Ilaquiloz.

If the characters ask about the house with the eggs, the warriors explain that it belonged to the tlamacazqui's youngest son, Metzpil. They suspect Metzpil was killed during the attack, but they have yet to recover his remains.

Those inquiring further into the nature of the dragon or dragon-summoning rituals are told to speak to the village storyteller. She explains that dragons are the offspring of the Drowned Serpent, the Emperor-God Tlatoani, and they were driven off after the gods defeated him by drowning the world. Beyond that, she admits ignorance — as such knowledge is far older than mortals. She then adds that if they require more information, they should seek Nahualipazotic. Gifted with great longevity, Nahualipazotic is a witch-priestess said to be the sea bride of the hero-god Itztliteotl. Legends say that the sea bride lives off the eastern seacoast in a floating temple-barge (see **Chapter 2: A Tangled Fate**).

The Jaguar Cuauhocelotls performed a ritual sacrifice often associated with Quiahuitl, a hero-god of the Aztlis often associated with the neighboring city-state of Mactli.

While the ritual appears to honor Quiahuitl, it is inauthentic and was staged. Instead, the deception is an insult to Quiahuitl, and the rites are more reminiscent of those performed to honor Tlatoani rather than the Aztli hero-gods.

If asked which way the gnolls fled, the warriors tell them that the hyena-men took the paths to the west, then headed off through the woods.

If asked which way the Jaguar Cuauhocelotls fled, the Poqoza explain that the Aztlis paddled their boats back into the canal and headed north, likely toward the city-state of Mactli.

WRAPPING THINGS UP

This section concludes when the players decide which course of action they want to pursue. If they choose to follow the gnolls, continue to **Chapter 1: Run Through the Jungle**. If they choose to seek the sea bride, go to **Chapter 2: A Tangled Fate**. If they choose to attempt to track down the dragon, proceed to **Chapter 3: Yoaltica Ilaquiloz**. If they attempt to follow the Jaguar Cuauhocelotls, go to **Chapter 4: The Secret of the Fallen Son**.

If the characters continue to follow the tracks, they soon encounter a quickly rigged trap set by the fleeing villagers to slow or deter anyone pursuing them.

STINGING INSECT TRAP

During their flight, the villagers found a wasp's nest and decided to set a small snare that might cause any pursuers to anger the stinging insects. A tripwire strung across the forest path triggers the trap. If touched or cut, the wire snaps, releasing a second cord holding a weighted log that swings into a nearby wasp nest, which causes the insects to erupt in a frenzied **swarm of insects** that viciously attack the nearest living creatures. Anyone actively searching the forest floor has a 1-in-6 chance to spot the wire. A thief can safely and easily disable trap.

Stinging Insect Swarm: HD 3; HP 22; AC 7[12]; **Atk** swarm (1d8); **Move** 9 (fly); **Save** 14; **AL** N; **CL/XP** 4/120; **Special:** immune to all but blunt weapons.

A band of **25 Poqoza escapees** fled down this road, but they were forced to veer off into the jungle and hole up in the brush when they heard the gnolls chasing after them. Wounded and weary, they were forced to stop and tend to the injured. They hid themselves a short distance off the trail and set perimeter defenses around their makeshift camp. Scared and cornered, the Poqozas fight back against anyone pursuing them, attacking first and asking questions later. Nonetheless,

Kurn Domladur
Turew
Octli
Ixtla
Tamazoli
Nepalta
Shassal
Balandrur
Ipaconoytl
Capual Desert
Nochtli
Xalpit
Hana'aloa
Mactli
Omehual River
Quannaqa River
Ouatulli Lake
Omiex
Droomph
Teocua
Cuahtla Forest
Yoaltica Ilaquiloz
Necocyaotl
The Great Canal
Quizaloa
Amilotetl
Ixchicta
Huitzineo
Azuato
Good fortune
Ezhuacoza
Zacatl
Quitlacatl
Cotza
Toxana
Mimicapoli
Ezhuitotl
Blibleblup
Ahuacua
Cuiateotl
Hilaya River
The Spring
Mototoloa
Ixnenatl
Zinacan
Xoxoquetzpali
Moyome
Atoyaxalli
Tlococua Marsh
Mauhque
Iachacina
Hamachi
Yolqui
Ixtama
Temetzin River
Yoyoliton
Mulla Chanacu
Hualcitzen
Xicotli
Onacina
Cuanintli
Nezcatayotl
Eei
Rommpf
Caxcalli Grasslands
Yuri
Tlahapina
N
CAXCALLI GRASSLANDS
1 Square – 20 Miles

Accommodating Alternate Plans

If the characters insist on returning, use the following encounter with the wood apes to cause conflict on the return journey. You can also run an alternate encounter for the Children of Itzcuin in which a group of **10 aquatic ogres** spots the gnolls loading their boats from the water. The sea ogres attack and devour most of the group, preventing the last few from leaving. In this event, the characters arrive to face the ogres who have the remaining **4 gnolls** cornered up a tree. The gnolls attempt to flee once the merrows turn their attention to the characters.

Ogres (Aquatic) (10): HD 4+1; HP 31, 27, 26x2, 23, 22, 21x2, 18, 13; AC 5[14]; Atk spear (1d10+1); **Move** 9 (swim 12); **Save** 13; **AL** C; **CL/XP** 4/120; **Special:** amphibious. (*Monstrosities* 356)

Gnolls (4): HD 2; HP 14, 12, 10x2; AC 5[14]; Atk bite (2d4) or weapon (1d10); **Move** 9; **Save** 16; **AL** C; **CL/XP** 2/30; **Special:** none. (*Monstrosities* 209)

they are weak and pose little threat to anyone, especially the adventurers. If the characters convince them they are here to help them, they quickly yield. Similar to the warriors in the village, offering assistance or healing gives the characters advantage on Charisma checks made to interact with the escapees.

Fleeing Poqoza Commoners, Male or Female Half-Elves (25): HP 1d6hp; AC 9[10]; Atk spear (1d6); **Move** 12; **Save** 18; **AL** Any; **CL/XP** B/10; **Special:** darkvision (60ft). (*Monstrosities* 254)

While little remains of Atoyatetl, the villagers want to return home. The characters are free to continue in pursuit of the gnolls or to lead the villagers back to Atoyatetl. However, make sure the players are aware that time is of the essence if they hope to catch the fleeing assailants.

The Woods Apes

If the characters have been wandering the jump for a while, or if they decide to take an alternate path, they run across an angry patrol of **4 carnivorous woods apes** who have had their fill of trespassers wandering across and disturbing their lands. Although blessed with sentience, these irate beasts are tired of watching humanoids despoil their forest. They have no patience for chatting with the interlopers and instead violently attack them on sight. In the event the characters successfully negotiate a peaceful resolution, the woods apes point the characters in the right direction in their pursuit of the gnolls.

Carnivorous Woods Apes (Gorillas) (4): HD 4; HP 30, 27, 23, 21; AC 6[13]; Atk 2 strikes (1d3), bite (1d6); **Move** 12; **Save** 13; **AL** N; **CL/XP** 4/120; **Special:** hug and rend (if both strikes hit, additional 1d6 damage). (*Monstrosities* 17)

The Children of Itzcuin

Before the characters break from the forest's edge, the characters hear the rough guttural barks of the gnolls shouting directions at each other as they rapidly load their boats to flee north, back across the canal.

When the characters reach the edge of the forest, read or paraphrase the following description:

> The forest breaks into a rocky plain that slopes down toward the bulkhead of the Acaotilihuei canal. Along the edge of the bulkhead, a large band of scraggly hyena-like humanoids scramble about packing sacks with loot, tying them into bundles, and lowering them over the seawall.

Traveling the Canal

Characters traveling to the various locations in this adventure are likely to use the canal at some point to reach their intended destination.

Because it connects to the surrounding ocean, the water levels in the canal ebb and flow with the tides. The **Children of Itzcuin** encounter starts at low tide. At this time, the waters at the bulkhead sit at a shallow 3–1/2 feet deep with a three-mile-per-hour current moving east. The depth drops off moving toward the center of the canal, which is deeply dredged to accommodate safe passage for larger ships.

If the characters arrive at the canal at a later point in the adventure, determine the tide randomly by rolling 1d4 on **Table 5–1** below. Start the tide at the determined position but continue to mark the shifts as time passes.

Table 5–1: Tides in the Great Canal

1d4	Tide
1	Ebb tide (tide is going out). Determine tide speed in miles per hour by rolling 1d8.*
2	Slack tide (tide is switching from going out to going in). Tide speed is zero.**
3	Flood tide (tide is going in). Determine the speed in miles per hour by rolling 1d8.*
4	Slack tide (tide is switching from going in to going out). Tide speed is zero.**

* Both ebb and flood tides last approximately 10 hours.
** Slack tides last about two hours each.

Characters moving with the tide increase their speed by the speed of the tide. Characters going against the tide decrease their speed by the speed of the tide.

At least once during their travels, the characters attract the attention of the canal's most fearsome predators. A hunting party of **10 aquatic ogres** spots their boat. If possible, they attempt to redirect the crafts by latching on underneath and swimming them off course. Once they isolate a boat, they flip or smash it and greedily attack the nearest target floundering in the water.

Ogres (Aquatic) (10): HD 4+1; **HP** 31, 27, 26x2, 23, 22, 21x2, 18, 13; AC 5[14]; Atk spear (1d10+1); **Move** 9 (swim 12); **Save** 13; **AL** C; **CL/XP** 4/120; **Special:** amphibious. (*Monstrosities* 356)

The tree line sits about 10 feet from the edge of the canal, exposing a small clearing that runs for 30 yards parallel to the water. The manmade bulkhead of piled logs and concrete rests 15 feet above the waterline.

Just beyond the tree line, **18 gnolls** work feverishly, binding up packages and crates of loot with coarse ropes and then lowering them down the bulkhead.

Below the bulkhead and out of the characters' sight, another group of **6 gnolls** stands waist-deep in the water to load the packages into the canoes. Once finished, they intend to head back across the canal.

Overly confident in their numerical superiority, the gnolls work loudly and clumsily. They exert no effort to keep an eye out for trouble.

Gnolls (24): HD 2; HP 16, 15x3, 14x4, 13x2, 12x4, 11, 10x3, 9x4, 8x2; AC 5[14]; Atk bite (2d4) or weapon (1d10); **Move** 9; **Save** 16; **AL** C; **CL/XP** 2/30; **Special:** none. (*Monstrosities* 209)

Ultimately, the craven hyena-men fear defeat. If the heroes reduce their numbers by half, the surviving gnolls break formation and attempt to flee. The gnolls are poor swimmers. If the characters corner them and force them over the bulkhead and into the canal, they wade along the water's edge until they find a safe location to climb up the bulkhead and flee into the forest.

If the characters prevent a gnoll from fleeing and call for its surrender, the monster drops its weapon and stops in its tracks.

Characters may interrogate each gnoll they capture and ask 1d4 questions, which the fearful beasts answer to the best of their ability.

The gnolls convey the following bits of information if asked why they raided the village or if faced with a similar inquiry:

• A man calling himself Cuanmitztlactl bribed them into participating in the raid by promising them the spoils.

If pressed for a description of Cuanmitztlactl, they reveal he is a Poqoza with distinctive tattoos, which he covered with clay paint before the attack to presumably disguise his identity. Anyone who speaks Aztli knows that the name Cuanmitztlactl loosely translates to Jaguar Lord, suggesting it is likely an alias. If the characters convey the Poqoza's description to any resident of Atoyatetl, that person identifies Cuanmitztlactl as Metzpil. If the characters accurately describe the tattoo to the village priest, the skein witch, a similarly trained person, or any Poqoza, that individual identifies the man as the son of the tlamacazqui.

• If the characters raise questions about the dragon, the gnolls divulge that the dragon is not a true ally nor was it magically summoned. Instead, Cuanmitztlactl (Metzpil) manipulated the beast into leading the attack against the village to retrieve her stolen eggs. They also pin this plan on Cuanmitztlactl, explaining that he stole the eggs and then sent one of them to tell the dragon that they had witnessed the humans stealing the eggs. They told the beast where to find its missing eggs.

WRAPPING THINGS UP

This section concludes if the characters defeat the gnolls. At this point, they can use any information they discovered to follow other leads or return to the village. The gnolls stole a number of tools, cloth, food, and other items from the village. The characters can travel on foot; however, they may also use the gnolls' dugout canoes to paddle along the canal. The dugouts have the same statistics as a rowboat for purposes of speed and other statistics.

The drop to the water is 15 feet, although the ropes and grappling hooks the gnolls used to land their dugout canoes and scale the bulkhead are still in place. The gnolls set spikes into the face of the logs to create makeshift cleats to which they tied off the six large dugout canoes. If the characters decide to take the canal, use the **Traveling the Canal** sidebar as a reference.

CHAPTER TWO: A TANGLED FATE

The temple barge of Nahualipazotic floats 5,000 feet off the coast, just east of the mouth of the canal. The chillier northern winds hammer against the warm, sun-soaked coast to create a dense and almost unnatural fog infamous among sailors and mariners who ply these waters. These waters just offshore are particularly dangerous to large vessels, as what lies just beneath the surface was once the top of a large mountainous region before the gods sank Tehuatl under the sea. Dozens of jagged rocky spires patiently wait to rip ships' hulls into splinters. The notoriously desolate shoreline consists entirely of pebbles and stones that churn angrily in the rolling surf.

The dense fog prevents the characters from spotting the concealed barge from the mouth of the canal. The vapors lessen and ultimately dissipate when the characters move approximately 1,500 feet away from the shoreline. However, finding their way through the fog poses a challenge. When the characters exit the fog and scan the water for Nahualipazotic's barge, read or paraphrase the following description:

GETTING TO THE TEMPLE

The temple drifts less than one mile off the coast. The characters may attempt to reach the barge in several different ways. A boat is probably the simplest option, though characters at this level are also likely to have some flight capabilities as well. While the current can be tricky due to the area's close proximity to the canal, a ranger or druid has a 3-in-6 chance (1-in-6 for all others) to determine when the currents are optimal, particularly if the tide is going out. Swimming (while also an option) is slightly more difficult, particularly if the character is swimming against the tide (see **Traveling the Canal** sidebar.)

When the adventurers near the temple barge, it becomes visibly obvious that the worn pumice blocks that hold it afloat have grown sodden with age. The temple barge floats low and at a slight angle and only the crest of the upper steps still struggles to stay above the gray water. A jungle of seaweed clings to the blocks and bobs slowly in the waves, sending it into a swirling hypnotic dance.

To get aboard and enter the barge by mundane means, a character must succeed at a saving throw to climb the steps without slipping and taking 1d4 points of damage. Once aboard, the character can search for the entrance. The water-slicked stone floors of the barge sit at a slightly uneven pitch, which is made worse by the constant rocking motion caused by the ocean waves. While four main entrances are at the base of the temple, all of these are now submerged and overgrown with seaweed. The only exterior entrance sits at the top of the structure.

The sea bride has **4 eel hounds** (see **Encounter T1**) that actively keep watch over the barge, entering and leaving through the submerged entrances on the lowest floor. Within 1d4 minutes after the characters' arrival, the hounds pick up their scent and start howling ominously to alert their mistress that there are intruders. They swim a few times around the barge to see if they can spot the intruders before calling off their search. They try to remain hidden while alternating their howls to distract the characters. After circling the barge twice, the creatures enter through the submerged entrances and go to meet with Nahualipazotic. At this time, allow the characters to react and plan whatever actions they intend on taking. As they do so, Nahualipazotic allows her eel dogs to lead her to the intruders. When the characters finish their actions, she arrives to confront them as described in **Encounter T1** below.

ENCOUNTER T1: THE SEA BRIDE

Nahualipazotic is a **marid** who served as the sea bride of the hero-god Quiahuitl. Before he ascended into godhood, the mortal Nahualipazotic gave her life to save her husband from drowning during a tidal wave spawned by Tlatoani. The forlorn Quiahuitl searched the outgoing tide but could not find her body. After several days, he presumed she died and was washed out to sea. However, her heroic act of self-sacrifice caused her lifeless body to fuse with the Plane of Water, giving her a new existence as a genie. The marid initially remembered nothing about her former existence, though faint glimpses and memories of her past slowly crept back into her mind over the centuries. Meanwhile, the widower Quiahuitl later married Atoyatl, who still bristled at the mention of her husband's first great love and the woman who sacrificed herself to save him. Now thousands of years old, the venerable genie largely keeps out of sight to avoid attracting Atoyatl's jealous glare, which rears its ugly head every few centuries. She secrets herself away in the decrepit remains of a half-sunken Maldraht maht temple-barge, where she simmers with anger toward the humans who forgot about the sacrifices her husband, and more importantly, those she made, to liberate them from the oppressive Tlatloani.

When she meets the characters, the haughty genie berates them for dishonoring her husband and warns them that if they do not leave immediately, she will order her **4 eel hounds** to feast on their flesh. The characters have one round to act before she makes good on her promise. If the characters do not flee, agree to leave, or adequately convince her to listen to them, she commands her eel hounds to rip out the characters' throats. The eel hounds then rush to attack as she attacks the characters with her trident.

Nahualipazotic, Marid: HD 11; HP 79; AC 5[14]; **Atk** 2 fists (1d8) or trident (2d6); **Move** 10 (swim 16); **Save** 3; **AL** N; **CL/XP** 13/2300; **Special:** spell-like abilities, whirlpool (sink boats in 1d4+4 rounds). (*The Tome of Horrors Complete* 268)
Spell-like abilities: at will—*create water, invisibility, polymorph self.*

Eel Hounds (4): HD 7; HP 51, 48, 43, 40; AC 6[13]; **Atk** bite (1d8); **Move** 12 (swim 15); **Save** 9; **AL** N; **CL/XP** 7/600; **Special:** amphibious, slick spittle (30ft range, target must save or fall prone from slippery ground). (see **Appendix A: New Monsters**)

To gain the sea bride's assistance, the characters must convince her of their integrity. They can accomplish this in several different ways. The characters could take non-hostile actions on their turn, such as dodging her attacks or throwing their weapons to the ground in an obvious sign of their willingness to negotiate with her. Next, they must promise an offering, sacrifice, or some other suitable tribute to her husband. The gift must be worthy of a deity, though if the characters are stumped in this regard, they may plead ignorance as to an appropriate sacrifice, leaving her to decide what they must offer her. In her temperamental mind, a gift of blood, such as a powerful enemy's heart, or precious objects, preferably with a connection to the sea or the rain, worth at least 1,000 gp will suffice. However, if the characters killed any of her eel dogs before beginning the negotiations, she demands additional compensation for her losses.

Alternately, any character who explains they came to seek her assistance to slay a black dragon that lives in the swamps immediately gets her attention. Nahualipazotic despises the black dragon Aaq'eq' because as a serpent, she considers her one of Tlatoani's daughters and by extension a sworn enemy of her mortal husband.

Once told about the dragon, clever characters can easily convince Nahualipazotic to aid them by vowing to seek out and kill the creature. If they do so, the sea bride asks them to wait for a moment and then disappears into the inner chambers of her temple. When she returns, read or paraphrase the following description:

If the characters agree to retrieve the black pearl, Nahualipazotic gives them further instructions on how to find the pearls.

At this point, allow the players to discuss and determine how they intend to get to the pearl beds as well as to ask further questions of Nahualipazotic if they deem it necessary. If the characters swam to the temple, Nahualipazotic offers them the use of several small pontoon canoes, ghastly crafts crafted from human skin and bone left behind by the Maldraht maht. If the characters ask Nahualipazotic about the wraith of Quiahuitl, she tells them that the sacrificial victims of the god of storms guard the sacred pearl beds and warns them to steer clear of their sodden corpses.

Once the characters are ready to depart, read or paraphrase the following description:

Upon seeing the corpses, the eel hounds stop and begin snarling. They refuse to go closer.

The floating corpses are **4 drowned maidens**, women sacrificed to the gods to protect the sacred pearl beds.

If characters approach, the creatures attempt to stealthily use their kelp hair to entangle the vessel in an attempt to capsize the vessel so they can attack opponents floundering in the water. The drowned maidens have a 45% chance of halting and flipping a small boat or raft.

If the characters defeat the drowned maidens, they are free to explore the sacred pearl beds.

The oyster reef is eight feet below the water's surface. Characters have a 15% chance of finding an oyster with a black pearl in it, but they can increase their odds to 75% by spending two hours harvesting and shucking oysters. The pearl they eventually find is flawless.

Drowned Maidens (4): HD 7; HP 53, 50, 46, 41; AC 5[14]; **Atk** 2 claws (1d8), 3 hair strikes (1d6 + constrict); **Move** 12 (swim 12); **Save** 9; **AL** C; **CL/XP** 9/1100; **Special:** +1 or better magic or silver weapons to hit, constrict (if hair hits, 50% chance hair wraps around target, save avoids, automatic 1d6 damage until freed), immune to charm and sleep, kiss (3/day, 2d6 damage, save for half), spell-like abilities. (see **Appendix A: New Monsters**)
Spell-like abilities: at will—*polymorph self, silence 15ft radius.*

Treasure: The pearl is worth 500 gp.

WRAPPING THINGS UP

This section concludes if the characters return to the sea bride with a black pearl. Nahualipazotic uses the material component to recharge the *arrow of black dragon slaying* (see **Appendix B: New Equipment and Magic Items**). The process takes her the entire evening. The characters are free to spend the night in the temple, though she cannot offer them much in the way of formal accommodations beyond a hard floor to sleep on, cold fish, and rainwater. After Nahualipazotic presents them with the arrow, the characters may depart for the saltwater swamp known as Yoaltica Ilaquiloz. When they depart, the sea bride makes them a final offer, which you may deliver by reading or paraphrasing the following dialogue:

If the adventurers kill Aaq'eq' and later return to Nahualipazotic with proof of the dragon's death, she offers them a small stone bearing a carving of a face set inside a sun. The characters can use the small medallion to contact her to seek her advice. They may use it to contact her three times, after which it turns to dust.

While her powers of insight are not unlimited, Nahualipazotic possesses a substantial amount of information about demons, Tlatoani, the creation of Tehuatl, and numerous other details that might help them defeat the Drowned Serpent's Daughter in the final chapter. Characters must choose their word carefully. Treat any questions posed to the sea bride as if the characters had cast a *wish* spell.

CHAPTER THREE: YOALTICA ILAQUILOZ

Yoaltica Ilaquiloz is a saltwater swamp along Tehuatl's eastern shore that consists of almost 4,000 square miles of flooded lowlands. It stretches northward from the canal to an elevated plateau of eroded hills that forms a natural barrier preventing it from spreading farther north. The swamp is an ecological, manmade newcomer to the island. It formed 75 years earlier, after the Flood of Quiahuitl's Tears brutally battered the coastline, causing the partial collapse of nearly 20 miles of the canal wall bordering the northern part of the island.

The harsh and desolate saltwater swamp makes traveling on foot difficult. Those who need to travel through the swamp typically do so by poling flat-bottomed rafts through mazes of shallow channels that weave through small islands of mud and silt. These small islands hold little aside from clumps of shaggy reeds and stout stocky mangrove shrubs with long, broad leaves. The soft mush forms small hummocks, though these are barely stable enough to support more than a few pounds of weight. Any creature larger than a cat walking on them slowly sinks into the muck and finds it impossible to move more than 20 feet before sinking into a few feet of mud. The mud affects characters in the same manner as quicksand, although it is just four feet deep. The mud poses no immediate danger unless the character is not tall enough to keep his or her head above water, in which case the character may drown without outside intervention. The water in the channels is 1d4 feet deep, resting above three feet of soft silt that covers the bottom. The channels are 2d4 feet wide, meandering in a web throughout the swamp, where they occasionally form larger pools that are 1d4 + 6 feet deep.

Vermin thoroughly infest the tropical saltwater swamp. Swarms of mosquitos, large toxic-skinned salamanders, stinging mudfish, frogs, and serpents fly and slither through the muck. While undoubtedly annoying, few of these creatures pose any serious threat to the characters if they took the proper precautions. On occasion, travelers might also encounter larger predators such as crocodiles or some of the more hostile reptilian humanoid tribes that inhabit the region, such as the lizardfolk and tsathars.

The dragon's lair is at the northern edge of the swamp near the edge of the plateau, about 60 miles due north of Azuato on the regional map. If the characters travel at normal speed through the terrain, the journey takes approximately five days. During their travels, you can occasionally slow the pace and add further description with the following obstacles and encounters. Consider one or more of the encounters from about the midway point (about the second day or so into the journey) to the black dragon's lair, before you run **The Temple of Necocyaotl** encounter. You may also want to consider adding your own encounters to the list, as well as saving one or more of them for the return trip.

SWAMP ENCOUNTERS

Insect Attack: Near midday, the burning sun breaks through the haze, hot enough to pierce the dense tangles of the swamp thickets. Clouds of insects shoot into the sky, enticed by the heat to seek out warm-blooded creatures bold enough to violate their secret abodes.

The small stinging insects swarm the characters. Those exposed to the swarm are bitten and exposed to plague. Characters can easily drive the swarm off with fire or smoke. Those who thought ahead and slathered themselves with herbal poultices or swamp mud repel the irritating insects and avoid contracting the disease.

Shambling Mounds: At this location, something triggered the swamp's foul alchemy, releasing an overwhelming stench of decay and decomposition. Suddenly, the reeds bend as **3 shambling mounds** emerge from the vegetation and attack.

Shambling Mounds (3): HD 8; HP 61, 55, 51; AC 1[18]; **Atk** 2 fists (2d8 + enfold); **Move** 6; **Save** 8; **AL** N; **CL/XP** 11/1700; **Special:** enfold (if two fists hit, save or suffocate in 2d4 rounds), resists cold and weapons (50% damage). (*Monstrosities* 419)

Reeds: The channel empties into a wide pool filled with dense, spiny swamp reeds. The pool fills a 1,000-square-foot area surrounded by stumpy clots of tiny mud islands. The reeds' abrasive shafts slash and tear any creatures attempting to move through them. A creature must make a saving throw or take 1 point of damage for every five feet of movement through the reeds on a failure. A creature moving through the area at half speed does not need to make the save. Of course, you are free to add sound effects and other overt signs of trouble to hasten their movement through the tangled vegetation.

Wispy Clouds: The day drags as a low fog rolls ashore, followed by scattered light rain showers. The weather conditions drive away the insects, but it also reduces visibility and lightly obscures the area. After one hour, clothing and equipment becomes sodden and clings to the skin. Those wearing armor or carrying heavier equipment and poling or wading begin to tire and chafe from the exertion, heat, and humidity.

After a while, it almost appears as if the fog is breaking, and the characters spot flickers of light ahead. The flickering light is an effect created by a gang of **1d4+2 will-o'-the-wisps**. The mysterious creatures surround the characters and attempt to drain away their life energy.

Will-o'-the-wisps (1d4+2): HD 9; AC –8[27]; **Atk** shock (2d6); **Move** 18; **Save** 6; **AL** C; **CL/XP** 10/1400; **Special:** lights (brighten or dim, or form wraith-like form). (*Monstrosities* 512)

Orange Lotus: This intersection opens into a wide channel that seems to offer easy passage through the swamp. An enticingly sweet scent drifts from large clusters of water lotuses that line the edges of this waterway. Their bright orange petals are in full bloom, but the cloying honey and mint scent of their nectar belies their toxicity. Anyone exposed to the blossoms or nectar of the orange lotus is exposed to its poison. Characters must make a saving throw each hour while among the blossoms or fall asleep for 1d4 hours. They take 1d6 points of damage per hour they rest among the poisonous blooms.

Downpour: While crossing a wide pond, the sky suddenly opens and a loud thundercrack ushers in a torrential downpour. Characters who wish to avoid getting thoroughly soaked can seek shelter beneath a nearby outcrop of mangroves that line the shore. If the characters travel in a craft that can take on water, the rains begin to fill their craft at a rate of one inch per minute. The swift downpour lasts only for 3d10 minutes, after which the weather shifts into a glum mixture of intermittent fog and drizzle.

THE TEMPLE OF NECOCYAOTL

A large temple to the lesser-known hero-god Necocyaotl — the enemy of both sides — once stood at this location. The priest-warriors who occupied this temple remained neutral during the conflict between the Poqozas and the Aztlis. Their territory served as a buffer zone between the two sides, earning them the enmity of both. They vigorously defended their territory against trespassers belonging to either faction. When the canal walls that created the Yoaltica Ilaquiloz flooded the region, the temple tumbled and sank into the mire. The warrior-priests, unable to escape the destruction, sacrificed themselves to Necocyaotl using sacred potions to mummify their remains so they could continue to serve their god in death.

They are known as Necocyaotl's Chosen and appear as shriveled bodies wrapped in rotted leaves and sealed with mud. Their faces are covered with obsidian masks stylistically carved with hideous expressions with a single stripe of gold inlaid down the center. There are **10 mummies**.

Mummies (10): HD 5+1; **HP** 37, 34, 33, 30x2, 28, 25, 24x2, 18; **AC** 3[16]; **Atk** strike (1d12); **Move** 6; **Save** 12; **AL** C; **CL/XP** 7/600; **Special:** +1 or better magic weapons to hit, rot (prevents magical healing, wounds heal at one-tenth normal rate, *remove curse* lifts curse). (*Monstrosities* 40)

Treasure: Six of the masks are badly chipped and damaged and worth between 1d10 gp each. Three are in average condition and worth 55 gp, 40 gp, and 25 gp. One is in superb condition and is worth 350 gp.

THE BLACK DRAGON'S LAIR

The dragon's lair is found where the swamp meets the plateau, in a series of flooded caves that carve their way into the elevated ground. If the characters approach, they notice that the grassy clumps and mud islands that block the outer swamp thin, giving way to freshwater flora such as floating lilies, cattails, and rushes that favor the improving conditions. Near the entrance of the caves, the swamp waters deepen, pooling against the stony barricade. Before the characters enter the black dragon's lair, you should make note of the following general cavern features.

GENERAL FEATURES

The dragon Aaq'eq' and her brood inhabit a series of caves that consist of several large chambers formed of natural stone. The caverns have extremely high, natural ceilings that (unless otherwise noted) climb between 30 to 40 feet from the chamber floor. A series of partially submerged channels connects the individual caverns using entrances hidden below the water line (see map). This means that a soupy morass of four-foot-deep water floods the majority of the cavern floors. The water rests atop another few feet of goopy murk. If the characters enter, the murk has settled on the bottom. However, when turbulence disturbs the murk, it mixes with the water and causes it to turn cloudy, reducing visibility in the water to zero feet. The dragons use this knowledge to their advantage when they swim, deliberately stirring up the murk to mask their movements and locations. The murk also obscures the submerged tunnels that lead to the lair's outer caverns.

The caves are not lit, except for any daylight that happens to filter in from the main entrance. The caves reverberate sound easily, creating echoes from the constant lapping of water against the walls and condensation dripping from the ceilings. Inside, the air feels thick and still, unbearably humid, and carries a rank, fetid stench.

The caverns are inhabited by three dragons: **Aaq'eq'**, a **very old black dragon**, and her children, **2 immature black dragons**. This section assumes that each of these dragons is in a specific location when the characters arrive; however, the dragons move freely about the caves and respond accordingly to the actions of the characters and to each other.

The dragons are intelligent creatures and have specific strategies for protecting their lair as noted throughout this section. You are advised to familiarize yourself with their tactics and motivations before running the encounter.

Lastly, Aaq'eq' and her brood have little interest in the affairs of humans. Having completed her assault on Atoyatetl, the dragon has little interest or motivation to attack other human settlements (as she exacted her retribution and recovered her precious eggs). Still, she does not take kindly to trespassers and believes any humans entering her domain seek to abscond with her eggs or steal her riches. If the characters find a way of presenting her with the truth about the individuals who stole her eggs, she furiously seeks out the gnolls and reaps all manner of vengeance against those who "set her up."

D1: LAIR ENTRANCE

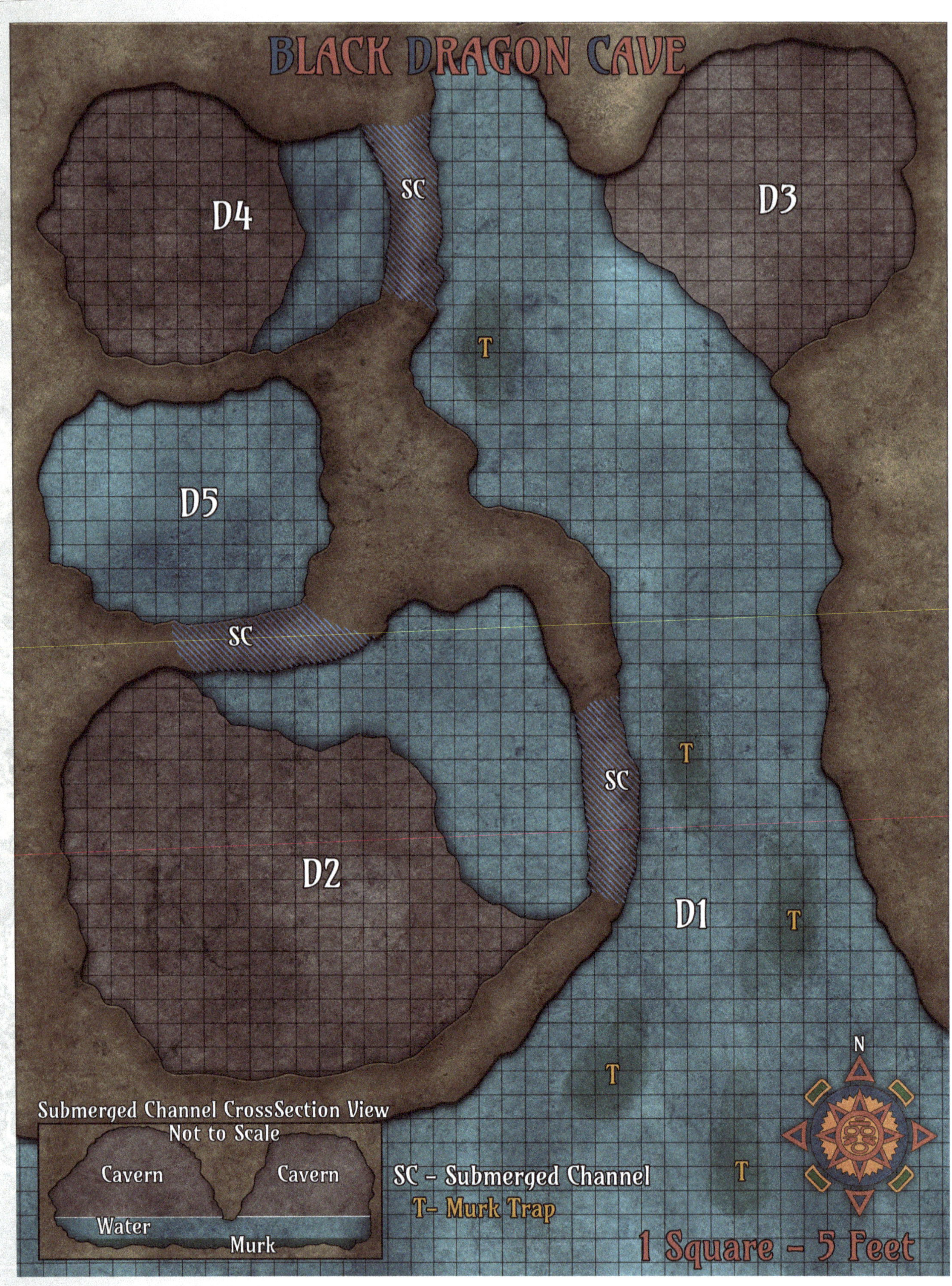

BLACK DRAGON CAVE
D4
SC
D3
T
D5
SC
D2
SC
T
D1
T
T
N
T
T
Submerged Channel CrossSection View
Not to Scale
Cavern
Cavern
Water
Murk
SC - Submerged Channel
T - Murk Trap
1 Square - 5 Feet

To defend the territory surrounding their lair's entrance, the dragons dug out several deep spots that hide unseen beneath the murky sludge. Those traveling on foot and unaware of their presence can easily stumble into them, making them extremely vulnerable to swimming dragon attacks.

Swamp Murk Traps

Those unwary or dimwitted enough to stumble into these hidden traps quickly sink into the mire as the dark waters force their way into their gasping lungs. Anyone stepping into a deep spot triggers the trap and risks becoming engulfed and suffocating in the mire. The triggering creature must succeed on a saving throw to avoid sinking into one. A successful save indicates the creature splashed its way back to shallower ground before sinking into the muck. On a failed saving throw, the target sinks into the mud and is restrained. The murk is 1d3 + 3 feet deep. If the creature cannot keep its head above the water, it must hold its breath to avoid drowning. Creatures submerged in the murk are blinded for as long as they remain underwater. The thick, soup-like water makes swimming difficult. Another creature can help a trapped creature escape.

If a character falls into a murk trap, the vibrations in the water immediately alert the nearest dragon, prompting the beast to swim forward and (if possible) try to surprise the character by swimming through the cloudy water and attacking the creature from below the surface.

When the characters enter the first cave, read or paraphrase the following description:

> The swamp spills into the broad mouth of the cave, covering the entire floor with its dark, fetid waters. Tiny clouds of small insects flitter along the surface, darting back and forth from the entrance and into the lightless passage beyond. The cavern appears to have formed naturally, despite its immense size and towering ceiling. The air inside hangs still and humid. Every so often, a stray water droplet falls from the ceiling and sends the faint sound of its splash echoing through the caverns. Proceeding deeper, the unmistakable stench that accompanies the lairs of most great wild beasts grows more pungent.

The western wall of the main entrance hides a submerged channel leading to the largest of the caverns. It serves as the inner sanctum for Aaq'eq', the adult female dragon that sired the entire brood inhabiting these caves. Characters actively searching the wall can detect the submerged channel. While the submerged channel appears only as deep as the rest of the caverns, it is carved slightly deeper and hides beneath another 15 feet of silt and murk. The 40-foot-wide, 10-foot-long channel empties into a broad pool that floods the northwestern portion of **Area D2**.

The passage continues for about 100 feet before intersecting with **Area D3**. There, it continues for almost another 100 feet at which point it appears to hit a dead-end. Here, a second submerged channel conceals **Area D4**. The channel is not as wide as the first one, but has otherwise identical properties. If the characters disturb the water, make loud noises, or otherwise perform actions that might alert the dragon of their presence, the dragons have a 45% chance to sense them.

If Aaq'eq' senses intruders, she waits for them to enter deeper into the cavern and then tries to slip behind them. She readies her breath weapon for when the characters confront either of her children.

D2: Aaq'eq's Sanctum

The submerged channel provides the only physical entrance to this cavern. If Aaq'eq' has not left the cavern, characters attempting to swim through the submerged channel risk disturbing the murk and alerting her to their approach. If this occurs, the dragon plunges into the water and flaps her wings to create a powerful current to sweep any characters caught in the passage back into the main entrance and toward the nearest murk trap. Creatures caught in the wall of water must make a saving throw or be pushed 3d10 feet backward down the tunnel, taking 1d6 points of damage per 10 feet traveled.

The cavern that serves as Aaq'eq's sanctum is pitch black; thus, individuals who cannot see in darkness must procure a light source. Cut off from the outside, the overwhelming reek of her foul stench permeates the entire cavern, and the air is twice as humid and stifling as the outer passages.

If the characters enter Aaq'eq's sanctum, read or paraphrase the following description:

> Emerging from the water, a foul pungent odor assaults your nostrils as you are enveloped within a blanket of humid hot air. Before you, a field of mud-slathered boulders rises from the water to form a makeshift lumpy platform that fills the southern two-thirds of this massive cavern.

While the boulder platform poses no difficulty for the larger feet of dragons, smaller creatures find it difficult to walk across the slippery surfaces without slipping or twisting an ankle. Any humanoid creature that attempts to cross the terrain at normal speed must succeed on a saving throw to avoid slipping and falling prone. Anyone who rolls a natural 1 on this check gets a foot stuck in a hole between the rocks. A character can stop for a round to free his or her foot, or the character can continue moving and take 1d4 points of damage.

If the characters have not yet alerted Aaq'eq' to their presence, she rests atop the stony platform feigning sleep. She waits for the intruders to get closer, then blasts them with acid hoping to force them to retreat back into the water. Aaq'eq' is a **very old black dragon**.

Very Old Black Dragon: HD 8; HP 48; AC 2[17]; **Atk** 2 claws (1d4), bite (3d6); **Move** 9 (fly 24); **Save** 8; **AL** C; **CL/XP** 16/3200; **Special:** spits acid (3/day, 60ft line, 48 damage, save for half). (*Monstrosities* 132)

D3: Main Cavern

> The cavern widens slightly to reveal a shallow and rocky incline of bloodstained boulders littered with piles of cracked bones. The incline rises from the murk and stops before a 20-foot-tall steep incline that ascends to a terrace. A high arching ceiling crowns nearly 60 feet above the terrace. The upper terrace opens into a wide cave that trails off into darkness.

The bones are a combination of livestock and humanoids. The rocky incline rises at a fairly steep angle but characters can ascend it if they are cautious. Characters have a 1-in-6 chance to notice a section of loose scree halfway up the cliff. Once spotted, it is easily avoided; however, characters attempting to climb over it jar some of the loose stones free, requiring them to succeed on a saving throw to reacquire their grip and avoid sliding back down the incline, which deals no damage but forces the creature to start its climbing attempt anew.

An **immature black dragon** hides in the far corner of the overlook. The eldest of Aaq'eq's spawn, the dragon uses this perch to watch over the cavern entrance. As soon as he senses intruders, he swoops down to attack, ushering a wailing screech that quickly alerts the other dragons within the lair. Upon hearing the screech, the others rush to his aid at maximum speed.

Immature Black Dragon: HD 8; HP 24; AC 2[17]; **Atk** 2 claws (1d4), bite (3d6); **Move** 9 (fly 24); **Save** 8; **AL** C; **CL/XP** 8/800; **Special:** spits acid (3/day, 60ft line, 24 damage, save for half). (*Monstrosities* 132)

D4: The Eggs

> This cave is centered on a curious mud and rock structure that resembles a sort of oversized hive or nest. A thick layer of mud slathers the walls and floor. The mud on the floor appears to be packed solid and heavily tracked with dozens of large reptilian footprints.

The nest stands about five feet tall and is 10 feet in diameter with an open top. Anyone peering over the top observes that it is hollow and filled with mud. Floating in the mud are three large ebony colored eggs. They are of course black dragon eggs.

Another of Aaq'eq's spawn usually dwells here to protect her eggs. If prior events have not drawn her from her duties (such as being called to battle by her brood-mate or her mother, or being drawn out by the actions of the characters), then an **immature black dragon** lurks here.

If any harm comes to these eggs or if anyone absconds with one or more of them, any surviving dragons swear a vendetta to tirelessly and mercilessly hunt down and slay whomever they believe to be the perpetrators of this act. They are singularly focused while hunting and use every available resource at their disposal. They refuse to be thwarted by any distance or opposing foe.

Immature Black Dragon: HD 8; **HP** 24; **AC** 2[17]; **Atk** 2 claws (1d4), bite (3d6); **Move** 9 (fly 24); **Save** 8; **AL** C; **CL/XP** 8/800; **Special:** spits acid (3/day, 60ft line, 24 damage, save for half). (*Monstrosities* 132)

D5: Dragon's Hoard

Chapter Four: The Secret of the Fallen Son

This chapter begins when characters decide they want to seek out Metzpil to determine what role, if any, he played in the destruction of Atoyatetl. If they are not sure where to track him down, they may return to his village and ask questions about his whereabouts. The local warriors inform the characters that in their absence one of their hunters captured a Jaguar Cuauhocelotl and is holding him for questioning. Alternately, if the characters do not return to the village, they may encounter the warrior and the captured Jaguar Cuauhocelotl while walking through the woods. Or they may run into a small band of the jaguar warriors themselves and capture one for questioning.

Once captured, it becomes obvious that the warrior is not a real Jaguar Cuauhocelotl. The man, who is disguised as a human, is really a half-elf Poqoza who exhibits more human traits than elf features. His body bears strange ritualistic scars that resemble scales. He is also in very bad shape — crazed, delusional, and badly weakened from some sort of poison.

Poqoza Cultist, Male Half-Elf (Clr5): HP 26 (currently 3); **AC** 6[13]; **Atk** macuahuitl (1d8); **Move** 12; **Save** 11; **AL** C; **CL/XP** 5/240; **Special:** +2 save vs. paralysis and poison, banish undead, darkvision (60ft), spells (2/2).
  Spells: 1st—*cure light wounds* (x2); 2nd—*bless, hold person.*
  Equipment: cipacahuipilli armor[B], macuahuitl[B].
[B] See **Appendix B: New Equipment and Magic Items**

Characters seeking to determine the details of his condition can either consult with Atoyatetl's storyteller or Nahualipazotic to learn that the man is suffering from withdrawal associated with a rare and dangerous hallucinogen known as maht. The psychoactive agent is most closely associated with the fearsome Slaughter Priests who indulge in the psychoactive agent before entering their violent and bloody sacrifice raids.

Fortunately for the characters, the prisoner's withdrawal symptoms are so intense that he is willing to tell them anything in exchange for maht. He gladly reveals that he serves Metzpil, who boasts that Tlatoani has gifted the Poqoza scion with powerful magic. He prophesies all will bow before Metzpil when he ascends into the Immortal Serpent Emperor. Beyond that information, he refuses to speak until he gets maht.

Maht is quite rare and its fearsome reputation causes most to shy away from it. While the Poqozas readily indulge in most hallucinogenic substances, they greatly fear maht, which is occasionally imported onto the island by Tulita traders from the distant Razor (see *Razor Coast* from **Frog God Games** for more details about this locale), where the grisly Slaughter Priests originate. If the characters ask where they can find the nearest possible source of maht, the reluctant residents tell them to see the tlamatini, an aged and wise Tulita man who serves several of the neighboring villages as a counselor, sage, and medicine man.

The sea bride probably has some as well, but the prisoner would likely die from withdrawals before they could reach her. The tlamatini is much closer and his knowledge of such things is good enough that he could probably procure some of the mystic root. The tlamatini lives in Ipaccanemiliz, Atoyatetl's sister village that languishes along the southern edge of the canal about three miles east of the Temetzin River.

Ipaccanemiliz

The small settlement of Ipaccanemiliz consists of 30 or so mud-brick dwellings along with a few larger structures augmented with broad thatched awnings suspended on wood post frames. The houses center on a great brick fountain connected to a subterranean well where the people get their water. Cooking fires burn in front of many of the homes, while the inhabitants bustle about performing various mundane tasks. A small moat of water piped in from the canal surrounds the village, but the settlement is accessible by four bridges that traverse the water. A statue dedicated to an ancient ancestor stands at the edge of each bridge.

When the characters arrive, the **town's warriors** immediately rush to receive them and take the prisoner into custody. The warriors and the townspeople are highly agitated by a terrifying recent event. The warriors seem as eager to interrogate the prisoner as the characters.

Poqoza Soldiers, Male or Female Half-Elves (as needed): HD 1; **AC** 7[12]; **Atk** tepoztopilli (1d10) or sling (1d4); **Move** 12; **Save** 17; **AL** Any; **CL/XP** 1/15; **Special:** darkvision (60ft). (*Monstrosities* 257)
  Equipment: tepoztopilli[B], sling.
[B] See **Appendix B: New Equipment and Magic Items**

The water in this cavern is five feet deep and floats above a thick stew of mud. A character who pokes around in the mud locates a sizable hoard of treasure buried in the silt-strewn morass. Uncovering the treasure also disturbs the silt, which means those looking for treasure are blinded while immersed in or looking into the soupy water.

Treasure: The buried hoard contains 20 large gold ingots worth 850 gp each, a carved jade statuette of a couatl worth 1,300 gp, a large gold bracelet emblazoned with images of the sun worth 600 gp, a gold lip plate set with bloodstones worth 125 gp, and a small stone coffer containing 12 teardrops carved from jade and obsidian, each worth 350 gp. It also contains a *ring of shooting stars*, a *potion of flying*, a *luckstone*, and a *macuahuitl of revealing* (see **Appendix B: New Equipment and Magic Items**).

Wrapping Things Up

This section ends if the characters defeat Aaq'eq'. If they slay the dragon and her children and provide proof of their victory (such as by taking trophies of teeth, eggs, or horns), they have the opportunity to earn the assistance of the sea bride as described in **Chapter 2: A Tangled Fate.** If they instead turn Aaq'eq' against the gnolls, she reveals that the individual she believed to have taken her eggs was Metzpil, the fifth son of the tlamacazqui.

At this point, the characters must travel back through the swamp. If they have yet to gather clues from other locations, they can use the canal to revisit or complete any of those sections. If they have enough information to seek out Metzpil, feel free to move on to **Chapter 4: The Secret of the Fallen Son.**

As soon as the characters ask about the tlamatini or recent events, one of the warriors divulges the following harrowing account:

Metzpil summoned a fiend to wield a powerful item to steal the tlamatini's soul, which he intends to present as a gift to the Drowned Daughter. She requires the soul for a ritual and prompted Metzpil to collect it for her. The tlamatini is now trapped in a horrific and torturous state between life and death, unable to continue in either direction and forced to confront both simultaneously, even though these realities are in conflict with one other.

If the characters possess magical means of speaking with either dead people (such as a *speak with dead* spell) or some means of communicating with him telepathically, the tlamatini explains his condition to them and reveals that Metzpil commanded a disguised fiend to steal his soul using a powerful item called the *seal of Miquito* that celestials and fiends use to guide souls on their journey to the afterlife. Essentially, his soul has departed on its journey while his consciousness remains in the present. No known human possesses the power to use the item to perform such a task, so therefore Metzpil has either transformed into an otherworldly creature or, more likely, he has a supernatural ally. The tlamatini can confirm with authority that Metzpil is responsible for the recent attacks and has fallen under the corrupt influence of a being he believes to be Tlatoani.

After speaking with the tlamatini, the characters might realize that they cannot acquire maht and may likely conclude that their prisoner is no longer of any use to them. The jaguar warrior has fallen deeper into his withdrawal but he begs the characters to let him go. If they do so, he makes a mad rush for Metzpil's encampment in a desperate bid to momentarily soothe his vicious cravings. At this point, he cares for nothing else and carelessly leads the characters on an easy and direct route to Metzpil who is roughly 20 miles north-northeast of Quizaloa in a locale known as a Nest of Serpents.

Alternately, Ipaccanemiliz's warriors can point the characters in the direction that Metzpil and his allies retreated. They are also willing to help track down their location and suggest that their dogs can easily track the scent now that they have a prisoner.

THE ASSASSIN

Metzpil ordered his agents to keep a careful eye on activities in Ipaccanemiliz. Unless they took precautions to enter the city undetected, his spies observed the characters arrive with their prisoner. Word of such activities piques his interest. His **2 spies** slip out of the village and report on the characters' activities. If Metzpil hears nothing from them for two days, he assumes the worst, and dispatches a **serpent's kiss assassin** to kill them. He arrives during the overnight hours under the cover of darkness to quietly sneak into the settlement to slit the characters' throats while they sleep.

Poqoza Spies, Male Half-Elves (Thf7) (2): HP 23, 19; **AC** 7[12];
Atk tecpatl (1d4) and shortbow x2 (1d6); **Move** 12; **Save** 9; **AL** N;
CL/XP 7/600; **Special:** +2 save bonus vs. traps and magical devices, backstab (x3), darkvision (60ft), read languages, thieving skills.
Thieving Skills: Climb 91%, Tasks/Traps 45%, Hear 5 in 6, Hide 40%, Silent 50%, Locks 40%.
Equipment: tlahuiztli armor[B], tecpatl[B], shortbow, 20 arrows.

Serpent's Kiss Assassin, Male Half-Elf (Asn12): HP 65; **AC** 5[14];
Atk tecpatl (1d4 + lethal poison) or longbow x2 (1d6); **Move** 12;
Save 5; **AL** C; **CL/XP** 14/2600; **Special:** backstab (x4), darkvision (60ft), disguise, poison use, spell-like abilities, thieving skills.
Spell-like abilities: at will—*polymorph self, magic missile* (3d4 damage); 1/day—*dimension door.*
Thieving Skills: Climb 94%, Tasks/Traps 70%, Hear 5 in 6, Hide 75%, Silent 85%, Locks 75%.
Equipment: +2 tlahuiztli armor[B], tecpatl[B], longbow, 20 arrows, 2 vials of poison (save or die).
[B] See **Appendix B: New Equipment and Magic Items**

A NEST OF SERPENTS

Metzpil and his disciples are holed up in the ruins of a forsaken temple compound dedicated to Tlatoani that lies 20 miles north-northeast of Quizaloa. The cataclysm and the hero-gods themselves razed almost all of the structures and monuments to the ground, but a handful of buildings survived the devastation. The early Tozcas attempted to rebuild what they could to no avail. The journey requires a hard trek through 30 miles of festering swampland.

Metzpil's demonic counselor gifted him these ruins as a token of their everlasting friendship. These ruins are approximately 20 miles from the Temple of the Serpent (Quizaloa) where the priestess resides. This locale now serves as a dwelling place for cultists and maht addicts she corrupted to create a living vessel for her father. At present, the ruins consist of three pyramids

WHO IS METZPIL?

Metzpil is the fifth son of the tlamacazqui, which gives him a measure of prestige but no inheritance rights. After his actual father left his mother behind and moved on to the next settlement before Metzpil's birth, the young woman married another man and raised Metzpil in the small trading village. This unpleasant fact coupled with Metzpil's lack of an inheritance has dogged him throughout his life. Metzpil presents himself as a supporter of the common people rather than as a haughty noble. Nonetheless, some villagers secretly wonder if he really is the tlamacazqui's son, though none ever openly expresses this opinion.

Metzpil grew up working trade vessels on the canal. About a year before the current series of events, he stopped in a small village along the canal where a priestess introduced him to a strange new substance that she called maht, a dangerous and highly addictive substance used by ancient warriors to induce battle fury. She knew Metzpil was the tlamacazqui's son and promised him that ritually consuming maht would reveal the young man's true destiny. In his altered state, Metzpil heard the whispers of Tlatoani in the chants of the priestess and experienced a vision where he transformed into a massive serpent and ascended to immortality to take the role of the new god-emperor of Tehuatl. When the maht's influence wore off, the priestess performed a baptismal ceremony upon him and then anointed him the mortal vessel and second coming of the Serpent Who Shall Devour the Gods.

The visions held more truth than Metzpil realized, for the priestess in fact was preparing his body to serve as the new mortal vessel of Tlatoani. What Metzpil does not — and cannot — understand is that Tlatoani needs only his flesh. When the time comes, the banished deity will devour Metzpil's mind and soul in the process of being reborn. Moreover, the priestess is far from what she seems. The demon daughter of the Drowned Serpent, she is orchestrating her father's return by turning Metzpil into a mere puppet, a sacrifice to alter the path of the cosmos.

In the years before their "chance meeting," the priestess seeded Metzpil's jealousy and ego until his disdain for his father and his secondary position in the family hierarchy filled him with greed and envy. Metzpil's arrogant delusions have now sealed his doom, as Tlatoani's haunted whispers slowly consume what remains of his mortal essence.

To his closest allies who act as his violent and murderous agents, Metzpil admits his ancestry and openly denounces his father as nothing more than a despot. He has forsaken Tlatlcolli and sworn himself to new gods who promise a different future that will emerge from the ashes of the old deities.

A NEST OF SERPENTS
1 Square = 50 Feet
E1
E2
E6
E4
E3
E5
N

and a ball-court. All other structures have long since crumbled. Metzpil and his disciples built a small encampment in the center of the ruins. He managed to corrupt 40 Poqoza warriors to his nefarious cause. In addition, he trained six serpent cuauhocelotls to serve as his elite commanders. These individuals move freely around the ruins in accordance with their needs or in response to the characters' actions or Metzpil's commands. However, they rarely congregate as a large group and are instead spread out across the ruins with specific numbers listed in areas where characters are most likely to encounter them. Warriors and cuauhocelotls noted in the location descriptions are part of the main group and are not additional enemies. It must also be noted that Metzpil and his disciples regularly indulge in maht and are highly addicted. Assume these individuals always have at least one dose on them at all times.

If given an opportunity, Metzpil and his disciples always attempt to eat maht before entering combat. If they succeed, they suffer from its effects (see **Maht** sidebar) until they wear off.

After the long journey, the characters reach the accursed region known as a Nest of Serpents. Here, the forest changes and becomes hauntingly quiet and the trees twist at odd angles. Use the strangeness to create tension just before the characters arrive. Once they near the ruins, read or paraphrase the following text box:

A wandering patrol of **8 Poqoza warriors** led by a **serpent cuauhocelotl** walk the perimeter of the encampment to keep a sharp eye out for any intruders. When the characters arrive, determine the patrol's starting location by rolling 1d8 to determine the cardinal direction of their current sector with 1 representing north, 2 representing northeast, and continuing clockwise around the compass culminating at 8 representing northwest. Thereafter, the patrol walks clockwise around the perimeter and explores each section for approximately 30 minutes.

If the warriors or their leader spot intruders, they initially attempt to drive them off. However, if they are unable to force the characters to retreat in four rounds, the warriors send half their numbers back to the encampment to get more reinforcements and to warn Metzpil. Alternately, if the Poqoza warriors and their leader drop to half their number in fewer than four rounds, the entire unit races back to the encampment to warn their allies.

MAHT

Maht is a highly addictive psychoactive plant originally brought to the island by the Slaughter Priests known as Maldraht maht. It is made by drying out a thick black root called maht and is frequently smoked in black coral pipes, though it can also be chewed or soaked in alcohol to create tinctures. When smoked, it smells like anise. Maht users experience extreme hallucinations that frequently cause violent and psychotic outbursts, which is why the Slaughter Priests hold it sacred and use it before embarking on raids. This also made it prized among more fearsome Poqoza warriors dedicated to Tlatlcolli.

Anyone who consumes maht risks such an episode or may willingly succumb to the full experience. After consumption, the user gains a +2 bonus to hit and damage for 1d4 hours but suffers a –2 penalty to saving throws for the duration. The creature is also highly susceptible to illusions and has a 50% chance to flee in fear.

After the effects of the maht wear off, the creature must make a saving throw, with a cumulative –1 penalty (maximum –5) for every consecutive day that the drug was used. If the save fails, the creature takes 1d6 points of damage each day thereafter until a *remove curse* is cast to end the ongoing damage. Consuming more maht reduces the ongoing damage to 1 point, but a creature that consumes maht for 10 consecutive days takes 2d6 points of ongoing damage if it cannot get the drug.

Serpent Cuauhocelotl, Male or Female Half-Elf (Ftr8): HP 54; **AC** 4[15]; **Atk** club (1d6 or 1d6+2 [maht user]) or tecpatl (1d4 or 1d4+2 [maht user]) or javelin (1d6+2); **Move** 12; **Save** 7 (9 maht user); **AL** C; **CL/XP** 8/800; **Special:** darkvision (60ft), immune to charm spells, multiple attacks (8) vs. creatures with 1 or fewer HD. (*Monstrosities* 256)
Equipment: olli armor, shield, club, 8 javelins.
Note: The serpent cuauhoceltl has a 45% chance of being addicted to maht (see **Maht** sidebar), which grants them a +2 bonus to hit and damage, but a –2 penalty to saving throws. They have a 50% chance of fleeing in fear from illusions.

Poqoza Warriors, Male or Female Half-Elves (Ftr4) (8): HP 30, 28, 25, 21x2, 20, 16, 14; **AC** 5[14]; **Atk** macuahuitl (1d8+1 or 1d8+3 [maht user]) or tecpatl (1d4+1 or 1d4+3 [maht user]) or sling (1d4); **Move** 12; **Save** 11 (13 maht user); **AL** C; **CL/XP** 4/120; **Special:** +1 to hit and damage strength bonus, blood sacrifice (3/day, slice own chest for 1 point damage to gain +1 to hit and damage for 1d6 rounds), darkvision (60ft), multiple attacks (4) vs. creatures with 1 or fewer HD. (*Monstrosities* 256)
Equipment: olli armor [B], macuahuitl[B], tecpatl [B], sling, 10 sling stones.
Note: The warriors have a 65% chance of being addicted to maht (see **Maht** sidebar), which grants them a +2 bonus to hit and damage, but a –2 penalty to saving throws. They have a 50% chance of fleeing in fear from illusions.
[B] See **Appendix B: New Equipment and Magic Items**

E1: PYRAMID OF THE LOST MOON

The ancients built this temple to honor the moon. They performed monthly rituals for the inanimate satellite during the new moon. It now sits in disrepair, encased in rubble and moss.

Metzpil now uses the temple as a vantage point for his lookouts. During daylight hours, **2 Poqoza Warriors** sit high atop the pyramid keeping watch over the surrounding area.

Inside, faded murals portray warriors undergoing several ceremonies that transform them into serpent cuauhocelotls. One mural shows a priest ritualistically scarring new recruits using obsidian shards and a bag of ash to cover their bodies in a scale-like pattern. Another depicts the warriors leading captured enemies up a giant pyramid topped with a stone serpent's head. Another depicts a man with a snake mask sacrificing a prisoner on a great black altar.

The depiction befits the description of a high temple of Tlatoani.

A primitive calendar set into the middle of the floor is surrounded by a series of circular patterns that represent the moon's phases. Characters can use the calendar to determine the moon's patterns. If the characters have been to the Temple of the Broken Ones, they can use the calendar to determine that all the events took place on the night of a full moon, probably during an eclipse.

Poqoza Warriors, Male or Female Half-Elves (Ftr4) (2): HP 27, 24; **AC** 5[14]; **Atk** macuahuitl (1d8+1 or 1d8+3 [maht user]) or tecpatl (1d4+1 or 1d4+3 [maht user]) or sling (1d4); **Move** 12; **Save** 11 (13 maht user); **AL** C; **CL/XP** 4/120; **Special:** +1 to hit and damage strength bonus, blood sacrifice (3/day, slice own chest for 1 point damage to gain +1 to hit and damage for 1d6 rounds), darkvision (60ft), multiple attacks (4) vs. creatures with 1 or fewer HD. (*Monstrosities* 256)
Equipment: olli armor [B], macuahuitl[B], tecpatl [B], sling, 10 sling stones.
Note: The warriors have a 65% chance of being addicted to maht (see **Maht** sidebar), which grants them a +2 bonus to hit and damage, but a –2 penalty to saving throws. They have a 50% chance of fleeing in fear from illusions.

E2: PYRAMID OF THE BROKEN ONES

Like the other ruins, this temple is speckled with moss and heavily eroded. To enter it, Metzpil excavated several feet of rubble from the main entrance. Inside, he discovered huge murals covering the walls that depicted the prophesy of the return of Tlatoani in mortal form. One panel portrays several priests anointing a man in some sort of oil amid clouds of incense and herbs. The man is naked except for a loincloth, and his body is covered in distinctive serpentine tattoos. A character who examines his panel recognizes the body ink as being consistent with serpent rituals that occurred before the hero-gods appeared. Furthermore, anyone studying the murals can make a saving throw to notice that the events in individual scenes correlate to specific times and dates.

Another shows the same man in the presence of a huge and terrible looking woman with six arms and whose bottom half is that of a great serpent. A series of runes carved below the panel reads "Titechcualtia Ianima," which is likely the creature's name. Titechcualtia Ianima is the name of one of Tlatoani's demonic daughters who was never banished from the world. Legends say she has existed for thousands of years. Every few centuries, she reveals her presence in an attempt to call her father back into the Material World.

The sanctum is never unguarded, as a **serpent cuauhocelotl** stands guard at the pyramid's entrance alongside **4 Poqoza warriors** and **4 wardogs**.

Metzpil waits inside this structure, which he uses as his personal sanctum.

Serpent Cuauhocelotl, Male or Female Half-Elf (Ftr8): HP 51; **AC** 4[15]; **Atk** club (1d6 or 1d6+2 [maht user]) or tecpatl (1d4 or 1d4+2 [maht user]) or javelin (1d6+2); **Move** 12; **Save** 7 (9 maht user); **AL** C; **CL/XP** 8/800; **Special:** darkvision (60ft), immune to charm spells, multiple attacks (8) vs. creatures with 1 or fewer HD. (*Monstrosities* 256)
Equipment: olli armor, shield, club, 8 javelins.
Note: The serpent cuauhoceltl has a 45% chance of being addicted to maht (see **Maht** sidebar), which grants them a +2 bonus to hit and damage, but a –2 penalty to saving throws. They have a 50% chance of fleeing in fear from illusions.

Poqoza Warriors, Male or Female Half-Elves (Ftr4) (4): HP 31, 28, 25x2; **AC** 5[14]; **Atk** macuahuitl (1d8+1 or 1d8+3 [maht user]) or tecpatl (1d4+1 or 1d4+3 [maht user]) or sling (1d4); **Move** 12; **Save** 11 (13 maht user); **AL** C; **CL/XP** 4/120; **Special:** +1 to hit and damage strength bonus, blood sacrifice (3/day, slice own chest for 1 point damage to gain +1 to hit and damage for 1d6 rounds), darkvision (60ft), multiple attacks (4) vs. creatures with 1 or fewer HD. (*Monstrosities* 256)
Equipment: olli armor[B], macuahuitl[B], tecpatl[B], sling, 10 sling stones.
Note: The warriors have a 65% chance of being addicted to maht (see **Maht** sidebar), which grants them a +2 bonus to hit and damage, but a –2 penalty to saving throws. They have a 50% chance of fleeing in fear from illusions.
[B] See **Appendix B: New Equipment and Magic Items**

Guard Dogs (4): HD 2; **HP** 13, 10, 9, 8; **AC** 7[12]; **Atk** bite (1d6); **Move** 14; **Save** 16; **CL/XP** 2/30; **Special:** none. (*Monstrosities* 127)

When the characters meet Metzpil, read or paraphrase the following description:

When the characters encounter Metzpil, they face off against an obnoxious, spoiled man who bemoans the fact that the circumstances of his birth deprived him of a loftier station in life. He bitterly complains about being passed over for his older siblings, though he now claims to have a greater purpose — one that exceeds any his tlamacazqui father could possibly imagine. With those words, he points to the murals as evidence of his greatness as he demands that the characters bow down and worship him just as every Poqoza and Aztli in Tehuatl soon will do.

Despite his arrogance, Metzpil does not take the intrusion lightly. If he hears the sounds of combat from the entrance, he summons **3 couatls** to his aid,

an irony that is not lost upon him. He also tosses his staff to the ground to transform it into a giant constrictor snake. The stress of combat also likely causes him to reach for and ingest a dose of maht (see **Maht** sidebar). Under the psychoactive agent's influence, Metzpil thoroughly and completely believes he is immortal and cannot die. Consumed with this notion, he fights until his mind or body finally give in to reality. If the characters capture him, he gleefully confesses to his crimes and tells the characters that a mighty priestess is preparing to turn him into a god within the confines of her sacred temple. He joyfully leads them to Quizaloa if they ask. If the characters accompany him there or discover the site's location, the journey takes them to **Chapter 5: The Daughter of the Drowned Serpent** of this adventure.

Metzpil, Male Half-Elf Priest (Clr14): HP 50; **AC** 4[15]; **Atk** +2 *ollitetlacotl* (1d6+2) or *staff of the snake* (1d6+1); **Move** 12; **Save** 4; **AL** C; **CL/XP** 15/2900; **Special:** +2 save vs. paralysis and poison, banish undead, darkvision (60ft), spells (5/5/5/5/5/2).
Spells: 1st—*bloodbath*[C], *counterattack*[C], *cure light wounds* (x2), *detect magic*; 2nd—*bless, hold person, snake charm, speak with animals, war cry*[C]; 3rd—*cure disease, flay skin*[C], *prayer, remove curse* (x2); 4th—*create water, cure serious wounds* (x2), *neutralize poison, sacrifice*[C]; 5th—*commune, create food, finger of death, insect plague, raise dead*; 6th—*blade barrier, palpitating heart*[C].
Equipment: *cipacahuipilli armor*[B], *+1 shield, boots of levitation, +2 ollitetlacotl*[B], *staff of the snake, ring of protection +1*, 2 doses of maht.
[B] See **Appendix B: New Equipment and Magic Items**
[C] See **Appendix C: New Spells**

Couatls (3): HD 8; **HP** 58, 55, 46; **AC** 4[15]; **Atk** bite (2d6 + poison), tail (1d6 constrict); **Move** 12 (fly 24); **Save** 8; **AL** L; **CL/XP** 11/1700; **Special:** poison (save or die), polymorph (at will), spells (3/2/1). (*Monstrosities* 73)
Spells: 1st—*charm person, magic missile, sleep*; 2nd—*ESP, phantasmal force*; 3rd—*lightning bolt*.

Metzpil ignorantly and mistakenly believes the mural portrays a prophecy that foretells his rise to power. What he has failed to notice or believe is that the panels describe the proper sacrifice of a human vessel. The dates and times coordinate with specific moon phases necessary to perform the ritual. The image resembles Metzpil because the ritual also requires that Tlatoani's vessel be the son of a tlamacazqui.

The interior of the pyramid is sparse, long picked clean of any treasures it once held. Aside from the strange murals, the only other object of possible interest is a basalt coffer inscribed with images of a man being devoured by a giant snake. Metzpil believes he shall be reborn from within and allows no one to touch it. The lid to the coffer is extremely heavy and requires a couple of characters working together to lift it.

Treasure: Metzpil hides his backup stash of maht (see **Maht** sidebar) in a large sack within the coffer. He has enough of the psychoactive agent on hand to keep his disciples at bay for three days. Fortunately for him, the Drowned Serpent's Daughter frequently shows up to help him with his transcendence, which means the arrival of more maht. Six smaller pouches contain more ritual components such as coffee beans, dried dog livers, herbs, owl feathers, cacao beans, and some tobacco leaves. A severed mummified human forearm is wrapped in a red cloth.

Treasure: Metzpil's golden serpent medallion is worth 2,000 gp. A character who examines it confirms that the jewelry was commonly worn by the emperor's snake advisors during the hero-gods' rebellion.

E3: Field of Redemption

The ancient and crumbling remains of what used to be a ballgame court now serve as an arena where Metzpil's disciples train to become serpent cuauhocelotls through ritual combat. During daylight hours, **1d4 + 6 Poqoza warriors** spar with each other on the court under the attentive gaze of a **serpent cuauhocelotl** who oversees the training. When night falls, only **1d4 Poqoza warriors** practice here. On rare occasions, Metzpil visits to observe their progress.

Serpent Cuauhocelotl, Male or Female Half-Elf (Ftr8): HP 48; **AC** 4[15]; **Atk** club (1d6 or 1d6+2 [maht user]) or tecpatl (1d4 or 1d4+2 [maht user]) or javelin (1d6+2); **Move** 12; **Save** 7 (9 maht user); **AL** C; **CL/XP** 8/800; **Special:** darkvision (60ft), immune to charm spells, multiple attacks (8) vs. creatures with 1 or fewer HD.

(*Monstrosities* 256)

Equipment: olli armor, shield, club, 8 javelins.

Note: The serpent cuauhoceltl has a 45% chance of being addicted to maht (see **Maht** sidebar), which grants them a +2 bonus to hit and damage, but a –2 penalty to saving throws. They have a 50% chance of fleeing in fear from illusions.

Poqoza Warriors, Male or Female Half-Elves (Ftr4) (1d4+6 or 1d4): HP 4d8; AC 5[14]; Atk macuahuitl (1d8+1 or 1d8+3 [maht user]) or tecpatl (1d4+1 or 1d4+3 [maht user]) or sling (1d4); **Move** 12; **Save** 11 (13 maht user); **AL** C; **CL/XP** 4/120; **Special:** +1 to hit and damage strength bonus, blood sacrifice (3/day, slice own chest for 1 point damage to gain +1 to hit and damage for 1d6 rounds), darkvision (60ft), multiple attacks (4) vs. creatures with 1 or fewer HD. (*Monstrosities* 256)

Equipment: olli armor[B], macuahuitl[B], tecpatl[B], sling, 10 sling stones.

Note: The warriors have a 65% chance of being addicted to maht (see **Maht** sidebar), which grants them a +2 bonus to hit and damage, but a –2 penalty to saving throws. They have a 50% chance of fleeing in fear from illusions.

[B] See **Appendix B: New Equipment and Magic Items**

E4: West Hill

A small hill overlooks the southwest corner of the ruins and offers an opportunistic view to whoever controls it. At all times, a **serpent cuauhocelotl** and **6 Poqoza warriors** keep guard over this location. A bonfire is here as well, but they do not ignite it unless they need to use it as an emergency signal.

Serpent Cuauhocelotl, Male or Female Half-Elf (Ftr8): HP 51; AC 4[15]; **Atk** club (1d6 or 1d6+2 [maht user]) or tecpatl (1d4 or 1d4+2 [maht user]) or javelin (1d6+2); **Move** 12; **Save** 7 (9 maht user); **AL** C; **CL/XP** 8/800; **Special:** darkvision (60ft), immune to charm spells, multiple attacks (8) vs. creatures with 1 or fewer HD. (*Monstrosities* 256)

Equipment: olli armor, shield, club, 8 javelins.

Note: The serpent cuauhoceltl has a 45% chance of being addicted to maht (see **Maht** sidebar), which grants them a +2 bonus to hit and damage, but a –2 penalty to saving throws. They have a 50% chance of fleeing in fear from illusions.

Poqoza Warriors, Male or Female Half-Elves (Ftr4) (6): HP 30, 27, 23, 22x2, 19; AC 5[14]; **Atk** macuahuitl (1d8+1 or 1d8+3 [maht user]) or tecpatl (1d4+1 or 1d4+3 [maht user]) or sling (1d4); **Move** 12; **Save** 11 (13 maht user); **AL** C; **CL/XP** 4/120; **Special:** +1 to hit and damage strength bonus, blood sacrifice (3/day, slice own chest for 1 point damage to gain +1 to hit and damage for 1d6 rounds), darkvision (60ft), multiple attacks (4) vs. creatures with 1 or fewer HD. (*Monstrosities* 256)

Equipment: olli armor[B], macuahuitl[B], tecpatl[B], sling, 10 sling stones.

Note: The warriors have a 65% chance of being addicted to maht (see **Maht** sidebar), which grants them a +2 bonus to hit and damage, but a –2 penalty to saving throws. They have a 50% chance of fleeing in fear from illusions.

[B] See **Appendix B: New Equipment and Magic Items**

E5: Tower of the Burning Eagle

The largest structure within the ruins is a 500-foot-wide, four-tiered tower that blocks off the jungle to the south. At night, Metzpil's disciples illuminate the tower's façade with two large bonfires set on either side of the main entrance.

The ground floor and the first tiers consist of large empty chambers covered with dust and the dried droppings of vermin that use it for shelter. A flight of stairs on the ground floor climbs to the other tiers, eventually reaching to the highest level. Metzpil and his serpent cuauhocelotl followers have cleared the top two tiers. On the third tier, a swath of sand covers the center of the floor. Several long sticks are propped against a nearby wall. Numbers and lines are scored in the sand, which on closer inspection seems to be some sort of diagram or map. It is a map of the surrounding region. In addition to their current location and markings indicating the general distance and directions to the raided villages, a path pointing south-southwest is marked with a coiled serpent. The pathway leads to Quizaloa and the high temple of Tlatoani, where the daughter of the drowned serpent awaits.

The top tier serves as a sacred space where Metzpil performs the extreme scarification rites and other body modifications that mark his most powerful disciples as serpent cuauhocelotls.

E6: The Encampments

Throughout the field, the vague outlines of weathered mud-brick foundations long buried and overgrown protrude from the ground. The encampment consists of makeshift wooden frame structures with thatched walls and rooftops that are supported by wooden poles pounded into the earth. Metzpil's disciples live here, using the huts for storage and sleeping.

Regardless of the time of day, there are always **2 serpent cuauhocelotls** and **1d4 + 4 Poqoza warriors** with an equal number of **wardogs** in this area. Half of them are prone on the ground resting, while the remainder loiter around the fire performing mundane tasks such as caring for their weapons, arguing, gambling, roasting meat on a stick, or taking maht.

Serpent Cuauhocelotls, Male or Female Half-Elf (Ftr8) (2): HP 60, 54; AC 4[15]; **Atk** club (1d6 or 1d6+2 [maht user]) or tecpatl (1d4 or 1d4+2 [maht user]) or javelin (1d6+2); **Move** 12; **Save** 7 (9 maht user); **AL** C; **CL/XP** 8/800; **Special:** darkvision (60ft), immune to charm spells, multiple attacks (8) vs. creatures with 1 or fewer HD. (*Monstrosities* 256)

Equipment: olli armor, shield, club, 8 javelins.

Note: The serpent cuauhoceltl has a 45% chance of being addicted to maht (see **Maht** sidebar), which grants them a +2 bonus to hit and damage, but a –2 penalty to saving throws. They have a 50% chance of fleeing in fear from illusions.

Poqoza Warriors, Male or Female Half-Elves (Ftr4) (1d4+4): HP 4d8; AC 5[14]; **Atk** macuahuitl (1d8+1 or 1d8+3 [maht user]) or tecpatl (1d4+1 or 1d4+3 [maht user]) or sling (1d4); **Move** 12; **Save** 11 (13 maht user); **AL** C; **CL/XP** 4/120; **Special:** +1 to hit and damage strength bonus, blood sacrifice (3/day, slice own chest for 1 point damage to gain +1 to hit and damage for 1d6 rounds), darkvision (60ft), multiple attacks (4) vs. creatures with 1 or fewer HD. (*Monstrosities* 256)

Equipment: olli armor[B], macuahuitl[B], tecpatl[B], sling, 10 sling stones.

Note: The warriors have a 65% chance of being addicted to maht (see **Maht** sidebar), which grants them a +2 bonus to hit and damage, but a –2 penalty to saving throws. They have a 50% chance of fleeing in fear from illusions.

[B] See **Appendix B: New Equipment and Magic Items**

Guard Dogs (as needed): HD 2; AC 7[12]; **Atk** bite (1d6); **Move** 14; **Save** 16; **CL/XP** 2/30; **Special:** none. (*Monstrosities* 127)

Wrapping Things Up

This section of the adventure ends after the characters defeat Metzpil and learn he is being manipulated by a greater evil that lurks in the high temple of Tlatoani. The characters can use the map in **Area E5** as a guide for determining the temple's location. Alternately, they might use magic or spells to find it. The temple is in a dense part of the jungle that marks the edge of the swamp about 20 miles to the south-southwest. It is known as Quizoloa on the regional map.

Chapter Five: The Daughter of the Drowned Serpent

Designated as Quizoloa on the regional map, the site where the temple resides was once a grand city until the hero-gods and the forces of nature and neglect virtually razed it to the ground.

> Dense clusters of trees and vines conceal the ruins of a bygone era. At the center of the tangled mass, a great stepped pyramid climbs skyward at a severe slope to a height of nearly 200 feet. A broad flight of stone stairs runs up the face to the summit where a large stone building carved in the stylized likeness of a gaping-mouthed head of a fierce demonic serpent awaits.

The ominous building atop the temple serves as its only entrance. A number of archways situated around the base and midsections of the temple served as entrances long ago, but they were filled with bricks and mortar and then plastered over with faded frescos of a skull with a coiled serpent emerging from both of its eye sockets. The stairs on the face of the pyramid are not difficult to climb, though the ascent can be tiring. About two-thirds of the way up, the path becomes littered with cacao seeds and spots of blood. Most of the seeds are so old they crumble into dust with a gentle touch. However, a character who examines the seeds notices that some were left here within the last week. Passing petitioners leave offerings of coffee and cacao beans to the gods on the temple stairs. When the characters reach the summit, the sun passes directly between the great serpent's fangs framing the entrance.

> A large round structure assembled from fitted stones sits near the edge of the open mouth, just between the two fangs where the sunlight spills in. It stands roughly three feet tall, is eight feet in diameter, and has a flat top with a one-foot-wide hole directly in the center almost like a well. A thick shellac of blood coats the entire surface. A series of images carved along the exterior of the stone structure depict humans wearing exotic serpent headdresses plunging daggers into the chests of victims prostrate before them. They tear out their vital organs and hold them aloft. Behind the stone structure, the hollow of the serpent's mouth forms a crude hallway that leads to a set of bronze-plated double doors embossed with a series of swirling patterns.

The stone is a sacrificial altar. A character attempting to decipher more from the carvings may confirm their worst fears, that the scenes are consistent with sacrifices made to Tlatoani, the Immortal Sun. Although it is not immediately apparent, the hole carved in the center of the altar is incredibly deep. If a character drops something into it (such as small stone or a coin), a faint, echoing splash emerges from the depths five seconds later.

A character may inspect the blood covering the stone. They can confirm that most of the bloodstains are ancient, but several are much more recent, perhaps from within the past several days. Anyone searching the stone has a 2-in-6 chance to discover a small aperture slightly disguised within the grisly carvings that hides two packages, both wrapped in thin pieces of cured leather. The first package contains a lacquered wooden dagger with an obsidian blade wrapped in a piece of leather. The second package contains a small black pipe carved from black coral. A sticky black residue that reeks of anise coats the bowl.

The double bronze doors frame an archway that is six feet wide and eight feet tall. The swirling etchings carved on the doors are coiled serpents, a fact the characters can determine upon close visual inspection without making a check. The doors are locked but can be unlocked with thieves' tools or magic.

Alternately, the characters can bash it open. The heavy doors swing inward to reveal a tunnel-like passage beyond the portal.

S1: Tunnel

Beyond the strange bronze-plated doors is a near-circular tunnel leading into darkness. The walls of the passage are carved from black stones and lined with bronze sconces holding torches consisting of wooden shafts topped with human skulls with the tops shorn off, presumably to hold fuel. The torches are enchanted so that as soon as any humanoid passes through the portal, the first pair of torches ignites. Thereafter, each time the individual continues for another 10 feet, a new set of torches ignites as the previous set goes out.

Angry Torch Trap

The torches are harmless unless a creature attempts to remove one. If a creature tries to pull a torch out of its sconce or otherwise physically manipulate it, the skull gushes forth a 10-foot cone of magical fire. Each creature in the fire takes 4d6 points of damage, or half as much with a successful saving throw. A thief who examines the statues can detect the trap and possibly disarm it. Each torch operates independently of all the others.

> At the end of the passage, the floor opens to expose a large shaft that drops into black, unknown depths. A curved stone staircase runs along the outer walls of the shaft, descending deeper into the shaft than one might care to guess. The stairs circle around a nauseating ornament: a chain of desiccated corpses preserved with lime that hang just above the shaft.

Anyone who inspects the stairs notices that they have a shallow curve to their surface and angle inward toward the shaft. Every seventh step bears the stylized carving of an ancient serpentine rune that a character associates with Tlatoani.

The 21st stair bears the mark of the Great Stone and acts as the trigger for a **rolling sphere trap**. If weight is put on the step, it opens a trapdoor that drops a 500-pound stone sphere at the top of the stairs. The sphere immediately begins crashing down the staircase. Anyone in the path of the rolling sphere must make a saving throw to dive out of the way or be crushed and take 4d6 points of damage.

The sphere stops when it reached the bottom of the staircase shaft.

Mosaics and Gemstones

Many of the inlays scattered throughout the temple's mosaics consist of gold and semi-precious stones such as jade, obsidian, and turquoise. If a room's mosaics contain these valuable metals and stones, they appear in the room's Treasure entry. Greedy characters may wish to pry out the stones as treasure. A character with a crowbar or similar tool has a 40% chance to remove the inlays from a single mosaic. Either way, performing the task requires 1d4 minutes. If the character fails, they may make a second attempt that takes another 1d4 minutes. A character who fails three times in a row removes the gems, but damages them, reducing their worth by half. If the character uses a dagger or knife to pry out the gems, you may also wish to rule that a failed attempt results in breaking the weapon. Each mosaic holds 5d10 assorted small jade, obsidian, and turquoise gemstones worth 5d6 gp.

S2: The Serpent's Entrance

About 20 feet above the bottom of the shaft, the spiral stairs pass four secret doors, each of which conceals a passage into chambers in the temple's inner catacombs.

S3: The Statues of Judgment

A large stone doorway blocks this passage. A worn clay fresco sculpted into the door depicts the face of an ancient warrior with its tongue sticking out.

The door is locked but can be opened by bashing it aside, picking the lock, or using magic. Alternately, if a character pours coffee, a warm cacao drink, or one of the preceding beans on the fresco's tongue, the door unlocks and opens. If the characters open the door, read or paraphrase the following description:

Rich mosaics depicting various stages of a ruler's ascent to power run the length of this entire chamber. Across from the entrance, a trio of alcoves enshrouds towering terracotta statues of warriors carrying small shields, brandishing macuahuitls, and wearing serpent-shaped feathered helmets. Their skin is carved to look as if they have scales.

The chamber is only 20 feet deep, but twice as wide. Two more alcoves house statues on either side of the entrance. Huge circular, gold-leafed frescoes on each of the far walls show images of various animals in coordination with curious phrases. They can be interpreted as a sort of chronological record of ancient events auspicious to the followers of Tlatoani. Adjacent to the frescoes, wide alcoves open along the south wall. A throne rests in each alcove (see **Areas 3A** and **3B**).

3A: Throne of Awakening

A towering throne chiseled from volcanic rock fills this small alcove. Its façade displays a grid of imposing images that detail the ritual sacrifice of a warrior having his heart cut from his chest upon the great altar. The alcove walls are painted to resemble a panoramic view of a forest-covered landscape.

While in power, Tlatoani used this throne to anoint his serpent cuauhocelotls and those priests entrusted to his order. Those pledging their lives to Tlatoani were forced to test their devotion by sitting on this throne to experience death and rebirth into the fold of the great serpent Tlatoani.

The panoramic mural is undeniably similar to the view from the top of the Serpent Temple.

Throne of Vengeance Trap

The throne emits a magical aura. As the handiwork of a god, the trap can be removed only with a *wish* spell. Any character bold enough to sit upon the throne is stricken with a graphic vision of lying on the altar at the mouth of the temple while a serpent-bodied creature with the torso and head of a human female brandishing several swords in each of her hands rips the character's heart from his or her chest. The character must succeed at a saving throw or take 2d6 points of damage and have their palms mysteriously scarred in the likeness of a coiled serpent on a failure. The symbol is that of Tlatoani. On a success, the character still experiences the terrifying vision, but takes half as much damage and is not physically scarred in the process.

3B: Throne of Vengeance

A great stone throne painted in a faded red color dominates this small alcove. The seat bears the carved image of a warrior standing atop a pile of skulls. The alcove walls are painted with a panoramic image of the phases of the moon, with the new moon appearing directly over the head of the throne.

Tlatoani used this throne to dishonor those among his chieftains who failed him in some way. In dark ceremonies, he would anoint them for their successes, bestow them an honorary title, and then offer them a seat atop the throne. Anyone who fell for the ruse or is now foolish enough to sit on the Throne of Vengeance quickly discovers it is trapped.

Throne of Vengeance Trap

Any humanoid daring enough to either sit upon the throne or to try to remove its glittering adornments triggers the trap. The throne emits a magical aura. Like its counterpart, nothing short of a *wish* spell can remove the trap. When triggered, two things occur. First, any individual seated upon the throne experiences a violent vision of serpents being flensed of their skins and flesh as they writhe in agony. The creature must make a saving throw or take 2d6 points of damage from the pain and be stunned for 1d4+2 rounds on a failure or take half as much damage and not be stunned on a success. Second, the throne releases the magical locks on the base plates of every statue in the room, causing them to unlock and release **5 spawn of Tlatoani**. The freed monsters immediately attack.

Spawn of Tlatoani (5): HD 7; HP 50, 47, 42, 38, 31; AC 6[13]; **Atk** bite (1d8 + poison) or barbed tongue (2d6 + constrict); **Move** 12; **Save** 9; **AL** C; **CL/XP** 9/1100; **Special:** constrict (automatic 1d6 damage per round until freed), fear aura (10ft radius, save or frightened as *fear* spell), immune to cold, poison (save or die). (see **Appendix A: New Monsters**)

Treasure: The mosaics on the walls are potentially salvageable. There are 12 mosaics in all (see the **Mosaics and Gemstones** sidebar).

S4: Trapped Corridor

Weathered, ancient paintings of serpents constricting men adorn the passageway's walls.

The paintings are barely visible after thousands of years of degradation and neglect. Nothing historically significant is concealed within the artwork, though the displays are not entirely benevolent.

Poison Dart Trap

If a character steps on the space marked as "T" on the map, the character triggers a **poison darts trap**. However, because of the discoloration in the artwork, characters have a 3-in-6 chance to detect the danger. The trap launches hundreds of poison darts in a 20-foot area. Any character in the targeted area takes 2d6 points of damage from the darts and must make a saving throw or be poisoned for an additional 1d6 points of damage.

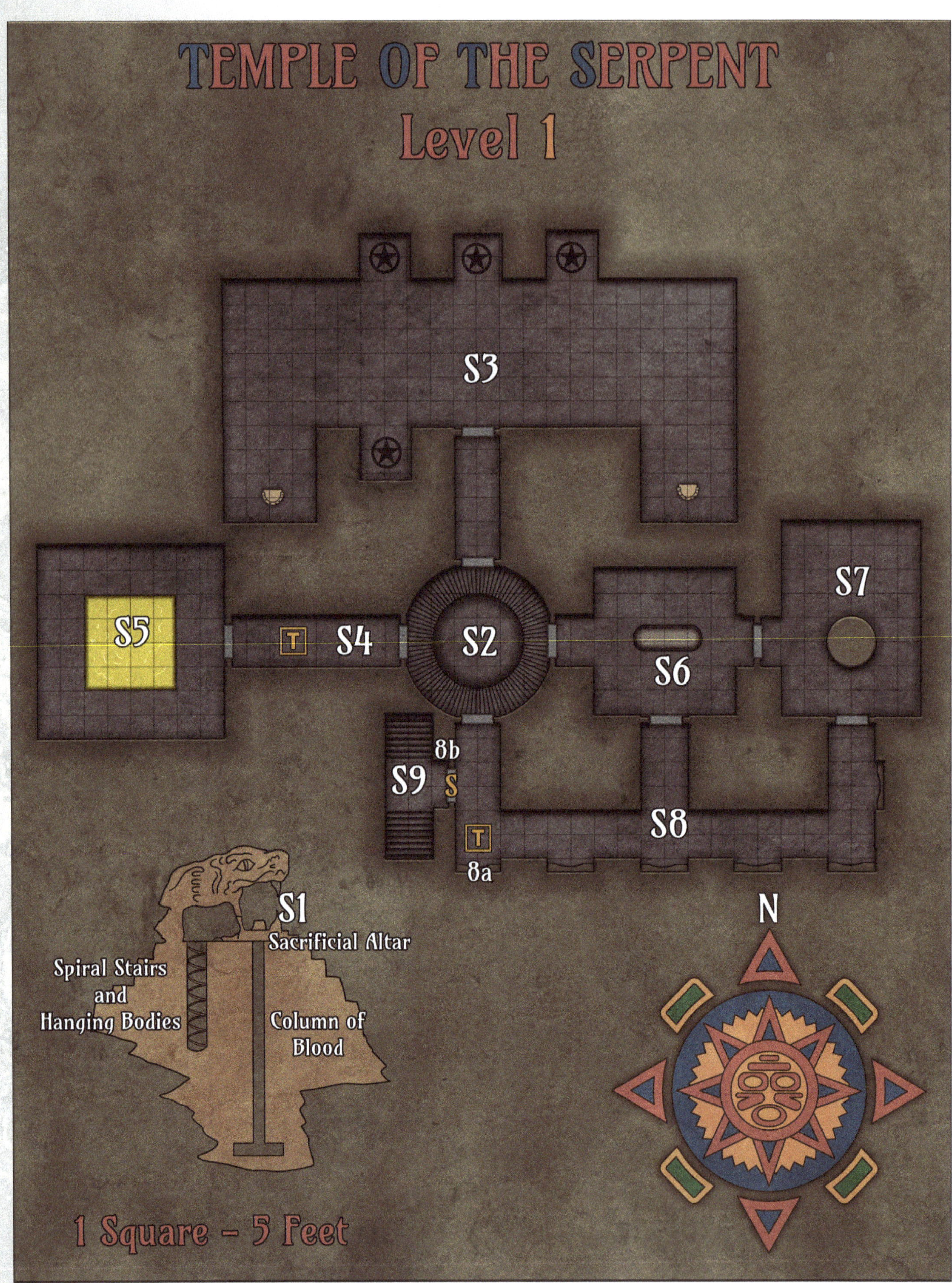

TEMPLE OF THE SERPENT
Level 1
S3
S5
S4
S2
S6
S7
S9
8b
8a
S8
S1
Sacrificial Altar
Spiral Stairs
and
Hanging Bodies
Column of
Blood
N
1 Square - 5 Feet

S5: Chamber of the Accursed

The door to this chamber is carved with a series of runes. Characters able to read draconic can easily decipher the ominous warning:

> Tlatoani demands sacrifice! Who are the accursed that would deny Tlatoani? The accursed shall be shown the truth! Tlatoani shall liberate the accursed of flesh and blood! Beyond this threshold lie the Accursed!

The door is locked, and its perimeter is sealed with wax. It can be opened with thieves' tools, magic, or by bashing it in.

> The door opens into a large square chamber. A 10-foot-wide walkway runs along the outer edge of the room around a large square pit. A disgusting substance resembling putrefied flesh fills the pit.

Any living creature staying in this chamber for more than one minute attracts the hunger of the undead monstrosities dwelling in the pit. When that time passes, **2 wraiths** emerge from the slime and attempt to drain the life of any trespassers. Every 1d4 rounds thereafter, another **wraith** emerges from the fleshy morass.

Tlatoani bound the tortured souls of those victims he sacrificed against their wills to this chamber and cursed them to prevent their escape. If the characters leave the room, the wraiths do not pursue them, as the curse prevents them from passing over the threshold. Characters can break the curse by sanctifying the pool of blood in **Area S7**.

Any character slain by a wraith is also bound by the curse and cannot leave the chamber.

Wraith (varies): HD 4; **AC** 3[16]; **Atk** touch (1d6 + level drain); **Move** 9 (fly 24); **Save** 13; **AL** C; **CL/XP** 8/800; **Special:** +1 or better magic or silver weapons to hit, level drain (1 level with hit). (*Monstrosities* 518)

S6: The Baths

> A wide stone trough occupies the center of this room. Piled inside, several tied bundles of large sticks rest on a thick bed of hard-caked ash. Along the edge sits a pile of large clay blocks, their faces black with soot. A basin chiseled from volcanic rock stands at the foot of the trough. A pair of worn benches dressed with crumbling mats woven from reeds and grasses frames a door in the south wall. A single large stone bench with a longer profile carved to accommodate individuals in reclining positions runs the length of the north wall. Two more doors offer additional egress to the east and west.

Anyone inspecting the basin notes a faint white line near the rim. It is some sort of mineral deposit indicating that the basin once held water that left a waterline.

This room once served as a purification room. Priests used the trough to create steam by heating the clay bricks and rapidly placing them in the basin.

The door to **Area S7** is locked and sealed with wax. It can be forced opened, unlocked with a set of thieves' tools, or by using magic.

S7: Blood Column

> An enormous column running from floor to ceiling bisects the chamber. Rings of stylistically carved faces of warriors cover the entire column. Each face displays an anguished expression, and streaks of dried black tears run down their cheeks and stain the floor surrounding the column's base.

Investigating more closely, the faces have tiny holes bored into the tear ducts, from which the black tears appear to emanate. The tearstains are very old dried blood.

The column lies beneath the sacrificial altar so when the victim's blood spills onto it, it runs down the center of the column and causes the faces to weep. The column is cursed and emits a magical aura. The weeping faces bind the spirits trapped in **Area S5**. If the characters sanctify the column with a *remove curse* spell, it breaks the curse binding the wraiths to **Area S5**. Thereafter, the creatures are no longer bound to their chamber.

S8: Portals to the Outer Worlds

> Arched doorways line the walls of this corridor and open into shallow, lightless alcoves no more than a few feet deep. The stonework framing each of the portals bears its own unique and intricate carvings that depict different animals and numbers.

The floor of the eastern end of the passage slopes slightly toward the west. Halfway down, the passage branches off to the north and ends in front of a carved stone door that leads to **Area S6**. The far ends of either side of the passage both take sharp turns to the north. The eastern passage connects to **Area S3** while the western passage connects to **Area S8**.

The iconography is related to auspicious dates and times on the calendar associated with aspects of the Immortal Sun during Tlatoani's reign over the southern continent. Tlatoani and his disciples used the alcoves as foci during rituals that allowed them to project their consciousness into other planes of existence.

S8A: The Arrow Cannon

This portion of the chamber contains an **arrow cannon trap**.

A plaster and clay mosaic in the floor conceals a pressure plate that, when stepped on, ignites an alchemical fuse connected to a long tube packed with explosives and fitted with scores of arrows hidden within the shadows in the back of the portal alcove. The trapped pressure plate has a curiously raised arrangement of the mosaic tiles. If more than 20 pounds of pressure is applied to the plate, the fuse ignites. One round later, the charge explodes and catapults the arrows down the corridor with a deafening boom. The arrows fly straight down the hallway. All creatures within 10 feet of the pressure plate are struck by 1d6 arrows and must make a saving throw or be deafened for 1d4 rounds. Each arrow does 1d8 points of damage.

S8B: The Secret Door

This portal conceals a secret door located at the back of the alcove that allows access **Area S10**. The stairwell beyond leads to the lower catacombs.

S9: The Secret Stairwell

This hallway hides a secret door. Characters who find the door can use it to access the temple's second level.

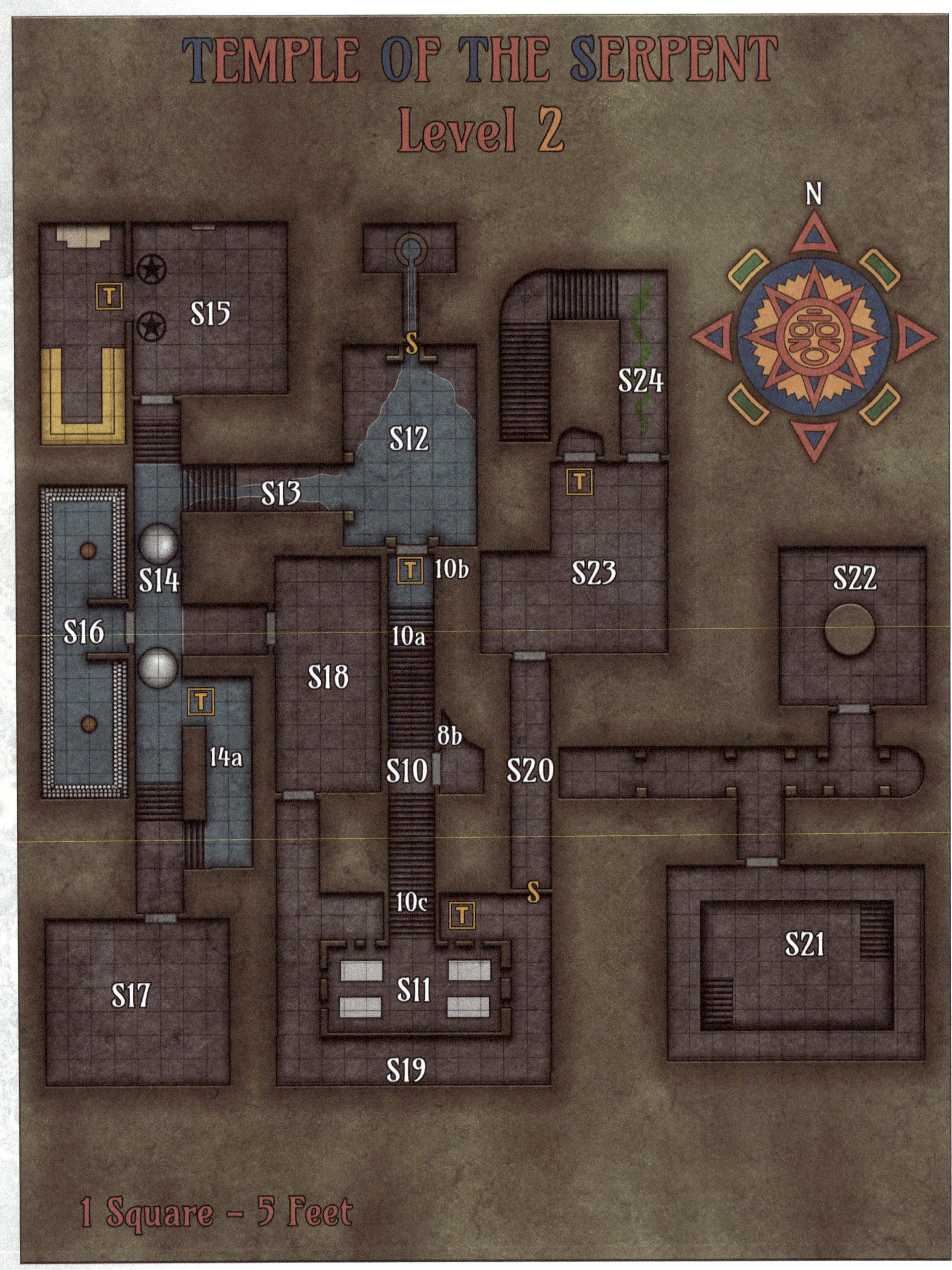

TEMPLE OF THE SERPENT
Level 2
N
S15
T
S12
S13
S24
S14
T
S23
S16
10b
S22
10a
S18
8b
S10
S20
14a
T
10c
T
S
S11
S17
S21
S19
1 Square – 5 Feet

Chapter Six: Temple of the Serpent (Level 2)

This chapter describes the temple's second level.

S10: The Serpent and the Mothers

The mural is crafted mostly from colored clay tiles. However, the serpent's two eyes are set with red garnets. If the characters successfully salvage them, they are worth 200 gp each.

S10A: Sunken Stairs

Approximately one inch of stagnant water covers the corridor floor. A strange door is at the end of the hall.

S10B: The Eclipse Door

The door is locked, sealed with wax, and magically trapped. The door radiates an aura of magic.

Anyone attempting to open the door triggers the trap. If that occurs, a powerful conjuration spell causes the image of the moon to animate, open its mouth, and vomit forth a **bog creeper**. The mindless plant attacks the nearest living creature in the room and continues fighting until destroyed. The magical trap can be dispelled vs. an 8th-level caster.

Bog Creeper: HD 7; AC 6[13]; **Atk** slam (1d6), 4 tendrils (1d4), or bite (2d4); **Move** 4 (swim 9); **Save** 9; **AL** N; **CL/XP** 8/800; **Special:** camouflage (hide among dead stumps and trees), constrict (2d4 damage if 2 tendrils hit target, save for half), spit acid (3/day, 15ft range, 2d8 damage, save for half). (see **Appendix A: New Monsters**)

S10C: Staircase

This long staircase leads to an archway opening into **Area S11.**

S11: Body Preparation Chamber

Tlatoani's priests used this chamber to prepare the bodies of deceased serpent cuauhocelotls to allow them to continue to serve their master in the afterlife.

Several quarter-inch holes are bored into the walls at eye level. A character who peers through a hole spots another hallway on the other side of the wall. The peepholes allowed observers in the outer chamber to watch the funerary preparations.

Although there are no exits, the walls are only one-inch thick and fashioned from wood and concrete sealed with lime and plaster. Anyone attempting to break through the wall can do so easily.

Treasure: The leather sacks hold different types of precision cutting stones, all made from razor-sharp obsidian. Priests used them to perform intricate cuts needed to prepare the bodies for the afterlife. There are four sets, each worth 150 gp.

If the characters remain in this room for more than a few minutes, they attract the attention of Cihuacoatl, one of the two spirit nagas that serve Titechcualtia Ianima. The reptilian creature spies on them through the peepholes long enough to gather basic information about the characters' intent and abilities. When she finishes, she deliberately makes noise to attract their attention while she slithers off toward the west. Then, she silently slinks back east to alert Titechcualtia Ianima, who awaits the characters in **Area S25.** If the characters block her path, she tries to lead them on a wild goose chase until she can slip past them and reach her mistress.

S12: Statue of the Weeping Serpent

Characters investigating the basin quickly determine leaves and other detritus have clogged it for what appears to be many, many years.

Characters searching the fountain can determine that it hides a secret door that opens into a narrow crawlspace leading into a small room. In the center of the room rests a shallow, two-foot-deep pool filled with rainwater funneled here from a chimney in the ceiling. Four small statuettes of two-headed serpents exquisitely carved from black basalt surround the pool, each poised to strike.

Anyone searching the bottom of the pool easily spots a collection of glittering gold ingots in assorted sizes.

Treasure: The four serpent statuettes are worth 500 gp each, while the 25 gold ingots are worth 3d10 gp each.

S13: The Flooded Corridor

The corridor leads to a short flight of steps. More water pools at the bottom and floods the adjacent hallways. About one foot of water covers the base of the stairwell and the entire lower concourse.

S14: The Long Haul

Characters attempting to traverse the hall soon discover their path blocked by a large round boulder that nearly fills the width and height of the entire passage. The boulder weighs several thousand pounds — easily enough to crush careless characters. Characters who work together with a combined strength score of 20 have a 20% chance to push the spherical stone 2d6 feet forward on each successful check. For every point above a combined strength of 20, add another 5% to the chance (so a combined strength of 25 has a 45% chance). To successfully navigate a way through the passages, the characters need to push the boulders out of the way. A side passage offers them a convenient place to push the ball out of the way. Unfortunately, just beyond the first boulder, another similar, inconveniently placed boulder blocks the remainder of the passage. Characters can simultaneously push both boulders in the same direction, though a successful check moves the two stones only 1d6 feet.

The secret to navigating around the boulders is to find intersections in the passage that provide the characters an opportunity to slip around the boulders. The best option is to squeeze around the corner at the intersection near **Area S16**, open the door to **Area S16**, and push one or two boulders into that room.

While it is possible to push both up the loop, the weight of both boulders causes the weakened floor to collapse.

If both boulders are placed in this section of the passage (marked with an A), the characters hear a sudden loud crack. The 40-foot section of passageway marked on the map collapses, plummeting any creature or object in the area 50 feet down into a large natural cavern unless the character succeeds on a saving throw to leap to safety. A character who fails his saving throw takes 5d6 points of damage from the fall and another 2d6 points of damage from the sharp stalagmites lining the bottom. If the floor breaks, the water from the chambers above drains into the cavern.

The large natural cavern at the bottom is sealed off from the rest of the temple structure and consists of a small complex of five caverns chained together by water-eroded tunnels. Characters can re-enter the temple by scaling the walls or by using another means to reach the top of the shaft, including flying, levitating, or teleporting. If the characters decide to explore this lower cave complex, they discover a labyrinthine tunnel that leads to an opening in the jungle about one mile west of the temple.

The cavern serves as the home of a clan of trolls. The characters have a 10% chance of encountering **2d4 trolls** for every 10 minutes they spend in the locale, up to a maximum of 29 trolls.

Trolls (up to 29): HD 6+3; **AC** 4[15]; **Atk** 2 claws (1d4), bite (1d8); **Move** 12; **Save** 11; **AL** C; **CL/XP** 8/800; **Special:** regenerate (3hp/round).(***Monstrosities*** 489)

S15: The Forum

The door to this chamber bears a mosaic of a ring of seven serpents, all biting each other's tails.
The door is jammed shut and sealed with wax.

A character who studies the plates interprets that the symbols appear to describe numerous judgments or sentences imposed for committing various criminal and heretical acts such as stealing, blasphemy, and treason.

If the characters walk past the statues and into the next room, read or paraphrase the following description:

Tlatoani's seers used this forum to perform and discuss divinations interpreting the stars, auspicious signs, and by performing haruspicy on animal and human sacrifices.

The handles of the knives include the images of a dog, an eagle, an ocelot, a deer, a crocodile, and a snake.

The animals are associated with days, months, and numbers used in divination. A common theme in divination included using ritual knives to draw blood.

Each animal determines the following information:
The dog represents the 10th day of the first week.
The eagle represents the second day of the second week.
The ocelot represents the first day of the second week.
The deer represents the seventh or eighth day of the first week.
The crocodile represents either the first day of the first week, or the eighth day of the second week.
The snake represents the fifth day of the first week.

Seers used these knives in accordance with their birth signs to draw blood and use it as an offering to Tlatoani before performing their rituals. Anyone using the knife associated with their birth sign to draw 1 hit point of blood as an offering successfully meets the sacrifice conditions for shutting off the magical trap that protects this room.

The terracotta statues radiate magic. Tlatoani enchanted them to protect the secrets of his seers and their secret council. They are firmly affixed to the floor, but ripping them from the ground and toppling them foils the trap. Likewise, a creature can spend 1d10 minutes bashing one into pieces with the same effect. If a creature approaches within five feet of the arch without paying the proper sacrifice, the statues immediately rotate and swing at the creature. Each statue attacks as an 8HD creature and does 6d6 points of damage with a successful hit. The statues pivot back to their original position after swinging and are poised to swing at the next creature who approaches within five feet of the arch without making the proper sacrifice. The trap does not trigger if the proper sacrifice is made.

Treasure: The two mosaics adorning these walls are salvageable (see the **Mosaics and Gemstones** sidebar).

S16: Racks of Skulls

The baskets appear to be filled with bones and ashes; however, if any living creature approaches within five feet of the basket, the contents begin swirling into an angry animated whirlwind of shattered broken bones. The **2 bone** swarms are immediately drawn to the presence of life and mercilessly attack the nearest living creatures.

Bone Swarms (2): HD 10; **HP** 74, 63; **AC** 6[13]; **Atk** swirling bones (2d6); **Move** 9 (fly 18); **Save** 5; **AL** N; **CL/XP** 10/1400; **Special:** immune to sleep and charm, resist slashing weapons (50% damage). (see **Appendix A: New Monsters**)

S17: The Foundry

Several small trenches scar the earthen floor. A basket near the trenches holds a collection of long tubes assembled from animal horn and bone. Three small flat boulders, two dusted with gold powder and one with bluish powder, rest in a wooden bench covered with scorch marks. A collection of granite stones, each about the size of a piece of fruit, sits next to the boulders. A cracked straw basket beneath the bench holds a pile of malachite. Another basket holds rocks threaded with gold veins.

Tlatoani's craftsmen used this room as a primitive foundry and were capable of smelting gold and copper items that were mostly used as jewelry and decorative items. Craftsmen used the granite rocks as hammers to crush malachite and other stones containing gold and copper ore on the large flat boulders. They used the trenches as ovens by filling them with charcoal, covering them, and then using the tubes to blow air over the coals as they used tools to work the extracted ore into jewelry and other items.

Tlatoani's slaves operated his foundry day and night, driven nearly to death daily by the two hulking obsidian creatures he used to enforce his bidding. In the years since, the serpent lord's slaves have died, though the elementals still remain.

The room is still operated and maintained by **2 obsidian elementals** made from the volcanic glass. If living humanoids enter, the elementals express surprise, but their shock quickly wears off as they immediately assign tasks to the new employees. If a character refuses to perform their bidding, the creatures condemn the individuals to death and then enforce their edict.

Obsidian Elementals (2): HD 8; **HP** 59, 52; **AC** 2[17]; **Atk** 2 claws (3d6); **Move** 9; **Save** 8; **AL** N; **CL/XP** 9/1100; **Special:** +1 or better magic weapons to hit, death throes (explodes upon death, 30ft radius, 3d6 damage, save for half), immune to fire, molten glass (1d6 points of damage to attacker, save avoids). (see **Appendix A: New Monsters**)

S18: The Plug Room

A long bench occupies about half of this chamber's eastern wall. The bench and shelves contain dozens of clay jars filled with powdered pigments and an assortment of bones, thorns, stone hammers, and a stingray spine that are readily identified as tools for scarring, branding, piercing, and tattooing. Above the bench hangs a series of wooden tablets containing images and words that describe the specific rituals for body modifications of the serpent cuauhocelotls, advisors, and priests. Six concrete and wood-slat boxes sit on the bench.

All the boxes are sealed with beeswax and held fast with a latch made from a mummified adder's head. One must break the seal to access the latch, but doing so triggers the trap.

Adder's Head Latch Trap

Opening the latch causes a **poison needle** to spring out from the adder's fang to deliver a dose of poison. If the trap is triggered, the needle extends three inches straight out of the latch. A creature within range takes 1d4 points of damage and must make a saving throw or die.

Treasure: Each box contains a small collection of miscellaneous jewelry, including numerous ear and lip plugs, labret plugs, jade plate, gold necklaces and bracelets, earrings, and nose rings. Each collection is worth 3d10 x 10 gp.

S19: The Peeking Hall

This curiously shaped hall encircles the body preparation chamber (**Area S11**). Holes set at roughly five-foot intervals along the interior curve of the corridor allow individuals to peek in and observe activities taking place in the other room.

A secret door in the northeast corner provides access to hidden chambers on this level as well as access to the lowest level where the daughter of Tlatoani hides.

One of the peepholes is trapped with an insidious device that the priests used on unsuspecting temple guests.

Any character attempting to peer through this peephole is in for a surprise. The moment they attempt to peer through the hole, a pressure plate in the floor releases a store of ground obsidian dust through a hollow within the wall and into the peephole. Anyone within five feet of the hole takes 1d8 points of damage and must succeed on a saving throw or be blinded by the crystalline shards.

A character who searches the peephole notices irregularities in the stonework that conceal the trap.

S20: The Intersections

A somber and unadorned hallway travels 40 feet north and ends at a single door. Along the eastern wall, an arched doorway provides a second exit. Overhead hang a trail of elaborately crafted feather and bone totems that run the length of the corridor. Plucked from exotic birds, the feathers have faded in color. The bones appear to be human and are intricately carved with images of skulls, birds, and serpents. Decorative columns constructed of lime and concrete line the walls beyond the arch, painted with red and green swirls.

The hall extends about 80 feet, finally ending before a recessed alcove. About two-thirds of the way down the hall, an exit leads to a door to the south. Near the end of the hall, a second door blocks another exit branching off to the north. All doors that lead from the hallway are locked.

Treasure: One of the fetishes hanging from the ceiling is a *chime of opening*.

S21: The Pit of Sacrifice

A deep recess, excavated nearly eight feet into the floor, marks the center of this large chamber. A five-foot-wide walkway encircles the perimeter of the recess. At opposite ends of the pit, a pair of carved staircases ascends to the sand-covered floor. Several stone disks of various sizes are strewn about the pit. Rough hemp ropes are threaded through a hole bored through the center of each disk.

Anyone making a quick and casual survey of the bottom of the pit spots broken shards of wood and other indicators of the violence and death that occurred here.

Warriors bound themselves with weighted disks while undergoing ritual sacrifice by combat. They used the weights to make it far more difficult to maneuver and to tire them out quicker.

Tlatoani constructed this chamber to serve as a ritual sacrificial fighting pit. He primarily used it to weed out initiates petitioning to serve as his elite serpent cuauhocelotls. Initiates were taken here, tied with weights, given clubs, and then bound with weighted stones. They would then face off against the pit guardian. Those who survived were granted status. Those who lost offered their deaths as a ritual sacrifice to maintain honor.

A **nalfeshnee demon** still serves as the pit guardian and waits to test the mettle of anyone who aspires to be a serpent cuauhocelotl. Although it would normally wait at the bottom, thousands of years of boredom prompt the diabolical creature to fly out of the chasm to attack any intruder.

Demon, Nalfeshnee, Fourth-Category Demon: HD 7d10; HP 64; AC 4[15]; **Atk** 2 claws (1d4), bite (2d4); **Move** 9 (fly 14); **Save** 9; **AL** C; **CL/XP** 12/2000; **Special:** +1 or better magic weapons to hit, +2 on to-hit rolls, immune to fire, magic resistance (65%), spell-like abilities, summon demons (60% chance, roll 1d6 for category). (**Monstrosities** 102)
Spell-like abilities: at will—*dispel magic, fear, polymorph self;* 1/day—*symbol of discord.*

S22: Column of Blood (Level 2)

This room is structurally similar to **Area S7**, which lies directly above it. Like **Area S7**, characters who cast *remove curse* on the altar free the spirits trapped in **Area S5**. The column connects this area to the altar in the serpent's mouth (**Area S7**) at the top of the temple and the blood pool (**Area 25D**) on the level below.

The sleeping beast is a **behir**, an ancient carryover from the age before Tlatoani's arrival. The beast's ancestors occupied the temple's deep caverns for thousands of years, but the current occupant seems content to feed on the fresh blood that recently stained the altar. The creature is currently sleeping. However, the instant the beast realizes she has an opportunity for warm meat, she rises and quickly lunges in for the feast.

Behir: HD 12; HP 89; AC 4[15]; **Atk** bite (1d8 + swallow whole); **Move** 15; **Save** 3; **AL** C; **CL/XP** 13/2300; **Special:** constrict and claw (wrap around target, save avoids, automatic 6 attacks, 1d6 damage each), lightning breath (once per 10 rounds, 24 damage, save for half), swallow whole (natural 20 to hit). (**Monstrosities** 44)

At this level, the column provides magical sustenance to the children and worshipers of Tlatoani. The column radiates an aura of evil and necromantic magic. The column was created to grant mystical energy to Tlatoani's followers

Clay Masks

These masks carry an ancient enchantment that allows any individual who dons the mask to see and comprehend the nature of magic attuned to the mask. Tlatoani's priests attuned each mask to a specific trap within the temple. If a creature wearing the correct mask gazes upon a trap to which it is attuned, then the wearer senses the trap's presence as if affected by a *find traps* spell. Although they are magical, the seers fashioned them from relatively fragile clay, which can break or crack if subjected to mild pressure.

Lizard: This mask attunes to the trap in **Area S10b**.
Monkey: This mask attunes to the trap in **Area S14**.
Death: This mask attunes to the trap in **Area S15**.
Vulture: This mask attunes to the trap in **Area S19**.
Serpent: This mask attunes to the trap in **Area S23**.

and disciples during their stay within the temple.

Each mask represents a different day on Tehuatl's ancient calendar.

S23: HALL OF SLOUGHED SKINS

A collection of eight stretched human skins adorn the walls, each marked with a gold mask decorated with a helmet of snakeskin mixed with feathers. The skins are heavily scarred and tattooed to resemble serpent scales. To the left of each skin hangs a macuahuitl and a round shield. The shields and macuahuitls are finely crafted and decorated with feathers, paintings, and carvings representing the power of their owners.

Two separate stone doors hang upon the north wall. They appear nearly identical, and both are carved with a rising serpent. On both doors, the serpents face inward toward each other.

This chamber served as the covert meeting area for Tlatoani's serpent cuauhocelotls. They convened here to discuss matters of importance, and it is also where they stored their prized weapons and armor.

The two serpent doors are locked. A casual inspection reveals that both doors were also sealed with wax, although the seal to the western door has been broken. The door to the east opens to **Area S24**. The door to the west is a false door. Any creature who breaks its wax seal (either by opening the door or piercing the seal) triggers the **poison gas trap**.

If the seal to this door is broken, an odorless toxic gas seeps into the room. A creature inside the room for three or more rounds becomes overexposed to deadly levels of the gas. Creatures in the gas must make a saving throw or take 3d6 points of damage and be blinded for 10 minutes. On a successful saving throw, the character takes half damage and is not blinded.

Treasure: The eight gold death masks are worth 300 gp each. There are also eight *+1 macuahuitls*[B], eight *serpent shields* [B], seven finely crafted helmets (100 gp), and a *helm of the ebon serpent*[B].[B] See **Appendix B: New Equipment and Magic Items**

The monetary and magical treasure in this room consists of items sacred to Tlatoani. Thus, all of them are protected by a curse. Any character removing one or more of the items from the room falls victim to the curse.

CURSE OF TLATOANI

After leaving the room with one of Tlatoani's sacred items, the cursed character must make a saving throw at the next dawn or become exhausted (half normal movement and –1 penalty to hit and damage) and take 1d6 points of damage that cannot be healed. Each dawn thereafter, the creature must make another saving throw with a cumulative –1 penalty per day (–8 maximum) or take the same damage (so a character three days removed from taking the objects would make a saving throw with a –3 penalty or take 1d6 points of damage and move at half speed). The curse can be lifted by using *remove curse* or similar magic or if the creature dies.

S24: THE HALL OF THE DESCENT

This hallway pitches noticeably downward. A large mosaic set into the floor depicts a slithering snake that runs the length of the passage. At the far end of the slope, the hall and arch on the western wall reveals a long, winding flight of stairs that twist and turn their way down into the darkness.

Characters can attempt to remove the gemstones from the large serpent mosaic to gain the treasure. It is big enough that it counts as two mosaics. The descending passage leads to **Level 3**.

Treasure: Players can attempt to salvage either of the two mosaics on these walls (see **Mosaics and Gemstones** sidebar).

WRAPPING THINGS UP

Characters who complete this section of the temple are ready to move on to the final chapter.

When they descend the staircase, read or paraphrase the following description to take them to the adventure's climactic encounter:

The stairs seem to descend forever, winding back and forth as they head deeper into the darkness until they lead to a long hallway. Light glimmers up ahead, and gouts of hot humid air waft up the passage, drastically increasing the temperature.

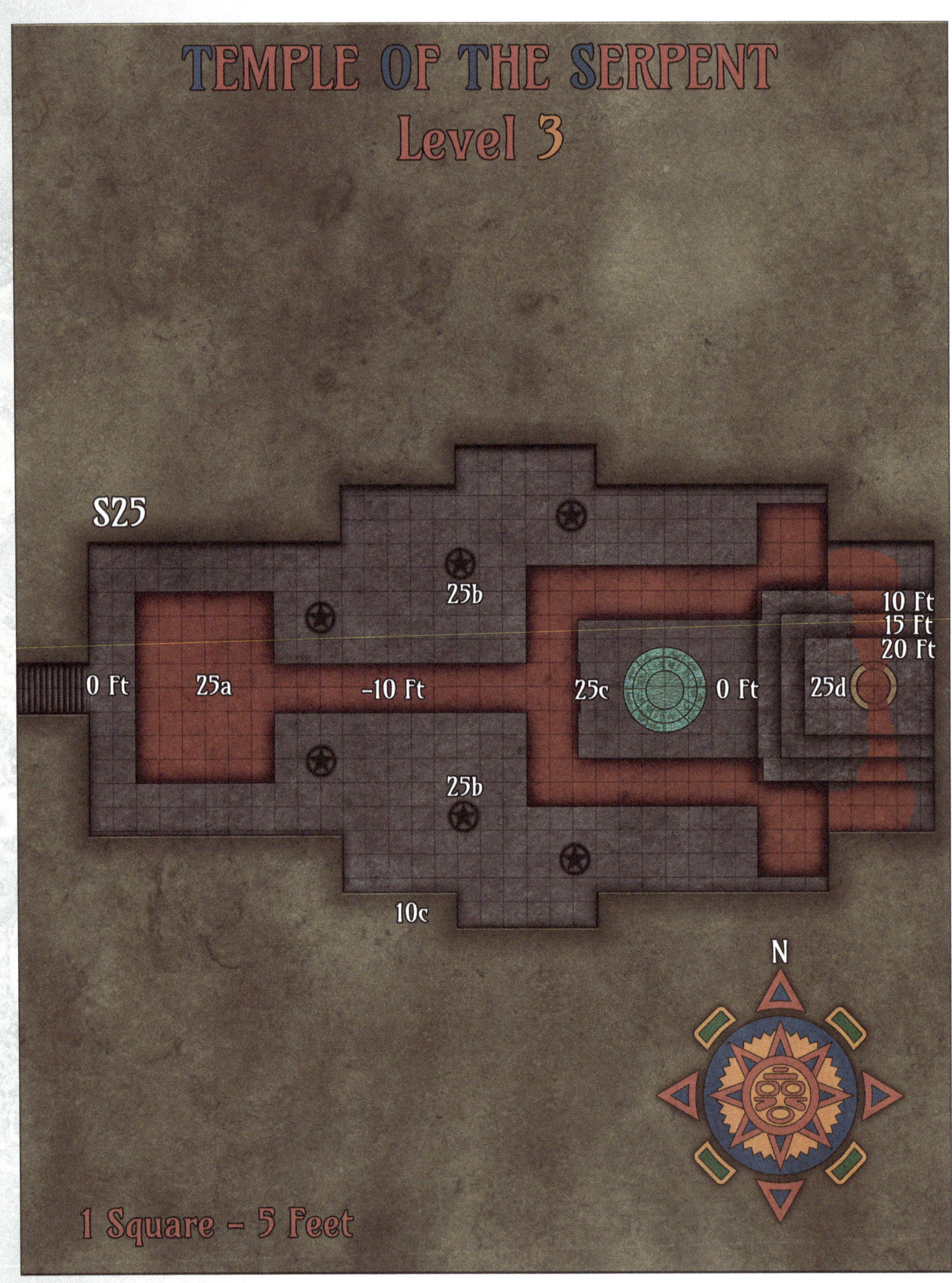

TEMPLE OF THE SERPENT
Level 3
S25
0 Ft
25a
-10 Ft
25b
25b
10c
25c
0 Ft
25d
10 Ft
15 Ft
20 Ft
N
1 Square – 5 Feet

Chapter Seven: Temple of the Serpent (Level 3)

One of the Drowned Serpent's most devoted daughters, a marilith called Titechcualtia Ianima, assumed dominance over the Serpent Temple and uses the lowest level as her personal sanctum.

This section of the adventure begins when the characters walk down the hall at the bottom of the temple staircase.

S25: The Drowned Serpent's Daughter

The arch opens into a grandiose hall consisting of several levels. Before the arch, a walkway encircles a deep pit filled with crimson blood. The blood flows into the pit via a canal that bisects the middle portion of the hall. Fire pits on either side sprout gouts of red and orange flames. Towering basalt statues carved to resemble striking adders line either side of the chamber, all facing the main entrance. At the far end, a small ziggurat rises, topped by a stone fountain that overflows with blood. The blood overflows from the fountain and spills into the moat that surrounds the ziggurat and flows down the canal. In front of the ziggurat stretches a wide platform, the floor of which bears a huge mosaic of a slithering serpent. Atop the platform rests a huge and hideous creature with the torso and face of a giant, six-armed woman and the lower body of a massive slithering serpent. Gemstones and other objects appear intertwined with her massive tail.

Titechcualtia Ianima, a **marilith demon** awaits the characters' arrival, hoping to corrupt them to her desires. In addition to the demonic creature, **2 spirit nagas** lurk in the wings ready to fight to the death alongside their mistress.

Titechcualtia Ianima, Marilith Demon, Fifth-Category Demon: HD 7; HP 52; AC 7[12]; **Atk** 6 macuahuitls (1d8), tail (1d8); **Move** 12; **Save** 9; **AL** C; **CL/XP** 13/2,300; **Special:** +1 or better magic weapons to hit, immune to fire, magic resistance (80%), spell-like abilities, summon demons (50% chance). (*Monstrosities* 101)
Spell-like abilities: at will—*charm person, levitate, polymorph self, teleport.*
Equipment: 6 macuahuitls[B].
[B] See **Appendix B: New Equipment and Magic Items**

Spirit Nagas (2): HD 9; HP 66, 59; AC 5[14]; **Atk** bite (1d3 + poison); **Move** 12; **Save** 6; **AL** C; **CL/XP** 13/2300; **Special:** charm gaze (as charm person), lethal poison (save or die), spells (MU 4/2/1; Clr 2/1). (*Monstrosities* 344)
Spells: 1st—*cure light wounds, detect magic, light, magic missile* (x2), *read magic*; 2nd—*bless, darkness 15ft radius, invisibility*; 3rd—*lightning bolt.*

Titechcualtia Ianima welcomes the characters to her abode. She invites them to share her power, tempting them with the following introduction.

"You have impressed Tlatoani with your cunning and skill, so why waste your abilities on mere mortals? Join with me, join with Tlatoani! You have proven yourselves. Metzpil is a fool whose only use is that of a vessel for the Serpent God's return. The other gods … what have they done for mortals? Tlatoani rose as a great emperor, he conquered Notos, including this miniscule island. He brought peace and order. The others rebelled out of jealousy. They demand sacrifices as well. How are they nobler than the Serpent? What can they offer mighty champions such as yourselves? Come now, we must not fight. We should join, rule the world together, and end this sorrow, end this slavery."

Her speech is merely a ruse to buy time for her allies to charm the characters before she attempts to destroy any mortals brash enough to thwart her plans. When they exhaust their spells or if the characters resist them, the spirit nagas cast *lightning bolt* and then move about the room, never staying in the same place for long. Likewise, Titechcualtia Ianima teleports out of danger when she can, darting around the chamber to gain an advantageous position in combat, use one of her traps, or drink from the waters in **Area 25C** to regain lost hit points. When engaged in melee combat, she always concentrates her seven attacks against a single target to quickly deplete that foe's hit points or to knock them unconscious. If the characters hold their own against the marilith, you may allow her to summon diabolical reinforcements as an action or have a demon watching her from afar suddenly appear on the scene. Titechcualtia Ianima is an impulsive creature rarely governed by logic and not prone to rigid thinking. If she finds herself in a dire circumstance, she puts her pride on the backburner and calls for aid.

Although she purports that she can resurrect Tlatoani, there is no evidence to support her claims that she truly is Tlatoani's daughter or that she can accomplish her stated goal. Instead, the characters may theorize that she uses this story to entice mortals to accept her diabolical bargain for another dire purpose of her own creation or that of another demon prince, such as Tsathogga who may be seeking to increase his influence in a domain completely surrounded by water and some of his allies. The characters can neither confirm nor refute her story, though the characters senses that the demon conceals or is omitting a crucial detail about her ties to the island's former master or her real motives for her actions, which you are free to create to fit into your plotline.

Treasure: Over the years, the demon and her minions have accumulated a wealth of goods and gear. There are 14 yellow sapphires on the mosaic worth 1,000 gp each as well as a a *tilmahtli of the owl*[B] and *xtabentun*[B].
[B] See **Appendix C: New Equipment and Magic Items**

25A: The Pool of Life

A pool of partially coagulated blood extracted from centuries of sacrifice rests within a 10-foot recess below the main level of this chamber. The blood helps Tlatoani maintain a connection to the mortal realms. The pool is five feet deep, but the blood in the pool is rank and decayed despite the enchantments of priests and demons to keep it from spoiling. If anyone falls into the pool or drinks from it, the character must make a saving throw or be sickened for 30 minutes.

25B: Lightning Adder Traps

The statues are enchanted to blast intruders with lightning. They are attuned to Titechcualtia Ianima, and when she touches one of the statues, she can cause that statue to unleash a bolt of lightning that targets any creatures in a 150-foot line directly in front of the adder statues' mouths. A creature in the line must make a saving throw or take 8d6 points of damage on a failure or half as much damage on a success.

25C: Altar of the Drowned

The mosaic on this platform depicts three serpents encircling a Tehuatl calendar. Tlatoani had multiple aspects and numerous children, at least according to legend. Titechcualtia Ianima claims she is not the only child of the Serpent, though she does not go out of her way to reveal this fact. She would rather die than reveal that she has other siblings. Anyone attempting to decipher the meaning of this mosaic can infer that Titechcualtia Ianima is not alone in her efforts to resurrect Tlatoani. However, the mosaic, if accurate, provides no clues about the nature, identity, nor whereabouts of her alleged siblings.

25D: The Font of Coagulation

The fountain is fed from above via the Serpent Altar that drains downward through the Column of Blood. A Chaotic creature who drinks from the fountain regains 4d6 hit points. However, the creature cannot regain hit points again in this manner until the next midnight. A Neutral creature gains no benefits but suffers no harm from drinking from the fountain. A Lawful creature who drinks from the fountain takes 4d6 points of damage. Unlike the fountain's beneficial effects, a good creature takes damage each time it drinks from the fountain.

Conclusion

The adventure ends if the characters defeat Titechcualtia Ianima. The characters can then ransack the rest of the temple or return to any of the villages to offer evidence of her defeat. If they killed Metzpil, they may seek forgiveness from his father, which he readily grants under the circumstances. The priest is curious to learn of the temples and the ruins. He implores the characters to lead him back to these locations so he can consecrate them and destroy any evidence of the rituals that others might use in the future to bring the Drowned Serpent back into this world. If Metzpil lives, allow the characters the opportunity to help him find redemption. His father may send the characters on an expedition to find a cure for his son's addiction or he may ask the characters to take Metzpil to find a cure. If a player's character died, the player may opt to assume Metzpil's role as a character and seek redemption through subsequent quests or expeditions.

If the characters return to either of the villages, the Poqozas offer the characters permanent residence, as well as food and restitution for their services. If they befriended the sea bride, she gratefully gifts them with a magic item of their choice for defeating her "husband's" age-old enemy.

Appendix A: New Monsters

The following new monsters appear in this volume.

Aboleth, Nihileth

Hit Dice: 10
Armor Class: 3[16]
Attacks: 4 tentacles (1d6 + withering touch)
Saving Throw: 5
Special: *charm monster*, drain zombie, ethereal form, immunities (cold, charm, poison, sleep), void aura, withering touch, telepathy (100ft)
Move: 6/12/12 (swim/fly)
Alignment: Chaos
Number Encountered: 1
Challenge Level: 13/2,300

A nihileth aboleth is an undead version of the monstrous subterranean amphibian. These undead creatures are no longer confined by their underground empires, however, and can slip between worlds in an ethereal state that allows them to fly as a dark purple outline with a blackish-purple haze contained within its ethereal form. Unlike a living aboleth, the nihileth doesn't secrete a mucus cloud. Instead, a chilling cloud surrounds the undead creature. Any living creatures within five feet of the aboleth takes 2d6 points of damage and is affected by a *slow* spell. A successful saving throw results in half damage and the creature is not slowed.

The aboleth can attack with its tentacles in its material form or while ethereal. Creatures struck by the undead aboleth must make a saving throw or one of their limbs randomly withers and becomes unusable. An injured nihileth aboleth can drain a nihilethic zombie within 60 feet to heal itself in the amount of the zombie's current hit points.

Aboleth, Nihileth: HD 10; AC 3[16]; Atk 4 tentacles (1d6 + withering touch); **Move** 9 (swim 12, fly 12 [ethereal only]); **Save** 5; AL C; CL/XP 13/2300; **Special:** *charm monster* (3/day), ethereal form (at will), drain zombie (heals number of hit points taken), immunities (cold, charm, poison, sleep), *phantasmal force* (3/day), void aura (chilling cloud 5ft around aboleth; 2d6 damage and slowed [as *slow* spell]; save for half and not slowed), telepathy (100ft), withering touch (save or random limb withers).

Alux

The aluxes are made up of several races of proto-humans whom the earliest gods created during the prehistoric ages long before the rise of Tlatoani and the hero-gods. Each of a different era, the aluxes were formed from the remains of the creations that came before them after their worlds were laid waste by cataclysm, war, and other apocalypses that befell the world before the age of man. They span thousands of years of creation and are the precursors to what the world recognizes as human. They walk upright, possess the ability to reason, and are human in appearance, though each age has identifiable traits that are distinctly non-human — some subtle, some hideous, or deformed. The earliest aluxes are more bestial than manlike. They are crude, barbaric, and barely able to speak. Aluxes hold a wide range of dispositions, though most have a chaotic bent. Some are kind and helpful. Others resent humanity, believing they stole the world from them and seek to reclaim it for themselves.

Few aluxes exist today. Those that escaped extinction remain hidden from the world, though they sometimes settle with their own kind. To exist in the realms of the living and the dead, the gods gave the aluxes souls. However, they can remove them when they pass into the land of the dead. For this reason, all aluxes are semi-immortal in that they do not age. Nonetheless, they can be killed by physical violence.

Alux of the First Sun

Hit Dice: 10
Armor Class: 7[12]
Attacks: bash (2d6)
Saving Throw: 5
Special: camouflage, darkvision (60ft), immune to fear, trigger rockslide, vulnerable to obsidian
Move: 15
Alignment: Any
Number Encountered: 1d4
Challenge Level: 10/1,400

Aluxes of the First Sun are great, nine-foot-tall giants with hideous proportions and dull wit. This large, muscular humanoid with mottled skin covered in mousy black hair has a protruding belly and bestial facial features. Its skull has a humanoid shape with a pronounced underbite, broad forehead, and jagged teeth, while its ears, nose, and mouth are slightly wider and longer than the typical humanoid. It wears little clothing and carries no weapons in its oversized, powerful hands.

Aluxes of the First Sun originally had a pleasant nature, as hurt and pain were unknown to them, yet as time passed, their outlook toward their world and their own kind evolved. Violence and aggression crept into their race, causing them to revel in bloodshed and carnage. The ancient gods who wagered on their brutal contests grew bored of their wanton bloodshed and terrible cruelty. They ultimately nearly ripped them into shreds, ending the age of the First Sun and the further development of the aluxes from this period.

An alux of the First Sun can hide in the hills and mountains (80% chance), and if discovered, is likely to trigger a rockslide to bury or at least hinder its foes. To do so, it slaps the ground repeatedly until the rocks begin to rush downhill from it in a 10-foot-wide slide that does 3d6 points of damage (save for half). It can trigger the rockslide three times per day.

Aluxes of the First Sun are vulnerable to weapons made of obsidian, and take double damage from such blades.

Alux of the First Sun: HD 10; AC 7[12]; Atk bash (2d6); **Move** 15; **Save** 5; AL Any; CL/XP 10/1400; **Special:** camouflage (80% chance to hide in hilly or mountainous terrain), darkvision (60ft), immune to fear, trigger rockslide (3/day, create 10ft wide rockslide, 3d6 damage, save for half), vulnerable to obsidian (200% damage).

Alux of the Second Sun

Hit Dice: 6
Armor Class: 7[12]
Attacks: bite (1d6), slam (2d4)
Saving Throw: 11
Special: camouflage, darkvision, vulnerable to obsidian
Move: 12
Alignment: Any
Number Encountered: 1, 1d3
Challenge Level: 6/400

Aluxes born during the second age of humanity were far smaller than the giants that walked before them. Light black hair covers the torso, arms, and legs of the bronze-skinned humanoid with an athletic build. The face appears distinctly human, with long black hair covering the scalp and falling past the shoulders. They were a gentle people who lived simple lives as gatherers of nuts and berries. They lacked the size and strength of their predecessors, which made them easier to kill when the gods ultimately swept them from the earth. The aluxes of the Second Sun that escaped the onslaught fled underground where they endured for centuries and had occasional contact with their Aztli successors in the Coyonqui.

An alux of the Second Sun can hide in the hills and mountains (80% chance), and unlike aluxes of the First Sun, they often use weapons to defend themselves. They are sneaky creatures, and if they attack from surprise, they can backstab their opponents for triple damage.

A few aluxes of the Second Sun specialize in ranged weapons, in particular longbows, and are deadly marksmen with these weapons. These snipers often hang back and pick off enemies from afar. They gain a +2 bonus to hit and damage with the longbow.

Alux of the Second Sun: HD 6; AC 7[12]; **Atk** weapon (1d8) or bite (1d6), slam (2d4); **Move** 12; **Save** 11; **AL** Any; **CL/XP** 6/400; **Special:** backstab (x3), camouflage (80% chance to hide in hilly or mountainous terrain), darkvision (60ft), vulnerable to obsidian (200% damage).

Alux of the Second Sun Sniper: HD 6; AC 7[12]; **Atk** longbow x2 (1d6+2) or bite (1d6), slam (2d4); **Move** 12; **Save** 11; **AL** Any; **CL/XP** 6/400; **Special:** +2 bonus to hit and damage with missile weapons, backstab (x3), camouflage (80% chance to hide in hilly or mountainous terrain), darkvision (60ft), vulnerable to obsidian (200% damage).

ALUX OF THE THIRD SUN

Hit Dice: 7
Armor Class: 7[12]
Attacks: Weapon (1d8) or 2 claws (1d4+1)
Saving Throw: 9
Special: darkvision (60ft), summon chom swarm, thieving skills
Move: 12
Alignment: Any
Number Encountered: 1d3
Challenge Level: 7/600

An alux of the Third Sun has a humanoid body shape with olive skin and a lithe, wiry physique. It has long, black hair on its head, though the rest of its body is hairless. Some simian and animalistic features can be seen in its eyes, ears, nose, and mouth. These aluxes most resemble modern Aztlis, though they appear more feral with mild simian or animalistic characteristics.

These aluxes survived the last cataclysm, and their road to continued existence proved more difficult than their prototypes because the gods attempted to erase humanity entirely. In their fear, the aluxes made pacts with the chom, a brightly plumed bird with a beautiful voice. When the gods discovered what the choms had done, they cursed them, stripped them of their colorful feathers, and bound them to the same fate as the aluxes for all eternity.

Aluxes of the Third Sun are stealthy and able to hide themselves away from those who would do them harm. The cursed alux are guides and transporters of souls, a grave responsibility they take seriously. Each alux of the Third Sun is bonded to a specific chom, which allows it to summon a chom swarm to aid it. The specific bonded chom holds the alux's soul, which gives the alux room to carry a departed mortal soul to the land of the dead.

Alux of the Third Sun: HD 7; AC 7[12]; **Atk** weapon (1d8) or 2 claws (1d4+1); **Move** 12; **Save** 9; **AL** Any; **CL/XP** 7/600; **Special:** darkvision (60ft), summon chom swarm (100%, arrives in 1d4+2 rounds), thieving skills.
Thieving Skills: Climb 89%, Hear 4 in 6, Hide 30%, Silent 40%, Locks 30%.

BEAST FROM BELOW THE BLACK

Hit Dice: 10
Armor Class: 3[16]
Attacks: bite (3d6) and tail (1d8)
Saving Throw: 5
Special: Breach hull
Move: 12/18 (swim)
Alignment: Chaos
Number Encountered: 1
Challenge Level: 10/1,400

Within the black waters of the Miquiatoyatl River that flows between the Great Void and Miquito lurks a tremendous reptilian beast known only as the beast from below the black. It is believed the creature formed at the dawn of time and serves to keep the balance of the cosmos by devouring those who would cross into Miquito unwarranted or without means of providing the necessary tribute demanded by the gods. Others claim the beast is the physical embodiment of the river itself — cold, uncaring, and violent. The beast from below the black lurks silently, biding its time before it strikes. The creature spends most of its time submerged, surfacing only sporadically before disappearing beneath the inky waters of the Miquiatoyatl.

Beast from Below the Black: HD 10; AC 3[16]; **Atk** bite (3d6) and tail (1d8); **Move** 12 (swim 18); **Save** 5; **AL** C; **CL/XP** 10/1400; **Special:** breach hull (25% chance to toss boat into the air and splinter hull).

BEAST OF ITZCUIN

Hit Dice: 2
Armor Class: 7[12]
Attacks: Bite (1d3)
Saving Throw: 16
Special: Darkvision, disease, misfortune
Move: 15
Alignment: Chaos
Number Encountered: 1d4, 3d4
Challenge Level: 2/30

Bearing the appearance of a mongrel dog, this coyote-sized beast has patches of fur missing from its coat along with an assortment of physical deformities including misshapen ears, a grotesque underbite, and a stubby, crooked tail. The beast attacks with a disease-ridden bite. Any creature bitten must make a saving throw or take an additional 1d4 points of damage each day until healed with a cure spell. Once per day, a beast of Itzcuin can cause misfortune in one target. The targeted creature must make a saving throw or take a −1 penalty to hit and saves for 24 hours.

Itzcuin's affinity with canines goes beyond the god's relationship with his gnoll minions. At some point in the distant past, the cunning deity transformed what most presume to be coyotes into the monstrous abominations bearing his name. During the metamorphosis, the beasts acquired numerous deformities and defects that made them appear more demonic than animalistic. Itzcuin's gnoll servants typically use these beasts as guardians within their communities and temples devoted to their malevolent god.

Beast of Itzcuin: HD 2; AC 7[12]; **Atk** bite (1d3 + disease); **Move** 15; **Save** 16; **AL** C; **CL/XP** 2/30; **Special:** darkvision (60ft), disease (save or 1d4 damage per day, healing ends damage), misfortune (1/day, save or −1 penalty to hit and saves for 24 hours).

BLACK ORC HIGH PRIEST OF ORCUS

Hit Dice: 7
Armor Class: 4[15]
Attacks: weapon (1d8) or two-handed sword (1d10)
Saving Throw: 9
Special: Spells
Move: 9
Alignment: Chaos
Number Encountered: 1, 1d3
Challenge Level: 9/1,100

Black orc high priests are the undisputed leaders of massive orc tribes. Black orc high priests cast spells as 10th-level clerics.

Black Orc High Priest of Orcus: HD 7; AC 4[15]; **Atk** flail (1d8) or two-handed sword (1d10); **Move** 9; **Save** 9; **AL** C; **CL/XP** 9/1100; **Special:** spells (3/3/3/3/3).
Spells: 1st—*cure light wounds* (x2), *detect magic*; 2nd—*bless, hold person, speak with animals*; 3rd—*cure disease, prayer, speak with dead*; 4th—*cure serious wounds* (x2), *sticks to snakes*; 5th—*finger of death, insect plague, raise dead*.

BOARFOLK HIT DICE: 6

Armor Class: 7[12]
Attacks: Club (1d8+2) or gore (3d6)
Saving Throw: 11
Special: darkvision (60ft)
Move: 12
Alignment: Neutrality
Number Encountered: 1d6
Challenge Level: 6/400

The boarfolk are humanoids that resemble the wild boars of the forest. They attack with massive greatclubs but can resort to a vicious gore to disembowel their enemies. They stand about seven feet tall and are covered in short, bristly hair. Two tusks protrude from their lips.

Boarfolk: HD 6; AC 7[12]; Atk club (1d8+3) or gore (3d6); **Move** 12; Save 11; AL N; CL/XP 6/400; **Special:** darkvision (60ft).

BOG CREEPER

Hit Dice: 7
Armor Class: 6[13]
Attacks: Slam (1d6), 4 tendrils (1d4), or bite (2d4)
Saving Throw: 9
Special: Camouflage, constrict, spit acid
Move: 4/9 (swim)
Alignment: Neutrality
Number Encountered: 1d4
Challenge Level: 8/800

The bog creeper is a creature native to the thickest, darkest swamps. It superficially resembles a man-sized rotted tree trunk sprouting several thorny tendrils each about 10 feet long and a single six-foot-long limb. Bog creepers are carnivorous, lurking amid dead trees and stumps waiting to ambush unsuspecting prey. When prey comes within range, a bog creeper lashes out with its single limb and slashes with its tendrils. If two tendrils hit the same opponent, the creature grabs the victim and constricts it for 2d4 points of damage (save for half) as it transfers the prey to its mouth. Three times per day, a bog creeper can vomit digestive sap up to 15 feet on opponents (2d8 points of damage; save for half).

Bog Creeper: HD 7; AC 6[13]; Atk slam (1d6), 4 tendrils (1d4), or bite (2d4); **Move** 4 (swim 9); Save 9; AL N; CL/XP 8/800; **Special:** camouflage (hide among dead stumps and trees), constrict (2d4 damage if 2 tendrils hit target, save for half), spit acid (3/day, 15ft range, 2d8 damage, save for half).

CADAVER

Hit Dice: 2
Armor Class: 6[13]
Attacks: 2 claws (1d4 + disease), bite (1d6 + disease)
Saving Throw: 16
Special: Disease, reanimation
Move: 6
Alignment: Chaos
Number Encountered: 1d3, 2d6+2
Challenge Level: 4/120

Cadavers are humanoids dressed in tattered rags. Rotted flesh reveals corded muscles and sinew stretched tightly over its skeleton. Hollow eye sockets flicker with an unholy fire of orange or yellow light. The cadaver's mouth is lined with jagged and broken teeth, and its hands end in wicked claws. The creature's claws and bite transmit horrible diseases that waste a victim's flesh (1d4 hit points damage; save resists). When killed, a cadaver regenerates 1 hit point per round. It stands up ready to fight again when it regains its full hit points. Damage caused by spells is not restored.

Cadaver: HD 2; AC 6[13]; Atk 2 claws (1d4 + disease), bite (1d6 + disease); **Move** 6; Save 16; AL C; CL/XP 4/120; **Special:** disease (1d4 damage, save resists), reanimation (regenerates 1 hp/round after death).

CARD SHARK

Hit Dice: 3
Armor Class: 6[13]
Attacks: Card slice (1d4)
Saving Throw: 14
Special: Drain, immune to sleep and charm, shape change, spell-like abilities, telepathy, vulnerable to fire
Move: 6
Alignment: Chaos
Number Encountered: 1
Challenge Level: 3/60

This miniscule, nearly two-dimensional creature is roughly shaped like an ordinary playing card. Two pairs of pseudopod extensions protruding from its lower half and sides function as rudimentary legs and arms. This tiny creature telepathically communicates with its humanoid gambler host, who can direct it to instantaneously transform into any inanimate object such as a playing card, a die, or a gaming tile to change the outcome of any wager (95% chance of a favorable outcome). However, any time the card shark tries to affect a game of chance, the gambler takes 1d4 points of damage (no save). Over time, the bond becomes unbreakable (requiring a *remove curse* to break the creature's hold on the gambler), and the card shark becomes more ravenous until it drains the gambler completely (with each successive use draining a higher amount: 1d4, 1d6, 1d8, 1d10, 2d4, and finally 2d6 with each use). The tiny card shark attacks by directing small, card-like razors up to 20 feet at targets.

A card shark communicates telepathically with its host (up to 30 feet), and can cast *invisibility* on itself once per day (usually as a defensive measure to escape). The thin card shark is especially vulnerable to fire and takes double damage from flames.

Card Shark: HD 3; AC 6[13]; Atk card slice (1d4); **Move** 6; **Save** 16; AL C; CL/XP 4/120; **Special:** drain host (with each use of luck, initial 1d4 damage), immune to sleep and charm, luck (host has 95% chance of success at games of chance), shape change, spell-like abilities, vulnerable to fire (200% damage).
Spell-like abilities: 1/day—*invisibility*.

CHILD OF THE BRIAR

Hit Dice: 2
Armor Class: 5[14]
Attacks: 2 claws (1d6)
Saving Throw: 16
Special: Entangle, spit thorns, vulnerable to fire
Move: 9/6 (climb)
Alignment: Chaos
Number Encountered: 1, 1d8+2, 3d6
Challenge Level: 2/30

Children of the briar grow in the thick briar patches of the world where evil and death contaminate the earth. A child of the briar attacks with its claws. If both claws hit, the target must make a saving throw or be entangled and take 2d4 points of damage per round. A child of the briar can spit a thorn up to 60 feet that does 1d6 points of damage to a target. Children of the briar are vulnerable to flame and take double damage from fire.

Child of the Briar: HD 2; AC 5[14]; Atk 2 claws (1d6); **Move** 9 (climb 6); Save 16; AL C; CL/XP 2/30; **Special:** entangle (if both claws hit, save or held, automatic 2d4 damage per round), spit thorns (60ft range, 1d6 damage, save avoids), vulnerable to fire (200% damage).

CHOMTZITZIMITL

Hit Dice: 6
Armor Class: 7[12]
Attacks: 2 claws (1d8 + bleeding)
Saving Throw: 12
Special: Bleeding, darkvision (60ft), detect living
Move: 9/15 (fly)
Alignment: Chaos
Number Encountered: 1, 1d4, 2d6
Challenge Level: 7/600

Chomtzitzimitls are powerful demon-like servants that wander the realms of Miquito. Some say they serve the lords of the underworld, while others contend that they act of their own accord. Chomtzitzimitls appear to be anthropomorphic crows with black or deep-green feathers edged with silver. Their faces are grotesquely human, with bulbous red and black eyes that dart wildly. They have a huge, 16-foot wingspan, and their gangly reptilian legs end in long, dexterously sharp claws. They smell like rotting corpses, and their flesh almost appears to flake with rot. Because of their physical similarities, chomtzitzimitls are usually associated with choms, the black birds that frequent their realm and act as liaisons between mortals and the gods of the dead. Chom often flock in numbers in locations where these fiends live, though the nature of their relationship remains unclear. Most likely the chom revere or even worship the chomtzitzimitl, and when the birds were first cursed, it may well have been the chomtzitzimitl who robbed them of their bright plumage and refashioned them in their image. Regardless of origin, the chom listen to the commands and will of the chomtzitzimitl with utmost fear and reverence.

A chomtzitzimitl's claws cause deep slashing wounds that bleed profusely if the target fails a saving throw. The target continues to bleed (for 1d3 points of damage) every round after being struck.

Chomtzitzimitl: HD 6; AC 7[12]; Atk 2 claws (1d8 + bleeding); **Move** 9 (fly 15); **Save** 12; **AL** C; **CL/XP** 7/600; **Special:** bleeding (1d3 damage per round after successful claw attack, save resists, healing ends ongoing damage), darkvision (60ft), detect living (60ft line of sight, 60% chance).

CIPATENHUA

Hit Dice: 3
Armor Class: 7[12]
Attack: 2 claws (1d4) and bite (1d6) or weapon (1d6) and bite (1d6)
Special: Camouflage, cursed
Move: 12/12 (swim)
Saving Throw: 14
Alignment: Chaos
Number Encountered: 1d4, 2d4
Challenge Level/XP: 3/60

The reptilian cipatenhuas resemble humanoid crocodiles. They attack with their claws and bite, but also wield weapons against their foes. They often hide in the waterways and strike fast from camouflage (1-in-6 chance to spot). The cipatenhuas are cursed and must always remain in contact with water, wet earth, or another wet surface. If they are not, they take 1d6 points of damage every 10 minutes.

Cipatenhua: HD 3; AC 7[12]; Atk 2 claws (1d4) and bite (1d6) or weapon (1d6) and bite (1d6); **Move** 12 (swim 12); **Save** 14; **AL** C; **CL/XP** 3/60; **Special:** camouflage (1-in-6 chance to spot), cursed (must remain on wet land or 1d6 damage every 10 minutes).

CIPATENHUA
DISCIPLE OF TSATHOGGA

Hit Dice: 6
Armor Class: 7[12]
Attack: 2 claws (1d4) and bite (1d6) or weapon (1d6) and bite (1d6)
Special: Camouflage, cursed, spell-like ability, spells
Move: 12/12 (swim)
Saving Throw: 11
Alignment: Chaos
Number Encountered: 1d2
Challenge Level/XP: 6/400

The cipatenhua disciple of Tsathogga is a humanoid crocodile spellcaster of the Frog God. They attack with their claws and bite, but also wield weapons against their foes. They often hide in the waterways and strike fast from camouflage (1-in-6 chance to spot). The cipatenhuas are cursed and must always remain in contact with water, wet earth, or another wet surface. If they are not, they take 1d6 points of damage every 10 minutes.

Once per day, the disciple can touch an opponent and cause them to babble incoherently for 1d6 + 2 rounds if they fail a saving throw. They can also polymorph themselves into a giant frog once per day. The disciple is a 6th-level magic-user.

Cipatenhua Disciple of Tsathogga: HD 6; AC 7[12] or 2[17] (missile) and 4[15] (melee) from *shield* spell; **Atk** 2 claws (1d4) and bite (1d6) or weapon (1d6) and bite (1d6); **Move** 12 (swim 12); **Save** 11; **AL** C; **CL/XP** 6/400; **Special:** camouflage (1-in-6 chance to spot), cursed (must remain on wet land or 1d6 damage every 10 minutes), spell-like ability, spells (4/2/2 MU), touch of madness (1/day, save or babble incoherently for 1d6+2 rounds).
Spell-like ability: 1/day—*polymorph self* (into giant frog)
Spells: 1st—*charm person, jinx*[C]*, magic missile, shield;* 2nd—*invisibility, phantasmal force;* 3rd—*instill madness*[C]*, hold person.*
[C] See **Appendix C: New Spells**

CIPATENHUA FROG PRIEST

Hit Dice: 6
Armor Class: 7[12]
Attack: 2 claws (1d4) and bite (1d6) or club (1d6) and bite (1d6)
Special: Camouflage, crazed croak, cursed, spell-like ability, spells
Move: 12/12 (swim)
Saving Throw: 11
Alignment: Chaos
Number Encountered: 1d2
Challenge Level/XP: 6/400

The cipatenhua frog priest of Tsathogga is a humanoid crocodile divine spellcaster of the Frog God. They attack with their claws and bite, but also wield weapons against their foes. They often hide in the waterways and strike fast from camouflage (1-in-6 chance to spot). The cipatenhuas are cursed and must always remain in contact with water, wet earth, or another wet surface. If they are not, they take 1d6 points of damage every 10 minutes.

Once per day, the frog priest can issue a crazed croak that causes anyone within 30 feet who fails a saving throw to be disturbed by horrific visions and unable to concentrate on a specific task (fighting, spellcasting, etc.) for 1d6 + 2 rounds. They can also polymorph themselves into a giant frog once per day. The frog priest is a 6th-level cleric.

Cipatenhua Frog Priest of Tsathogga: HD 6; AC 7[12]; Atk 2 claws (1d4) and bite (1d6) or club (1d6) and bite (1d6); **Move** 12 (swim 12); **Save** 11; **AL** C; **CL/XP** 6/400; **Special:** camouflage (1-in-6 chance to spot), crazed croak (1/day, save or lose focus for 1d6+2 rounds), cursed (must remain on wet land or 1d6 damage every 10 minutes), spell-like ability, spells (2/2/1/1 Clr).
Spell-like ability: 1/day—*polymorph self* (into giant frog).
Spells: 1st—*bloodbath*[C]*, cause light wounds;* 2nd—*hold person, silence 15ft radius;* 3rd—*flay skin*[C]*; 4th—cause serious wounds.*
[C] See **Appendix C: New Spells**

CIPATENHUA FROG PRINCE

Hit Dice: 8
Armor Class: 6[13]
Attack: 2 claws (1d4+3) and bite (1d6) or greatclub (1d8+3) and bite (1d6)
Special: Camouflage, cursed, immune to charm and fear, spell-like ability, Tsathogga's cursed touch
Move: 12/12 (swim)
Saving Throw: 8
Alignment: Chaos
Number Encountered: 1
Challenge Level/XP: 9/1,100

The cipatenhua frog prince is a humanoid crocodile. It attacks with its claws and bite but also wields a greatclub. It often hides in the waterways and strikes fast from camouflage (1-in-6 chance to spot). Cipatenhuas are cursed and must always remain in contact with water, wet earth, or another wet surface. If they are not, they take 1d6 points of damage every 10 minutes.

Once per day, the frog prince can target one creature with an attack that does an additional 3d6 points of damage and curses the target if it fails a saving throw. On a failure, the creature suffers a –2 penalty to hit, saves, and damage for 48 hours (or until a *remove curse* spell is cast on the creature). If a creature dies from this attack, its body turns to festering pustules of rancid flesh (*resurrection* or *wish* to restore). The frog prince can polymorph itself into a giant frog once per day.

Cipatenhua Frog Prince: HD 8; AC 6[13]; Atk 2 claws (1d4+3) and bite (1d6) or greatclub (1d8+3) and bite (1d6); **Move** 12 (swim 12); Save 8; AL C; **CL/XP** 9/1100; **Special:** camouflage (1-in-6 chance to spot), cursed (must remain on wet land or 1d6 damage every 10 minutes), spell-like ability, Tsathogga's cursed touch (1/day, successful strike, additional 3d6 damage + curse, save or –2 to hit, saves, and damage for 48 hours; if killed, body turns to festering pustules of rancid flesh [*resurrection* or *wish* to restore]).
Spell-like ability: 1/day—*polymorph self* (into giant frog).

CUEYATL

Hit Dice: 4
Armor Class: 5[14]
Attacks: Weapon (1d6) and bite (1d4), or 2 claws (1d6) and bite (1d4)
Saving Throw: 13
Special: Amphibious, camouflage, darkvision (60ft), leap, slimy
Move: 12/9/12 (climb/swim) or leap (20ft)
Alignment: Chaos
Number Encountered: 1d4, 3d6
Challenge Level: 5/240

A cueyatl is a humanoid frog-like creature with green, blue, or purple skin. They wield weapons but often attack with their claws and bite. Many claim these creatures share a common ancestry with the tsathar found on Akados and Libynos in the Lost Lands. The amphibious cueyatl is more suited for a jungle climate, however, and is difficult to locate in such terrain (85% chance to spot). A cueyatl can leap 20 feet (with a height of 10 feet) to surprise its prey. The creature's skin is slimy, which makes it difficult to grab and grants it protection from fire (half damage).

Cueyatl society has developed into different hierarchies, with lowly common cueyatls, warriors, sea priests, and moon priests.

Cueyatl: HD 3; AC 8[11]; Atk club (1d6) and bite (1d4) or 2 claws (1d6) and bite (1d4); **Move** 12 (climb 9, swim 12) or leap (20ft); Save 14; AL C; **CL/XP** 3/60; **Special:** amphibious, camouflage (85% chance to hide in jungles), darkvision (60ft), leap (20ft horizontal leap), slimy (half damage from fire).

Cueyatl Moon Priest: HD 10; AC 7[12]; Atk flail (1d8) and bite (1d4), or 2 claws (1d6) and bite (1d4); **Move** 12 (climb 9, swim 12) or leap (20ft); Save 5; AL C; **CL/XP** 12/2,000; **Special:** amphibious, camouflage (85% chance to hide in jungles), darkvision (60ft), leap (20ft horizontal leap), night's chill (3/day, 30ft radius, 2d6 cold damage, save for half; *dispel magic* in 30ft radius), slimy (half damage from fire), spells (2/2/2/2/2).
Spells: 1st—*cure light wounds, light*; 2nd—*bless, hold person*; 3rd—*cure disease, prayer*; 4th—*create water, cure serious wounds*; 5th—*finger of death, insect plague*.

Cueyatl Sea Priest: HD 8; AC 7[12]; Atk trident (1d8) and bite (1d4), or 2 claws (1d6) and bite (1d4); **Move** 12 (climb 9, swim 12) or leap (20ft); Save 8; AL C; **CL/XP** 9/1100; **Special:** amphibious, camouflage (85% chance to hide in jungles), darkvision (60ft), leap (20ft horizontal leap), night's chill (3/day, 30ft radius, 2d6 cold damage, save for half; *dispel magic* in 30ft radius), slimy (half damage from fire), speak with sea life, spells (2/2).
Spells: 1st—*cure light wounds* (x2); 2nd—*hold person, silence 15ft radius*.

Cueyatl Warrior: HD 5; AC 8[11]; Atk battle axe (1d8) and bite (1d4), or 2 claws (1d6) and bite (1d4); **Move** 12 (climb 9, swim 12) or leap (20ft); Save 13; AL C; **CL/XP** 5/240; **Special:** amphibious, camouflage (85% chance to hide in jungles), darkvision (60ft), leap (20ft horizontal leap), slimy (half damage from fire).

DAUGHTER OF CHALATIHUATL

Hit Dice: 15
Armor Class: 0[19]
Attack: *+3 flaming spear* (3d6+3 + 1d6 fire)
Special: +2 or better magic weapons to hit, cry of the damned, immune to cold and fire, magic resistance (25%), spells
Move: 15/18 (fly)
Saving Throw: 3
Alignment: Neutrality
Number Encountered: 1
Challenge Level/XP: 20/4,400

A daughter of Chalatihuatl manifests as a towering woman dressed in a cloak of black feathers and wearing an ornate tunic woven from the black petals. She carries round shields decorated with a stylized depiction of her mother and great black obsidian-tipped spears.

Chalatihuatl serves a queen over the outer realms of Miquito. She is allegedly married to Itzcuin. Their sons guard the City of Yellow Dogs in Miquito, while their daughters guard the secrets of the Obsidian Spire. She is sometimes called the Lady of Sacrifice, and some believe that she determines the worthiness of a mortal's sacrifice. Her daughters collect these sacrifices and then act accordingly as dictated by her judgment and the circumstance.

A daughter of Chalatihuatl can emit a hideous screech that causes all creatures within the sound of its voice to be stricken with *confusion* as per the spell for 2d4 rounds unless the creature succeeds on a saving throw. A daughter of Chalatihuatl casts cleric and druid spells as 15th-level cleric. The daughter of Chalatihuatl can be hit only by +2 or better magic weapons. They are immune to cold and fire.

Daughter of Chalatihuatl: HD 15; AC 0[19]; Atk *+3 flaming spear* (3d6+3 + 1d6 fire); **Move** 15 (fly 18); Save 3; AL N; **CL/XP** 20/4400; **Special:** +2 or better magic weapons to hit, cry of the damned (at will, screech causes *confusion* [as spell] for 2d4 rounds, save resists), immune to cold and fire, magic resistance (25%), spells (6/6/6/5/5/2).
Spells: 1st—*cure light wounds* (x2), *detect evil* (x2), *detect magic, light*; 2nd—*bless, heat metal, hold person, silence 15ft radius, speak with animals, warp wood*; 3rd—*call lightning, continual light, plant growth, prayer, remove curse, speak with dead*; 4th—*cure serious wounds, hallucinatory forest, neutralize poison, dispel magic, insect plague*; 5th—*commune, control winds, finger of death, quest, raise dead*; 6th—*blade barrier, word of recall*.
Equipment: *+3 flaming spear*.

Demon, Derghodemon (Cockroach Demon)

Hit Dice: 8
Armor Class: 6[13]
Attack: 2 claws (1d4+3) and bite (1d6) or greatclub (1d8+3) and bite (1d6)
Special: Camouflage, cursed, immune to charm and fear, spell-like ability, Tsathogga's cursed touch
Move: 12/12 (swim)
Saving Throw: 8
Alignment: Chaos
Number Encountered: 1
Challenge Level/XP: 9/1,100

The derghodaemon is one of the strongest of the demonic races, but its low intelligence has relegated it to a position of brute warrior and little more. It is a tall, bloated, insect-like creature with five arms and three legs. Each of its arms ends in a sharpened, clawed hand. Its legs end in four-toed feet. Its flesh is mottled green and black and its eyes are large and black with no pupils. A derghodaemon stands eight feet tall and weighs about 800 pounds. Twice per day, by clicking its mandibles, a derghodaemon can affect all creatures within 30 feet as if by a *feeblemind* spell. A derghodaemon's head can rotate 360 degrees, making it almost impossible to surprise the creatures or backstab them. In addition, they can see invisible creatures. At will, derghodaemons can cast *darkness 15-foot radius*, *fear*, and *sleep*.

Derghodemon (Cockroach Demon): HD 10; AC –2[21]; Atk 5 claws (1d4) or 2 claws (1d4) and 3 swords (2d6); Move 15; Save 5; AL C; CL/XP 16/3200; Special: +1 or better magic or silver weapons to hit, immune to acid and poison, magic resistance (50%), spell-like abilities, telepathy (100ft).
Spell-like abilities: at will—*darkness 15ft radius*, *detect invisibility*, *fear*, *sleep*; 2/day—*feeblemind* (30ft range).

Demon, Geruzou (Slime Demon)

Hit Dice: 4
Armor Class: 4[15]
Attacks: 2 claws (1d4), bite (1d6)
Saving Throw: 13
Special: +1 or better magic weapons to hit, goo spit, immune to electricity, magic resistance (10%), spell-like abilities, telepathy (100ft)
Move: 12/18 (fly)
Alignment: Chaos
Number Encountered: 1, 1d3
Challenge Level: 6/400

Geruzou are sometimes called slime demons because their sickly-gray, leathery skin constantly drips and oozes thick, jelly-like mucus. Like their brethren, they are fierce combatants and are often employed as hunters and trackers by greater demons. The typical geruzou stands nearly four feet tall and has a horse-like head with downward-curving horns. It has long, sharp teeth exploding from its mouth, stretching its lips back in a perpetual snarl, and taloned hands and feet. A pair of large, membranous wings jut from its back.

Three times per day, a geruzou can spit a stream of slimy goo in a 20-foot line. This spit attack requires a ranged attack. A creature hit by the slime is coated and slowed (as the *slow* spell) for six rounds if it fails a saving throw. A geruzou can cast *fear*, *darkness 15ft radius*, *ESP*, *invisibility (self)*, and *mirror image*.

Demon, Geruzou (Slime Demon): HD 4; AC 4[15]; Atk 2 claws (1d4), bite (1d6); Move 12 (fly 15); Save 13; AL C; CL/XP 6/400; Special: +1 or better magic weapons to hit, goo spit (20ft range, save or slowed for 6 rounds; save avoids), immune to electricity and poison, magic resistance (10%), spell-like abilities, telepathy (100ft).
Spell-like abilities: at will—*darkness 15ft radius*; 3/day—*ESP*, *invisibility*; 1/day—*fear*, *mirror image*.

Demon, Kishi

Hit Dice: 8
Armor Class: 3[16]
Attacks: Spear (1d6) or bite (2d6)
Saving Throw: 8
Special: +1 or better magic weapons to hit, darkvision, resistances (electricity, fire), spell-like abilities, summon kishi demon, telepathy
Move: 15
Alignment: Chaos
Number Encountered: 1, 1d4+1
Challenge Level: 10/1,400

Kishi demons are male humanoids with ruggedly handsome features that they use to lure the opposite sex into their clutches. The demon has a second hyena face on the back of its head, and anyone fascinated by the human face often ends up as food for the hyena side. They often keep these second canine faces covered so they can further their schemes without being discovered. This second head makes the kishi demon difficult to blind, charm, deafen, frighten, or stun (30% chance of being affected). Kishi demons attack with a bite and a spear.

Victims of the horrible jaws of the kishi often end up as grisly trophies on its shield. These trophies grant the kishi demon a +1 AC bonus against others of the same race.

At will, a kishi demon can cast *detect evil*, *detect magic*, and *suggestion*. Three times per day, it can cast *charm person*. Once per day, it can cast *confusion*. A kishi demon has a 35% chance of summoning another kishi demon. A kishi demon takes half damage from fire and electricity, and can be hit only by magic weapons.

Kishi Demon: HD 8; AC 3[16]; Atk spear (1d6) or bite (2d6); Move 15; Save 8; AL C; CL/XP 10/1400; Special: +1 or better magic weapons to hit, darkvision (60ft), resistances (fire, electricity), spell-like abilities, summon kishi demon (35% chance), telepathy (60ft).
Spell-like abilities: at will—*detect evil*, *detect magic*, *suggestion*; 3/day—*charm person*; 1/day—*confusion*.

Demon, Plaresh

Hit Dice: 4
Armor Class: 4[15]
Attacks: Bite (2d6 + poison)
Saving Throw: 13
Special: Immunities (charm, poison, sleep), infect corpse, magic resistance (10%), poison, resistances (cold, electricity, fire, slashing weapons)
Move: 12/12/12 (burrow/swim)
Alignment: Chaos
Number Encountered: 1d4, 2d8
Challenge Level: 6/400

Plaresh demons are swarming masses of writhing worms from which pseudopods and mouths emerge to snap at their prey. The demonic worms work in unison as a single being, but their undulating mass lets them slide around slashing weapons (50% damage). The worms can form snapping maws that allow them to burrow through wood, stone, steel, and dirt. Their bite delivers a debilitating poison that does an additional 1d4 points of damage if a creature fails a saving throw. Plaresh demons take half damage from cold, electricity, and fire. They are immune to poison.

If a plaresh demon kills a foe, it can burrow throughout the corpse's flesh for one round, irrevocably destroying the body. A new plaresh demon rises from the corpse within 1d4 rounds. A body destroyed in this fashion can be restored only with a *wish* spell.

Demon, Plaresh (Swarm): HD 4; AC 4[15]; Atk bite (2d6 + poison); Move 12 (burrow 12, swim 12); Save 13; AL C; CL/XP 6/400; Special: immunities (charm, poison, sleep), infect corpse (destroy body and cause new plaresh demon to rise in 1d4 rounds), magic resistance (10%), poison (save or additional 1d4 damage), resistances (cold, electricity, fire, slashing weapons) (50% damage).

DEVIL, SALT

Hit Dice: 11
Armor Class: 5[14]
Attacks: Weapon (1d8) or 2 claws (1d6)
Saving Throw: 4
Special: +1 or better magic weapons to hit, immune to fire, magic resistance (15%), spell-like abilities
Move: 12
Alignment: Chaos
Number Encountered: 1, 1d2
Challenge Level: 12/2,000

Salt devils are seven-foot-tall humanoids with scaly spikes covering their bodies in overlapping plates. These spikes gleam with salt crystals. They attack with weapons or with their sharp claws. The salt devil is immune to nonmagical weapons and fire. At will, the demon can cast *darkness 15-foot radius*. Once per day, it can cast *disintegrate* and *teleport*.

Salt Devil: HD 11; **AC** 5[14]; **Atk** weapon (1d8) or 2 claws (1d6); **Move** 12; **Save** 4; **AL** L; **CL/XP** 12/2000; **Special:** +1 or better magic weapons to hit, immune to fire, magic resistance (15%), spell-like abilities.
Spell-like abilities: at will—*darkness 15ft radius*; 1/day—*disintegrate, teleport.*

DRAKE, FEY

Hit Dice: 5
Armor Class: 2[17]
Attacks: Bite (1d6)
Saving Throw: 12
Special: Bewildering breath, spell-like abilities
Move: 9/18 (fly)
Alignment: Neutrality
Number Encountered: 1d3
Challenge Level: 6/400

Fey drakes are small purple-and-black dragons born with mischief in their eyes. These dragons are known tricksters but are also extremely loyal to the deities they follow. They are so trustworthy that deities often anoint them as their divine servants. A fey drake attacks with a dangerous bite that causes confusion as the spell in creatures that fail a saving throw. A fey drake can cast *invisibility* at will. Three times per day, it can cast *locate animals*, *phantasmal force*, and *suggestion*. Once per day, it can cast *polymorph self*.

Fey Drake: HD 5; **AC** 2[17]; **Atk** bite (1d6 + confusion); **Move** 9 (fly 18); **Save** 12; **AL** N; **CL/XP** 6/400; **Special:** bewildering breath (3/day, 15ft cone, save or charmed), confusion (as spell, save avoids), spell-like abilities.
Spell-like abilities: at will—*invisibility*; 3/day—*locate animals, phantasmal force, suggestion*; 1/day—*polymorph self*.

DROWNED MAIDEN

Hit Dice: 7
Armor Class: 5[14]
Attacks: 2 claws (1d8), 3 hair strikes (1d6 + constrict)
Saving Throw: 9
Special: +1 or better magic or silver weapons to hit, constrict, immune to charm and sleep, kiss, spell-like abilities
Move: 12/12 (swim)
Alignment: Chaos
Number Encountered: 1d4
Challenge Level: 9/1,100

The product of a failed romance, a drowned maiden is the corpse of a woman usually found floating facedown in a body of water with her hair floating around her in the current. After her death, the drowned maiden awakens with a thirst for vengeance. The drowned maiden attacks with her claws and three hair strikes that can hit an opponent up to 10 feet away. If a hair strike hits, the target has a 50% chance of being wrapped in the tresses if the target fails a saving throw. A trapped creature suffers an automatic 1d6 points of damage until freed from the constricting strands.

Magic or silver weapons are required to hit a drowned maiden. They are immune to charm and sleep. Three times per day, they can kiss an enemy (usually one held in their grasping hair) to drain them of their life. The target takes 2d6 points of damage, or half as much with a successful saving throw. A drowned maiden can cast *polymorph self* and *silence 15-foot radius* at will.

Drowned Maiden: HD 7; **AC** 5[14]; **Atk** 2 claws (1d8), 3 hair strikes (1d6 + constrict); **Move** 12 (swim 12); **Save** 9; **AL** C; **CL/XP** 9/1100; **Special:** +1 or better magic or silver weapons to hit, constrict (if hair hits, 50% chance hair wraps around target, save avoids, automatic 1d6 damage until freed), immune to charm and sleep, kiss (3/day, 2d6 damage, save for half), spell-like abilities.
Spell-like abilities: at will—*polymorph self, silence 15ft radius*.

DRYAD, DUSKTHORN

Hit Dice: 8
Armor Class: 6[13]
Attacks: Dagger (1d4)
Saving Throw: 8
Special: Control vines, speak with plants and animals, spell-like abilities, tree stride, vulnerability, wall of thorns
Move: 12
Alignment: Chaos
Number Encountered: 1
Challenge Level: 10/1,400

Duskthorn dryads are fey women with graying skin. They wrap themselves in vines and leaves, and live within dead and decaying trees. They cannot travel far from these trees and vines without suffering 1d6 points of damage per hour. However, the dryad can step into one dead tree and emerge from a second dead tree within 60 feet of the first tree.

The dryad can control the vines to attack and defend her. A vine is AC 7[12] and attacks as a 4HD creatures. It does 1d6 points of damage and has a 50% chance to tangle around its target (save avoids). A tangled creature takes an automatic 1d6 points of damage per round.

At will, the dryad can cast *faerie fire* and *sleep*. Three times per day, she can cast *charm person*, *invisibility*, and *magic missile*. Once per day, she can cast *dispel magic*, *obscuring mist*, and *suggestion*. Once per day, she can also cause a wall of thorns to rise out of the ground (with dimensions similar to the *wall of stone* spell).

Duskthorn Dryad: HD 8; **AC** 6[13]; **Atk** dagger (1d4); **Move** 12; **Save** 8; **AL** C; **CL/XP** 10/1400; **Special:** control vines, speak with plants and animals (at will), spell-like abilities, tree stride, vulnerable (must stay near tree and vines or take 1d6 damage per hour), wall of thorns (thorn wall as a *wall of stone*).
Spell-like abilities: at will—*faerie fire, sleep*; 3/day—*charm person, invisibility, magic missile*; 1/day—*dispel magic, obscuring mist, suggestion*.

EEL HOUND

Hit Dice: 7
Armor Class: 6[13]
Attacks: Bite (1d8)
Saving Throw: 9
Special: Amphibious, slick spittle
Move: 12/15 (swim)
Alignment: Neutrality
Number Encountered: 1d4, 2d6
Challenge Level: 7/600

The amphibious eel hound is a grotesque combination of a slimy eel and a misshapen canine. It has a bulbous, short-snouted head, four webbed paws, and a muscular tail. An eel hound can spit a globule of slick spittle up to 30 feet. Any creature struck by the spittle must make a saving throw or fall prone on the slickened ground. An eel hound attacks with a vicious bite.

Eel Hound: HD 7; AC 6[13]; **Atk** bite (1d8); **Move** 12 (swim 15); **Save** 9; **AL** N; **CL/XP** 7/600; **Special:** amphibious, slick spittle (30ft range, target must save or fall prone from slippery ground).

ELEMENTAL, OBSIDIAN

Hit Dice: 8, 12, or 16
Armor Class: 2[17]
Attacks: 2 claws (3d6)
Saving Throw: 8, 3, or 3
Special: +1 or better magic weapons to hit, death throes, immune to fire, molten glass
Move: 9
Alignment: Neutrality
Number Encountered: 1d3
Challenge Level: 8 HD (9/1,100), 12 HD (13/2,300), 16 HD (17/3,500)

Obsidian elementals are hulking humanoids composed of razor-sharp volcanic glass. Their form is dark and smoky, evidence of their violent creations. They attack with two jagged-glass claws. Anyone striking an obsidian elemental must make a saving throw or take 1d6 points of damage from the molten glass that bursts from the elemental's wounds.

If an obsidian elemental is killed, it explodes and showers everything within 30 feet in shards of volcanic glass. A creature takes 3d6 points of damage, or half that with a successful saving throw.

Obsidian Elemental: HD 8; AC 2[17]; **Atk** 2 claws (3d6); **Move** 9; **Save** 8; **AL** N; **CL/XP** 9/1100; **Special:** +1 or better magic weapons to hit, death throes (explodes upon death, 30ft radius, 3d6 damage, save for half), immune to fire, molten glass (1d6 points of damage to attacker, save avoids).

Obsidian Elemental: HD 12; AC 2[17]; **Atk** 2 claws (3d6); **Move** 9; **Save** 3; **AL** N; **CL/XP** 13/2300; **Special:** +1 or better magic weapons to hit, death throes (explodes upon death, 30ft radius, 3d6 damage, save for half), immune to fire, molten glass (1d6 points of damage to attacker, save avoids).

Obsidian Elemental: HD 16; AC 2[17]; **Atk** 2 claws (3d6); **Move** 9; **Save** 3; **AL** N; **CL/XP** 16/3500; **Special:** +1 or better magic weapons to hit, death throes (explodes upon death, 30ft radius, 3d6 damage, save for half), immune to fire, molten glass (1d6 points of damage to attacker, save avoids).

ELUSA HOUND

Hit Dice: 3
Armor Class: 7[12]
Attacks: Bite (1d6+1)
Saving Throw: 14
Special: Detect magic
Move: 15
Alignment: Neutrality
Number Encountered: 1d4, 2d4
Challenge Level: 3/60

The elusa hound is a powerful wolf-like dog with coarse, pale white fur (though some recent breeds have whitish-gray fur) and a short, bushy tail. Its eyes burn with a ghostly yellow glow and its teeth are ivory white. The dog is attuned to magic-users and can track them unerringly using its ability to detect magic at will.

Elusa Hound: HD 3; AC 7[12]; **Atk** bite (1d6+1); **Move** 15; **Save** 14; **AL** N; **CL/XP** 3/60; **Special:** *detect magic* (at will, as spell).

FIRE PHANTOM

Hit Dice: 6
Armor Class: 6[13]
Attack: Slam (1d4 + 1d6 fire)
Special: Fire blast, immolation, immune to fire
Move: 6
Saving Throw: 11
Alignment: Chaos
Number Encountered: 1d2, 1d4+2
Challenge Level/XP: 7/600

Fire phantoms appear as humanoids with raging fire for hair, flame-encased fists, and elemental fire playing across their bodies. A fire phantom's eyes are tiny balls of molten fire, as is its tongue. Fire phantoms attack with fiery fists that deal an extra 1d6 fire damage. Once every 1d4 rounds, they can hurl a globe of concentrated flame up to 30 feet (2d6 damage, save avoids). As a last resort, a fire phantom can detonate itself in an inferno that does 6d6 points of damage to all creatures within a 10-foot radius (save for half). The explosion kills the fire phantom if it fails a save, and causes its flames to extinguish for one round if it succeeds.

Fire Phantom: HD 6; AC 6[13]; **Atk** slam (1d4 + 1d6 fire); **Move** 6; **Save** 11; **AL** C; **CL/XP** 7/600; **Special:** fire blast (every 1d4 rounds, 30ft range, 2d6 damage, save avoids), immolation (1/day, 6d6 damage to all within 10ft radius, save for half, kills phantom if it fails save or extinguishes flame for 1 round if successful), immune to fire.

GHOUL, CINDER

Hit Dice: 6
Armor Class: 4[15]
Attack: Slam (1d8 + 1d6 fire + level drain)
Special: Fire, level drain
Move: 12 (flying)
Saving Throw: 11
Alignment: Chaos
Number Encountered: 1d3, 2d4
Challenge Level/XP: 8/800

A cinder ghoul is a ghost-like spirit in the form of a swirling humanoid cloud of burning ash and charred body parts. Its dark, smoky shape is lit here and there with the red glow of perpetually burning embers, and the grisly remains of scorched body parts can occasionally be glimpsed floating within the mass. These baleful undead creatures reek of smoke and burnt flesh. A cinder ghoul's touch drains 1 level. Any creature struck by the ghoul's vicious touch also suffers 1d6 fire damage and must save or catch on fire.

Cinder Ghoul: HD 6; AC 4[15]; **Atk** slam (1d8 + 1d6 fire + level drain); **Move** 12 (flying); **Save** 11; **AL** C; **CL/XP** 8/800; **Special:** fire (additional 1d6 damage, save or catch fire), level drain (1 level with hit).

GOLEM, WITCH-DOLL

Hit Dice: 10 (65 hit points)
Armor Class: 2[17]
Attacks: 2 fists (2d8)
Saving Throw: 5
Special: +1 or better magic weapons to hit, immune to most spells, linked damage
Move: 10
Alignment: Neutrality
Number Encountered: 1
Challenge Level: 10/1,400

A witch-doll golem appears to be crafted from stuffed human skin dressed in a patchwork of ill-fitting clothes. Large needles and pins pierce the creature's body where a humanoid's vital organs would be. A witch-doll golem stands twice the height of a human and weighs about 1,000 pounds.

A witch-doll golem can be commanded to target a specific foe. Against that foe, the witch-doll golem deals an extra 1d8 points of damage with each fist. Once the golem hits its intended target, half of any further damage the witch-doll golem takes is transferred to the victim so long as they are within 60 feet of each other. Only the linked target can attack a witch-doll golem and not take "linked damage." Witch-doll golems take full damage from fire and do not pass this damage to their linked target. They are immune to all other spells.

Witch-Doll Golem: HD 10; HP 65; AC 2[17]; **Atk** 2 fists (2d8); **Move** 10; **Save** 5; **AL** N; **CL/XP** 10/1400; **Special:** +1 or better magic weapons to hit, immune to most spells (all but fire spells), linked damage (additional 1d8 damage to chosen foe, which also takes half damage done by others to golem [except fire damage]).

HUECUVA

Hit Dice: 2
Armor Class: 2[17]
Attacks: 2 claws (1d4+1 + disease)
Saving Throw: 16
Special: +1 or better magic or silver weapons to hit, change self, disease
Move: 12
Alignment: Chaos
Number Encountered: 1d4
Challenge Level: 5/240

Huecuvas are the undead spirits of good clerics who were unfaithful to their god and turned to the path of evil before death. As punishment for their transgression, their god condemned them to roam the earth as the one creature all good-aligned clerics despise: the undead. Huecuvas resemble robed, worm-ridden skeletons and are often mistaken for such creatures. Three times per day, a huecuva can disguise its appearance with an illusion that makes it appear to be a normal cleric.

A huecuva attacks relentlessly until either it or its opponent is dead. During combat, if a Lawful cleric attempts to turn a huecuva and fails, the huecuva concentrates all attacks on that cleric, ignoring all other opponents until the cleric or the huecuva is dead.

People struck in combat by the huecuva's claws must succeed on a saving throw or come down with a fever. The fever incubates for 1d3 days before its symptoms appear. Once the incubation period is over, the disease inflicts 1d3 points of constitution and dexterity damage each day until the diseased victim passes a saving throw at a –3 penalty.

Huecuva: HD 2; AC 2[17]; **Atk** 2 claws (1d4+1 + disease); **Move** 12; **Save** 16; **AL** N; **CL/XP** 5/240; **Special:** +1 or better magic or silver weapons to hit, change self (3/day), disease (save resists initial onset; symptoms appear 1d3 days after failed save, 1d3 points of constitution and 1d3 dexterity loss each day, save at –3 penalty to overcome ongoing damage).

ICE MAIDEN

Hit Dice: 5
Armor Class: 7[12]
Attacks: Ice dagger (1d4 + 1d4 cold)
Saving Throw: 12
Special: +1 or better magic weapons to hit, chilling presence, flurry form, immune to cold, invisibility, kiss of the frozen heart, magic resistance, snowblind burst, spell-like abilities, vulnerable to fire
Move: 12
Alignment: Chaos
Number Encountered: 1
Challenge Level: 9/1,100

Ice maidens are solitary creatures born of powerful ice creatures. Despite their solitude, their desire for affection leads them to dominate creatures to serve as their servants. An ice maiden's flesh and hair are as white as snow, and their piercing blue eyes are like scintillating flecks of glacial ice. An ice maiden normally attacks with a frozen ice dagger, but once per day she can change into a swirling flurry of ice and snow for three rounds to deal 2d6 points of damage to targets caught within 20 feet.

Any creature within 15 feet of an ice maiden takes 1d4 points of damage from her freezing aura (save avoids). Her icy nature allows the ice maiden to walk freely in snow and ice without being hindered, and she can see perfectly through the heaviest blizzard. At will, she can turn invisible while in a snowy environment. Once per day, the ice maiden can cause a burst of snow to explode around her in a 30-foot radius. Any creature caught in this burst must make saving throw or be blinded for 1d4+1 rounds.

Once per day, an ice maiden can kiss an individual to freeze their heart. The target must make a saving throw or fall under the ice maiden's sway as a *charm person* spell. An ice maiden can have up to three servants at a time. *Dispel magic* can free a servant.

At will, an ice maiden can cast *detect magic* and *light*. Five times per day, she can cast *fear* and *obscuring mist*. Three times per day, she can cast *polymorph self* and *wall of ice*. Once per day, she can cast *ice storm*. An ice maiden is vulnerable to fire and takes double damage from flames and fire-based spells.

Ice Maiden: HD 5; AC 7[12]; **Atk** ice dagger (1d4 + 1d4 cold); **Move** 12; **Save** 12; **AL** C; **CL/XP** 9/1100; **Special:** +1 or better magic weapons to hit, chilling presence (15ft radius, 1d4 damage per round [save avoids], 45% chance to dispel cold protection magics), flurry form (1/day, 20ft radius, whirling snow cloud for 3 rounds, 2d6 damage), immune to cold, invisibility (at will in snowy environments), kiss of the frozen heart (1/day, freeze heart of target to create servant, save avoids), magic resistance (15%), snowblind burst (1/day, 30ft radius, save or blinded for 1d4+1 rounds), spell-like abilities, vulnerable to fire (200% damage).
Spell-like abilities: at will—*detect magic, light*; 5/day—*fear, obscuring mist*; 3/day—*polymorph self, wall of ice*; 1/day—*ice storm*.

ICHNEUMON

Hit Dice: 9
Armor Class: 5[14]
Attacks: 2 claws (1d6), bite (3d6)
Saving Throw: 6
Special: Mud armor, resistances (acid, cold, electricity, fire)
Move: 15
Alignment: Neutrality
Number Encountered: 1d3+1
Challenge Level: 10/1,400

An ichneumon resembles a rodent-like weasel grown to the size of a grizzly bear. The ichneumon is a dangerous opponent, with powerful jaws and sharp teeth that it uses to cut through the thick scales of dragons, whom it attacks on sight. They have a natural resistance to all dragons' deadly breath weapons, gaining a +3 bonus to their saving throw.

An ichneumon can roll in mud to coat itself. When this mud covering hardens, it adds a +2 bonus to the creature's armor class.

Ichneumon: HD 9; AC 5[14] or 3[16] from mud armor; **Atk** 2 claws (1d6), bite (3d6); **Move** 15; **Save** 6; **AL** N; **CL/XP** 10/1400; **Special:** mud armor (mud coating grants +2 AC bonus), resistances (acid, cold, electricity, fire).

JACULUS

Hit Dice: 5
Armor Class: 4[15]
Attacks: Bite (1d8), 2 claws (1d6)
Saving Throw: 12
Special: Charge, darkvision (60ft), immune to electricity, leap.
Move: 9/12/9 (fly/climb) or 30ft leap
Alignment: Chaos
Number Encountered: 1d3
Challenge Level: 6/400

A jaculus is a small, light-brown dragon that has feathered wings to propel it in flight. However, the creature prefers to leap at its prey, using its powerful back legs to cover up to 30 feet in a single bound. A jaculus uses its darkvision to sneak up on prey. It attacks with its bite and claws. If it charges at least 10 feet toward a target and makes a successful bite attack, it deals an additional 1d6 points of damage if the target fails a saving throw. A jaculus can be distracted with shiny objects, which infatuate the dragon. Despite its dragon-like appearance, the jaculus has no breath weapon. It is immune to electricity.

Jaculus: HD 5; AC 4[15]; **Atk** bite (2d6), 2 claws (1d6); **Move** 9 (fly 12, climb 9) or 30ft leap; **Save** 12; **AL** C; **CL/XP** 5/240; **Special:** charge (successful bite after 10ft move deals additional 1d6 bite damage, save avoids), darkvision (60ft), immune to electricity, leap (30ft).

MIQUITO ADDER

Hit Dice: 2
Armor Class: 5[14]
Attacks: Bite (1d8 + poison)
Saving Throw: 16
Special: Poison
Move: 12/12 (swim)
Alignment: Neutrality
Number Encountered: 1d4, 2d4
Challenge Level: 4/120

At first glance, this tiny black and gray snake has the appearance of a normal venomous snake. It can easily be mistaken for a small adder or another species with extremely intricate patterns embedded into its scale. However, on closer inspections the patterns bear strange symbols and stylized markings that indicate its supernatural origin. Miquito adders are almost exclusively confined to the Realm of the Dead unless a powerful being brings or summons them into the mortal world.

Miquito Adder: HD 2; AC 5[14]; **Atk** bite (1d8 + poison); **Move** 12 (swim 12); **Save** 16; **AL** N; **CL/XP** 4/120; **Special:** poison (save or die).

MINOTAUR, OBSIDIAN

Hit Dice: 12
Armor Class: –2[21]
Attacks: 2 claws (2d8 + 1d6 fire)
Saving Throw: 3
Special: Breath weapon, burn, immune to magic
Move: 9
Alignment: Neutrality
Number Encountered: 1d4
Challenge Level: 16/3,200

An obsidian minotaur stands 12 feet tall and weighs roughly 2,000 pounds. It appears to be a minotaur carved from a single block of obsidian and then animated via some eldritch ritual. Small pinpoints of blue light can be seen in its eyes.

Once every 1d4 + 1 rounds, an obsidian minotaur can expel a cloud of gas directly in front of it. The cloud fills a 10-foot cube and lasts for one round before dispersing. Any creature in the area must succeed on a saving throw or be slowed (as the *slow* spell).

The burning claws of an obsidian minotaur deal an additional 1d6 points of damage each time they hit if a creature fails a saving throw. The creature continues to take 1d6 points of fire damage for 1d4 + 1 rounds as its clothes ignite and its armor becomes searing hot.

An obsidian minotaur is immune to most spells although certain spells and effects function differently against the creature as noted below:

A *transmute rock to mud* spell slows it (as the *slow* spell) for 2d6 rounds, with no saving throw, while the reversed *transmute mud to rock* heals all of its lost hit points.

A *stone to flesh* spell does not actually change the obsidian minotaur's structure but negates its immunity to other magic for one full round.

Obsidian Minotaur: HD 12; AC –2[21]; **Atk** 2 claws (2d8 + 1d6 fire); **Move** 9; **Save** 3; **AL** N; **CL/XP** 16/3200; **Special:** breath weapon (every 1d4+1 rounds, 10ft cloud of gas, save or *slow* as spell), burn (after hit, save or take additional 1d6 damage that continues for 1d4+1 rounds), immune to magic (*transmute rock to mud* slows it for

2d6 rounds; *transmute mud to rock* heals all damage; *stone to flesh* negates its immunity to other magic for 1 round).

MOBAT

Hit Dice: 4
Armor Class: 3[16]
Attack: Bite (1d8)
Special: Sonic screech
Move: 9/15 (flying)
Saving Throw: 13
Alignment: Neutrality
Number Encountered: 1d3, 2d4
Challenge Level/XP: 6/400.

Mobats are large brown bats with razor-sharp fangs and green, glowing eyes. The mobat has a wingspan of approximately 15 feet. It is a nocturnal creature, cruising silently through the night sky in its never-ending quest for food. A mobat can blast an ear-splitting screech that affects all creatures within a 20-foot spread. The screech stuns any creature in the area for 1d3 rounds if it fails a saving throw. Mobats use echolocation to pinpoint creatures within 120 feet, allowing them to attack invisible opponents with no penalty.

Mobat: HD 4; AC 3[16]; **Atk** bite (1d8); **Move** 9 (fly 15); **Save** 13; **AL** N; **CL/XP** 6/400; **Special:** sonic screech (3/day, 20ft spread, fail or stunned for 1d3 rounds).

MONOLITH FOOTMAN

Hit Dice: 6
Armor Class: 5[14]
Attack: Longsword (1d8+1)
Special: +1 or better magic weapons to hit, fey flame, immunities, vulnerable to blunt weapons
Move: 12
Saving Throw: 11
Alignment: Neutrality
Number Encountered: 1d3
Challenge Level/XP: 8/800

Monolith footmen are the golem-like creations of the fey. These six-foot-tall creations are often carved into fantastical images by their fairy creators. They attack with a longsword (or a different carved weapon). Three times per day, the footman can imbue the weapon with cold or fire to deal additional damage. The footman is immune to normal weapons. Because of their delicate fey origin, a magical blunt weapon that hits with a natural 20 instantly destroys the footman (no save).

Monolith Footman: HD 6; AC 5[14]; **Atk** longsword (2d6) or slam (1d8+2); **Move** 12; **Save** 11; **AL** N; **CL/XP** 8/800; **Special:** +1 or better magic weapons to hit, fey flame (3/day, enhance longsword with additional 1d6 fire or cold damage), immunities (charm, fear, and sleep), vulnerable to magical blunt weapons (natural 20 destroys footman).

MUDBOG OOZE

Hit Dice: 3
Armor Class: 5[14]
Attack: Engulf
Special: Acid, engulf, immune to blunt weapons
Move: 3
Saving Throw: 14
Alignment: Neutrality
Number Encountered: 1, 1d2
Challenge Level/XP: 3/60

Mudbogs are slow-moving, pudding-like creatures that are brownish in color, resembling nothing more than brackish mud. The average mudbog is roughly 10 feet across and three feet deep. Mudbogs dig holes in the swamp and wait for creatures to blunder into their bodies. A mudbog secretes a digestive acid that dissolves organic material (leather armor, wooden clubs, etc.) and deals 1d6 points of damage. Any being that stumbles into a mudbog is considered engulfed and automatically takes 1d6 points of damage from the creature's acidic nature in the rounds thereafter.

Mudbog Ooze: HD 3; AC 5[14]; **Atk** engulf (save avoids); **Move** 3; **Save** 14; **AL** N; **CL/XP** 3/60; **Special:** acid (1d6 damage, dissolves organic material), engulf (automatic 1d6 damage per round), immune to blunt weapons.

PHOOKA

Hit Dice: 4
Armor Class: 5[14]
Attack: Weapon (1d3)
Special: Alternate form, magic resistance (16%), spell-like abilities, tree stride
Move: 6
Saving Throw: 13
Alignment: Neutrality
Number Encountered: 1d4
Challenge Level/XP: 5/240

A phooka is a small hairy creature resembling a cross between a goblin and a child's fuzzy play bear. Phookas have wide-set, glowing, golden eyes and long, pointed ears like those of a donkey. They have a mouth to match their ears, complete with buck teeth. Phookas are tricksters and jokesters that revel in playing tricks on unwary travelers. A phooka's trickery may include turning itself into an enchanted pony and offer a stranger a ride, only to run through brambles and thorns at top speed. Or it may lead travelers to enchanted springs that cause them to fall into a deep slumber and then strip them of all their belongings and clothes, although it then leaves behind clues as to where their possessions are hidden. A phooka can assume the shape of a mountain lion or wolf. They can create dancing lights three times per day. A phooka can enter a tree and move from it to another tree within 50 feet.

Phooka: HD 4; AC 5[14]; **Atk** weapon (1d3); **Move** 6; **Save** 13; **AL** N; **CL/XP** 5/240; **Special:** alternate form (mountain lion or wolf), magic resistance (16%), spell-like abilities, tree stride (50ft range). **Spell-like abilities:** 3/day—create dancing lights.

PURPLE SLIME

Hit Dice: 5
Armor Class: 8[11]
Attacks: 2 spikes (1d8 + 1d6 acid)
Saving Throw: 12
Special: Acid, immune to acid and cold
Move: 9/9/9 (climb/swim)
Alignment: Neutrality
Number Encountered: 1d3
Challenge Level: 5/240

Purple slime is an amorphous slime that propels itself on pseudopods. It can transform these limbs into hardened spikes that it uses to attack its prey. Any foe struck by a spike must make a saving throw or suffer an additional 1d6 points of acid damage. The slime is usually a dark color that tends toward purple.

Purple Slime: HD 5; AC 8[11]; **Atk** 2 spikes (1d8 + 1d6 acid); **Move** 9 (climb 9, swim 9); **Save** 12; **AL** N; **CL/XP** 5/240; **Special:** acid (additional 1d6 damage with strike, save avoids), immune to acid and cold.

RETCH HOUND

Hit Dice: 3
Armor Class: 5[14]
Attacks: Bite (1d8)
Saving Throw: 14
Special: Breath weapon, stench
Move: 18
Alignment: Neutrality
Number Encountered: 1, 1d6
Challenge Level: 4/120

Retch hounds are large, muscular dogs with sickly brownish-yellow fur that is often matted or torn in places. Small sores cover its body, each oozing a thick, yellowish-green liquid. Its mouth is filled with long pointed yellow teeth, some broken off on the ends. A retch hound has four large yellow eyes evenly aligned across its canine head. A typical retch hound stands 4 to 4-1/2 feet tall at the shoulder and weighs about 150 pounds. A sickening stench surrounds a retch hound, nauseating opponents who approach within 30 feet unless they make a saving throw. Once per round, a retch hound can belch forth a blast of digestive acid in a 10-foot cone (2d6 damage, save for half).

Retch Hound: HD 3; AC 5[14]; **Atk** bite (1d8); **Move** 18; **Save** 14; **AL** N; **CL/XP** 4/120; **Special:** Breath weapon (1/round, 10ft cone, 2d6 damage, save for half), stench (30ft radius, save or nauseated, −1 to hit and saves).

SIGHTLESS SERVANT

Hit Dice: 8
Armor Class: 6[13]
Attacks: Weapon (1d8)
Saving Throw: 8
Special: Life drain
Move: 12
Alignment: Chaos
Number Encountered: 1d4
Challenge Level: 9/1,100

Sightless servants appear to be humans except with faded bluish skin. They keep their eyes wrapped in gauze, though their bandaged eyes leak a black fluid that stains their cheeks with ebon streaks. These waning souls refuse to travel to their final resting places, but instead wander the Great Void, seeking the pieces of their dismembered savior, Ixqumilli, the blindfolded one. They collect these pieces and then feed them the life essences siphoned from other beings to fully restore their god's divine powers.

Three times per day, a sightless servant can drain the life essence of a single creature within a 30-foot radius. The target must make a saving throw or take 2d6 points of damage. The sightless servant gains the damage done as hit points.

Sightless Servant: HD 8; AC 6[13]; **Atk** weapon (1d8); **Move** 12; **Save** 8; **AL** N; **CL/XP** 9/1100; **Special:** life drain.

SKELETON, BLACK

Hit Dice: 6
Armor Class: 4[15]
Attack: Weapon (1d6) or 2 claws (1d4)
Special: Shriek
Move: 12
Saving Throw: 11
Alignment: Neutrality
Number Encountered: 1d4, 3d6
Challenge Level/XP: 6/400

A black skeleton is a six-foot-tall skeleton with glistening black bones seemingly constructed of blackened steel. Small red pinpoints of light burn in its hollowed eye sockets. Black skeletons wear any clothes or armor they had in life, and some still carry their gear and weapons. A black skeleton can shriek a hellish sound that causes fear (save avoids).

Skeleton, Black: HD 6; AC 4[15]; **Atk** weapon (1d6) or 2 claws (1d4); Move 12; Save 11; AL N; CL/XP 6/400; **Special:** shriek (30ft radius, save or flee in fear).

SKELETON, VINE TROLL

Hit Dice: 7
Armor Class: 6[13]
Attack: 2 claws (1d6), bite (1d8)
Special: Immune to sleep and charm, regenerate
Move: 12
Saving Throw: 8
Alignment: Neutrality
Number Encountered: 1d4, 2d6
Challenge Level/XP: 8/800

A vine troll skeleton is wrapped in the living vines created by a duskthorn dryad. The vine-covered remains are often found lurking in the shadows of dead trees, where they serve their dryad creators. They are immune to sleep and charm spells, and regenerate three hit points per round.

Vine Troll Skeleton: HD 7; AC 6[13]; **Atk** 2 claws (1d6), bite (1d8); Move 12; Save 9; AL N; CL/XP 8/800; **Special:** immune to sleep and charm, regenerate (3hd/round).

SPAWN OF TLATOANI

Hit Dice: 7
Armor Class: 6[13]
Attack: Bite (1d8 + poison) or barbed tongue (2d6 + constrict)
Special: Constrict, fear aura, immune to cold, poison
Move: 12
Saving Throw: 9
Alignment: Chaos
Number Encountered: 1d4
Challenge Level/XP: 9/1,100

The spawn of Tlatoani are huge, mummified serpents that slither in the darkness. Withered and desiccated flesh stretches tightly across its skeletal frame. The origin of these foul, undead abominations remains shrouded in mystery, though religious scholars believe the former lord of Tehuatl and the whole of Notos crafted these undying horrors from pythons. The ritual used to make these creatures has been lost to time, as the only known specimens are found in places closely associated with the southern continent's former master.

Measuring roughly 10 feet in length from snout to tail, the monster attacks with its fearsome bite and its surprisingly supple tongue that somehow survived the mummification ritual largely intact. The tongue can strike a target up to 15 feet away from the spawn. If it hits, the target must make a saving throw or be constricted and take 1d6 points of damage per round until freed. The spawn of Tlatoani cannot use its bite attack while it is constricting an opponent.

Spawn of Tlatoani are immune to cold. Anyone within 10 feet of the undead serpent must make a saving throw or flee (as per a *fear* spell).

Spawn of Tlatoani: HD 7; AC 6[13]; **Atk** bite (1d8 + poison) or barbed tongue (2d6 + constrict); **Move** 12; **Save** 9; AL C; CL/XP 9/1100; **Special:** constrict (automatic 1d6 damage per round until freed), fear aura (10ft radius, save or frightened as *fear* spell), immune to cold, poison (save or die).

SPÖKVATTEN

Hit Dice: 8
Armor Class: 5[14]
Attack: Cold touch (2d4 + paralysis)
Special: Cold touch, icy fog, immune to cold, paralysis, shape change
Move: 12/12/12 (swim/fly)

Saving Throw: 8
Alignment: Neutrality
Number Encountered: 1d3
Challenge Level/XP: 10/1,400

The wicked fey known as the spökvatten lives in lonely ponds, streams, and waterfalls, lying in wait for its prey. In its natural form, a spökvatten resembles a beautiful elven woman with pale skin, long black hair, and pupil-less black eyes. When prey (animals or humanoids) approaches, the spökvatten can transform into a cold, clinging mist. When hunting animals, the creature can simply envelop its prey in a chill grasp to paralyze and kill it. Intelligent prey requires more subtlety, and in such cases, the spökvatten can take on the shape of any animal or humanoid — impersonating an especially impressive target for hunters, a lost child, or an especially attractive individual to draw its quarry closer.

A spökvatten's freezing touch causes paralysis in a creature that fails a saving throw. Three times per day, the fey can breathe forth an icy fog in a 15-foot cone that does 6d6 points of damage (save for half). The spökvatten can shape change at will into a mist form, an animal, or a humanoid.

Spökvatten: HD 8; AC 5[14]; **Atk** cold touch (2d4 + paralysis); Move 12 (swim 12, fly 12 [mist cloud only]); **Save** 8; AL N; CL/XP 10/1400; **Special:** cold touch, darkvision (60ft), icy fog (3/day, 15ft cone, 6d6 damage, save for half), immune to cold, paralysis (save or frozen for 1d4 rounds), shape change (at will, cloud of mist, beast, or humanoid).

SWARM, BONE

Hit Dice: 10
Armor Class: 7[12]
Attacks: Swirling bones (2d6)
Saving Throw: 5
Special: Immune to sleep and charm, resist slashing weapons
Move: 9/18 (fly)
Alignment: Neutrality
Number Encountered: 1
Challenge Level: 10/1,400

A bone swarm appears to be a pile of scattered bones until it rises up as a single entity. Bone swarms move along the ground in large heaps until prey causes the jagged bones to swirl into the air to attack. The mindless swarm is immune to sleep and charm spells and takes half damage from edged and slashing weapons.

Bone Swarm: HD 10; AC 6[13]; **Atk** swirling bones (2d6); **Move** 9 (fly 18); **Save** 5; AL N; CL/XP 10/1400; **Special:** immune to sleep and charm, resist slashing weapons (50% damage).

SWARM, CHOM

Hit Dice: 5
Armor Class: 5[14]
Attacks: Swarm (1d6)
Saving Throw: 12
Special: Cast omen, mimicry, soul steal
Move: 4/18 (fly)
Alignment: Neutrality
Number Encountered: 1d4
Challenge Level: 7/600

Choms are supernatural raven-like birds that the gods punished by taking away their once bright and colorful plumage after they betrayed them. They appear during auspicious times. Sorcerers and witches portend their appearance as a grim omen, for their arrival never occurs by happenstance. As further punishment for their misdeeds, choms must serve the deities and other supernatural beings of Tehuatl. They possess the ability to pass between the realms of the living and the dead, and frequently carry messages between the gods or deliver them in the form of omens to mortal humans. They can also transport mortal souls. Despite the lies and deceptions that led to their undoing, choms habitually speak in half-truths and riddles, and attempt to deceive anyone they encounter, including powerful supernatural beings whom they often serve.

Any creature meeting the gaze of a flock of choms must make a saving throw or be cursed with an evil omen. For the next 24 hours, the creature suffers a –1 penalty to hit, damage, and saving throws.

If the chom swarm encounters a sleeping or incapacitated creature, the flock attacks and attempts to steal the creature's soul from its body. The target must make a saving throw to resist this theft. If the target fails, the chom takes its soul and consumes it. The soul resides within the chom, which can carry it about and regurgitate it, typically as a gift to a more powerful entity tied to the Land of the Dead that choms often serve. If the chom perishes or if the soul is destroyed, the creature to whom the soul belonged also perishes with his immortal soul forced to exist for all eternity in the level of the Land of the Dead where the chom's servitor entity resides. Similarly, should the individual whose soul has been stolen perish, his soul is forced to the servitor's plane. A being whose soul has been taken cannot be raised, resurrected, or otherwise saved from this fate (even via a *wish* spell). A chom swarm can hold only a single soul at a time.

Chom Swarm: HD 5; AC 5[14]; **Atk** swarm (1d8); **Move** 4 (fly 18); **Save** 12; **AL** N; **CL/XP** 7/600; **Special:** cast omen (1/day, targets meeting gaze of flock, save or –1 to hit, saves, and damage for 24 hours), mimicry (simple sounds), soul steal (against incapacitated or sleeping foe, soul is stolen and held within the flock, save avoids).

SWARM, POISONOUS FROG

Hit Dice: 4
Armor Class: 8[11]
Attacks: Swarm (1d6 + poison)
Saving Throw: 13
Special: Poison
Move: 9
Alignment: Neutrality
Number Encountered: 1d6
Challenge Level: 4/120

Poisonous frog swarms are composed of small, fierce, poisonous frogs. A single poisonous frog is small and dark green, with black bands or stripes on its hind legs. These stripes function as a warning to predators that the frog is poisonous. The skin of a poisonous frog is very smooth to the touch. The middle digit on each of its extremities is slightly shorter than the others. A poisonous frog swarm delivers its poison with a successful swarm attack. Creatures that fail a saving throw die from the deadly poison.

Poisonous Frog Swarm: HD 4; AC 8[11]; **Atk** swarm (1d6 + poison); **Move** 9; **Save** 13; **AL** N; **CL/XP** 4/120; **Special:** poison (save or die).

TROLL, SWAMP

Hit Dice: 3
Armor Class: 3[16]
Attack: 2 claws (1d6), bite (1d8)
Special: Surprise, swamp dependent
Move: 12
Saving Throw: 14
Alignment: Chaos
Number Encountered: 1
Challenge Level/XP: 3/60

Swamp trolls are large, stocky, dark gray or brown hunched humanoids with large, upward-curving fangs jutting from their lower jaws. Their flesh is slick and slimy like moss. Swamp trolls make their lairs deep in swampland and marshes away from more settled areas, but not far enough away where they cannot hunt humans if game and other food runs scarce in the swamps. Swamp trolls are seven-foot-tall hunched humanoids and weigh about 400 pounds. Swamp trolls speak the language of trolls.

Swamp trolls keep their bodies covered in a thick coating of mud and swamp water. Without such a coating, they eventually suffocate. They can survive away from their murky home for 10 hours. After that, they suffocate.

Troll, Swamp: HD 3; AC 3[16]; **Atk** 2 claws (1d6), bite (1d8); **Move** 12; **Save** 14; **AL** C; **CL/XP** 3/60; **Special:** surprise (1–2 on 1d6), swamp dependent (suffocate after 10 hours away from water).

T'SHANN

Hit Dice: 4
Armor Class: 9[10]
Attack: Strike (1d4)
Special: Alien thoughts, spew
Move: 5/5 (burrow)
Saving Throw: 13
Alignment: Neutrality
Number Encountered: 1d6, 2d8
Challenge Level/XP: 4/120

The slug-like t'shann has a cylindrical body and a mass of dripping, writhing tentacles at its head. It is brownish gray, with patches of green and black blotches scattered unevenly over its body. Its underside is pasty off-white in color and ripples with the muscular contractions that move the creature along. T'shanns burrow through earth and stone to consume the minerals trapped in the rock. They range anywhere from two to four feet long.

The alien brainwaves of a t'shann have a bizarre effect on intelligent creatures. All opponents within 30 feet of a t'shann must save or be affected as if by a confusion spell. If opponents approach to within 10 feet, they must succeed on another save or suffer 1d4 points of damage for as long as they remain within 10 feet of the t'shann.

A t'shann can emit a spray of powerful acids from nearly every pore on its body, affecting any creature within 10 feet of it. This acidic spray does 1d4 points of acid damage (save for half damage).

T'shann: HD 4; AC 9[10]; **Atk** strike (1d4); **Move** 5 (burrow 5); **Save** 13; **AL** N; **CL/XP** 4/120; **Special:** alien thoughts (30ft range, save or affected by *confusion* spell; within 10ft, save or 1d4 damage), spew (10ft range, acid spray, 1d4 damage, save for half).

TUKKURU GARGOYLE

Hit Dice: 3
Armor Class: 6[13]
Attacks: 2 claws (1d4), bite (1d3)
Saving Throw: 14
Special: +1 or better magic weapons to hit
Move: 9
Alignment: Neutrality
Number Encountered: 1d6, 2d8
Challenge Level: 3/60

Standing only two feet tall, Tukkuru gargoyles appear to be living stone, yet the stocky creatures waddle about with a playful air. These sentient beings are distant relatives of ordinary gargoyles that have formed strong bonds with several remote humanoid communities, most notably the residents of Alataq. They display no malevolence like most of their kin, and some even become adopted family members. The jovial creatures perform basic household chores for their humanoid companions. People who gain the affection of a tukkuru gargoyle generally have a friend for life. Unfortunately, these gargoyles have the same lifespan of domesticated pets such as cats and dogs. Unlike the latter animals, they neither eat, drink, nor breathe.

Tukkuru Gargoyle: HD 3; AC 6[13]; **Atk** 2 claws (1d3), bite (1d4); **Move** 9; **Save** 14; **AL** N; **CL/XP** 3/60; **Special:** +1 or better magic weapon to hit.

UNRESURRECTED WRAITH

Hit Dice: 6
Armor Class: 3[16]
Attacks: Spectral touch (1d6 cold + level drain)
Saving Throw: 11
Special: +1 or better magic or silver weapons to hit, breath of the dead, immune to sleep and charm, level drain, resistances (cold, electricity), spell-like ability, vulnerable to sunlight
Move: 18 (fly)

Alignment: Chaos
Number Encountered: 1
Challenge Level: 9/1,100

An unresurrected wraith is a sinister incorporeal figure with malevolent red eyes that can expel a cloud of black mist from its open mouth to incapacitate its foes. These woeful beings remain bound to the mortal world, trapped for all eternity in the perfectly mummified corpses of their former bodies, only to be awakened and transformed into incorporeal horrors under specific circumstances. They cannot voluntarily transform into their incorporeal form and thus remain bound forever to the pacts and magics of their creators.

Many of these creatures willingly enter bargains to serve as the guardian of a sacred place only to learn in death that the fate bestowed to them is not an honor but a cruel curse. They remain trapped in their mummified forms until someone triggers the conditions set by their creator (such as violating the sanctity of the master's tomb). However, when the task is completed, the unresurrected wraith rises to reap its vengeance upon the living whose very presence mocks its sorrowful existence.

The wraith's touch deals 1d6 points of cold damage but also drains a level if the target fails a saving throw. Three times per day, the wraith can exhale a deadly breath that creates a 30-foot line of black mist that does 3d6 points of damage (save for half) to creatures caught in it. Once per day, an unresurrected wraith can cast *finger of death*.

The wraith can be hit only by magic or silver weapons. It takes 1d6 points of damage per round if exposed to sunlight.

Unresurrected Wraith: HD 6; AC 3[16]; Atk spectral touch (1d6 cold + level drain); **Move** 18 (fly); **Save** 11; **AL** C; **CL/XP** 9/1100; **Special:** +1 or better magic or silver weapons to hit, breath of the dead (3/day, 30ft line of mist, 3d6 damage, save for half), immune to sleep and charm, level drain (1 level with touch, save resists), resistances (cold, electricity, 50% damage), spell-like ability, vulnerable to sunlight (1d6 damage per round, no save). **Spell-like ability:** 1/day—*finger of death*.

WAHUAPA (MAIZEFOLK)

Hit Dice: 7
Armor Class: 7[12]
Attacks: 2 claws (1d6 + blood meal)
Saving Throw: 9
Special: Blood meal, camouflage, entangle
Move: 9
Alignment: Neutrality
Number Encountered: 1 or 1d10
Challenge Level/XP: 8/800

Wahuapas (which are also known as maizefolk) are stalks of corn or maize that move on tendrilled, fibrous legs. One ear of maize at the top of the plant's central stalk seems to function as its crude brain, though the monstrosity lacks eyes, ears, or any other discernible sensory organ or orifice. They are often indistinguishable from normal stalks of corn or maize in which they hide (1-in-6 chance to spot if motionless). Wahuapas attack with their sharp, serrated leaves, which slash their opponents. If the target fails a saving throw, it takes an additional 1d4 points of damage. The wahuapa feasts on the spilled blood to heal itself (gaining hit points equal to the damage done). Three times per day, a wahuapa can cause plants to grow in a 10-foot radius within a 60-foot radius of the creature. A creature caught in the tangle of plants must make an Open Doors check to escape.

Wahuapa (Maizefolk): HD 7; AC 7[12]; Atk 2 claws (1d6 + blood meal); **Move** 9; **Save** 9; **AL** N; **CL/XP** 8/800; **Special:** blood meal (save or additional 1d4 damage, wahuapa gains hit points equal to damage), camouflage (1-in-6 chance to spot while standing still in maizefield), entangle (3/day, plants grow in 10ft radius within 60ft range, save or restrained, Open Doors check to escape).

XOCO TEPEYOLLOTL

Hit Dice: 9
Armor Class: 4[15]
Attacks: Weapon (1d8+2) or bite (1d8)
Saving Throw: 6
Special: +1 or better magic weapons to hit, fearful visage, immune to charm and fear, Jaguar God's sacrifice, magic resistance (20% and reflects spell at caster), spell-like abilities, telepathy (60ft)
Move: 15
Alignment: Neutrality
Number Encountered: 1 or 1d4+2
Challenge Level/XP: 11/1,700

The xoco tepeyollotl are towering jaguar-headed woman warriors whose bodies are decorated with scars and the ancient mystic tattoos that mark them as the daughter of a god. Their long fangs gleam with jadeite inlays. The xoco tepeyollotl are the surviving daughters of the deceased god Tepeyollotl, the great jaguar whose children destroyed the first race of aluxes. Neutral in countenance and devoted to their father, they serve as the guardians of the Pale Portal and similar divine gateways that the dead and the divine use to traverse the many diverse layers of existence. They possess great martial prowess as well as a fair amount of knowledge concerning divine law and magic, though they are wise and intelligent enough to reason with those who seek passage through the portals that the hero-gods have granted them the authority to watch over.

Xoco Tepeyollotl: HD 9; AC 4[15]; Atk weapon (1d8+2) or bite (1d8); **Move** 15; **Save** 6; **AL** N; **CL/XP** 11/1700; **Special:** +1 or better magic weapons to hit, fearful visage (30ft radius, save or flee as *fear* spell), immune to charm and fear, Jaguar God's sacrifice (the heart of slain being has a 45% chance of exploding and healing xoco tepeyollotl for 1d8 hit points), magic resistance (20% and reflects spell back at caster), spell-like abilities, telepathy (60ft). **Spell-like abilities:** at will—*detect evil, ESP, phantasmal force*; 3/day—*nohpalli^C, jaguar spirit^C*; 1/day—*palpitating heart^C, teleport*.
^C See **Appendix C: New Spells**

ZOMBIE, NIHILETHIC

Hit Dice: 2
Armor Class: 9[10]
Attacks: Strike (1d8 + 1d6 withering touch [3/day])
Saving Throw: 16
Special: Ethereal, immune to charm and sleep, withering touch
Move: 9/12 (swim)
Alignment: Neutrality
Number Encountered: 1d6, 3d4
Challenge Level: 3/60

Nihilethic zombies are undead created by nihileth aboleths. Their skin is translucent and shiny. These zombies are excellent swimmers that move faster in the water than on land. A nihilethic zombie attacks with its claws and bite. Three times per day, the undead can deliver a withering touch to a target it strikes to deliver an additional 1d6 points of damage, or half that if a creature succeeds on a saving throw.

At will, a nihilethic zombie can assume an ethereal form that appears as a dark purple outline of its material form, with a blackish-purple haze within. It can be struck only with magical weapons while in this ethereal form.

An injured nihileth aboleth can drain a nihilethic zombie within 60 feet to heal itself in the amount of the zombie's current hit points. This destroys the zombie.

Nihilethic Zombie: HD 2; AC 9[10]; Atk strike (1d8 + 1d6 withering touch [3/day]); **Move** 9 (swim 12); **Save** 16; **AL** N; **CL/XP** 3/60; **Special:** ethereal (+1 or better magic weapons to hit), immune to charm and sleep spells, withering touch (3/day, 1d6 damage, save resists).

APPENDIX B: NEW EQUIPMENT AND MAGIC ITEMS

The people of Tehuatl rarely sit still, physically or mentally. Their intellectual curiosity inspires them to constantly search for knowledge, while their ingenuity allows them to apply their newfound discoveries to aid them in their endeavors. A miniscule handful of technological advances are predominately confined to small corners of the island for various reasons, but the overwhelming majority of groundbreaking inventions spread across Tehuatl at breakneck speeds as local artisans and scholars devise innovative ways to enhance the original creation. The following chapter presents a broad overview of these wondrous devices ranging from armor, weapons, clothing, gear, and, of course, magic items.

NEW ARMOR

Steel and heavy armor fare poorly in Tehuatl's humid, semitropical climate. Over time, frequent rainfall and the moisture in the air take a toll on the ferrous metal's durability. Magical equipment ignores the ravages of rust, but being encapsulated within a thick shell of metal on a hot, sticky afternoon under the sun's relentless glare feels like a hellish torment. The island's weather conditions and environment generally lead most warriors to value flexibility and comfort over maximizing protection. Of course, some individuals choose the latter options, most notably the Firebrand dwarves of the Tepepan Mountains, the elves who still prefer chain shirts, and the Tlotls who closely guard the secrets of forging steel. Nonetheless, the bulk of the new armor and shields presented in the following section adheres to the principles of providing lightweight defensive options without compromising stealth and mobility.

LIGHT ARMOR

This defensive equipment typically consists of thin, flexible material stitched together in layers to provide stopping power against projectiles and sharp implements as well as deadening the impact of bludgeoning weapons that strike the armor.

Ichcahuipilli. This two-inch-thick light armor resembles a vest designed to protect the wearer's torso from the neck to the hips against arrows and sharp blades. It consists of layers of cotton and vegetable fiber stitched together in a network of interconnected diamond-shaped patterns and then soaked in brine or another saline solution to harden the materials.

Tlahuiztli. Made from cotton or linen supplemented by hide or leather, this light armor covers the wearer's arms and legs and is worn over the ichcahuipilli. Unlike the basic undercoat, the tlahuiztli almost always boasts elaborate decorative features such as feathers, dyes, and other ornamental accoutrements. The armor's intricate and beautiful designs flaunt the wearer's wealth and status. The tlahuiztli presented in **Table 3–1** incorporates the underlying ichcahuipilli in its cost, weight, and game statistics.

MEDIUM ARMOR

Protective gear falling into this category provides added defense at the expense of mobility. Supple materials are generally combined with more rigid, durable components to allow the wearer to better fend off attacks while not bogging him down with overly heavy gear.

Cipacahuipilli. This unusual armor follows the basic schematics for creating ichcahuipilli armor with a few modifications. Surprisingly, this armor is thinner than its lighter counterpart, but the flat pieces of hide and bone strategically sewn into the fabric adequately compensate for its lesser thickness. The armor's name comes from the flat sections of crocodile vertebrae and hide stitched into the material at vulnerable spots to improve toughness without adding tremendous weight and bulkiness. Most importantly, the armor's lack of metallic pieces or parts makes it immune to rust and suitable for druids.

Olli. Armor smiths combine latex and the juice from a morning glory vine to create a flexible and resilient material resembling modern rubber. Although typically used to create the tlatchli, clever innovators use the durable substance to protect warriors from injury. The lightweight suit includes a jacket and leggings. An inner and outer lining of breathable linen provides added comfort. While wearing this armor, you reduce any falling damage you take by 1d6 points, though you cannot reduce the falling damage below 0. Because it is made from plant-based products, druids are permitted to wear olli, and it is immune to rust.

HEAVY ARMOR

Those willing to sacrifice mobility and comfort for added protection ultimately turn to heavy armor. This category of defensive equipment covers the entire body with hard, sturdy materials with the strength to deflect projectiles and even powerful blows from a melee weapon.

Ollixalli. One day, Atoyapaca, an innovative botanist and renowned jeweler, heated olli and combined it with ground quartz to enhance its strength. His bold experiment exceeded his wildest expectations, leading others to follow in its footsteps by adding other silica-based and sulfurous components to the liquified olli mixture. The delicate and laborious process of creating ollixalli is a tightly guarded secret confined to those who have the technical expertise and specialized equipment required to set the ollixalli mold. Unlike conventional heavy armor, a suit of ollixalli consists of a lightweight jacket and pants that protect the torso and limbs. Ollixalli has no metal components, making it suitable for druids and immune to rust. Because of the specialized training and equipment needed to create ollixalli, the armor remains extremely expensive and rare.

TABLE B–1: TEHUATL ARMOR

Armor Type	Effect on AC from base 9[10]	Weight[1] (pounds)	Cost
Light Armor			
Ichcahuipilli	−1[+1]	4	15 gp
Tlahuiztli	−2[+2]	6	200 gp
Medium Armor			
Cipacahuipilli	−3[+3]	15	75 gp
Olli	−4[+4]	12	75 gp
Heavy Armor			
Ollixalli	−5[+5]	25	1,000 gp

[1] Magical armor weighs half normal

Weapon	Damage	Weight (pounds)	Cost
Melee Weapons			
Itztopilli	1d6	2	4 gp
Macuahuitl	1d8[1]	2	10 gp
Ollitetlacotl	1d6	1	35 gp
Ollitztli	1d6	1	40 gp
Tecpatl	1d4[2]	1	2 gp
Tepoztopilli	1d10[3]	6	25 gp

Weapon	Damage	Rate of Fire	Range[4]	Weight (pounds)	Cost
Simple Ranged Weapon					
Atlatl	1d6	1	30 ft.	1	1 sp

[1] Deals double damage on roll of 19–20; deep cut does 1d4 additional damage per round; second deep cut raises continual damage to 1d6; roll of 1 damages weapon and imposes –1 to-hit penalty; second roll of 1 destroys weapon

[2] Deals double damage on roll of 19–20; deep cut does 1d4 additional damage per round; second deep cut raises continual damage to 1d6; roll of 1 destroys weapon

[3] Deals double damage on roll of 20; deep cut does 1d4 additional damage per round; second deep cut raises continual damage to 1d6; roll of 1 damages weapon and imposes –1 to-hit penalty; second roll of 1 destroys weapon

[4] Shooting or throwing beyond this range is at a –2 penalty to hit. The weapon cannot reach farther than twice this range. Outdoors, these range increments are tripled.

New Weapons

The lack of iron and steel has never hampered the island's weapon designers. The craftsmen who build implements of war emphasize creativity over components. Used properly, wood, stone, and other natural materials can be deadlier than a metal sword. Obsidian, a viciously sharp volcanic glass, takes a prominent role in this arms race. Its edges are keener than any steel blade, allowing the hard, brittle material to slice through flesh and bone with surgical precision. Yet achieving this incredible cutting edge also makes obsidian vulnerable to fracturing when it comes into contact with a hard object. Despite these breakthroughs, some of Tehuatl's inhabitants, most notably the Firebrand dwarves of the Tepepan Mountains, still place their trust in the forge's molten steel.

Atlatl. This easily made wooden device uses javelins for ammunition. To use this javelin launcher, you must place the javelin's butt into a cup, groove, or spur at the top of the atlatl. With your forearm perpendicular to your arm and the atlatl and javelin both parallel to the ground, you let the javelin rest atop your fingers while you hold the atlatl's base in the palm of your hand. When you are ready to release the javelin, you fling your forearm and wrist forward, which in turn pushes the javelin out of your hand toward the intended target.

Itztopilli. This axe has a wooden haft with a bronze head fitted into a groove built into the haft. The head is long and narrow, and its cutting surface is only slightly wider than the axe's flat back. The itztopilli's versatile design allows you to hack into flesh as well as chop wood with remarkable accuracy and comparable ease. Indeed, most woodworkers incorporate the weapon into a standard set of carpenter's tools. *Macuahuitl.* Made from hardwood such as oak, this weapon resembles a long, flat paddle with obsidian or flint chips embedded into the weapon's edges. The insertion of these incredibly sharp stones gives the weapon unmatched cutting power at the cost of increased fragility. When you attack a creature with this weapon and roll a 19 or 20 on the attack roll, the weapon deals double damage. Furthermore, the creature struck loses 1d4 hit points each round due to the blade gouging a deep laceration through its flesh. The damage increases by 1d6 if you inflict another deep laceration during a subsequent attack. However,

when you attack a creature with this weapon and roll a 1, you damage the weapon. Your attacks with the weapon suffer a –1 to-hit penalty, and you can no longer inflict a deep laceration. If you damage an already damaged weapon, the weapon breaks, rendering it useless. *Ollitetlacotl.* This hardened rubber club is difficult to manufacture yet greatly valued among Aztli warriors for its lightweight punching power. Because of its unusual components and unique feel, the weapon requires more skill and training to wield than an ordinary club.

Ollitztli. Almost identical in its size, shape, and general appearance to the ollitetlacotl, this vicious weapon has an important added enhancement over its similar counterpart. When the olli starts to harden yet retains some malleability,

the makers embed obsidian slivers into the weapon, riddling its surface with dozens of slightly raised spikes that puncture flesh like fine needles. Unlike the macuahuitl, which uses obsidian chips to form a contiguous edge, only tiny slivers of obsidian protrude above the weapon's surface, giving it a rough texture akin to a vine covered in tiny, fine-yet-rigid needles. Although the weapon lacks the ability to rip through flesh and bone like the macuahuitl, the tiny needles excel at delivering poison to a victim.

Tecpatl. Carved from flint or obsidian, this double-edged knife has a pointed tip and a decorative wooden, stone, or mosaic handle. Although an effective, close-quarters combat weapon, the tecpatl is predominately used in religious rites and revered for its multitude of symbolic roles. When used in battle, it may open a deep laceration in the same manner as described under the **macuahuitl** entry (see above). However, because the knife itself is made entirely of flint or obsidian, the weapon irreparably breaks instead of being damaged when you roll a 1 on your attack roll with the weapon.

Tepoztopilli. This polearm has two components: a five- to six-foot-long wooden shaft carved from a single piece of wood and an oblong wooden head attached to the end of the shaft. The head ends in a sharp point, and like the macuahuitl, obsidian fragments are glued into grooves cut into the head to increase its deadly cutting power. When used in battle, it may open a deep laceration as described under the **macuahuitl** entry (see above). However, because such a blow requires greater precision than the macuahuitl, you inflict a deep laceration only when you roll a 20. Despite its surface area being much smaller than the macuahuitl, you still damage the weapon when you roll a 1. A second roll of 1 destroys the weapon.

Adventuring Gear

Like their armor and weaponry, Tehuatl's adventurers capitalize on the ingredients at hand to create potent concoctions and wondrous instruments to give adventurers more than a fighting chance in a dangerous world. These tools of the trade incorporate the designers' understanding of botany, astronomy, mathematics, and other scientific disciplines into these creations.

Table B–3: Tehuatl Adventuring Gear

Item	Cost	Weight (pounds)
Cempohualxochi (vial)	50 gp	—
Chilli (vial)	50 gp	—
Coanenepilli (vial)	50 gp	—
Copal glue (flask)	100 gp	1
Cuitlapan	3 gp	5
Iyollo (vial)	75 gp	—

Item	Cost	Weight (pounds)
Kindling sticks	1 cp	1
Mictlampa	100 gp	1
Ollicactli	50 gp	—
Ollixima (vial)	25 gp	—
Passiflora (vial)	50 gp	—
Rust dust (vial)	25 gp	—
Tecuaniz (flask)	25 gp	—
Tlilitl (vial)	25 gp	—
Uictli	2 gp	5
Xochitl (vial)	50 gp	—
Zoyoyatic (flask)	20 gp	—

Cempohualxochi. A creature that drinks this vial of liquid made from marigolds gains a +1 bonus on saving throws for 1 hour.

Chilli. Made from the spiciest peppers on the island, this vial may be used as a food additive to enhance flavor and add heat to a dish when used in small doses — or it can be used to harmful effect. If you add the entire vial to food or liquid, the creature who eats or drinks an item containing chilli must succeed on a saving throw or be blinded for 1d6 + 2 rounds and unable to speak. Alternatively, you can splash the contents of this vial onto a creature within five feet of you, or you can throw it up to 20 feet to shatter on impact. When you splash the chilli or throw it, make a ranged attack against a target creature. A creature struck by chilli must succeed on a saving throw or be blinded for 1d4 + 2 rounds. A creature struck by chilli can still speak, unlike a creature who ingests chilli.

Coanenepilli. A creature can apply or administer this salve to an injury or wound to heal 2d6 points of damage or to halt ongoing injury from a physical attack that poisoned the creature.

Copal Glue. When mixed, this amalgamation of cooked resin from copal and pine trees creates a strong and durable adhesive. When found, a container of this glue contains 1d6 + 1 ounces of the substance. One ounce of the glue can cover a one-foot-square surface. It takes 1d4 + 1 rounds to set. You can use the glue to repair a damaged or broken item (such as a macuahuitl or tecpatl). When applied to a surface that can be opened, such as a door, lid, or gate, the object becomes more difficult to force open, requiring an Open Doors check with a −1 penalty (minimum 1). The bond lasts indefinitely, though once a bonded surface is forced open, or a paired object becomes broken again, the glue is destroyed.

Cuitlapan. Primarily used to carry heavy loads long distances, this device consists of a wooden frame slung over the back. A cord affixed to the frame is then wrapped around the waist to keep the load secure, while a second strap loops just above the forehead for added balance. The cuitlapan has a volume of 1–1/2 cubic feet and a weight capacity of 50 pounds of gear.

Iyollo. A creature that drinks this delicious, chocolate-flavored drink experiences exhilaration and euphoria for one hour. The creature gains a +1 bonus to saving throws for the duration. ***Kindling Sticks.*** Without steel, most people use kindling sticks to start a fire. Enough sticks are in the kit to start 10 fires.

Mictlampa. Icons and symbols cover the face of this flat, round wooden board. The contraption has three movable hands corresponding to fixed points in the sky. When the hands are aligned correctly, it reveals your current position in relation to the four cardinal directions. ***Ollicactli.*** These sandals contain rubber padding and soles wrapped between two layers of leather for enhanced durability and cloth for added comfort. The shoes offer protection against the terrain and the elements, and reduce any lightning damage by 1d6 points.

Ollixami. This vial of black, clay-like material can cover a one-foot-square surface. Made from a mixture of latex, juice from the morning glory vine, and lime juice, it takes 1d4 rounds for this substance to set. The material can create a watertight seal or patch a hole in a canoe, roof, or other surface by forming it in the desired shape before it hardens. The bond can repel water and act as a sealant, but it lacks the adhesive strength to repair a broken object.

Passiflora. A creature that drinks a vial of this liquid made from passion flower gains a +1 bonus on saving throws against being paralyzed for one hour.

Rust Dust. The contents of this vial are spread onto an unattended manufactured object. The vial contains enough dust to coat a single object measuring one-foot square. If the object is made of a ferrous metal such as iron or steel, the dust chemically reacts with the metal for one minute. When the oxidation process ends, patches of orange rust appear on the object's surface.

The item must succeed on a saving throw or crumble and become useless. The dust has no effect on magic items, constructs, or objects affected by a spell or magical effect.

Tecuaniz. The contents of this flask can be splashed onto a creature within five feet or thrown up to 20 feet to shatter on impact. In either case, the wielder must make a ranged attack against the target creature. The flask contains a mixture of herbs that distracts animals. If the target is a beast, it suffers a −1 penalty to hit and saving throws for one turn.

Tlilitl. A creature that drinks this vial of vanilla-flavored liquid with hints of chocolate gains a +1 saving-throw bonus against magical sleep for one hour.

Uictli. The wedge-shaped wooden or bronze blade attached to the end of this five-foot-long wooden pole is used to burrow into the earth to till, remove, or carve irrigation channels through soil and loose stone. A creature using an uictli can dig at twice its normal rate.

Xochitl. A creature that drinks this vial of vanilla-flavored liquid suffers a −1 saving-throw penalty on saving throws against magical sleep for one hour. Alternatively, a creature that drinks xochitl less than one hour before going to sleep falls into a deep slumber. A creature that normally needs eight hours of sleep awakens refreshed after only four hours of sleep.

Zoyoyatic. The contents of this flask can be splashed onto a creature within five feet or thrown up to 20 feet to shatter on impact. The wielder must make a ranged attack against a target creature. The flask contains powder made from the crushed seeds of the sapodilla herb. If the target is a mouse, rat, or wererat, it takes 2d6 points of damage from the poison.

MOUNTS AND VEHICLES

Beasts of burden are few and far between in Tehuatl, while wheeled vehicles are merely an oddity. Its people have undertaken little effort to domesticate the wild animals roaming across the island. Despite taming turkeys, ducks, and dogs, none of these creatures has the strength or stamina to haul wagons or carry large loads of goods long distances. Instead of expediting travel across Tehuatl, heavy wagons would constantly get bogged down in mud and standing water. Furthermore, the island's small size in comparison to Akados and Libynos does not create tremendous need or demand for a transportation network stretching across thousands of miles. Instead, commerce centers around the island's numerous waterways, including the Great Canal separating the Aztlis from the Poqozas. While most of Tehuatl's residents haul goods by canoe or by foot when traveling overland, there are some circumstances where people turn to a novel solution. Although not domesticated, the ilhuitecuani, a massive member of the pinniped family, can be used to lug an apanimacal, a hybrid aquatic-land craft, across relatively flat and stable ground. The following mount and waterborne vehicles are available throughout Tehuatl:

Acalli. This large vessel made from spruce wood measures 10 feet across and 75 feet in length from its upturned bow to stern. The waterborne vehicle can accommodate a combination of up to 60 passengers or three tons of goods. It takes a crew of six to 10 oarsmen to propel the vessel.

Apanimacal. The apanimacal combines several technologies to create a vehicle suitable for aquatic and land travel. The sleek vehicle is 30 feet long and 10 feet wide with an elevated deck atop its cargo hold and a tapered bow and stern. It can accommodate a combination of up to 20 passengers and 3,000 pounds of goods. It takes a crew of four to operate the vehicle. Its hull is completely flat, which allows it to float on the water or be pulled across the ground as if it were a sled. Some models have a series of ski-like rails that can be attached to the vessel's undercarriage while it is still underwater. The apanimacal is always propelled by an ilhuitecuani tethered to its bow.

Canoe. Carved out of the trunk of a single tree, this waterborne vehicle has an upturned bow and stern and is 15 feet long. It can accommodate three passengers, including its driver, or transport the equivalent weight in goods. The driver propels the vehicle with a long pole or paddle.

Ilhuitecuani. At a weight of nearly 5,000 pounds and almost 20 feet long, the massive ilhuitecuani looks more like a whale than an enormous member of the seal family. This carnivorous wild animal can be temporarily tamed or at least placated with abundant quantities of food — roughly 100 pounds of meat per day — and the proper coaxing. The ilhuitecuani is predominately used to haul the hybrid land-water vehicle known as the **apanimacal** (see above).

TABLE B-4: MOUNT

Item	Cost	Move	Swim	Carrying Capacity
Ilhuitecuani	175 gp	9	15	800 lbs.

Item	Cost	Speed
Acalli	4,000 gp	1 mph
Apanimacal	1,500 gp	2 mph on flat land or water
Canoe	150 gp	1–1/2 mph

MAGIC ITEMS

Courage and ingenuity alone can sometimes bring you only so far. When all seems lost, adventurers frequently turn to magic to even the odds and win the day. The sages and scholars who create magic items on Tehuatl frequently enchant readily available objects, items, and materials. The magic items in the following section embody such principles.

ARMOR AND SHIELD

ARMOR OF ELUSIVENESS

Warriors hoping to avoid being captured covet this armor, which appears to be coated with an oily sheen. This +1 armor (any type) grants the wearer an additional d6 for grapple checks. In addition, the wearer cannot be paralyzed or restrained by magic.

FEATHER SHIELD

This shield is made from tightly packed layers of eagle, falcon, or condor feathers bonded together with pine resin. Three times per day, the wielder can speak its command word to cause the shield to sprout wings and talons. The talons can slash or grab an opponent. A slash does 2d6 points of damage with a successful hit. The grab restrains a target if it fails a saving throw and can carry the creature up to 20 feet. The shield releases the target on your command. Any creature dropped takes 1d6 points of damage for each 10 feet it falls.

SERPENT SHIELD

The small, round *+1 serpent shield* is crafted from a wicker and wood frame covered with lacquer and serpent's skin and adorned with feathers and various patterns of color to denote the status of whoever carries it. The wielder gains a +1 bonus to saves vs. poison.

MAGICAL MISSILE WEAPONS

ARROW OF BLACK DRAGON SLAYING

This magical *+1 arrow* is a *+5 arrow* vs. black dragons. In addition, the arrow has a chance of automatically slaying any black dragon it hits. The dragon is allowed a saving throw; if successful, the dragon takes 4d8 points of damage from the strike. If the save fails, the dragon dies.

ARROW OF FLESH FINDING

The *+1 arrow of flesh finding* has the unusual ability to avoid striking inanimate objects in its path. The target does not gain any bonuses granted by cover or a shield. If the target's body is made of flesh, the arrow deals an additional 1d6 points of damage on a successful hit. Once the arrow hits a target, it becomes nonmagical.

STONE OF STUNNING

Made from hard rubber, these spherical sling stones are designed to debilitate rather than kill an enemy. When the stone hits a creature, the target takes no damage but must succeed on a saving throw or be stunned for 1d4 rounds. Once a stone stuns a creature, it becomes nonmagical.

MISCELLANEOUS MAGICAL ITEMS, LESSER

COCOA BEAN

This dried and fermented seed from the cocoa tree is usually found in a small pod containing 2d6 cocoa beans. When a seed is eaten, it heightens awareness, improves mood, and grants extra energy for 10 minutes, and the creature gains a +1 bonus to saving throws against being charmed, frightened, or confused. If two or more beans are eaten before resting, there is a cumulative 25 percent chance for each bean after the first that the target falls into a deep sleep for at least four hours. Usable by all classes.

SANDALS OF THE MITOTE

These durable sandals are made from maguey fibers and have woven fabric straps that fasten the shoes to the feet. Anyone wearing these sandals can move normally through terrains that would normally slow their movements. While the sandals let the creature walk through dangerous areas, it offers no protection against damage caused by these dangerous locales. Usable by: All classes.

TANGLED GOURD

This roughly spherical green, orange, or bright yellow gourd is three inches in diameter and weighs one pound. If thrown, the gourd rips apart on impact and fills the area with fibrous vines. Each creature within a 10-foot radius of where the gourd lands must succeed on a saving throw or be restrained by the vines. Creatures that enter the area must succeed on a saving throw to also avoid being restrained. Restrained creatures take 1d6 points of damage each round. A creature restrained by the vines can make an Open Doors check to escape. The effects last for 1d4 + 2 rounds. Usable by all classes.

TURQUOISE NACOCHTLI

Originally given to esteemed midwives, these ornate earplugs magically adjust to painlessly elongate and then fit inside the earlobes. Any spellcaster wearing them heals an additional 1d6 hit points of damage when casting *cure light wounds* or *cure serious wounds*. Usable by clerics and druids.

MISCELLANEOUS MAGICAL ITEMS, MEDIUM

DEATH WHISTLE

Three times per day, this whistle can be used to emit a horrific sound resembling hundreds of terrified voices screaming in unison in a 20-foot cone that is audible 400 feet away. Every creature in the cone must succeed on a saving throw or take 2d6 points of damage and become frightened (as per a *fear* spell). On a successful saving throw, the creature takes half damage, is not frightened, and is immune to the whistle for 24 hours. Usable by all classes.

EAGLE HEADDRESS

Eagle feathers adorn the sides and top of this headwear, while a long, slender beak covers the wearer's forehead. The wearer of this headdress gains a +1 bonus to ranged attacks. Once per day, the wearer can also cast *polymorph self* and transform into an eagle. Usable by fighters.

LUCKY FINGERS

These hideous trinkets appear to be a collection of 1d4 dried human finger bones held together only by hard, dry cartilage. They are usually found tied in a bundle hanging from a leather cord or stuffed in a pouch. Snapping one of the bones gives a character a +1 bonus on the next to-hit roll or saving throw. When snapped, the magic in that digit is released, rendering it worthless. Usable by: All classes.

Tlachtli Ball

This solid, rubber ball weighs nine pounds and has black and red swirling patterns painted on it. Three times per day, a command word can be spoken to cause the ball to fly in a 120-foot line. Each creature in that line takes 2d6 points of damage and is knocked prone. Creatures that succeed on a saving throw take half damage and are not knocked down. When the ball reaches the end of the line, it falls harmlessly to the ground, but the wielder can instantly summon the ball back to their hand. Usable by fighters and thieves.

Miscellaneous Magical Item, Greater

Box of Rocks

This small rectangular wooden box features decorative mosaic artwork depicting meteors streaking across the heavens on its exterior. It has no latches or hinges, yet it stays tightly sealed. The wielder must speak a command word to spill the box's 3d4 pebbles on the ground. Each pebble instantly fragments into a cloud of tiny rocks that swirl in a 10-foot-high, five-foot-diameter cylinder. Creatures that enter a swirling cylinder take 3d6 points of damage (or half as much with a successful saving throw). The rocks swirl for 1d3 rounds before they fall harmlessly to the ground. The box can be used three times per day. Usable by magic-users.

Cuacalalatli of the Beast

These wooden helmets are shaped into the likenesses of various beast heads. The protective device fits over the head and covers the top and back of the skull as well as the jawline. Anyone wearing one of these helmets gains the animal's abilities. The type of beast associated with the helmet determines its specific properties:

Crocodile: The wearer can slam its target for 1d6 points of damage.

Eagle: The wearer cannot be surprised.

Frog: The wearer can hold his or her breath for 15 minutes and gains a +1 to-hit bonus when fighting underwater.

Jaguar: The wearer gains a +1 bonus to attacks and damage against injured foe.

Monkey: The wearer can scale vertical walls (Climb 9).

Serpent: The wearer can slide through gaps half his or her size.

Usable by fighters and thieves.

Helm of the Ebon Serpent

Fashioned in the shape of lashing serpent's head, this light helm is crafted from lacquered wicker covered in black snakeskin. The wearer's face is framed by a gaping mouth with fangs in each corner. A crest of ebony-colored feathers adorns the top and runs down the neck. Three times per day, the wearer can spit venom 15 feet with a successful ranged attack. The venom does 2d6 points of damage and blinds an opponent. The target must succeed on a saving throw for half damage and to avoid blindness. Usable by fighters and thieves.

Jaguar Cloak

Stitched together from the pelts of Tehuatl's largest cat, this spotted garment also serves as a status symbol among the Aztli nobility. Anyone wearing it gains the following:

A Climb speed equal to its normal Move rate (fighters only).

A 20% Hide in Shadows bonus while hiding in grasslands, forests, or swamps (thieves only).

+1 to-hit bonus against a creature that is surprised and any successful hit does double damage.

Usable by fighters and thieves.

Mask of Smoke and Mirrors

This decorative turquoise mask is most commonly associated with the worshippers and priests of Tezcatlipoca. Deerskin straps attached to the sides of the mask keep it securely fastened around the wearer's head while completely covering the face. The mask lets the wearer see normally in fog, mist, or smoke. When worn in such an area, the wearer can also teleport up to 30 feet to an unoccupied space within the fog, mist, or smoke. Usable by all classes.

Mask of Quiahuitl

This stylized mask of lacquered ebon wood has long fangs and wide eyehole carvings that make the wearer appear to have oversized bulging eyeballs. The mask is topped with an elaborate headdress made from heron feathers. The mask lets the wearer see clearly through fog, rain, sleet, wind, and other forms of precipitation. Three times per day, the wearer can also use a gaze attack on a creature within 30 feet. The target must make a saving throw or be affected by *charm person*. Usable by all classes.

Pumpkin Seed

The eyes of anyone eating a pumpkin seed glow, emitting a faint yellowish glow in a 20-foot cone for one turn. An undead or fiend caught in the glare takes 2d6 points of damage, or half as much on a successful saving throw. Alternatively, the eyes can pulse with a bright light for one round. Anyone caught in the pulse must succeed on a saving throw or be blinded. Usable by all classes.

Seal of Mictlán

This strange stone vessel is circular shaped, about six inches in diameter and three inches tall. The sides bear thousands of ancient runes while a grinning skull is carved into the top. The seal separates into two pieces and feels unusually light (it is hollow). The wielder can force the soul of any humanoid within 100 feet to depart its body and enter the seal. The target must succeed on a saving throw to resist the pull of the seal. On a failure, the target's soul is trapped within the seal. Once used in this way, the seal cannot be used again for seven days. The seal can hold only one soul at a time.

When the soul is removed, the target's body falls into a catatonic state. If the seal is destroyed and the target's body is less than 100 feet away and is still alive, the soul returns to the body and the target regains consciousness. Otherwise, the target dies. Usable by clerics and magic-users.

Tilmahtli of Flowers

This white linen cloak features red, yellow, and blue flower petals stitched onto the fabric. When worn with the hood up, the flowers release a subtle yet perceivable sweet aroma in a 20-foot radius that beasts and humanoids find pleasurable and soothing. Any creature smelling the scent must make a saving throw or be charmed (as a charm person or charm monster spell). Usable by all classes.

Tilmahtli of the Owl

This dark linen cloak bears the image of an owl with outstretched wings stitched onto the fabric. The wearer can grip the edges with both hands and raise and lower them to simulate an owl in flight. When done in an area of bright or dim light, the cloak casts an ominous shadow in a 20-foot cone. Each creature within the shadow must succeed on a saving throw or flee (as a fear spell). Usable by all classes.

War Paint

Typically stored in clay jars, each container holds 1d3 applications of viscous pigments made from dyes and other colorful components. A creature can wear no more than three different colors of paint at a time, and only one color of war paint can be applied to a weapon. Any attempt to apply more colors fails. Each application of paint lasts for one turn regardless of color. The *war paint's* color determines its effects:

Black: The wearer is infused with a dark energy that deals 1d6 points of damage to any creature touched or struck.

Blue: A frigid chill courses through the wearer's body and causes frost to form on any weapon. The cold is harmless to the wearer and the weapon. This cold deals an additional 1d6 points of damage with a successful strike.

Green: The wearer cannot be restrained or paralyzed.

Orange: The wearer is immune to fear.

Purple: The wearer gains a +1 to-hit bonus during combat.

Red: Warmth radiates through the wearer's skin and causes one weapon to glow red-hot. The heat is harmless to the wearer and the weapon. This fiery weapon deals an additional 1d6 points of fire damage.

White: The wearer's weapon deals an additional 1d6 points of damage to undead and fiends.

Yellow: Energy surges within the wearer's body and causes one weapon to crackle with electrical energy. The electricity is harmless to the wearer and the weapon. The weapon deals an additional 1d6 points of electrical damage.

Usable by all classes.

POTIONS

BALCHÉ

This mildly intoxicating concoction is a mixture of tree bark soaked in honey and water. When found, a vial contains 1d4 + 1 one-ounce doses of the fermented liquid. When used, the imbiber gains a greater understanding of nature and cannot become lost or surprised while outside. The effects last for one turn. Usable by all classes.

XTABENTUN

This fermented beverage made from honey, tree bark, and corn allows the drinker to momentarily defy reality. When found, a vial contains 1d3 + 1 one-ounce doses of the prized liqueur. The imbiber experiences a sense of euphoria and gains a +1 bonus on saving throws for one turn. Usable by all classes.

RINGS

RING OF IRON

The Firebrand dwarves originally forged these expertly crafted iron rings as tokens of appreciation for trusted allies and loyal friends, yet over time they came to realize that the rings' usefulness outweighed their ceremonial purpose. The wearer is immune to fire and lightning damage. Usable by all classes.

RING OF PURSUING

This undecorated bone ring made from the vertebra of a large, predatory animal appears more fearsome when worn as a nose ring. The wearer can choose a creature within 30 feet and know its exact location for one turn. The targeted creature must succeed on a saving throw when it attempts to move more than 30 feet from the wearer; on a failure, it is magically restrained and cannot continue beyond that distance. The wearer cannot select a new target until the current target drops to 0 hit points or the turn expires, whichever happens first. Usable by fighters.

STAFFS

CHICAHUAZTLI

This *+1 quarterstaff* made from a long bone of a large beast or humanoid has a hollow interior filled with tiny shards of bone that rattle when shaken. While holding it, the wielder can expend one or more charges to cast one of the following spells: *bloodbath* (1 charge), *dance miquiztli* (4 charges), or *war cry* (2 charges). Usable by clerics, druids, and magic-users.

STAFF OF WILDERNESS EXPLORATION

The wielder of this staff always senses the direction of true north. In addition, one charge can be used to learn the direction of the nearest natural hazard, such as quicksand or a volcanic pit, within 500 feet, although the dangerous obstacle's actual distance is not known. The wielder can also expend one or more charges to cast one of the following spells: *detect snares and pits* (1 charge), *find the path* (3 charges), *locate plants* (1 charge), or *speak with animals* (2 charges). Usable by druids.

WEAPONS

MACUAHUITL OF REVEALING

The *+2 macuahuitl of revealing* does an additional 1d6 points of damage to shapechangers. If struck, the shapechanger must succeed on a saving throw or revert to its original form.

Legends claim the hero-gods used these weapons to unmask the emperor's serpent-advisors.

MACUAHUITL OF QUIAHUITL

The +1 macuahuitl of Quiahuitl is carved from heavily lacquered dark wood and set with rows of gleaming obsidian teeth. The flats of the club bear engravings of a serpent coiled around a cornstalk set above a flooded plain. A tightly wrapped snakeskin covers a long wooden handle tipped with a collection of six heron feathers dyed orange and blue that dangle from a woven string. Three times per day, the weapon can siphon 1d4 hit points from the wielder as a sacrifice to Tlaloc. When this occurs, the weapon deals an additional 1d6 points of damage on a successful hit.

OBSIDIAN DAGGER

Carved from a single shard of razor-sharp obsidian, this magical blade differs from the ceremonial daggers often used in sacrificial rites. Its blade fits into a cedarwood handle carved into the likeness of a pouncing jaguar. If the wielder rolls a 19 or 20, the attack rips open a vicious gash. If this occurs, roll another attack roll. On another roll of 20, the blade pierces the target's heart, killing it. If not, the blade deals 2d6 points of damage and the target's wound bleeds for an additional 1d4 points of damage until magically healed.

Appendix C: New Spells

The compulsion to create and innovate flows through the fiber of nearly every sentient being born and raised in Tehuatl. While most express themselves through mundane mediums such as painting, song, sculpture, and dance, some steer their imaginations toward the mystical arts. These practitioners devise new cantrips and incantations ideally suited for their unique environment. Their ingenuity appears in the new spells presented in this chapter.

Cleric Spells

1st-Level Spells
Bloodbath
Counterattack
Detect Corpse

2nd-Level Spells
Cremation
Floral Bouquet
War Cry

3rd-Level Spells
Aura of Altruism
Flay Skin
Jaguar Spirit

4th-Level Spell
Sacrifice

6th-Level Spell
Palpitating Heart

7th-Level Spell
Volcano

Druid Spells

1st-Level Spells
Bloodbath
Counterattack
Detect Corpse
Nohpalli
Pulque Infusion

2nd-Level Spells
Floral Bouquet
Heat Stone
Rust
Steam Bath
Wall of Smoke
War Cry

3rd-Level Spells
Falling Logs
Jaguar Spirit

4th-Level Spell
Magnetize

5th-Level Spell
Chinampa

6th-Level Spell
Flesh to Maize

7th-Level Spells
Black Hole
Uncoordinated
Volcano

Magic-User Spells

1st-Level Spells
Babble
Bumble
Compulsive Step
Jinx
Numb
Slither
Stumble
Superstitious

2nd-Level Spells
Floral Bouquet
Parasitic Bond
Steam Bath
Wall of Smoke

3rd-Level Spells
Falling Logs
Flay Skin
Instill Madness
Triplicate

4th-Level Spell
Time in a Bottle

5th-Level Spell
Dance Miquiztli

6th-Level Spell
Palpitating Heart

7th-Level Spells
Black Hole
Uncoordinated

Aura of Altruism

Spell Level: Cleric, 3rd Level
Range: 30 feet
Duration: Immediate

This spell causes healing energy to radiate around the caster in a 30-foot radius. Every ally within range of the caster is healed for 1d4 points of damage. The cleric heals an additional 1d4 points of damage for every 3 levels of experience (to 9th level). Thus, at 6th level, the caster is able to heal 2d4 points of damage, and a maximum of 3d4 points of damage at 9th level.

Babble

Spell Level: Magic-User, 1st Level
Range: 30 feet
Duration: 24 hours

A creature within range of the caster finds it impossible to communicate verbally or in writing. The target must succeed on a saving throw or any words it speaks or writes come out garbled and incomprehensible. The target is unaware of the spell's effect, as it hears and sees its own words as it intended to say or write them. The target finds it impossible to cast spells or transcribe any documents, including spell scrolls and spells. Anyone listening to the target or reading its written words cannot understand what it is trying to say. Even spells such as *read languages* and *read magic* cannot translate the target's words, as it communicates with nonsensical sounds and indecipherable symbols. *Dispel magic* ends the effect.

Black Hole

Spell Level: Druid, 7th Level; Magic-User, 7th Level
Range: 500 feet
Duration: Immediate

This spell creates a tiny yet immensely dense object known as a black hole that appears at a point within range. The immensely powerful object pulls creatures and objects weighing less than 2,000 pounds within a 100-foot-radius toward it. Any creature that fails a saving throw is pulled toward the black hole and crushed within its event horizon, taking 1d6 points of damage per level of the caster.

Bloodbath

Spell Level: Cleric, 1st Level; Druid, 1st Level
Range: 30 feet
Duration: Immediate

This spell creates 10 gallons of blood to either fill an open container or to splash onto all creatures and objects in a 30-foot cube within range. The blood extinguishes exposed flames in the area and is identical in composition to the caster's blood. Each creature within the area must succeed on a saving throw or be disgusted and drop whatever it is holding. Disgusted creatures cannot willingly move closer to the caster and avert their eyes. Creatures that make a saving throw are still doused in blood but are otherwise not affected.

Bumble

Spell Level: Magic-User, 1st Level
Range: 30 feet
Duration: Immediate

After casting this spell, a creature of the caster's choosing within range must succeed on a saving throw or its initial attempt to interact with an object fails. This spell affects only a creature's first attempt to interact with an object rather than end an existing interaction. For instance, the spell can prevent the target from drawing a weapon from its sheath or picking a weapon up from the ground, but it cannot cause the target to drop a weapon it is holding in its hand.

The spell prevents the target from interacting with the same object for a longer period of time at higher levels: 2 rounds at 3rd level, 3 rounds at 6th level, and 4 rounds at 9th level.

Chinampa

Spell Level: Druid, 5th Level
Range: 120 feet
Duration: Up to 1 hour

This spell creates a one-foot-thick parcel of solid, dry land that springs into existence atop up to 1,600 square feet of water (an area 40 feet square, or 64 five-foot squares, or 16 10-foot squares). The parcel of land consists of bare earth devoid of any vegetation or life. The chinampa cannot cover any existing landmass at or above the water's surface, though any existing landmasses can be incorporated into the created parcel. At the end of the spell's duration, the caster can decide if the land becomes permanent. Otherwise, the land disappears when the spell ends.

If a creature is partially submerged beneath the water when the land appears, it must make a saving throw to emerge atop the dry land if it so chooses. On a failed save, the creature is pushed into the water beneath the dry land.

The land otherwise supports the weight of any creatures atop it, though structures made from stone or other heavy materials cause the ground directly beneath it to sink underneath the water's surface until it settles on the bottom.

Compulsive Step

Spell Level: Magic-User, 1st Level
Range: 30 feet
Duration: Immediate

This spell forces a creature to make a saving throw or move five feet into a space of the caster's choosing. The creature cannot be forced to move into a space with an obviously deadly hazard such as a chasm or open flames. The target continues to move in the chosen direction each round until it makes a saving throw to end the effect. Creatures immune to *charm person* are not affected.

The number of creatures affected increases at higher levels: two creatures at 4th level, three creatures at 8th level, and four creatures at 12th level.

Counterattack

Spell Level: Cleric, 1st Level; Druid, 1st Level
Range: Touch
Duration: 1 turn

The caster touches an ally who for the duration of the spell can immediately return a melee attack by a foe who attacks and misses. The spell ends once a counterattack is made.

Cremation

Spell Level: Cleric, 2nd Level
Range: Touch
Duration: Immediate

The caster touches a corpse or other remains, which is instantly reduced to a pile of fine gray dust that cannot be raised or turned into an undead. The creature can be restored to life only by means of a *resurrection* or a *wish* spell.

Dance Miquiztli

Spell Level: Magic-User, 5th Level
Range: 60 feet
Duration: 1 round/level

This spell compels up to 12 creatures within range to perform a frenetic dance routine. Each target must make a saving throw or feel an irresistible need to dance. The target incorporates the dance's violent, pounding motions into its movement, causing it to take 1d4 points of damage each round. Any attack on a dancer ends the spell.

Detect Corpse

Spell Level: Cleric, 1st Level; Druid, 1st Level
Range: Caster
Duration: 1 hour + 10 min/level

For the duration of the spell, the caster can sense the presence and location of humanoid corpses and bones that are not undead within 30 feet. The spell also allows the caster to identify the decedent's race and gender in each case.

The spell can penetrate most barriers, but it is blocked by one foot of stone, one inch of common metal, a thin sheet of lead, or 10 feet of wood or dirt.

FALLING LOGS

Spell Level: Druid, 3rd Level; Magic-User, 3rd Level
Range: 120 feet
Duration: Immediate

This spell causes three 10-foot-long logs to appear vertically 50 feet up in the air above three spots chosen by the caster. The spots must be at least 10 feet apart and within a 40-foot radius of the first log's location. The logs immediately fall in a vertical line. Any creature directly beneath a log must make a saving throw or take 1d6 points of damage per level of the caster (higher-level casters create larger-diameter logs that do more damage). On a successful saving throw, the target takes half damage.

FLAY SKIN

Spell Level: Cleric, 3rd Level; Magic-User, 3rd Level
Range: 30 feet
Duration: Immediate

This spell flays portions of skin from a chosen target within range. The target must make a saving throw or take 1d6 points of damage per level of the caster (maximum 12d6 points of damage). The target takes half damage on a successful saving throw.

FLESH TO MAIZE

Spell Level: Druid, 6th Level
Range: 60 feet
Duration: See below

This spell turns one creature within range into a maize plant. The target must succeed on a saving throw or it drops everything it is holding as its flesh transforms into fibrous plant material. Its legs turn into roots and a lower stem; its torso into a central stalk; its arms into leaves; and its head into an ear of maize. Its equipment melds into this new form. Creatures who succeed on a successful saving throw are not affected.A transformed creature can make a saving throw each round. If it makes three successful saving throws, the effect ends. If, however, it fails three saving throws, it permanently becomes a stalk of maize. These successes or failures do not need to be consecutive; keep track of both until the target accumulates the required number. *Dispel magic* also ends the effect.

FLORAL BOUQUET

Spell Level: Cleric, 2nd Level; Druid, 2nd Level; Magic-User, 2nd
  Level
Range: 120 feet
Duration: Immediate

A flower bulb streaks from the caster's finger to a point within range and then bursts open to release floral aromas and pungent scents. Each creature in a 20-foot-radius sphere must succeed on a saving throw or be stunned by the sensory overload for 1d6 + 1 rounds.

HEAT STONE

Spell Level: Druid, 2nd Level
Range: 150 feet
Duration: Immediate

This spell causes a 20-foot square contiguous stone surface centered on a point within range to instantly become searing hot. Creatures touching the slab take 4d6 points of fire damage unless they make a saving throw for half damage. Despite the stone's warm temperature, it radiates little heat and shows no outward signs of being hazardous.

INSTILL MADNESS

Spell Level: Magic-User, 3rd Level
Range: 120 feet
Duration: 1 hour

This spell causes a creature to succumb to madness if it fails a saving throw. While in the throes of madness, the target can only move or attack. It cannot activate magic items.

The target is free to decide whether to move or attack, but after it does so, it acts randomly. If it moves, it wanders in a random direction until it reaches its maximum movement or until it encounters another creature, obstacle, or obviously deadly hazard in its path. Roll 1d8 to determine the random direction. If it decides to attack, it can use only natural weapons or any weapon it held when it succumbed to the madness. It randomly attacks any creature within range.

JAGUAR SPIRIT

Spell Level: Cleric, 3rd Level; Druid, 3rd Level
Range: 60 feet
Duration: 1 turn or until dispelled

The spell calls into existence a floating, spectral jaguar. The jaguar (3 HD creature with AC 6[13]) attacks a target chosen by the caster and deals 3d6 points of damage. The target must make a saving throw or be held and take an automatic 3d6 points of damage until it is freed. The jaguar does an additional 1d6 points of damage at higher levels: 4d6 points of damage at 8th level, and 5d6 points of damage at 12th level.

JINX

Spell Level: Magic-User, 1st Level
Range: 30 feet
Duration: 1 hour + 10 min/level

A target the caster can see receives an ominous feeling that something bad is about to happen. The target must succeed on a saving throw or be jinxed. A jinxed creatures suffers a −1 penalty to hit, damage, and saving throws for the duration of the spell. Additional creatures can be affected at higher levels: two creatures at 3rd level, three creatures at 6th level, and four creatures at 9th level.

MAGNETIZE

Spell Level: Druid, 4th Level
Range: 120 feet
Duration: 1 turn

A metal object of the caster's choosing becomes a powerful magnet that attracts metal objects within a 40-foot-radius sphere. Any unsecured metal objects are pulled toward the magnet. A creature carrying metal items must make a saving throw to hold onto an object. Creatures wearing armor who fail the saving throw are pinned to the magnet. Anyone pinned to the magnet can make a new saving throw each round to pull away and move 20 feet from the magnet, but must make another saving throw in the next round if still within range. A weapon can be pulled free with a saving throw, but might be drawn back to the magnet in the next round if still within range.

Nohpalli

Spell Level: Druid, 1st Level
Range: 90 feet
Duration: Immediate

This spell causes a four-inch-diameter cactus ball with one-inch-long needles to materialize and streak toward a chosen target. The caster must roll to hit. On a hit, the target takes 1d6 points of damage per caster level (maximum 7d6), and the ball sticks to the creature. The target takes 1d6 points of damage for two additional rounds unless the ball is removed.

Numb

Spell Level: Magic-User, 1st Level
Range: 60 feet
Duration: 1 turn

This spell numbs a creature to pain if it fails a saving throw. The spell suppresses the target's pain receptors, causing the creature to believe its wounds and injuries are harmless scratches requiring no immediate attention. The target never willingly heals itself and refuses assistance from others. If an ally attempts to heal the target, the creature becomes enraged and attacks. The creature takes 1d6 points of damage each round it refuses treatment. The target can make another saving throw with a –1 penalty each round to shake off the numbness. Aztli priests sometimes use this spell on sacrificial victims to ease their suffering.

Palpitating Heart

Spell Level: Cleric, 6th Level; Magic-User, 6th Level
Range: 60 feet
Duration: 1d4 + 1 rounds

This spell causes a spectral hand to reach into a living creature's torso and appear to rip out the creature's still-beating heart or other vital organ, which then instantly appears in the caster's hand. Blood and other bodily fluids gush from the creature's chest. The illusion is perceivable only to the caster and the target. The target must succeed on a saving throw. On a failure, the target believes the illusion is real and is stunned for the duration of the spell, taking 1d6 points of damage each round it is affected. When the effect ends, the target makes another saving throw. On a failure, the creature falls unconscious from the imagined pain.

Parasitic Bond

Spell Level: Magic-User, 2nd Level
Range: 30 feet
Duration: 1 round/level

One target chosen within range must make a saving throw or become a conduit to heal the caster. Each round thereafter for the duration of the spell, the target must make a saving throw or take 1d8 points of damage. The spellcaster absorbs this damage through the bond as an equal amount of hit points. If the target succeeds on a saving throw, the spell ends.

Pulque Infusion

Spell Level: Druid, 1st Level
Range: 30 feet
Duration: 1 turn

This spell infuses pulque directly into a creature, which must succeed on a saving throw or become intoxicated, suffering a –1 penalty to hit, damage, and saving throws. A creature immune to poison is not affected by the spell.

Rust

Spell Level: Druid, 2nd Level
Range: 60 feet
Duration: Immediate

This spell causes a chosen metal object to rust if it fails a saving throw.
Weapons affected by this spell crumble into dust when they hit a creature or object, while armor and shields affected by the spell disintegrate when an attack hits the creature wearing or holding the protective device. The spell does not affect magic items.

Sacrifice

Spell Level: Cleric, 4th Level
Range: 30 feet
Duration: Immediate

The caster selects one target, usually an ally.
The target of the spell takes no damage from the next attack that strikes it. Instead, damage that would have been dealt to the target is dealt to the caster of the spell instead. This spell must be cast before damage is rolled.

Slither

Spell Level: Magic-User, 1st Level
Range: Touch
Duration: 1 turn

A creature touched by the caster can crawl at its normal movement. It can also squeeze through small spaces a creature half its size would normally be able to maneuver through.

Steam Bath

Spell Level: Druid, 2nd Level; Magic-User, 2nd Level
Range: 120 feet
Duration: Immediate

The spell creates a 20-foot-radius sphere of steam. Any creature in the sphere takes 1d4 points of damage per level of the caster, or half as much if it succeeds on a saving throw.

Stumble

Spell Level: Magic-User, 1st Level
Range: 30 feet
Duration: Immediate

This spell causes a chosen creature to fall prone if it fails a saving throw.
The caster can target additional creatures at higher levels: two creatures at 4th level, three creatures at 8th level, and four creatures at 12th level.

Superstitious

Spell Level: Magic-User, 1st Level
Range: 30 feet
Duration: 12 hours

A creature of the caster's choosing obsesses over superstitious rituals if it fails a saving throw. While affected, it dwells on real and imaginary omens around it. When the target misses an attack roll or fails a saving throw, it takes 1d4 points of damage. *Dispel magic* ends the effect.
The spell's damage increases at higher levels: 2d4 at 4th level; 3d4 at 8th level; and 4d4 at 12th level.

Time in a Bottle

Spell Level: Magic-User, 4th Level
Range: Self
Duration: Up to 1 turn

The caster saves a brief moment of time for future use. The caster can use the extra time to take an extra turn, even if he or she already took an action. The spell ends when the extra turn is taken or if the time limit expires.

Triplicate

Spell Level: Magic-User, 3rd Level
Range: 60 feet
Duration: 1 hour or until destroyed

The spell creates three illusory duplicates of the caster, which appear at unoccupied points chosen within range. Neither the caster nor a duplicate can occupy the same space.

The duplicates imitate the caster's actions but remain stationary. However, the caster can move one duplicate up to 20 feet in a round, but any duplicates outside the range of the spell are destroyed. A duplicate is also destroyed if it is physically struck, but spells do not affect it. One of the duplicates can also be designated as a point of origin for the spellcaster's magic, as if the spellcaster was standing at that spot. The duplicates last until the spell ends or the caster dispels them.

Uncoordinated

Spell Level: Druid, 7th Level; Magic-User, 7th Level
Range: 150 feet
Duration: Immediate

The spell overloads the central nervous system of a creature, disrupting its motor skills. The target takes 4d6 points of damage, or half damage if it succeeds on a saving throw. On a failure, the creature's movement is also halved, and for every five feet it travels, there is a 50% chance that the creature moves in a random direction. At the end of 30 days, the creature can repeat its saving throw against this spell. If it succeeds on a saving throw, the spell ends.

The spell can also be ended by *restoration* or a *wish*.

Volcano

Spell Level: Cleric, 7th Level; Druid, 7th Level; Magic-User, 8th Level
Range: 500 feet
Duration: 1 hour

This spell causes liquid magma from the planet's core to surge to the surface, giving rise to a volcano. The 60-foot-tall mound of molten rock and stone with a 10-foot radius instantaneously emerges from the ground. The volcano destroys any buildings in its path when it rises.

The small yet potent volcano belches pumice, lava, and pyroclastic gases within a 100-foot-radius sphere.

Each creature or object in the area takes 4d8 points of damage from the falling pumice and 8d6 points of damage from the falling lava. Creatures that succeed on a saving throw take half damage. When the spell ends, the volcano collapses in on itself and sinks into the ground.

Wall of Smoke

Spell Level: Druid, 2nd Level; Magic-User, 2nd Level
Range: 120 feet
Duration: 1 hour or until dispelled

This spell creates a wall of thick, black smoke up to 60 feet long, 20 feet high, and five feet thick, or a ringed wall up to 20 feet in diameter, 20 feet high, and five feet thick. The wall is opaque and cannot be dispersed by high winds despite being composed of wispy vapors. Creatures caught in the smoke take 1d6 points of damage per caster level and are blinded. Creatures who succeed on a saving throw take half damage and are not blinded.

War Cry

Spell Level: Cleric, 2nd Level; Druid, 2nd Level
Range: 30 feet
Duration: 1 turn

This spell whips the caster's allies into a frenzy for the duration of the spell. Up to three creatures within range gain a +1 bonus to hit, damage, and saving throws. At higher levels, the spell grants greater bonuses: +2 at 6th level, and +3 at 10th level.